Lemprière's
Dictionary

LEMPRIÈRE'S DICTIONARY

Lawrence Norfolk

HARMONY BOOKS

NEW YORK

Copyright © 1991 by Lawrence Norfolk

Published by Harmony Books,
a division of Crown Publishers, Inc.,
201 East 50th Street, New York, New York 10022.
Member of the Crown Publishing Group.

Originally published in Great Britain by Sinclair-Stevenson Limited in 1991.

HARMONY and colophon are trademarks of Crown Publishers, Inc.

Manufactured in the United States of America

Library of Congress Cataloging-in-Publication Data
Norfolk, Lawrence, 1963–
Lemprière's dictionary/Lawrence Norfolk.—1st American ed.
p.   cm.
1. Lemprière, John, 1765?–1824—Fiction.   2. London (England)—
History—18th century—Fiction.   I. Title.
PR6064.065L4   1992   92-17434
823'.914—dc20   CIP

ISBN 0-517-58184-1

10 9 8 7 6 5 4 3 2

First American Edition

To
S B-H

Barbarus hic ego sum, qui non intellegor ulli

*Lemprière's
Dictionary*

CAESAREA

The winds blew high over Jersey, clearing the sky for the stars to glimmer down on the island below. Its gentle beaches and high cliffs were barely distinguishable from the dark water. The moon had sunk from view hours before. Some nights it shone bright enough to read by, but not tonight. The oil lamp which stood on the desk at which he sat threw a soft, yellow light. A book lay open before him and he studied it intently, his face only inches from the characters. His head followed the movement of the lines, turning slightly from left to right and back, moving slowly down the page. Outside, the murmur of the waves just reached his ears as they washed in and slapped against the cliffs of Bouley Bay.

After some time, the hunched figure brought his head up from his labors and rubbed his eyes with his knuckles. His tall, angular body was cramped, legs twisted around the chair, elbows seeking a resting place among the clutter of papers on the desk. He shifted position awkwardly. When he brought his hands away from his eyes, the room had dissolved. The patch of dull red he was able to make out would be his bed and the lighter area beyond it the door. The floor he could feel with his feet and the window he identified by the slight gusts and breezes which blew coolly against his face. At this distance, yards rather than inches, the rest was lost to him in a flux of shadows; nothing but "air deprived of light"; he recalled the formula. Lucretius, matter-of-fact and unhelpful. As the objects about him drifted, disappeared, and shaded into one another, John Lemprière felt the slight panic in his stomach to which he had become inured, an unwelcome sensation even now. He bent to the page, trying to focus his eyes once again.

The blurrings of sight had begun when he was fourteen or thereabouts and grown more and more frequent as he had entered his late teens. The world came to seem as it did now. Objects fogged and merged with other objects. Outlines broke and seeped into their surroundings. His myopia dissolved the world in a mist of possibilities and its vague forms made a playground for his speculations. His youthful panic had later become acceptance and, later still, something akin to pleasure. Only the faintest vestige of unease remained, and he allowed his speculations, his day-dreams, and his visions free rein. The island itself could not compete with the routs of demigods and heroes, the noisy unions of nymphs and animals, with which the young scholar populated the fields of his imagi-nation. His head had only to leave the pages of Tully, Terence, Pindar, or Propertius to see their most delicate or lurid descriptions made flesh in the wavering dusk outside his window. Galatea had made sport with Acis in that land of visions. And Polyphemus had made sport with them both. There the last Punic war had been fought and lost by the Poeni whose Carthage burnt for seventeen days before twenty miles of its walls crashed in to quell the flames. Scipio Africanus was nothing but a trick-ster, but got the consulship he craved. *Delenda est Carthago*. The ancient kings whose lives flickered between natural and supernatural worlds, the ordinary loves of shepherds touched for an instant by hands that trans-formed flesh to wood, hamadryads and nereids, what vision was it that saw in the simple flames of an Athenian hearth the gory torture of Prometheus, in the nightingale's song the rape of Philomel, in every tree a face, every stream a voice? And behind them lay the ukases which commanded not with reason, but with the simple certainty that it was their place to do so; perhaps the gods too were victims of that savage simplicity, he wondered. Victims to that clarity with its steel logic, its sentence without redress. Princes and heroes, nymphs and satyrs stalked the antechambers of the young classicist's mind, disporting and dis-membering, playing and replaying the scenes he chased through the pages of the Ancients.

"He tripped over a bucket. It was plain in view, Charles." His moth-er's querulous voice brought his head up from the page of Thuycidides, and the Greek characters swam as his ears caught snatches of the nightly dialogue.

"What of it? Did he hurt?"

"Must he snap a leg before you'll see it, Charles? You're as blind as the boy." They spoke in the hush reserved for worry or intimacy. Lem-prière's fingertips brushed the chalky surface of the page before him. Three feet from his face he could not read it, inches and the letters were hard-edged and distinct. His parents were not intimate.

"He'll be a fine scholar, perhaps the finest of his age. What need for him to step over buckets?"

"It's the reading's ruined his eyes. Ruined *him*." This last hissed, answered by Charles Lemprière's snort of disbelief.

"He's grown strange to us, Charles, you know it."

"He's simply fond of his studies, the balance will come in time. I was the same, I remember it well."

"Oh yes, the Lemprières have ever been the same, that much I know. Nothing changes, does it, Charles?" Her voice was bitter.

Lemprière caught only muffled words after that, his mother's soft sobbing. The debate was a familiar one to him. He stayed awake waiting for it, enjoying his central role. He felt intimate with his parents as they unknowingly told him all they felt regarding him. Normally his mother seemed to understand little of what he said, while his father held himself in reserve, harboring feelings his son could only guess at within a stern outward aspect. This, however, was to be the last of these particular discussions, for the next morning it transpired that a resolution had been reached. John Lemprière was to have eyeglasses.

So it was that a week later two figures could be seen making the four-mile trek across the island from Rozel to Saint Helier. Taller, and walking half a pace ahead of his son, Charles Lemprière picked his way through the ruts of the road with a practiced ease. An occasional glance at the sky reassured him that though they would be spattered with mud to the knee, they would at least reach their destination dry. His son stumbled frequently, and each time he did so Charles would forbear to look back but would stiffen and wince inaudibly to himself. His wife was right, of course, but blindness, of the eye or mind, had its benefits. It was possible to see too much. The path was passing through a wood. He ducked an overhanging branch and lifted it for his son. The pair walked on. Passing Five Oaks, they gained the brow of the slope, and Charles saw Saint Helier laid out ahead, beyond it Elizabeth Castle improbably afloat in the harbor. It was only five years since Rullecourt and seven hundred men had got the governor out of bed to sign away the island. And, rubbing the sleep from his eyes, he had signed. Elizabeth Castle stood firm then. Poor Moses Corbet, running through the marketplace with musket balls peppering his hat. There were more Martellos than cottages now.

His son heard Saint Helier long before he saw it. The town clamored at him, open arms brushed at his jacket, and the din of human voices as they transacted, bickered, or greeted each other enfolded him in an anonymous, urban welcome. He caught his father's arm and was hurried through the crush as its sounds crested and broke over his head. Charles Lemprière, son in tow, carved a passage through the business, gossip, and grind of Jersey. The market crowd thinned as they took a sidestreet past the Peirson and walked through streets which seemed unnaturally silent after the hubbub of the marketplace. Another turn and they arrived, breathing heavily, at the workshop of Ichnabod Bonamy, glassmaker and lensgrinder. Charles was reaching for the bell when a voice boomed from within.

"Come in, Lemprière!"

They entered and found themselves face-to-face with Ichnabod holding a coal shovel in one hand and a large stuffed owl in the other.

"Welcome, welcome you both. Are you well, Charles? The boy I know of already, he of the stiff eyes, hmm? Forgive the owl." He put down the shovel. "I've been dusting." He pointed to the walls. There, perched, poised, or nailed, were fixed rows upon rows of stuffed owls of varying widths and heights, beaks hooked downward, eyes (of glass) fixed straight ahead in attitudes of mute disdain at the indignity of their position. It was rapidly becoming clear to Charles that many of them were not completely cured.

"I have errands to run, Mister Bonamy. Will two hours suffice?"

"Splendid, splendid," rejoined the other as he polished an eyeball here, wiped a talon there.

"Two hours then, John." But his son did not reply as Charles Lemprière hurried to the door in anticipation of the fresher air beyond it. The lensgrinder turned to his subject.

"A legacy from the former occupant," explained Ichnabod to the young man.

John Lemprière was not listening. The glint of owlish eyes impinged dully upon him. Hundreds of them, paired and focused on his dim attempt to return their gaze, his mind adrift. Was this Cecrops's Hall writ small? They would call softly to each other, forming the delicate skein of wisdom's ligaments as the light faded in the room. The gaping wound, the birth. Ichnabod, a name without precedent . . . sprang fully armed.

"In here, John Lemprière!"

He walked slowly past the long counter to the small door at the back of the shop from which the voice had issued, and entered. The room was square, its walls formed of the granite which in the shop proper had been concealed behind wooden paneling. The ceiling was disproportionately high and contained a skylight, which threw a beam of light down onto a large mahogany chair. At the far end of the room was a large stove, a workbench, and several cupboards through which Ichnabod was now searching. The stove burned hotly.

"Sit on the chair." He did so, shifting uneasily in the unfamiliar surroundings. Pallas's antechamber to Hephaestus's forge, thought the sitter. What is he doing? The lensgrinder seemed to find whatever he searched for and advanced on his subject carrying a large tray.

"Hold this." And Lemprière's arms were effectively immobilized as he sat facing the stove and holding the tray of glass disks before him. "Now for the frames." Ichnabod loomed toward his subject holding a large wooden contraption.

Trapped in the chair, Lemprière felt flutters of panic in his stomach, and his bladder tightened. He had a strong desire to throw the tray to the floor and fend off the apparatus, which now seemed to have extended two large claws toward his face. Ichnabod fitted the bulky test-frames over his head and clicked the fastening shut.

"My own invention," he explained proudly. The frames formed a kind of cube encasing the irregular sphere of Lemprière's head. Singled out from the rest of his body, his skull felt acutely vulnerable in its wooden cage. He stared fixedly ahead, suppressing a strong urge to get up and run, wooden cage and all, for the street outside. The lensgrinder took no heed of the young man's anxiety. Focal length, dynamism, ease of accommodation: These were the subjects that concerned him as he dropped different lenses in front of the defective eyeballs.

The lens: a talisman for Ichnabod, who did not believe in such things. Had not Archimedes used one to fry the Roman force at Syracuse? And did not Ptolemy set one on the tower at Pharos wherein he saw the ships of his enemies, six hundred miles distant? The simple disk, its smooth surface tapering gently to the rim, unchanged in two millennia.

It had taken him many years to master the basic processes of lens manufacture. But the processes themselves reached back through the centuries. Oh yes, Newton may be the man with his *Opticks,* but he could never apply his own rules. The simple glass ball, the careful cutting into disks with the emril stone. A dunce might do that, but not the gluing on of the handle (Colophonia gave the smoothest join), the heating to the prescribed temperature, the pouring into the iron dish. And then began the long polishing. His upper arm ached at the memory. First with saldame, later with water of Depart and powder of Tripolis, the glass would begin to shed its coat of irregularities and the perfect lens within the brute hunk of glass would eventually emerge, its properties locked into its dimensions. He remembered the manufacture of each smooth disk as he dropped them into the slot before the boy's eyes. Some nights he would press one between his palms, until its slick cold yielded to the heat of his hands and he exchanged it for another.

For Lemprière, the world was not so much composed of lenses as ceaselessly dispersed by them. As fast as his eyes adjusted to the new world heralded by one pair, it was replaced by another trumpeting its claims, only to be banished in its turn. He would signal his approval or disapproval by saying "better" or "worse," as befitted each case. Ichnabod, after perhaps two dozen pairs had been tried, stopped. He looked down at the tray, mumbled, and seemed to make some brief calculations.

"John Lemprière," he announced in magisterial tones, "prepare to see."

Reaching down to the tray, he picked up one of the few remaining pairs. Lemprière heard them click against each other and then against the frames. The stove glowed a malevolent red. The lenses dropped noisily down. His knuckles whitened around the tray.

"Aagh! Get me out! Get me out!" The tray crashed to the floor. The lenses grasped the room and hurled it at the speed of light into the captive's face. He let loose a cry of fear. The lenses sucked his eyeballs through the frames, dashed them into the first elected object. The stove. He was in the flames. They were licking greedily at him. He wrestled with the wooden cage. The fire burned hot in his face; behind the flames two eyes caught his, a horrible, misshapen face, a twisted body, eyes black with ancient cruelties, the legs curling and unfurling at him, like serpents. "I see you, John Lemprière" hissed from each mouth. Erichthonius. Curling and unfurling, like snakes. Like flames. Just flames. Flames in a stove in a room. A room between Minerva's shrine and Vulcan's forge.

"Welcome to the visible world, John Lemprière."

On the floor between them lay the scattered lenses. They punctuated the gray flagstones like precious stones, gazing up mutely at the two men. Lemprière shivered and blinked. The stove was but a stove, the room but a room. And Ichnabod . . . Ichnabod was a man with a limp, a genius for glass, and too many owls. Lemprière could see.

• • •

Icy waters surged silently eastward beneath the waves, shooting their jets forward, blunting and falling back to be gathered by the tidal force behind. Waters charged with a blind purpose streamed from the unlit, stony basins of the ocean floor, stabbing through the placid sea ahead, feeling vague, coastal constrictions to either side before slamming against the stubborn peninsula at Cherbourg, scudding against its coast and slipping away into the channel.

Down from the slate-gray North Sea, channeled through the Dover Straits, raced the rival westward tides. They gathered force, swerved and fought their way through the eastward waters, gouging whorls in the sea's surface. Sucking currents were shot sideways from the force of the conflict. The mass of two seas met to slice one through the other, and in the midst of their battleground, registering the force of each blow and counterblow against its cliffs, stood a rock of granite. Twelve miles long and six miles wide, it surveyed the subsurface drama of current and crosscurrent, tidal ebb and flow, and seemed to stand firm against the treacherous waters. The waters might climb forty feet, the tides hauling up the coast, or rage against the cliffs to the north, but the red granite was old and hard. It broke through the turf in outcrops all over the island like scars from some elemental battle.

Hedgerows parceled out the land amiably, scarcely disturbing the green vista, which now and then would shade into drifts of purple heather or the darker green gloss of the ferns. On the southern hillsides, the grass was beginning to brown in patches under the late summer sun. Innumerable tracks and lanes crisscrossed the verdure like cracks in a fine glaze. Where roads met, a few cottages might cluster about the crossroads, sometimes a church, a new villa, or one of the older seignorial manors. The twelve parishes of the island, from Saint Brelade's to Saint Ouen's, Saint Clement's to his own Saint Martin's, traced their invisible boundaries on the island's face, and these were subdivided further into vingtaines. More ostentatious evidence of the old desire to mark the earth littered the island. The druids had left their menhirs and poquelayes, the Romans their houghes, although raised fortifications seemed superfluous on the inland sites where they were to be found. Around the coast, Martello towers, observation platforms, castles, and forts bespoke more recent fears of invasion from France, whose coast, not fifteen miles distant, was beginning to appear as the sun burnt the morning sea mist out of the air.

To Charles's right was Rozel windmill, where, in a few weeks, apples from the new orchards would be brought for pressing. Below him, the hill fell away in côtils, each carefully cut shelf overgrown with couch grass. The slope had not been worked for six or seven seasons now. On the far side of the hilltop, a flock of four-horned sheep started at some brief, private terror and wheeled en masse before stopping just as suddenly. He turned back to the scene before him. The scent of cider apples was blown in and away by the southerly breeze; each seventh wave was just audible from the bays at Bouley, Rozel, and Fliquet. The sound was carried and checked in the air, reaching him in sustained, sibilant whispers. Their dull repetition seemed to carry the ghost of a message that may once have been vital, but now spoke only of attrition and defeat.

Do not take comfort in our sound. Do not believe you can discover the least purpose in our action, they seemed to say. When your rock is worn flat as the ocean bed, do not imagine it marks our triumph. It marks nothing but the beginning of the same action elsewhere. We go on, we continue, that is all. The sea rippled and chopped around the island; its surface crawled like the skin of an immense beast, flexing and readying its muscles for violence. It brooked no dissent against its ancient murmur: To be is justification enough. And the man on the hill struggled with that maxim. His grandfather, clutching at his throat and crying out "Rochelle!" before his tongue thickened and the poison turned it blue. His father, who had left shore in an open boat and returned, face down, on the tide. Old anger, tempered hard with grief, had turned to revenge. And now it was alloyed with fear. The fight would continue a little while yet, just time enough to finish it. He would not see those he brought down, he did not even know their names, but the wheel only required a nudge now to bring them blinking into the light. The line of ancestral casualties arrayed itself at his back to urge him forward to the act. The long-kept secret had found them all. And will find me too, he thought. But not yet, not on this fine summer's morning, not on this island where my life has been spent. He looked down at the stream that raced through the shallow dale. Silvery black they had dammed it as boys, but to what purpose he could not remember. There were no fish in it. Beyond it the copse of elms and oaks where—he smiled at the memory— Marianne had led him fearlessly, stripped, and lain with him in the hard tufts of grass among the tree roots. To his left was the church where he had married her a fortnight later. And there, on the track between the two, was the offspring of that union cutting an eccentric path toward the same church.

. . .

The offspring seemed to be making repeated and unsuccessful efforts to scale the steep bank on the far side of the path. He would run at it, allowing the gathered momentum to drive him up its face to within a foot or two of its summit. He would hang there for perhaps a second, still, before thundering down to the track again. Zigzagging: an appropriate manner in which to approach one's god, thought Charles Lemprière as he watched the distant figure from his study window. The eyeglasses had been worth the outlay, though not an absolute insurance against mishap, he reflected as his son lost a foothold and sprawled chaotically in the road.

John Lemprière spat dust and gingerly picked himself up. No damage, good. Was that the second or third bell? Dust covered him from the waist down. He brushed vigorously and touched his spectacles. They had returned him at the ripe age of twenty-two to a second childhood. Running, jumping, making the steep climb down to the strand and throwing stones at the sea; he liked the ache in his muscles that told him his body was reawakening. He stopped and stretched, feeling the pleasurable tension crawl up his spine. Ahead of him, the church beckoned. Normally, his mother and father came, but they had stayed home this day. To discuss something, they had said. He marched on; the faint discords of the church band tuning up reached him as he drew nearer. Saint Martin's, already ancient at the time of William the Conqueror, extended its long nave out to catch all comers, its spire pointed up toward heaven. *Amor dei,* subjective and objective genitive, Quint's lesson, echoed in an obscure chamber of his memory. Whose love indeed? God's for me or mine for God? He breathed in the scents of apples and grass. The sky was blue without limit. Or mine for another? He savored the forbidden taste of the thought. "Another." Who might she be? An outlandish woman from beyond the pale of this world. A strange woman, an unfathomable woman. He would save her. He stopped at the lych-gate to let fat Mother Welles through. And worship her.

Lost in this random stew of thoughts, the young scholar allowed his favorite musings a silent parade before his inner eye. White, distressed limbs and golden tresses mingled with vague heroic deeds. Strange beasts slavered before his sword, turned their spit red. He dried the tears of ox-eyed women and broke the chains which bound them to the black rock. Their flowing skirts were so white against that adamant surface. . . . It went on and he did not see the carriage trundle slowly down the lane to

8

the church. Pebbles cracked and skeltered out from beneath its iron-banded wheels. A nostalgic regret was already forming in his mind as the pleasing thoughts fled from the noise. They left only their silhouettes, whose lines wavered before breaking and settling back into the scenery, which recomposed itself before the young man's gaze. The blue sky threw its light down onto the fields below.

The carriage wheels came to a slow halt, intruding more subtly into his daydream now, the two merging as John Lemprière watched the image of Aphrodite descended from ether to earth in the guise of Juliette Caster-leigh. The sunburnt Cyprian, eyes wide and fishing nets forgotten at the sight of the goddess's birth, had his counterpart in the young Lemprière. His gaze unreturned, he watched slack-jawed at the vision of Venus Epistrophia in a spume of cream linen placing a delicate foot on the cracked footplate of the Casterleigh carriage.

Twenty years out of date, the gilt on the rails shouting 1760 to anyone who could ascend the height to listen; this bothered Juliette Casterleigh not a whit. The importance of the carriage lay not in the discomfort its seats afforded, nor even the ample evidence of its increasingly frequent repairs (Jersey's thoroughfares being pitted with ruts and potholes), but in its relative position (foremost) among the muster of vehicles that assembled each Sunday mutely to affirm their owners' degrees of standing in a community that valued the testimony a pound well spent might buy.

"Good morning, Miss Casterleigh."

"Good morning, Pastor."

"Good morning, Miss Casterleigh, your father not gracing us today?"

"Good morning, Mister Carteret."

A nod to the farmers' wives, a tilt of the bonnet (and nothing more) to their sons. Intricate scales of greetings and good-days accompanied her passage to the most forward pew of the church, where she was lost to Lemprière's adoring gaze. Settled in her seat, she reflected on those behind her and resisted firmly, this week as every other, the impulse to turn and watch the slow files of worshipers as they made their way in. The accents of Jersey French reached her ears from the back of the church, mingled with snatches of English. The conversations of Saint Martin's parishioners were garbled together in the vaulted ceiling of the church.

Not so below. From the front pews, the protocols of island life sorted and cataloged the worshipers according to wealth and standing. Landowners shaded into tenant- and fee-farmers, who mingled with the cannier artisans. Behind them jostled the bulk of the congregation, farm and orchard hands, shepherds and vraikers who, along with their wives and children, were busily exchanging the choicer anecdotes from the preceding week. The church echoed with this bustling hum, from which Juliette was excluded. She sat on the front pew, a solitary figure.

And why should it be otherwise? she thought to herself. Because I am flesh and blood, no more or less than they? She pondered this. Yet they doff their caps and bonnets, their brats make clumsy curtsies and bows. What do they see? Take away my fine clothes, my coach, the manor and the acres which surround it. What would be left? A wretch fit only for the fields or the backstreets? Perhaps.

The last members of the assembly were taking their seats. The church settled toward hush. She remembered the day Lizzie Matts had insulted her in the street in Saint Helier. The slut had made a comment and her friends had laughed. Juliette had slapped her in the face without thought or hesitation. She had caught the girl's lip with her ring and it had bled a little. When she told Papa, he had laughed. And he reminded her of it when they had spoken some weeks later. "Remember this, my jewel," he had said, "shepherds may change, but sheep will always be sheep. The shepherd may be a lowly creature, scarcely better than his flock. But to the sheep he is a god, they are certain of it. And if one runs off, it is not because he does not believe in its god. Precisely the opposite, the sheep is pleading for the god to show his face, his power. We play to the pit, my love. . . . Remember that." She had laughed then, to please Papa. Later she had come to understand his words better. And so I strut before them, she thought. And I enjoy their envy.

Indeed there *was* envy; "new money," it was whispered, as if the slight edge of hostility in the island's deference to the man she called her father had no precedent in the serf's curse on his seignor, the serf's son on his heir. The Casterleigh thousands, obscure in origin to be sure, spoke as loud as any decayed dynasty's ailing fortunes. And where we end will scotch the lowliest beginnings, is that not true?

Is that not true? His cool hand on her white neck as he had planted that sentiment in her mind. Oh yes, it was true. His other hand showed her the spread of their lands on a map spread out on the hall table. His forefinger ran along contours and boundaries.

"They were ours for the taking, my Juliette, mine by force often enough. You have played your part in all this, played it to perfection. But now there are other parts for you to learn. Can you do that, I wonder?"

"Of course, Papa." Why should he ask?

His thumb massaged the nape of her neck, tenderly, and the frescoed ceiling hurtled into view as her head went back. Little cupids.

Lemprière's neck underwent more strenuous convulsions as he craned and angled from several rows back for a view past her bonnet. Aphrodite played her part to perfection, though, her head never turning more than a few degrees to either left or right. He had never seen anything or anyone quite so beautiful as Juliette Casterleigh in his whole life, and now, stranded in voyeuristic frustration, he felt already the pangs that he believed to be the pangs of love. After all, what was a goddess without her unacknowledged devotees? Indeed, he was not alone in these devotions, even if the fantasies concocted about Juliette by the sons of the wealthier farmers were alloyed with rather baser motives. The sermon dragged on; the Reverend Calveston's bald pate glistened with sweat as his favorite metaphors and parables issued from his lips.

"We are all foot soldiers for Jesus' army. . . . And sin, which is our inward foe. . . . For is that not just as it is in life?"

In keeping with his practice the last six weeks, he seemed to be directing the whole sermon at the Matts family. It was rumored that Lizzie Matts had punched him in the eye, but no one, as yet, knew why. Nobody had the nerve to ask the priest. Lizzie would not tell. It went on. Juliette's eyes never left the reverend's face. Lemprière wrestled half-heartedly with his inward foe. His neighbor's stomach growled in anticipation of lunch. The service ended.

"Move along there, John, move along." He wanted to stay, to watch her as she made her way out, but the hunger of Pierre Dumaresque and family would not wait. He moved along the pew and was carried down the aisle on the newly penitent tide.

"A true crapaud at last."

"Tell us about Ovid, Lemprière."

"Toadeye!"

The unwelcome tones of his ex-classmates greeted him as he emerged, blinking furiously, into the strong sunlight.

"Good morning, Wilfred. George." He tried to hide his timidity behind formality, but his tormentors were having none of it. Edging past them, he felt something about his ankles, stumbled, and fell headlong in the path. Wilfred Fiedler withdrew his outstretched boot. A moment later he withdrew too the grin that was threatening an affected peal of laughter.

"O brave Mister Fiedler!" Lemprière heard a girl's voice, but hard. The sarcasm wiped Wilfred's face blank.

"Heroic Mister Fiedler! To fight such mighty battles, Major Peirson would be green with envy. Allow me to wish you well in your forthcoming campaign against the bailiffs. Now, move along." And summarily dismissed, Wilfred Fiedler departed, pondering, among other matters, how Fiedler père was going to react to his offending the daughter of his principal creditor.

The dust on the churchpath tasted, if anything, slightly worse than that of the lane. Lemprière replaced his eyeglasses just in time to see his tormentors moving down the lane at a brisk trot. He began to gather himself together, and as he did so, a delicate white hand grasped his forearm and hauled him to his feet. For a moment she held him. He smelt scent, mingled with a faint tang of perspiration. Her cheeks glowed red still with her late annoyance, and her black eyes gazed concernedly into his. When she asked if he was fit to walk, he felt the slight wisp of her breath on his cheek. "Out of me way, you both. Come now." Fat

Mother Welles demanded passage and was not to be denied. Her imperious bulk was followed down the path by the slighter figure of his savior, "Take care, John Lemprière" cast carelessly over her departing shoulder. How did she know his name? He watched openmouthed and absently dusted his clothes as she stooped to enter her carriage. A sharp tone to the coachman, and they moved off. If Lemprière had not vigorously suppressed his strong desire to run after the carriage and peer into the shrine of the goddess, he would have seen Juliette Casterleigh leaning forward, elbows on knees, with an expression of studied contemplation on her face.

But he did not. He had imagined the goddess and she had come. He had fallen at her feet and she had elevated him. He had been beset by enemies and she had protected him. He was Paris faced with the outrage of Menelaus, the cuckold's horns tipped with bronze to gore him. The sweaty fear of pain, the dull throb of thickened blood in his temples, the strength-sapping wrench in the pit of his stomach, the smell of anticipated harm: and then Aphrodite with a cloak of sea mist. To wrap it round him, hide him and spirit him to safety, yes, he was hers for the taking. He walked on toward home, imagining the goddess furling him in cloud. It touched his skin with cool, electric fingers, stealing under the folds of his clothes, touching him. If he tried to cry out she would stop him, she would place her hand, which was nothing but the mist of thought and yet it was her hand . . . over his mouth. He would kiss that hand, being borne upward through the ether, safe in her close embrace.

Lost in these thoughts, he began the climb up the hill toward Rozel. Sandy-colored dust exploded out from his feet as he kicked aimlessly. His spindly legs stood out like a marionette's, and from a distance the reflected backlight from the track shaved them to pins. They danced, kicked, and sprang as Lemprière decided to run the last half mile home.

He was greeted at the door by his father.

"Good morning, John. Were we missed at church?"

"Father Calveston had his eye on the Matts girls. . . ."

"Ha! And you had an eye on Father Calveston. That leaves one eye for the road." His son's strenuous brushing had not been completely successful. "So at what was this surplus eye directed, I wonder? The Matts family too, perchance? Ha, ha! Come now, lunch awaits." This last was almost bellowed. His son was more than a little taken aback at this hearty badinage. Charles Lemprière's manner was normally more reserved. On entering, his mother's constant sniffing hinted broadly at the reason behind his father's dissembling jollity. What *had* they been discussing? The meal proceeded similarly. His mother sat in virtual silence while his father carved mutton, commented on the vegetables or the weather, joked and made small talk. The son did his best as his father, in the space of an hour, doubled the number of words he had spoken to him in the past year. But his mounting bafflement did not fail to discover the tension behind this charade of good humor.

The meal over, John Lemprière escaped to his room in some disarray. He picked a book at random from the small stack by the bed on which he had thrown himself and held it, his arm dangling over the side, like a talisman. Solid and cool to the touch, its compact weight obscurely reassured the young man. If he brought the book up and opened it, he would immediately find himself in a—what was it?—an elsewhere. Yes, an elsewhere that was here, that was also him. There for him at any moment, an anchorage of memories; a nice phrase. The book warmed in his hand and the moisture from his fingers smoothed its passage as it slid in leisurely fashion from his grasp to land with a thud upon the floor. And why had he not said that he had exchanged greetings with Juliette Casterleigh? Normally he would. Secrets bred secrets bred secrets; secret pleasures. She had saved him, perhaps, he groped hopefully, for a purpose? He dragged himself away from the tempting vistas to which this speculation might lead and fumbled on the floor for the book. He bent his arm round to display the title on the spine: *Sextus Propertius, Opera*. The Roman Callimachus. They all claimed that.

He remembered his first meeting with the poet. Not a meeting, a passing glance exchanged between countrymen on soil foreign to both. Quint's classroom entered his thoughts and revisited its tedium upon him. The dull monotone throbbed in his memory as he recalled the airless room and its malcontent inhabitants. Quint's views on the Ancients were eccentric and applied as dogma. Endless afternoons reciting grammatical rules by rote and learning passages of Latin prose had been the schoolmaster's stock-in-trade. He had resented the boy's precocious ability and derided his youthful taste for the lyric poets. In return, the boy had gleefully pointed out the most minor of Quint's mistakes and argued interminably against the merits of the prose writers whom Quint professed to favor, and in whose defense he might even have been said to wax lyrical. His exaltation of Tully, whose pompous, inflated rhetoric might run for pages unhindered by punctuation, knew no bounds. Tully was the "complete master of oratory," he contained "a compendium of figures that may dance for us if we construe them correctly," his "eloquence was unbounded." The young Lemprière had wondered when Mister Quint had had occasion to hear Mister Tully. In such a schema neither Lemprière nor Propertius had fared well. Propertius "was of some interest for his archaisms, but to be esteemed far below Tibullus," while Lemprière, master at the age of fourteen over any text Quint was likely to teach in the foreseeable future, was fast becoming an embarrassment. He had left school the following year to pursue the *Novi Poetae* on his own. The train of thought petered out and he lay there with his mind blank for a long time. Familiar sounds of domestic activity reached him vaguely from below. His room was very still, the only movement his arm swinging almost imperceptibly at the side of the bed, his hand still holding the book. Like a pendulum, counting nothing, and the hours passed empty-handed.

Outside, the sun was setting and the young man turned again to his book. He read idly as the vast red disk seeped out of sight. Flicking from page to page, scarcely conscious of the breaks between the end of one poem and the beginning of the next, he savored the lateness of the moment. A final sliver of red narrowed to the graying blue behind it and dusk fell. He turned the page.

Qui mirare meas tot in uno corpore formas,
accipe Vertumni signa paterna dei

The impossible choice. Lemprière matched verbs, subjects, and objects one to the next, arranging and revising, and relished the slow movement into clarity as he construed the lines.

Who marvels, no, whoever marvels, or supply a pronoun, more dramatic. . . . You who marvel at so many forms, shapes, better, in one body, a single body, accept the fatherly signs, no, ancestral signs of the god Vertumnus. Accept into your mind, learn. Yes, learn was right. Formae, corpus, a good tension for late Rome, the first city of deceits.

The gold grayed and turned leaden, the sky darkened. Clouds of insects swarmed in the dusk and fed hungrily on the soft necks of the cattle grazing under the trees. The fields were untended; lead turned to iron, turned to rust on the plow as the light decayed and released the forms of night. The single light of a cottage some two miles away weighed anchor and drifted in the gloom, trees shifted and merged with the sky behind. The fields rolled and rippled. He was sweating. The trench the stream had gouged for itself down the slope before the trees seemed to suck the sheets of turf into its maw. Learn what? The last light floated down to the fields on either side to be snatched by some tremendous undertow toward the long, thin mouth which snaked away into the dark, wavered, and now, his hands whitened around the bedframe, widened. Opened, a monstrous, formless mouth, like the victim of a hideous burial, the face decayed and interlaced with roots which writhed and tore through its surface, falling away in clods. The face was crumbling away, and beneath it a dull glint shone feebly. He tried to work his tongue, his throat was knotted and dry. The black slash of its mouth writhed, its lips splitting in tatters, peeling away until the bronze figure beneath began to emerge. It melted, then recomposed. It softened, then redefined. It formed, only to collapse. Its aspects shifted second by second, each complete metamorphosis being the herald for the next. But through it all the bronze eyes remained fixed and focused on the young man who breathed in quick, shallow gasps, chest tight, limbs rigid on the bed.

And the eyes too melted, after a fashion. For they cried. The shining drops gathered in the corners of his eyes and fell soundlessly to the earth below. Huge, sad eyes spoke soundlessly through the voided air that closed around them, of youth, courting Pomona through the orchards inland from the shores of Laurentum, winning her. Garlanded, handsome I was when the crown of plenty dangled from my fingers, and the songs sung of me, and how they were sung less, later not at all. . . . Of my silence! The black earth which reclaimed me, I would speak of it. . . . And yet the dark interment weighs heavy on my thoughts, too long in silence, too long. . . . And through his rambling melancholy the tears fell, until the darkness thickened around him. His eyes fell back into the forgetful, sad centuries of which they spoke, narrowing to points, to pinpricks, until they vanished mutely into the dark. The tears of an abandoned god, a last appeal before dark.

Lemprière jerked violently as every sinew in his body snapped out of tension. He was shaking. He drew his knees up and rocked on his heels. His breath came quickly and his neck ached. What have I witnessed? he wondered. It cannot be, it cannot. . . . Better that I am mad than it be true. He looked out of the window. The stream, trees, and fields looked much as they ever had. No trace remained of the vision he had witnessed. The god may have returned, may have risen and mourned his neglect, but no sign remained to betray the fact. And what of me? he thought then. It is I who read of him. Did I call him? But the other possibility hammered insistently in his skull, the thought that could not be faced for fear that it was true. I called him, I must have called him. He clasped his head in his hands. His temples pounded and a low groan gathered in his throat. Hammers in his head. He threw himself off his bed, ran to the window and, drawing breath, shouted into the dark,

"I called him!"

The darkness was blacker than he could ever remember. An absolute silence followed the falling off of his voice. But the sound within was still there, barely audible, there, like the drops of water which as a child he had seen falling from the glistening roof of the cave at Rozel Bay and which, given time, produced the squat stalagmites on the cave floor. One might catch a hundred, a thousand, a million of those drops, they would produce the stalagmite just the same, each tiny deposit adding its layer until it reached the roof. He turned from the window and walked back to his bed. Lying there, staring into nothing, he opened the gate in his mind.

"It is I." He spoke the words aloud and would have chuckled at how simple and how terrifying a statement he had just made. Somewhere within me, he thought, is a god who tears his face out of the ground, who has not walked the earth for two millennia and who walks outside my window. Then, he wondered, what else walks within me?

The room was silent for some time. A few splutters were heard, which gradually grew more frequent until they became recognizable as high-pitched giggles. Alone and in the dark, Lemprière laughed to himself without the least idea how or why he did so. The laughter rose and fell. Gaps of silence between the outbursts grew longer, until, exhausted at last, he fell into a deep and dreamless sleep. Outside the window the moon broke through the clouds and cast a bleaching light over the young man's face. His limbs twitched periodically as his body released its inner tensions; his face was white in the moonlight and calm. He slept on.

• • •

Father Calveston applying grease to his contraption, dammit, he hadn't wanted to be a priest anyway, a shepherd for wayward sheep. He snorted. Constant interruptions, cretinous old women asking if they'd go to hell for being rolled in the hay forty years previously, a miserly stipend. Every week the sermon, every other week another puking, screaming brat that would piss in the font while its cloddish parents trod mud down the aisle and pondered, "Should we call him Ezekiel?" when there were already four in the parish and four too many at that. He wasn't suited for the job, he had no vocation. They'd told him as much at Oxford. "Calveston," they'd said, "have you considered fully the fact that many are called but few are chosen?" Considered! Dammit, he'd thought of little else. Except he'd been sent, not called, and when the sender was his father he was destined for the Lord's service whether the Lord wanted him or not. On balance, he reflected, He probably did not, but what choice was there? Dear brother Michael had the land, and sold it with father's body still warm. He had the church. Dammit! He cursed aloud, not so much at brother Michael, conniving little spendthrift runt that he was, as at his own clumsiness—he had jammed his thumb in the complicated piece of machinery he was cleaning and it was proving hard to extricate. Aah! It came loose and he stood back to survey the object of his labors.

It stood about four feet tall, its cast-iron sides gleaming dully. It looked something like a waterpump except that the cylinder through which the water would have been drawn up was partially cut away. A complicated mechanism of meshes and cogs could be seen together with the end of a pistonlike object, which presumably extended the length of the cylinder to the handle. It was his own invention, the first he had seen through successfully from conception to existence. His chicken-plucking engine had been too ambitious a project. It had worked well as a chicken disemboweler, but a disemboweled chicken with feathers had proved a commodity without a market on Jersey. The haircutting engine too had had its problems. No wonder the Crewe boy had made such a noise. Still, the hair had grown back to cover the marks. But his latest and greatest invention was of a different order. Ouch! He pulled his thumb out of the mesh which had pinched it for the second time and sucked it ruefully. He would be a great Inventor, a Man of Science yet. If only his duties were not so time-consuming.

Thoughts of his flock did not soften his mood. Dammit, only this morning that priggish young ass had burst in demanding that he exorcise the field behind his house. Exorcise it! There hadn't been an exorcism on Jersey for two hundred years, and if John Lemprière wanted one he could damn well do it himself. The little twit, babbling on about ancient gods rising out of the ground and grinning or crying, one of the two. If the idiot wanted a pope, there was always Italy. That should have shut him up, but in the end he fobbed him off with one of those pamphlets *On the Right Guidance of the Rectal Soule* or somesuch. Old Eli kept printing the damn things and delivering them by the crateload. God might know why, but he didn't. He doubted if Eli did either, stupid old . . . But his machine awaited, there were more important things to occupy him than Eli's stupidity. It was high time to operate the engine.

He picked up one of the five potatoes which lay on his workbench, feeling its smooth, cold skin in the palm of his hand. Father Calveston braced himself and took a firm hold on the handle. An expression of pleasurable anticipation spread across his face, making him seem, for a moment, rather younger. His bald head shone gloriously as little beads of oily sweat percolated up through his skin to form a reflective sheen on its surface.

· · ·

Lemprière walked back from Calveston's cottage, and only occasionally did his thoughts stray into the forbidden areas of which he had spoken to the minister. The priest had seemed preoccupied when he had walked in, had seemed skeptical when asked for guidance, and scornful when Lemprière had brought himself finally to tell of what he had seen. He had not raised his expectations overmuch.

The sun shone down. On impulse he made a run at the venerable and ancient tree about which the lane ahead curved respectfully. Without stopping, he shinned up the trunk and swung himself into the cage of branches, where he sat and enjoyed the novel prospect the height afforded him. The baying of hounds could be heard faintly from some miles away, and the sun broke through the leaves in vivid flashes as the breeze rustled the canopy of leaves that shaded him. A long line of ants was making slow progress along the branch to his left. He perched there and watched them for some minutes. He had not thought of ants as tree dwellers. What determination was it that marshaled them in so orderly a file? He heard the sound of light footsteps below. Lemprière turning and angling himself to get a view. His hand reached out for a branch to steady himself. Alarums and calls to battle among the ants go unheeded by Lemprière. Fat white insect larvae crawling with ants are exposed briefly as Lemprière's hand takes hold of the rotted branch and it crumbles like paper beneath his touch.

The sun was suddenly very bright as Lemprière made an uncontrolled descent from the tree and landed heavily in the dust of the track. As he struggled to right himself, an unknown hand took firm hold of his collar and helped him to his feet.

"Your liking for the soil befits a farmer, not a scholar," said a familiar voice.

Stumbling and dusting at the same time, he brought his head up with a start at the sound of her words. Juliette smiled her sweetest smile. A strand of jet-black hair had escaped the clutches of her bonnet and lay across her cheek, dimpled. Lemprière was shaken and tongue-tied. How ridiculous he must seem to her, five years her elder at least and behaving like a truant. No wonder she wanted to laugh at him. But she smiled with, not at, him. He coughed and managed a smile in return.

"Good morning, Miss Casterleigh." That seemed acceptable. A silence followed. They looked at each other. He should try something else, a compliment.

"Your hair . . ." And he stopped. Anything he said about her hair would border on the scandalous, so black and thick. . . .

"Oh dear." She caught the loose strand and tucked it beneath her bonnet. "I would not have noticed," running her fingers over her ears, her head tilted back a little.

"No, no, I didn't mean to . . . I mean, it looked very nice, at least I think it was very . . ." It was all going terribly wrong. Perhaps he should feign madness and run. Madmen could make the most appalling indiscretions and be excused. But Aphrodite, with the experience of two and one millennia behind her, seemed to understand John Lemprière well enough.

"Your fall has saved me a journey," she announced brightly. "Father has a favor to beg of you. . . ." And Lemprière listened, as much to the sound of her voice as to the message, while Juliette explained that the Casterleigh library, which had been bought wholesale from a bankrupt estate on the mainland, had a very curious omission.

"Of the several thousand volumes . . ." She dropped the figure lightly but saw from the expression on his face that the hook had caught. Several thousands! An almost unimaginable figure in Lemprière's experience. "Of the several thousands of volumes," she continued, "there are none of those in whose study *you* have distinguished yourself, Doctor Lemprière."

"Not yet a doctor," Lemprière murmured.

"Among them all, the Ancient authors go unrepresented and Father believes this is a matter for concern, you would understand, and that you are the man to redress it." She talked on lightly. Her father would be grateful if Lemprière might advise on some suitable editions, he had heard that Lemprière was a scholar of great promise, his advice would be invaluable. He would be free to use the library whenever he desired. . . . Could he come next Thursday? Had it been a century hence in the East Indies, Lemprière would not have refused. He blushed at the compliments and fidgeted with his eyeglasses as Juliette said that they would expect him after lunch. She offered him her hand, bade him good-day, and walked off down the lane. Ten paces and she turned.

"John Lemprière!" she called after him. "Tell me, is Father Calveston home today?"

• • •

Five potatoes all in a row. How hungry would he be that night? Three-potato hungry or only two-potato hungry? Only two-potato hungry, he thought. Good, three for the engine. Humming to himself and moving purposefully in quick strides, the Reverend Calveston gave the first potato an affectionate squeeze and popped it into the cylinder.

"Pull down," he said aloud as he did so. In the bowels of the engine, a complicated system of pistons and cogs ground the meshes together in a blur of metal. They clattered against each other for a moment before biting into the fibrous potato flesh. At the bottom of the cylinder, a gleaming metal tray collected first a drip, then a large glutinous dollop of the thoroughly mashed potato. Father Calveston regarded his invention with pride: It was a potato masher. But now he was getting that tickly, prickly sensation all over his sensitive white skin. . . . Just the sight of the cool purée. He popped another potato into the cylinder and pulled down hard.

• • •

How foolish Lemprière had looked, all arms and legs in the middle of the road. Why was he up a tree? Papa had said he was very clever. Very learned, even if he did go red as a beet every time he looked at her. Red as a beet. But she liked that too. Papa would be angry if he knew that. He would guess anyway, she knew. Papa knew everything. He had known John Lemprière would fall for her head over heels, and there he was, falling and grinning and stammering every time she tossed her head.

"Ho, there!" She barely glanced up. The farmhand hailed her again. Silly man in a silly cocked hat. How could they do that, work in the fields all day? But everyone has to do things they don't like sometimes, she thought. Why else would I be going to talk to the egg-pate? There was the rectory cottage ahead. Her feet dragged her reluctantly onward.

• • •

Cool, squelchy, pulpy potato. White and gooey, gray and gluey. Handfuls and dollops and slimy slurps of splodgy, sweaty mashed potato. He loved to slap it on, a great generous handful of it. Father Calveston, naked. With potato. He writhes, he slithers, he oozes potato paroxysms of joy. A freezing wad on the nape of his neck trickles down his spine to disappear between quivering, globular buttocks. Slimy coatings all over his chest harden his nipples, tighten his navel. Gelatinous gloops slap and splat all over his nakedly naked body. *All* over his utterly naked body. How he loves it, so exciting and disgusting, how his sap rises to join with the potato sap, to join, as the doorknob turns, unseen on the far side of the room, to join, as the hinge creaks, alerting him too late, he turns, to join . . .

"Good morning, Father Calveston."

The Reverend Calveston, defrocked, froze. Slowly, and with a patience only possessed by the insentient, a modest dollop of mashed potato eased a passage down his stiffened penis and trickled off his right testicle to land with a muted slap on the floor. Its passing revealed the fiery, shiny red head of that erstwhile exulting (now wilting) implement which, within the taxonomy of reds currently offered by the Reverend Calveston's naked body, was only exceeded in radiance by the very top of his head. He blushed from the cranium down, as if his very humiliation threatened to burst the bounds of his body like a chick from its egg.

"Sit down, Father Calveston. Please." But the iron tone of that voice, sounding almost grotesque from one so young, belied any notion of this being a request.

"Now." She paused, leaned back against the workbench, and folded her arms. "Let us talk." He seemed to have no choice.

• • •

He was in love. There was no doubt as he made his way back up the lane toward his home. She had charmed him and he would follow her anywhere. He would range widely over what territory he might, pursuing her wishes over seas and oceans, through lands where strange and fierce peoples lived, the Hyrcanians, Sacians, and Parthians who twisted backward on their horses to fire arrows in retreat. He would follow the Nile until it split in seven and tinged the Middle Sea, scale the utmost peaks of the Alps from where he would view the monuments to his victories and beyond, the alien seas which lapped at the outermost isles of Britain that even now he heard faintly as their whispering reached him across the hospitable curves of the lush summer landscape which held him safe to its bosom while his imaginings sought out the most perilous corners of the earth in tribute to his Aphrodite. His Aphrodite. That thought was bittersweet, tainted with the accompanying thought that it would never be true. She had invited him to her house; that was something. The Lemprière household came into view. He would tell his mother of the invitation first.

The front door, in fact every door, was open. His mother was airing the corners, as she put it.

"I met Juliette Casterleigh in the lane today."

"Yes, John?" She walked past him carrying a large spider by one leg and threw it out the door.

"We talked of books."

Marianne Lemprière squashed a woodlouse which was attempting an entrance over the windowsill.

"Her father wants help in his library." Marianne caught another spider, stamped on an ant, and smote a small, brown beetle with an edition of Menander that had been lying on the table.

"What exactly is the request?"

She turned from her insecticidal labors for a moment and smiled at him. Her son, she admitted to herself, was an odd child. She loved him very much.

He smiled back and explained to her about the library and his vital role in its completion. She pretended reluctance, as much for the pleasure of hearing her son cajole her into acceptance as any real misgivings. But he had already carried the day. A stray thought struck her.

"Why does Mister Quint not do it?" she asked, suddenly remembering her son's former teacher. "After all, he is engaged by the Casterleighs now, is he not?"

Her son looked up.

"Of course you should go," she said. "But you must ask your father, John."

Charles Lemprière, upstairs in his study, surrounded by papers of every description, heard all. He wrote quickly on the sheet lying before him: "With regard to your letter, and your objections to my assertion that . . ." He paused, then crossed out the last clause and wrote, "I beg to differ. A vessel of such a tonnage might indeed put in at a port as I describe. Lorient perhaps, or Nantes, Rochelle, or even another. Might charts be procured? Tonnage against harbor drafts may well confirm Philips's account. . . ." He stopped again. Captain Guardian, his correspondent, did not believe in Philips.

It was Philips who had requested the meeting. Facing each other over a table at the dingy inn in Saint Helier, Philips had spoken of a ship. He knew neither its name nor its purpose. According to Philips (and this was a phrase Charles would have frequent recourse to in the years which followed), the ship made a twice-yearly voyage up the western coast of France to a port where her cargo was unloaded; on her return voyage south she rode high in the water. Philips had introduced himself as a marine surveyor. He was a young man with a clever face, dressed in black. He spoke with a peculiar intensity of this ship and offered two peculiar details. First, she was said to displace above four hundred tons. A large ship then, too large for the coastal trade. And second, her design: for she was an Indiaman. A Company ship.

Philips told his story with compelling candor. But what business had a Company ship putting in at a French port? Their meeting had lasted less than an hour. John, barely six at the time, sat in solemn silence throughout. His own excitement had mounted. He listened and nodded. The meeting concluded, he had returned to his study and searched through the very papers that faced him now. He had found the account he sought, written in his father's hand. "I have found the ship," his father had written. "She sails by the Pillars of Hercules and north, up the coast of France to a port I must discover." But he had never found the port. Within the year he was dead, drowned in calm seas off the coast of Jersey. And Charles Lemprière had not seen Philips since that day at the inn.

He had taken up the search for the vessel, drawing in correspondents the length and breadth of the mainland. Ebenezer Guardian was only the first, but Eben suspected this Philips. It was as if he had been brought into existence only to fire Charles's curiosity and, that task accomplished, had vanished into thin air.

Still the search went on, and though this "ship" was still a phantom, no more than a handful of unrelated facts, there had been other facts since then, incidental discoveries, enough to draw him on. Somewhere in the morass of receipts, bills, bonds, affidavits, and orders of acquisition which lay strewn about the room, there was a pattern. Somewhere within the pages of handwritten accounts, diaries, letters, and notes ran a thread. But he could not find it. A single memorandum, a scrawl on a dog-eared endpaper might supply the link, the key to the pattern. It was here, buried here somewhere. Perhaps he had already seen it and missed its significance.

The voices in the kitchen below were silent. He looked over his half-completed letter and thought of the ship. Why could his son not plug this gap instead of Casterleigh's. No, no, he checked the thought, remembering his wife's angry tears of Sunday last. Let the boy get on, let him follow his own path.

Charles Lemprière reached for a stack of papers on the far side of the desk. Keep him away, he thought. Keep him away from all of it.

Papa would be pleased with her. Papa would kiss her and compliment her. She was his jewel. He needed her as nobody else. Papa loved her. Clever Papa. Poor, stupid Father Calveston. How funny he had looked, especially when the potato had started to dry, all those little cracks. How he had cringed to her! She made him play a game. He had to crawl and fetch her handkerchief whenever she dropped it. He said "sorry" so much, she told him to be quiet in the end. He told her everything she asked. He seemed so eager to talk, to please her. Even when he blubbered he went on and on about things, things that she knew Papa would want to hear. She would tell him how foul and filthy Father Calveston was, for it was surely true, but not about her feelings when he picked her hand-kerchief up. She would not tell Papa about that. She would not anger him. Father Calveston had had those feelings too; when she left his thing had gone up again. She would tell Papa about that. Yes, she thought, as she climbed the stairs.

Facing east, the window threw a slanted lattice of shadows across the floor and over the brilliant white wall behind. A frame for the figure which moved into that light and threw its image on that wall. Arms raised and braced against the folding shutters, its body broadened in girth by the angle of the light, the figure looked like a primitive man turned to stone. Slight movements shook its upper arms and shoulders as if pitting its strength against the solid wooden frame: a slow testing of familiar thoughts, as rope is tested and paid out foot by foot. A coarse, rough braid of thought. And on the day the floor gives way beneath, you may hang by it for your very life. How firm are the most trusted foundations, and what are the things which must be done to protect them? These were slow, visceral questions, asked in the flexing of the arms, the straining of the shoulders. The time had come to answer those questions, to provide the answers. Not as palliatives to some mood of inquiry, but as tablets of marble: answers that would eradicate the very possibility of such questions being asked again. Never asked again. Behind the house, the pack was barking and wailing. Why had they not been fed? Casterleigh turned from the window in some annoyance, just as Juliette burst into the room.

"Papa! Papa!" She was laughing and out of breath. "Sit down, Papa, let me tell you of my day." His annoyance rose to anger at her intrusion.

He turned as she ran to him holding her skirts.

"Silence!" he barked.

Instantly, she was quiet, her face blank. He looked at her, saw the dependable fear in her eyes. He was soothed. He rested against the desk, then spoke again.

"Tell me of the boy," he said.

Summer was announcing its end in the sky, sending small, dark clouds over Jersey. Compacted and black with rain, they looked unnatural against the deep, continuing blue behind. A brisk southwester was whipping the tops of the taller grasses. The clouds passed quickly and silently overhead, their shadows racing across fields, lanes, and houses. Despite the sun's intermittent appearances and the strong breeze, morning dew still clung to the stems of the grass through which he tramped. The path was not walked often and had become overgrown. His shoes were wet through, yet he hardly noticed this. He came to the stile, climbed it, and made his way up the lane toward the Casterleighs' home.

The house stood in open lawns, but two screens of trees, staggered at angles to each other, concealed it from casual view. Lemprière rounded the second line of trees and came upon his first sight of Casterleigh's country house. Only half a century old, its plum-red bricks had withstood the corrosive effects of the sea air well. The color stood out violently from the gentler greens of the surrounding lawns and made the house seem larger than it was. Even so, it must be thirty or forty yards across, he estimated. The four angles were rounded and set with bay windows, giving the edifice the look of an oval. All the many large windows were set with scarlet-gauged bricks, and pilasters ran the height of the building between them, ending in elaborately carved stone capitals which, in their turn, supported an entablature extending, so far as he could tell, all about the building. Two of the pilasters rose higher than the others to define an attic story on the center of the roof, and on their tops stood two intricately carved stone figures. But even with his eyeglasses he was unable to distinguish their exact features. Two stone staircases ran up in parallel to meet on a balcony in front of the main entrance, the doors of which now flew open as if pulled violently from within.

"Enter, John Lemprière, your doom awaits!"

Intoned in mock solemnity, the words betrayed Juliette's presence in the cool shade of the entrance hall within. He made his way up the staircase to his left. Juliette advanced to greet him, smiling, as his eyes adjusted slowly to the dimmer light in the entrance hall. On the ceiling, chubby cupids aimed playful arrows at each other.

"Come, Papa wishes to see you." The look of alarm on his face prompted her. "Don't fret. He only wants to thank you."

In his pocket was a list of ancient authors he had compiled two days previously. He clutched it like a charm. Juliette chattered over her shoulder as she led him through the house. Her voice lilted and Lemprière fancied he heard a cadence beneath her words not truly belonging on Jersey. French perhaps. They passed through an antechamber to the drawing room beyond it.

"Papa, Doctor John Lemprière has arrived to set our world to rights." And with that introduction, she left him alone with the Viscount.

Casterleigh stood over the writing desk at the far end of the room. Even in the frock coat the man was wearing, Lemprière noticed the powerful shoulders, the thickness of his arms. He gave an impression of strength only barely held in check by his surroundings. When he turned to greet his guest there was a quick, strong control to his movement which was echoed in the lines of his face. His graying hair was swept back over his head, and his eyes, fixed on whatever object they chose, seemed not to blink. A large Roman nose gave him a hawkish appearance.

"Thank you for coming to our aid, Mister Lemprière. It is quite fortuitous that an island of Jersey's size should hold the man for the task." He toyed with a paper knife on the desk. "I have given instructions to Mister Quint, with whom, I believe, you are formerly acquainted?" Lemprière nodded. The Viscount stared him squarely in the face. Lemprière was beginning to feel he was being scrutinized more thoroughly than the situation demanded. "To work then. Until later, Mister Lemprière." He extended a large hand.

"Yes," replied Lemprière. His hand was gripped, then released. The Viscount watched as a maid appeared and conducted him through a door in the wall adjoining that through which he had entered. They crossed a corridor, then paused at a second door. The maid knocked and, hearing no reply, ushered Lemprière into the room which housed the library.

"Thank you," he murmured as she left him. The door clicked softly shut.

The shelves were stacked from floor to ceiling. The highest, six or eight feet out of reach, were served by a ladder mounted on castors which ran in brass tracks set into the floor. A long table of polished walnut ran almost the length of the room to a large window which admitted a pale light. At the other end of the table, a mahogany long-case clock softly ticked away the seconds. The air was heavy with a dry, musty odor. Essence of books, Lemprière breathed.

He looked around the room and his eyes widened. Moroccan leather bindings of red, blue, and olive, elaborately tooled and inscribed in gold and silver. Enameled cloisonné bindings from Germany, pointillé bindings from France, perhaps even the work of the Gascon, he speculated, before the gleam of parcel gilt silver caught his eye, the hand of Gentile? The collector of this library was a rival to Grolier. Juliette had given the impression that the collection was the rag-ends of a country seat fallen on hard times. He was unprepared for a latter-day Alexandria.

He stayed stock-still, his back to the window while the silent rows of books regarded him from their shelves. He closed his eyes and imagined he heard them murmuring. A deep, low babel of accents and languages, merging, indistinct. And, he opened his eyes wide, he *did* hear them. He heard their voices! But his amazement was short-lived as the explanation for this phenomenon walked into the room in the shape of Juliette and, a second later, Mister Orbilius Quint.

Gray-haired, stooping slightly Quint advanced stiffly across the room, his movements oddly birdlike. Juliette sat herself unceremoniously on the edge of the table.

"Well, well, if my pupil hasn't returned to aid me in my labors." His voice grated on Lemprière's ears.

"Good, good, shall we work, hmm? Or are we to stand idle and wait for the Mongol hordes? Come now, John. . . ."

Orbilius Quint was rapidly easing himself into the role of magister, but his former pupil was not going to submit to an authority which had irked him ten years ago and merely irritated him now. No, my dear Quint, he thought, I'll not be your amanuensis, this is my arena, the library, it is you who will pass under the yoke this time. But aloud, he said only that he hadn't expected to see Mister Quint, that he would welcome his help (which had not, in truth, been offered), and of course the sooner they began the better. They both busied themselves preparing pens, paper, and blotters, and it was Lemprière who, having readied his implements, took the initiative.

"Let us begin at the beginning," he announced, "with Homer."

"The question, I think, is of the edition rather than his inclusion, hmm?" countered Quint.

"The best edition being of course—"

"That of Heyne," Quint capped his sentence.

"No, that of Eustathius of Thessalonica is without doubt the best. But, being almost completely unavailable, Heyne will do in its stead."

Honors were shared on a roughly equal basis, and they proceeded to Hesiod, where Lemprière argued successfully for Parma's edition, published the previous year, and won his cause chiefly by the fact that Quint had not heard of it. Juliette, without the least understanding of the varying merits of the Ascraean Bard's editors, understood well enough the varying merits of their advocates. She fanned the flames of their rivalry with exclamations of support or caution as they jousted over abstruse points of grammar, corrupted fragments, and the finer distinctions of classical paleography. Their pages were littered with the corpuses of dead authors and the air grew thick with disputed emendations.

Lemprière fought hard for Oppian on fish. Quint conceded the *Halieuticon,* but was adamant on the *Cynegeticon.* Quint insisted on quoting twenty lines of Bacchylidês.

"Bravo!" exclaimed Juliette as he finished. Lemprière responded with six possible construals of a line from Anáxilas and drew a similar commendation. Each maintained a rigid politeness with regard to the other, but both knew that this was what they did best, this in a sense was what they were. Their catalyst tossed her head and slapped the table with her hands as the battle raged from Athens to Rome. In vain did Quint try to quell her enthusiasm; she drove them on, perched there at the end of the table. Lemprière contended that Caesar had no place in the literary pantheon.

"Either they were notes or he understood not the first principles of grammar," he argued impatiently. Quint was familiar with that line of thought but would not be drawn.

"He justifies his place as a strategist," he declared flatly.

"And the *Aeneid* as a travel guide," rejoined the younger man, exposing the argument.

"Ah, but not, not the same thing at all, you see. . . ."

But Lemprière was gaining the upper hand. Cato's *De Re Rustica* provoked a tussle, Quint favoring Ausonius Pompona's edition, Lemprière the more modern one by Gesner. Lemprière eventually gave way, but stood firm on half a dozen more. His thoughts had never been so clear, his arguments so incisive. He quoted long passages with ease, halting only to explain a textual crux here, a corrupt reading there. All was clear, and as he moved toward proving this point or discrediting that, he kept the old man in sight, the real object, the target of his endeavors. Juliette now was openly favoring his advances. It spurred him on.

The light was fading outside when they arrived at Sextus Propertius. Quint was sweating while his adversary wore a half-concealed smile, as if savoring a private joke.

"The edition of Santenus, I have heard, is excellent. Concise, learned—"

"I think not." Lemprière cut him off.

"That of Barthius then—"

"No, Propertius is unworthy of inclusion."

And Quint found himself in the strange position of defending a poet he detested against the charges of one whom he knew to be his passionate advocate. But Lemprière would not be swayed: The poems were lascivious, colloquial, ungrammatical, and filled with clumsy archaisms.

". . . and if we love him for his learning we may as well be satisfied with Ovid," he finished dismissively. Quint was tempted to agree with all these charges, but committed to the opposing view, he argued fiercely against each. Still, Lemprière would not be persuaded. Juliette was growing clamorous.

"Unless," the young man conceded, "he be represented by his fifth book alone, for the first four seem quite inadmissable."

Quint jumped at the compromise.

"Quite, quite, the fifth book, yes, I quite . . ." tumbling the words out in flustered agreement. Lemprière held back for a moment, then leaned forward at his former teacher.

"There is no fifth book."

He dropped the fact like a stone into a calm pool which swallows it and sucks it down out of sight, leaving only ripples that lap gently toward the bank and fall back in silence before reaching it. The room was instantly very still.

"It is late, I must go," muttered the old man. Without looking at either of them, he turned to make his way out. It was only as he was closing the door that Lemprière saw the humiliation on his face. And in that instant he was sorry. Sorry, with a deep regret for what he had done and confirmed in the certainty that he was wrong. The door closed and, for a moment, only the soft ticking of the clock could be heard in the library. But Juliette did not think he was wrong. No, Juliette did not think he was wrong at all. She ran to him as he hung his head. She placed her cool palm against his cheek and, for the barest fraction of a second, touched her lips to it.

"Bravo, my warrior."

Her hot whisper in his ear.

• • •

My thanks to you, Mister Lemprière, and this token of my satisfaction at your labors. Between us we will keep the booksellers of England in pocket for a decade.

The note was signed only with a "C." For Casterleigh. He turned the book over in his hands. It was beautiful. "Publius Ovidius Naso *Metamorphoses*" stenciled in silver on the black calfskin. He opened it at random:

> *Rumor in ambiguo est; aliis violentior aequo*
> *Visa dea est. . . .*

Four days had passed since he had emerged the victor from the library. Four days in which he had thought of little but the brush of lips against his cheek. He had come over absentminded again, but happier, his mother thought. The rustle of papers from his father's study had been unceasing, the level of activity rising and falling all hours of the day and night. Normally, his son would have taken this activity as an object for intense study, another clue to the enigma his father presented, but for now he was absorbed in his own thoughts. Thoughts of the girl in the house across the valley, thoughts that were more like devotions, devotions that were more like love. Like love, yet somehow he was held back from that. When he had looked into her eyes, that first time, outside the church, he had seen the image of all that was desirable, all that he *might* love. But he saw no farther. Beyond those deep black eyes, he did not know. It baffled and inflamed him. An appropriate gift, he thought.

Lydian women, maidens from Thebes and Haemonia changing into trees, birds, and streams in their efforts to evade the gnarled hands that grasped at their ankles. He turned the pages without method, the familiar stories of Ceix and Alcyone, Jupiter and Europa, and the revenge of Althaea trod lightly through his thoughts. But the book itself was strange. The text, so far as he could see, was free from errors, yet no editor was credited. There was no date, nor any printer's mark to indicate its provenance. The only clue was an oddity in itself. In the middle of the frontispiece a circle was printed, obviously a symbol of some sort, but the imprint was poor, the circle was cracked on one side. In most editions this would not have detained his eye for a second. Fouled type was common enough. But here the type was uniformly excellent, every cusp and point perfectly formed. Such an obvious error, surely it would have been spotted by the printer. . . . It puzzled him. But he did not let this mar the pleasure he took in leafing through its pages. Almost every tale was illustrated. Small lithographs interspersed through the text; they complemented the fine Roman type well enough but did not hold his attention. Until he came to the legend of Actaeon and Diana.

This one was different. It occupied a whole page, contained far more detail than the others, and looked as though the artist had made only a halfhearted attempt to ape the style of the others. He noted that the page numbers did not account for it. The artist had obviously thought long and hard on the folly of Actaeon. Poor Actaeon, condemned by his own ill luck to witness the fierce chastity of Diana in her nakedness. She has just been surprised in the pool, her bow is unstrung. But this does not save Actaeon: His head is already a stag's head and his own dogs are clawing at his legs and rib cage. One arm extended for support from the tree behind him, the other raised in futile supplication to the heavens, he bellows painfully with his stag's head; to no avail. Diana seems calm, her soft arms, adorned only by leather bracelets set with turquoise, hold the bow out as if to show it to some hidden, but permitted, onlooker. One breast is exposed. An avenue of trees extends a perspective into the background of the picture, and in the shady tones and halftones a figure that could be a man on horseback surveys the scene. The picture gripped the young man. He did not know why. Actaeon's fate had held little interest for him before. But now he pored over the tale, half consciously looking for clues as to why it should fascinate him. But all he found was what he had always found: Ovid's rather leaden sense of irony, a strange cohabitation of beauty and violence in the descriptions, and an abstracted kind of compassion for Cadmus's grandson laid low by *crimen fortunae*. Whether Actaeon deserved his gruesome fate or not was a hackneyed debate in the classical world. He remembered he had argued it through with Quint once, and at the end they had changed sides and argued it in reverse. That was a happy memory and he felt suddenly regretful again at his triumph over the old man. Yet Juliette had sweetened him and more. She kissed me, he thought to himself, then turned back to the outrage of Diana at Actaeon's prying eyes.

. . .

There was no key. Not here at any rate. And not yet. . . . Charles Lemprière paused in his labors. Time was not on his side. The path had come to an end with the destination still out of sight. He was close, he knew that much, close enough perhaps. Perhaps he would stir the waters even if he did not flush them out, or maybe they would emerge of their own accord? He did not smile at this thought. He would be bait for creatures of which he knew nothing but that they waited for him in the dark spaces where he could not see. But was it time to entice them into the light . . . or a time to die? He feigned annoyance with himself at the melodrama of this thought. But somewhere within him lurked the knowledge that it might only be the truth. It waited for him to uncover it and he dodged it. When would he be ready for that knowledge? When is anyone? he thought. The breeze through the open window lifted the corners of the papers piled in disarray on the desk before him. From time to time one would float gently down to the floor. There were quite a number there now. How long have I been here? They would know from Chadwick the solicitor by now. He must assume so. . . . The rest was an easy guess. He wished his own were so. It was late, the stars gleamed down on him from the summer night sky. Somewhere among those points of light was an order; somewhere, said the theologians, was the shape which explained them all. And perhaps I will find it, he thought.

. . .

"This may be the last fine day of summer," Marianne Lemprière greeted her husband and son the next morning.

"It may, Marianne, it may indeed," replied her husband through a mouthful of egg. Her son nodded. The two men had the same thought at the same time.

"No, Marianne. It's simply not necessary."

"The house has never looked, never looked—"

"More palatable," Charles improvised an ending to his son's sentence. Marianne Lemprière waited for silence.

"The last day of summer is the day the house is cleaned for winter," she announced, smiling as their faces dropped.

"And I do *not* want the two of you under my feet. You've finished your breakfast, John? Good. Charles?" He handed her the plate. "I don't want to see either of you until five at the earliest. And then I want to see you both." She laughed as she pushed them through the door.

"Five o'clock!" she shouted after them as the door slammed.

Outside, they looked awkwardly at each other. Within their joking protests at their expulsion from the house lay a rare vein of intimacy which, stripped of its humorous camouflage, now embarrassed them both. No matter. They had shared a joke as any father and son might do. The son grinned.

"I think I might take a walk to Saint Lawrence's," he said.

"And I to see Jake Stokes," rejoined his father. They both smiled; these were their habitual refuges in times of Marianne's cleaning crises. The sound of pots and pans being marshaled for the day's activities arose from within. The house sounded like a smithy and Marianne would, they knew, soon emerge for water.

"Until tonight then, John."

"Farewell, Father." And with this they parted company.

Across the intervening fields of Saint Martin's, a matter of two, perhaps three miles away, Viscount Casterleigh led his horse around to the kennels by its bridle. The animal snorted and tossed its head, unnerved by the sudden baying and barking. His face was set, determination mixed with the first trace of excitement. The plan had taken shape when the solicitor had come to them. At some time, all of them, even Jaques, had known it would come again to this. It always had. Always would.

Where was the girl? Already the dogs were clawing to be loosed, sensing the off. He lifted the latch and they spilled out into the yard, scrambling over one another in an ill-tempered melee of tails and legs, snapping at one another's ears, brief, vicious skirmishes taking place as each fought for its place in the hierarchy of the pack. He mounted and the dogs became more frantic, milling about in expectation of the chase. Where was the damned girl? He called her, his anger rising, as she came at a run around the corner. She would have to take her place first. There must be no delays.

"Get up!" he ordered her as she waited, apprehensive and costumed for the piece.

The dogs had grown no quieter. Heavily built animals. He felt the horse steady itself under the girl's slight weight. Her hands closed about his waist. She would play her part as instructed, even unknowing. He smiled to himself at the irony. The manufacture of the scene might not be his, he might even resent his being cast within it, but the part itself, that was something to savor. Suddenly his thoughts closed in on this, gripping hard on what he was about to do. The horse, its riders, and the eager pack all wheeled about, readied themselves for a second, then surged out the gate for the fence and the fields beyond. The dogs fanned out ahead, wanting the kill.

The son and the father had parted, Charles taking the lane for Saint

Martin's church, his son cutting across the field to the cliff tops which rose around Bouley Bay. Once the church was reached, Charles too took to the fields, following the hedgerows eastward toward La Vallée and the house of Jake Stokes at Blanche Pierre which was his goal. Jake would be expecting him. He knew as well as Charles that Marianne's housewifely campaigns were conducted according to a rigid regime. And it was becoming more and more obvious, as he strode along through the fields, that this was indeed the last fine day of summer.

The sun had risen high, and the still air held the morning heat. To the southeast he saw a lowering, black bank of cloud that seemed to thicken and darken as he watched. Jake would see it too and guess at Marianne's reaction. The thought of his wife suddenly stabbed at him. She had looked so pretty, holding back her smiles in pretend sternness. So desirable, and it occurred to him that they had not lain together for weeks. How many weeks? He had forgotten, and the impulse gripped him to turn back then and there. To turn back and throw open the door of their house and kiss her hand and say that he was a brute to neglect her so. And she would laugh and say, as once she had, that she had a hankering for brutes and lead him upstairs by the hand.

But Marianne was busy and would not welcome intrusion. He knew that, and walked on. Birds sang in the hedgerows. He thought he saw a magpie and heard the baying of dogs in the distance. He loved his wife. He hoped there would be time to make up for his indifference, for she must see it as that, he thought. The turf felt unyielding beneath his feet, dried out by the summer sun. Cracks had appeared in the fields on higher ground, worrying some of the farmers. "The soil's giving up its ghost," they said, without believing it. He caught the sounds of the dogs again. Casterleigh's curs, he thought to himself. The Lord knew why he ran them on Jersey. There was little enough to hunt.

He took a random path through the fields, following a general direction rather than any particular route, and so perhaps it was an unlucky lie of the hedgerows which substituted for the normal southward bias of his direction a northward one. Or perhaps he simply lost his way. But what is certain is that whenever he veered south he heard the sound of Casterleigh's hounds. At least, he assumed they were Casterleigh's. He never actually saw them. He did not like dogs, but his half-conscious efforts to skirt around the pack only resulted in his emerging some distance to the north of Quetivel Mill, when he would normally expect to be half a mile from Les Chasses. He was three or four miles from there. Damned animals. But it was his own timidity which vexed him most. He resolved to cut straight down into the Saint Lawrence Valley and follow the stream down to Blanche Pierre which lay to the south.

The pack quickened. Through Champs Clairs, cutting the Chapel Road to Handois, circling and moving down to Quetivel and the valley, their trail led across scrub and pasture, over hedges and ditches, walls and fences, meadows and fallow fields, through undergrowth turning to woodland until the roots reared up to trip the dogs as they made their way down a steep incline. The man on horseback picked a more deliberate path, guiding the horse down to the bushes he knew lay below. The dogs panted and their tongues hung out. They no longer barked.

The steep sides of the valley were composed of dark earth which the canopies of trees had not prevented from drying out. It crumbled away beneath Charles's feet as he half ran, half slid down the slope. He was in little danger of falling. The trees threw up elbows of thick, gnarled roots which served as handholds for his descent. As the slope began to level out, the trees thinned and thick brambles took their place. Charles knew their supple, barbed stems from berry-picking outings when a boy. No one had picked berries here, though. They had shriveled to tight, brown buds on the branch. He picked his way carefully around the dense bushes until he found, a little to his surprise, a viable path. It must have been cut recently, he thought. By whom? He made his way through, unsnagging the thorns from his clothing as he went. The sound of running or falling water reached his ears, but a patch of tall ferns blocked any view of it. He pushed them aside and strode through. It *had* been falling water, but the sight that met his eyes then dropped him to his knees as surely as if his hamstrings had been snapped. His heart pumped a thick pulse through his body.

"Good Christ," he exclaimed at the scene before him.

About now, yes, thought the man on horseback. His mind was very clear. And the boy too. Soon. He gathered the dogs as they reached the bank of the stream. They knew the object of their pursuit was close. He held them, waiting, tracing in his mind the path the boy would have taken, gauging distance and terrain against time. The sun blazed down on him. Soon, he calculated, the boy would come to the place marked out for him and find his own part in the scene. Then the need to finish it rose irresistibly. He rallied the hunting pack and aimed his horse upstream. Now.

John Lemprière had dawdled along the cliff tops of Bouley Bay as far as Vicard Point before heading inland to Cambrai, then west to the Mont Mado quarries. From there he had trod southward, past the Wesleyan Chapel and into Saint Lawrence Valley. Warm sunlight sparkled through the leaves above and dappled the ground around him. With his eyeglasses he had little fear of the slope, and in any case the west side of the valley was less steep than that which faced it. He walked along, taking his bearings from the sound of the stream which flowed, out of sight, below and to his left.

He loved this valley. Undisturbed by human habitation, it might be anywhere in time; a place where ancient figures might run unchecked, might be seen fleetingly, the glint from a headpiece, a quick movement on the very edge of his vision. His face ached from having spent the night pressed against the book that Casterleigh had sent him. Twice in the night he had jerked his head out of sleep in a dreamed panic that the characters had shifted beneath his eyelids. Twice he had fallen back into sleep, reassured. But the memory of the huge face with its tears of molten bronze still pursued him. And in Ichnabod's shop too, he thought to himself. He moved on, toward his most favored place in the valley, the waterfall, where the quick stream took a drop and widened to a shallow pool before narrowing again and running on down the valley to Blanche Pierre. Somewhere he had visited at other times to do nothing but sit and listen to the water.

He heard its light roar long before he saw it, and attuned his ears to the sound as though it were a beacon. But as he made his way down at an angle to the slope, he heard a short cry followed by a loud splash. Someone had found his pool. Someone was *in* his pool! He strode forward angrily, rounded a copice of trees, and stopped dead in his tracks at the sight of Juliette Casterleigh, naked beneath the waterfall.

He might have run forward then. He might have run forward and knelt and kissed where the waterfall kissed her now. On her stomach and breasts, on her lips. But it was all he could do to breathe. Desire dried his tongue, and he felt every muscle in his stomach tighten. Shining, silvery water glistened on her skin. She threw back her long black hair, and glittering drops of water rained out in an arc. Her cupped hands sluiced water up her legs, over her stomach, and onto her breasts whose nipples, stiff with cold, dripped shiny droplets back into the darker water which swirled at her feet. The waterfall cascaded down onto her and she reached up with her arms to embrace it, opened her mouth to taste it, arched her back to feel it tingle down her spine, between her buttocks, and on the backs of her legs. She stood as if fixed by the gazes from either side of the pool, the father and the son. As she took the cold kiss of the water-fall on her body, John Lemprière's eye was caught by a faint birthmark on her upper arm, but before he could make out what it was, she had turned.

Skin of alabaster, eyes of jet, the girl's body swung from son to father. On the other side of the pool, Charles Lemprière had seen all his son had seen. All but one detail. White flesh in the black water and the dark glitter of water drops as they skated from her skin. And when she turned, he saw those drops scatter about her like a silver noose rising out of the pool. He saw the black triangle between her legs, and her breasts, and her eyes which were blacker yet, and the breath caught in his throat. And as her body turned for him, he saw the mark, the imperfection his son had glimpsed a moment before and not recognized. But the father recognized it and he knew it as a sign he dreaded above all others, burning into him as once it would have been burnt into her. A broken circle, the signature of all he had fought against. And he knew then that his patient, faceless adversaries had bested him, that all his efforts, and his father's, and his father's before him had again come to nothing. The account against him would be settled now and his life was forfeit to it. They had found him. For a moment he knelt as if entranced by the recognition of defeat, and then he rose, the protest welling in his throat, to scream mindlessly.

"No, no! Not now! Not here!"

Then he heard the pack. He stopped dead, the words dying in his throat as he realized *he* had been their prey from the beginning, from the very first. But the time for any kind of thought was past.

The dogs broke cover forty yards downstream, moving fast and low over the ground. He turned to the naked girl who now watched him from the pool. Her black eyes glittering, sinking into him. He told himself not to run, to face whatever might come. But run he did, flailing wildly at the ferns and bushes in his way, while on the other side of the pool, under cover of the overhanging trees, a pair of legs tried to run, and could not. A pair of hands tried to claw their way out of the emerging nightmare, and could not. A voice tried to scream, and heard only the screams of his father as the dogs pulled him down.

The long, dark cloud bank moved silently overhead, shading the hills, fields, and valleys as it went. It shaded the gashed and twisted body by the pool. It shaded his son, wrapping its gray shroud about him. A gray shade touched his skin with cold fingers, like mist. He felt dry, racking sobs force their way up his throat. There were no words at first. Deep inside him, at his center, a black gland was already leeching its transfiguring thought through his body and its channels, observing its own slow seepage into the basin of his brain, offering its mouth to him in his grief, and as it coupled with him, it was accepted. In his mind's eye, the book was still open on the table in his room. Actaeon was still alive, still waiting for the dogs to reach him. Here, half lying in the pool, was his father's torn cadaver. Between both these bodies was his own, which connected them, turning one into the other.

• • •

The oil lamp held ten wicks. An unusual design, it flickered and gave off a fitful light. One was a lighting wick; of the other nine, three were lit.

"We hear Dundas's bill may be debated next month. We hear there is support for it."

"An inquiry has been made. There should be no difficulties, although—"

"A little leverage might ease a conscience or two. Have it done. If there are still difficulties, we shall think on it again." He paused. "The other business?"

There was a short silence.

"Carried off as we planned."

"Jaques can be sent to France now. We must not delay further. The girl can go with him."

Assent was indicated.

"The boy?"

"Matters are in hand. I cannot foresee any difficulties, not at the present."

"Your place is *precisely to* foresee. Do so. Remember what is at stake."

A third voice sounded. Deeper, slower than the others.

"Everything. Everything is at stake."

. . .

Small waves slapped the side of the boat. Above, gulls wheeled. To them, the sea was transparent. The boat, a tiny point in a vast uniformity, a flaw in the pattern. They caught the thermals as they rose and rode up with them until they saw both islands, Jersey and Guernsey and beyond them the coast of France. And they flew higher still until the coast of England was just visible, a gray smudge on the horizon.

Far below, the pacquet sailed slowly into the harbor of St. Peter Port. The young man swung his trunk up and carried it high on his shoulder, down the gangplank to the jetty. He stopped at the end and looked back, just once, before turning and walking on. Gulls flew up into the clouds, up until they were lost to view in the gray expanse of the sky.

Farewell Caesarea.

LONDON

Gulls screech and wheel overhead. They can be heard inside the coach as it bumps and slides through the muck and mud, its beveled wheels cutting deep, thin ruts in the road which leads on toward London. From Southampton by way of Guildford and the Holmesdale vale, it has struggled through mud, rain, ice, a broken shaft, and the foulness of the North Downs in November. For the moment, the sky is fine. The horses pull hard against the shafts and snort as the driver cracks them on. Their breath comes hard in the cold air. Through shrunken hamlets and empty fields, past abandoned farmhouses, shining green streams, steaming hayricks, and churches decked with elder trees they have come in their drive for the metropolis. The road has cut through valleys, low hills, moors, and marshland. Now it moves through George's Fields.

Meadows and dry stone walls are being replaced by more businesslike fences enclosing terraced cottages with red pantiled roofs, chimneys coughing smoke. The driver pulls his hat down and gets to work on the tired horses again. They pick up and pull on through Southwark to the Borough as the houses gain a story, then another, growing taller and narrower all the way up to London Bridge where the crowded piles break, suddenly, for the river.

". . . lifeblood of my trade, import-export. Any way to turn a penny," Cleaver is explaining to his audience as they pass over the sluggish water. Nobody cares. A woman and her young child nod politely; the young man is asleep, lolling on his shoulder. Cleaver shrugs him off.

"Nobody'll say Ned Cleaver don't love the river," he declares. The young man knocks himself awake just in time to hear this. The woman nods again.

"The river? Where's the river?" he asks as he comes to. His voice is thick with sleep.

But they are across it now, rattling over the cobbles of Lombard Street.

"Back there." Cleaver jerks his thumb over his shoulder. The carriage slows for the crowds which thicken and grow noisy as they continue down Cheapside and around Saint Paul's at a snail's pace. Cleaver sneezes without troubling to cover his nose.

"Just look at her!" he exhorts them. "No city like her, you know." Above, the driver pulls in his reins. The horses stop immediately.

"Journey's end!" he shouts down. Cleaver clambers out, pulls his case from up top, and is off without so much as "good-day." The woman and child follow, then the young man, less steadily, still rousing himself. The woman clasps her valise in one hand and offers him the other.

"Thank you, Mrs. Jemmer."

"Good-day to you, Mister. . . ." She struggles with the name which has been offered her only once, three days previously. "My condolences, sir," she says instead and takes her leave.

"This yours?" asks the driver, handing down his chest. He takes it and feels in his pockets. His hand closes in error about the miniature of herself his mother had pressed into his hand as he boarded the pacquet from Jersey. People are pushing and shoving past him. He fishes again and pulls out the paper upon which she had laboriously drafted a map laying out directions from any point on the Thames. He has only to find the river from the midst of this crush. He cannot fail.

"Whoa there!" He jumps back as a handcart rattles past. The chest is hoisted onto his shoulder.

"Oi!" He is propelled forward as a burly individual demands passage behind. The thoroughfare is crammed with vendors and their customers who have spilled out of Fleet Market to fill the neighboring streets. Stall-holders cry their wares at the throng which mills and presses all around. Car-men force their way through with kicks and curses, load-carriers the same. The din fills his ears as mistresses haggle pennies and farthings and the sellers protest at their stinginess. Small boys dodge between the legs of the punters. Dogs get in the way.

Across the street, a man sells oranges, a penny apiece from a barrow with his name upon the side.

"Excuse me, sir?" he begins.

"You know me, sir?"

"No, I—"

"You want oranges?" He proffers one.

"No, I—"

"Then don't waste my time." The rebuff throws him, but no matter. Other fruit-sellers are farther up the street. They will know where the Thames is. They do, but none will tell him. They offer him fruit: persimmons, apples, and pears at fourpence, a penny, and tuppence. He moves on, chest high upon his shoulder, farther into the mart where the crush is at its thickest, buying and selling, bartering and bargaining.

"Could you direct me to the Thames?" he asks passing strangers. They look at him as if he were mad. He is offered swedes at a shilling the bushel and turnips for the same. Fishwomen carry on a passing trade, jostling him deeper into the market, where a lad urges him to take a box of snuff for a shilling, or three for two. A customer overhears, knows a good thing when he sees it and takes them, catches a woman by the elbow as she passes to give her thruppence for a turbot. Thruppence from a guinea, a guinea for a watch. She cries on, basket on her back from Billingsgate at six. Her companion will sell you a sausage for less but wouldn't touch a turbot for a shilling, unless to eat it. Passing the matchseller she drops a penny in his box but leaves the matches with him. Both legs off at the knee, by night he dreams of buried treasure; "I buried it but thirty paces from here!" he rages on his stumps at the young man who declines to ask the question that was on his lips. Business is good for the tripe sellers, fourpence the pound and all you need is vinegar. Vinegar from the chandler's at tuppence a bottle. The soap-boiler's stench clogs the nose of Mister Gyp, knifegrinder, before that bunter and bellows-mender. He ground the knife that slit Kieran Healey's throat and appeared before Sir John to explain it. Healey's widow is destined for the pox, his son steals perukes from a basket, in contribution to the wigmaker's business. No commission paid, though. Milady Alice de Vere wears them and is carried in her chair, her spaniel trailed from a lead, languid hand out the window, six tarnished pennies from Albemarle to the Piazza, working out at five hundred and two paces the penny. "Careful there, boy! Those spectacles for show?" Alice's carrier checks his stride for an instant, then on. Guinea punks have the market tight as Millicent Martyn's whalebone corset from Stapes of Picadilly, twenty-three shillings by way of Greenland. Guzzling pie and porter makes her the darling of the vintner at a penny a pint, fourpence ha'penny for gammon and bacon. Her father, sign-carver, made good at three hundred pounds the year previous, this one better, despairs of a suitor, blanches at the dowry, applications invited from any with polish on their boots. Candidates to see, the scamp Willem (parents unknown, parish unwilling) who'll fit them for whatever they can afford. Willem's brushes are manufactured by Simon Kirkby and Sons of Spitalfields. The sons do a roaring trade with the footpads of Deptford Fields, pewter a speciality, the proceeds to be speculated at Jonathan's coffeehouse and lost in the shadowy columns of figures drawn on the accounts of his numerous clients by Marmaduke Oates who took a bet of a thousand to walk every street in the city within a week, lost, and had his creditor deported. Now he walks Change Alley, playing the market in saltpeter and China tea, no, young sir, rivers not my line. Consulting his watch, it is close to a quarter past ten. He fingers the gold of its case. 31*l*.17*s*.10½*d*. per oz., the price that morning. It races toward midday. Soon, the druggists' and grocers' factors will do their briskest business between the Turkish merchants and the statue of Charles II in the courtyard of the Royal Exchange. They barter furiously, making the odd foray over to the West India interest on the south side, but the real business is done on the benches lining the walks. Obadiah Walker has taken an option off Ducane for twenty tons of sugar, the balance to be discounted at the bank from the biscuit-bakers of Lambeth. Today the run is on tea, the *Nottingham* is due in, cargo intact. Those who ran with the rumor that it was nine-tenths spoilt and hung on to their stocks are losing tuppence, tuppence ha'penny in the pound. No one's interested, except some bewildered idiot asking if the Thames is still in London, and they'll spend the afternoon upstairs at the Antwerp where the talk will not be of tea, unless the glass-sellers choose that afternoon to spread their interests. An anxious trader sighs, touts for buyers another farthing down and, finding no success, stalks out the North Gate into Threadneedle Street. Now, down the table at the Jerusalem, a group plying the inland coastal trade cock half an ear as the shopkeeper turns out a gangling joker who, would you believe it, wants to know where the river is, tumbling his baggage down the stairs behind him, the cheeky sod. A woman looks up at the commotion, sucks on her flask, and looks down again as her companion walks past to offer the quester his best advice. "Go west, young man." He points, is understood, and marches on, pursued by that fool question about the river, will he never learn? The advice at least is free and the young man takes it, moving through the bewigged crowds of Holborn, toward the Oxford Road, along which a lad leads an enormous pig toward its ritual slaughter the Saturday next while his sister herds a goose. An approachable pair, they don't rightly know where the water-way is, nor the road to it neither. All they know is pig and goose. He turns back toward the maze of alleys running north and east by Charing Cross. His stride has become a trudging pace. His feet are aching. The chest digs into his narrow shoulder and his arm throbs. He moves on, slowly, through the alleys where the cobbles can barely be seen for dirt. Women shriek from tenement windows and common sense tells him not to look back as his feet drag on through Sheath Alley toward the Piazza. Will he ever find the river? Despair courts him as he skirts the square, inching through the crowds to follow a short street southward. Halfway down he comes to a halt, exhausted as he lowers the chest to the ground and leans back against a door. A man carrying a large blue bag weaves an unsteady path toward him. Lemprière shifts position. The man staggers, then lurches. They collide.

"Damn you!" Lemprière's frustrations are suddenly heaped upon his drunken assailant, who falls at his feet. Lemprière thrusts his map before the man's face.

"The river," he demands. "I want the river." The man looks up at him fearfully.

"Where on the river, sir? Where exactly did you want?" he asks, as he is pulled upright. The hand-drawn map is brandished.

"There," the young man stabs at it, "Southampton Street."

"Ah now, there's no need to mock me, sir. I'm in my cups and I'll own it, but there's reason enough for that—"

"Tell me!"

"I had no mind to knock you like that, you know. . . ." The young man raises the chest.

"Just tell me," he repeats, slowly, with what he hopes is cold menace. His captive looks from side to side, hesitating; is this an excuse for violence?

"Why sir, this is Southampton Street. You're in it!" he blurts desperately.

"In it?"

"This is it, sir. It is."

He had found it, better, was in it! He let go the man and let his breath out slowly, feeling nothing but relief.

"Thank you, my man," he says as he bends to brush absently at the mud on his breeches. The other makes no reply, and when the young man looks up to discover the cause of his silence, finds he has fled. He glances quickly up and down the street but the unfortunate is nowhere to be seen. A little way down, on the far side, he sees his lodging house. He crosses, takes the pavement in his stride, and knocks upon the door. Footsteps thud down the stairs and the bolt flies back.

"Welcome, Mister Lemprière!" exclaims the old woman who has opened the door and led him in. He follows, dragging his chest and abandoning his search to the mercy of the street outside. Where is the Thames? He does not care less.

. . .

The currents met in confusion about the dead water marking the mouth of the estuary. The waves threw up brief, white crests, and on the choppy surface a gull bobbed uneasily. Its wings grabbed the air in exploratory fashion, hauling itself into flight as the tide began to heave the thoughtless currents into its channel and the sea's agitation ceded to a deep, purposeful swell. The waters stirred vaguely at first, then, catching the insistent tug, united in a determined flow toward the city.

On the half-defined horizon, just visible in the winter light, a royal sail signaled the approach of a ship under full sail before the light wind, cutting through the water in an effort to catch the tide. The gallants, then mainsails, appeared as she entered the estuary and the currents began to draw her into the mouth of the river. Tamasa, dark river, Tamesis. The Thames.

Twelve hundred tons unladen, her maiden voyage. Aboard, the lascars worked quickly to slacken sail as the flow of water began to draw her on. She progressed, the Indiaman *Nottingham*, late of China and the Cape of Comorin. The caulkers, carpenters, and joiners of Thomas Brown's yard had done their work well; she looked untouched by the voyage, tackle mostly stowed and ports sealed. Pride of the East Indian fleet, the *Nottingham* sat low and profitable in the water which carried her inland. Her timbers were sound, had weathered well, the futtock hoops still tight, pumps barely used. With little tumble home, the *Nottingham's* topsides grew sheer out of the water. She wore her size grandly as she progressed in mute pomp up the Thames.

It was partly masked by the larger ship, partly it seemed to merge with the undistinguished gray of the sea. Even lightly laden, the vessel wallowed in the swell. Half the tonnage at most, it steered a guileful course along the wake of the *Nottingham*, a spent prodigal trailing the acknowledged heir. Aboard, there were no lascars, but the weather-tanned faces of the crew might have been taken for them. They worked hard and in ill-humor at the demands of the antiquated rigging. The shiny ropes afforded little purchase, sliding quickly through blocks worn thin with use. Straining timbers creaked and this, along with the slapping of the water on its hull, was the only sound to be heard on board, for the men worked in silence. The two ships continued on.

Soon, the first few houses could be seen. At Gravesend, a longboat met the *Nottingham*, ferrying the pilot who would guide her draft the last stage of the voyage through the channels of the Thames to Deptford.

Both ships moved out to midstream now. The pacquets, pleasure boats, and ketches which crowded the upper reaches of the river acknowledged the draft of the great Indiaman and cleared the deepest channel. The Upper Wet Docks were approached, then entered.

"Hove to!"

The mooring lines were thrown and the ship made fast. The long voyage was at an end.

Nazim left the ship with the others; home for the last nine months, he did not give it a backward glance. His attention was fixed upon the nondescript vessel which had trailed them to port. It moved slowly up the river, piloted by its captain, toward Rotherhithe. Nazim watched until it rounded a bend in the river to be lost from his sight. It continued on, wallowing upstream toward its berth where it docked without incident and lay at anchor, creaking, taking on water. No stevedores rushed to greet it, only a grizzled and crippled old seafarer cast more than a glance as he hauled himself slowly along the quay. And a face appeared briefly at the attic window of Captain Guardian's house farther up. The ship's crew shuffled belowdecks, heads down, hands jammed in pockets. Their vessel rocked gently with the Thames tide, its return long overdue, long beyond the faith or patience of any who might be expected to await it, tap, tap,

tap against the wharf, a drab tattoo for the homecoming of the *Vendragon.*

. . .

Sir, your attendance is respectfully requested on the morning of the twenty-second of this month of November at our offices in Chancery Lane. At this time, those effects of your father's, that is, of Charles Lemprière, kept on his order by Chadwick, Skewer, and Soames, will be delivered over to your keeping as his son, agent of his heir, and executor of his estate, henceforth. I remain yours with regret at this sad time,

Ewen Skewer (solicitor)

He had journeyed west. He had arrived. John Lemprière sighed as he eased off his boots. His feet ached. The letter had been waiting for him. Underneath the main body of the message, written in a different hand, was a note stating firstly that the majority of the effects were papers and that there would be no need to arrange any particular transportation. Secondly, that an interested party would call on him the next morning and direct him to the solicitor's office. This note was not signed and Lemprière wondered who the interested party might be. Interested in what?

He took off his spectacles and worked the skin on the bridge of his nose. Afternoon light draped the room in gray. It was sparsely furnished: a chair, a small writing table, the bed on which he sat, and a chest of drawers. His traveling chest lay open on the floor beside the last, the papers through which he had lately rifled in disarray within it. The object of this brief search sat like a lifeless presence beside him. A letter. The excitement of his adventure had already faded to be replaced by a more familiar fatigue. He stared gloomily out the window at the drab sky.

"London," he said aloud and to no one. The din from the street below reached his ears, street-traders and their clients. A dog barked.

He had barely spoken a sentence in the six days since leaving Jersey. His great voyage had been marred by nausea that had seen him puke from Saint Peter Port to Southampton. There was something rotten inside him. The coach had scarcely been better. A ruddy-faced man with beer on his breath had told him over and over again that he was in the "import-export" trade; each time with a broad wink, as if this was of some secret importance. A middle-age woman and her child had sat opposite and nodded a lot. He had not been sick, even on the worst of the turnpikes, but his dull unease had reared up more vigorously. He felt it now as he looked down at the letter beside him, his father's letter. Lemprière toyed with it, sinking back into the thoughts that had snapped at his heels the fortnight past. Thoughts that, should they catch him, he felt, would not wait for his readiness to confront them.

The door had been flung wide. An old woman had chattered about the other tenants as she led him up the stairs. The basement held Welsh girls who worked in the market. The ground floor was empty, but the first was taken. His own room was on the second floor, and above him was a tailor, his wife, and family. She was eager to be off. Leaving him by his door, she clattered back down the creaking wooden stairs.

He had waited there, listening to her noisy departure, and it was when the door to the street outside had slammed shut, at that moment, he felt the first inner prick of conscience, familiar since the day of his father's death, increasingly dreaded, which had grown over the last hour or two into the feeling that descended upon him now with its fullest and most drab force. He had come to recognize its slow arrival, its obstinate, alien residence. The last weeks had seen him take long, exhausting walks along Jersey's cliff tops. Several times, he had found himself running, coming to himself and not remembering why. But he knew why.

Lemprière rose and walked to the window. Closing the casement, he looked down at the men and women who jostled in the street below. All of them would, one day, give up the ghost and leave their leaden lives for the ether above. And my father, as harpy, siren, or sphinx; different incarnations of the ker. It left the body through the mouth, flying on black wings. It had a woman's face. Miasma. They had believed it caused plagues, that it fouled the fields; a jealous creditor dunning the carefree debtors below.

Above, the tailor's youngest had begun a recitation, "Ethelred the Unready, Edward the Confessor, Henry the Fifth. . . ." The unadvised, and he pondered again the letter he had replaced on the bed, his father's words. *Currite fusi*. . . . Snip, snip. Voices from the past and future, "Henry the Seventh, Henry the Eighth . . ." Someone in the street shouted, "Good Beef!"

When its teeth had met in the calf it had made a sucking sound, surprising how loud, *suck*, like a boot pulled out of thick mud. February was the month of appeasement, too early, he thought. Or too late. Exactness was the heart of the rite. When a man died, his remains were placed in a large earthenware jar, a pithos, buried with some ceremony, and the family of the dead man would practice rites to soothe the ker, the spirit of the dead man. Sometimes their observances would have no effect, but this did not shake the faith, or fear, of the Athenians. They knew that the ker was a frightened spirit, outliving the trauma of death, and that when, much later, Charon's coin was to be paid, the waters of Acheron crossed, and the shaded land reached, it took with it still the remnant fear. It was a bitter residue in the mouths of the living, the taste of anticipated reunion. "You too will follow," beckoned voices without bodies.

The reek of the river still hung in the room. The small fire at the far end was almost out. He walked over to poke at it listlessly, adding a few coals. Even the fires burnt differently here. He squatted down and watched fitful flames lick at the coals without conviction. The letter still awaited him. He was filled with foreboding as he turned to fetch it, yet what could he fear? Questions to which he had no answer, accusations from which there was no redress. Nonsense; but its very being there was an accusation of sorts. He rubbed his shoulder and resumed his place on the bed. The envelope in his hand, he thought of Hipponomus, the Bellerophon, sent from the supposed bed of Sthenoboaea to the court of Jobates bearing his death sentence unwittingly in Proteus's letter. Yet he had survived, he observed to himself. Charles the First floated down from above. His father's carefully formed characters stared up at him. He began to read.

• • •

Nazim had made his way to the Ratcliffe barracks with the others. Once inside the ramshackle building, the older men huddled together in groups, talking among themselves. He sensed their despondency but, as had been the case many times before, he did not share in the mood. Certainly, the barracks was a foul place; cold, ill-lit, it had lain uncleaned for months. What did it matter? He kept his own counsel and did not join the muted discussion. Some were already talking of finding a berth back to Madras or Goa. The Company would not permit that, he knew. And in any case, few ships would be sailing for the Indies in November; the risk made a nonsense of it. Nazim looked at the lascars. His fingers drummed deliberately on the planked floor, one, two, three, four, the thumb. Flexing of each finger-muscle, one, two, three, four, the thumb. Strings and levers. There were worse places than this. And better.

Across from where he sat the men grumbled on. His fingers ceased their slow movement. It was only the other side of the coin. Their griping would be replaced by joy, equally inexplicable to him, if the Company's promises had turned out to be true. A worthless coin. Had it gained him anything, he would have puzzled over their behavior, but he had lived apart from such concerns for long enough. He had seen the other side. Men struck dumb by what they thought was their desire. Their vanity. Years ago now, when his uncle had still lived, he had made his first visit to the palace of the Nawab. He had seen much that day, much he had not understood, but the point of the visit, one of the points as he had later come to understand them, was a lesson in vanity.

His thoughts drifted back. He and his uncle stood together outside the huge building. He remembered the burning heat, the glare of red sandstone. And then the cool marble inside. Their feet had slapped on the floors, the sound echoing off the walls and high, gilt ceilings. As they walked through the entrance bazaar, his uncle had pointed at the music pavilion beyond it. He had stared dutifully. They had traversed the audience hall, past the private rooms and the zenāna, the hot baths and gardens where water channels and waterfalls sprinkled the swimming pools. Domes and roof pavilions looked down on them as they disappeared into the inner chambers where embossed doors of brass and silver closed silently and faint whispers were heard behind the perforated screens. The two of them had continued down long, shadowed corridors which had led them, finally, to a reception room decorated with arabesques and inscriptions, designs inlaid with agate and carneol, others painted in gold, turquoise, and purple, all the most precious colors. Here, a small, shrunken man sat, attended for this occasion by a single servant.

His uncle had addressed him respectfully. They had talked for some time and he, a gangling twelve-year-old, had been presented to the little man. He had not guessed it then, and had not been meant to, but at that meeting a bargain had been struck, a succession assured, and from that moment, even unknown to himself, he had become the servant of the Nawab. Eventually, after hours in which his uncle and the Nawab had spoken in a low tone, they had paid their respects and turned to take their leave.

Before they left the palace, his uncle had taken him to see the Mirror Room. He had heard tell of it from others, it was said to be wondrous. Myriads tiny glasses mounted in stucco ledges and slabs formed a strange, shifting mosaic. He had seen himself in thousands of tiny pieces, all dislocated from each other. It was a marvel, was it not? He had nodded politely, unmoved by the spectacle. It would have made neither more nor less an impression upon him if the walls had been plain. What was it for? His uncle had watched him carefully and later, much later, he had realized it was a test of sorts. No flicker of interest had passed across his features.

His uncle had smiled then and led him back through the audience hall where the palace servants cleared a path before them and averted their eyes. Nazim had not thought his uncle was a man of such import. He had peered at their faces and seen in all of them the same expression. There was respect, certainly, and something else. His uncle had reprimanded him for curiosity, but still he stared, taking quick glances as they passed and seeing then a trace of distaste in the servants' eyes, and more, unmistakably, a strong and ill-concealed fear. He tried to think why they should fear a man such as his uncle, a man who, so far as he knew before this day, wielded little influence with anyone. Later, he would smile to recall this misapprehension, but then, as they made their way back through the bazaar and the ornate palace gates, his curiosity had grown. The courtiers, the favored servants, the professional dissemblers of the palace, all had watched with unobtrusive care as they walked slowly out of the grounds. The two of them: the divinely appointed assassin to the Nawab of the Carnatic and, appointed only that day, his twelve-year-old apprentice. Hand in hand together, Bahadur-ud-Dowlah had led his young nephew home. . . .

The barracks door flew open suddenly, startling Nazim from his reverie. The first of his countrymen had returned. He spread his blanket over the boards and lay down, angling his head toward the door as was his habit. The door banged open at irregular intervals. Each time, his eyes blinked open, then, seeing no threat, closed once more. His shipmates wandered back in twos and threes; none returned alone. The first lesson, he thought to himself. A few put a brave face on things, but most returned downcast, some were bloodied. He sighed and tried to settle on the hard floor. His sleep was fitful, broken by the sound of the night's stragglers as they stumbled to their places. Tomorrow, the task with which he had been entrusted would begin.

. . .

"*My son,*" began the letter, "*by the time you read this, my first and last letter to you, I shall be dead. If the mode of my passing follows the precedent set by our ancestors, then you will be left curious, besieged by doubts and unanswered questions. John, pursue them no further. Your curiosity will not be appeased, your vengeance never enacted. If the history of the Lemprières has resembled that of the house of Atreus, it is because this advice has been too rarely offered, never taken. It is my thought that you will be reading this letter in London, or on your way to that city. Complete any business you must and leave. Of my papers,*" at this, John looked across the room at the traveling chest which overflowed with these, "*burn them. Do not trouble to read them. I fear to say more, merely do as I say and I will be at peace.*"

It was unsigned, but the hand was his father's without doubt. What had he meant by vengeance? And how had he known that his death would be a violent one? The more he thought of his father's words, the more these and other questions assailed him.

He lay back on the narrow bed, gazing up at the whitewashed ceiling, now yellowed by firesmoke. He thought with mixed feelings of the woods and fields of Jersey, briefly of his mother. Above him, the tailor's family could be heard preparing for bed, while outside, the din of the street was undiminished, although changing in character. The noise of the journeymen, market-workers, which had provided a steady hum of commerce, insults, and greeting, faded, as now the broken rhythms of evening asserted their different dominion in sudden shouts, footsteps which approached and receded.

He thought of his father. Why had he screamed? Had he simply lain there it would not have happened. Had Casterleigh chosen any other day to go hunting it would not have happened. Had Juliette not been bathing, had Juliette not been playing in the water, had Juliette not . . . had I not committed Actaeon's sin. . . . No, he refused that thought. Not now.

But yes, another voice persisted in him, *had you not let another take your place* . . . It would not have happened, he concluded wearily. So many ways for it not to happen.

Had I not read the tale, invoked it, had I not been given the book, had I not tried to prove myself in the library. So many things I might not have done. Watching her in the pool.

His thoughts kept returning to the girl. Outwardly, he seemed calm, while within, his waking senses drained slowly down like the white sand in an hourglass. The night moved on. At length, his eyes closed and he slept.

Long, long ago, something huge pounded the rocky substrata on which the city would be founded. Unmindful and arrogant in its mortality, here its shadow fell across whole plains and scarps. Here its footprints were craters and here it sank down into the soft loam which slowly closed about it. Here it died. And here the soft, accepting earth drew it down to the beds of stone. A slow accommodation began. Gradually, so slowly, it succumbed to the patient stone which seeped into its limbs and organs, preserving it perfect in every detail. Its form hardened and became more than a corpse; almost imperceptibly, it became the monument to its own passing, a riddled lode which now plays silent host to five intruders.

Deep beneath the sleeping city, there is the slightest quickening in this structure. At five points in its fossilized remains, there is movement. Five men creep through arteries of granite, adamantine galleries, and brittle plates of crystal. They advance by separate routes. Their paths twist and curve but never cross. All have made this journey many times before. No one knows the path of the others. Their destination is all they hold in common as each picks his way through the network of tunnels. At times, they might be only inches from one another, separated by the merest, paper-thin membrane of flaking limestone, but they would never know. Each takes his own path to the chamber at the very center of the vast corpse, a chamber which might once have been its heart. The door to it may once have been an aorta, pounding with hot blood through arteries and veins that now harbor only the faint echo of shuffling footsteps as the five men draw nearer. The lamps they carry close to their chests light the way before them while their bodies throw shadows which lengthen away into the darkness at their backs. On entering the chamber, each extinguishes the lamp he holds and lights a wick in a lamp mounted upon the wall. There are nine of these wicks, not counting the lighter. When five of the nine are lit, they throw a stuttering light on the chamber's roof and walls. It is the only illumination this place has known. The chamber is cold and the air very still. The Cabbala is in session.

Dim though the light is, their leader avoids it, drawing back into the shadows of the chair. Two figures stand behind, flanking him like pillars. A little way down the table, a thickset man takes his seat. He has the air of one more accustomed to movement and shifts uneasily. Beside him, his companion, a wiry, compact figure, settles more quickly.

"Sit down, please," he says, as the last takes his place opposite them. There is no air of expectancy, no excitement. Gravity perhaps, as if they are assembled for the final signing of a treaty whose terms have been agreed upon years before. He leans forward almost imperceptibly, his face remaining in shadow. It is a signal. The company attends to him with a practiced manner. There have been many such meetings before this one. The thickset man leans his elbows on the table before him and clasps his hands. The tip of one finger taps noiselessly on a ring he wears on his left hand. It is gold, crudely made, with a device upon it. He studies his nails as if the words of the other take up only a fraction of his attention. The contemplative pose is so foreign to him, however, that the effect is almost comical. The speaker repays his assumed indifference in kind.

"Word reaches us that the Nawab has dispatched an emissary. . . . He will be identified. A decision can be taken—" he pauses for breath, "at a later time. He is at any rate only part of our larger problem—"

"Why wait?" The larger man unclasps his hands. "Why not deal with him now, his presence cannot profit us, surely?" He looks around the table for assent but, as always, the faces are impassive. The other continues by way of an answer to the interruption.

"He will be watched. It may profit us to know his identity before we—" he pauses, "before we act. There are no simple distinctions."

Across the table, the individual originally indicated toys nervously with a sheaf of papers. He glances quickly at the man opposite, whose smaller companion catches the look and holds him unblinkingly.

"The problem lies at the center of the web," says the older voice. "Go on."

"Yes, the Nawab himself plays a more devious game than was anticipated. By agreeing to honor all debts, both those of the government and the Arcot interest, he plays the claims of one against those of the other and pays neither. The Nawab has proved himself very agreeable; he will agree to anything."

"Which amounts to agreeing to nothing. He is virtually powerless but holds all parties to a sort of ransom by virtue of his own debts!"

"Quite." The voice came from the unseen one. "An empty center at which all interests converge."

"Including our own?" The man flexed his muscles as he spoke.

"There is no reason to believe our own arrangement is altered, or even implicated. Nevertheless, the attention drawn is—" he deliberated, "unwelcome. Provision should be made. We will await the emissary; this is not, after all, a situation we need to resolve." He smiled to himself. "Merely . . . contain. It will be done?"

One by one, all present nodded their agreement. The assembly shifted in its seats before settling back. The resolution had to be ingested. One by one, they signaled this and then a mood of the faintest expectation, the drumming of fingers on the table, an inclination of the head. The older voice spoke again.

"Word has reached us from Jaques. He has spoken with our colleagues in France." A slight tension was felt by the company as Jaques's mission was touched upon.

"He returns within the month, we will hear more fully on his return."

"The girl?" the larger man asked, not looking up.

"The girl will return too, of course. We have uses for her yet." This train of thought led him on. "Of the other affair, we can anticipate no difficulties at this time. From your silence I take it that the boy has arrived."

The heavily built man looked up in mild surprise. "Arrived and installed," he confirmed.

"Good," he said. "The Lemprières have been outside the fold too long. The game, gentlemen, has truly commenced."

The meeting moved on to other, lengthier matters. Later, when the rest of the business had been discussed, decisions taken or deferred, courses of action resolved, when most of those present had filed out, only two wicks remained and the light in the room was even poorer than before. The large man paced restlessly while the unseen one stayed seated. His eyes followed the other's every movement.

"You do not like the business with the boy, that much is plain, my friend."

"The manner of its execution is wasteful," he retorted. "Charades, games for children."

"That is your only worry?" The larger man stopped, rested his hands on the table, working hard to keep his expression neutral.

"It is worry enough," he replied. "We could accomplish what we want more simply. We should act directly."

"It is perhaps a little late to be setting precedents."

"Only the practicalities concern me—"

"Of course, but we are not dealing with a peasant. Decorum has its place in this matter."

"Decorum. What's that to do with it?" A hint of contempt could be heard in his voice. Tread carefully, my friend, thought the other.

"The Ciceros and Socrates of this world rarely dispute the verdict," he said, laying emphasis on the last word. "It is the manner of its execution that offends them, the wording, the precise detail of the ritual. It is not what we do, it is how we proceed that matters." The larger man seemed to accept this. He nodded and moved toward the lamp. As he snuffed out one of the wicks he was surprised to hear the other's voice again.

"I grow old, Nicolas. And tired. There will be time for change." He fell silent again. Nicolas Casterleigh turned on his heel and left without answering. The leader was left alone at the head of the table.

The coming months stretched ahead of him as the last idea took on the shape he had prepared for it. For there will be change, he thought as the last wick guttered. The old city rose in his thoughts, twin towers like sentinels guarding the inner harbor. There will be a return.

. . .

Nazim awoke with the dawn and began to prepare for the day ahead. Reaching into the bag that had served him as a pillow, his hands found the broad-brimmed hat and cloak that he had stowed there months before. He dressed quickly, his breath sending small clouds of vapor into the cold air. He pulled his hat down over his face as he gained the street. The Ratcliff Highway was still quiet as he walked westward toward Smithfield. As he rounded a corner of the Tower, his steps became more purposeful and he took the Minories at a brisk pace. The sky was cloudless. The sunlight from the wet cobbles dazzled without warming the air. As he cut through George Street, a small crowd of children flowed about him; he felt a hand brush his hip and swatted it away casually. The offender, a boy of eight or nine, taller than the rest and ghostly thin, caught his eye briefly. Nazim moved on and a chant went up instantly.

"Black Bird! Black Bird!" He quickened his pace but they skipped along behind him, singing the monotonous refrain over and over. The unsuccessful thief led them, dancing in front of him in time to the tuneless chorus of his companions. He wore nothing on his feet. The stall-holders and passersby began to take notice, shouting good-natured abuse at the gamins. Nazim felt the focus of unwelcome attention and his mind began to work furiously. They went on, showing no sign of giving up their sport. He spied an alleyway a few yards ahead and turned into it. It was empty. A little way down, he slowed his pace. Instantly, he was surrounded by the chanting children. The ringleader was to his left.

"Black Bird! Black Bird!" he screamed.

Nazim turned and reached with deceptive speed. Grasping the boy by the back of the head he drove the palm of his other hand into the nose.

The boy was too shocked to cry out; the grate of cartilage on bone was suddenly the only sound. He held him still for a second, pulling his head back farther to show his companions the blood. The children stood dumbfounded as he turned to continue swiftly down the alley and out of sight.

. . .

Lemprière had slept well. He rose reluctantly, put on his eyeglasses and boots quickly before the bed's warmth deserted him. No expert in fire kindling, he shivered through two unsuccessful attempts before the sticks caught the coals and their flames began to take the chill out of the air. He washed, flinching as the cold water raised goose pimples, and arranged his hair into something like order. Moving to the window, he saw that the street below had come to life with porters and car-men elbowing their way through the crowds. A dray was coming to a halt opposite his lodgings and a woman of forty or fifty years was shouting vigorous abuse at its driver. Farther up, the street was even more congested. The wigs of the gentlemen looked very fine, he thought.

As Lemprière watched, his eye was caught by a figure dressed completely in black who moved quickly through the crowd in an assured manner. The figure walked down the street toward his house and turned abruptly into the doorway which was obscured from his view by the ledge of the window. The solicitor's "interested party," he thought to himself. It must be, no one else would have business at the house at this hour. He waited by the window, expecting an entrance at any moment. A minute passed and he heard nothing. It was possible that the man had gone up to the tailor's room. Lemprière walked to the door and threw it open. There was no one in sight.

"Hello!" he called, feeling faintly ridiculous and craning his neck to see farther up the staircase, which was narrow and badly lit. There was no answer. I must have been mistaken, he thought as he retreated, pulling the door shut. But as the catch clicked in the lock he fancied he heard a distinct creak, as if the wooden stairs were being climbed or descended by stealth. Lemprière put his ear to the door and listened intently. Almost instantly he heard another, similar sound, louder this time. His irritation got the better of him. He flung open the door and this time was confronted by a man, his fist raised ready to strike. Lemprière slammed the door shut before the fist fell, ran to the hearth, and snatched a burning stick from the fire. He braced himself, legs apart and firebrand raised, in the center of the room, ready to strike. He waited, poised. He waited, coiled. He waited.

Nothing happened. Lemprière remained in his pose. Then, two knocks were heard on the door, and a voice, slightly muffled, inquired, "John

Lemprière?" The door opened a foot or so and a head appeared around it.

"Is this the lodging of John Lemprière?"

"Who are you?" demanded the young man. "Why are you here?" He was gradually relaxing his gladiatorial pose. The firebrand had gone out and was filling the room with smoke.

"Septimus," said the face, "Septimus Praeceps. I am here from Chadwick, Skewer, and Soames. The solicitors." And with that he entered the room, his hand extended in greeting. Lemprière shook it, coughed, and returned his stick to the fire.

"Why was your fist raised?" he asked more calmly.

"I was about to use it upon your door. My apologies if I startled you."

"Not at all, not at all." Lemprière coughed again, then turned and examined his visitor. Mister Septimus Praeceps stood perhaps an inch taller than himself and was dressed, as he had observed, almost completely in black. His hair, which was short and loosely curled, matched his clothes, and only the white of his face, his shirt, and his stockings interrupted his dark attire. His face was striking, with high cheekbones and dark brown eyes. Lemprière's own eyes were still watering from the firesmoke, and he dabbed awkwardly under the lenses to dry them with his handkerchief.

"Are you recovered?" asked Septimus solicitously. Lemprière nodded.

"Good, shall we go?" Lemprière nodded again, put on his coat, and followed his companion down the stairs. They paused for a moment at the doorway before plunging into the crowd. Septimus walked slowly while Lemprière did his best to dodge the bodies which threatened to separate them. He thought of the marketplace in Saint Helier, and of his father.

"Take care!" warned Septimus, pulling him by the elbow. A generous mound of horse manure was sidestepped. Carriages sped past. The two of them avoided the refuse underfoot, Lemprière keeping close to Septimus, whose pace had increased. They progressed down the Strand, past Somerset House toward Temple Bar where the human traffic seemed less frenetic in temper.

Lemprière began to gather his thoughts and was about to deliver a choice remark on the obstructive habits of the citizens when Septimus suddenly darted off to the left, hissing for him to follow. Lemprière's path was blocked by a large individual carrying a brace of bewildered chickens. He tried to duck around his back but a young man, clearly drunk, swayed in his path, eyes unfocused.

"Septimus!" he called.

The drunk swiveled disjointedly at him. 'Sebdimus?' he parroted.

"No, I . . . A friend of mine, excuse me." Lemprière had lost sight of the black figure.

"A friend of *mine,*" retorted the drunk. "Where is he?" Both men scanned the crowd in vain.

"Here," said a voice, and they both turned to see Septimus smiling at them. "You're drunk, Walter," he addressed Lemprière's accoster. "Tight, raddled, and cut."

"And drunk," agreed Walter. "Lend me a guinea. Good evening" (this last to Lemprière).

"Go home, Walter," said Septimus.

"Good night and good luck and good riddance," slurred Walter. "Can I borrow your spectacles?"

He giggled and staggered off through the crowd.

"I didn't realize you knew him . . ." began Lemprière.

"Walter Warburton-Burleigh, drunkard, whoremonger, and my dear friend but no sport at this time of the morning. I was trying to avoid him." Lemprière nodded and they continued in the direction of Chancery Lane where the offices of Chadwick, Skewer, and Soames were to be found.

As they turned into the great highway, Lemprière noticed that the buildings differed from those which had gone before. A greater uniformity, a difference of temper were apparent. Set within the white walls of the buildings which lined either side of the thoroughfare were small, latticed windows behind which copy-clerks diligently practiced their fine hands and, from the higher ones, bewigged gentlemen peered down briefly from time to time as though to check that their own particular cubicle was still attached to the whole. Similarly attired gentlemen made up a large proportion of the passersby, moving in animated clumps of four or five by choice, although solitary ones also were spotted.

Septimus seemed to take particular delight in forcing passage through the middle of such colloquies. Protests followed in his wake. Lemprière was left to follow behind, trying, with scant success, to convey the impression that he was not party to his companion's antics. When they had reached almost the top of the lane, Septimus turned into an entrance. A stone staircase faced them, but instead of ascending, they walked around it to one side and emerged through an identical doorway at its back into a small courtyard. Their destination lay via one of the staircases on the far side which Septimus climbed taking its steps two at a time. Septimus knocked purposefully on the door at the top, which was opened by a small, plump individual who carried a quill in his hand.

"Yes?" he inquired absently, his mind clearly on other matters, then, coming to himself, invited them in. Septimus was obviously acquainted with the clerk, clapping him on the shoulder as he walked into the anteroom and introducing him to Lemprière as "the worthy Peppard."

The worthy Peppard's workplace was a short corridor which looked out onto the courtyard. A large desk stood in the center; behind it, the worthy Peppard's chair. A long pew extended the length of the opposite wall. Peppard thus worked with his back to the window. At the far side of the room a door bore the legend "Ewen Skewer, Solicitor." Septimus strode toward it.

"He has a visitor," exclaimed Peppard, half rising from his chair as Septimus reached for the doorknob. "I am afraid you will have to wait," he apologized.

Septimus swore and Lemprière sat down on the pew. Septimus paced in an agitated manner up and down the floor, plainly infuriated by the delay. He put his ear to the door.

"Are you certain the man's engaged?" he asked in exasperation. Peppard looked up from his work. "Oh yes, quite sure, you see he had an appointment with two gentlemen at ten, but they arrived late and so when the lady arrived who is in there now, she was unannounced, you see, she had to wait too, and—"

"Yes, yes quite, thank you; dammit." He resumed his pacing.

"You arrived a little early, you see," Peppard continued to Lemprière, "and what with the two gentlemen and the lady and your arriving early, the morning's become quite muddled." This was said in such melancholy tones that the young man forgot Septimus and felt some little sympathy at the difficulties of the worthy Peppard.

"We quite understand," Lemprière said. But Septimus was having none of it.

"Pox on understand!" he exclaimed, but as he did so the previously inaudible occupants of the far room began to make themselves heard.

"You filthy scamp! You thief! Curse you!" These words were shouted furiously in a woman's voice and swiftly followed by a loud crash. "You creature! I'll beat the truth out of you!" A man's voice could also be heard, trying to adopt a conciliatory tone, but an abrupt change in temper was signaled as the woman presumably began to carry out her threat.

"Peppard!"

Bang!

"Peppard, where . . . ow! Peppard!"

But Peppard was already running to the door. He threw it open to reveal a woman in late middle age holding the beleaguered solicitor by the collar while using the other hand to beat him over the head with her shoe. Her bonnet was awry, her face flushed. She froze at her discovery in this undignified operation. Septimus had watched these proceedings with an amused detachment which suggested this painful farce was the least the solicitor could do to alleviate the tedium of delay. He took charge of the situation. He walked over to the woman, who remained poised above her victim, evidently in two minds as to whether she should allow herself the satisfaction of one more blow or preserve what remained of her decorum by desisting. Inexplicably, Lemprière hoped she would hit him again.

"Madame?" Septimus offered his arm in polite fashion to the woman, who accepted it, and together they made their way to the far door. Only semi-shod still, she limped across the room. Intuiting that any acknowledgment of the previous violence was likely to mark its resumption, Lemprière paid the simple courtesy of standing up as she passed.

She stopped and turned to him. Her voice was quite calm, although the eyes still blazed.

"Thank you, sir," she offered as he rose. "My actions are not those of a madwoman. My mind is clear. Clear as a bell, and that man"—she did not trouble to point—"is a liar and a thief in the pay of knaves yet more vile than himself. Good-day to you, sir."

With that she replaced her shoe, opened the door, and left. They listened to her footsteps until they faded from earshot.

The solicitor seemed not to have suffered any grievous hurt. A spindly individual with a thin, pinched look about his face, the high color, which did not suit him in the least, was rapidly being replaced by a pallor, which did. He mopped his brow. Peppard was engaged in setting his master's office to rights. Large folios lay scattered on the floor. A chair was overturned.

"Excuse me, gentlemen," he explained. "Most unseemly, the poor woman's deranged, a widow, you see, never got over the loss. Please." He ushered them into the office. "Mister Lemprière, I take it?"

Lemprière nodded. The solicitor indicated the chairs before his desk and they sat down, Septimus crossing and uncrossing his legs several times before coming to rest. Ewen Skewer faced them from the other side of his desk, his thin lips pursed. He toyed in an agitated way with the blotters, quills, and seals before him. Lemprière noticed that none of the quills had been cut.

"A widow, did you say?" he asked, still curious as to the woman's behavior.

"Mrs. Neagle, yes. Her husband was captain of an Indiaman. It went down with all hands—"

"How terrible!" interrupted Lemprière.

"A risk of the trade," said Skewer matter-of-factly, then, catching Lemprière's look of reproach at this presumed callousness, continued, "This was some twenty years ago; but the woman's never been the same. To begin with, it was grief, but now the memory has faded and she is plainly mad still. She truly believes there is a conspiracy to blacken her late husband's name and that I, this firm rather, have proof of his innocence, documents, maps, or some such."

"What kind of conspiracy?" persisted Lemprière.

"In truth, I do not know." He paused. "Something to do with whales, I believe. As I said, the woman is deranged. However, we are not here to discuss the fantasies of widows." He rose and fetched down a large envelope from the shelf behind him. It was yellowed on one side as though exposed to the sun, bound with tape, and dotted with bright red seals. Skewer broke them and untied the tape. A quantity of papers fell in disarray onto the desk before him. He searched briefly before singling out a smaller envelope sealed in the same manner as the first.

"The will," he announced, cracking the seals. Lemprière had been diverted in his thoughts by his encounters with Septimus, the unfortunate

Widow Neagle, and the city itself, but now he experienced a similar sensation to that of the previous evening. Foreboding, curiosity, and, behind both, the tinge of guilt. He wished that the solicitor would cease his cursory inspection of the signatures and begin reading. Skewer looked and declared that the will exhibited no obvious irregularities and was valid, at least in form. At length he cleared his throat and began to read.

> I, *Charles Philip Lemprière*, do by this my will dispose of such worldly estate that it hath pleased God to bestow upon me: First I will that all my debts be paid and discharged and out of the remainder of my estate I give and bequeath unto my wife, Marianne Wroxley Lemprière, my house and its adjoining lands within the parish of Saint Martin's on the island of Jersey, and I further give and bequeath unto said woman the contents of that house with the exception of my private papers not pertaining to the ownership and management of that house and its lands, namely its deeds of title and surveys, which shall go to my son, John Lemprière, and if my son should die without issue then to Jacob Romilly Stokes of Blanche Pierre on the island of Jersey. . . .

The will continued in long, elaborate periods, its sense all but lost in convolutions and repetitions, and Lemprière soon gave up his attempt to follow the path of its thought, letting his mind wander where it would. The drone of Skewer's voice smoothed over any intended inflections or emphases, and his intonation sounded oddly soothing. Only the names disturbed the anodyne flow. Septimus confined his natural impulse to somehow speed the ritual along to frequent consultations of his pocket watch, whose case he snapped loudly shut at each full stop. The will proceeded to the accompaniment of these reports while Lemprière day-dreamed idly, half-listening, half-waiting for Skewer to finish.

". . . signed, sealed, published, and declared as and for his last will, in the presence of us . . ."

The will had been attested to by his mother and Jake Stokes. He faintly remembered a solemn little meeting between his father and the last two, and another man. It had not been Mister Skewer. He had been little more than an infant then but wondered now if that meeting had been the occasion of the faded signatures he saw at the foot of the will. It surprised him that he had not remembered that before, but in his heart he knew that he had confronted nothing yet and that such remembrances were often the preludes to battles he was ill-prepared to fight. And he recognized that the floating sense of detachment that he felt from all around him was another side to that coin by which he paid off the past with half-promises and grudging regrets; another day, one more day, but the coin was running low. The solicitor broke in upon these thoughts.

"These are very old," he declared as he handed a sheaf of papers gingerly across the desk. Lemprière looked up distractedly.

"What are they?" he asked.

"Heirlooms, I presume, history of the family, that type of thing . . ."

"I think you will find they include an agreement between an ancestor of yours and a man named Thomas de Vere," predicted Septimus, and Lemprière remembered that his official status at the gathering was that of "interested party."

"Yes, this is it, I believe."

Lemprière carefully unfolded a parchment document that the years had yellowed and dried. A complicated arrangement of serrations marked two of its edges; it crackled alarmingly as he smoothed it flat on the desk. Then, standing over it, he began to read.

At an assembly of the persons hereunder named holden on the twenty fifth day of April in the sixteen hundredth and third year of Our Lord.

Agreement betwixte *Thomas de Vere* fourth Earle of Braith and *François Charles Lemprière*, merchant. Whereas the first person abovenamed by the suffrance of almightie God after Royal assent of our Soveraigne Lord the Kinges most excellent maiestie first thereunto had and obteyned, does entend for the honour of our native Country and for thadvancement of trade and merchaundise within this Realm upon his severall adventures, undertaken with others according to the severall proportions of the sommes of money by them severally sett downe and inregestred under ther owne hands, To make over that portion of his share with those moneys accruing thereto, those benefits and goodes that come of it as of the vyages set forthe to the Est Indies and other the Ilandes and Countries thereaboutes and moneys coming from the sale of suche commodities as uppon further deliberation shalbe resolved to be provided for these partes or otherwyse by buying or barteringe of such goodes wares jewelles or merchaundise as those Ilandes or Countries may yeld or afforthe to the abovementioned second named *François Charles Lemprière*, merchaunt, who shall retain the service of the abovenamed *Thomas de Vere* forth earl of Braith at the rate of one tithe of those monies and benefits accruing to that portion of the late-formed Joynt-Stock Companie made over and given freely apart from this portion agreed betwixte both partyes, as his neutral agent and representative in the abovementioned Joynt-Stock Companie trading to the Est Indies and that this agreement shall stand notwithstanding any desuetude or the death of either or both partyes to it, namely *Thomas de Vere* and *François Charles Lemprière*, merchaunt. In witness whereof we have caused this letter to be an agreement betwixt us

Witness ourselves at London the twenty fifth day of April in the sixteen hundredth and third year of Our Lord,

Thomas de Vere
François Charles Lemprière

Lemprière looked up from the document at the solicitor.

"Rebarbative phrasing," pronounced Skewer. "Quite outlandish."

"Certainly odd," agreed Septimus. "Perhaps Peppard might be prevailed upon for an opinion?"

"Hardly necessary," Skewer retorted. "An interesting relic, certainly, but its appeal lies in curiosity—"

"What is your interest, Mister Praeceps?" Lemprière asked.

"None at all—"

"But the letter clearly stated that you were an *interested* party—"

"I have none at all for myself," Septimus continued, "but the twelfth Earl of Braith, that is Edmund de Vere, has an interest in this document's acquisition, that is he would wish to purchase it . . . on favorable terms, of course."

"It is a course of action I would advise," added Skewer. "As your father's solicitor, the disposal of his effects falls within my province and . . ."

"A moment, gentlemen, one moment, please." Lemprière straightened and gestured silence with his hands. "First of all, you, sir, are not my father's solicitor, my father's solicitor was Mister Chadwick, as is plainly written there." He pointed to the original envelope. "In fact, I would like to know where is Mister Chadwick?" he demanded.

The solicitor's face took on a grave expression. "Mister Chadwick passed on, it grieves me to tell, not eight months ago." He sighed. "I am truly sorry that my efforts have not been satisfactory, if I might—"

But Lemprière cut him short. "Please accept my apologies. I meant no offense. Your efforts have been laudable."

"A hundred guineas for it," Septimus cut in crassly.

"Mister Praeceps!" exclaimed Skewer.

"Two hundred."

"My father's bequest to me is not for sale," Lemprière answered rigidly and without looking at Septimus.

"Not strictly a bequest," murmured Skewer.

"Good then, that's settled," Septimus said in conclusion.

"What on earth do you mean?" Lemprière was fast becoming outraged.

"You refuse to sell, yes?"

"I do."

"Good."

Lemprière hardly knew what to make of this conclusion. Septimus's crude bandying of figures seemed to desecrate the solemnity of the occasion, while his ready acceptance of the refusal was so jovial as to make a mockery of his earlier eagerness. He recalled himself. "Why on earth would the Earl of Braith wish to buy this document? What is his interest?" Lemprière demanded.

"Oh, family archives," Skewer answered. "The earldom of Braith is not a particularly ancient one. Recent additions to the peerage, at least in my limited meetings with them, like to, how should I say, firm up the foundations, lay stress on the historical side of things. . . ."

"But the matter's closed," said Septimus.

"And how would the Earl know I, I mean my father, had this document? Would Mister Chadwick have told him?"

"Good gracious, no." Skewer sounded appalled at the thought. "The confidentiality between a solicitor and his client is absolute."

"Unless Mrs. Neagle is to be believed," Septimus threw in.

The solicitor ignored this and continued. "It is quite beyond the pale to believe that—"

But Septimus interrupted him again. "He knows because he holds the other one."

"Other one?" Lemprière echoed.

"There are two," Septimus continued, "obviously; one for the Earl and one for this man, your ancestor. It is an agreement, is it not? Two copies, one for each."

This seemed a plausible explanation to Lemprière. "At any rate, I fear it is not for sale. My apologies to the Earl." He was resolved. Septimus looked at Lemprière. The solicitor looked at Septimus.

"The other effects are all in order, I believe. The inventory lists all the contents. Of course, if you feel that there are any questions you wish answered, any assistance, please return."

Lemprière had the impression that Mister Skewer was relieved at the meeting's being over. He glanced down at the inventory. Most of the entries began, "A document . . ."; some stated that only. His finger paused on the column.

"A seal is listed here: 'A gold seal of our estate,' " he read aloud. Skewer searched through the papers and handed an object to Lemprière. It was a gold ring, heavy and crudely fashioned. Affixed to the band was a signet whose design was a circle broken on one side. This was set within a square face, and the whole shone as if newly minted. There was not a scratch or mark of any kind to be seen. Clearly it had rarely or never been worn. Lemprière looked long and hard at the design, but the faintest sensation of remembrance it evoked in him would not surface.

"A ring," he said blankly.

"A seal ring," Skewer corrected him.

On impulse, he put the ring to the seals on the envelope. They did not match.

"It has never been used," said Septimus.

"No," said Lemprière without thinking. He placed the ring in his pocket and stood up. "Thank you, Mister Skewer."

"My condolences, sir." Skewer escorted him to the door and handed over the envelope. Septimus followed.

"Your father was a fine man," the solicitor said, by way of parting.

You did not know him, thought Lemprière, although you are right. "Thank you," he said again and suddenly felt a deep sadness as if the closing of this ritual marked the end of something that he had valued more than he would have guessed possible. He choked it back.

"Shall we go?" inquired Septimus.

"Yes, yes, of course." He moved toward the door.

"Good-bye, Mister Peppard." The clerk looked up from his work as if surprised at being addressed at all.

"Good-bye, Mister Lemprière, Mister Praeceps," and he bent diligently to his task once more.

As they descended the staircase, their footsteps echoed loudly. The meeting with the solicitor seemed to have passed off without trouble. Earlier forebodings of his father's voice exacting vengeance from beyond the grave had proved baseless and he had dealt with Septimus's and Skewer's demands as if born to it, so he thought. And yet there remained, if not unanswered questions, at least answers that begged further questions. Septimus had not explained why his interest in the document had waxed and waned so quickly, and he observed that Skewer had supported the case for its sale with suspicious vigor, as if he too had some interest in it.

Crossing the courtyard, Lemprière felt his suspicions mount as he added the elements of their late meeting one to the next. Septimus's crude expressions of interest, then disinterest, and Skewer's to-ings and fro-ings turned his puzzlement to exasperation until he caught Septimus by the arm.

"Why on earth would you speak of my father's affairs in such a tone?" he demanded more sharply than he had intended. Septimus came to a halt. "Speaking in that manner, what did you hope to gain? I mean, what did you want in there?" Lemprière demanded with diminishing vigor.

But Septimus's face told him nothing. "I am sorry," the other spoke quickly, "if my manner should cause you discomfort. I did not intend it so and will not make the mistake twice. Forgive me, Mister Lemprière. Let us part on good terms. We shall not meet again." His face was the image of injury as he held out his hand in parting. Lemprière took the hand, somewhat taken aback by the sudden turn of events. "Naturally I am sorry for your loss. My slight service was inept and I apologize for that too. I wish you luck, Mister Lemprière, but now if you will excuse me . . ." He did not finish his sentence and was already turning away.

"Wait." Lemprière caught his arm again. "I only meant—"

"And I too 'only meant,' Mister Lemprière. I meant to bring two parties together to their mutual advantage, to facilitate, to help, in a word. No matter. You seem an amiable sort, resourceful, hardly stupid, but do not think this city will welcome you. You are alone here, friendless and ignorant of custom. You are the barbarian, and your familiar words have different meanings. That is all. You are probably right to mistrust me, so good-bye, Mister Lemprière, and good luck." He offered his hand in parting. Lemprière took it, wavering now, then coughed to clear his throat.

"I believe I may have misunderstood you, Mister Praeceps. My apologies," muttered Lemprière. The two of them stared at each other. Lemprière felt an hour pass in the second before the other's wooden expression broke into a broad grin.

"Septimus, please," said Septimus. "You can hardly call me by such a mouthful, if we are to be companions after all."

"John," said Lemprière.

"Good, very good." Septimus's wounded expression had already evaporated. "Come now," he said, pulling Lemprière forward, and the two of them left the courtyard together.

Lemprière walked in silence past the staircase they had encountered earlier. There was a further detail that niggled at the back of his mind. It had to do with Peppard. They crossed the road, dodging the ridges of muck piled up by the cartwheels, and continued down. Septimus was unusually silent. Lemprière kept pace more easily than before, mulling on the questions that bothered him. They had taken a different route from before, cutting around the back of Lincoln's Inn, and as they reached Portugal Road he turned to his silent companion.

"Why did you ask for Peppard's opinion on this?" he asked, proffering the envelope. Septimus stopped and looked at it.

"Skewer's a fool," he said shortly, and then was off again, faster than before. Lemprière struggled to keep pace.

"And Peppard is a fool's clerk, then?" He secretly agreed with Septimus's estimate of the solicitor. Unfair, he rebuked himself.

"That is Peppard's misfortune."

"So why ask him?"

"I did not ask him."

"But you would have asked him," Lemprière persisted. Septimus kicked at an imaginary obstacle.

"Yes, I would have asked him," he conceded. "Skewer barely recognized that it was an agreement at all. Peppard . . ." and he stopped.

"Peppard what?"

"Peppard is the brain of Chadwick, Skewer, and Soames. Or so it is said. It would make sense." He sniffed. "Dammit, I'm starved."

"Make sense?" Lemprière prompted.

"Yes. Peppard was thought one of the finest legal minds in London at one time. He was tipped for success, high office, but there was a scandal. This was many years ago, twenty perhaps." Lemprière thought back to the clerk and the chastened demeanor he had taken for meekness.

"What kind of scandal?" he asked in frank curiosity.

"That I am not sure of, something to do with insurance. Maritime insurance, I believe. It was a long time ago." Septimus dismissed the subject with an irritable wave of his hand. "I need to eat," he declared, as if Lemprière's questions simply dissolved in the face of such a pronouncement. "In fact, I need both to eat and"—catching sight of a tavern on the corner ahead—"drink." Lemprière realized that he too was hungry. Tempting cooking smells wafted from the inn were sending messages of enticement to its potential customers. Septimus turned to his companion and spoke quickly.

"Listen, I know that a great deal of all this"—he waved his arms expansively—"is strange to you. If you want to know why Edmund, the Earl, wants this scrap of parchment, why not ask him yourself? What I mean is meet him and me both. Yes?"

Lemprière was somewhat taken aback by this invitation.

"Come this Saturday. We meet at the Craven Arms, at eight o'clock, or thereabouts. You'll come?"

"Yes, I will," resolved Lemprière in a rush.

"Good." Septimus turned as if to leave, then checked his stride suddenly. "If you wish to know more before then," he said quickly, "you know the man to ask," and he nodded back at the building behind him.

"Skewer?" Lemprière queried disbelievingly. Septimus was already walking away. He turned and continued backward to answer him.

"His clerk."

. . .

Peppard's grandfather had had a craving for the stage and so, naturally, he had become a barrister. His mother had had a craving for a solicitor but had married a grocer. After the wedding she had been delivered of a boy and, disappointed in the first instance, was resolved to be rewarded in the second. Peppard cursed silently: One more blot and he would have to copy it afresh. She had bought volumes of case law, battered and bound in red leather. Peppard had read them voraciously. By the time he arrived to study law at Cambridge, he was ready to take his final examinations. His indenture with Mister Chadwick was a formality.

He had been attracted to commercial law for reasons that even now he could not fathom. His lifelong inability to grasp the value of money was, oddly, a boon to his career. The wealthier merchants and financiers felt secure with a man whose eyes did not widen when the counting was done in thousands, and his less fortunate clients appreciated those same eyes not closing in boredom when the talk was of shillings and pence. The offices of George Peppard attracted clients in droves, he was courted by several levels of society, and there was talk of his being "too good for the law." A post in the treasury was in the offing. He began to think of marriage.

But there the dream faded. Recalling the days that followed still hurt and he did not like to dwell on the events that filled them. His pen moved quickly, tracing expert strokes over the complex document before him. He finished the last clause, leaving a good footer for the signatories to add their names, blotted the whole, then placed it carefully in his drawer. Looking up, he saw Mister Skewer leaning against the open door of his office.

"You may go if you wish, Peppard."

"Very well, sir." He was both surprised and pleased. Instances of Skewer's generosity were few and far between. He looked out of his window and saw that the light was failing already.

The air was cold outside, and he walked quickly through the courtyard toward the street. As he did so, he fancied that he heard footsteps somewhere behind him, but when he looked about there was no one to be seen. He turned and quickened his pace. In the usual run of things he would have dismissed it with little hesitation. But the last few days had not conformed to Peppard's idea of the usual run of things.

Twenty-odd years had elapsed since the scandal which had reduced Peppard to his present station. In that time, he had often fancied himself under the scrutiny of the very men who had so successfully ruined him. He had good reason. Faces in crowds had grown inexplicably familiar. He had grown conscious of men who lounged at the corner of his street to little obvious purpose. They would station themselves at this and other vantage points for a few days, then disappear, never to be seen again. Twice his room had betrayed traces of subtle examination: a book left open, a basin of water emptied and refilled to a different level. How many details such as these had he missed? When first he had grown aware of their attention, the occasions had seemed quite random. Later he had realized that these intrusions had coincided with crises of one sort or another in his old adversary, the East India Company.

On impulse he turned about again. Nothing. The courtyard was dark. Anything might hide in the shadows. He wondered what upheaval afflicted John Company now. His curiosity had never left him. Something was afoot, that much was a certainty. Three days before, he had been walking home as usual when, for the first time in all those years of half-confirmed suspicions, he had been confronted directly. In truth, it was trivial. He told himself that it was nothing. He had been walking home by his normal route when a man had fallen into step beside him. He had had a thin face and had been dressed in black. Peppard had ignored him. Perhaps he was a prankster, or a madman of some sort. But after a minute or two the man had stopped him, put a hand to his shoulder, and looked him in the face. Peppard had said nothing. The thin-faced man had said only one word, "Peppard." A voice like metal. Just one word, but the message for him was clear: We know who you are, where you are, you are ours if we wish it at any time. . . . Not this time, not now, Peppard had wanted to protest. He had managed to keep silent. The man had looked him full in the face for several long seconds, then walked back into the crowd to be lost from sight. When Peppard had reached his home, his clothes were drenched in sweat and his hands shook for an hour. He had been given a warning. Now, as he gained the street, he wondered if the visits of Septimus, or his companion, or the Widow Neagle might be the occasion which had prompted it. He could not know. Damned curiosity. He had imagined the footsteps. It was nonsense, all of it, and here was the street before him. Thousands upon thousands of footsteps.

Chancery Lane at that hour thronged with clerks and their masters bent, as he was, on their homeward journeys. They jostled and shoved to avoid the filth of the gutter and Peppard was hard-pressed in this struggle to maintain his pace. Slowing, he fell in behind a group of young men who moved in an aggressive group through the crowd, refusing to yield passage to any and jeering at those unfortunates who were relegated with little ceremony to the roadside muck or worse. Peppard felt protected. Holborn was just as crowded, but at Saffron Hill the mass of people thinned. Turning into Vine Street, he chanced to look back and as he did so a figure perhaps a hundred yards behind him froze conspicuously. Peppard held his stare for a second or two, then walked quickly down Vine Street and across Clerkenwell Green. From the far side, he scanned anxiously for the figure, but did not see him. No one had followed him. Why should they? He wished now that he had returned home on his more usual route by Cheapside and up. In this part of the city the main thoroughfares ran north to south, and thus the safety their numbers afforded was short-lived as he negotiated from one to the next by means of the network of alleys that served as streets in the northeast quarter. He cursed his timorousness, but the narrow paths of Clerkenwell were ill-lit at the best of times and their twists and turns so frequent that he could rarely see twenty yards before or behind. His pride would not let him run, but he imagined the footsteps of his unknown pursuer every time he slowed his pace, and his breath came quickly as he picked his way east.

Emerging on Golden Lane, he calmed down and even felt somewhat foolish. He was only a few hundred yards from home now. He stepped back as a dray laden with planks trundled noisily past. His eyes followed its passage up the road and there he saw, distinctly and without doubt, the same figure as before, not fifty yards distant.

Peppard panicked. He ran headlong across the road, his sudden movement alerting the figure farther up. He ran into the first opening he found and turned right into another. The footsteps followed him, louder now, and faster than his own. It was not until he reached the dead end at the bottom that Peppard remembered Jermey Row had only one entrance.

For a moment there was silence and he looked about him for some means of escape. But the blind alley was bare of doors or even windows. Only a single buttress provided any possibility of cover. He cowered behind it, flattening himself against the wall. Then he heard the footsteps again. His pursuer had overshot the alleyway in his haste, but backtracking had found it. Gravel ground underfoot. The footsteps slowed. They advanced down the alley, slower and slower. Peppard tried to make himself believe that he would spring at his unknown opponent, that he would somehow break clear and escape. Slower and slower. He shut his eyes. They were almost upon him now. He cringed as they stopped, awaiting whatever fearsome act was to follow. He could hear deep gasps of breath. His pursuer looked down.

"Peppard," he said simply, gulping air. Peppard looked up, his mouth falling open.

"Mister Lemprière!" Peppard exclaimed.

• • •

Five thousand, four hundred and fifty-two vessels lined prow to stern stretched through the mind of Captain Guardian, over the horizon and out of sight. Triremes, barges, brigantines, and tugs; carvels, carracks, and cogs. Captain Guardian had built every type of ship known to man, it was his pleasure. Every night since the one fifteen years back when he had bade his farewells to the sea and first found his thoughts as empty as the deck he had left, he sat down before a roaring fire, closed his eyes, and built a ship. He had read Bouguer, Duhamel Dumonceau, and Leonard Euler (although, for himself, any vessel designed by a Swiss mathematician would not have inspired confidence). He had visited boatyards and talked to their shipwrights. He had even visited France.

On matters of shipworm, he lent cautious support to the advocates of copper sheathing, but would not run down the virtues of fir board, hair, and tar, an amalgam whose prophylactic qualities had, after all, served him well for close on thirty years, six of those in the West Indies. He favored plans rather than models, although the shipwright's habit was more important than either, and believed in the calculation, not guessing, of drafts. A small engraving of Anthony Deane which rested above the mantelpiece attested to this credo and he allowed himself an occasional chuckle when the high spring tide fell short of the launchers' expectations.

After all these years, the comings and goings of the Thames's traffic still held a fascination for him. The sea had never really let him go. Only the previous day, the late afternoon, he had watched as the latest arrival docked and its crew mooched belowdecks. From the window of the Crow's Nest (for so he styled the attic room of his house), Eben had strained his old eyes against the thickening gloom of dusk to watch the hustling watermen as they went about their business. The fire he had stoked warmed his back from the other side of the tiny room. Along its walls, bookcases held well-thumbed volumes. A desk of disproportionate size, far larger than the small door through which it had once presumably negotiated a passage, was strewn with papers, charts, and plans. Looking down from the window, he was able to make out the lines of the shabby vessel berthed a hundred yards down the wharf from his house. He had looked once, then again.

There was something familiar about it. He had seen it somewhere before. . . . He craned and squinted for a better view. He would go down to the dock later, or perhaps in the morning. The room had been warm and the window was misting over. Eben had retired to his desk, sinking into his chair, thinking, as he always did at this time, that he was glad to be warm, dry, and ashore.

That had been the previous evening, and he had yet to take the closer look he had resolved upon. Tomorrow morning, perhaps. Tonight he was indulging his passion which was for the imaginary building of ships. Tonight he was building a hermaphrodite brig.

He had already got the keel on its blocks, the stem and stern posts up and scarfed, the keelson bolted onto the floor-timbers. He bent to his task, planking up to the gunwales, nailing in the decks. Tap, tap, tap, the knocking of mallet on nail, wales on jetty. . . . Somewhere before, he knew it. It nagged at him, it would not let him go. He cut in the grates. Tap, tap, tap, there was something missing, something niggling like the object taken away in a memory game. Tapping at him until remembrance or fury should plug the gap. Captain Guardian propelled himself out of the armchair, up to the casement, and, looking down the quay, realized that this was not the memory game he had thought, for there was the object and here was still the gap. The ship berthed a hundred yards down the quay was called the *Vendragon*. Something in that name, or in that ship, jarred with him. Somewhere in all this, something was wrong.

· · ·

"Here, here, here, and here. Here and here and here!" Peppard's forensic finger stabbed downward with precision. "Also here," he added, the digit moving up.

A white enameled bowl, half filled with grayish water or perhaps it was the light; books, worn red-leather bindings with dust; a bed, a desk, two chairs. No fire and the room was cold.

"But what is it?" Lemprière asked, looking back to the little man.

He had been waiting by the outer entrance to the courtyard only a few minutes before Peppard's compact figure was spotted. But only for a second; the stream of passersby had swallowed the little man immediately and Lemprière had crossed the road several times in search of him. A glimpse, fifty yards up, more a guess. He had used the road, sprinting up to the spot, looking around quickly. Nothing.

Then he had seen him again, frozen for a second with the bustle behind him, and he was off, watching as his quarry disappeared from the highway, marking the point and making for it. But Peppard might have taken any one of the offshoot alleys. No sense trying to pick the right one, he dove in at a run.

Soft dirt underfoot, flagstones the exception rather than the rule. He tripped, almost fell, but regained his feet just in time. The alley had twisted and turned, but each time he thought he was being bent too far off his bearing, it veered back. He heard the raucousness of the highway ahead.

He must have reached the road before his prey. Lemprière moved back and forth, dodging the passersby and looking out for Peppard. He must emerge soon. . . . Yes, there! He shouted, but Peppard had moved quickly and Lemprière drew a curse or two as he shoved his way into the road, across and down the path opposite. He could see nothing. It was impossible, Peppard could simply not have moved that fast. Then he noticed the narrow opening to his left.

"Odd, very odd. Wouldn't have been a professional . . . but perhaps." He paused. "Very odd." Peppard bent closer to the document, using his hands like compasses to bridge the paragraphs, linking word to word.

"Peppard?" Lemprière reminded his companion.

"George, if you like, a moment please. . . ." He was still reading.

"Skewer thought it a curiosity, but not valueless," Lemprière prompted again.

"Certainly not valueless," murmured Peppard, intent in his examination.

Peppard pushed himself back from the table, still staring at the document. The cowering air which he had still worn when they had entered his rooms had now disappeared. He had reentered a world where he was the orchestrator, and now he exuded the confidence of one who had the measure of his task.

"Not valueless, although it begs the question of value," he said at length.

Lemprière's face remained blank.

"Pardon me, that was ill-phrased; if perhaps you told me what you wished to learn?"

What he wished to learn? Lemprière's thought had spun outward in his waiting, and now, as Peppard's offer drew him back to circle in upon that question, discarded possibilities threw out their tangents. He would have liked to learn what a man of Peppard's ability was doing serving someone like Skewer. He would have liked to learn more of the scandal which seemed to have some bearing on this fact. He would like to know a great deal more about Septimus. He warmed to the question. There were whole catalogs of things he wished to learn. The meaning of the sibylline leaves; the location of the omphalos. Why had Alexander killed Hermolaus? The nature of the channels between the living and dead, did they exist, who was the fairest of them all, might she love him, her long, black hair, the water. . . . Enough?

"What is it?" he asked.

Lemprière had looked down the passage. It was only a few feet wide and the walls of the buildings rose up on either side, giving the impression that really they should have met and the space between them existed only by default. The alley appeared quite empty.

Peppard the fleet of foot, he thought to himself. The name of the miserable passage had been scrawled on the wall, but the rain, or whatever liquid fell from the sky in these parts, had partially scoured it. Now it read "er ow." He walked a few yards up, the same few yards back. Then he saw the buttress. His feet crunched on the gravel as he approached the only hiding place possible. Sure enough, there was Peppard.

"Peppard," he said.

"Mister Lemprière!" exclaimed Peppard in astonishment.

Lifting Peppard up, legs none too steady, the mutual explanations, Peppard cowered in embarassment. They had walked back together, Peppard muttering directions, Lemprière apologizing for this and that, he might have waved more vigorously, called out, all the while harboring guilty thoughts that he had enjoyed the chase. They were close to the lodging house in Blue Anchor Lane that Peppard called home.

"That depends upon how you view it, do you see?"

He did not.

"It is a crude sort of covenant, an indenture, a blackmail note, even a charter-party, or nothing at all, or all of these." He smiled. "All to varying degrees and proportions, of course."

"Basically though, it is an agreement, isn't it?" Lemprière ventured hopefully.

"Absolutely correct," confirmed Peppard, "but then, almost every legal document is an agreement. An order for execution is an agreement, although on considerably less favorable terms for one party than the other. I do not think we can leave it at that. The law, remember, is an imprecise instrument, hence lawyers. It finds *in favor*, or not, of course; the truth is excluded so far as is possible. Tends to complicate things. Shall we take some tea?"

They sat nursing the hot cups, warming their hands by them. Peppard had ensured that he took the chipped one. The two men hunched over the desk with the document laid out before them.

"An indenture is the simplest explanation," began Peppard.

"An indenture?"

"These," he ran his finger along the fringe of serrations at the parchment's edge, "they indicate the presence of another copy, or copies, most probably one, though."

"The one held by the Earl of Braith?"

"If it is still in the family, yes." He slurped. "It is a kind of security; you see, if the two sets of cuts do not match then one must be a forgery." He bent to examine the serrations more closely. "Cleanly cut, this would be the top copy, not that that means anything. Of course," Peppard changed tack, "cutting up bits of paper has no force in law, it is only for the convenience of the parties." He paused. "Puzzling really, it may have been drafted in a hurry, whatever was to hand . . ." and he drifted into some private speculation at which Lemprière, for the moment, could only guess.

"You see, the agreement was between the two of them," Peppard was explaining. "The recognition of one copy by another was subsidiary to their recognizing each other, unless both were using agents, but I think that unlikely."

"Why?" the other broke in.

"I'll come to it. But if they recognized each other, why do the documents have to confirm it? Unless one or both were to change in appearance. They may have met only very rarely." Peppard's fingers drummed. "It would make sense."

Lemprière felt that something had been explained, but his question remained unanswered.

"I know," said Peppard, reading the thought, "I was coming to it." Both slurped. "As you said, it is an agreement."

"And as you said, that means everything and nothing."

"Well, yes. In its essentials, it is this. Thomas de Vere agrees to act as your ancestor's representative in matters which aren't specified exactly, but have some bearing on foreign trade, East India trade." Peppard pored over the paper. "Your ancestor will be the recipient of all . . . ah yes, all his share and will pay a tenth of this sum back to the Earl for his services. This is only half the story, unless the Earl was an idiot. As the arrangement stands, the poor Earl simply gives nine-tenths of his share—"

"Share of what, though?" Lemprière demanded.

"Why, the Joynt-Stock Company, of course, the dear old Joynt-Stock Company, the forerunner of that good and great institution, that safeguard of our foreign interest." Peppard's voice was acid. "That benevolent fund of the distressed and down-at-heel, that, that," he spluttered, his mouth working. "Damn me."

"That what?" Lemprière quizzed gently, wondering what raw nerve had been exposed here.

"The Company," his companion said at length in calm but strangled tones.

"The East India Company?"

"The same." Peppard seemed to be fighting for self-control. His face was red. He choked something back, then continued unconvincingly as if nothing was amiss. "At any rate, your ancestor must have offered the Earl something, and we can only guess at what that might have been."

Lemprière would like to have heard some of these guesses, but held his tongue. The little man's voice was even now. Only a slight rigidity in his manner suggested his earlier outburst.

"This paragraph, 'Whereas the first person' and so on, this is all quite irrelevant. It does not matter how the Joynt-Stock Company was formed, its charter has no bearing at all; I would hazard that it has been lifted from a previous document; padding, no more. Of the rest, there are four points which indicate clues." Peppard was nothing but business now. His guest relaxed.

"I was saying that the first is this word 'vyages,' 'the vyages set forth to the Indies' and so on, the question being how many, and to that there is no answer. Not here at any rate. The second is the 'service' that Thomas de Vere offers," Peppard went on. "There is no mention of *what* service, although I could guess at that, given the third point, this 'his neutral agent and representative.' Why neutral? Rather, why the need for 'neutral'?" Lemprière had no idea. Peppard's thoughts had some pattern, they led to something, he could see that much, but he was lost.

"The fourth point begs all these questions; you see this, 'notwithstanding the desuetude or the death,' the death, mark you, 'of either or both,' et cetera, et cetera. Now the agreement is between these two men, how can death *not* end it? The vagueness is not in the phrasing, it is in the idea of the thing." He tapped irritatedly with his finger.

"Extension."

"Extension," echoed Lemprière.

"How many voyages? How much of an agent? How neutral? For how long? These are the questions," Peppard vigorously insisted.

"The questions, yes, they are."

"You see, there is a supposition here that cuts two ways. First, the future is taken for granted, the deal is in perpetuity, 'notwithstanding' and all that, here." He pointed for Lemprière's benefit. "Second, that this is so because the whole thing is too vague to be at all binding. The key areas are undefined. And the style is odd. I've seen many documents— deeds and wills, mostly, but it's all of a piece—roughed out by both parties with a legal handbook and a little common sense. The poor devils take immense pains. All the phrases are there, but something invariably goes astray. They are rarely legal, properly speaking, that is."

"And this is like that; there is a flaw?" said Lemprière.

"Quite the opposite. This is perfect. What they are trying to agree to is, I think, impossible, unless they were immortal, but the form is quite legal. The impression I get—" He stopped, rubbed the bridge of his nose. "The impression I get is that a lawyer was employed and told to cover his tracks, make it seem an amateur's job."

"But why on earth—?"

"It ties with the second point, the vagueness as to what they are agreeing. A contingency plan, I should imagine—"

"Contingency, contingent on what?" Lemprière was thrown again. Peppard looked across the table at him.

"Why, treason, of course. When this agreement was signed, your family was French, I take it?"

"I suppose so, I don't know, yes, I still don't see—"

"The government of the day, or even now, might well take the view that acting as the agent of a Frenchman was not the duty to"—he checked the date—"Queen and country expected of a loyal citizen. Of course, it's treason. That is the binding force of the document. Obvious, really."

"George, it is not obvious. It is not obvious at all."

"Listen, the terms of the document are so ill-defined as to be capable of almost any construction, correct?"

Lemprière nodded.

"Therefore there must be some hold, without the legal, to bind the parties, are you with me?"

Lemprière nodded again.

"If De Vere had reneged, this document could have been used as his death warrant; therefore it is binding. I would imagine that the vagueness of the terms were his attempts, fruitless ones I might say, to guard against indictment." He paused and looked more closely. Then he chuckled. "Do you know what the most binding feature of this document is?" Without waiting for an answer, he stabbed at the middle of Lemprière's ancestor's Christian name. "That," he said, "that is what would have hanged Thomas de Vere."

Lemprière peered across at François Lemprière's faded signature, noticing for the first time that the hand was uncannily like his own.

"A 'c'?"

"Not the 'c,' its appendage: the cedilla. Decisive proof the man was French. No Englishman would spell his name with a cedilla. Poor Thomas de Vere, this was the hook for the rope he feared." Peppard grew more serious. "Of course, none of this answers why the Earl signed it. We do not know what he was offered, but it must have been something worthwhile. The risks were enormous."

His companion was mulling on questions closer to home. "That was why Septimus wished to buy it: treason. . . . Reason enough."

"Not quite, the agreement only binds the fourth Earl. It would be a minor embarrassment at worst today."

"But 'notwithstanding the death of either party' and all that?"

"True, but no one would pursue such a case. Unless the agreement was somehow revalidated." Peppard was tempted to pursue this line of thought, but no, Skewer was probably correct about the Earl's motives, and why raise the boy's hopes? If the document were valid and the share or portion had been reinvested each time the Company had amalgamated, then Master Lemprière would be a very rich young man indeed. . . . And the Company so much the poorer, a thought which pleased him. They talked on, going over the points Peppard had explained, poring over the old parchment together.

"The essentials are these," Peppard said. "François Lemprière takes a ninth share in the Company and pays Thomas de Vere a tenth from that sum. In return, Thomas de Vere acts as his agent, a front to conceal his ownership. How did Thomas benefit? I do not know." Lemprière stared somberly at the document before them.

"There is more to the business than that," he said. Peppard only nodded.

It began to grow late. The two of them talked on, but Peppard had little to add to his explication. At length, their conversation drew to its close. Lemprière folded up the parchment with care and buttoned his coat. Peppard had opened the door. Lemprière thanked him.

"Good-bye!" called Peppard after his guest. Lemprière waved his farewell, then turned to begin the journey home.

Tucked away inside his shirt, the parchment crackled as he drew his coat about him and headed down the street. He tramped along thoughtfully, the feeling gathering that some onus was testing him for strength weighing pleasantly about his shoulders. The flood of people on Golden Lane was undiminished; a mass that moved with powerful, divided purpose, it gathered him and bore him along buoyed up in thought. A little way ahead, an osier plodded, panniers slung from his hips and a chest dragged behind. He cleared the path for Lemprière, who followed.

Lemprière puzzled over Septimus. Skewer he understood, at least as much as he wanted to. Peppard, he felt, he not only understood but liked as well. Septimus, though . . . It was not that he had the air of a concealer, more that there was too much on view. Why had he wanted the agreement? And why had he directed him to Peppard? True enough, the lawyer had told him more than he might ever have divined alone. The advice had been a boon, and the matters revealed. . . . Well, he would look into them further. Septimus and Peppard: his allies. The rest? Septimus's admonition resounded in the confusion of the whole city. *Here, you are the barbarian.* . . . And, if not Septimus, who else in this city would help him?

So he continued, a scurrying dot in an ant army of scurriers, winking in and out of view of all but the watchful, silent buildings. They awaited his performance, their serried balconies and storys stacked one on another, on and up, each succeeding the next in dispassion until only a mosaic of jostling heads was available to the eyes of stone above. The bustling street had its own needs, the street creatures their desires, but somehow from up here it was all too remote, too faint. Perhaps it was lost somewhere in the ascent. The buildings registered it in the jumbled noise of the street, an always-decreasing but still fervent possibility that the shapelessness below might suddenly coalesce. They sensed a drift away from the marked-out paths and toward the tingling prickle of cold water down the spine, the tang of vinegar, and a thousand other, minor derelictions from the proper route. Toward, in fact, the lesson of their cousin, the ziggurat, on whose eighth and highest plane there is no image, only yourself, and the doubts that dance attendance on your sufficiency.

Lemprière's doubts milled and whirled about him as he carried his thoughts homeward.

He had allies; and he had mysteries. Already he was thinking of Saturday when more of both might be revealed. *Suck.* He was watched as he made his way along Fleet Street, trudging west to gain the Strand. Weary steps into Southampton Street, watched until he disappeared from view.

• • •

The thin man who watched from the far side of the quay, yes, without a doubt. The chain of porters lurching on board with the cases, no, also without doubt. The cripple was too obvious, discount him, but the face that had appeared twice now at the attic window a hundred yards up the quay would have to be taken into the reckoning. A plan was taking shape in Nazim's mind, a provision. The *Vendragon* was watched, but not guarded—a weak point. If he failed in his first mission, he would triumph in the second. Some might have argued that the way to stop a river was at its source, that the rule of the Nawab was in some way undermined by this kind of expedient. But Nazim knew, indeed had been told by the Nawab himself, that there were larger issues involved. There was a need for secrecy, and beneath the confiding tone the injunction to be caught dead if at all was unspoken and understood by both. The thin man would not look in his direction. This was part of the game; Nazim knew he had been noted and remembered. You too, he thought back. He tipped his hat at the thin man, saw the eyes flicker. His quarry turned and walked eastward along the quay. Nazim hoped he wasn't giving too much slack: If the thin man left before he could double back he would be left with nothing but the old man in the window, who might well have nothing to do with it. . . .

• • •

Untimely Anthesteria, bitter fruit out of season. His elation had proved short-lived as he sifted through his father's papers, sitting there on the hard floor. Another, more substantial pile of papers lay in the trunk awaiting inspection. A map of the world with a question mark scrawled on the Mediterranean, a series of monthly receipts *"reçue par Mme K., 43, Villa Rouge, Rue Boucher des Deux Boules, Paris,"* old letters from people whose suffixes (retr.d, Capt.(ex), miss) told tiny stories of disappointment. There were sketches of ships, long columns of figures,

74

plans of buildings, and a map of some structure he could not identify. Also: a notebook with all the pages torn out, the second half of a sonnet, a list of the ten most numerous butterflies on Jersey with brief descriptions and sketches, a memoir of his grandfather, and some doodling. He had read through most of these, poring over the contents, trying to match handwriting, ink color, types of paper, all in an effort to find the one detail, phrase, jot that, he felt sure, would reveal whatever his father had been searching for. So far, he had discovered nothing.

Septimus had paid a visit the following day, ostensibly to draw a diagram of where the Craven Arms was.

"I would guide you there myself, but as Master of Ceremonies I must arrive early." Lemprière had wondered exactly what ceremonies were being alluded to, but Septimus had already become disruptive, making paper darts out of the more frail-looking documents and offering to teach Lemprière the art of boxing. When he had begun propositioning women from the window—"Come on up!"—Lemprière had asked him to leave.

"Saturday then!" he shouted as he went, practicing his left jab down the stairs.

Now Saturday had come and he knew no more than before. He turned pages listlessly, barely looking at them now. Remains. Could it matter that much? Here was a ship's inventory, here was a broadsheet ballad like one Father Calveston had given him (by mistake?), here was one that Septimus had ruined. He swiped at the papers in irritation. As they settled and came to rest only a few feet away, it occurred to him suddenly that these were the first words he had read in weeks. Strange. Why had he not thought of that before? Of course he had not packed any books (of course?), but then . . .

He had set off on this line of thought and now he did not wish to follow it through. Peppard had read the covenant; he had only glanced at it himself. He might have read it, had he wanted. He had not wanted. Books had led him to all this; already further than he wished to go. All books, though? No. Only the books he had loved most, books with gilt letters on the spine, rag-paper leaves, the Ancient books, the stories that had stayed. Stories of times when the deeds done meant nothing more than they pretended to, when the world could be plotted from its center. He thought of his father's body as it lay by the pool. He thought of the story he had read idly. The dogs ran low over the ground. He never dreamed it could come true. And yet he *had* dreamed. The cloud above turned the waters gray and his father's blood turned them red. The dream was his and no one else's.

It was getting too late for all this, it was getting too dark and far too late. Lemprière rose, put on his coat and boots, and stamped downstairs to the street. Cold? *Your father?* No. His feet tap on the cobbles, the street oddly empty and very little to distract his thoughts as he hurries along, coat wrapped tight against possible rain. Quicken up now, don't want to be late. Why do the feet curl in like that? Must be why boots wear through at the instep, a good anatomist could put England's cobblers out of business, skeletons never his strong suit. . . . Left, right, left at the Henry VIII and Seven Bells, onward and upward; why, we're all Protestants, seminal baptism of the new faith.

Puddles reflect his face as he keeps his head down, avoiding the pilasters with their Doric bottoms and fussy Corinthian capitals, the gaze of caryatids, other relics and remnants. He turns into Hogg Street, walking faster still. Excessively baroque masonry might fall and crush him to death at any moment, no one can say the streets are safe, tap, tap, tap on the cobbles. *Your father?* No, not yet, better to wait, or a passing eagle might drop a tortoise on his head like Æschylus, better to work round to it, press-ganging makes the worst sailors, the triremes manned by freedmen, galley slaves a thing of the future. . . . This is more like it, wondering now about the ceremonies Septimus mentioned. He is in the mood for company, and singing (although he can't) no, yes, and perhaps drinking too, cantilevered here between something approaching hysteria, walking even faster now, and that other voice that he hopes he has lost somewhere in the backstreets to be found murdered the next morning; death by tortoise bombardment.

Above, the moon is being unnaturally silvery, cloud illumination high on its agenda tonight. Well to its rear, several particularly pluvial specimens are making their way eastward over the shires to demonstrate cloud functions (moon eclipse, rain, symbolic needs of one kind or another) to the city that chance has dictated as their destination. At the moment, though, compact, woolly puffs (strictly scenic) amble around the sky, dissolving as they pass the lunar face and providing it, momentarily, with a wispy fringe of hair.

Had Lemprière looked up, he might have drawn an analogy between this phenomenon and the steel-gray leonine head of the ranter who appeared to be waving a flag in fury at an invisible opponent at the other end of the street. The flag-waver is very angry as he shouts about vanity and the exchange of goods and the land of our fathers. Really, Lemprière thinks, it is too late for this kind of thing, but a crowd of fifteen or twenty people are standing around listening, excuse me, excuse me, as he finds a way through, ". . . and the worst of it, the worst of it is this" (more flag waving) . . . But Lemprière never hears the worst of it, at least not until too late, because now he's through them, around the corner, and anticipating his entrance at the inn, whose sign he has spotted just a matter of yards away, hurry up now, nearly there and distractions aplenty, find out all the things I, fumble the door, all the answers, all the questions. . . . *Your father?* No-oo, here we go. . . .

"*Wel*-come to the *Pork Club!!*" Septimus, mountebank, impresario, is in full flood, jigging on the table. The place is heaving. Is this what he agreed to? Around and about, a herd of brocaded fops conducts intercourse of several sorts with sozzled and unbuttoned beauties.

"Oink!" They turn as one to acknowledge their heralding master of ceremonies. No one (except Septimus) is actually shouting, but the din is horrible. Lemprière blinks nervously; this is not what he expected at all and now Septimus has spotted his entrance and decided to leap *over* the assembled Pork Club members in a greeting designed at once to draw attention to his bespectacled friend and confirm this bundle of first-night nerves as party to all this, one of the gang. As he attempts this maneuver, a shrieking chit and her swain feel that this is the moment to propose a toast. Bottle waving and leaping coincide as Septimus boots the vessel inadvertently, crashing into the crush where bystanders break his fall.

"Ha!" He bounces up. The bottle, meanwhile, has continued along Septimus's aborted trajectory, over the crowd and ends up, *slaap,* in Lemprière's hand.

"Have a glug," a voice from somewhere down near his hip. He glugs.

"So you've met?" Septimus has disentangled himself from a melee of arms and legs, rejected the importunings of something with too much mascara, and approaches with perfect composure, one hand fishing in his pocket.

"Bacon?"

"What . . .?"

From the folds of his coat Septimus produces the longest, reddest, greasiest piece of bacon that Lemprière has ever seen. It has to be a yard in length. Is this the first of tonight's ceremonies? A pig the size of a horse died for this monster but Septimus doesn't actually expect anyone to eat it, does he?

Seems not. It dangles lewdly as Septimus makes the introductions.

"Teddy, John Lemprière. John, Edmund de Vere." So this was the Earl. First impressions were not always the best.

"We're playing together later, John," he continued to Lemprière, then lowered his voice," "Don't drink too much. Hold yourself in reserve."

"Playing together? Playing what?"

"Foolish boy, the Game of Cups, of course," beams Septimus.

"Er . . . Septimus?"

But Septimus has already disappeared back into the crush to find that little redhead he's promised a sure-fire piquet cheat, the one where the Knave of Clubs is tucked inside the garter. . . .

"S'alright," the lordly slur near his hip issues in boozy gulps which, being slightly warmer than the surrounding air, rise to his twitching nostrils and mingle there with the odors of smoke, fire and pipe, sweat, half-stifled farts, Bergamot snuff, Jessamine hair-butter, and something else. . . .

Septimus has retreated (is, in fact, draping his flaccid rhabdos about the neck of an unsuspecting maid at the far side of the room, the piquet trick can wait), so it can't be that. His nose scans the olfactory scene until, there, he lights on the fireplace from which delicious porky fumes are lacing the air with memories of bacon-for-breakfast and sausage-for-supper, sizzling chops, and glistening gammon steaks. Yum. Suspended over the fire, trotters touching one side of the chimney, snout grazing the other, a pig of obese proportions oozes fat into the flames below. The spit bends under its lolling weight, and on its face (apple in snout notwithstanding) is an expression of ironic martyrdom recalling Saint Lawrence who, after twenty minutes on the griddle, asked to be turned for fear one side was becoming rather well done.

This pig obviously holds some numinous significance for the assembly. The revelers nearest it are tending toward the racy-conversation-and-pipe-smoking side of indecency, leaving the far side of the room to the more gymnastically inclined, while the crone giving it an occasional prod with her stick is treated with the greatest respect; nods and gentlemanly offerings of "good-evening" are coming her way thick and fast.

Meanwhile the voice at his hip has been replaced by a hand. He swivels about; an apparition in creamy satin and red ringlets is already explaining, no, sorry, mistook you for someone . . . so sorry, before gliding away, leaving only the scent of rosewater and a short trail of cards that drift to the floor from their lodging somewhere beneath her aprons.

"Spectacles!" The leering Warburton-Burleigh reels up. "Grog?"

"Thank you, no, I—" Lemprière stiffly.

"Don't mind if I do," and with that he snatches the bottle, heading back for the seething swell in which Lemprière catches sight of Septimus demonstrating a spirited *pas de chat* while, in the corner, someone has attached eight bottles on strings to the banisters above and is trying to pour *just the right amount* of beer into each one to get doh, ray, me, etc. Unfortunately, every time he pours too much in, he is having to drink it down to the right level; success looks remote, and the cooing wench who, just half an hour ago, expressed a wish to hear a song from the auld country played in this manner is bitterly regretting ever opening her mouth while Monsieur with the mustache over there is showing his shiny, yellow teeth and winking at her in just the way she likes.

For Lemprière, everything seems to be happening *over there* while he is ghettoed *over here*. No matter, he is here on business. He sits down next to the Earl, and instantly knows he has done the wrong thing. The Earl is playing "find the bean" on the table, switching the three tumblers with surprising deftness given his addled state. The bean has been lost for several rounds now and his opponent wandered off some time before that. Besides, all the tumblers are glass. . . . The evidence convinces Lemprière that the Earl is in no fit state to divulge anything much, but, he reasons, this is going to get worse rather than better, it's now or never so here goes.

To start with, the Earl doesn't respond at all. Lemprière prods him, which gives rise to some nonspecific flailing around and lots of slurring. Nothing of use so far, but he keeps at it, explaining about the meeting between their ancestors and so forth. True, this was a century and a half ago, not of immediate relevance, but didn't the Earl want to buy the record of this ancestral tête-à-tête? Gradually he garners that although the Earl knows what he's talking about, he's not even remotely interested, and why isn't Lemprière drinking anyway?

"Drinking not my strong point," he explains to the drunkard.

"Good man, never start," the Earl commends him, offering a glutinous, green substance with one hand and supporting his head with the other.

"You see, this agreement—"

"A thimbleful wouldn't hurt, though, would it?"

"No really, thank you."

"Here, try this. It really is very, very . . ." The Earl searches for an adjective. "It really is very," he concludes. Lemprière declines again, which seems to depress the Earl.

"I think you might tell me why you won't drink," he demands in injured tones. "Only courteous, I'd say." The Earl's elbow has hit a patch of pork grease, probably dripped there earlier by Septimus's outsize rasher, and now every time he tries to rest his head on his hand, the arm is shooting out sideways, dumping his head, *bang,* on the tabletop. The conversation proceeds to the accompaniment of these collapses.

"Of course, quite," Lemprière is obliging the Earl's request. "It's very simple." *Bang.* "I was warned not to—" he pauses, "by my parents." He looks down for a moment. "Now, as to this agreement—"

Bang!

The quiz continues on a more equal basis with Lemprière providing a justification for not drinking every time he asks a question but not much is coming of it and he's down to doctor's orders when he throws in a last gambit (the Earl can't last much longer) and offers to sell the document. At this the Earl offers thruppence and the advice to try "Sebdimus, he's much more interested anyway. . . ." Lemprière had been half-expecting this and would have pumped the Earl for more, but the booze-to-body-weight ratio is against him and the Earl seems about to slide. . . .

In point of fact, this observation of Lemprière's, despite being founded on the soundest inductive principles, is quite mistaken. All appearances to the contrary, Thomas de Vere is not getting drunker, but more sober. There is something in these ruinous gatherings that brings out the progressive in him. A mutant strain of the dissent whose viral ancestor might well have had something to do with the little get-together Lemprière's so curious about is lurking someplace about Thomas de Vere's lymph system and now, between sporadic phagocyte attacks, is busy oozing its idea of happiness through his membranes and venous capillaries. As symbioses go, it's one-sided. The leucocytes are reserving judgment.

Hard to say just what it is or even where it comes from, but there's an

79

austere tinge of self-denial about it. A touch of the Prussian, streaming over like influenza from Königsberg and covering its trail. Only
a sprinkling of umlauts give the game away, whispers of a cousin
somewhere called Friedrich, or Emmanuel, the faint whiff of bratwurst
and a dim, hereditary yearning for black, rained-on forests with the
steam rolling down the hillsides in the morning sunlight, everything very
fresh. . . .

There's something very *onward* about it too, a belief implicit in the
Earl's intimate biochemistry that somehow things are always going to
improve. His drinking exploits are the stuff of legend, but it is a recent
legend. It has nothing to do with prowess, and downing a flagon of sack
merely to reach sobriety has often seemed to him a cruel reversal. To his
friends, the Earl's habit of turning up drunk and leaving sober is nothing
but a quirk; he doesn't need a motive but *schadenfreude* will do.

Had Lemprière known all this he might have deferred his questions till
later in the evening, but his recidivist heart is set on things getting worse
rather than better, and indeed they will, for Monsieur the Mustache has
got the girl while her erstwhile companion is still dinging away in frustration, just another quarter-tone, the tonic's a little out and on top of that
people keep coming up and drinking vital parts of the instrument. The
crone has left her place at the fire to show Septimus how the step should
be done, toe in and *flick!* her shoe whirls off across the room to crash
against an oil lamp which spills a sinuous tongue of flame across the floor,
but everything's under control as the Pork Club rallies in common crisis,
spraying the conflagration with beer, cider, and the nastier wines (glad
for a refill anyway), and no one is so much as singed.

Everything starts up again, but a general and complex movement is
taking place, a vague, concentric urge radiating out from the center of the
debauchees, from, in fact, the Crone. She has given up the dancing lesson
as a bad job and is turning around, putting the eye on the smoochers,
snorters, and swiggers who, under this weird pressure, begin to separate.
Hands are discreetly removed from bodices, temptingly steatopygous
posteriors are no longer being slapped, the sexes are parting like the Red
Sea, and fond farewells, blown kisses, and entreaties to be true fill the
melodramatic air like limp translations of a libretto by Calzabigi. An air
of expectation begins to take their place. Fops, cads, toffs, and swells are
now corralled on Lemprière's side of the room while wenches, damsels,
nymphs, and baggages take up positions on the other; a few look somehow familiar but there's no time to ponder that now because the Crone
has pounded her stout wand three times upon the floor and retreated back
to the fire. The stage is bare and into it bounds Septimus.

His face is grave. Serious matters are impending as he addresses the
bacchanals.

"My friends," he begins, "dear ladies," turning behind him, "in this
most excellent and convivial of clubs—" (cries of "Hear, hear!" and

"None better!") "we have all spent many happy hours which, could we but remember them, would most certainly never be forgotten. We have drunk—" (mutters of "Very true" and "No doubting that") "we have sung, we have—" a pause for obscene effect, "roistered!" ("Ha! We have at that" and "Best roistering in town." Mutual phrases of "Well roistered, sir!" are exchanged.) "But—" Septimus holds up his finger, they know what's coming, "above all, we have eaten—" they're poised for it, "huge quantities of Pork!"

At the mention of pork, the place erupts, whooping and hat throwing are general, a fight breaks out, and the combatants are separated amid scenes of license and celebratory lewdness. From the fireplace, the Crone acknowledges the compliment by throwing a sizzling strip of crackling into the midst of the rejoicers, who fall upon it with frenzied gnashing and drooling.

"Madame!" Septimus salutes her, and the company raise their glasses.

"Drink hearty, my boys!" she throws back and attempts a brittle pirouette which is noisily applauded. Septimus has caught them in an appreciative mood.

"My friends," he continues, "we have with us tonight a very dear acquaintance of mine." (Curious glances among the assembly, who is it?) "A young man cast adrift on life's river. If he is too young to be an orphan, he is old enough to be our friend. Welcome with me my partner in the game this night, Mister John Lemprière!" There is polite applause as Lemprière acknowledges the introduction. Septimus switches to mock-lecture tone.

"Now, as all good cooks know, the most succulent, fragrant, the most sublime flitch of pig flesh is deemed to fall short of its acme, to hurtle down from the zenith of Eumaeus's pen when deprived of its natural companion, its liquid bedfellow. . . . My friends, I speak, of course, of drink."

The Pork Club bangs its glasses three times on the table.

"Yes, my friends, drink. The solace of abandoned wives, the lubrication of our fleet; if it is good enough for sailors and their tarts"—hands outstretched in appeal, plangent he goes on—"surely, *surely* it is good enough for us?" A few grunts of "Certainly is" confirm the truth of this.

"And so we have a game." At this, Septimus falls silent and paces the floor, fingers to the bridge of his nose, all of a sudden in deep thought. An act.

"It may not be the most athletic of games, it may not be for the scholars or even the *hoi polloi*, but it has two great qualities. First, it involves jeroboams, nay salmanazars of drink—" (the Pork Club rumbles its collective appreciation, he's gingering them up) "and second, it is at least *our* game." Dying fall, aah . . . Sentimental glances are exchanged, the strong and the dissolute gaze down at their feet. Tears might be welling in their eyes.

"My friends," Septimus recalls them before this gets too maudlin, "our thanks are due to two dear people: our gracious hostess—" (cheers for the Crone) "and perhaps, tonight, her husband-to-be, that stalwart progenitor . . . King Archon!"

This is a setup. The Pork Club boos and hisses, death threats are offered, and hideous expressions of loathing can be seen on every face. Lemprière is nonplussed, looking around for the object of so much hatred.

"Over there," the Earl whispers to him between shouts of "Cut his shriveled ballocks off!" and "Crush his face in!"

Sitting in a chair by the side of the fire at the foot of the stairs which run at a diagonal up the far wall is King Archon. His once-majestic face falls in unmuscled folds, expressionless, his lips twitch and drool, and the drool smears a trail down his shirt. He seems unaware of the Pork Club's vociferous disgust. The years have burnt away his life from within until only this remains, and whatever once sustained him has been eked out further than nature should allow; abomination, old scum, he deserves death but his punishment for living, being life itself, is crueler and more drawn out than that. Filthy, scabrous remnant: Long live the King! The compassion of his subjects dictates his life's endurance although, in some other shape or effigy, the King will be killed tonight.

Septimus is quieting the mob now, readying them for the off. The Crone hobbles center stage to acclamation as the gallants begin to pair off.

"Bon chance," the Earl offers sportingly to his late interrogator.

On the far side of the room, two of the more venerable courtesans have opened a book and are busy shouting the odds, taking bets in coin and credit notes of one sort or another. Lemprière's on offer at sixes (and only that generous because of Septimus), while Walter Warburton-Burleigh and the Pug (a barrellike individual with squinty eyes) are strong favorites at 13–8. Lemprière drifts to tens. The smart money's ignoring him. The bookmakers look familiar but before he can think about this he sees Septimus hand them a purse of coins which is accepted after some hesitation and the price comes in suddenly to fours.

The Crone, meanwhile, is doling out lumps of pork to the contestants and setting up an array of bottles on the table in the center. There are bottles of all shapes, sizes, and colors, some bound in raffia, some sealed with wax, and in front of each she places a small earthenware cup with a letter stamped upon it. There are twenty-six of these. On the other side of the room, a small table supports a bowl of black beans. Something is stirring inside Lemprière, some inarticulate response to the iconography, but he doesn't know quite what and before he can think about it Septimus swaggers over, about time too. Lemprière starts hissing his doubts, what is he doing here, what is going on? But his fellow player dismisses this as too metaphysical to be taken seriously.

"That's not what I meant," he hisses.

"Just watch what the others do," advises Septimus, chomping on Lemprière's pork, "and stop hissing."

Most of the contestants have found their partners, final bets are being taken, and the games seem about to start. The Crone has raised her rhabdos for silence.

"The Game of Cups!" shrieks the Crone.

"Oink!" oink Septimus, the Earl, and the other contestants.

"The prize awaits the winner, let the game begin!"

"Pythoigia!" shouts everyone except Lemprière. Pythoigia?

"What *is* the prize?" he asks Septimus when the noise dies down.

"You'll find out," Septimus replies.

The Crone has retired to the fire. The first contestants rush to their places.

"Eat more pork," Septimus advises, and the Earl nods sage agreement.

"The more pork, the better your chances," he confirms.

The first pair are well into the first round of the game. One drains the cups before him in order, arrack, brandy, cider, and so on, while his partner takes up station by the bowl of beans.

"Watch the rhythm," urges Septimus, "the rhythm's the key."

At every third cup drained, the player by the beans picks one out and spits it in a controlled parabola into the empty cup which the drinker holds up while reaching for the next. From nine beans spat, only three found their way, *ding!* into the allotted empty cup, all of which are immediately refilled in readiness for the next contestants.

"Weak round," adjudged the Earl.

By the time they have finished, the drinker is reeling and there is some jeering at his modest capacity.

"Choes!" screams the Crone.

This heralds the second round, and the first two take up positions on bended knees, one by King Archon, the other by the Crone herself. They seem to be pleading with them, but to little avail. Meanwhile, the second team is in position, drinking and firing, firing and drinking, eggnog, furmity, *pfft, ding!* gin, hock, Irrois, and on, five beans out of six so far, pretty good.

Lemprière's attention is on the first team as they entreat the Crone and her scraggy appendage, King Archon.

"Don't worry too much about the Choes part of the game," Septimus says.

"But what are they doing?"

"One persuades King Archon to marry the Crone, the other the same in reverse; but forget it. It's an interlude, treat it as a breather."

"Won't we lose if—?"

"No, not at all. In all the history of the Pork Club, no one has ever succeeded in persuading either of them. It's considered sportsmanlike to try but save your energies for—"

"Chytroi!" shouts the Crone as the second team's drinker drains the last cup. They have managed seven beans out of nine and the drinker is still standing, better than expected. They move on to the game's final part, a mime of some sort.

"What's this?" whispers Lemprière.

"Where the Game is won or lost," Septimus replies. "The hopefuls improvise a dramatic entertainment along broadly tragic lines; the only hard and fast rule is that it must end with the death of King Archon. Look, this is it now."

One of the contestants looked as though he were trying to erect a ladder while the other brushed frantically at imaginary bees. Suddenly, both rush at King Archon with something that might have been a caldron, one on either side, and empty its imaginary contents over his head. There is scattered applause for this.

"Spirited, but nonsensical," comments Septimus.

The Game of Cups is in full swing now. Impassioned entreaties, elaborately coded body language, and beans fly around the room. The contestants who have finished are munching on pig meat and swapping compliments on one another's performances.

"Darling! *Loved* your killing."

"How many did George get? Good God, really?"

"Oh, you're too modest. It was *simply* Plautine!"

Bean-spitters are swigging rapidly to catch their partners; there is a feeling of camaraderie among the finishers. The Earl has wandered off to find his partner. The Game goes on and it is not until Walter Warburton-Burleigh and the Pug have arisen to take their places at Pythoigia that Lemprière realizes he and Septimus are going last.

"We're last!" he says to his partner, but Septimus is exchanging hostile looks with the Pug.

"They'll be the ones to beat," he confides.

"You don't seriously expect us to win, do you?" Lemprière is aghast at the responsibility.

"You better hope we do," Septimus ripostes. "I bet all your money on us."

Whaat?

And sure enough, the lining of his coat is empty . . . an apparition in red ringlets and creamy satin, clever fingers in his pockets, oh you fool. . . .

There is a certain predictability in the lunge Lemprière throws at Septimus. And something very inevitable about its missing. Lemprière is outraged. He outstares Septimus for several long seconds, should he try and hit him again? Lemprière is furious, but surprised at himself; a half-pleased feeling mixed in with the still-strong urge to break Septimus's nose is leveling him out and Septimus is apologizing anyway. . . . Hell, we can win, and suchlike sentiments are rising in crescendo; an irresistible urge to do something really rather stupid and pull through is the right stuff for the occasion.

The Pug and Warburton-Burleigh are going like clockwork, slurp, slurp, slurp, arm out, *pfft . . . ding!* Warburton-Burleigh is sending the beans over in arcs of all descriptions, drawing high proscenium arches, perfect semicircles, and flat-out bean-to-cup beelines in the pungent air, child's play. They're on for nine out of nine.

"Remember, rhythm," hisses Septimus as they get up. "Get it down at your own pace, but get it down whatever."

"Perhaps I should spit the beans," suggests Lemprière, who doesn't remember agreeing to the drinking role.

"No time to discuss the tactical fine points now. Look, see those two? Know why they're smiling? They saw me put that bet on, they want us to lose, do you see? Smug bastards, we'll wipe their faces in it. For God's sake, *come on*, John. It's your money. . . ."

The other contestants are applauding Warburton-Burleigh's acrobatics, but everyone has half an eye on Septimus; how can he pull this one out of the fire? Especially with that half-blind lame duck as his partner. . . . Confidence is not high but best wishes will be with them. No one really wants to see the Pug and Warburton-Burleigh win the prize, Septimus is the last bastion.

"Come on, John. Let's go to work." And with that, Septimus is up, flexing and swallowing, while Lemprière bumbles behind him.

"You know what to do?"

He nods.

"Every third cup."

"I know." Lemprière takes his place at cup "A," Septimus by the beans, a look is exchanged. No "Good luck"; this is business. They're off.

Lemprière's worries up to this point have been mostly along the lines of some unspecified failure and consequent public humiliation. He has thought about the difficulties of bean-catching in a vague sort of way, but the notion that he may not be able to physically swallow the potions in front of him has not occurred. Until now. The earlier swig should have forewarned him of this. The stench of arrack fills his nostrils as he raises the first cup to his lips; a few titters start up at his hesitation. He is certain that if he swallows this, if he allows this noxious poison down his throat, he will puke instantly. The titters are turning to insults now, oh no, it smells of death, only one thing for it. . . . He swallows, and by some intestinal miracle, he holds it down. The brandy burns but is less disgusting. The cider he might almost have drunk voluntarily, almost forgets to turn, just in time, *pfft . . . ding!* One out of one. Somewhat encouraged, he tries to remember to keep the rhythm, furmity, *pfft . . . ding!* gin, hock, and on he goes, glugging and turning, the other contestants are cheering him on, who'd have thought it, slurp, slurp? The drinking is definitely getting easier, first is worse, oh yes, julep, kümmel, lethe, turn and catch, porter, quassia, rum, *ding!* He catches a sight of the Pug from the corner of his eye and tries a hostile grin. Wassail runs down his chin, no matter, Xeres sack, turn and nine out of nine, yellow-root, force it down, one more. He pours the last down with a flourish, splashing it all the way back to his eager tonsils, zythum, pyramid juice. *Slurpp.*

Lemprière bangs the cup down on the table and turns to acknowledge the cheers of the Pork Club. The alcohol has brought tears to his eyes but he only needs his ears for this.

"Good work." Septimus claps him on the back. Warburton-Burleigh and the Pug have (as expected) failed to persuade King Archon and the Crone of each other's charms and are sneering across the crowd. Septimus and Lemprière limber up for the next round.

"How are you feeling, John?"

"Very well, nine out of nine, eh?" True, he is feeling a little flushed and his stomach is shifting about in unfamiliar ways, but it is not exactly unpleasant, yet.

"Take the next stage slowly, all right? You take the King, I'll deal with the Crone. There's nothing to it, John." This last as Lemprière's anxieties begin to surface on his face. "Just describe her in the most favorable terms you can think of. If you get stuck, tell lies."

"Right." Lemprière is warmer than he was a few minutes before and loosens his collar as they take their positions, Septimus kneeling at the feet of the Crone, his partner by the King.

The Pug and Warburton-Burleigh are impatient to commence, and the Pork Club agrees with them. At a signal from the Crone, all begin, Pug and Warburton-Burleigh instantly into a pretty snappy sword fight while Septimus assails the Crone with gamomanic protestations of King Archon's progenitive capabilities and all-round, nuptial dark-horse characteristics, ". . . appearances can be deceptive," he's saying.

But Lemprière is stuck. He looks across at the Crone, then back to the King. Nothing complimentary springs to mind.

"She'd probably feed you well," he begins lamely.

"She feeds him anyway!" shouts a freckled porker behind him. His tonguetiedness is attracting unfavorable attention and Septimus is shooting him glances. The Pug is imitating a boat now, while Warburton-Burleigh seems to be vaulting over it and slaying things in an unspecific but convincing manner. Lemprière decides to try lying.

"Her eyes are . . . her eyes, she has wonderful eyes," he bursts out. A few onlookers nod to each other approvingly, this is certainly untrue.

"Wonderful eyes, and a generous heart," he goes on. "A heart full of, of milk, the milk of human kindness!"

Warburton-Burleigh is in alligator death throes now, writhing and thrashing, murmuring *habibi* in waltz-time pulses while the Pug mimes the genocide of the titans, not one but hundreds crashing to the floor, fingers the size of Chesil Spit.

"She loves you, at least that's true," Lemprière lies and now, as he looks over at the Crone for fresh, well, any inspiration, there is a flicker of her features that might say, *Yes, it's true; he doesn't deceive.* This cannot be right but . . . He continues with a conceit on the curve of her cheek, something about the sway of long violin notes as they ripple the air (a little florid? ponders the Pork Club) and looks over again. No, this cannot be right. Right before his eyes there is, faint but unmistakable, a definite modification of the Crone going on. To be exact, there is a change in the shape of her cheek, no room for doubt. What is worse, or better, the shape has a visibly violin-ish quality about it. Certainly, the Pug and Warburton-Burleigh are doing a synchronized imitation of the Lisbon earthquake blindfolded, but can this compete with a genuine, if slight, metamorphosis? Lemprière looks around for acclamation, amazement, a dash of dismayed respect even. The Pork Club is busy making up its mind about the earthquake, though: "Is that the harbor draining?" "The Alhambra, maybe," and "What?" are random samples of the reaction. Only Septimus looks across at him. Can they all be blind?

"Observe her fulsome, red lips." He is fired to this. "The bloom of her dimples, the pools of her eyes." That should do it and, yes, it seems it does. All these things are actually beginning to happen. Not grotesquely, but as if the years were peeling off in layers and time was always meant to run this way, the other way was a mistake and things should get better, at least not so bad.

The Crone is passing presentable, indeed verging on the desirable, and Lemprière is spurred to yet greater heights of eloquence. Taut rhetorical figures and fervid apostrophes reap immediate rewards. A thousand third-rate sonnet sequences are cleaning out their closets; Lemprière just has to blow the dust off and tidy up the orthography a little for the words to become tangible flesh on the person of the Crone, breasts like ripe fruit, a neck of white marble.

"O lucky man!" he hails King Archon, and by Jove he means it; the Crone is ravishing now, her staff crackling and sparking with unattributable thoughts of lust. Any man worthy of the name would be mad to pass up the chance of getting his snout in her trough. He tries a few lines from Anacreon and her newfound beauty takes on a boyish tinge, quite pleasing but best not to take it any further. Now, when he turns around, Lemprière notices that the Pork Club is becoming less articulate than before. A larger proportion of the background buzz is taking the form of grunting and snuffling. A few are down on their hands and knees rooting around in the empty bottles, uneaten gristle-gobbets, and busted glasses that litter the floor. The Pug and Warburton-Burleigh are reaching the climax of their act, the latter on the former's shoulders, contorting his fingers in animal shapes—a rabbit, a vole, a large snake, an alligator (again,

what is the iconography here?)—which throw huge, successive silhouettes on the wall behind while the Pug approximates jig-steps, tap, tap.

Lemprière adds a couple of dimples and looks around again. A
transformation is taking place behind him. Most, if not all, of the spectat-
ing revelers are showing signs of piggish metamorphosis, noses thickening and flattening, bellies extending taut, rounded contours. Oinking and
snuffles are general, and not a few seem to be eating the tablecloths. This
is not what he means at all, he hasn't mentioned pigs, could it be
coincidence? It's definitely hotter now and someone has set the unlit
chandelier above his head in wheeling motion. On top of this, the Crone
is reverting to type, blurring and wrinkling, his stomach feels a little
volatile, and unwelcome memories, other transformations, other places,
he has held them off all evening and it's only a game, isn't it?

Certainly is. The Pug rips King Archon's head off and feeds it to the
grunting herd behind while Warburton-Burleigh pulls off his wig to
release seven snow-white doves which beat upward through the pork-
fumed smoky air, dissolving through the ceiling in quest of innocence on
the floor above. Somewhere, a goose cries. Septimus smiles over at him,
thumbs up. The round is at an end.

The Earl taps Lemprière on the shoulder.

"Well done. Do you need a hand?" Lemprière lurches up. The Earl
doesn't look porcine at all, a little hazy maybe, but the haziness belonging to a quite different order than before. His knees ache. Comments
reach his ears about the Pug's and Warburton-Burleigh's performance:
Consensus is boiling down to ingenious, well-executed, but just a little
obscure and tricksy. The papier-mâché Archon-head is acknowledged as
a *coup de théâtre,* albeit smacking of professionalism. A few congratulations are being passed his way, none by pigs, and the Crone is as
scraggy as before. Lemprière stands dumbfounded, did he dream it all?
No, you did not. . . .

"No, you did not. . . ." Septimus is explaining to him that the Crone
and King Archon have decided, after all, not to tie the knot although his
suasive verses have created a favorable impression on all who heard them.
King Archon is as impassive as before, but not to be discouraged, this is
the norm. Everything is as it should be.

Lemprière hangs on to this, and Septimus. Involuntary genuflections
are afflicting him and the room is growing less distinct. Louder too,
dimmer. Perhaps this is because of the smoke which striates and layers
the air in lazy drifts, confusing the issue.

"Pull yourself together, John. Come on, man," Septimus breaks in on
these unwelcome thoughts.

"Do you suppose he might have had too much to drink?" asks the
solicitous Earl.

"Come on, John. This is where we win the day, get up! Let's go!"
Lemprière tries to ignore the leaden ichor creeping through his body.

"Get 'em!" he blurts.

"That's the spirit. Just follow my lead."

The Pork Club have ingested the previous performance and are ready-ing themselves for the next. Their paramours have rejoined them after long abstinence and recouplings are being negotiated in raised eyebrows, fan-fluttering, pert and winsome smiles. Collective anticipation is the palpable mood. Septimus is already giving them what they want, pacing up and down with occasional short runs at the spectators who spill back—"Whooo!"—playing along with it. Lemprière is at a loss until Septimus begins waggling his fingers over his ears, an unnatural addition; a monster of unknown pedigree is being implied here, which is enough for Lemprière. He goes into heroic mode (every monster implies a hero, or vice versa), dibbing with an imaginary javelin at Septimus, who is now waggling more urgently. At this point, it dawns on the dibber that Septimus's fingers must be meant to represent snakes and that his flashing eyes are approximations of Medusa's petrifying glance. The Pork Club is going with it, hooting him on between swigs. Lemprière hopes that Septimus-Gorgon is following the Ovid version; he certainly is, carefully using a nonexistent shield as mirror, thrust and parry until he slays the beast, crash! and spectacular dying agonies from Septimus.

Matters start to get a little confused now with Septimus swooning and wringing his hands, mimicking a character that Perseus-Lemprière cannot identify. He decides to go on a Hero's Journey to gather his thoughts, wandering about at random while trying to ignore the shouts of the Pork Club, "Left, left! No, go right! Go right!" Andromeda! Of course! But he's running out of time now, hurry up, slay the dragon in double-quick time and get the girl. The girl doesn't want to be got, though, and more confusion arises; could Septimus-Andromeda be alluding to the cele-brated (but lost) Iolus-fragment in which the Perseus story (it is rumored) is almost exactly reversed? It seems unlikely, but the show must go on. Lemprière decides on a bold ellision: Leaping over the business with Phineus (too complicated in any case) and not giving Atlas a second thought, he arrives at the Larissan Games. Septimus is undulating now, probably the Larissan crowd, thinks his partner. Picking up an invisible quoit, he winds up the dramatic tension, swinging his arm up high, then low, ready to release it on its fated journey to the fragile skull of Acrisius. Applause breaks out among the Pork Club, scattered clapping at first, then louder, louder still, and when it reaches its peak he releases the missile, watching its path into the distance, its inevitable destination the head of Acrisius-Archon.

He holds the pose as tumult turns to congratulation.

"Bravo, Theseus!"

"Hurrah!"

"Victory to the Athenian!"

Some of the Pork Club seem to be a little confused as to the exact content and characters of the performance, but now they are all about him, shaking his hand and slapping him on the back.

"Wonderful, John!" The Earl separates himself from the mass. "Solves the essential problem of old Archon's noncooperation, brilliant conception, quite brilliant. . . ." A certain Lydia (she of the cream silk, red ringlets, and fingers) offers him an apologetic kiss as he pushes toward Septimus. All is well and Septimus is all smiles.

"Did I get the impression you were doing Perseus?" he asks in a low tone as Lemprière approaches.

"Yes, my quoit-throwing." He demonstrates (there are adjacent whoops at the reprise). "Not bad, eh? The quoit." He holds out an empty hand but Septimus interrupts.

"We were doing Theseus," he hisses. "The finger-waggling was the Minotaur, and you were meant to be abandoning Ariadne, not marrying Andromeda. The last bit was your return to Athens in the black-sailed ship—"

"Which the aging Ægeus takes as a sign that I am dead." Lemprière's late confusions are being cleared up.

"And so commits suicide, yes. Luckily your quoit-throwing bore some resemblance to Theseus waving from his ship, thus deepening the dramatic irony, et cetera. In short, my friend, they fell for it, so keep it under your hat. Oh, and John." Lemprière turns back. "We've won. Well done." He smiles and hands his companion-in-arms a bottle. The Pug and Warburton-Burleigh are somewhat peevish, but the Pork Club is unanimous, the laurels are theirs. Septimus pulls a cork for himself, *mgnk, mgnk, mgnk,* in tandem, the liquor most reminds Lemprière of cup "R," with perhaps a dash of "J," *mgnk, mgnk,* it slips down like syrup.

At this point, the Crone forces her way into the circle that has formed about the victors. Lemprière focuses unsteadily on her. The bottle in his hand is half-empty and it is dawning on him that drinking it might have been a mistake.

"The prize! The prize!" cackles the Crone.

"Oink!" confirms the Pork Club.

"The prize?" slurs Lemprière.

"The prize," endorses Septimus.

"Who's first at the trough, my little piglets?" shrieks the Crone at the two of them. The Pork Club mumbles to itself. Septimus resolves the issue.

"John shall go first," he announces. "In recognition of his inspired amateurism."

"For his sea legs," shouts someone, for Lemprière is swaying now in time with the walls, which are swaying too.

"Don't knock his legs," bawls the Crone. "He's going to need them!" Several horribly exaggerated winks and obscene arm movements blow the innuendo's scant cover.

"Not sure if I'm quite ready, just now. Feeling a mite, you know," murmurs Lemprière.

"You'll be absolutely titanic, John!" bellows Septimus. "Onward Theseus!"

"Are you well, John?" asks the Earl.

It is a measure of Lemprière's deterioration that he is convinced by Septimus's exhortation. Yes, titanic.

"Absholutely. Never better," he answers and lurches toward the stair-case on the far side of the room. By the time he reaches it, the staircase is lurching toward him. They dance a quadrille of Shandean slowness (the staircase taking three parts), and when it is over he is at the top.

"Bon soir, sweet prince," calls Septimus to the inadvertent hero, who attempts a mock curtsy in return. The din from the mob below sounds like an orchestra tuning up, and the light is coming in waves, more and more intense. He isn't feeling very well at all. A squawking bassoon hovers about waiting to become audible and the air is filled with tiny soap bubbles that pop at the rate of millions per second, a fizzing mass suicide that bleaches the air white as the sky when the cloud cover is perfectly even and it hurts to look at any part of it. He is feeling distinctly odd.

Downstairs, his victory is being celebrated with toasts. Someone has insinuated a peacock feather down Lydia's cleavage and she is shrieking with laughter. Even the Pug has found a playmate and holds her above his head while she drops small morsels of pork into his opening-and-closing mouth, leavening the diet with splashes of Negus when his chewing rate slows and fellating the bottle betweentimes. A general urge to form close and affectionate links with someone, anyone, is diffusing itself through the Pork Club; not quite lust, but not quite brother-and-sister stuff either. The mood of arousal percolates through everything; even the furniture has a new flirtatiousness about it, and upstairs, Lemprière catches on to it, confirming the gist of his speculations as to just what his prize is.

This is not to say *he* is aroused. At the moment he is standing up, which is enough to be getting on with, for ventrally speaking, things could be better. A rather substandard vintage is slugging it out with the kümmel, the brandy and cider have hit it off, but all are ignoring the yellow-root which sits in painful concentration somewhere near his abdomen. The rum he knocked back only lately is still making its way down, but its arrival is as imminent as it is unwelcome. Nevertheless, as he makes slow progress toward the far door (wasn't it nearer than that a minute ago?) there is no question but that this is the way. There are aspects of this disorientation, grim though it feels, that he likes, chief among them being the fact that it did not originate with him. He isn't thinking about the Crone's metamorphosis now. He is not thinking about the story he just acted, its accidental parallels. . . . The inadvertent hero, would Septimus have known, anticipated the connection? Surely not. Too devious, professor. Not yet. Not thinking about (another step) that, just another step he takes, determined not to think. Door shouldn't bend that way, the knob, use it as a support, like that yes, look to the future and onward Perseus. Theseus, whoever. Eyes up. Not that. Eyes up. No, he refuses, staggering, swaying, sliding, staggering, definitely no to that as the door opens to spill him inside.

Downstairs, Jemimah is explaining that she didn't mean to do it. No she didn't, so sorry, ouch! as the Crone cracks a spatula on her robust bonce, and again for good luck, good lord anyone'd think it was all on purpose. How was she to know the girl would sell such an ill-tempered bird as this one that'd fetch the mistress such a clip with its wing (tee hee)? Jemmy's got the goose firm under her arm now, nice and tight, mitt around its beak, peering round the door here as the Earl explains to Lydia why it would result in serious injury to one or both of them, dislocation of the hips at the very least, patiently, what a good, kind man he is. And so sober. Marry me, thinks Jemmy. Make me Earless of Braith! Someone is making a bottle-noise, *ding, ding,* over there and the floor will take some sweeping later. Goosey won't settle. A wash too, by the greasy look of it. Jemimah takes a firmer grip on the bird, *ding,* that is struggling artfully to get loose.

Ding. Very faint in Lemprière's ears upstairs. Perhaps a silver fountain is dripping music into a silver pool where fabulous white birds are bathing and drinking? No. Heavy-looking dogs with sad faces mooch up and plash about in the water, stirring the mud, is that it? No again. It is a bedroom. Black, red, white. A fire burns, carpets cover the floor. They break Lemprière's fall. A room with a bed in it. It has that frisson: of being placed here for a purpose. Horizontals and perpendiculars. The carpet is a very dark red. The bed is made of black wrought iron. Posts at each corner rise straight up. They are made of the same black iron. There are no pillows. Lemprière lurches upright. The stillness of this room and its sense of waiting for him, prepared for him (by whom?), add another tension to the cross-hatching of drunkenness and evasion which are still his main thoughts. The setup is doing its best to throw him. He resists. The room may be wavering and swaying, urging somnolence. Lemprière grasps the post nearest him and looks down. Yes, he thinks, as his eyes focus on the prize laid out before him. It had to be this.

The girl is fastened, spread-eagled and facedown, to the black iron of the posts. She is naked, of course; only the red ribbon binding a central tress of her hair has been permitted. A sheet of raw white silk has been thrown over her. Although this conceals the precise extent of her nakedness, it's understood nevertheless. There are details which have escaped the cover's touch. Her ankles and wrists are visible, strapped to the bed's ironwork with leather bracelets. The bracelets are set with turquoise.

Lemprière knows these ankles. He has seen them before. Bright water-drops flashing off them and the streak of red, the red colors the water. . . . Leaning over the foot of the bed, his legs good as useless here, holding on and it cannot be this, not this, everything very slow and deliberate,

92

concentrate now. Pulling back the sheet, one hand still holding him up but only just, uncovering first the shock of her black hair with its scarlet ribbon, jet on her milky back, arched slightly, it cannot be, he has to know, swimming in a lake of milk, muscled and shimmery, the smooth buttocks, cleft and expectant, the sinews in her legs rippling the surface of her skin as her body shifts in the cooler air, how many hours has she lain like this, awaiting the attentions of her violator? The white of her flesh is dazzling, a liquid white flowing out and around him, everything blurring in it as he hangs there, losing his grip.

"Juliette?" His voice sounds weakly. But he knows the scene is incomplete. *Your father!* He stumbles forward, falls, and is still.

Downstairs, meanwhile, and not too surprising given the proximity of Christmas, the goose has got wind of its fate and escaped. Or, half-escaped. When it comes to long-haul continent spanning (with inexplicable pinpoint navigation to boot), there is a wide consensus that the goose is your bird. But, it is further acknowledged that certain maneuvers are not strongpoints of the goose, and chief among these is cornering. This goose is flying about downstairs, cheered on by the Pork Club, wearing a kind of dazed expression which is not too surprising given that it's trying to fly straight through the walls. It's a miracle it's still airborne, *clunk,* staggering about three or four feet above everyone's heads.

The Crone doesn't see it in quite these terms. She is lobbing up bolsters, trying to create a barrage of the things that will bring the goose down. So far, it's not working, but on the walls there are certain nails on which once hung some rather nasty watercolors in the manner of John Opie, the Cornish wonder, executed by a onetime regular, now dead. The goose has yet to encounter these nails (another miracle), but a couple of the bolsters already have and goose down is showering down like snow on the Pork Club. With all the bacon and pork grease yet to be abluted, most of it is pretty adhesive and so now there are a lot of feathered people leaping up and down, imitating the goose which is none too pleased at the attention. (Plus, it's putting two and two together as to the origin of this weird white stuff.)

Amid all this, only Septimus hears the crash which comes from upstairs. Perhaps he felt it was inevitable. Racing up and bursting in, he comes upon Lemprière collapsed on the floor. Slapping him elicits nothing coherent, only a hawking sound from the back of his throat. Septimus picks him up without effort, and as he turns to leave Walter Warburton-Burleigh slides in the door.

"Thought you might need assistance," he grins. "She been touched?"

"Clearly not," says Septimus shortly as he bundles up Lemprière and quits the room, edging past two women in blue who are peering into the room with proprietorial interest. Lemprière is being carried, the backs of his knees slung over Septimus's shoulders, his arms trailing almost to the floor. The older of the two women stops Septimus.

"Your winnings," she says.

"His." Septimus indicates the upside-down body. The woman tries to put the bulging purse in Lemprière's hands, but it is no good. He will not hold it. Eventually she stuffs it in his mouth. Warburton-Burleigh, meanwhile, has extracted his own purse and is laying a cold line of coins down the girl's warm back, one for each vertebra. She jerks a little.

"Keep still, Rosalie," he murmurs silkily. "The first is always worst."

Lemprière comes to, descending the staircase, *muhbubh,* gagged with his winnings. He is floating upward, toward the people whose feet are glued to the ceiling. Below, a crystal tree tinkles its leaves and a large white bird circles it clumsily. His head is light, so light it draws his body up to within inches of the ceiling. Everyone is upside down, poor devils.

The Pork Club have not lost interest in the goose. They have decided to serenade it and divide for this purpose into chorus and verse, ranged about here like opposing teams of so many standing patterers. It has been pointed out that the goose's flight is (very) roughly circular, and someone has trotted out the old music-of-the-spheres theory. There is a feeling that with the right song the goose will descend. It is a weak argument, but the will is there and they have decided after an informal show of hands to sing what amounts to the Pork Club anthem. It is called "The Inheritance Song" and goes like this:

> Who stalks the courts of t'poorer sorts
> Who's known as The Open Purse?
> Who hands out alms to punks and charms
> The widows 'hind the hearse?

(descant)
> Your father! Your father!
> Your rampant, fleshly sire.
> Your father! Your father!
> The spendthrift of the shire.

> When the heir is left of all bereft
> Save bastards, bills and slatt-erns,
> He gambles, drinks, and marries a minx
> D'you recognise the patt-ern?

(descant)
> Your father! Your father! &c.

Lemprière spits the purse into Septimus's boot.

"Get me out, Septimus. For God's sake . . ." trying to inject the urgency he feels into his voice, not even sure if it is audible. *Your father! Your father!* Septimus has heard, or just knows. They lurch toward the door, which the Earl holds open for them. Septimus and he exchange a few words after which the Earl kneels in front of Lemprière.

"Sir?" The Earl taps Lemprière on the shoulder. "Mister Lemprière?"

"Grnnh?"

"Mister Lemprière!" The Earl's face looks very strange upside down.

"The agreement of which we spoke earlier . . ." The Earl's voice, indeed his whole person, has changed. There is no trace of a slur as he speaks and his eyes are focused. The Earl seems suddenly all business as he outlines the gist of their earlier discussion, pointing across the room to where it took place, when and how, before launching into an involved story quite beyond Lemprière's present level of understanding. Why is he doing this?

". . . between the investors. Sixteen hundred was to be the De Veres' *annus mirabilis,* the first voyage was set to yield vast returns. We borrowed. . . . The stake was beyond everyone; but the returns, the returns would be so huge. . . . De Veres have always been traders, always an eye for the salable cargo. When the venture failed, Thomas, the fourth Earl, had nothing. The family might have been ruined but for your ancestor. François Lemprière was our savior, the stock worth nothing, you understand. Of course, he sold. And when the Company prospered again, the De Veres grew rich on their share. Your ancestor must have reaped ten times that. Thousands upon thousands! Of course, when the agreement was broken, our fortunes declined once more. But we never knew why. The siege, or treachery of some sort. It's all in the past. . . . But the agreement was valid in perpetuity, forever, I presume you know that. In theory, it would just go on and on. . . ."

Ancestors, agreements; clearly, the Earl is talking about something that should concern Lemprière. But what?

". . . who knows where that share is now? The Lemprières' and De Veres' . . . It would be millions, piling up over the centuries, almost unimaginable," continues the Earl to Lemprière's queasy indifference. His eyes begin to glaze over behind his spectacles.

"Millions!" shouts the Earl in Lemprière's face. This is provocation.

"Pizz off," says Lemprière, trying the phrase for the first time. The Earl's face wavers a little but remains in position a few inches from his own. Then the vague remembrance of a similar scene drifts back to him. Agreements, ancestors, Earls of Braith. But that was hours, years ago, some time at any rate, who would remember all that? It was all too late and in the past and it didn't matter, no, not now. *Your father!*

"Your ancestor!" yells the Earl. But Lemprière will not grasp the point of all this. The Earl is a very noisy fellow, he thinks. Drunk perhaps. Lemprière considers vomiting on his boots. The Earl is shouting something again, but it's all too late, too noisy, too drunk, and please go away now, just go far away. . . .

The Earl will not go away. He is demanding a reply. Lemprière gathers all the resources at his disposal.

"Ask Sebdimus," he manages at length. The Earl turns away for a moment.

"Addled," he comments to Septimus, then turns back.

"Another time, Mister Lemprière!" bellows the Earl. "Farewell!"

"Pizz off!" Lemprière tries again. This time it seems more successful, for the face disappears. The Earl's voice is audible in the near vicinity, then that of Septimus, garbled together with the background burble and the horrible singing. Above him (or below) something large, white, and presumably winged collides *clunk!* with the wall. The goose was still flying.

"Good-bye, goose," mumbles Lemprière as Septimus hoisted him up and kicked open the door.

Fatherkiller, hissed the goose. They left for the night outside.

The clouds had broken. Freezing rain fell into the black streets, beating down in rods on the roofs and gables. It fell in sheets on the slates and tiles, bursting the gutters and washing down the walls to the street. It danced on the flags of the pavements and ran into the ditches and drains. Rain scoured the cobbles, dissolving the muck, scum, and scurf, sending it down the street in a thick wave of slurry. It sluiced through the rookeries, irrigated the great thoroughfares, baptizing the courts, rising as it ate into piles of horse dung, picked up fish heads and old meat wrappers and rats drowned in the open sewers, driving them along in a rich, liquid mulch. Tomorrow it would stink. But now, the rain brought its violence down to purge the city, drilling into the stonework of breached walls and the stumps of columns, each raindrop exploding in white as it conceded the dissolving city its forms. The details of the buildings seem to blur and the downpour replaces them with wretched waterfalls and fountains, broken pipes and seeping minarets; templates of appeasement to the preterit, just the weather again to the elect, for the sky absolves nothing, of course.

Standing clear of these accretions, a dim recognition of the need below hardly disturbs the weather's deep composure. Its cycle turns and the cities fall. Rain today, tomorrow none. For as long as these structures have offered their pathos or their gray arrogance it has been like this. Seven hills surrounded the paludium, remember? An interim empire, its center already malarial, spreading the seizures and relapses whose masquerade of health will later conceal the drain of that need, its exile. Now the outlines of its form is discernible through the fabric, like the girl on the bed, its indistinctness part of the game as it reaches through, fingertips light and icy, insinuating its return. Each cold raindrop a reminder of his debts, every freezing drop arcing out in silver cusps *an appropriate manner in which to approach one's god. . . .*

"The rain . . . So cold." They stumbled on, Septimus hauling him along upright now, his feet dragging and useless. The rain comes in waves, washing in and out of his hearing. They had reached the river. Lemprière tried to turn to his friend.

"What do you know?" he demanded. "Damn you, what do you know of any of it?" He could hold back no longer.

"What do you know of me? Of what I've done? Of what I am!" He could be crying. It is raining so hard now one cannot be sure.

Septimus's face was still, the first time Lemprière had seen it so, like marble, a statue's face.

"Tell me," he said, putting his arm about Lemprière's shoulders. "Tell me everything."

• • •

But the rain fell harder, drowning the two of them out. They were inaudible almost to each other as Lemprière sat heavily in the wet, almost invisible from the mire of the road where, now, the two women in blue muddied themselves as they tramped leaden-footed through the muck of the storm, homeward. The streets ran with mud: the Strand, past Fleet Market to Ludgate and up, the heavens beating down and drilling into the city. Rain.

From Ludgate to the women's destination, not to be reached for an hour yet; a house stood with darkened windows in Stonecutter Lane. From within the cellar, the rain sounded in lackluster, irregular waves. Nazim could see it being slapped down into the street by the wind through the narrow grille which gave a worm's-eye view onto the pavement and the deserted street beyond. Waterdrops slapped in a quick pulse from the sill just above. Peering through the chinks in the boards above his head, he could make out the dim light of a window in the room directly over his head.

Morning was hours off yet, the dawn and its gray light by which his dockside vigil would continue. The ship would be there, the *Vendragon*, with its complement of shunters and porters, and he would watch as the cold took the sweat off their backs in clouds. Coker, had that been the name? Coker, the gangleader whose words he had caught from his hiding place among the piled gear on the quay. The thin-faced man had watched him as he tipped his hat forward and made off around the corner at a pace. Fake farewells, covert returns. Coker, yes. He meant nothing. Not significant. He had doubled back and crept along the quayside, plenty of cover, easy for him to get in close, to overhear the two of them.

". . . within weeks. As the loads arrive you will be advised. You will be to hand?" But it was not a question. Nazim heard calculations in the thin-faced man's voice. Coker had twisted his hands. He would be available, his men too. The crates Nazim had spent the last days watching as they were loaded were arriving irregularly. But from where? And when? Nazim had strained to catch details, but the two had only touched on it. Somewhere in London, in the city. Stop the river at its source. Nazim fancied himself tangled in tributaries and offshoots, lost, attend-

97

ing the surface hum of the machine. He could not expect to learn much more from keeping watch over the *Vendragon*. The crates, the men, the ship, they all marked a trail leading him away from the Nine. "Mizzer Mara," Coker had called the thin-faced man. "Mizzer Mara" was one of them.

The older face which had appeared in the attic window a little way up the quay that first day had reappeared several times since. He thought their eyes had met once, but the distance was too great. The face exercised him, but he was inclined to dismiss it. They would not send two of their own to supervise the loading. "Mara" had given his orders to Coker in a grating monotone. There was almost no inflection in his voice, and its timbre had shocked Nazim. It was the accent which leveled away fear or crowing triumph or pleasure and left only the act. Men and women heard that voice only once, in the moment before the Nawab's assassin took away their lives. But Nazim, hearing it spoken by another, was momentarily unnerved. He knew what "Mara" did. Mara was a killer too.

"*Le* Mara," came the voice again. He was correcting the other man. "Mizzer *Le* Mara," Coker repeated like a child and "*Le* Mara" muttered again to himself as he shambled back toward his men. Nazim had looked up and caught in the corner of his eye the curtain falling across the attic window up the quay. The cripple had moved off in the opposite direction and was fifty yards distant already.

The days which followed had added nothing to his understanding. He had watched Coker and the other men carry cases back and forth, and Le Mara watched them too. Ships had passed up and down the river before him, the sun had shone or not, but he had learnt no more, and now, listening to the steady drip of water into the cellar and the unrelenting rain outside, he began to wonder at his next move. Unfamiliar ground, and then, "You may not fail," the Nawab simple and direct, which was a mark of respect to him; admittance to the inner sanctum of the Nawab's unmediated wishes, him and him alone. Nazim, his chosen tool for a task. "You may not fail, or fall short," the Nawab had told him. He would not fail. He would not fall short. That had been the core of their meeting months before.

The Nawab's thoughts ran thus: He would go into the partnership, accept the caravans arriving by night, close his ears to the advice of his courtiers (who knew nothing), dispatch the locked chest to a destination hundreds of miles distant which he would never see, to the ship which would take them on across the Mediterranean, which too he would never see. Was he a fool? He would turn his palace to use, a glorified clearinghouse, he no better than a moneylender, no better than that, and the ridicule of his ancestors was easily imagined, easily heard in the shadows of the corridors and sunless corners. . . . The Nawab, a tenant to his title, and later, a borrower from the British whose sweating nabobs dunned him politely, handkerchiefs to their brows, with all the correct observances of rank and custom and without relief. And he could not pay. He could not.

That was when he had turned, when he had gone to the locked chests with the air of a thief and first thought how it might be done. The Company would scarcely conceive the scale of the fraud, the numberless insignificant leaks from the coffers of the Indies and the tributaries they formed as they flowed, inevitably, unaccountably, to the strong room beneath his palace. There were nine men in England, only nine, and they controlled the whole with subtle touches and twists that the Nawab himself, their servant, could only admire. A partnership, yes, in which he was paid a fee and a large fee, but now they were breaking the contract. The chests, which gradually accumulated in the palace, always arriving by different means and routes, which were collected and dispatched each year to his anonymous masters, had arrived less frequently. He suspected that if he threw them open and peered within he might find only rocks and sand, a mocking note. His use was ending and he felt the full weight of the wealth which had passed through his hands to those of the nine, hundreds and thousands of miles distant, wealth which was indistinguishable from the power he had yielded, which had been stolen from him and what was he now? A puppet and plaything, the butt of the English, his usurpers. No, he would not fall to that, and he thought again of the locked chests and their contents, the finest gemstones, the most pure precious metals, silver and gold clouding and coalescing in his vision, almost within grasp, almost even now. For he knew more than they thought.

They thought they had the measure of him. They had caught Bahadur and returned him changed, a stranger. But he was a stranger bearing gifts, the wherewithal of the Nawab's restoration and the retrieval of his fortunes. Poor Bahadur, a faithful servant tested on the cliff top and found wanting. Now Nazim would take up the torch, and flush them out, the nine of them. . . . Nazim would do what his uncle could not do.

Nazim stood up as the Nawab entered the room. He bowed and the Nawab motioned for him to be seated. The instant he was settled, the Nawab began to speak. The words came out in a long, flat speech, point leading to point, redoubling over this or that passage, crossing lines already taken up and followed through without a single break until Nazim began to grasp the larger pattern taking shape and echo it in his own mind as he listened to the tale of the Nawab and his nine trading partners, their subvention of the Company's profits, their betrayal of the Nawab, the treasure's long journey from the palace in which he sat to the distant island where the Company made its home and from where the Nawab's partners, his betrayers, controlled it from houses of secrecy; find them out—his injunction was unspoken so far, but it would come, and Nazim traced the story as it issued from the Nawab's mouth, of secret deliveries, consignments and stockpiles, broken contracts and ensuing penalties, a story in which he was now already a character and player.

"When Bahadur was sent to France, I believed they made their den in Paris. But, I was . . . mistaken. They are vicious, and clever. Bahadur found that out, and more. . . ."

The mention of his mentor's mission awoke memories of that time in Nazim—Bahadur's absence, he was still a boy then. Seventeen years ago, a point he marked, for Bahadur was a different man on his eventual return. He had been in France, in Paris.

"He found out my error"—the Nawab colored a little—"for they make their home in England. Only by chance did he come across them, only by his wits and courage did he return. He was an exceptional man." The Nawab's voice bathed Nazim in its warmth. "And you too, Nazim-ud-Dowlah."

Bahadur had been changed into something cold and distant. He had never truly returned. He had spoken little of his time away, it seemed to exist as a gap in which something of himself had been lost. They had caught him, and let him go. Perhaps it was his pride.

"Yet he had given his word," the Nawab was speaking again. "He would find the men who betrayed me. . . . He kept his word."

The Nawab talked on, telling Nazim how the steady passage of the treasure through his palace had become less steady, had slackened off, and finally, some months before, had stopped altogether.

"They believe I am something to be discarded," he said dismissively. Nazim smiled at the lunacy. "They are taking it to England, and thence. . . . They must be stopped. We must take back what has been taken from us. You must find them, and kill them, all nine. You must find what is mine, get it back. . . ." Nazim gazed curiously at his master, who was looking up distractedly at the corner of the ceiling as he spoke, turning his head as if he expected something to be there that was not.

"There are nine of them." He looked down again. "They are in the city of London. You must go there, find them." He fell silent, then suddenly: "And the ship! The ship, it is called the *Vendragon*. That is how they will move it, yes. You must find the ship, do you understand? The ship is how you will find them." The Nawab picked at the hem of his sleeve, then looked Nazim in the face. "You will do it." Only that. Yes, my master. "Yes," replied Nazim.

It was done. The audience was at an end and Nazim rose to leave. But as he did so, the Nawab reached out and clutched his arm, astonishing Nazim.

"There is more." He spoke urgently. "A moment, more, a name. One of the nine perhaps, Bahadur was not certain . . . but a name." Nazim waited for the Nawab to say it, but he must come closer, closer, yes, like that to whisper it in his ear and Nazim inclined his head as asked. The Nawab leaned over, Nazim catching the scent of something sweet on his breath, waiting for the word; then he heard it and committed it to memory as the Nawab relaxed the grip on his arm and moved back quickly for his servant with an odd shuffling motion.

Nazim left the palace that evening, deep in a single thought. Finding the nine men, the ship, his master's wealth, somehow they must all become the same thing, a single act. He had assented to it already. Now he must learn its nature. And around that central preoccupation the whispered name hovered like an insect drawn toward the web.

"You don't! You bloody don't." A voice jerked Nazim out of his reverie and into the present in an instant. He started, breathed in. His body tensed. His ears pricked as a second voice was heard.

"I cannot be sorrier, Bet. Did I say I wished it so?" Two women were in the street, above him and outside. The second with an accent. Not English. Nazim looked out through the grille but caught only a glimpse of blue, a dress, before they had exceeded the spy-hole's scope, and then he heard them fumbling at the door. The house was unfurnished and boarded up. He had believed it deserted. He had entered through the coal hatch. They had opened the door and now Nazim heard their boots echo on the floorboards just above his head. They were arguing. Nazim listened, pondering the measures he might have to take.

". . . this filthy place. My bones ache with it," the one called Bet was complaining. "Why did you take the bet? We had money enough, and now we have nothing. Now we are here." The voice was venomous, suggesting previous acquaintance with cold, hard floors.

"Anything within reason, you told me, you told me that." The foreign woman sounded close to tears. "You told me that," mimicked the other harshly. And indeed, seconds later a soft sobbing sound reached Nazim's ears. The complainer relented, walking over to her companion and comforting her.

"Karin, come now. We shall make a fire, dry our clothes. Don't cry." Karin allowed herself to be quieted. Presently, a candle was lit and Nazim could make out the two figures by its faint glow, their bodies distorted and cut across by the angle and narrow slits through which he spied the two of them, both in blue above him.

"Poor Rosalie!" Karin was saying. Her accent softened or thickened with her emotions.

"The poverty is all ours . . ." and a few clinks were heard, a few coins dropped to the floor between them. ". . . all my fault." Karin was beginning to sob.

"No one could have guessed the boy would win, even with Septimus," her friend said soothingly, but it was no good.

"And Rosalie was . . . she was a daughter to me, and now what becomes of her?" Karin was crying in earnest now. "We sold her, like meat, and she was our own." Her friend's voice hardened.

"She was not our own, she was no one's. Now she is someone's. . . ."

101

Whose? Nazim wondered, allowing the drowsiness he felt to advance through his body. ". . . and there will be more work there. He pays well, this joker man. The boy fell for it too, thought she was someone else, didn't he?" But Karin was still sniveling. "It was all in play. There'll be others." Poor Rosalie, as the two of them mooched differently around the roles they had played and, despite himself, Nazim cocked half an ear for the sound of their voices above him and listened as the sequence of events emerged from their respective sides. A transaction, a girl, girl as a prop in some masquerade for the benefit of a young man, that evening in another place. A bet taken, and paid, and the money lost in that way, thus grief. Hope came in the form of more work from the same source.

"We meet at Galloways, tomorrow," Bet was explaining to her companion. "Galloways," Karin repeated, but her voice was drifting. It didn't matter.

Nazim turned back to his own thoughts, of the ship, the nine men, and the name Bahadur had gleaned years before. Above, the women laughed.

"He couldn't walk! Couldn't piss in a pot. . . ."

"Who?" Karin not paying attention, poking at the fire. Far below, the two figures on the cliff top seemed to move nearer the edge, one was trying to pull away from the other.

"The boy, the dupe," Bet explained. "It was a joke, I tell you. Perhaps he weds tomorrow. . . ." Nazim could hardly see the two of them at all, he was trying to get back to before, but the women were in the way, their voices.

"Who, though? Septimus's friend, I know. But who was he?" Suddenly, then Nazim was back in the cellar and, at the same time, in the rose-colored room with the Nawab whispering the name to him, the name Bahadur had won so that he might later find its owner, and he was hearing the name again, in answer to her question: Who was he?

"Septimus called him Lemprière," said Bet. Lemprière, the name the Nawab had whispered in his ear. He was alive, living in London. He could be found.

The night dragged on with its secrets and its weather, growing frayed as the hours moved it on and dawn made the first ragged inroads into the dark. Showers were falling haphazardly when the sun finally rose, and a light, high wind blew the last clouds out toward the sea. The city glistened in its sleek sheen of rainwater and the early risers that Sunday morning had to shade their eyes to see its glittering surfaces. Nazim's heart had thudded like a piston when he heard the name. Lemprière, the dupe of a practical joke, a drunkard, a friend of "Septimus," which was a name he did not know. Lemprière, whose own name had traveled from Paris to the Indies, then back from the Indies to London to meet him here, seventeen years later, and confront him. One of the Nine, perhaps; one who would lead him to the other eight. Lemprière was here, in

London, and Nazim would find him. He promised himself that in the cellar, and again in the morning when he awoke, rose, and climbed through the outside hatch to the pavement beyond.

The air was cold and Nazim shivered. He took up station in a doorway opposite and waited for the women to emerge. An hour later, he was walking quietly twenty yards behind Bet, who had appeared in the same bedraggled blue dress as before and now strode toward her rendezvous through a hodgepodge of alleys and runs which taxed Nazim as he followed her. Church bells masked the sound of his footsteps. When they reached Galloway's Coffee House, Nazim remembered its name from the night before. This was where she was to meet the man who had paid for the trick on Lemprière, who would pay again for other services, who had paid for the girl Rosalie. This was Lemprière's enemy, perhaps. Perhaps his, Nazim's, greatest ally. Nazim watched as the woman entered. After a few minutes, he followed her inside.

The interior of the coffee shop extended farther than he had thought and was lined with high-sided booths, each with a table and facing benches. The woman had chosen one toward the rear of the shop and was sitting in such a way as to keep watch over the entrance. She looked up as Nazim walked the length of the shop to take the last booth behind her, then resumed her vigil. Nazim sat with his back to the door, his head leaning against the partition. Presently the shop's proprietor appeared and Nazim ordered a mug of coffee. When the man turned his attention to the woman's booth, it was to order her out: "No women." A short argument followed, the man was firm, but suddenly it seemed an accommodation had been reached. The woman remained seated as before while the man retreated behind a counter at the rear of the shop. Nazim heard coins drop into the drawer.

A clock mounted on the back wall ticked away the minutes as he waited for Bet's assignation. Another coffee followed the first. Minutes turned into hours and the shop gradually grew crowded. It was sometime after midday when a movement in the booth behind told him that the woman had risen to indicate her presence. Someone had walked in the door, and though the shop was now almost full, Nazim picked out his footsteps from the general hubbub as they moved to the woman's booth, then stopped.

"I thought you had abandoned us. . . ." The woman's voice. Nazim's head was only inches from the recipient of the complaint, but he could not make out the reply. A man's voice, but indistinct, shielded by the wooden partition and talking away from him. He could hear only Bet as their opening remarks grew more businesslike, money was handed over at one point, more coffee was ordered. It seemed Bet was asking after Rosalie, the girl mentioned and lamented by the other woman the previous night, but that transaction was complete, it did not concern her now and she gave it up. A new offer was being made. Her own participation was required, and would be paid for. It was a masquerade of sorts but Nazim could not hear the details, only the woman's assent. Nazim controlled his frustration and fought down the strong urge to peer over the top of the booth and discover the man's identity. The woman's voice was querulous; she wanted more money and was protesting that her services did not come cheap on Christmas Eve. Christmas Eve, Nazim clutched at that. A place, he urged her silently, name the place.

"My family come first." She was still wheedling. "How can I tell them I must work on Christmas Eve?" But the man had lost patience, his voice came louder and harder than before, audible at last to Nazim.

"Whores have no family," he told her flatly, and rose to leave. In the booth behind, Nazim heard the voice and his arm jerked in shock, upsetting the coffee mug before him. He knew who the man was. The voice was the same flat voice heard at the docks two days before. The woman's savior, her paymaster with a pitiless, thin face, was Le Mara; Le Mara was the architect of this Lemprière's first deception. Now he was preparing a second with this woman as its centerpiece. At the sound of his enemy's departure, Nazim rose to follow, and what he saw confirmed his guess.

• • •

Anarcharsis of Scythia, inventor of anchors, tinder, and the potter's wheel, observed that every vine brings forth three kinds of grape: the first producing mirth, the second drunkenness, and the third repentance. A door slammed; bells rang; boots banged up the stairs. The warm bedclothes, impregnated with his own faint odors, enveloped the sleeper who burrowed into the pillow in retreat from the racket. John Lemprière awoke to find his eyelashes sutured by a crust of dried sleep and his skull lined with brittle, crackling paper. His eyes watered, dissolving the sleep, then opened, and sunlight hit him in the face. Blood pounded under his skull, pressing on his brain. He rolled over and groaned. When he moved his head, it felt oddly heavy at the sides, pulling down his jowls, and his skin seemed to be covered in an oily sheen. When he moved, it hurt, and when it hurt, he stopped. He fell back into something that looked for all the world like sleep, but was not sleep. For the moment, he thought to himself, I will do nothing at all. But the banging of boots grew louder and louder until Septimus burst into the room to rouse him, grinning and stomping and immediately urging him to rise. The previous night had nurtured strange and bitter fruit.

"Awake, awake!" bellowed Septimus, banging about and throwing Lemprière's clothes at him. The brightness of the sunlight seemed to intensify, heating his insides. A cramp gripped his stomach, and for a moment he thought he was going to be sick. But he was not, and when the cramp subsided, Lemprière realized that he was very hungry. It hardly seemed appropriate, but then he remembered he had been sick last night, copiously. Last night . . . that was why Septimus was here. He had agreed to something. Another cramp gripped him and he clutched his stomach in misery. He had told Septimus something the previous night and it was a mistake. He was putting on clothes still damp from their recent soaking and that was a mistake too. It was Sunday morning after the Saturday night before. . . . The sun shone brightly and it was not raining. All mistakes.

"We shall call upon the gentleman of whom I told you last night," Septimus explained carefully.

Last night. Much of it was a mystery to Lemprière, the latter part particularly. They had won the Game of Cups, he remembered that. He had won a prize, he remembered that too, her white back, smooth, and her jet-black hair. But it could not be her, not in the cold light of morning, not there or like that, not Juliette. Later, he had found the Thames. He had sat down on a bridge. Septimus had asked him a question.

Then he remembered his mistake. He had told Septimus everything.

"Ernst and Elly are friends of mine . . ." Septimus was telling him as they strode up the street. This was a phrase Lemprière was learning to distrust.

"We are going there now?"

"Now, yes. You did agree to this, in a way it was your idea." Lemprière's idea. He had no recollection of it. Presumably he had agreed to it when he had spoken to Septimus on the bridge, or perhaps before, or after, or not at all and it was some form of practical joke, or something worse. What *had* he told Septimus? Everything, everything.

"You'll like them; at any rate, they will like you. Ernst is quite brilliant, after a fashion. . . ."

"Yes, but what are they? Why are we going there?"

An hour later, they were walking past a terrace of modest houses. Septimus suddenly came to an abrupt halt and knocked loudly on a bright red door. Then he turned to his questioner. "They are doctors of the mind, John. And we are here because you are not sane." Not sane . . . Lemprière's face momentarily dissolved. Then the door was being thrown open and he recovered himself in time to see a bulbous, smiling man greet Septimus like a long-lost son.

Introductions were dispensed with and both of them ushered directly to the drawing room, which doubled as a consulting room for Elmore Clementi and Ernst Kalkbrenner, men who, in their time, had been called heretics, sodomites, amateurs, quacks, seditionaries, and, most lately, friends of Septimus.

"Victims of calumny," Septimus confided as they entered the room. "Good friends, damned good friends."

The drawing room was overwhelmingly red. Dark crimson bokhara rugs lay on the floor, red velvet curtains and oils on the walls in magenta and vermilion. The piano on the far side had been stained a dark rust-brown. Their usher stood expectantly as they came to terms with all this. A pinkish striped clothcoat lined with scarlet silk, scalloped cuffs à la marinère and death's-head buttons, overlaid a double-breasted waistcoat of crimson velvet embroidered with orange fleurs-de-lys, both being topped by a lace-trimmed cravat wound multiply about his neck. His face was powdered and rouged beneath a carefully coiffured ramillies plait whose tail swung freely as he bobbed from side to side, awaiting an introduction.

"Septimus?" he warbled after a few seconds had gone by. Septimus came to.

"John, my learned friend, Elmore Clementi."

"Call me Elly." The creature offered his hand.

"And I," came a voice from behind them, "am Ernst Kalkbrenner." A tall, thin figure dressed in grey appeared in the doorway. "Welcome again, Mister Septimus." He offered his hand to Lemprière, who returned the handshake.

"We seek your opinion," Septimus announced.

"Splendid, splendid. Elly, tea, I think?" At this, Clementi threw up his hands in a fluster and disappeared. Septimus and Lemprière took places on the mauve divan in the center of the room. Clementi soon returned with tea.

"There's a little camomile in it," he confided to Lemprière. "It will help clear out the system. Awful stuff, drink . . ." Lemprière was secretly impressed by this diagnosis. He sat sipping tea, which did indeed make him feel a little more robust than before. The red was becoming more bearable. Ernst Kalkbrenner had taken up position by the piano while his patient occupied the velvet armchair opposite. He turned to the pair on the divan.

"It would be best if you explained to me the exact nature of the problem," he began.

Lemprière turned to his companion.

"John was rather drunk," began Septimus.

And it was raining, thought Lemprière. They were on the bridge.

His legs had given up. He sat heavily, finally in the wet. He could hear his own voice breaking up in the downpour, the unstoppered heavens pouring down on them both. Two women in blue dresses were being drawn slowly out of sight, moving clumsily like rag dolls past the far end of the bridge. Septimus was saying, "Tell me everything," and his own voice was lurching forward to meet that question, stumbling and picking itself up and going on with the story, its characters dissolving like ink in the rain and the scoured fibers of the page emerging clean and snowy white, pristine and candid, perfectly blank. He could not remember. "Go on," said the voice at his side. The ink was dissolving in reverse, coming back as grays and dark blues, irregular patches merging and emerging out of the blank tablet, returning for a second scene, a simulacrum of the first except now the tangle of surds and glyphs was a tangle of arms and legs, motile cells and released agents running over the surface, fast and low over the ground *suck* the nightmare scene was seeping back not as a tame tale in a book but a gray contagion, a seepage of his brain's soft sponge *suck* the story he had read was unfolding in his father's flesh, a famished parasite bursting out of its host, the expended body rolling over in the water and far away on the far side of the island the story settled back into innocuous paper and harmless print. The sound when the teeth had met in the calf. *Suck*.

Septimus had finished his recitation. Ernst Kalkbrenner pursed his lips in thought.

"Reads things?" Kalkbrenner cogitated aloud. "They happen? Can't quite see it."

"Not everything," Septimus said. "It's happened twice for certain, perhaps twice more." Lemprière nodded. Septimus was at least direct; he could imagine taking all day telling it himself. "First there was a four-teenth-century—"

"Fifteenth," Lemprière corrected him.

"A fifteenth-century Athenian king in a stove on Jersey; then a local deity, the Vertumnus, who stalks about the fields outside his parents' house; then Diana, with her dogs, also on Jersey." Lemprière looked away. "Lastly, there is the transformation of a Covent Garden madam into Circe. This was last night."

Lemprière cringed with embarrassment at this recitation. It sounded ridiculous even to himself. Kalkbrenner, however, was deep in thought, Clementi watching him with the air of one confidently expecting revelation. Septimus had already begun to fidget. At length the good doctor signaled his readiness to diagnose by beginning to pace up and down before the piano.

"I believe," he announced, "that I have discerned a common thread running through these incidents. Correct me if I am mistaken," he continued, in a tone which forbade such presumption, "but is there not at work here an *antique* element? A touch of the Ancients, no?"

Lemprière wondered if this was meant to be a quip, perhaps to set him at his ease. Septimus was nodding without a trace of irony.

"Very astute," he commented.

"Of course, we might describe this unfortunate condition. We are able to do that—"

"Describe it, Ernst!" Clementi burst out.

"But it would be pointless. We must begin from first principles, compare and contrast; symptomatic classification is for the *encycloped-ists*." Lemprière was beginning to lose the track of Kalkbrenner's reasoning, a fact which brought with it a feeling of security.

"The mind only exists by virtue of the qualities it shares with other minds, thus." He flipped open the lid of the piano and struck the keys:

"Happy or sad?"

"Sad," replied Lemprière promptly.

"Just so, a universal response."

"Alcmaeon might have pronounced you perfectly sane simply from that, but we have moved on from Crotona, isonomy will not suffice. Empedocles would have concluded that you were part piano and Protagoras would agree, adding that the piano be part Lemprière, of course. This brings us to Aristotle. . . ." Kalkbrenner moved on, through a fluid series of dismissals to the accompaniment of Clementi's endorsements. Plotinus, Augustine, and Aquinas were incidental travelers along the highway he had chosen, Descartes's fixation with the pineal gland was risible and Linnaeus was a scribbler, an oneirodyniac who only dreamed he was awake. . . . Kalkbrenner had the measure of them all, his Teutonic demolitions left nothing but the ruins of buildings built in outmoded styles. He admitted a partial admiration for Locke but excused himself on sentimental grounds. It was only when he began intoning the name of Etienne Bonnot, L'Abbé de Condillac, that his tirade ended and panegyrics took their place.

"Le divin abbé" (for so he addressed him) had had a profound effect on the young Kalkbrenner. He had the apostate's zeal and as a young man had been observed sucking the toes of a marble statue in Darmstadt, but the authorities ("Cartesians to a man, damn their hybristic *sums*") had refused to understand.

"How could they, their experience being conditioned by the very system I proved to them was false? 'Sedition! Exile!' they cried, and thus began my years of wandering, alone but for dear Elly here, through the Low Countries and France; this was before the troubles began, thence to your own fair shores spreading the words of le divin abbé as I went."

He paused in his story and allowed his fingers to dally once more on the piano. Two or three notes rose up. Kalkbrenner picked out a well-thumbed book from the shelf behind the instrument.

"This. The *Traité des Sensations*. Your story brings to mind its dedication. 'We cannot recollect the ignorance in which we were born. It is a state which leaves no traces behind it. We remember our ignorance only when we remember what we have learned. We must already know something before we can attend to what we are learning. We must have ideas before we can observe that we were once without them.' " He sighed. "Sublime . . .

"The statue becomes fully sensible, fully alive, only through knowing its own former emptiness, through seeing the construction that came to be itself. This is what we must divine in you, sir," he said, looking at Lemprière. "We must take your story and trace its cogs and levers back to the original fault; we must make the screw adjustment, the crucial quarter turn that sets you ticking properly. . . ."

But despite this prolegomenon, Doctor Kalkbrenner had not the slightest intention of hearing the story of Lemprière's life. He continued to expatiate on the principles of the human mind, to sing the praises of "le divin Abbé de Condillac," and now and again would touch on Lemprière's case as if it were quite incidental to these favored themes. Occasional questions were asked and answered by Lemprière, whose nausea was returning, replacing his headache, brought on, he suspected, by the redness which surrounded him. After digressions on the case of the pregnant woman and the porpoise, a remarkably shrunken pineal gland he had come across in Aix-la-Chapelle, and a "Monsieur Sienois" whose obsessive urinary retention had only been cured by his neighbor setting fire to his house, the good doctor at length arrived at his diagnosis.

". . . and so it is clear from these examples that the condition you suffer from, a peculiarly rare one, I might add, is none other than projective-objective palilexic echopraxia. Palilexia I first came across in Salzburg, a gentleman there had read a handbook on obstetrics, in reverse, of course." He gestured with his hand as if the results of this were too terrible to speak of. "Echopraxia is more normally associated with mass hysterias. The tendency to mirror the bodily motions of those about one is commonplace in military environments. L'Abbé de Condillac does not treat of those matters directly, you understand. . . . You seem to function as a conduit of some sorts: read, secrete, excrete would be the pattern." Kalkbrenner frowned.

"Perhaps a diversion," offered Septimus.

"Exactly the solution I was coming to," Kalkbrenner affirmed.

"A hobby, perhaps—"

"Which would provide an outlet for this excessive reading," Septimus completed the sentence.

"An outlet? Oh. Yes, an outlet. I was just going to suggest the same. An outlet would be the thing, a valve, yes, an outlet." Kalkbrenner's cure was taking shape. "Now the form of this outlet; surgery offers us several alternatives—"

"Which only a man of your own experience, Doctor Kalkbrenner, would have the confidence to reject. As your admirable Condillac advises us, it is the mind which probes the mind," Septimus intervened.

"He does indeed, he does indeed. Ah, the mind. The mind needs a mental outlet—"

"An activity," interrupted Septimus again. "Something to do to exorcise this *reading*."

"To exorcise it? Well, not that quite, but these are the general lines of my diagnosis, yes, Septimus." Kalkbrenner was groping for the answer: "The mind," "the outlet," "the reading," shunting these counters around, the shape was coming into focus. . . . "To write!" he exclaimed. "He needs to write!"

"Of course," said Septimus as if stunned by the sheer rightness of Kalkbrenner's prescription. "The answer was staring us in the face, but only you could have unearthed it. Well done, Ernst. Well done!" Kalkbrenner was mopping his brow and smiling, half embarrassed—had his brilliance been too ostentatious? His instincts told him no.

"To write?" Lemprière's voice was lost in a self-congratulatory hubbub. "Write what?"

An hour later, in the same place, the four of them were moving toward an answer to this question by a process that had become one of elimination. On the criteria, they were agreed: It must embrace Lemprière's love of the Ancients, and at the same time, it must treat of all the ways in which this love might return to haunt Lemprière's waking hours, including those instances already mentioned. "Lay the ghosts of Antiquity to rest!" Ernst had exclaimed. "Do it to them before they do it to you." Septimus had endorsed the sentiment. "But what?" Elly had asked.

Rejected so far were: *an almanac* (too late in the year), *a breviary* (pointless), *a cadastre* (too bourgeois), *an encyclopedia* (would take too long), *a fescennine verse-dialogue* (only Lemprière knew what it was), *a glossary* (too many already), *a homily* (no), *incunabula* (too late), *juvenilia* (also too late), *a kunstlerroman* (too early), *a log* (Lemprière hated boats), *a manual* (boring), *a novel* (too vulgar), *an opera* (overambitious), *a pamphlet* (too humble), *a Qu'ran* (already was one), *a replevin* (too arcane), *a story* (too simple), *a treatise* (perhaps, but little enthusiasm), *an Upanishad* (too fanciful), *a variorum edition* (of what?), *a weltanschauung* (onanistic), *a xenophontean cosmology* (out of date), and *a yearbook*.

Lemprière, Kalkbrenner, and Clementi were sunk in gloom, stony ground for Septimus's suggestions whose rate had slowed to the occasional thought thrown out with little conviction or chance of acceptance.

"No," they said to the latest (*a zetetic tract*). "Too inquisitive." Even Septimus seemed disheartened for a moment. Abruptly his expression changed. He stood up and strode briskly to the bookshelf opposite. He had spied two large, identical books. The author's name gleamed in gold on their spines.

"I have it," he said, picking one out. "This is it. This is what you must write, John. Write one of these." The name stared up at him. "Samuel Johnson."

"Samuel Johnson," he read aloud.

"Samuel Johnson," echoed Kalkbrenner. "Of course! How could we have missed it? You are indeed correct, Mister Praeceps; Mister Lemprière, you must emulate the good Doctor Johnson, that is my final and certain prescription." Septimus brandished the book like a club, then threw it across to Lemprière, who caught it and peered curiously at its frontispiece.

"What is it?" asked Elly.

"You wanted a work which covered everything, did you not? This is that!"

"Right," said Lemprière, his head in the book.

"How clever of you, Ernst, but may I ask what it is?" cooed Clementi.

"The answer at last. Do you think you can do it, John?" Septimus asked.

"Yes," replied the other, still reading. Septimus marched across to shake Kalkbrenner's hand.

"Knew we'd find it."

"Well done, Ernst!"

Clementi was bobbing up and down, offering congratulations and praise to both. "Well done, all of you! Really, everything seems to be quite put to rights. Might I ask now, terribly ignorant of me, might I ask, exactly what is it, do you think?"

Lemprière looked up from his reading.

"It is a dictionary," he replied. He would write a dictionary. But as he was about to announce his decision, Lemprière had the strangest sensation. The events of his life, his infancy, childhood, and youth, his love for

Juliette, his father's death, even his tattered memories of the previous night, all of these seemed suddenly to come into view. The events and travails of his life hurtled forward, closing on one another like a hundred chariots with their horses and charioteers crashing together in a tangle of limbs and broken shafts. Lemprière was at its epicenter. From a stillness that lengthened, gathered pace, and moved on, he watched them ride off once more, fanning out over the plain like the spokes of their wheels. They were his emissaries, agents of the dictionary.

"Angels of the dictionary?" Septimus's tone was suddenly sharp. Lemprière had mumbled the title aloud without knowing.

"Agents," he corrected his friend. "Nothing." The three of them were watching, waiting for him. It was quite clear.

"I will write a dictionary," he told them, and they closed upon him, suddenly celebrants of his decision.

A little later, after mutual congratulations and prolonged leave-takings, Lemprière and Septimus were retracing their earlier steps, past the same terraces and through the same streets as before. Lemprière recalled his friend's account of his own outburst the night before. True, he had listed all that had happened to Lemprière, yet Lemprière knew he had told him more. How much more? He agonized over this as they continued their progress in silence, Lemprière stewing in uncertainty, Septimus preoccupied with thoughts which remained opaque. At length, Lemprière could contain his curiosity, or dread, no longer.

"You did not mention the girl," he challenged Septimus.

"The girl? Which girl? When?" Lemprière had framed the question ambiguously, Juliette perhaps, or another. The girl on the bed, whom he had drunkenly mistaken for the one he loved, but that was impossible. It had not been her. Now Septimus had called his bluff.

"I believe I was . . . confused."

"Yes, I believe you were," Septimus readily agreed. They walked a little farther, but the silence, which earlier had been somehow agreed upon, was now onerous. Lemprière felt compelled to speak again.

"I don't believe either of them credited a word of it," he burst out.

"Ernst and Elly? What does it matter? After all, it is still possible you imagined all these things. I don't say you did, but it is possible. Monsters and gods in fields, in stores, Circe in the Craven Arms. You read of them, certainly, and they appeared. But only for you, perhaps. They were real to you, but imaginary, you see?" Red on gray, pool, sky.

"Not the dogs," Lemprière said. "I didn't imagine the dogs."

"No," Septimus conceded. "The dogs were real. And the girl, of course."

"The girl?" Lemprière turned on Septimus sharply.

"The girl in the pool, bathing, like Diana. That girl."

"Of course." Lemprière began walking again. That girl. Juliette, naked in the pool.

At the end of the street they came to a halt. "The dictionary, then," he said as if it were a toast. This seemed to focus Septimus.

"The dictionary, yes. The dictionary is very important." The last two words were enunciated with some emphasis. "You must begin just as soon as possible."

"I shall begin this very evening," Lemprière promised confidently. Septimus looked away. He seemed lost, detached somehow. The moment dragged on.

"Well, good-night to you, then." Lemprière clapped him on the arm.

"Yes, good-night, John," he returned. Lemprière smiled, then turned on his heel and strode out into the street, on a determined path homeward. Septimus stood there for a few seconds longer, looking about, then wandered off in the other direction.

That night, Lemprière sat at the desk in his room. Ranged before him were his pen, an inkwell, and a single sheet of white paper. He dipped the pen quickly in the well, then held it still and watched as three black beads of ink slid down to drop back silently from the nib. He looked down at the sheet of paper on his desk. The pen moved quickly in rehearsal just above its surface. Lemprière paused; then, in the top left-hand corner, he carefully inscribed the letter "A."

· · ·

Now down through the city's tight skin to the hodgepodge of rocks and earth beneath. Through blue-gray and stiff red clay, crumbly slabs of sediment, black granite, and water-bearing formations, past fire-damp flares, shale, and veins of coal to pierce a second, more secret skin and enter the body of the Beast. Here, long fluted chambers twist away into honeycombs and open into caverns the size of churches with cradles of silica hanging from brittle calcified threads, ridges, flanges, and platforms all frozen in stone to wait for centuries beneath the city. Once it was a mountain of flesh, red throbbing meat, and muscle. Now it is dead stone with its veins sucked dry as dust and all its arteries blown out clean by time; an ignorant monument playing host to nine, then eight, men who crawl through its passages like parasites and who differ in their understandings of its chambers, tunnels, and lattices, not unnaturally—it can be accounted for in so many ways.

Boffe, vast and red in his bathtub, splashed vigorously and tried to imagine the stone creature which surrounded him on all sides. He sat now in his liquids, contemplating the chamber, as was his custom during bathtime, faintly aware of the millions of tons of ground, rocks, and earth pressing down on him from the surface, hundreds of feet above. Sheer weight, a deep bass rumble in his badly orchestrated thoughts. Damn

Vaucanson, who had called him "the weak link" and who was nothing without him, he the show's imperator, the pilot of illusion. Boffe sploshed and gurgled through his ablutions, then emerged to towel his steaming bulk dry in the chamber's colder air. Vaucanson, Boffe's surface irritant, rose like a rash, deepening Boffe's irritation. His theatricals (marvelous things), his spectacles and seances, composed, planned, passed, and performed, were dependent on the other man's genius, his mechanical contrivances. Boffe needed engines and machines, occasionally actors (though the latter, being invariably stiff-limbed and speechless, taxed his invention so that he had to remind himself that all great art is produced in the face of resistance from the medium). Boffe! He regarded himself in the mirror at the far end of the chamber. He was unmistakable.

Behind him stood the table with his models and plans, little clumps of trees hand-fashioned from sponge and wire, figures modeled in clay, and Vaucanson's engines reproduced in matchwood and string. Boffe was no weak link, the plan before him proved it. Vaucanson disliked him, Cas de l'Île hated him. His poor, abused, prostituted talents could barely stand it, with Le Mara creeping about like a machine of death, and the caves, the horrible caves, he hated it, could hardly bear it, it was too terrible. Boffe patted his stomach in self-regard, and dressed. When accoutred he was magnificent, his legs perhaps a little thin in proportion to the rest of him but still serviceable as he walked to the table where he hovered over the miniature mansion and its gardens, the lawn (made of stretched baize), the scrubby ground beyond (dyed hog's bristles set in papier-mâché), the trees, and the centerpiece which was a pyre where the woman would burn in excruciating torment, suffering unimaginable agonies that even Boffe's ingenuity had found no means to prolong beyond a minute or two.

Vaucanson's business would be set up behind the trees. Boffe's thick digit pressed lightly on the top of the leafy canopy, as he saw it. From here the blinding flash of molten torture would be raised, swung over, and deposited as though from the heavens down on the unfortunate woman, into her even. It would be spectacular in the best possible way, giving an illusion of necessity usually only achieved by God.

Boffe readjusted his crotch which had become snarled in the imagined excitement, then turned his attention to the house whence the boy would emerge. His same finger traced a path over the lawn and scrub into the trees, thence to the pyre, mentally reviewing the methods of enticement and distraction he had designed which would lead the boy to the required place at the required time to play his role as witness and (so the leader assured him) oblique participant. Boffe conceived the space around the pyre as an extravagant Chair of State in which the boy-king might sit, at once to see and be seen. Boffe glanced again at his brief, the open volume which lay to one side and told of the flaming conception of Perseus, a fabulous visitation of the virgin by Zeus the cloud-propeller, raining down in guileful drops upon her, a shower of gold. The brazen pit would have to be faked up, of course, and there was the woman to think of, though her active participation was not required. . . . Most of all it was the boy who troubled Boffe. He would be unrehearsed, naturally, ambiguous in his relations with the production, perhaps resistant to the whole affair, hmm. But Boffe had built in leeways, resistances, counter-weights, and suggestive encounters which should keep him on track, while allowing latitude too, for every skeptic must have his bone of reason. Boffe stood back and admired. So many niggly, logistical pro-blems, and he had found solutions to them all! He acknowledged the rude vigor of Vaucanson's engines: The crane was good and he liked the dog-machines, splendid contraptions.

Boffe gathered up his plans and thought of the other seven, but Jaques was in France, six then, their shocked surprise at his cleverness. Boffe reached for his lamp and strode toward the chamber's door. Soon the meeting would begin. His entrance was awaited.

The Cabbala were gathering. Casterleigh stood on the fringes of a pool of light afforded by the oil lamp marking the meeting room's entrance. The door a few meters behind him was airtight. There was no chink of light. Before him, one of the Beast's flat areas extended away into darkness. In reality, it was a huge, semicircular platform carpeted with dry gravel that crunched loudly underfoot, a sound amplified by the vaulted roof almost a hundred feet above. The wall of the meeting room bisected the area, leaving the gravel plate as a kind of apron onto which several passages opened. To one side was a high, sloping wall which eventually became the roof, on the other a sheer drop. The apron was seventy or eighty yards across and unlit for the most part. Most of his colleagues were already within. Not Jaques, who was still in Paris, with the girl. . . . Not Boffe, who was tardy, dead weight, Casterleigh thought. And not Le Mara, whom he awaited now.

After some minutes he heard a shuffling sound in the darkness, in front of him and to his left. That would be Le Mara. There was little point in calling out. The acoustics of the cavernous space which opened out in front of him were peculiar. From his station close to the door it was possible to pinpoint sounds from the surrounding area with unerring accuracy. Le Mara was heading straight toward him, toward the door, in fact. The Beast seemed to Casterleigh a haven for anomalies, pushed from the ragged fringes of theory to pose their problems here. Other caverns were utterly silent, the walls soaking up sound like a sponge, and unless you spoke directly to the other person, the sound failed, leaving you mouthing inaudibly, to no one. Temperatures were odd too. You could pass from freezing, bitter cold to sweltering heat in a matter of minutes. Some parts of the Beast were too hot to enter, the lower parts mostly, but there was no order to it. Le Mara advanced, his footsteps growing louder as he emerged from the gloom and saw Casterleigh for the first time. He stopped, blinked. Casterleigh gestured for him to approach. Casterleigh looked for curiosity in the other man's face. There was none.

"The first consignment is aboard?" he asked. Le Mara nodded.

"The Indian is still content to watch?" Le Mara nodded again, then spoke.

"He should be stopped. He follows our movements. Searches for something." Casterleigh hated the monotone of Le Mara's voice, the voice of a dead man. He towered over the assassin. The wait had been oppressive.

"I agree." Casterleigh knew the leader was against it; moreover, opposed it adamantly. This fact hovered between the two of them, potential conspirators. Neither spoke. Le Mara turned abruptly and looked back into the darkness behind him. Then Casterleigh heard the sound which had prompted his movement, footsteps. Boffe's footsteps, as he clambered across the gravel toward the door and the meeting beyond it.

"Shall we go?" Casterleigh indicated the door. It was time. Le Mara nodded and moved, then stopped. The assassin spoke as if it were the logical outcome of some process that had taken a set amount of time to complete.

"The Indian should be killed." There, it was said. "The clerk too."

"Not yet, we wait a little." Casterleigh stayed him. Le Mara turned again. Casterleigh smiled. The decision was his. He walked with Le Mara to the door and watched as the smaller man passed through ahead of him. Le Mara was his too.

Six candles lit the inner chamber. Boffe's breathless arrival a minute later added a seventh. Jaques's chair remained empty, and the one to the left of the leader, naturally. The leader sat back, as always, his face hidden in the shadows. The hours dragged by in desultory talk, plans. Le Mara reported on the loading of the *Vendragon*. Coker and his men were proving satisfactory. The next consignment was approved.

"The Indian remains—"

"Not to be touched," the leader's voice cut sharply across Le Mara's. Vaucanson looked up. Casterleigh caught his eye. They were thinking the same thought. The Indian was not the first to come, not the first "emissary" from the Nawab. They had hesitated over the earlier incident, they had compromised. Boffe fingered his plans impatiently. That had been a mistake and it had been made at the leader's insistence. The spy had been sent back. Changed, certainly—Vaucanson had seen to that with his pincers and silver wire—but returned nonetheless with the little he had learned. Now his successor was here, knowing more than he should, a threat.

"He is not to be touched," the leader reiterated. Le Mara gazed back steadily, then looked away, the order accepted. "The clerk too," he spoke abruptly.

"The boy has met with him," Casterleigh addressed the leader, then went on to describe the meeting between Peppard and the object of their attentions. "The boy might be misled. Peppard knows more than he ever admitted." The memory of the Neagle scandal occupied all their thoughts. The risk was unacceptable.

"If there is further contact, more than cursory contact," the leader spoke carefully to Le Mara, "then we must act finally." Le Mara nodded. Casterleigh watched as the compromise was reached. He would have imposed his wish without discussion. "The boy must be shielded from such people," the leader continued in paternal tones. "He is vulnerable, impressionable. . . ." Several of the men smiled. Casterleigh thought of Juliette.

"Are we prepared for him?" The question required no answer. From the shadows which masked his features, the leader searched the faces around the table.

"The woman is prepared," Le Mara said. Casterleigh nodded in confirmation. He and Le Mara exchanged glances.

"The Indian was there, when we took her, he saw—"

"Not to be touched!" The leader's voice rasped harshly. The assembly fell silent. Boffe considered presenting his plan at this point, but the leader spoke again.

"Our own friend brings better news. . . ." Casterleigh scowled. This was the part of the plan he most detested. The endless elaboration, subtleties, the sheer impracticality of it—all these rallied the doubts in his mind, but to bring in an outsider and place him at the very heart of it all, this struck at the root of things. Not just an outsider, but one seemingly without a past. Their best efforts had discovered nothing, nothing at all. They knew only what they saw, and he volunteered no more. The arrangement stank of haste and incaution. The leader saw mistrust written clearly on Casterleigh's face as he told of the boy's drunken mistakes, the evening's chaos. Juliette's name was mentioned. The incident raised smiles and the leader's tone was almost affectionate.

". . . the girl will be kept safe for the moment. The resemblance will prove useful." Le Mara nodded assent at Rosalie's reprieve. The account moved to the following day, Lemprière's movements about the city, his visit, his resolution.

"He will write the dictionary," the leader announced, and perhaps there was a tinge of relief in his voice. The others looked up in approval at this fact. "Now, we can proceed . . ." and Boffe knew his moment had come. "Two weeks from today, we shall plant a second demon in him," the leader continued. Boffe shuffled the papers before him, his plans.

"Two weeks?" Vaucanson queried. Boffe cleared his throat in readiness.

"Yes," confirmed the leader, as Boffe rose at last to begin his peroration. "Christmas Eve."

• • •

The fortnight following Lemprière's decision brought Septimus and several of his friends. Lemprière forgot his friend's distraction at the coffeehouse in the confusion and bustle of their arrival. They came singly, escorted by Septimus, who grinned as he introduced them—men of varying use to the project.

A Mister Stone undid his canvas sack to show Lemprière pieces of paper, little grubby scraps and larger sheets, all dog-eared, which he had scavenged and saved up over long years for just such an occasion.

"To write on," explained Septimus. Mister Stone mumbled as he laid out the scraps and poked them about to display their best aspects.

Two days later, Septimus introduced Tom Cadell, bookseller. Mister Cadell spent an hour or more looking through the completed entries in Lemprière's dictionary. He took snuff, and after scrutinizing each sheet of paper would pick it up and flick it so that the loose grains floated invisibly to the floor. Every time thereafter that Lemprière sneezed in the room, he would think of Mister Cadell.

"You are a man of some learning," he addressed Lemprière, after he had replaced and degrained the last sheet. "I would be happy to buy your book, and sell it too." The "but" implied by his "would" grew huge in the silence that followed. "A touch more humanity," he said at length. "It must be readable above all. Your readers need the man as well as the work." Lemprière was baffled. "Bring a blush to their cheeks, a smile to their lips."

"Make them laugh?" he said.

"Make them pay," Mister Cadell said with finality. "I will be happy to buy, print, and sell your book, Mister Lemprière," he said, and the two of them shook hands. It was agreed. Septimus would hammer out the fine points, and he gave a clenched fist salute behind Mister Cadell's back as they both left.

There followed Jeremy Trindle of the Porson Trindles, who offered to bring Lemprière the books he needed on loan and at a reasonable rate. It was an irregular arrangement, but he would do it for a friend. Septimus looked pleased with himself.

"Thank you," said Lemprière, and, a day or two later, "No, thank you," following Lydia's sideways look, an offer of unspecified services through the long winter nights. Septimus kissed her as she left, bringing a practiced blush to her cheek.

Lastly and most puzzling of all, there was a nondescript fellow, tall, dressed for the times, with brown or black hair, not so tall perhaps, but certainly not short, and gaunt rather than full in the face, although neither description wholly missed the mark. Septimus brought him in with a minimum of fanfare and at first said nothing at all. Lemprière looked at the man suspiciously.

"Who are you?" he asked at length.

"This is Mister O'Tristero," said Septimus. There was a second long silence.

"I am your rival," said Mister O'Tristero. That was the substance of all that was said.

After he had gone, Lemprière turned to his friend for explanation. "Keep you on your toes," explained Septimus. He was particularly sprightly that day.

"Do two more entries." He pointed to the manuscript already piling up on Lemprière's desk. "Are these all signed and dated?" He leafed through the sheets.

"Signed? No."

"And dated. Sign and date every entry. That's very important, do you understand? Sign and date everything, absolutely of the first importance."

"Certainly," agreed Lemprière.

"Proof," Septimus said. "Cadell has no scruples about such things. Everything . . ."

"Of course," said Lemprière.

"Two more entries then, no more than that for the present. I will collect and deliver them the evening of Edmund's ball. Do you have a costume?"

But Lemprière had no memory of Edmund's invitation, whispered over his reeling, drink-soaked head the night of the Pork Club two weeks back. It was there somewhere, in the whirl of shining faces, chandeliers, the goose, the girl who was and was not Juliette, the drink, victory, and the teeming rain—somewhere beyond recollection. He had no idea what Septimus was talking about.

"Costume?" Septimus explained that they had both been invited, along with most of the Pork Club and many others, men and women, young and old. They were expected. The De Veres' seasonal gathering was an occasion, even if it had fallen off a little in recent years.

"But where is it, and when?" demanded Lemprière.

"They have a pile in Richmond," Septimus told him as he moved through the door. He was late.

"Be ready at three." He was clumping down the stairs.

"But when? What day?" Lemprière called after him.

"Three days from now," Septimus shouted back. "Christmas Eve!" And he was gone.

Lemprière sat down at his desk and took in the news. Already he was apprehensive. He knew no one, or almost no one. He would be expected to dress his part, and he did not know what that part should be. Most of all, he wondered why he had been invited at all.

The street noise drifted up chaotically, but he was used to it now. When he wrote, he heard nothing. The Earl, as he recalled, had seemed approachable. A little drunk, perhaps . . . and hardly forthcoming. Perhaps he was wrong. None of his questions would find answers before Monday in any case. Monday was Christmas Eve.

Lemprière looked now at the pages piled before him, his dictionary—at least the beginnings of it. He took up the first page, with its competent "A" scrawled at the top. "Aaras'sus, a city of Pisidia." It was difficult, sometimes, to imagine anyone even interested in such facts, let alone making them laugh or cry. "It is probably the Ariasis of Ptolemy," he had added. So it was. Who cared? The answer to that was that he cared. It was all whirling around inside him, he had to care. He wrote his name carefully beneath the entry and dated it "twenty-first day of December, 1787." After his decision to start the book, after his parting with Septimus, who had been very odd at the end, Lemprière had returned and begun work immediately. The coffee he had drunk made him tireless and nervy. He wrote through the night and took to his bed at dawn, glass-eyed and aching from the head down. After that, he tried to write during the hours of daylight only, but his sleep, which had always been regular, began to choose its own times and occasions. He would take three hours at midday, and another four sometime after midnight. Or he would wake and sleep, two hours at a time, or not sleep at all for a day or a night and a day. Then sleep for an age. It felt unnatural. More and more of his waking hours were spent at night, and several of Septimus's visits had found him sound asleep in his bed or slumped on his desk. It was as if his dictionary preferred to be written at night, and this made obscure sense to Lemprière, anxious about it but with little choice in the matter. He had worked on for two weeks, put up with Septimus's interruptions, and the results of his efforts were here before him: thirty-eight closely written leaves, full of holes and errors which he would later have to plug and correct, from Aaras'sus in Pisidia to Cyzicus in the Sea of Marmara.

Now he sat signing and dating, signing and dating like an automaton as the results of his efforts brought back their old antagonisms and fragile graces: the stories, characters, and places revisited upon him over the fortnight past, and Actaeon especially, which was no surprise to him, nor his own dread of it, the dogs and the prone figure as his pen scurried quickly over the candid paper, "John Lemprière, twenty-first day of December, 1787." There. He had put his name to it, and though when he shut his eyes and let his mind go blank it was the same lowering bank of cloud moving above, the corpse his father underneath, he felt the truth of what Kalkbrenner had said. To write it all down, write it out of himself; that was his task, and now the true nature of what that meant was becoming clear. His early optimism had all but evaporated and been replaced by something harder and more durable, determination, perhaps, for the work was to prove harder than he thought, more involved, and in ways he had not imagined. What began, only a fortnight ago, as a simple list of persons, places, and events, had since grown strangely, with odd nodules and tendrils sprouting in all directions and linking up with one another to form loops and lattices, the whole thing wriggling under his nib like a mess of worms on a pin. It looked in all directions, spoke scrambled languages, and made wild faces at him, an Argus-eyed, Babel-tongued, Chimera-headed catalog of all the true things that had turned to dreams and the men who had turned to their dreamers. All dead now. "John Lemprière, twenty-first day of December, 1787." Again.

Even this early, the dictionary had become its own beast, with little twitchings of life carrying out their own commerce, quite apparent to him as he worked steadily, tediously, through the entries. Reappearances by major and minor characters folded the story back on itself, places recurred, accruing and expending significance, events paralleled one another. It was a serpentine thing, hardly a list at all. Lemprière paused over his entry on Acrisius, the ill-omened grandfather who had met his appointed death at Larissa, who had shut his grandson in a chest and his daughter too, the vessel of his destruction in a vessel of her own (for which *vid.* Danae); but they had survived, returned to Argos, and the boy had joined the list: Adrastus, ally of Theseus; Ægisthus, lover of Clytemnestra; and Agenor, father of Crotopus—kings of Argos as he, Perseus, would be, Lemprière's alter ego in the Pork Club mime, his Persiad of errors. Perseus had rescued Andromeda ("John Lemprière, twenty-first of December, 1787"), married her with the blessings of Cepheus and thanks of his wife, Cassiopeia, and Argos had called him back. Argos, city of altars and usurpations, Admeta's to Juno and Danaeus of Galenor, whence perhaps the name Danae. He did not know. It was for Admeta that Chiron's pupil brought back Hippolyte's girdle, and it was he again, Augeus's stableboy, who brought Alceste back from the regions of hell, who caused Charon's yearlong confinement, and tamed Cerberus, the triple-headed dog. And Alceste was to marry Admetus, who won her with a chariot given him by exiled Apollo, his shepherd and ward of sorts. . . . . Admetus, Admeta. Danaeus, Danae.

As Lemprière had written, he had, from time to time, stepped back and seen accidents and coincidences join lazily to form stories that twisted, broke up, and formed new, yet more bizarre chains of circumstance. The whole of his effort shifted. With the Acheron at his back, Antaeus's killer defied the judges of hell, Æacus among them who was conceived by Ægina after Jupiter took her in the guise of a tongue of flame, reminding Lemprière of Danae once more, and the same hero, Alcmena's son (Buphagus, as the Argonauts called their gluttonous friend), broke off one of Achelous's horns, the river god who fought him as a serpent, then an ox, then a one-horned ox, for the horn was given to Copia to fill with grain, and Lemprière grew further confused as Jupiter took a horn from Amalthea, the goat who suckled him, and gave it to the nymphs. A second Cornucopia, or the same one somehow, Lemprière puzzled. And did it have anything to do with Agrotera, the goat sacrifice at Athens, so lavish it caused famines? Probably not, he thought, and signed "Agrotera" as the rest, then dated it "twenty-first day of December, 1787" again. Perhaps he needed an amanuensis. Talk of horns reminded him of Electryon (though he had yet to reach "E"), who was Alcmene's father, and grandfather of her twins, conceived through her husband and another, Jupiter again over three nights (her triple moon sign admitting as much), whose efforts produced Achelous's slayer himself, him again but . . . Horns, yes. Electryon had been killed by horns (the Ceraton was a temple made entirely from *antlers*), cow horns on the cows which Amphitryon gave him and herded for him to the extent of throwing missiles at one which strayed until the missile rebounded from its horns to Electryon's skull with such force that it killed him. And Amphitryon became king of Argos with Alcmene as his bride. And, of course, Electryon was the son of Andromeda, and his grandmother the woman who had floated on the middle sea, imprisoned in Acrisius's chest until washed up in the Cyclades: Danae, again. Somehow she seemed to Lemprière to be at the center of things, though his dictionary had yet to reach her. Danae.

Electryon's death seemed the most unlikely of all to Lemprière, until he remembered Æschylus, killed by a blow to the head from a tortoise dropped by a passing eagle, and then Capaneus's celebrated opinion that a good Cappadocian orator was as common as a flying tortoise. Unfortunate perhaps, but Capaneus had invented the siege and there were monuments enough to that: Carthage with Cato baying for destruction in the Senate, Babylon with its hundred gates of bronze and walls two hundred cubits high cemented with bitumen, and, greatest of all, Alexandria where the books burned. . . . A clatter on the stairs outside his door. The tailor. He had yet to set eyes on the man. Lemprière returned to the drudgery of signing and dating the work he had completed.

Over the following two days, he checked the pages carefully and found time to write a further two entries as instructed. He was not surprised to find that the name left after these labors, hanging over the page, the entry which would have been his third had he written it, was that of Danae.

· · ·

"Move over, Lydia, that's it." Lemprière squeezed onto the seat.

"Spectacles!" Walter Warburton-Burleigh seemed delighted to see him. The Pug sniggered. They were sitting opposite him in the coach. It was almost four, Christmas Eve, and the light was failing. Septimus clambered in, slammed the door, and banged on the woodwork. The coach set off.

Warburton-Burleigh smiled at Lemprière. "Rosalie disappeared, you know? Saturday last. I came around and she was gone. Got you a souvenir, though," and he reached into his pocket. It was one of the anklets.

Lemprière said something dismissive; Lydia looked sharply at him and he felt he had betrayed the girl in some way. Sisters in arms. Where *had* she gone? On his other side, Septimus said something about her legs, and Lydia laughed suddenly as if trying not to. The atmosphere grew more friendly. The Pug lit a pipe and puffed odorously until Warburton-Burleigh snatched it from him quickly and threw it out the window. After a very short discussion, the coach was stopped, and they all got out to look for the thing. No one was sure if it was still alight or not. Septimus claimed that he would be able to find it by smell alone. The city was some miles behind them and the sky was overcast. It was almost dark. They separated and scrabbled about in the road for some minutes. It had snowed the previous night. The fall still filled the ditches on either side of the road and lay on the fields beyond like surf at night, pale and faintly luminous, somehow misplaced. Several roads were still blocked and the mail was late. They were fortunate to find the turnpike clear. Lemprière could see nothing.

"John." He turned. It was Lydia. "Have you found it?" he asked.

"No, listen. Did Rosalie visit you? She was dragged off by someone. Strange voice," Lydia said. "Bet and Karin knew something about it, but they have disappeared too. It's not my loss, but still . . ."

"Bet and Karin?"

"Aha!" from farther down the road.

The Pug was bellowing that he had found it, that it was broken, and Warburton-Burleigh was the son of a whore. They returned to the coach and the journey continued with the Pug in a sulk. He would emerge from it periodically. Warburton-Burleigh would wave the broken pipe about and the Pug would submerge once more. It was amusement of sorts. Lemprière's apprehension grew as they drew nearer the De Veres'. He was wearing a new frock coat and cloak provided by Septimus earlier that day, a loan.

"Very good," Septimus had said when he had tried it on, and the same thing as he had leafed through the completed sheets of the dictionary. Their collection had been his main business. "Danae?" He had been reading the final page.

"Not yet . . ." Lemprière was ready to reprise Septimus's earlier instructions in explanation, but was cut short.

"Good, good . . ." from Septimus. It had been very businesslike. No trace of the puzzling vagueness when they had parted after the consultation with Ernst and Elly.

"So who will be there, I mean, exactly?" Lemprière asked brightly during a lull in the talk. But the coach jolted violently and when all had righted themselves the question was forgotten. He had to ask again.

"Everyone," Septimus told him. "Teddy's friends and acquaintances, his mother's." Septimus caught the need for reassurance in Lemprière's silence.

"There is almost always music, eating, of course, and a display of some sort. . . ."

"Fireworks," added the Pug. Lemprière nodded.

"Then there's the meat," said Walter Warburton-Burleigh. Lydia sighed theatrically. "Fat girls whose paters own things up north."

"The late Earl had shipping interests, lots of old sea men, Company boys," Septimus went on. "Military types . . . Teddy knows them all. His mother packs the place with widows and dowagers, but they bring their own friends. Strange mixture, truly; I noticed Dundas last year—"

"Dullest man in England," interjected Warburton-Burleigh.

"And Byrne, Byrne was there, who else?"

"Chadwick?"

"Not this year," said the Pug. "He died." Lemprière looked up in surprise at the name of his father's old solicitor.

"And that creepy little fellow, said nothing the whole evening . . ." Walter Warburton-Burleigh tried to recall a name.

"Who was he with?" asked Septimus.

"Alone, I believe, no, no, he was with Croesus."

"Croesus?" Lemprière was being startled from several directions by the exchange.

"As in rich as."

"Viscount Casterleigh," Septimus deciphered, taking a look at his friend. Casterleigh.

"And the Pork Club," Warburton-Burleigh shouted.

"Oink!" Septimus and the Pug shouted back, raising an imaginary toast.

"Everyone," Lydia said in conclusion to this.

"Of course! You would know Casterleigh. His Jersey house . . ." Septimus said suddenly to Lemprière, who was sitting back with his face tight and expressionless, Casterleigh's name and Juliette already rising in his thoughts, but he had time also to think of his drunken confession on the bridge in the rain. He had not mentioned Casterleigh to Septimus after all, nor his daughter. A sort of relief flooded privately through him.

"Yes, yes! I know the man," he admitted readily and explained about his role in the library on Jersey. Warburton-Burleigh looked at him with renewed interest.

"Naturally you were introduced to his daughter?" he questioned slyly. Lemprière thought for a moment; he was giving nothing away.

"Naturally," he agreed.

"Aha," said Warburton-Burleigh shortly, and Lemprière saw from the expressions on his companions' faces that he was flatly disbelieved. He protested, describing her in persuasive detail, her manners and habitual gestures, all of it etched indelibly in his memory.

"We've all *seen* her," said the Pug.

"He guards her like Acrisius," added Septimus. Lemprière looked sharply at him.

"Think what you will," he said. And abruptly he hardly cared whether they believed him or not. She might be present that evening. The prospect already raced in his brain. His companions were forgotten. He could see lights in the darkness beyond the window, spelling Juliette, Juliette, perhaps.

"We are here," said Lydia as they approached.

"And late," said Septimus.

It was true. Coaches filled the courtyard and spilled down the drive. Hedges and fences extended out into a darkness that harbored trees and scrubland, wild shrubs, rootless brambles, and other sprawling plant life: all of it out there, unseen, waiting, and being secretly green. Lydia, Lemprière, Warburton-Burleigh, the Pug, then Septimus clambered out of the coach stiff-limbed, yawning and stretching into the cold evening air. The night sky was blacker than before.

As Lemprière rounded the coach, the house came into view. A tall construction of white plaster and timbers with transoms and Gothic quatrefoils studding its face, more of it kept appearing as his eyes were drawn to either side by gables and straggling roof lines which twisted back into the darkness where they were lost in a scrum of haphazard additions, low galleries, and outbuildings. The front at least was impressive with mullion windows flanking a massive black door, country oak and a large knocker on it, which Septimus took charge of and rapped, one, two, three reports echoing in the hall beyond like a huge stone drum.

All five waited for the door to be opened, silenced for the moment by their different anticipations, and Lemprière thought again of Mister Chadwick, whom he had never met and would never see. "Froze," hissed the Pug between clenched teeth.

The door was opened. Mister Chadwick had stood here too and wondered at the reason for his invitation. A small bald man in a red coat was being buried under cloaks. The man was asking him, "Sir?" Lemprière handed the man his coat and walked through behind the others. Why had his father's solicitor been wanted here?

"Through here, sir." Lemprière nodded. "Quite a night, I would imagine, sir." But Lemprière only caught the thread of the butler's patter as he was led within the house, until that voice was replaced by a more general murmur, a different thread. The general hum grew louder and broke up into a jumble of tones and accents, with odd voices breaking through like heads popping up out of a maze, more and more of them until the sound seemed to reach a new level and then another as the butler threw open a pair of double doors and the gathering beyond was unmuzzled.

The noise crashed out and broke over Lemprière in a rich cackling babble, a roaring noise of chitchat with glasses and cups chinking together, and the scene was full of sculpted women jabbering to each other, their menfolk lining the walls disputing among themselves, with lines of servants nudging their way through the crowd carrying trays and decanters, crates of bottles, table linen, and chairs, 'scuse, 'scuse, in apologetic procession. Cabriole chairs snarled themselves and hindered the servants' progress. Garish ormolu side tables resisted any sensible usage. Trays filled with empty glassware littered the floor, inducing mild anxiety in the revelers, and a focus for conversation among the women. The men disdained their chitchat, preferring to talk of Godolphin Arabian, Mendoza's next bout, and the curious late explosions aboard a slave ship, the *Polly*, off Bristol, followed a fortnight later by explosions at Mister Hervey's gunpowder works in Battle, both something of a mystery.

"It's in the nature of the beast," said Mister Lifter of the Tenth Foot. "Never any evidence." He was on edge, a captaincy was in the offing.

"*Dar*ling, she was quite the *la Chudleigh*. One wonders why they dress at all. . . ." The speaker all hip pads, bustles, and layers of linen as Lemprière squeezed through the crush after Septimus until they reached the far side together and looked about for the others, who were lost to view. The hall was large, its vaulted ceiling providing a great sounding chamber for the hundreds of guests below. Lemprière watched as the women swirled about, gradually prizing the men out of their resistant huddles and swapping them about in a freer commingling of the sexes. Elderly ladies hobbled about on silver-topped canes, wearing huge floral hats and *malades imaginaires,* while their stiff-gaited consorts followed in train, clutching their sticks. Younger folk clutched glasses to their chests, as the oldsters picked beady-eyed paths through their midst at a snail's pace. Their eyes rolled heavenward in mock impatience. Gallants put on little displays. Girls peeked out from behind their nosegays.

Lemprière recognized faces from the Pork Club, the toothy fellow with a mustache, the bottle-banger, and others. No Rosalie, but Lydia's friends and then the Earl, who looked over and waved. "Come over," mouthed across the crush of bodies. No Septimus either. He had slid away some little time before, waylaid by a po-faced dowager to whom he was now recounting his adventure in a Sicilian bordello while the woman's skittish teenage nieces listened wide-eyed in silence.

"Appalling!" barked the dowager after the recitation, and a small chunk of her face powder dislodged itself to fall in her glass. The nieces bit their lips and looked away. Septimus winked at them. Lemprière floundered. He had pressed determinedly toward the Earl at his signal but somehow had been deflected. Suddenly, the Earl was nowhere to be seen.

He set off again, but the hall had grown even more crowded with conversations and informal greetings, little frigid exchanges between polite enemies, and hearty embraces going on all about him, distracting him so that he found himself eavesdropping on the party chatter of his fellow guests.

". . . and the cook shuts the dog in, as she was told, gets on with the tripe, and when she looks around again, the dog's gone."

"Gone?"

"Gone. So she nips out and starts shouting for the dog, but the bloody thing is hiding, or it's run off. So she puts down a lump of meat and just waits for its stomach, thinks, dog'll follow."

"No stomach, no dog."

"Right, so she puts down this lump of meat . . ."

A dark little man with a dipped mustache carrying a music stand carved a path between Lemprière and the story, forcing him sideways, where a flamboyant gentleman in a purple cravat pitched up a word that fell on him like long-expected bad news.

". . . tortoises."

"Absurd!"

"Tortoises, I tell you. Hundreds of gigantic tortoises. Read your Livy. The siege of Sparta."

"Marmaduke, are you certain?"

"Of course, I'm certain." Lemprière was certain too, sniggering to himself at the confusion of the tortoise battle formation with the animal itself. Marmaduke was now miming the approach of the massed tortoise ranks. The dark little man was returning with a large heavy chest, dragging it with difficulty through the least tractable part of the crowd. He barged through, red in the face and panting, as Lemprière stepped out of the way for the third time to hear Marmaduke explain how the heroic Roman tortoises had smashed through the Spartan lines to win a great victory.

"Never heard that before, eh? Well, everyone will be hearing about it soon, everyone'll be *seeing* it, the whole thing . . ." His companion looked blank, then aghast.

"You are not proposing to put this spectacle on the stage, Marmaduke." An actor, thought Lemprière.

"It is my stage," Marmaduke came back at him, then noticed the horrified expression. "But no, not *on* the stage. Above it."

"Above?" A theater manager, Lemprière revised his earlier thought, then imagined the giant tortoises swinging from the wings above a production of, what, the *Oresteia*? A maniac.

"On the roof!" Marmaduke exclaimed. I've already commissioned them, the Coade manufactory will cast them six feet across, four guineas each, less if I take more than a dozen."

"More than a dozen!"

"I thought perhaps two dozen or so, with one on the parapet, a

127

tortoise-rampant. We could have tours of the roof before each performance, notices in the newssheets, that sort of thing. . . ." Marmaduke's companion was shaking his head and murmuring, *oh dear, oh dear, oh dear,* very softly to himself while Marmaduke clapped him on the back and Lemprière thought of Æschylus and the tortoise predestined for his skull, then lurched as the mustachioed man passed by again, this time carrying a sheaf of papers and a small brass screwdriver. Lemprière watched him disappear and thought perhaps he should follow and make another attempt to find the Earl, or Septimus, or Lydia, the Pug even, even perhaps Warburton-Burleigh.

"John! Good man!" A great clap on his back knocked the wind out of him so that Lemprière coughed and spluttered, then turned to see Edmund, the Earl of Braith, with a broad grin on his face and a funnel-shaped object in his hand which he raised to his lips then bellowed through it, "Good to see you!" Several people turned, including Marmaduke.

"Have you met Marmaduke Stalkart?" The Earl took them both by the elbow and drew them together. "Marmaduke is the proprietor of the Haymarket Opera House, sadly dark at the present—"

"Soon to reopen." Marmaduke offered his hand, which Lemprière took. The conversation flagged immediately. The Earl looked from one to the other. "You must be wondering why you came?" he said breezily to Lemprière in mock apology for the evening.

"Yes, why *am* I here?" demanded Lemprière.

"You are here on your merits," said the Earl. "But I believe my mother, Lady de Vere, wanted to speak with you."

"Your mother? I have never met your mother. Where is she?"

"Upstairs. She never attends these affairs, not since father died. Truly, I am as much in the dark as you. She is very old, you know." The Earl kept looking over his shoulder as he said this, then abruptly his explanations came to an end. "John, I must announce the display. Monsieur Maillardet seems ready at last. Forgive me, we will talk afterward. It's all rather silly, I know. . . ." The Earl was sidling off, in the direction of the little man who had taken up a position with his paraphernalia at the far side of the hall nearest the double doors. Lemprière launched a shot into the dark.

"Mister Chadwick!" he called after Edmund, and the Earl turned, his face showing bewildered recognition at the name. "Mister Chadwick is why I am here!" Lemprière repeated with more emphasis and knew that he had scored a hit. He had no idea why.

"Later, John," was the best the startled Earl could manage as he struggled through his guests to reach Monsieur Maillardet, who was now kneeling with his head inside the box doing something with his screwdriver.

"It'll never work," said a soft Scots voice, and Lemprière turned to find himself addressed by a tall man with a mat of jet-black hair.

"Mister Byrne" he introduced himself, and Lemprière reciprocated.

"Maillardet's a bloody toymaker; brilliant mechanic, but he wouldn't know a command structure if it hit him in the face."

"Yes, I suppose. . . . I don't know." Lemprière began but was interrupted by a loud banging sound. The Earl had climbed on a chair and was begging silence of the company.

"A merry Christmas to you all," he began rather oddly, and having taken this initial wrong turn, the speech never really recovered. After long rebuttals and qualifications of things he had already said, long embarrassing pauses and fake stops and starts, he waved his glass about in happy confusion while his audience made appreciative noises or murmured "Hear, hear!" at various junctures.

"Much improved," said a familiar voice in Lemprière's ear. It was Septimus. Marmaduke and Mister Byrne nodded their hellos. "Last year was far worse. Went on for hours."

". . . and far be it my intention not to wish to deny, rather *wish* to deny, on the contrary that is, until we are ready . . ." the Earl was saying, ". . . which, I would hope, there is no doubt surrounding, we are." The last word was emphasized, prompting affirmative grunts from those sections of the audience construing his sentence in the positive, while others, believing the opposite to be the case, mumbled "Not at all" or "Have no fear." Then, when no more was forthcoming, both camps raised the pitch of their support in the belief that the speech was ended, and a polite shouting match ensued. In the middle of this, Edmund resumed his sentence, most of which was lost in the hubbub until his audience realized he had started up again. They stopped in time to hear ". . . Monsieur Maillardet, and thank you all," which really was the end. There was some confused clapping. Cappadocian, thought Lemprière.

"Right as ever, Mister Praeceps," Mister Byrne was saying. "A markedly better effort." Something was happening at the front. The little man with the mustache was speaking through the horn Lemprière had earlier seen the Earl carrying, squeezing alien vowels through its funnel and firing them up into the roof where they crashed about and returned as a jumbled echo. Then he stopped.

"Shall we move nearer?" Mister Byrne entreated the other three, and they followed him as he wormed his way through to the front of the crowd who were watching Monsieur Maillardet, now assembling his machine. "What is it?" asked Marmaduke.

"A demonstration," said Septimus.

"Rank amateurism," added Mister Byrne. "I've built machines that could design a better toy than that." Lemprière raised his eyebrow at Septimus. "A rival," whispered Septimus. "He gave the demonstration last year."

Monsieur Maillardet raised his horn again and spoke briefly, pointing to his contraption. It was a chest upon which a life-size doll dressed in the uniform of a French soldier knelt. In front of the doll was a desk with writing paper on it. One of the doll's arms hung down at its side, the other raised and crooked at the elbow as if warding off a blow.

"Rather wonderful, don't you think?" said Marmaduke.

"No," said Mister Byrne.

A small group of men in their sixties, naval types by their bearing, shuffled forward to take a closer look.

"What is it?" asked Lemprière.

"Part of you and me," said Septimus.

"An automaton," Mister Byrne answered him. "A moving statue. An imitation of humanity."

"Ernst should see this," Lemprière whispered to Septimus. "It fits all his theories." Septimus laughed noisily at this, drawing an angry look from Monsieur Maillardet.

"Pipe down there," said one of the naval company, who was paying close attention to the goings-on.

Lemprière looked back to the automaton and its maker, who was kneeling at its back, winding something and muttering to himself. It seemed he was ready to begin. A few more turns and he stood to one side, quite near to Mister Byrne, who was studying his fingernails. Everyone else watched the automaton. A few seconds passed in which nothing happened, a slow smile spread across Mister Byrne's face, then suddenly, a shrill squawk was heard from one of the women. The automaton was moving. Monsieur Maillardet gave Mister Byrne a look that suggested he had only just noticed him. The head swiveled sideways and looked up into the faces of the crowd. Its false hair was black under its helmet and its eyes an unnatural blue. A fixed smile was carved on its face. The doll looked down at the paper on the desk and its arm jerked, stopped, jerked again, then moved slowly down, the fingers opening, then closing with a snap on the pen. Lemprière noticed that the position of the pen was marked exactly on the desk. Toward the rear of the crowd a few individuals clapped. When they fell silent, Lemprière heard a low whirring sound interspersed with irregular clicks. As the demonstration proceeded, these were joined by several muffled reports from within the chest, less frequent than the other sounds. "Didn't even damp the camsets," whispered Mister Byrne in his ear.

Within the machine, control passed to and fro between the drive and servo-motors as the index-wheels regulated the program cams and fuses passed coded power through the gears to jointed levers moving silently inside the automaton's limbs. Dipping its pen in the inkwell, the doll went through a series of tiny mechanical shivers before its arm moved down to write and the information flow was resumed. The arm seemed to move very stiffly, but Lemprière noticed the pen itself gliding smoothly over the paper. After twelve or fourteen lines of script, Monsieur Maillardet removed the sheet and handed it to a woman who was standing near the front.

"A love poem! Oh, mon amour!" she hammed to the machine. Her companions laughed and clapped their hands together. Monsieur Maillardet accepted these compliments on behalf of his creation. The doll itself stared fixedly ahead. The performance was repeated twice more, each time to similar delight, with the ladies comparing the automaton's efforts and vying with each other for a place in its affections. After this, Monsieur Maillardet held up his hands for quiet and spoke through his horn as incomprehensibly as before. Then he replaced the pen and paper and rewound a crank behind the chest. Everyone watched in silence. The machine began to move, more quickly this time, the internal clicks and hums louder than before.

"He's geared the motor too high," said Mister Byrne to Lemprière. The automaton was producing an image with quick slashes and jerky stabs of its pen. It was a ship, a three-master with all its rigging and every detail down to the rail-stanchions and the join of the stempieces. The naval men edged closer to gain a better view, one in particular moving right up to the machine, obscuring Lemprière's view. He had a weather-tanned face which looked as though it were not much given to extravagant expression, but now, as the man peered down at the emerging image, his look was one of astonishment. Monsieur Maillardet moved protectively toward his creation as it put the last halyards on the ship.

"Good God!" the man exclaimed. "I tell you I know that ship!" And with that he reached to snatch the paper just as the doll started inscribing the name on the ship's bow.

"Monsieur!" remonstrated its inventor. He was too late. As the man's hand closed about the paper, the doll brought over its left arm, the hand opened and closed tight about the man's wrist. The left side of the machine seemed to freeze as the man tried to prize himself free.

"Damn," he muttered, then suddenly shouted loudly as the right arm descended deliberately and with the pen inscribed the name of the ship in the soft skin of his palm. A mess of blood and ink welled up.

"Good Christ, get it off!" shouted the man, shaking the thing furiously. His companions were pulling at the metal arm.

"Messieurs! Please!" cried Monsieur Maillardet. Mister Byrne acted. Walking over to his rival, he snatched the screwdriver which was still in his hand. He knelt behind the automaton, braced himself, then drove the screwdriver in at the back. Instantly, both hands splayed their fingers, releasing the man, and a shrill, ear-piercing whine started up within the machine. The arms flew apart, then slowly, very deliberately, the left hand came over, took hold of the right and twisted. The hand came off at the wrist. Several people looked away. Little brass levers twitched inside the stump. Then the same hand rose up as if to touch its nose. Lemprière watched as the movement simply continued and the automaton drove five fingers through its plaster face. The hand tightened on something inside the head and the arm began to pull back. There was a tearing sound, then a loud snap, and the head broke off at the neck. The motors inside were screaming, the cams clacking furiously, but the automaton's movements showed no lack of control. It sat there with its smiling head dangling from its hand, and began to bang the head on the desk, once, twice, three times. The motors screamed louder as the unseen machinery pulled itself apart. The automaton twitched violently and then it was still. The head dropped from its fingers and rolled across the floor. Attention turned to Monsieur Maillardet who was standing theatrically with his hands over his ears and who now rushed to his stricken creation. He picked up the head and hand, then slumped to the floor in despair. The headless automaton had fallen forward, face down over the desk.

"Why?" cried Monsieur Maillardet to the company at large, then "Why?" again, louder, at Mister Byrne who was handing him back his screwdriver.

"Things fall apart," said Mister Byrne in laconic tones. "It's scientific."

The show was over. The Earl's guests looked about for the next spectacle. The injured man was surrounded by a small group of his companions, dabbing at his hand with a handkerchief.

"Damn it, that damn ship. I *know* that ship," he was saying, still shaken by his encounter with the wrecked machine.

"Pipe down, Eben," said an elderly lady in imperious tones.

"I tell you, it's moored right here," the man was protesting. "Here in the Thames." He was sixty or more with steel-gray hair and solidly built. Solicitous advice began to pour down on him from all sides as the guests transferred their attentions to his plight. Some of the younger fellows were nudging each other. It was agreed that the hand should be cleaned and dressed. Eben suffered himself to be led away behind a serving girl, still muttering about ships and shocks of recognition, but more quietly, aware perhaps of the spectacle he had provided.

"It's the *Vendragon*, I tell you, the damn *Vendragon*. . . ." he was saying as he passed Lemprière.

"Why?" asked Monsieur Maillardet from the floor again. No one answered him.

"John?" It was the Earl, and Lemprière's thoughts turned forensic again, remembering the Earl's shocked expression at the mention of Chadwick, his own doubts, and a hundred other questions he wanted to ask.

"My mother expressed a wish to see you," said the Earl. Mister Byrne had joined Maillardet on the floor. Together, they were retrieving tiny brass screws, washers, and pieces of motor-housing. The weather-beaten face of the injured man was disappearing through one of the doors to the side of the hall. Septimus was nowhere to be seen. Neither was Casterleigh, Lemprière noted. Nor his daughter. "Did you like Monsieur Maillardet's demonstration?" asked the Earl, to which Lemprière replied that he thought it unique.

The two of them made their way to the back of the hall. The Earl seemed boisterous, passing comments back and forth with his guests, laughing a little louder than they did.

"This way," he said, and the two of them passed through a door into a long corridor. The racket from the hall died away and their footsteps were the only noise.

"As I said, she *is* very old." The Earl talked over his shoulder as he led the way. "She wants things just so. You understand me?" Lemprière shook his head. "She wants things as they were, or how she imagines they were." They climbed a staircase and moved through a long room with chipped stucco work depicting various mythological scenes, hydras and men with swords, women in towers. The room beyond it was lined with empty shelves. They were moving back through the house, its geography becoming piecemeal and more confusing. Oddly shaped rooms, rooms without windows, and innumerable short flights of steps argued a haphazard plan, as if the house had accreted rather than been designed. Edmund kept up a running commentary as they passed through, explaining to Lemprière that the original edifice had been built by Thomas, the fourth Earl, in Elizabeth's time, with money from his trading interests.

"But, of course, you would know all this. . . ." he was saying as Lemprière thought of the agreement with Thomas's name upon it, and François's.

"Tell me more," he said, but the Earl only resumed his domestic travelog, telling Lemprière of the later additions which seemed not to match the scale or grandeur of the original house, bits and pieces bolted on as necessary through the intervening centuries, the shoddiness of the workmanship evident in some parts of the building. Nevertheless, Lemprière felt compelled to pass appreciative comments as they moved through its interior.

"Oh, it has some fascinating corners," the Earl said airily. "I only wish I was able to show you the gardens. I have a drainage project underway you might find interesting. Something of a family tradition. All the De Veres have added something." The Earl's speech began to grow a little slurred during this recital, though still comprehensible. "My father built the new stables before he died, but of course we cannot keep the string *he* maintained. Between the two of us, the whole place is close to collapse. Mother cannot accept it. She thinks of little else. Try to understand, John." Lemprière assented to this in all sincerity. They continued into a wing where the walls were paneled and the furnishings in better repair than before. Pictures lined their route, stiffly posed men and women in odd costumes. The Earl paused before one of them.

"Thomas de Vere, the fourth Earl, as a young man," he said. "Odd, is it not?" And Lemprière agreed that it was. But for the yellowing varnish and the garishly discolored flesh tones, the picture might have been of Edmund. The resemblance was quite disturbing.

"In here." The Earl opened a door next to the fourth Earl's portrait, and they stepped into a long salon with sofas, a piano, and several bureaus pushed against the far wall. A fire burned briskly in the hearth. "If you would wait here for a moment . . ." The Earl walked across the room and disappeared through a second door. Lemprière began to look about him, but it was only seconds before the Earl returned. "John Lemprière, let me introduce you to my mother, Lady Alice de Vere," he said. As he spoke, a figure appeared in the doorway, a woman, very thin, dressed in very pale blue. Her face was powdered white, a dot of rouge on each cheek, and her hair was piled very high, quite unlike the women in the hall. She stopped and held up a pince-nez to peer at Lemprière. Lemprière made a little bow, and the eyeglasses were lowered.

"So, this is Lemprière," she said in a clear voice. "The De Veres welcome you, Mister Lemprière, as they did François, your ancestor." Lemprière blinked behind his spectacles. "One hundred and fifty years may have changed our circumstances, but our welcome at least remains the same."

"Thank you, Lady de Vere," said Lemprière.

"The snow did not trouble you?"

"No, no."

"Edmund? Perhaps Mister Lemprière will take some wine." The Earl had been standing next to an overstuffed chair, but was now leaning on it as though for support. When he moved to fetch the decanter he stumbled slightly. Lemprière sipped at his glass. The Earl gulped, then took another. His mother looked at him.

"I should return to the guests," he said. His speech was clearer than before. "I will tell Septimus you are here," he told Lemprière, then left by the door they had entered.

Lemprière found himself alone with Lady de Vere, who now moved nearer.

"You are a young man," she said. "Children?" Her steps were fragile, tottering affairs. Lemprière wanted her to sit down.

"No, none," he said. Close up, she was even thinner than she'd seemed before, hollowed out somehow. Her eyes were very dark and fixed unwaveringly upon Lemprière, or at some definite point behind him.

"It was Skewer," she spoke quickly and sat down, indicating that Lemprière should do the same. "You are puzzling over your presence here. It was Skewer, not Chadwick. Mister Chadwick is the old school. It was Mister Skewer brought us word of the agreement."

"Was," said Lemprière. "Mister Chadwick *was* the old school. He died some time ago."

"Dead?" said Lady de Vere. "Yes, of course." This last was spoken more to herself than her guest. "Your father is dead too?"

Lemprière nodded, faintly offended by this flat statement of fact.

"Your father had some commerce with Mister Chadwick a year or more ago. Skewer was his assistant then. It was he who told us of the agreement. You will have wondered at our late interest. One year ago to this day we invited Mister Chadwick to reveal what he knew. He refused, was even offended that we should ask, but we had to ask: It was in your interest as much as our own." Lady de Vere had grown more animated. "When your father died, Mister Skewer came to us once again—"

"That is how you knew of the agreement—" said Lemprière.

"We knew before," she replied sharply. "As I told you. But the changed circumstances led us to a further attempt, Mister Praeceps's involvement and our offer to buy the document." Lemprière thought of Skewer's face across the desk, full of solicitude, telling him it was a curio. The image of the Widow Neagle hitting him with her shoe. "In the pay of knaves," her angry words. All true.

"You wished to purchase the agreement," he said bluntly. "You want to buy it. It is something you need."

"No, Mister Lemprière," she said more softly. "The agreement told us of matters we had imagined long past." Lady de Vere contemplated the young man for a second or two, then spoke again. "What we need, as you put it, is quite other. The object of our commerce up until now, Mister Lemprière, is not the agreement. It is yourself."

Lady de Vere rose from her seat as she said this and walked quickly to a bureau cabinet at the far side of the room. Even in his surprise at her last statement, Lemprière noted her improved stride. The tottering entry, the impression of frailty, had all been an act for his benefit. Or hers, he thought as the woman rummaged through the bureau, then another, to return with a large pile of papers and several roughly bound books.

"Indeed, why should we want your agreement," said Lady de Vere, handing him a sheet from the pile, "when we do after all have our own." It was the agreement, identical in every respect down to the signatures and the serrations along the lower edge. Thomas de Vere. François Lemprière.

"My son told you of its significance," Lady de Vere was saying, but Lemprière's face was blank. A garbled speech mixed in with the Pork Club's drunken noise, his nausea, the Earl's face upside down before his own saying, "a tenth part . . . millions by now . . . in perpetuity . . ." There was more, much more than that, but it had slipped away like water through his fingers. He could not remember.

"The fourth Earl was a venturer, one of the original investors. . . ." The words were falling from nowhere. ". . . a merchant. The first voyage was the key to all that befell him later. It was an adventure in every sense." Alice de Vere had been rearranging the pile of papers as she spoke. Now she handed Lemprière a dog-eared pamphlet, yellowed with age, and the young man read aloud, "The voyage to the Indies and adventures of Captain Lancaster of the *Dragon*, together with the *Hector*, the *Ascension*, and the *Susan*. A true account."

"That was the first voyage." Lemprière nodded, turning the pages over

135

before him, reading idly of the expedition's trials and triumphs. Lady de Vere spoke again, the facts coming with a quick fluency, a familiar recital.

"There were many investors at the start. The ships left in 1600. All they knew was that beyond the Cape were the spice markets of the East. The Dutch merchants were bringing spice back by the shipload. It was enough. The ships went off and nothing was heard for over two years. Two years, Mister Lemprière. Most of the investors lost their nerve. Only a few kept their stock, and bought the stock of the faint hearts, of course. At the last there were only nine of them."

"Including Thomas de Vere," Lemprière said.

"Naturally. All nine were mortgaged to the hilt. The De Veres owed thousands of pounds. The shipwrights had not been paid, nor the victualers. Their households were living on the patience of the City lenders. All nine had huge debts, but between them they owned all the stock, and they had faith." Lemprière was still leafing through the account.

"The ships returned," he said. Even over all the years Captain Lancaster came through the stilted prose as an extraordinary man.

"Oh yes, they returned. There was an early report from a Frenchman, Beaudeguerre. Then all four ships were sighted off the west coast of France. The value of the stock doubled, tripled, then tripled again, and Thomas could have sold then and there. There were offers. But his nerve had held so long, two years had gone by. As the facts stood, he would have been foolish to give it all up." Lady de Vere paused and wiped her mouth.

"The ships were empty?" ventured Lemprière.

"No! They were full! Their holds were stuffed with pepper. Lancaster had done everything that was asked of him."

"So, everyone was rich—"

"Everyone was ruined," said the woman. "The Dutch had been flooding the market for months. Indeed, there was no market. The pepper was all but worthless. No buyers could be found here, nor on the continent. God knows, Thomas tried to sell his share, but . . ." There was a short silence. "That was how our families first met, Mister Lemprière."

The clock ticked softly in its case. Four oil lamps threw an even light over the room. Lady de Vere sat very straight with her hands in her lap. Her fingers twitched about her rings, twisting them round and round as she spoke.

"That was the worst time Thomas de Vere would face, in truth. He himself would later think differently, but that was the worst. The voyage had been successful, and still it had failed. His family had been assured of riches and were all but bankrupt. Creditors were hounding him. He owed sums he knew he could never repay. Worst of all, he knew he had been right all along. Lancaster had proved that the Indies were a stuffed purse, richer even than he had imagined. All the profit in the world was

136

waiting for him, but he could not get to it. No one would advance any one of them the cost of a second voyage. He was stranded, marooned; like Tantalus, the waters receded just when he bent to drink. Can you imagine that, Mister Lemprière?" Lemprière thought of his dreams, matters half-known to him, the very story she was telling.

"Yes, I believe I can," he said.

"All nine of the investors were in similar straits, all in the same boat, ha!" The laugh was bitter. "But they were saved, after a fashion."

"François?" hazarded Lemprière.

"And others. Nine in all, a mirror image. They were merchants and venturers themselves, a kind of club. They sailed from Rochelle some months later, but read for yourself—" And with that she handed Lemprière a bundle of papers which had once been a book, but the spine was cracked and the pages were spilling out. Lemprière took the bundle of papers and glanced down. Columns of figures, lists.

"An account book?" he said.

"Of sorts," Lady de Vere agreed. "But read on." She looked over as Lemprière bent his head once more, then pointed to the top of the page.

"The date, you see? The winter of 1602, shortly after the expedition's return." Lemprière nodded without replying. He was reading a list of names.

"The servants were always paid, even if months in arrears," Lady de Vere said, with a touch of pride. Lemprière read on, noting the sale of some sheep early in the following year, then a parcel of land, then another. "February 1603. Mister Woodal called upon me again today for the seventh time, but could give him no pledge. Thomas Wilbert, the same."

"His creditors," said Lady de Vere. The entries grew more frequent, along with "Meeting. Philp. Sm. and the others" five times in March alone.

"Philpot and Smith," explained Lady de Vere. "The others were the other six venturers. They were all in trouble together." Toward the end of the March accounts was an inventory. "All the goods and chattels in the Long House in our parish here. In the large chamber: Item, a standing bed with a covering, a coverlet, a pair of blankets and the hangings, a feather-bed, a mattress, a bolster, 2 pillows, 3 curtains, a *teaster*, a chest and a *teaster* with 2 chairs. For these, £9 9s. In the Chapel Chamber, Item . . ." and on, through the middle and main parlors, the hall, the buttery and kitchen, two more chambers, each suffixed with "For these" and a figure. As far as Lemprière could see, it was the only money received that month.

"He sold the furniture?" he asked.

"He had no choice. The long house was the old part of the building. The family closed it up and moved into a wing. Hard times." Lemprière looked down again, but Lady de Vere was smiling grimly. "Not just the

sins of the father, Mister Lemprière, the misfortunes are revisited too."
He could feel his cheeks burning, but a moment later all such thoughts
were banished. The next page contained a single word scrawled across it:
"Saved"; and underneath, in a calmer hand: "Met with the french-man
today, a merchaunt, by name François Lemprière."

The next few days recorded a number of further meetings, though now
they were marked only "F.L. Met and talked for some hours" or "F.L.
Talked further until very late."

"They were negotiating the agreement," said Alice de Vere.

"Of course," Lemprière murmured, somehow caught up in the urgency of their business, conspiratorial meetings in the dead of night, hushed
voices, fatigue.

"Taken with us unto Norwich, Eighteenth day of April, year of Our
Lord 1603, Cloves, 3 oz. at 6d. per oz. 1s. 6d. *Long Synamon*, 2 lb. 2 oz.
at 3s. 3d. per lb. 6s. 11d. White starch, 12 lb. at 4d. a lb. 4s. *Trenchers*, 2
doz, 11d." The list extended down the page: silk, thread, ribboning, tape,
pins, rosewater and sweetwater, long mace and middle mace, Beaser
stone, ambergris, saffron, and Horsespice. Pepper. It had been quite an
expedition. Then Lemprière remembered the last words of the agreement, *Signed this day in Norwich.*

"Thomas went there to meet François and sign the agreement," he said.

"Yes," said Lady de Vere. "It was signed on the 25th of April."

"Why Norwich?"

"It might have been anywhere. But not London, and not here. They
had to keep it close, things were not as they are now. France was our
enemy in more than name, it was—"

"Treason," said Lemprière, remembering the evening spent with Peppard, listening as the little man had unstitched the agreement, phrase by
knotted phrase.

"Treason, yes," replied Lady de Vere. Her eyes were on him.

"Skewer mentioned some such thing," he said.

"He did." It could have been a question. Their eyes met. She knew he
was lying.

"But I cannot see *why*," Lemprière said. "Not the secrecy, but the
whole partnership. François could have sent his own ships. Why should
he enter into such an agreement at all? Thomas would act as his agent and
gain a tenth of all the profits for his trouble, that I understand, but not the
need for an agent in the first place. Why did these men not sail from
Rochelle in the first place?"

"They had their own difficulties. Remember, they were dissenters,
Huguenots. . . . Protestants," she expanded, "and the French court was,
is, Catholic to its bones. You see, the English Joynt-Stock Company had
nothing but impounded ships and their charter: but that was what
the Rochelais lacked. Their own king would never have granted
them that and they knew it. The charter protected the monopoly

138

of the route. If they were not Company ships sailing around the Cape, they were none. That was what the Rochelais bought from Thomas, Philpot, Smith, and the others."

"But the Dutch sailed the route, or did they use another?"

"No! There *is* no other route. If there were, every ship afloat would be plying it, believe me. The Dutch were a nuisance, but they had no army or navy to speak of then as now. They could not guarantee the route if challenged."

"And they were challenged?"

"Oh yes," and the woman gestured again to the account book. "Read."

The pages which followed the signing of the agreement told quite a different story from before. Creditors were paid off, land bought back, craftsmen engaged for this or that project, money invested in other, smaller ventures, new servants taken on.

"The greater part of this house was built around then." Lady de Vere spoke again. "The arrangement ran smoothly for close to a quarter of a century. Of course, tongues wagged when the second voyage set sail, people wondered how it was financed, but none of their gossip was as strange as the truth. And the truth made our family very wealthy; the other investors too. Voyages were mounted one after another, trading stations set up. Nothing to the size of the Company now, but still the rewards were huge. Your own family must have been rich as Croesus. It even became a problem; gold in those quantities becomes a cargo in itself, visible."

"What did they do with the money? If it was all supposed to be secret, the arrangement, that is?"

"I do not know," said Lady de Vere. "The Rochelais handled it, that much I *do* know, but how . . . The fourth Earl never wrote of it, and I have looked, believe me. Thomas was paid his tenth by your ancestor, but I do not even know how *that* was accomplished. Thomas never recorded the amounts, though they can be estimated from his expenditure, thousands upon thousands."

"Hard to conceal," said Lemprière.

"Not impossible," said Alice de Vere.

Outside the room in which they spoke, the snow-cloaked country was still. Damp air lay heavily about the house and gardens. Beyond, in the rougher terrain, all sounds were deadened and soaked up by the snowfall. The machines lay about like sleepers. All traces of activity were buried in the night. Boffe had caught his foot in roots, or something. It would not come loose. He took a step backward, then tried again. It was still caught. He brought his other foot over, then stamped down. Something cracked and his foot came away with a jerk. He had lost all feeling below the knee, he thought. He should not be here. He hurried over to the other man, standing still, waiting for him.

"All ready," he announced a little breathlessly as he came closer. The larger man turned and began walking back. "I said it is all ready," Boffe repeated, hurrying to catch the other, who swung around suddenly.

"I heard you!" Casterleigh barked.

"So the Rochelle merchants gained control of the Honorable Company. The agreement was honored with Thomas de Vere and the others. All was well," ventured Lemprière.

"Yes, François and the others returned to Rochelle, I presume. All was well for close to a quarter century. The Company grew and grew. Then it all blew up."

The fire had burnt low and the cold was creeping into the room. Lemprière shivered. The carpet on the floor between the two of them had a diamond design in red on gray. If Juliette were to arrive at all, she would have arrived by now. The snow, perhaps. "Blew up?"

"The siege." But he knew nothing of that. A blue sprite flickered in the grate, dancing back and forth on the black ironwork, back and forth. It drew his eye along, past the old woman who was talking to him: ". . . encircled all about, by land and sea, Mister Lemprière!"

"Yes, I heard, I . . ." Rochelle, the siege of La Rochelle. That was what blew up, and they had all been caught, so intent on their commerce they had not seen it coming, waiting for them in their neglect.

"It went on for months, a year and beyond. All the payments were halted, caught up somehow. Presumably the money was routed through Rochelle. At any rate, it stopped. The Company could run itself by and large, but the profits were another matter entirely. Perhaps they were lost. Perhaps not."

"So François and his associates died in the siege?" Lemprière interrupted her.

"It all becomes very complicated," said Lady de Vere. "The siege itself was terrible. The French king wanted no quarter given. He wanted them crushed, every Huguenot life taken, the city razed to the ground. There were stories of massacres in the countryside round about the city, terrible stories. . . . The English mounted an expedition, common cause supposedly, all Protestants together, but it failed or was designed to fail. The siege dragged on into the next year, 1628. The Catholics under Richelieu built some sort of seawall and that was the end, really."

"The city was taken?"

"What was left of it. Most of the Rochelais were dead of starvation and those that were not soon followed them."

"Slaughtered?" Lemprière asked.

"They killed themselves"—Lady de Vere's voice was cold— "rather than be captured."

"But you said François and the others escaped."

"Perhaps the only ones to do so. I do not know how. They were resourceful men. But something had happened, something among themselves, I believe. It was a few months after the siege, the spring of 1629. No payments had been made for close to two years. The investors in London believed their partners had perished. Thomas, the fourth Earl, was convinced of it. It was then he was contacted again by your ancestor. Remember, they had not seen one another for twenty-five years. François was in London and they met there. It was a strange meeting, but see for yourself." Lady de Vere took the battered bundle of papers from Lemprière's hands and turned its sheets five or six at a time. "He recorded the meeting in his accounts," she was saying; a few more sheets were glanced at, then the whole mass was thrust back at him. "There." She pointed to where Thomas de Vere's account began. "The spring of 1629." Lemprière took the papers and began to read.

On this day I became the wealthiest man alive or the meanest beggar and I know not which. I have met the man who once before found me ruined and burthened me with riches, and now promises the same. I mean François Lemprière, merchant. Five and twenty years have passed since last we met and we both are much changed. François carries a stick, for his leg is damaged and will not mend. He is gray but still his countenance is full of expression and his speech is full of extravagance, and truth too I pray, else I am ruined and my own family shall seek dinner with Duke Humphrey.

Our meeting was a thing of chance, and yet recovering from our surprise we fell to talking at once and dined on beeves and ham. A thousand mysteries beset me but I stilled my tongue from useless wagging and patience was never a better valued virtue than then, for François was pumped up like a bladder with talk, much of it terrible. He spake of the siege and its horrors whereof I was aghast, his words were so vivid and countenance so wild, but I will not write of them here. We supped further and drank of a bottle of Negus and François spake of his adventure in escaping from that fated place, Rochelle. His leg was all smashed within and he bears a scar. He had been sent, a kind of envoy to the good Duke of Buckingham and the Court in England, but it availed the poor men and women within the walls nothing for I knew the Duke had not broken the siege and when the Duke came back François had sailed with him, fain as he was to leave his friends. But when I asked if he mourned his fellow-merchants still for it is now some months since the final slaughter he told me nay, for they lived yet and were they burned to death with the rest his answer would even then be nay for he detested them as he would birds who eat their young and worse. All this was said in a grete rage like a madness but he calmed again and talked like a sane person. He has lodged in the island of Jersey, the months past the siege. He has broken with his fellow-merchants and challenged them. He will not say why but says only that the spirits of Rochelle know why and that is enow. I did not press him more, but rather told him of mine own privations though they were nothing to his own, his wife and six children were all dead. François was full of spirit when I spoke, and told me soon I will be richer than any man bar himself for he made an Agreement with me and will keep it. I believe he means mischief to his old fellows the other eight merchants but talked only of marking their papers or having marked papers, saying *mark you* and making a grete play with that word *mark* in his accent. For myself I kept my peace and we talked of other matters, like the vile attacks by hacks on the Company. When I said this my outrage was a kind of Comedy to him for he laughed very loud and his madness came back though in another joking way. I asked him how it could come about that we would be so rich as he said but he would say no more then but to trust or know, the choosing was for me. I am home now at my small-table and my head has an ache from the hour and the wine. The Lord guides me in this matter though I would wish his direction plainer and François is a strange man, but no stranger to me. I will trust him. That is my decision.

"And he was wrong," said Alice de Vere. "For he never saw François again and never received another penny." Lemprière let his eye wander up and down the hastily formed characters: "like the madness . . . and his madness came back . . . I will trust him."

"But what happened? If François had a plan against the others, some sort of revenge—"

"If, if," said the woman. "I have never discovered what it might have been. It came to nothing, at any rate. I have combed the fourth Earl's papers for a clue, and I believe he knew no more than I do now. Less . . ." But Lemprière was thinking of François's madness, imagining his eyes rolling and the uncontrolled laughter, the rage. Something had thrown him into that, something at Rochelle.

"What were the attacks?" he asked. "And the business with marked papers, or marks? When François laughed like . . ." Lemprière hesitated. "When he laughed?"

"The attacks were pamphlets," said Lady de Vere, burrowing among the papers once more and handing over a shabby production with irregular type printed off the center of the page. "A Primer for John Company, wherein he might find his letters writ large and learn of them his true nature."

"They were a series," she said. "This is the second."

"Hell-hound. These are the vermin who perjure, rob, and blind the common weal with talk of trade, by which name they know their own profit and gain and we know them as the Company. . . ." "I" was for "infection" and "J" for the "Just War I wage against them, like germs they are in need of a purgative, a scourging," and so on, through "K" and "L" and "M," the whole thing a catalog of abuse and invective against the Company written in the most shocking language. There was much talk of unmasking, but no unmasking was done, nor were any specific charges made. It was only when Lemprière saw the pseudonymous signature on the final leaf that something rang very faintly inside him, *Asiaticus*. He brought his head up, as if the elusive memory might be revealed in the cracked plaster of the ceiling. The chest. That was it. His father's chest contained such a pamphlet, *Asiaticus;* he had glanced at it on the night of the Pork Club and now told the woman so.

"Ah yes," said Lady de Vere. "The mysterious *Asiaticus,*" and she seemed about to say more, but checked herself. "The point is," she took up on a different note, "that François had disappeared without a trace. His family had been killed in the siege, and after the meeting you read of, we heard no more. Perhaps he was killed, or simply died of his malady, or ran away. Likewise, the months between the end of the siege and their meeting were a mystery to Thomas. François had appeared from nowhere so far as he was concerned. François must have spent the best portion of those months on Jersey. The fourth Earl never thought to travel there, though if he had, he would have found François's second family and everything might have been different."

"Second family? How can you know François began a second family? He was only there for—" Lemprière peered once more at the account, "a few months."

"You have been here only a matter of hours, Mister Lemprière. Nevertheless, I am quite certain you exist. However long he was there, François Lemprière took time to begin a family. When Skewer brought us his scrap of news, it was not the agreement which interested us, Mister Lemprière. It was you."

"Me? But—"

"The family begun by François in those months was your own. You are a true Lemprière, the other half of the partnership, do you not see? The agreement is in perpetuity. Mister Lemprière, a full ninth of the Company is rightfully yours and a full tenth of that is ours. Read it for yourself." Her hands had a life of their own, jerking down with each point on the low table. Her ring rapped on the frontispiece of the pamphlet which lay there before them on the tabletop.

"Forever, do you not see?" Lemprière saw the earlier meeting between Thomas de Vere and his own ancestor in a new light, the edge in Thomas's need to know what was happening, the urgency of it and the dammed-up restraint, waiting to be told his lot with François reeling like a drunkard, a madman. It was there in Alice de Vere's eyes, the same thing, her arm was on his arm and he knew it was absurd. All those men were long dead and their mad hopes with them. "Millions upon millions," she was saying, and her hand was like a claw holding them together over the agreement. He could hear himself saying, "No, no, impossible," saying the things Peppard had said, that she would have heard before and known in any case even before that. It could not be done, it was too late. Her house might crumble about her ears as she claimed and still no one would listen. They were all dead. Lemprière was shaking his head and repeating himself. "Whoever owns the Company will not simply give it up. Not for this." And he held up the agreement which Lady de Vere suddenly snatched from him.

"Then to hell with it!" She stood upright quickly and almost ran to the fireplace. "To hell with you!" she cried, as she threw the document into the flames where it was consumed and burnt to ash in an instant.

The old woman stood over the fire. Lemprière stared at her, then looked down. A piece of ash whirled out on a tiny thermal and lodged in the prickly brocade of her dress. "I must apologize, Mister Lemprière," she said after a long silence. Lemprière mumbled something at his feet, sorry. Lady de Vere looked down too, then turned to him once again. Her carriage was as erect as before. When she spoke again, her voice was even, almost as if nothing had taken place.

"I would like to tell you about the drainage of the west pasture," she said in a different, clearer tone. Lemprière looked across at her, still startled as she held up her hand for forbearance. "Before you rejoin the guests, Mister Lemprière, if you would."

"Of course," Lemprière said, although mention of the other guests sharpened his impatience. He wanted to be gone.

"This house stands on a slight rise," Lady de Vere addressed him. "You would have noticed the incline in your approach." He had not, but was nodding. Pug's pipe had occupied his attention, that and other thoughts. "The gardens surround it, and beyond them, to the east and west, are two pastures, each of several acres. They are identical in most respects, both were cleared in the time of the fourth Earl, the soil is similar, they suffer the same weather and both are low-lying. When they were cleared, the east pasture formed good springy turf and was used for grazing within a year. But the west pasture turned out to be a bog swarming with all sorts of flies in summer, freezing over in the winter. Quite useless. The fourth Earl accordingly decided to drain it and, with some labor, managed to do so. The west pasture was now good grazing ground, the whole operation a success. But after some weeks, Thomas's man noticed that the east pasture was becoming wetter, and in fact, before the year was out, it was as marshy as the west pasture had been before."

"They were connected by a channel underground?" Lemprière speculated.

"Quite possibly," said Lady de Vere. "Now, Edmund, being rather more practical than his mother, was determined to undertake the same project and a year ago did indeed drain the east pasture."

"The west pasture flooded?"

"Of course. Now he has a small army of engineers with their machines in the west pasture. When the weather lifts he will pump out the west pasture, and then, I presume, the east again, then the west. When I ask why he wants to spend his life moving a swamp back and forth over half a mile, he tells me it is progress. He is bringing the land back into use. The local farmers understand this lunacy, Mister Lemprière, they commend him and believe him exceptionally farsighted. Neither I nor my son chose to act as fools, and yet I do not understand it. I only understand that both our families, the Lemprières and the De Veres, were once powerful forces and now we are spent. That is all I understand now, Mister Lemprière."

Lemprière wrestled with this peculiar story, trying to force a bearing on their previous discussion. It was somewhere in their not being fools. "If Edmund, the Earl, drains the land, what will he then—"

"Very good, Mister Lemprière." Her voice was steel-hard. "He will sell it, and the servants will be paid. If not, not. We all make our choices as we see them." Then Lemprière realized that the whole story was in explanation for her outburst; an apology, and he was full of regret that he could not go along with her, but it was impossible. Insanity.

"Thank you for listening, Mister Lemprière." She was walking over, extending her hand to him, no, picking something off the table. "Take it, Mister Lemprière. A memento." He was being guided to the door and handed Asiaticus's pamphlet. She was dignified. He was cowed. He could change his mind, tell her that they would fight the Company through every court in England and win too.

"Thank you," he was saying, and would have said something more, but what? The door was closing.

"Good-bye, Mister Lemprière," spoken in a voice which hung in the air as the door closed, *click*, softly, and he was alone in the corridor outside.

Thomas de Vere looked down on him from his gilt frame. The corridor was lit by girandoles whose light brought a spectrum of dingy yellows and browns out from the woodwork, linen-fold paneling, squabs, and plain chairs finely carved from Grenoble wood. The floor was carpeted and Lemprière padded its length with François's imagined face a gargoyle eyeing him out of gilded amorinos: merchant, venturer, refugee, re-venger. Madman. Something had happened to prize him out of sanity, to turn him against his former colleagues and friends, something at Rochelle.

He took the short flight of stairs at the corridor's end and followed the unexpected angles of the passage beyond. What was the plan which he had laid out in his head and kept there, a hidden gift for the fourth Earl, hanging in his shadowy thoughts? Nothing at all perhaps, or something vast, sprawling and invisible, waiting, somewhere out there. He was walking through a high-sided clerestory whose glittering floor of *pietra dura* suggested another, abandoned use. A staircase at its end led Lemprière down to an area where the passages were narrower, with lower ceilings, and the doors off them were plain wood. Unplastered stonework. He did not remember it, but continued, looking into the rooms he passed which all seemed to have different functions. Some were quite empty, some crammed with kitchen furniture or packing cases. There was not a soul in sight, and Lemprière was beginning to realize he was lost when a soft *pop!* sounded in the passage from somewhere outside, then another and another. The sounds rolled around him in the passage, suggesting now one direction, now another. He moved forward, then remembered Septimus's telling him what to expect during the evening. The sounds he was hearing were the fireworks, but whether they came from in front, behind, or to either side he could not tell. He seemed to have wandered into a basement and now set about retracing his steps. Lemprière turned and walked back toward the staircase, around the corner, then another, both of which he had expected to reveal the steps which would reunite him with the guests, Septimus, and the others, Juliette. He continued, but the corners would show him only more of the same: echoing reception rooms, empty salons, long gloomy corridors, and doors. Scores of doors.

Standing at the head of the latest passage, Lemprière was beginning to wish himself back in the safe embrace of his dictionary, home, when in the semilight at the end of the corridor he noticed an object like an outsize pair of legs. He walked closer.

It was a stepladder. Directly above it, cut into the low ceiling, was a trapdoor. Lemprière looked at the trapdoor. He had wandered aimlessly about the corridors and passages for what seemed like hours. He had become more despondent by the minute. The choices as he saw them were simple. Reluctantly, he began to climb the stepladder, which veered from side to side and back and forth as he reached the top and pushed at the trapdoor. It was unlocked and moved a few inches, but something was on top of it, something which seemed to increase in weight the harder Lemprière pushed. Added to this, the angle of his head dictated he should squint over the top of his spectacles and the whole effort was effectively conducted blind. He was sweating inside the borrowed coat, and the stepladder had adopted a wild gyration all its own as Lemprière raised the trapdoor at last and slid it to one side. A crash sounded somewhere above him and his head came into contact with something rough, some kind of fabric. He pushed against it and suddenly heard quick footsteps moving toward him, then the ladder gave way; he had kicked it out from under himself. Why? his thought as he crashed down into the ladder wreckage below. The answer: Someone in the room above had clubbed him violently over the head; someone, in fact, his last quick thought as he settled into a welcoming bed of splintered stepladder, had knocked him out.

· · ·

"Hold still, sir, there now," the servingwoman told him. Gruff thanks were in order and Captain Guardian gave them. As the vile toy had drawn its lines he had become increasingly certain, matching them in his mind's eye with the image of the *Vendragon,* they were one and the same. No two ships were exactly alike, really there could be no mistake, and he might have trusted his own judgment too—would that he had— but he had taken a closer look to see it plain. Identical down to the angle of the hold-covers, the same ship. Guardian had known then for certain that he recognized the vessel from somewhere, and that was odd too for it was an Indiaman, almost the only ship he had never sailed in. But from where? His palm had begun to throb and he clutched the handkerchiefs more tightly. The prospect of handing these blood-soaked badges back to their owners did not enthrall him. The sniggers and covered smiles of his fellow-guests. . . . There might even be sympathy, but that was too awful to contemplate.

It would not come—the name. Not *Vendragon*, the true name, there somewhere, locked in the lines and angles of the vessel which formed a template to some elusive original. Where? And when? Captain Guardian snorted in irritation and banged his fist against the door by his side, a mistake. He swore loudly as pain welled up in his bandaged hand once more, shooting up his arm and jolting his shoulder. The door had swung open at the impact to reveal a room beyond. The lamps were lit.

"Pardon me, I seem to be . . ." Guardian was taken aback, abashed his outburst might have been overheard as he offered these apologies and peered cautiously around the door. But, the light notwithstanding, no one was there.

"Hello?" he called again. There was no reply. He padded in gingerly and looked about, a strong air of trespass hanging about his actions, but curiosity had ever been his weak point. Besides, who would know? The room contained a bureau, a writing desk and chair, it was carpeted, and at the center of the carpet stood a low table with chairs clustered about it. A larger desk on the far side of the room was strewn with plans and charts which drew Eben's gaze. He shut the door behind him quietly and walked over for a closer inspection. There were plans of the estate with dotted lines drawn from east to west and enlarged details on separate sheets, along with drawings of machines, huge impractical things to Eben's untutored eye, with notes about soil composition and water levels scrawled across them. It appeared to be a drainage project. Casting his eye over all these, Eben could not help but notice a bottle of wine which stood half-empty on the cabinet beside the desk. A moment's thought convinced him that a tot would not be overstepping the bounds of hospitality, and he opened the cabinet in search of a glass, only to find it full of identical bottles, all empty. Odd, he thought, as he swigged direct from the bottle. The evening was improving. Captain Guardian settled back in the chair, took another gulp, and resumed work on the imaginary barge whose keel he had scarfed earlier in the day. A rather dull project, truth to tell, but he would enliven it somehow. An outrigger perhaps. Lots of pennants . . . hmm.

An hour or more passed in this matter, the only event of significance being the end of the bottle and Eben's discovery of another in the desk's drawers. A series of dull reports announced the beginning of the fireworks somewhere outside. The world began to take on a roseate glow and the chair supplied all the curves and angles his old body demanded. A barge began to take shape within his imagination. A royal barge perhaps, with buglers on a little platform toward the prow and little heraldic things dangling over the side. And more pennants. The barge was a good thought after all, drifting down a river under a purple sky with rain visible far off in the distance where it would never fall on him, *mmth*, another swig, and cheering crowds along the bank waving pennants which might be designed to complement the colors of those on his boat, a signaling system of sorts whose only word would be harmony, intricately fleshed out in all its meanings by a thousand happy wavers, yes, he was drunk and didn't care. *Thump!* And canoes! Ornamental canoes towed in strings behind the—*Thump!* This time it registered.

Eben brought his head up, already rehearsing apologies and taking his feet off the desk, he had got lost, safe haven and the rest of it, but as he looked about the room, it was still quite empty. An intruder? Repel boarders! Eben kicked his feet off the desk, and looked about for a weapon. No chance of a belaying pin but, but, the empty bottle, one of them anyway, yes. Now the target . . .

He was a little drunker than he had thought. The floor in the center of the room seemed to be moving. The chairs arranged about the low table were creeping toward each other and the table itself was moving up and down. Suddenly the table seemed to leap into the air and fall with a thud on its side. It was the carpet, it was swelling in the middle. Something was coming up through the carpet.

Captain Guardian acted. He marched smartly over to the bulge erupting out of the floor, raised the bottle, and brought it down, rapping the thing a glancing blow on its highest point. The swelling disappeared and a moment later there was a loud, crashing sound. Then silence. The carpet now dipped where the table had stood. It was a square cavity which Guardian recognized belatedly as a trapdoor. Perhaps he should have waited before hitting whatever, whoever it was had attempted entry, and mild anxiety began rolling back the alcoholic haze as he shifted the chairs and table to pull the carpet away from the hole in the floor.

An open trapdoor was revealed, and as Guardian peered down into some kind of passage below, he saw his victim, a spindly-looking youth lying splayed out among a lot of broken wood.

"Hey!" Eben called and waved down at the young man, forgetting the wad of handkerchiefs and the bottle which he held in his right and left hands and which now he let fall, the bottle smashing safely a few feet from his victim, the blood-soaked mess landing squarely in his face.

But Eben paid them no mind. All his thoughts were suddenly on his hand where the name of the ship had earlier been inscribed by Maillardet's wretched contraption and was now revealed to him, a ragged tattoo of the name he had known all along, of course, but twenty, twenty-five years ago or more, and he spoke it aloud as if to confirm it, the *Falmouth*.

Hey! A yellow fog was rolling back, becoming red, and wet. There was something on Lemprière's face. Someone above shouted "Falmouth!" The thing on his face was preventing him from breathing. Soon he would remove it. Now, perhaps. There was something on his head too. Lemprière's body rose from the pieces of ladder, something red and wet fell into his lap, and above him a bearded face peered through the ceiling and told him that the *Falmouth* was berthed not one hundred yards from his home. "Not the *Vendragon* at all. I guessed as much. . . . Just think of it! Lost for twenty years and here it is once more. The *Falmouth*, I knew it, just knew it. Never forget a ship. . . ." His head had an egg-shaped bump on it. The man above had hit him and now he was talking about ships, *Falmouth, Vendragon*. He had fallen off the ladder, that was why it was broken. Now the man had extended his hands down through the trapdoor. One of them had the word "Falmouth" written on the palm. Painful. Then he recognized the weather-tanned face, which was asking if he was injured.

"The automaton," said Lemprière. His tongue felt thick. "You were attacked by the automaton. Your hand . . ." That was enough for now.

"Catch hold," said the man. "I thought you were—I thought it was an attack, you see. I'll pull you up." Lemprière rose, but there was three or four feet between them, it was simply not possible. "Wait," said the face. "I'll fetch a rope." The face disappeared, then returned with an astonished expression upon it. "There's no rope here," it said. "Someone must have removed it." It was an impasse.

"I'll stay here," said Lemprière after a moment's thought, and this seemed to solve the problem. He rubbed his head. "Who are you?" he asked the face.

"Apologies for striking you. Guardian, Captain Ebenezer Guardian. Retired." The name, something inside Lemprière. His face was still wet. He ran a finger down his cheek and saw blood. His nose? No, the cloth. It lay on the floor between his feet. Guardian would have thrown it to revive him. Good idea. He threw it back.

"Lemprière," he told the man whose face broke into a smile.

"Lemprière! Well, why did you not tell me? I was expecting an older man. Good God, how are you?" The man knew him, but how? Then Lemprière remembered the letters in his father's trunk, Captain Ebenezer Guardian (retired), a name he had glanced at the night of the Pork Club. Guardian thought he was his father.

"John," said Lemprière, "not Charles. My father died, some months ago. . . ." The face above took on an expression of deep regret.

"Your father knew more about the western coast of France than any man alive," Guardian said warmly. "We corresponded, you know?

Charles dead. I am truly sorry, young man." His face grew sorrowful.

"How is your hand?" Lemprière changed tack.

"Hand? Oh, very well, I suppose. All rather embarrassing. It was the ship that did it, the *Falmouth*, or *Vendragon*. She's moored a little below my house, but that's a long story. Listen, we shall talk further. I have letters of your father's and a book he needed in his studies. Everything he asked had a purpose." Lemprière's neck was going stiff from looking up at Captain Guardian.

"We could meet at the front of the house," he suggested.

"Excellent," Guardian replied. "Until then, then." His head disappeared, Lemprière heard his feet move toward the door and the door slam shut. He looked about him; then he remembered he was lost.

An hour later, an hour made up of minutes which stretched like long, pointless corridors, returning Lemprière to places he had left only moments before, he had grown heartily sick of the sprawling pile the De Veres called home. Passages: As fast as he eliminated them, the house seemed to grow new ones, with rows of suites leading to enfilades, which led to further suites and more possibilities and so on until he stood finally in a large empty room which might have been on any one of three floors as far as he knew and cursed Septimus for dragging him here against his will like this, damn him.

"John?" Septimus? From beyond the door opposite. And footsteps. He heard footsteps.

"Septimus!" Through the door, an identical room, with an identical door, which was closing as he entered.

"Septimus!" He ran across and pulled it open to reveal yet another room, but this one was different, more like a short corridor, and the door led directly outside. It had been left open. He had reached the back of the house. Where on earth did Septimus think he was going? The snow had banked up against the door whose opening had pushed it back in a perfect semicircle. Lemprière saw footprints stamped in the crisp fall, leading away across the flat area of the lawn.

"Septimus!" he shouted once more, but there was no reply. Lemprière stepped outside and began to follow the footprints. The snow crunched under his feet and the light from the doorway faded rapidly, making the task of following the trail more difficult. The footprints themselves grew ill-defined, lighter, and a few paces later they could not be seen at all. Lemprière found himself staring at a perfectly even blanket of snow as if his quarry had been winched clear from above. Impossible. There was nothing for it but to return, and this he did, only to find the door was closed. And locked. He had heard nothing. An overofficious servant, or perhaps he had missed Septimus in the pale gloom behind him and his friend was now inside, wondering where he, Lemprière, had got to. Accordingly, Lemprière hammered on the door and shouted, but there was no reply. It was rather cold. Assignations piled up in his mind: Septimus and the others, Guardian, Casterleigh, and he speculated absurdly that the house itself had grown dimly conscious and was now rejecting him, like some foreign body that must be expelled. He knew where he was: the back of the house. It would be a simple matter to walk around to the front and enter as before. The fireworks might still be in progress. Everyone would be outside. Lydia, the Pug, Walter, and the rest. Juliette.

With the door closed the whole house seemed dark, and its jumbled perspectives merging in the gloom seemed even more confused than before. The snow-covered lawn stretched out in front, enclosed by neatly clipped box hedges. He thought, keep the house to the right, and then set off on his trek through the white landscape.

As Lemprière's eyes adjusted to the darkness, it seemed the snow itself gave off a very faint light, each flake locked in its own tiny ice-cage to produce minuscule glimmers. The scene was very quiet, apart from Lemprière's boots, which squeaked as they sank in the snow, and a low rustling sound, branches rubbing together somewhere out of sight. The snow covered everything: lawn, hedge, stone ornaments, topiary trees. Paths lined with the same high hedges ran off every few yards to left and right, and Lemprière took one which ran, as he imagined, parallel to the side of the house. The house itself was lost to view.

The night air hung between the hedges thick with damp. The path swung Lemprière out in a tangent, away from a destination that he now imagined ringed with faces: reds, blues, and greens in the firework light. The garden was silent. Lemprière listened to the noise his feet made as they scrunched the snow, attempting various leaps and specially angled hops to produce slightly different sounds. A bizarre trail stretched away at his back. Ahead of him the path funneled out. The ordered lines of the formal garden were giving out, the neatly clipped hedges becoming more shaggy. Not even the snow could conceal it, no longer a smooth blanket as the broken ground beneath puckered and rucked up, rejecting the past violence of gardeners, improvers, projectors, believers in the ideal of extent. Little ridges snaked off like questions: *claire et distincte? claire et distincte?* off into a wild, non-Euclidean yonder.

Lost in his snow music, Lemprière only looked up when his feet drew discordant clumps from the frozen ground. The covering of snow had thinned. It was dark. The house was invisible. There was the line of the hedge perhaps, behind him, but the night pulled the ground up like a sheet all around and he found himself staring into walls of silent white which sloped away from him up into the sky. Like limbo, he thought, or the paradise of the Persians. *Pairidaezo:* an enclosure. But Alice de Vere had told him the land fell away from the house. He must have walked in a wide semicircle, his constant margin of error first taking him away, then turning and bringing him back along the same lucky parabola. As he looked ahead, the white slope grew in substance until he saw it extend away to either side, a long low hump beyond which would be the house. But the ground began to slope downward in a gentle incline that was only interrupted by a straggling ditch which Lemprière scrambled down and then up without difficulty. The low white hump grew nearer, and extended back farther. The going grew rougher and Lemprière had to place his feet more deliberately to avoid low snow-covered shrubs. He began to hop from tussock to tussock, a new game, then struggled through a cordon of juniper scrub which encircled the white promontory. It was not a hill. It was trees, preceded by low bushes and saplings on which the snow had settled in a deceitful white canopy, suggesting ground actually lying some feet, or yards, or many yards below. Lemprière forced a path through a patch of dead elder which rose in height about him, as though he were wading into a lake of white powder. His waist, chest, then finally his head were swallowed up until he found himself beneath the canopy.

Densely tangled upper branches held the snow suspended above like the roof of a tent. Beneath it, the woodland dripped with life. Wild hawthorn caught against his legs, and the trunks of invading beech trees reached up, splitting and proliferating into a mat of branch-work high above as though the snow had been peeled off the earth leaving these filaments and threads to mark its earlier adhesion. Great boles swelled out of the trunks. The ground steamed as Lemprière's feet crunched, crashed, then squelched in a mulch of decaying grasses, rotten leaves, and branches. A slow combustion seemed to be taking place all around him. Stinking hellebore, dropwort, and henbane surrendered to more virulent life forms. The forest-floor detritus piled up in small, potent volcanoes of steaming compost. Large drops of water formed from condensation fell from somewhere high up in the branches onto the slithery ground. The snow above him seemed to have taken on an orange tinge and the land's incline was still taking him down. The ground itself was becoming even more squelchy than before, wetter, less pungent, and Lemprière found himself dodging large, stagnant puddles. The wood was changing in character, becoming colder and quieter, less secretly active. The trees here were stunted oaks and hazels which had fallen at crazy angles against one another; some were standing, some not, but they were all dead in the water which, the occasional gurgle of marsh gas aside, lay in still, black pools. Lemprière's feet were soaked through before he realized that he must be in the flooded pasture to the west of the house. Alice de Vere had not mentioned a century and a half of undergrowth. Obviously it had not been cleared since the fourth Earl's day, and Lemprière wondered if she knew. He had gone wrong. He should turn back.

But he did not turn back, he went on, thinking to emerge on the other side and skirt the forest, back toward the house which must lie at his back, or to either side, or even before him. Just conceivably, yes, for the orange tinge to the snow canopy was growing stronger the farther he advanced.

There was his cussedness too, and the recent memory of other disjunct journeys: his country-boy helplessness amid the barrow-boys and fishwives of London when he had first arrived, subsequent meek acquiescence to Septimus's determined forays through those same streets, and at the back of both a path which had led him to the pool above Blanche Pierre on Jersey, but no farther. Then, he had not gone on. He had watched like a coward as the story he had read and imagined and brought out and made flesh had unfolded its violence on the twitching corpse who was once his father. Go on, that scene said. Go farther.

The bog was deeper, the dead undergrowth even thicker, but he plunged ahead through it all. The orange glow grew less diffuse and he could hear something, a faint roaring sound. He was streaked with muddy black water which his efforts had thrown up. So many things unanswered, unfinished, meetings yet to take place. He was revisited by his earlier thought; cold, alone, frightened, he wished fervently he were back at his desk and the empty page was before him again, headed "Danae." Below her name the blank page: immaculate as alabaster, or flesh, or the snowfield itself. Then his spidery handwriting would put the story down in a mass of tiny black stitches. Danae, in her brazen tower, or pit, as Apollodorus had it. Danae, visited by the violence of Zeus, disguised as a shower of gold.

The orange glow was closer now, a fat diffuse pillar rising out of the ground. The roaring sound had stopped. He splashed closer, walking faster now, wading through the pools and straddling the fallen tree limbs until he noticed the substance of the color was a kind of mist and it was more yellow than orange. Lemprière almost tripped on a submerged root, righted himself, pulled aside a rotten curtain of ivy, then saw the source of the strange light.

It was sunk into the ground; a hole, three or four yards across. The waterlogged ground should fall into it, but it did not. The orange-yellow glow was coming from the hole in the ground, a neatly cut circle whose perfection seemed to contradict the decaying logic of the surrounding terrain. It was something that did not belong. His mouth was dry. He knew he would look. The legs which walked to the edge did not seem his own, nor the eyes which looked down. He saw the dull gleam of bronze, and in the pit, a woman. He felt hot. The blue satin dress was in shreds, remembered now from the Pork Club and the street outside the coffee shop. There were things holding her there in the pit, and something in her mouth. A metal ring holding her mouth open. Her eyes were worst, looking past him to something above. Then a roaring sound was in his ears and he looked up suddenly, following her gaze, to see the huge black shape swing over and down out of the black sky and open and the sky was not black but full of light. The heat was in his face, the yellow blur so bright it blinded him to everything else as it hissed past him, a cascade of molten metal down into the pit. Gold. His ears heard flesh crackle; his eyes saw her struggle, her limbs thrashed like a doll's as the scalding gold fell. Not his eyes. Not his ears. How could she scream like that? Her mouth was filled, her throat. How? His limbs flailed through the marsh before he realized the screams were his own and he could not stop them. Already, his fears were spreading and extending into the wider context. The jailers will come, lock you up. He heard her stomach burst. She was alive for a long time. Lock you up. Little drops of gold like torches moved in a cluster, miles away. He ran forward. The night was a black mouth huge enough for them all. The woman was already dead, burned miles and miles away. Little drops of gold. Lock you up. Bright drops of golden light like fireworks and torches miles behind him as he fled into the night.

· · ·

The search party was beginning to lose heart when the shouting was heard. A high wailing sound distorted somehow as though the night air were overloaded and there were certain sounds it would no longer carry. Septimus pricked his ears. "Over there." He pointed to their left.

The Earl groaned. "It's a bog," he said. The band dutifully turned and trudged toward the source of the noise. Flames from their torches flickered in the damp air.

"He said we should meet at the front. Could he truly have wandered all the way out here?" Guardian's feet were wet through, his mind on the *Falmouth*.

"Yes," said Septimus, "he could." They fanned out and, as the Earl predicted, quickly found themselves splashing through the sodden west pasture. The shouting had stopped and the searchers moved quietly. The only sound was their feet as they advanced through the wet. They spread out farther, then one of them said, "Olr," as if slightly taken aback by something. The others moved toward him and gathered around. Together they looked down into the pit.

"Merciful God," said Captian Guardian. The large man at the back of the group was the only one not to peer down. There was a long silence. The Earl broke it.

"We shall return to the house," he said. It seemed the right decision. He turned to the large man next to him.

"It was good of you to help, Viscount," he said. The man moved forward and looked down at the body.

"Not at all," said Casterleigh. He looked about him at the faces, read and yellow in the torchlight. "Who could do a thing such as this?" No one answered.

• • •

He moved left, then right, then left again. Snow on the high ground was thinner. He stumbled and fell, crawled forward, got up, fell again. He moved but without *toward* or *from*. Seen close, his breath came quickly. All around, the snow lay quietly on the ground.

Lemprière's lungs burned from the cold air. His face still felt hot. He had no idea where he was. He had run, and he had lain here. For how long? Presently, he got up and began to walk. His own footsteps seemed alien to him, the way his legs moved. He went on, he might walk forever on and on like this. He reached for the miniature of his mother, but it was in his own coat. This was the borrowed one. Finding it missing somehow filled him with dread. No one knew he was here. No one would know to look. And if they did look, did find him, he would run. If he stopped, he would freeze. His footprints stretched away into the dark.

Sometime later he began to shiver. His head felt larger than it should. His hands too. He began to stomp his feet and the noise cheered him. No going back. Lemprière dragged himself forward, feeling the cold creep into his bones. He wondered how cold he would get before ceasing to feel it. He had collided with something. The clouds had lowered, become mist. A fence post. He climbed over, then his ears caught a sound, a dim pounding ahead of him. Lempriére moved forward, still listening, then heard a second sound beneath the first which he recognized. Wheels. The pounding was horses. A coach was moving toward him. For a moment, he saw nothing. Then it was there, a black shape, thirty, forty yards in front of him to his left, moving fast over the road. Lemprière ran forward as a black coach drawn by four snorting horses thundered suddenly out of the fog. He would not be seen, faster. He was shouting. The coach was heading straight toward him, its steel-rimmed wheels were almost on him. But it was not going to stop.

He hammered at the doors with the palms of his hands and a white face rose up within the black interior, framed in the glass of the window as the coach sped past. Lemprière let his hands drop and stood gazing, panting, openmouthed at the coach until it was swallowed up again by the night and the mist, leaving him alone on the road with the image of the face only inches from his as it was pulled back into the dark, lost to him. The coach was gone. Juliette's face.

• • •

Sir John Fielding, portly and bandaged, stepped out on Christmas morning at the insistence of Mister Rudge. Immediately his guide-boy was running ahead.

"Cease!" he roared, and gave the string a sharp tug.

"S'John." The boy's tones were sheepish. He would be tugging his cap. Sheepish boy, but better than the last, who deserved hoisting. Church bells were ringing. The streets would be crowded. He sensed bustle and adjusted the bandage which covered his eyes.

"On!" he commanded, and the two of them continued. He heard snatches of conversation, odd words, noises, the usual urban hum, and Sir John pricked his ears. His old enemy was in town—he had reports—stirring up trouble from the top of an orange crate, agitating, misrepresenting the great and the good and, more dangerously, the not so good. Sir John could feel him in the streets, in the growing complaints, harangues against imports or the Company or both, an undertone of dissatisfaction that would boil up, bringing street-robbers, highwaymen, shoplifters, cardsharps, cheats, pickpockets, and pilferers of all kinds out of their kennels and rookeries to disturb the good order which was *his* business. Sir John was the magistrate at Bow Street, the blind beak they called him behind his back, and other names. He knew them all and forgot nothing. A grinding sound. "Gyp!" he bellowed across the street.

"Sir John." Yes, it was Gyp. Another sheepish fellow. He had questioned Gyp over the Healey case and disliked him. Too clever for a knife-grinder, too clever by half.

"Honest trade, Gyp!" he enjoined the man before moving on. Nasty piece of work. Sir John preferred an out-and-out rogue, a proper scamp. There was a part of him loved a murderer. Thieving brought the venal out of folk, victim and guilty alike. But a murder, a murder had clarity. It made sense. Murder presented itself as a puzzle begging solution. His forensic powers were famed, he knew this. (He could, after all, recognize every lawbreaker unlucky enough to cross his path by voice alone.) But fame was garnish. It was the process of solution he relished. There was the body, or the report, a witness or two, or not, and out of that he was supposed to draw motive, means, and murderer, all three. He did it too, slowly drawing in the threads, clipping off irrelevances, red herrings, and outright lies until some otherwise undistinguished wretch stood before him invested with a black aura that, at the last, was of his, Sir John's, own fabrication. Then he would hang the man. A waste really, but there was nothing Sir John relished more than a murder. Even a horrid one. Even an insoluble one, come to that. It was almost like coitus. No, that was wrong, but innocent and vicious pleasures were commingled in it. Sir John took no pleasure in death. It was a frightening and nasty business, his business. He would have it no other way.

They continued, man and boy, on their journey to Mister Rudge. People's eyes were on him. He could feel it.

"Farina!" A shout out of the crowd and Sir John stiffened. A goad, a bait, and if he took it, retorted with a sharp "Come forward, that man!" and no one came forward (no one would), he would suddenly be a ludicrous figure, a fat blind man led by a boy on a piece of string, bellowing at embarrassed strangers. Restraint, huge restraint, silenced him. Farina was his enemy; also known as the second Wilkes, as the Liberty Man, the People's Shield. A certain rogue, in Sir John's opinion. He must not respond, not be a fat blind man. He would pull Farina off his orange crate in time. The voice had come from behind, which pleased him. There was a lurking suspicion among the rogues and trouble-stirrers that Sir John's blindness was feigned. It was almost superstitious; himself, the presiding bogeyman. Sir John did not discourage this belief. Farina was in the city, somewhere, popping his head up here and there, denouncing the things he had always denounced. A worthy opponent, but the dish he served was complex, overspiced. There was the politics. It was not half so appetizing as a murder. Too, Farina had the advantage of being loved by the people, which brought Sir John to the matter of Henry.

Half-brother Henry had similarly held the magistracy at Bow Street. Sir John was respected almost universally. He held loyalties in some quarters, but he was not loved. Truth to tell, Henry had not been a good magistrate—executing Peulez under the Riot Act, dear me, a mistake— but still he had been loved. Why? Henry's shadow fell over Sir John like an onerous example beneath which all his efforts fell short. Little brother John, the efficient one, the born lieutenant. He might have resented this, but life was short. In times of crisis he touched on it like a talisman: This situation, that situation brought it out like a losing advocate's leading question, What would *Henry* have done? What *would* Henry have done?

The boy had settled, his pattering footsteps coordinated more exactly with Sir John's heavier gait. They were almost at Rudge's, and Sir John wondered what mystery it was the pathologist would serve up for him this morning.

"Here, sir," said the boy.

"Good lad." Sir John mounted the steps and entered the building. Strange chemical smells made his nostrils twitch.

"Good morning, Sir John." Perse, Rudge's assistant, a genius at scrubbing. "Mister Rudge is in the laboratorium, Sir John."

Laboratorium? "Thank you, Perse." Sir John had the boy wait and descended to the morgue.

He enjoyed his encounters with Rudge. Rudge was methodical, his brain working by cancellation. In another man it might have been called deduction, but Rudge was a plodder. In all the years of their acquaintance, everything the pathologist had said had been true. An extraordinary feat that, though it had to be said that Rudge's utterances became increasingly pedestrian the further they were removed from the subject of dead bodies. He was a bachelor.

"Sir John! Good morning to you." The morgue was a still, quiet place; a haven where all the violent flurries of death came to rest, thought Sir John.

"Mister Rudge." There was a body on the table, he could smell it under the carbolic. He suffered himself to be led to the corpse.

"Murder," said Mister Rudge. "A peculiar case, perhaps the most peculiar I have come across, Sir John." Peculiar: That meant violent, horrific, repulsive, obscene, bizarre, uncanny, any, some, or all of these in Rudge's limited lexicon. *Most* peculiar, though. Their game was beginning.

"She was brought in last night, the early hours." Sir John rested his hand gingerly on the corpse. "I have yet to open her," Rudge went on. The flesh was cold, colder than the room.

"She was found outside."

"She was." First point to Sir John. He began with the feet, then the ankles which were swollen. Some sort of constriction, the skin was unbroken, rope perhaps. The legs were thick, a heavyset woman. Sir John paused over the left thigh, which moved loosely when touched.

"Broken?" he asked.

"Dislocated," said Rudge. "I have never come across it before." Sir John reached the stomach and felt the ragged edges of a huge wound. But Rudge had not opened her, and this was not knifework of any sort. It was a tearing, a ripping open. Then it came to him. The stomach had burst, and that meant heat, a great deal of heat. Sir John moved his hands quickly over the corpse's skin. It was smooth, not burnt at all. Several ribs were fractured. Cold hard ridges of something seemed to be stuck to her sides, and the flesh around these was puckered. Heat again. The ridges were made of some kind of metal, and Sir John thought of outlandish jewelry, some whorish adornment. But Rudge would have already removed any such articles. His mind raced. Heat, metal . . . No, it was too horrible. Not that he was squeamish, but it was too strange, too peculiar. He continued up the body.

The rules of their diagnostic game allowed a certain latitude. Thus Rudge, in the past, had once presented him with a heart, just a heart, found in Poplar and brought to him amid talk of ritual slaughter and Moorish practices, even grave robbing. It had vexed Sir John, as he turned the clammy organ over in his hands, much to the amusement of Rudge who had later told him that the heart had indeed belonged to a victim of ritual slaughter. Specifically, a pig. On the other hand, Sir John had once walked in, spent a few seconds feeling the unnaturally constricted waist of a young woman, then announced that she had been killed by exhaustion and want of water brought about by her being tied by the waist to a doorknob so that she could neither sit nor lie, probably over a period of three to four days. Further, she had been found in a gully hole, probably in Chick Lane or thereabouts, and the murder had actually been committed some weeks before. He had not told Rudge that a Mister Rooker, tea dealer, had informed on the girl's employers, her murderers, that very morning. Rudge had been impressed, and suspicious. It was an excellent contest, though grisly.

His hands reached the woman's shoulders. Both dislocated. Her struggles must have been very fierce. One of her eyes had come out. Sir John let the tips of his fingers run over the face, which was dotted with hard nodules of metal like smooth studs.

"Her expression is violent?" he queried.

"Very violent," confirmed Mister Rudge.

His early suspicion was coming true; nevertheless he started in shock when his fingers touched her mouth. Rudge would be smirking. The mouth was blocked, filled with the same cold metal which here protruded up like a stump rooted in her throat. Sir John took away his hands. He knew enough. Rudge passed him a cloth.

"You were right," he said, wiping his hands. "Most peculiar. She was killed very horribly." He handed back the cloth. "Her mouth was held open. If you dig away the metal in her mouth you will probably find the device. Molten metal was poured into her mouth, a great quantity of it and from height. The splashes on her face." He made a gesture. "The metal boiled her innards, causing her stomach to burst. More, it burnt through her organs and skin from the inside out. There are traces on her sides. All the wounds would have been cauterized by the heat, thus no blood, am I correct?"

"You are," said Rudge.

"More than peculiar," Sir John went on. "Quite the most barbarous murder I have encountered. Her agonies . . ." but he left that sentence unfinished.

"There is more, a further puzzle," said Rudge. Sir John brought his head about, what more? "It is the metal used . . ."

"Yes?"

"Gold," said Mister Rudge. "This corpse is worth a small fortune."

Minutes later, Rudge was writing down the details of the corpse's discovery at Sir John's request.

"Below Richmond?"

"The De Veres', a mile or so to the west of the house."

"How was she found?"

"There was a ball. A guest went missing. The search party came across the corpse in a bog on the estate."

"She would not have been killed there."

"It seems that she was."

"The search party . . ."

"I have a list. Edmund de Vere."

"The Earl?"

"Yes."

"I knew his father, and mother. A formidable woman, though infirm nowadays."

"The Earl then, Mister Warburton-Burleigh, a Mister Septimus Praeceps, Captains Pannell, Guardian, and Stokeley, three servingmen, and Viscount Casterleigh."

"Casterleigh, eh? Odd company for him to be keeping." Sir John Fielding reviewed the list in his mind, but the corpse on the table pulled his attention away.

"None of them knew who she was, so they said."

A dead woman. Gold. Both common enough, but combined like this they became something different. Like sulfur, saltpeter, and charcoal. Sir John Fielding was filled with unease. And the woman was nameless. Public order was an instinct with him. He could feel disturbances welling up under the city's surface already, shooting up in destructive jets. Gold in her mouth. What would Henry have done? Contain it, make it make sense. Farina built revolts out of such things, the mob trampling appeals to reason, torches in the street. No, not while he could put his stamp on the business. Not while the body politic numbered himself among its servants. A body stuffed with gold. He would not countenance it.

"Mister Rudge?"

"Sir John."

"Who besides ourselves know of this unfortunate's death?"

"The search party. I told them to keep silent, not to put the investigation in jeopardy."

"Good. I may speak to them myself. I believe there is a need for discretion, for secrecy, not to put too fine a point on it. It is a horrible murder, bad enough, and yet, I fear, more than that if it were known. A focus—"

"I understand."

Rudge understood. Of course, he did. Like himself, set off to the side of the crowd's passions, with a perspective on them. Of course, he understood.

"For whom were they searching? De Vere and the others?" he asked abruptly.

Rudge's thoughts had been running along similar lines to Sir John's. He was thrown momentarily. "It was mentioned. I wrote it down." He looked at his notes. "Lemprière," he said. "A Mister John Lemprière."

"Lemprière." Sir John echoed the name in an absent tone. "I may speak with Mister Lemprière too." He moved toward the stairs, troubled. Then suddenly he turned and spoke urgently. "Mister Rudge, tell no one of this. Conceal the body. You have my authority." He paused, his anxieties gathering inside him. "Tell nobody, Mister Rudge. Tell no one at all."

PARIS

To Paris, by pacquet-boat from Saint Helier to Saint Malo, by coach along the stages of the Normandy road, wheels clattering over a metaled surface rolled out of Trésaguet's tripled-tiered genius and the corvée labor system like carpet through mile after mile of flat gray skies and avenues of plane trees and Lombardy poplars, with outriders making up an escort though no one is encountered for leagues except capped and smocked peasants toting sickles and scythes for the late harvest who wave the mail through by reflex, grinning, waving, scything: Le Nain country.

On, into the interior, Île-de-France, where the terrain becomes more intensely rural, pigs, cows, sheep, fields of sorrel shaking in the slight gusts that freshen the shallow slopes the road cuts through, and clouds of chickens thrown up by the coach's commotion tumbling about in the air, apple trees too and stunted vines pushing branches out of the earth like the arms of the dead, flat lawns and neglected *parterres*. It all helps, even the skies which are still lead-gray, even the peasants though they contribute less, scarcely looking up as the coach approaches the metropolis, their oppidan indifference a sign meaning the city is not far off, and a little later a purple-gray smudge up ahead on the horizon confirms this, four or five hours away at the most. It is late autumn.

Inside the coach, the two passengers sensed its approach as it crept closer toward them, Paris, city of white plaster walls, leaning tenements, and the Palais Royale where the two of them will later stroll and admire the treillage and horse chestnut trees, guess at the humbler structures which will turn out to be extraordinary, though in different ways, trumpet schools, a wallpaper factory, or an entrance to the catacombs which riddle the city guts with passages and channels, for the soil is very chalky and buildings have been known to disappear overnight, or even in broad daylight—it is a city of sudden collapses and rumors of collapse which turn out to be true. Paris. City of lovers, which the coach has entered by the Rue de Sèvres, its pace slowed to a walk by the drovers and carters. Juliette angled her head against the glass to watch the city as it lumbered toward them, its spires and rooftops drawing her eye this way and that until there was nothing but buildings all about them; the driver was passing through the tollgate and they were inching through streets crammed with flower-sellers, letter-writers, women selling pastries, and men selling herrings spiced with vinegar and chives. The smell made her remember everything. The coach came to a halt in Rue Notre Dame des Victoires and she stepped onto the ground which became hard and real beneath her feet, crystallizing into Paris, suddenly the city of her return.

Behind her, the other passenger climbed out more slowly. They had been on the road from first light and now it was late in the afternoon. Jaques watched the girl as she strode about at the back of the coach gabbling in French, pulling the men this way and that as they unloaded the cases, hailing an open carriage. Her activity came in flurries, he had noticed, with periods of lethargy when nothing would animate her but a barked command. Casterleigh's work, he thought, or the past encounters he had not witnessed and at which he could only guess. The journey from Jersey had exhausted him, though smooth enough compared to the last. He was growing tired of it, but this was the last time, if all went well.

"Wait!" Jaques shouted across to the girl, who froze and looked back over her shoulder with the face of a thief. Casterleigh again. Leaving his stamp. Jaques pointed to the girl's own case which still sat on the cobbles at the rear of the coach. Battered canvas, a cheap thing. She had hugged it to her all the way from Saint Helier; it had blue flowers painted on its side which were all but faded away.

The house lay a quarter of a mile away, across the Rue Montmartre in a court off the Rue du Bout du Monde. It was entered via a courtyard. The porte-cochère's heavy gates were closed behind them as the carriage rolled through, a three-story villa, plastered white with the lower windows protected by iron grilles set into the stonework. The footmen were waiting to unload the baggage. Stable lads unharnessed the horses. Inside, the maids curtsied to Juliette before going about their business. A faint smell of dust hung in the air. She could hear pails and mops clattering somewhere out of sight. The house had lain empty and was now being opened for the two of them. Other than the servants, they were the only occupants. Jaques had already disappeared. She was alone in the entrance hall with her cases and a footman who waited quietly at the foot of the staircase, the familiar scene, tens, perhaps hundreds of such halls, cool echoing interiors with alabaster columns and Japanned urns, intricate stucco work, and herself, waiting for the servingman who would fetch her upstairs in silence broken only by their footsteps.

This time it was he who waited for her, but the silence was unchanged as she motioned him to guide her to her room where a maid stood in attendance, curtsied, and began to unpack the cases. She clutched the canvas bag to her chest. High windows looked south, out over the city with its rooftops which looked like scales, the river, and the spire of Notre Dame, until the detail was lost in distance and the onset of evening. Between her vantage point and the spire lay the Marché des Innocents, just beyond that the tangle of streets bounded by the Saint Denis highway and Quai de la Mégisserie. She might have reeled off every street in that quarter, every alley, court, even the nameless passages that connected some of the establishments with discreet back entrances onto the quieter thoroughfares. She knew them all, running through with her playmates who stank of the river, scabs on her knees and her hair cut like a boy's, pretty even then. They had watched as the floods brought small boats crashing down the river and cheered as they splintered against the stones of the Pont Neuf. Her mother had cuffed her till she saw double, but she had forgotten why, almost forgotten when. Almost forgotten Maman.

"Mademoiselle?"

"Yes, yes, of course." The maid was finished. A pier glass mounted on the wall between the windows threw back her reflection. There she was, brought back for a purpose. The Viscount knew but would not tell. She had known better than to ask as they took the carriage down to the waiting boat. He had spoken with Jaques on the jetty. She had watched through the window, then Jaques had taken her back to the house. The Viscount's departure sharpened her vague sense of betrayal, for she already sensed a new phase in their relations and heard the clatter of gears changing. She thought of the pool. The water had been very cold, and when the man, barely a man then, had flopped over and his arm had come up with its hand shredded to rags, she had thought of her own body, white, naked in the water which held her like weights around her ankles. More and more he was the Viscount; not Papa at all. He would be one then the other, she could not follow and was left floundering in his disapproval, a coquette, a precocious harlot all out of step, but in the pool she was frightened in a new way. Later, he had shot the dogs. She had sat in her room. It had taken an hour, and each time the gun cracked she had jumped, then tried to settle, but all the time waiting for the next report which would jerk her back to the moment in the pool when she had looked up at him on the horse and he had looked down at her and she saw the aftermath of a decision in his face. She was alone and naked and the dogs were there, aimless, waiting; the decision had gone her way. The gun cracked and she jerked again. It was the boy's father, but she had guessed that. Later, when she went to the Viscount, he had told her that the boy had seen it all. That was the point. She was ashamed he had seen her. Casterleigh had become Papa again, tender or stern as the situation demanded, no longer the Viscount, just as he had been when she had told him what Father Calveston had told her, what Lemprière had told him.

"Visions?" he had demanded.

"He reads things. He believes they come true—"

"What things?"

The man turning over. The dogs eating him. Letters had been sent to men in London and he had become the Viscount once more, raging and cursing. Children's games. He wanted to kill the boy, and the letters told him no. Juliette spied on him hunched over his desk like an animal with the letters in his fists, little bits of paper telling him no, and the boy was still alive. Jaques had told her during their weeks together on Jersey. The boy had sailed for England, for his father's will. She and Jaques had left for France a fortnight later. There would be a reason for both these things. There was a reason for the dogs drifting harmlessly back through the stream toward their master, leaving her there shivering, unmarked in the water; reasons like the bits of paper in his fists keeping Lemprière alive. The men in London, his partners, had told him no.

"He reads them. And he believes they come true." The dogs rounded and trotted back to their master. Lemprière: His thoughts were in the trees of that scene, in the pool, the dogs, even in Casterleigh and herself. All his dreams came true, they were all here. In the pool she was at their center. The Viscount's decision and Lemprière's dreaming her there shuttled her this way and that at their behests while the dogs pulled the body apart. She was them both somehow, all their choices. It was a new phase. Papa was gone. There was only the Viscount now, and Lemprière.

Her search had taken her to the top of the house. From there, she heard a coach enter the courtyard far below. Juliette slipped from her perch on the desk and ran lightly down the corridor and stairs.

When Jaques entered the entrance hall she was preparing for bed, seated at her dressing table, picking pins out of her hair. They made tiny clinking sounds as she dropped them one by one into a small glass tray on the table. She was combing her hair. Jaques was in the doorway, she saw him in the mirror. Jaques was almost bald, he had a soft intelligent face. He was hanging there, neither in nor out of the room. She turned to look at him, surprised, she had not thought this required of her. Her comb caught, and she had missed a pin and drew it out carefully with her head bent down. Her hair hung down her back, *click,* she looked up once more at the slight sound. He had closed the door. The pin fell with the others, *ting,* into the tray. She looked around. Jaques was gone.

The following morning found them strolling arm in arm in the triple avenue of the Cour de la Reine. She was his daughter, his ward, a favored niece, some or all of these as they drifted back along the Port aux Pierres and up into Place de Louis Quinze. Later they admired the arcaded houses which had gone up on three sides of the Tuileries. The next day was much the same, walking along the Quai de Pelletiers with the gamblers playing *passe-dix* and *biribi* seated on folding stools among the herring racks.

Other days, other sights. When the November skies threatened rain, she had her hair dressed at Baron's. They ate at the Véry or Beauvilliers and watched the learning riders fall off their mounts at Astley's. Juliette, for whom routine was a series of coincidences strung together, found it unsettling. In the evenings they played *trente et un* at Madame Julien's, or dominoes at the Chocolat Café, or they went to the theater. Sometimes she was left alone. There was a calculated aimlessness to their days. Each one, somehow, was a facsimile of the last. Only the details varied.

The days became weeks. Their vague rambles through the streets became vaguer still as though any sort of planning or forethought was forbidden, and they found themselves in the Halles or Courtille districts where Juliette would never have ventured of her own accord, or walking through streets where the sewers were choked with straw, animal droppings, and offal. There seemed no point or design to these tours, except that not once did they venture into the area below the Marché des Innocents, which she had viewed at a distance on her first evening. They would take long exhausting detours to avoid it, and the sight Juliette dreaded was never encountered. Casterleigh would have told him, must have told him. "Papa" once more, perhaps.

They were watched. She could not be certain—they were always different—she caught them in the corners of her eyes just within earshot and at irregular times, in places which signified nothing. She kept her peace about them; another component to be weighed up and fitted into the puzzle with the others, like Lemprière's list of books turning up in the study. Their aimlessness, their waiting, their watching; some central task, some event would link them, but she did not know what. Her role was changed, she was a stranger now. Her first embrace, when the city pressed itself right up against her as she stepped from the carriage, that was gone. She was drifting and floating. Somewhere in these repetitious dawdling days, the two of them had come apart. Even the watchers were falling away, or blending more successfully into the crowds. The time was filled with events and diversions, things they had done, or avoided doing. Somewhere in it all was a point.

December came and nothing was changed. Through salons and lobbies and spacious reception rooms with chandeliers of heavy crystal they went on with their listless promenade. She hardly knew the city, she was lost in it as she made fleeting conversations with people she would meet once and never again and was swept this way and that by the crowds who pressed against her in the streets, but they were far away too, already in the next street, already at their doorways, already there, waiting for her the next day when she would join them once again, the same face hundreds and thousands of times a day. Only Jaques was constant. He was waiting for something and she clung to that. The winter bled color out of their faces. The white buildings were not white but grayish brown, streaked with soot and muck thrown up by the wheels of carts and coaches as they passed by. The city began to freeze. The men and women moved slowly, more slowly through the lanes and byways. The life of the metropolis was a sluggish suspension of liquid solidifying around them. In the Alley of Sighs, dead-eyed creatures lifted limp wrists as they passed shivering with the others, their teeth glittering like paste. The drunks could dream of ice and the bitter cold. Their breath rolled into the gutters.

To all this, the cold, the dreary threats and lackluster whispering, the stranger's glassy flesh, the Palais Royale said *No!* The coaches rolled up along Rue Saint Honoré to fill it with high and low, Comtesse and commoner, journeymen and food-sellers, balladeers and musketeers, child actors and pornographers, bankers and their clerks and their wives and their mistresses who were always dancers and singers dressed in levités, light silks, and chintz, bright sashes, their fingers sparkling with stones. There were magic-lantern shows and players on the *parterre,* cafés, booksellers, and eating houses. Gentlemen in citron jackets and striped satin spoke with kohl-eyed demi-mondaines in feathers and Italian gauze in language that twisted like smoke through candlelight. Red cheeks, white gloves fluttering about their mouths, bands of velvet, and the swish of silk as they glided and jostled against one another, their gossip seeming to burn the very air.

Juliette roamed through it all like a veteran. Jaques held her by the arm, she was an animal in a jeweled collar. Even at this time of the year the gardens were packed with tight clusters of men and women talking quickly in knots. It was an orchestra of voices, undertones mixing with piercing shrieks, hissing sibilants and deep, gurgling laughter. The two of them sliced through all of it in a diagonal, left to right, and Juliette half-caught, half-saw, she was unsure, there was the staircase and it was jammed with women. She looked again. They passed a group of chevaliers who doffed elaborate hats to her so that she turned away and then she knew that she was right. A man in plain dress. He had moved parallel with them across the length and breadth of the gardens. She caught his silhouette flickering through gaps in the crowd. Then he was gone. He wore a small black hat. They were in the Great Gallery where the women's heads bobbed and nodded, the movement amplified by their piled hair and the colored feathers. Suddenly, he was there again, ahead of them now. It was impossible, and she twisted about so that Jaques had to pull her back. He was to their right, but he could not have moved so rapidly through the crush. There were two of them, suddenly clear, two of them. Or more. They were inching toward the point where she had glimpsed the first. Juliette looked up at Jaques and saw his face was changed, tight now, his eyes flicking from side to side. She began to open her mouth, to raise her arm and point, but he caught her wrist quickly and forced it down.

"Say nothing!" he hissed at her. The man to their right was converging on them, they would beat him to the doors at the far end of the gallery, but not the other who was ahead of them and slowing. They were closing on him as they threaded a path through the idle talkers and powder-cakes, and when they reached the door he was only yards away. She could hear the sharp reports of the second tracker's heels moving at a pace behind them. The first was moving more quickly than before. Jaques was pulling her along by the wrist. They were almost running across the court, her breath coming fast in the cold air, and then they *were* running, out into the street beyond, and the steps behind them were louder still, closer. Ahead of them, the man moved into the center of the street as a coach moved past them, slowing, the first man pulling open the door, and Jaques was pulling her in behind him as he scrambled into the coach and the second man threw himself in behind, then the first, the door slammed shut and the coach gathered pace quickly with the four of them inside and the horses broke into a gallop.

The two men were facing them, seated opposite. One of them leaned across and Jaques clasped his hand. The other man was impassive.

"Nine weeks," said Jaques. "Nine weeks we have been here."

"I know," said the other. "You were watched." And Juliette knew suddenly that the meeting with these men, whoever they were, was the event for which Jaques had been waiting.

Their destinations rushed toward them. The coach made a clacking racket as it sped east down Rue Saint Honoré. Juliette looked out of the window as the town houses slid by and crowds spilled off the pavements into the road. Their faces were white blurs right up against the glass. *Keep them out*, she thought.

The coach turned left before the Marché des Innocents as though to cross the river by the Pont Neuf, but no, they were slowing to a standstill. Juliette's skin was prickling. Jaques glanced down at her and caught her eye. The maze of streets and alleys they had skirted like a hostile fortress during their time in the city was now to their left. Ahead of them a dray was overturned, blocking the road with timber. A horse was dead. Juliette heard the hooves of their own horses clatter awkwardly as the driver had them wheel about, and even without looking, Juliette knew the road which would form their detour. Then she did look, as the coach turned into the Rue Boucher des Deux Boules and she felt something rising in her throat. There was the bakery, and a few doors along the Hôtel where she had watched little Restif stand on the parapet and scream—they all had—as he pissed on the heads of the passersby below. Past that was the alley which had no name but they called it the "Black and Green" from the colors of its walls, which glistened with a mold they had found nowhere else. The street bent midway along its length and the angle came suddenly, giving her the houses farther along for a second before the coach gave a violent jolt, found its bearing, and that was when Jaques reached across to draw the curtain.

But she had already seen it, the lights were blazing behind the red drapes—the same ones—and she could see the long room within, remember it vividly, with sofas and chaises dotted about and fires burning in the hearths at either end. In the mornings the sunlight had streamed through the high windows and she had played on the floor while Oudin, Petit Pas, Minette, Grosse Bonne, and the other girls had lounged about, talking, yawning, scratching. And Maman too. Upstairs were the bedrooms and above them the attic room where she had kicked and screamed with every ounce of her strength but it was no good. Then a year or two later, the same window, Maman had strode down the street swinging her blue canvas bag, not looking back. She banged on the pane, but no one heard. Petit Pas had run after her and later returned with the same blue bag. A keepsake. Then she had known that Maman would not return. Madame Stéphanie would not take her back again and she was gone for good. The bag was good-bye and she was left with the long afternoons and her memories of Maman spinning out rambling stories about her lovers, one of whom was Juliette's father.

"A fine man. A man of his word." But she only said that because he sent money every month, money for Juliette which she gave to her mother, taking for herself only the fact that somewhere her father knew of her existence. He would not come for her, she told herself. She would hunt for him. It was a rage inside her, she let no one see it.

Now the coach would be passing the heavy front door which she had last seen four years before when it had closed finally behind her and the Viscount's coach had stood waiting in the street. She had sat in it while he had concluded the business with Madame Stéphanie. Her face was white, then as now, and she twisted her skirts in her hands. When he joined her in the carriage she learned that she was to leave the city. For Jersey.

"Papa?" That faint possibility had run out at the island's name in a rush of false hope. The money was sent from Jersey, her father was on Jersey if he was anywhere. "Papa?" She knew it was not this man who was built like a bull. There was nothing in his face, and it was confirmed to her anyway almost as soon as the coach moved off. He had dealt with her there and then, roughly, on the seat of the carriage. Papa: At his insistence she would call him that. She had thought to run, even in her disarray. But when she had burst out that he was no father of hers, that he had tricked her (though he had claimed nothing), the Viscount had laughed at her misery.

"Your father? Absurd! Your father and I are utterly unalike." The words had been almost tangible. He might have strung them about her neck as a leash. She remembered her mother slipping away from her down the familiar street, her own days of waiting in the halls of Madame Stéphanie's acquaints and clients, the business which would follow and its late repetition within this same coach. Her father's absence stood over these scenes and others like them. His return was the faintest of hopes, her finding him a long-postponed task, but now at last she was embarked. She saw her passage laid out as the coach rattled down the street, a simple quitting of this for that. But "that" was still faceless and nameless, not yet "him," not yet the father she sought. Her pursuit was underway, fueled with a passion that was all her transmuted loathing of the Viscount and rage at the woman who had slipped away to leave her here. And the Viscount too was adept at transmutations, turning her petty ignorance into allegiance, her willful struggles into docility. She watched him gazing idly out the window. Her father. *We are utterly unalike.* . . . Of course. Her quick hatred was already sinking. She could not leave him then, or misunderstand his needs. He would ask more of her than that and she would surrender what he asked. That much was clear as he saw the implications of his phrase register in her expression. He knew the identity of her father. That made her his.

One of the men rapped on the woodwork and called, "Stop!" She had lost all notion of where they were as her thoughts had drifted over the events of four years past. She felt Jaques's hand on her elbow. The two strangers followed them out. They were in a backstreet bounded on one side by a high wall. The coach moved off and a low door opened in front of them. All four ducked through to find themselves in a large garden. It was quite dark, and the carefully clustered trees looked like black mountains against the night sky. Juliette could feel clipped grass beneath her feet. They moved around a copse in silence, and a large house, larger even than the Viscount's, was suddenly visible. The lights within were blazing and Juliette could see through the windows that a banquet was going on in a long room on the ground floor. Twenty or thirty men were seated around a table, talking, eating, and drinking. They moved across the lawn and the scene slid from view. The two men led them to a door at the side of the house. An unlit corridor led to a drawing room, beyond it a larger chamber where the lamps had been lit.

A long table ran down its center. Jaques took a seat and motioned for Juliette to do the same. The more impassive of the two men sat opposite them. The other was closing the door as his companion addressed him.

"Duluc! The Cardinal should be fetched now." Duluc nodded and rose. The three were left together. Juliette noticed that Jaques, who had been abstracted and distant during their weeks together and tight with nerves during the journey to this mansion, had now assumed a third guise. He lounged in his chair. He was at ease, nonchalant even.

"Are you well, Protagoras?" he asked casually. The other nodded as though the matter were of great import. Jaques cast his eyes round the room. He might have been seated on a bench in the Elysée Gardens, watching the promenaders go by. The door opened and Duluc reentered followed by a man dressed in gray robes wearing a scarlet skullcap.

"Cardinal." Jaques offered his hand across the table.

"Jaques." They shook hands briefly. "You seem well." His eyes roamed over Juliette, who sat bolt upright in her chair.

"You took my advice, I see. The reports which reached me identified her as your niece, was that the story?"

"We are tourists, naturally." The Cardinal smiled. His teeth were small and yellow.

"My apologies for the delay. You were watched until very recently, Duluc explained?"

"Of course. Delay is inevitable. Only risk is unacceptable."

"Yes, yes. Watched closely too." The Cardinal's voice had an edge in it, he was nervous. "Even tonight . . . Do you know my guest tonight?"

"We saw."

"An irony. He would appreciate it, were it not to cost him so dear." The Cardinal smiled again.

"You should introduce us," Jaques said. His tone was serious. The Cardinal did not smile. "In any case, we shall meet later. When circumstances are changed."

"A toast to that, perhaps?" The Cardinal turned to Protagoras, who began to move toward the decanter on a sideboard table.

"Perhaps not," said Jaques. Protagoras stopped and resumed his seat. The Cardinal smiled again. Juliette realized suddenly that he had deferred to Jaques, in his own house. Did the Cardinal fear Jaques, even here?

"The Viscount could not be with us; a pity."

"We have other affairs to manage," Jaques replied. "Our business here is not negotiation; the negotiations have ended, are we agreed upon that?" The Cardinal assented. "And we are here only to clarify the matters which are already part of our agreement, is that clear?" Yes, it seemed. "When I address you, Cardinal, it is with the undivided will of the Cabbala. Likewise, you represent here each and every member of *Les Cacouacs,* am I right?"

"The *Conseil aux Conseils,*" the Cardinal amended. "Yes, without doubt. There were, however, a number of small points which some members wished to stress, the schedule of repayments, for instance . . ." Jaques's manner changed immediately.

"Listen to me, Cardinal." He leaned forward over the table, almost pushing his face into that of the Cardinal. "There will be no talk of points. When you and the other patriots"—he stressed the word insultingly—"came to us, you brought nothing but a simple fact: If your country were sold lock, stock, and barrel, it would not pay its debts. You do not even know your debts! Monsieur Necker believes in a surplus that is in truth a deficit of forty million livres. Monsieur Calonne believes it is eighty, and we think it closer to one hundred and twenty millions. Which of us is right, Cardinal? You and I and every other man in Europe with a head for the figures know that France bleeds from a million holes. The debts even within her boundaries are greater than all her efforts to repay them. Beyond those frontiers, her debts are greater still, and every Dutch banker knows they are paper, a house of cards. You are standing on nothing. We, the Cabbala, will take your debts and honor them. No longer will you pay dividends to a million creditors, but only to one. Ourselves. We place all our reserves at your disposal. Our wealth will lie like granite beneath the whole of France. And for this we ask nothing but that you allow us to do it, and you will allow us, Cardinal. No one else will come to you now. France is the whore who sold her favors too often and too cheap. You see, Cardinal, when you lose who you are, there is only money."

Duluc and Protagoras wore faces of stone. Too often and too cheap. Juliette turned the thought over in her mind. The Cardinal subsided into a craven silence. Duluc spoke.

"We have accepted all these strictures. The *Conseil aux Conseils* recognizes all you have said. Yet when your reserves become the reserves of France, what is to stop you from withdrawing them and bringing our country down in ruins?"

"Your country is already in ruins, but to answer you, why, once it is given, should we wish to withdraw our support?"

"For any number of reasons, Monsieur Jaques, a policy which displeases you, an edict—"

"Then you shall not pursue such policies, nor pass such edicts."

"In effect, you will govern our country."

Jaques sat back once more. "In effect, you have directed us to do so."

"We do not even know who you are," the Cardinal rallied. "You might be agents of any power. We do not even know if you can fulfill your promises. Where would such sums come from? How have they been concealed?"

"Cardinal, we know of your efforts to discover our identity. You will cease those efforts, you will discover nothing in any case. How we have amassed such sums is our own business, likewise their concealment. But the bulk of our wealth is already in France, you need know no more. We represent no power beyond ourselves, no nation nor faction within any nation. We have no interest in your politics. We are investors, no more nor less. You will never know who we are except that which we tell you. We will become patriots just as you, the *Cacouacs*, are. The sum of our wealth will be revealed to you as it will be to the whole of France when the time is right, when the change has been made. And the change is something we must discuss, for we will not meet again until it is done."

"Duluc has undertaken the task," the Cardinal replied, and looked around at his comrade. Duluc had been searching through the contents of a cabinet at the far end of the room while Jaques was speaking. Now he advanced, untying a large scroll which was laid on the table to reveal a map of France. He pointed quickly to several areas which were marked in mauve ink.

"From these cities, any disturbance will spread as fast as its report. We have our own men in place, they will merely have to stand back, to do nothing at the right moment." His finger had come to rest on an area marked more prominently than the rest. "It is here," he tapped, "that the revolt will succeed or fail. Here in Paris—"

"It will succeed," Jaques said flatly. "Our only concern is the delay until that time. A year and six months; everything can change in such a period. Your revolt, if it fails, will fail in the aftermath. You will need to feed your partisans, clothe them, arm them. There will be a thousand expenses. As we agreed, we will meet them all. A ship is being loaded in London even now. Its cargo represents only a fraction of our wealth, but it will suffice. It will sail seven months from now and will reach your shores on the thirteenth day of July. I will be aboard to oversee the transfer. You, Duluc, will be waiting for me on that night." Jaques leaned across the table and placed his finger on a point on the western coast. "Here. You will need men and a jetty. The bay is isolated and there is only an anchorage. On that night, you will show three green lights from a hillside to the left of the bay, do you follow?" Duluc nodded. "The slope of the hill is such that the signal will be seen only from the sea. The gold will be unloaded there."

"Gold?" Duluc raised an eyebrow.

"Have no fears. It is well disguised. A customs vessel would find nothing of note." Jaques paused, then indicated the decanters. "We shall take that drink now. A toast." Protagoras saw to the glasses. Juliette was not included. Jaques raised his arms. "To the overthrow, and the new France." The four men drank.

"I must return to my guests," the Cardinal spoke.

"We shall meet again in July," said Jaques, and the Cardinal withdrew as though dismissed. "Our coach has been arranged?" Protagoras confirmed that it had. Duluc was already at the door, the map in his hand. The four of them followed the same path through the house and gardens. Jaques saw Juliette peering curiously across the lawn at the lighted window where the dinner party was still in progress. The Cardinal was visible, smiling and speaking with a tall, richly dressed man in a cascading wig. Duluc and Protagoras accompanied them only as far as the coach.

As Jaques climbed in, Duluc caught his arm. "Jaques. I do not know the name of the ship."

The backstreet was deserted but he must not be seen here. "The ship is called the *Vendragon*," he answered quickly. "Do not fail to be there."

As the coach moved off, he realized that Duluc had no need of the ship's name. He had been hurried into revealing it. Duluc was more adept than he had thought. The coach gathered speed. Juliette sat opposite him, lost in her own thoughts. Jaques leaned back in his seat and breathed out a long sigh.

The evening had drained him. Now, as he looked through the carriage window, the darkened streets which flew past as shadows began to merge in his mind with the earlier street. He had avoided it, all their walks had skirted it. But now the Rue Boucher des Deux Boules was creeping like a ghost from the lines of slatted shutters, the fussy ironwork, and high, narrow doors which they passed now, and Jaques felt the events of seventeen years ago leap out at him and chase through the streets after him. Earlier that evening, he had snapped the curtain shut, but the girl had blanched. Duluc had noticed and pretended not to. As they passed Madame Stéphanie's, or the Villa Rouge, as it was known, the coach had lurched and it seemed to him that he had been thrown up and left hanging in midair. He had struggled with the rush of memories, forcing them down under the neutral gaze of the two men opposite. But now they were climbing back, crawling back, reminding him of that night. He could not resist.

All night it had rained. He and Charles had been in the city a week, touring paper factories, one of which they would later buy and, later still, sell for a loss that would ruin Charles. That was the plan: Necessity would drive the man into their arms; but necessity had not proved strong enough for the task. It had ended in the fields above Blanche Pierre on Jersey, and Jaques had foreseen that ending seventeen years before. That was why he had been in Paris with Charles, why he had lied to him, deceived him, ruined him. And when, years later, he had seen the ripped corpse on the slab in Saint Helier, he had known in equal measure that he had been right and that he had failed. Charles had been too proud, and too enterprising. The Lemprières had not been poor for long. As they had toured Paris that week, Jaques guiding his friend through the streets and alleys, the cafés and inns, the gardens, he had felt that he was right to do as he did. The deception was justified. He had believed it then and still believed it now. But the night it had rained changed the nature of Jaques's belief, made it complex and more dark.

They were eating at Puy's when the downpour began and stayed on there through the afternoon, waiting for it to subside. The factory they had seen that morning was perfect for them. They toasted each other with glasses of Gannétin and Condrieu until evening. The rain had not decreased, indeed it was worse when they eventually left. Already they were quite drunk. Charles had stuffed his pockets with virguleus pears from the table and they ate these as they tramped through the streets which were running with the overflow of rainwater from the open gutters. Both were quickly soaked, but still in good spirits as they sang "Tod's Buckler" walking down Rue Saint Martin, Charles clowning and Jaques oddly irritated by this.

They took their bearings at the Rue de Venise and decided to walk west. But the Rue de Venise led only to a churchyard and they retraced their steps to turn right at the next opportunity. Charles was saying something about paper or watermarked paper. Jaques tramped through the downpour with his hat pulled down in unresponsive silence while the rain fell in rods. The street they took led them to a corner of the Marché des Innocents where uniformed terraces stretched away to the south and west, shuttered against the weather. The square was deserted and rain curtained the far corner. Sight of the flat expanse of black cobbles and desultory mud pools sobered Charles and they marched across in silence.

At the far corner, Jaques looked back at the dismal square, then turned to Charles and pointed back at their route. Both peered into the rain. There was an indistinct outline that might have been a man, thirty or forty yards behind them. In the dark and the wet it might have been any kind of thing. Charles thought they should find the river and orientate themselves by that. They began to thread a path through the maze of narrow streets and alleys below the market square. A drinking shop claimed them in Rue de Déchangeur. Blowing on cups of hot wine, the two of them sat there in contented silence while their clothes dripped on the planked floor. That was when, too late, Charles told him of the man who had followed them from Rue Saint Martin, his decision prompted suddenly by the same man's appearance across the crowd from them, there in the tavern.

He was soaked like themselves, a tall man with a dark, oval face. Jaques rose unsteadily to gain a better view. The man was well dressed, even with his clothes bedraggled, sitting alone at a table in the corner. He was staring up at nothing in particular. His manufactured ease had the opposite effect on Jaques, who stamped out of the room to the jakes with his mind racing. There were any number of possibilities. Charles might have been mistaken, but Le Mara's warning about "the Indian" was ringing in his ears. The Nawab's man was coming for them, so the intelligence went, and Jaques was burdened with Charles, who could be told nothing. A narrow corridor led to the outhouse, with a door off the passage to a kitchen. A fat woman began to squeeze past him carrying a steaming dish of leeks high above her head, but she had forgotten something and ducked back into the kitchen. Jaques moved back into the corridor but the Indian was waiting for him at the other end. Jaques froze, all his doubts suddenly resolved. The Indian was moving toward him. Jaques could not think, glued there, but then the fat woman backed out of the kitchen once again, blocking the passage between them. His mind worked again, and he moved up to the woman, who advanced with a pile of dishes stacked precariously in her hands. The Indian was confused. The woman was forcing him back out of the corridor and he could not get to his man. As the corridor became the tavern, Jaques edged sideways to keep the woman between them and saw the hilt of a knife in the Indian's hand. But now he was in the crowded room, and he grabbed Charles by the elbow, pulling him up and propelling him toward the door and the street beyond it.

The two of them crashed into the street, Jaques with his visions of a cold tickle in the ribs, blood running down the corridor, and the rain was still coming down, Charles still mumbling about the river, drunker than Jaques had allowed for. Should have left him, he thought then; and would think the same again much later, and with better reason. They made a stumbling run down the street and took the corner as the tavern door opened again behind them. The houses were battened down and lightless as Jaques pulled Charles along by the collar. Jaques saw quick ugly movements, a quick movement in the street. Another corner, and a glance over his shoulder. The Indian was still there, loping around the last corner as they ran into Rue Boucher des Deux Boules. And there was their refuge, lights blazing behind the blood-red curtains: Villa Rouge. Charles was talking disjointedly about a boat down the river, he would buy a boat and carry it to the river. Jaques hammered on the door as the Indian came into view, saw them at the door, and broke into a run. But he would not reach them. The door was opened by a woman of forty or fifty dressed in lilac who would have closed it again at the sight of them but Jaques was already pressing coins into her hands and they were inside, bent over, panting in the entrance hall, dripping on its tiled floor. The woman offered them her hand, she was Madame Stéphanie and she welcomed them to her establishment. Jaques realized that their refuge was a brothel.

In his later consideration, Jaques would think of Charles in the hours that followed as an escaped detail, a tiny area of neglect in the wider canvas, which would grow to overwhelm all the other elements, like missing one's own name in a list of other, unknown names and signing the order blind. The Madame spoke in an exaggerated manner and asked them both to sign a visitors' book. All her gestures were extravagant. For the moment, Jaques was only glad that Charles was too drunk to require explanations. Already he had drifted into the long salon beyond the hall where two fires burnt briskly and a limp hand pulled him down onto one of the sofas. Jaques paid the Madame some more money. Le Mara, Vaucanson, and their men were a tantalizing few streets away. The Indian would be waiting somewhere outside, out of sight. Jaques spoke quickly to Madame Stéphanie, telling her a nonsense about practical jokes, lost in the streets, and worried friends; the essential point, a messenger. It could be done and Jaques concealed the relief which flooded through him. The Indian had missed his best chance in the corridor, and he had allowed them too long a leash in the streets. Now his own patience would work against him. A boy was fetched. He would use the rooftops which straggled away almost to the ground at the back of the house. No one would see him, no, he shook his head at the suggestion. The message was scrawled quickly and the boy left. Jaques moved through to the salon to wait, feeling that the evening's events were slowing and turning in his favor.

An hour or two hours later, Madame Stéphanie ushered in a short, thickset man, and Jaques knew that the episode was concluded. It was Vaucanson. The message had been received. The Indian had been caught somewhere in the streets outside and was safe in Vaucanson's custody. Already the man had a design on his captive. The Nawab would be repaid in his own coin. Vaucanson left then, and Jaques walked back into the salon to take a glass of wine. The girls and their clients were engaged in low, halting talk, a soothing sound as he sipped at the liquor, with his back to the fire. Charles, whom he had last glimpsed entwined in the thin arms of the establishment, was nowhere to be seen. Jaques finished his wine and asked one of the girls if she had seen him. She had not, but another called over that he was with "the little Contessa." They had ascended to the privacy of the first floor some half an hour earlier.

Jaques climbed the stairs and opened doors, until at the end of the passage he came to a room in which a young woman with a sour expression on her face was sitting up in the center of a large iron bed. Jaques noted her hair which was thick and black and fell in tresses over her shoulders. Charles lay beside her, mostly undressed, quite unconscious. The woman was naked and did not trouble to cover herself as he stood in the doorway. Details, small details.

The next morning brought nausea and a shivering fever to Charles who accepted them as his lot and sat in bed as small islands of memory floated past him in a sea of rain and drink. He remembered the streets and the tavern, scenes from the brothel, a woman's face. He swore Jaques to silence on the whole matter. They had departed for their return to Jersey some days later and neither of them had given that part of their adventure another thought until almost a year later when Charles stood in Jaques's doorway, holding a letter from Paris, stammering that the woman had been got with child that night, the night it had rained. Charles had written his true name in the register in the brothel, another detail. Now the woman wanted money for her baby girl. Jaques stood there in a rage that was all his own, telling his friend to ignore the demand, she would assume from the silence that his name was false.

"Send it back unopened" were his words. But Charles, in his obstinate decency, had sent the money. And more money. Every month without fail, his payments would be sent "Villa Rouge" in the Rue Boucher des Deux Boules, a paper trail of payments and receipts leading back and forth between Paris and Jersey. And that, of course, was how Casterleigh had found the girl, seventeen years later, a whore like her mother in the same establishment. No more than a child, older than them all. Now Jaques was looking at the same girl seated opposite him inside the coach, no longer a child, almost a woman.

Juliette gazed out of the window as the streets sped by and the low clouds which had lowered overhead all day and were now invisible in the dark sky delivered at last their promise of rain.

It was still raining the next morning when the two of them watched

177

their belongings being loaded onto the coach which would take them out of the city. They climbed in and Juliette began settling herself for the long journey. Her canvas bag lay beside her on the seat. Jaques sat in silence opposite. When the coach moved off, she thought of the last time she had made this journey. Then, it had been the Viscount. Rain turned the city gray and the hawkers on Pont Neuf huddled for shelter. Paris slipped away under the wheels of the coach until it was only something at their backs, buried in the outlying gray-green sward of their thoughts. The downpour attended their jolting progress through small towns and staging posts, uncomfortable nights in unfamiliar beds, and at the last, when the boat from Calais was rolling in the swell and its captain looking up at a sky that told him snow, Paris was a limping memory that had fallen back irretrievably, crippled in the forethought of its ashes.

Their crossing was a slow, unsettled affair. The wind blew in gusts, and the crew were sent scrambling to tack or slacken sail according to its caprices. Juliette, who had not felt sick on the Saint Malo pacquet, felt sick now. Jaques fed her something sweet and treacly from a dark brown bottle, and within the hour her nausea had vanished. The choppy little waves looked to her like polished glass, jagged and moving, of course, but the movements came as a series of jolts, quick as lightning one after the other. The yaw of the boat was strange too. If she concentrated on the horizon, a dark strip far off somewhere, the movement could disappear altogether. Or if she shifted her weight from foot to foot with its rhythm, the rolling seemed to grow more and more extreme. With a little effort she felt it would be possible to roll the boat over in a complete revolution, and perhaps it could approach the shore in this manner, sideways on, rolling over and over in the water like a tree trunk. The sky had a purple tinge. The sun was hidden somewhere in the low clouds, but Juliette found that by electing a particular part of the cloud cover, her eye could gather the dispersed light in a pale disk, not the sun but like it. Or even two of them, which hung like huge eyeglasses in the sky. Her face felt cold and prickly as she looked up at her creation and thought of their owner looming into view behind them like a hesitant giant, just the head. Then she was sick. It was extraordinary stuff. Then she passed out.

Again. No. Someone was shoving her. Jaques. He was shaking her by the arm, waking her. Her mouth was foul and she was shivering. The legs of other passengers were walking around them. Juliette rose unsteadily and saw jetties, a low line of buildings with men walking about carrying things, and a steep hill, almost a cliff. The sky was still gray and the face she had seen pushing its vague features down on her out of the clouds was gone, though now she put the name to it as Jaques guided her to the gangplank and put her hand on the rail. She was outside all this, looking down on it like the young face in the sky. Her bag. On the quay, a line of men were carrying sacks and loading them onto a cart. Beside the cart a black coach was waiting. Beside the coach stood the Viscount.

Roads, tracks, drovers' paths, turnpikes, straining climbs and gentle descents, two freezing nights in rooms closed up for the winter months, a flurry of snow and all the miles between Dover and their destination, which she did not know. Jaques was gone, by horse to London, their baggage by coach. Not London then, she deduced. The Viscount eyed her in silence. His inquiry as to her time in Paris was hours ago. He told her nothing. Paris was an old dream. The miles dragged by and it was almost dark. Their progress slowed further, the snow lay thicker, and the horses pulled the coach at a snail's pace. In places the snow had drifted and they would stop altogether before a path was found, then continue on through the still night.

Juliette was quiet with her thoughts. The Viscount's legs were stretched out and he shifted position from time to time as though the state of rest was alien to him. He was part of the interior too. Paris was still tagged to the journey and Casterleigh was part of that too: the same silent presence who had escorted her in this familiar space four years before. The two of them had sat there, components in the same system with their different criteria and goals while the environment flashed past as land-scape. The coach was neutral, a box on wheels, nothing more. But how to account for the overlaying of the earlier scene? She had assigned him his attributes then, his brutishness and air of brooding confinement. They were inmates of the same logic. Their shadows broke out of postures assigned each by the other. Casterleigh's parody of fatherhood was always drifting into other modes, the autocrat, the confidence trickster, the rapist, others also. Could they all be parts of this fatherhood? He seemed physically to swell and grow in the four years of her use as his personality grew new projections like tumors. The lines around "Papa" were floating, new construction was underway, and she waited to see what would emerge. "The Viscount" was something en route. He was exceeding himself. Her understanding of her own role in this process was growing too; she was an agent somewhere within it, as was the boy about whom their late maneuvers seemed to revolve. Her role was changing. Her relations with the Viscount were skewed in some way and Lem-prière, even in his absence, was part of that change. Even ignorant he was their central interest now, a cipher of them both, so that when the Viscount leaned across her and indicated the lights of the house up ahead which marked their destination, she felt sure that he would be somewhere within it.

There were many coaches already in the courtyard when their own drew up. Casterleigh guided her to the door which was opened by a little man in a scarlet suit, and they were ushered along a long corridor to a hall which was filled with people. She was told to amuse herself and concealed her surprise as Casterleigh took the elbow of a fat man she did not recognize to disappear with him through a side door. The guests in the hall were clustered around in a large horseshoe, all watching someone

who announced himself as "Monsieur Henry," a maker of brilliant Philo-
sophical Fireworks. He was apologizing for the inclement weather and
the cancellation of his outdoor show. Nevertheless he would endeavor
not to disappoint.

The crowd were still talking among themselves. Juliette moved
through the crowd to gain a better view.

"First," Monsieur Henry was saying, "I shall show a Vertical Sun and a
North Star which will alternately display the colors of the British Navy."
An appreciative murmur went up. Behind her, Juliette could hear a man
talking about a dog and a rabbit. Someone said "tortoise."

"Allow me to reassure all those of a delicate disposition that there will
be no smoke or scent or powder in my pieces; and above all there will be
no detonations."

"Thank God for that," said a large lady standing a little to Juliette's
left. A cluster of her younger charges giggled into their hands. The piece
went off.

"And now, a Turning Sun with twelve points which form a variety of
colors, particularly lilac and a lively red," continued Monsieur Henry.

"And now, two Saxons, turning different ways—let me draw your
attention to a fine golden spark. . . ."

Juliette grew bored. She looked around at her fellow-guests, many of
them familiar faces from other such occasions, but then she had never
been more than yards from the Viscount's side. She turned her head as the
thought of this slight freedom ran through her mind and saw Casterleigh
as he reentered the hall by the same door. He was walking up to a small
group of young men who were clustered about a gray-haired man with a
bandaged hand. Casterleigh's earlier companion was no longer in evidence. There were eight or nine of them, all engaged in an animated
discussion. She had a clear view of three only: the man with the bandaged
hand, a young earnest-looking type who was waving his hands, and one a
little older, three or four years, dressed all in black with well-made
features. This last turned at the Viscount's approach and extended his
hand. The Viscount did not look over. He joined the discussion which
went on for a minute or two before it seemed a resolution was reached.
The whole group moved toward the side door which was opened to
reveal, she thought, a servingman holding a bundle of torches in both
arms. Each of the group were taking one as they passed him, then the
door was closed once more.

Few of the guests noticed, or paid their departure any mind. Most were
still held by Monsieur Henry, whose lackluster pyrotechnics had de-
veloped their own forward momentum. A double catherine wheel was
being set off. Juliette moved away through the individual spectators who
were reuniting in little cliques. A threadbare hour was passed in gossip
with women half-familiar to her from past introductions. She was avoiding the eye of a snub-nosed young man when a tap on her shoulder
brought her up short.

"Yes?" The servingman had been sent across and over his shoulder she saw the tall figure of the Viscount once more, beckoning her over. He was red-faced from the cold.

"Come, we leave now. Hurry," he said as she drew near. His boots were muddy. She followed him out of the hall and into the corridor where the rest of the search party were carrying something as though they were pallbearers. It was five or six feet long and wrapped in their cloaks. They were straining under the weight. Juliette walked quickly toward them, in step with the Viscount. She thought of the ones who had frozen in the streets each winter and were carted off like logs on the municipal wagon the next morning. As they walked past, she saw grim expressions on the bearers' faces. They were unused to such work, and their cloaks did not quite cover the load.

"This way," the Viscount directed her. Once outside, they walked between the carriages to their own. Casterleigh held the door as she mounted the step. A figure was already sitting inside, waiting for them. It was the fat man she had seen earlier talking with the Viscount, the one with whom he had first disappeared.

"Well?" asked the man as the coach left the courtyard. The Viscount nodded.

"And the boy?" Lemprière. Juliette felt her fingernails dig into the palms of her hands.

"No trace."

"This is no night for walking. The cold creeps into you, you hardly notice—"

"If he lives or dies is not my concern," the Viscount said shortly.

"The leader would not—"

"Not my concern," Casterleigh repeated, but in harsher tones. The coach moved off. Juliette kept her face averted, her cheek pressed against the glass. The coach's rough movement could not keep her awake, not even when it gathered speed and carried her dreaming, speeding through the white fields, their surroundings. The light was almost blue, coming off the snow. She was racing along at the coach's side with long, shallow leaps. It was easy to keep up. There were low fences which she took cleanly, then more and more of them. There was nothing but snow as far as she could see and she could see as far as she wished. Then the snow began to break up with little jagged crevices appearing before her, sometimes a split second before she was about to land and leap once more. They grew more and more frequent, but the road was unaffected and the coach was tearing along. She wanted to look down into the crevices, but she was falling behind. The coach was pulling ahead of her. She was calling out to the driver to slow down, dim cries, then to the occupants of the coach. She could not see them, but they were in there, watching as her progress became more desperate. She tried to hammer on the sides of the coach, then looked inside but saw only the monotone of the Dover skies and the luminous disks she had hung there like huge lenses, then came the face behind them. It swooped down at her, it was pressed right against her, and the hammering was deafening like a hand slamming against the side of her head, Lemprière's angular face with its owlish glasses, his mouth open like a fish's behind the glass, moving, someone shouting, "No! Stop!" Suddenly she was awake, his face falling away into the night. It was not a dream. The shouting was her own. As the coach sped away, she looked at the Viscount whose face registered the effect of her outburst as astonishment, then rage. Papa was gone, ripped away like a cloth mask. Somewhere behind her on the freezing road she imagined Lemprière, standing there alone as the coachlights disappeared into the darkness, taking her away from him. She looked back at the Viscount, then out into the night. She was between them now, and she realized that she too was alone.

. . .

An hour, perhaps two had passed. The coachlights had faded to points and been lost in the gloom. Lemprière had given up walking. He had stopped shivering. Sitting by the side of the road, he could hardly be bothered to turn his head at the faint noise rising behind him. He had walked and found nothing but the road and the surrounding darkness. And the snow. The noise was a little louder. It would be a coach. A coach, he thought. The cold was a dull ache in his bones. His face was numb, his head lolling. A coach, no doubt now. His legs were stiff and heavy. There it was, in front of him. It had halted. People getting out. Septimus. Asking, "What was he doing here?" Something on top. Blue. Hello? He should answer at least. Being carried. Lydia's lap. When he woke up.

"He is asleep," said Lydia.

"Unconscious," said Septimus.

"Five-to-one his toes are black." Warburton-Burleigh was tugging at his boots. The coach hit a pothole concealed beneath the snow and they all jumped in their seats as something thudded loudly against the roof. Lydia looked up and blanched.

"Could not Casterleigh have taken her?" she asked. "After all, he was the first to leave."

"We should have bound her faceup," said the Pug. The coach jolted again, and again there was a harsh thud.

"Horrible!" said Lydia, covering her ears to shut out the sound. Lemprière's head lolled in her lap. The other three were quiet. The coach continued on over the rough London road with the woman's body lashed to the roof. Every time the coach rode a bump, the head jerked and the stump of metal from its mouth banged on the roof of the coach. Collapsed in the interior, Lemprière dreamed of women leaping through the fields over streams of burning gold. The coach went on through the fields of ice and snow, back toward London.

. . .

" 'Danae, the daughter of Acrisius, King of Argos, by Eurydice. She was confined in a brazen tower by her father, who had been informed by an oracle that his daughter's son would put him to death. . . .' " Septimus's voice, there, standing over his desk. Lemprière knew he was awake and struggled up.

" 'His endeavors to prevent Danae from becoming a mother proved, however, fruitless; and Jupiter, who was enamored of her, introduced himself to her bed by changing himself into a shower of gold.' Hmm, good. Didn't you kill Acrisius at the club that night?" Septimus imitated quoit-throwing. But his friend was still barely awake. Sometime in the night, his own shivering had awoken him. He had risen and written the entry. His sleep was full of strange interruptions.

"How does it end?" Septimus was asking. The inquisition would begin soon. He might have died from the cold.

"Badly," Lemprière managed after a long pause. Septimus was still standing over the desk.

"We looked for you, you know? Search party, torches . . ." He remembered a coach, the road, a thudding noise.

"You found me," Lemprière said.

"No, we found a woman. . . ." Lemprière had let his head fall back into the pillow. Septimus would not be able to see his face. "A dead woman . . ." Lemprière thought, tell him.

"A dead woman?" and before he could catch himself, "How did she . . . I mean . . ."

"Out in the west pasture, more like a bog. Quite horrible. You were miles away." How could he read the entry and not guess? "Miles away," an instruction?

"I became lost, thought I was going back to the house. It was dark."

"You were outside the house to begin with?"

"Yes, of course . . ." Of course, led by fresh footprints in the snow on the lawn, by a glimpse of Septimus. "I thought I saw you, a corridor at the back of the house, a room," Lemprière said.

"Yes," said Septimus.

"On the lawn."

"Yes. I took a turn round the lawn, then went back inside. I was looking for you. You missed the fireworks." Turn round the lawn. Fireworks.

"I tried to go around the house," Lemprière said. The footprints had not come back.

"Shall I take this? You have already signed it." He was holding the entry. Take it, yes, yes, take it away. The lolling eye, the mouth, take them all away.

"If you like," Lemprière said. The footprints had just stopped. Septimus was folding the entry carefully.

"You could have died, you know? From the cold."

"Yes, I know." Lemprière looked over at Septimus who was walking toward the door. "Thank you," he said. Septimus was leaving.

"Alice de Vere's a queer bird, isn't she?" he said.

"An extraordinary woman," replied Lemprière carefully.

"And you missed the Casterleigh girl." This was shouted as he clumped down the stairs. And then, "More fool you!" The front door slammed shut. Exit Septimus, thought Lemprière, *cum mea culpa*, for which my thanks.

In the days that followed, Lemprière wrestled with the letter "D." He sat at his desk disentangling the thirteen Domitii from one another. There were over twenty people called Dionysus. He had distinguished twenty-four so far and had a nagging feeling there was another. The librarian of Atticus was one, Cicero mentioned him, but there was some business about book stealing, also to do with Cicero—the same one? As the references piled up, walking back and forth between his desk and the pile of books on the far side of the room became a tiresome ritual. Accordingly, he opened all the books and arranged them on the floor in a sort of bookcarpet. Gaps were left for his feet when he wished to walk from one part of the room to another. It was a far superior arrangement and eliminated drafts. He remembered the twenty-fifth Dionysus. Lemprière hopped over the Stoics and part of Euripides to confirm the source. "A slave of Cicero's who plundered his master's library of several books, *Cic. Fam.5. ep.10 1.13 ep.77*," he scribbled, that was it. He was rather sick of "Dionysus," all twenty-five of them. He worked on haphazardly. He had forgotten Daedalus had built mechanical men, *automata*. And assisted Pasiphae in her unnatural passion. Everyone knew about the flying; his edition had a small picture of Daedalus and Icarus flapping up toward the sun. Perhaps the flying and the automata had become confused in some way and they were flying machines, not flying men. It was possible, though he would rather believe in the flying men. Flying: an extraordinary idea, really, *whoosh!* Lemprière made a clumsy soaring motion with his arms. Heavy carts rumbled down the cobbled street outside. He had an idea that there was another Dionysus, a twenty-sixth, but it would not come. He returned to the Doberes, Dobunni, and Dochi, peoples of northern Macedonia, of Gloucestershire, and Ethiopia all jammed together in his dictionary; a new geography. Docimus had had too many hot baths.

Through the days and nights that followed, his sleep remained troubled: three hours here, twelve hours there, and all at strange times. The dictionary seemed still to impose its own unfathomable schedule. If he forced himself out of bed, on the dot of seven or eight as he should, he would later find himself staring into space, daydreaming, drifting on other currents. It was at one of these times that he found himself thinking of Alice de Vere, Lady de Vere rather, who Septimus thought was "queer," and he did too, really. "An extraordinary woman." That was good. Had the ring of authority. Pontificating from the mantelpiece: phrases such as "or so one is led to believe," and "If one thing convinces of the truth of the matter, it is this," they would say, "that Lemprière knows more than he says." Alice de Vere, Lady de Vere rather, who Septimus thought was "queer," and he asked, after all. Give me this small thing and you will have all the wealth and power your ancestor enjoyed. More, whatever you wish. Lemprière remembered Peppard's pause: "in perpetuity . . ." The little man would have said more but had stayed his words. "In theory the agreement would go on and on. . . ." Alice de Vere had offered him that theory's practice. He was a Lemprière, he was entitled to a ninth of all the Company. The agreement told him so. Had that been the message his father sought in his long hours in his study? His father had had some business with Mister Chadwick, and that business had involved the agreement. He knew this because Alice de Vere had told him. And she knew because Skewer had told him. The solicitous Skewer. The shyster.

So the Widow had been right, and Lemprière had thought her mad. Peppard should have told him of the agreement's implications, even if they were fanciful. And Skewer. Skewer had lied to him, had deceived his father. Had run to Alice de Vere and sold his knowledge for a pittance.

Lemprière watched the crowds in the street below as he struggled into his coat. He had brushed the worst of the mud off when it had dried. Now it had large mottled areas. His boots followed and he checked his pockets: key, coins, the miniature of his mother, whose presence reminded him of Rosalie; and Lydia asking him about her, and, ghostly memory, the thuds which had reached him even through his exhaustion in the coach. Days ago. Her head banging on the roof. But when he reached the street, his thoughts turned back to Skewer, and Peppard too, but most of all to Skewer. Mister Skewer had extended to him an open invitation, "any problem, however small." Those were his words. As Lemprière entered Southampton Street he reflected on that invitation. He *had* a small problem. It concerned betrayals of confidence and he would take Ewen Skewer up on his offer.

His second journey to the solicitor's office followed the path of the first. Here Septimus had pulled him off a collision course with some dung, the Strand had seen crates of chickens and Warburton-Burleigh's slurs, good-bye, and the continuance of their hurried progress along Fleet Street, up Chancery Lane, a promenade of side steps until the courtyard which he now entered, crossed, and mounted the stairs on the far side. As before, he took them two at a time, but then the parallel shifted and the first schedule ghosted the second, a matter of the minutes which he had earlier spent kicking his heels in the outer office, for as Lemprière approached the door at the top of the staircase, a familiar sound started up. Angry voices. The door opened and he was confronted with the Widow Neagle. She should still be in Skewer's office, the shoe poised above his head, but she was not; the shoe had been replaced though her fury was evident.

"Why are you here? Did I not tell you?" She directed herself at Lemprière. On the other side of the door, Peppard would be settling back into his chair, flustered from the encounter. Skewer would be nursing his head. Lemprière grinned.

"There is nothing amusing, young man," the Widow continued. "I am well aware of the impression given by an elderly woman in a temper. You, on the other hand, are blissfully unaware of the reasons for it, Mister Lemprière. Until you are, keep your own counsel. You have problems enough of your own." Lemprière no longer grinned. The Widow pushed past him and stamped down the stairs. Lemprière was about to knock on the door. He stopped, turned, and hurried back down the stairs. The Widow was crossing the courtyard.

"What problems?" he demanded as her angry words caught up with him. "I was not laughing at your misfortunes. It was Skewer, you see, before—"

"Do not make the mistake of patronizing me, Mister Lemprière." She turned again and would have continued but Lemprière caught her arm.

"I am not patronizing you. I am not laughing at you. I am trying to explain." He had the same sensation as in the coach when they had disbelieved his acquaintance with Juliette. The Widow was looking at him, not in the least intimidated by this outburst. Her eyes were searching his. His hand dropped from her arm.

"You ignored my advice. I told you not to trust Skewer, now if you wish to explain yourself, explain yourself to him." What problems? Lemprière thought.

"You were right," he said quickly.

"Of your affairs, I know only this," the Widow said. "Skewer serves only one master, and you are not he. Nothing he does will benefit you. Now, if you will excuse me—"

"One master?" Lemprière wanted to hear more.

"It is a long story, Mister Lemprière, if you wish to hear it."

"Might I call on you?" Lemprière asked. "This afternoon, perhaps?"

"After your meeting with Mister Skewer? I fear you would not be welcome then."

"Another day, tomorrow?"

"Make a choice, Mister Lemprière, either come now, or do not trouble me again," said the Widow and turned to leave. The tone of her voice left no room for doubt. Skewer's perfidy. One master. She was disappearing through the opening on the far side of the courtyard. Lemprière hung there, strung between curiosity and mild revenge. The Widow was out of sight, only footsteps.

"Wait!" he shouted and ran after her.

. . .

"When they write their history books, my name will burn a hole in the page. Farina!"

Lemprière recognized the ranter as they skirted the crowd in the street outside the inn. He and the Widow sat at a table by the window.

"They have lit the fuse, my friends, not I, not you all. They think of their fat daughters, their fat fortunes, while the blackbirds of Saint Giles gobble the bread from our mouths and the mothers of Spitalfields uncover their infants on the parish step. . . ." The crowd rumbled about him. Lemprière had seen him outside the Craven Arms the night of the Pork Club, brandishing a length of silk, shouting to a smaller mob. This time the crowd was larger. More ill-tempered. The Widow looked away from the window.

"If you hate Skewer so, why do you visit his offices?" Lemprière asked.

"Not hate," answered the Widow, "despise. Skewer is a little man, a nothing, hardly worthy of hate. In any case, Skewer's office holds more than just Skewer."

"He keeps something of yours, a document?" hazarded Lemprière. The Widow smiled and looked down at the table.

"In a manner of speaking," she said. Lemprière waited for her to continue but she added nothing.

"Skewer said that you had lost your husband," he prompted.

"Also that I am mad with grief," the Widow came back at him. She said something else but the crowd had grown noisier, a low roar drowning out her words. ". . . popular story in the taverns. I still hear it from time to time: Neagle's Whale. There was even a ballad. But that was more than twenty years ago." She smiled to herself. "Neagle's Whale. My husband would have appreciated it."

"So he is dead?"

"Oh yes, Skewer told the truth about that. The questions for me are how and why. Skewer might know the answers, though I doubt it. But he knows more than he tells, as do the insurers, and the insurers' lawyers, and my late husband's colleagues, and, most of all, the Company. Perhaps you know more than you tell, Mister Lemprière?"

"I only know what you have told me . . ." he began to explain, but the Widow was smiling, teasing him.

"I married at eighteen and was a widow at twenty-four," she told him. "Alan, my husband, was almost ten years older than I. It hardly mattered. He was one of the youngest captains of an Indiaman ever to take a command. We made a fine couple. He beat off all his competitors, wooed me, won me." The Widow flicked a loose lock of her hair back in a coquettish gesture, then replaced her hand quickly.

"Anyway, we were married, Alan and I, and took a house in Thames Street. I still have it. The next part of the story is Alan's, Commander Neagle's, rather. I have it by his report. His ship sailed in 1763 for Madras, it had been refitted and it was late in the year, but he believed he could catch the tail of the Trades and convinced the Company too. By anyone's account he was an expert sailor, but the voyage ran into all sorts of troubles. He had to put in at Lisbon for repairs—the Blackwall shipwrights had been hurried, you understand—and a squall hit them a few days afterward. All they could do was run before the storm. They were blown east toward the Gates of Hercules, through the Straits of Gibraltar, and into the mouth of the Mediterranean. They had their share of fortune too, though. When the storm passed they found that they had moved safely through the Gates and were sitting in the Sea of Alboran. The lookouts had not seen either coast. It was something of a miracle. Alan gathered the men on deck and told them all of their good fortune, there was a prayer, and then soundings were taken. It should have been a ritual, they were in open seas, after all, but when the readings came back, the whole ship fell silent. They were all but aground. Alan had no charts, but he could not believe it. A second sounding was taken. This time, the starboard side was clear, but the port gave a depth less than the draft of the ship. In other words, they were aground. But they were not. The ship was floating freely. The crew became nervous, peering over the side but seeing nothing. Alan could not understand what was happening. More soundings were taken, but no two were alike. Some of the men began to panic and Alan had stationed his officers around the whole of the ship when the mystery suddenly resolved itself. There was a low rushing sound to port, and great whorls began to appear in the water. Then the same on the starboard side. A huge spout of water gushed up, soaking everyone aft of the mainmast, and almost as one, a school of whales surfaced all about the ship. Ten or fifteen of them at the least and they were huge, more than half the length of the vessel. The soundings had been taken off their backs. For a moment, the ship was silent, then everyone cheered, although the danger was hardly over. But the whales circled the ship for a minute or two, then swam off close to the surface, heading east. The ship was safe." The Widow peered across the table at Lemprière.

"Alan returned with his ship and cargo intact the following year. When he told me the story of the whales I was only filled with relief. But it is a strange story and for a number of reasons. Why did the whales not damage the ship, or even sink it?" Lemprière shook his head.

"I had no idea there *were* whales in the Mediterranean," he said.

"Exactly!" the Widow exclaimed. "There are very few, or so it was thought. But the most extraordinary thing was the direction the whales took when they left the ship. Whales do not swim without purpose, and these whales swam east. Away from the opening of the Mediterranean, toward Arabia."

"Arabia, and then where?" But the Widow waved the question away.

"My husband had made sketches showing the fins and flukes, even some notes on how they swam. He showed these to friends of his in the whaling fleets, but he was no draftsman and they all identified them differently until he mentioned the size, close to one hundred feet. Then they were unanimous: The beasts were blue whales, the greatest of all the whales. But when he was asked where he had seen these leviathans, they scoffed. There were no blue whales in the western Mediterranean, and no whales at all to the east. You see, there was nothing for them to eat. The nearest feeding grounds were in the northern Indian Ocean, and there was no route from there, unless they could somehow cross the deserts of Egypt. My husband became the butt of a number of jokes, a new kind of whale was dubbed Neagle's Whale. It was supposed to have legs. But Alan knew what he had seen and, more to the point, what it meant. His request to the Court of Directors to investigate further was turned down flat, and when he persisted he was warned off. We discovered an old account of a voyage which convinced us we were correct, the same place, the same whales. A Company ship had made the sighting almost a century and a half ago."

"But what *did* it mean?" Lemprière asked. "Where were the whales going?" The Widow said something in reply, but a roar from the crowd outside drowned her out again.

". . . the Company's charter gives them the monopoly of the route, you see. Anyone can trade with the Indies provided they do not travel by the tip of Africa. So long as there is only the single route, the Company's trade is safe." The Widow paused, and realized that Lemprière had not heard. "The Indies," she said. "The whales were heading east to the Indian Ocean, to their feeding ground. They had discovered a second route to the Indies, probably through the Red Sea. That is why the Company had to silence my husband."

Lemprière sat back, trying to imagine schools of whales passing unseen through uncharted channels between the Mediterranean and the Red Sea.

"It is an unlikely enough story, I will own," said the Widow. "But not so impossible as it appears, and it does not end there."

Abruptly, the table was thrown into shadow. The crowd had swelled to fill the street until the backs of the men on its periphery were pressed right up against the window.

"Does not end there?" Lemprière prompted, but the Widow was looking out of the window. The crowd was growing rowdier. Farina's voice was only just audible to them inside the tavern.

". . . this is for the Spitalfield's weavers. . . ." Even above the crowd, a loud tearing sound could be heard and a deafening cheer went up. ". . . and this for the woolpackers who have buried their skills with their children. . . ." Another tearing sound, and this time the cheer was louder, angrier.

"We shall continue our talk elsewhere," the Widow spoke quickly to Lemprière. "Come." He hesitated, bewildered by the turn of events. She spoke sharply. "Hurry!" He rose and the Widow pulled him to the door where the full extent of their situation was revealed.

The crowd, which earlier had consisted of two dozen spectators, now numbered two hundred or more, rough customers too, it seemed to Lemprière as he was pulled along the front of the tavern by the Widow, squeezing past the men's backs. Farina was visible, raised up at their center, standing on something. At his side, Lemprière noticed, a small balding man who was referred to from time to time—"Give me the figures, Stoltz!" or "True or not, Stoltz?"—at which the man would reply or nod. Stoltz. His demeanor rendered him almost invisible beside Farina, who now held a length of red silk. Stoltz was doing something to it, kneeling?

"This way!" The Widow yanked his arm, and he edged past more of the men who now raised a shout, then another and another. He was deafened and the mob was punching the air. Farina was standing with his head thrown back, the silk tight in his hands, the mob jostling one another, growing more frantic, and flames were licking up the cloth when Farina ripped it in two and he was standing there with his head bent back, arms outstretched, in each hand suddenly the silk went up, two burning banners framing him like an unholy avenging angel. The mob's noise seemed to go on and on. "Indian spies!" Then another voice. "Spies! Indian spies!" The silk was ash. The Widow shoved burly journeymen out of their way. The call went around the mob and Farina looked down. A punch was thrown, then another.

"Farina!" A voice like gravel stamped its authority over all the noise of the mob. A man was standing on the far side of the crowd, his stick raised and pointed unwaveringly at the ranter. His eyes were bandaged. A man had gone down and was being kicked.

"Push!" the Widow shouted back at Lemprière.

"No!" Farina yelled at the mob but the fight spread through them like the flames up the silk.

"Indian spies!" The call to violence went up as the blind man pointed and shouted once again. It was too late, the brawl was all about Lemprière, who ducked, tripped, fell, then felt a hand like steel close around his wrist and pull him along the ground. Not the Widow's; a broad-brimmed hat, cloak. He was on the edge of the crowd. The Widow was turning. She had seen him, was hauling him up, and when he looked around for his rescuer, the man had gone. All he had seen was the hat and cloak. And the hand, which was tanned and brown. A sailor, thought Lemprière.

"Come," said the Widow, then pulled him by the arm and he stumbled after her. Behind them both, the mob's ferocity was waning. There were men lying on the ground. The blind man shouted "Farina!" once more and his stick still pointed to the center of the mob. But Farina had disappeared.

"Hurry now." The Widow was talking breathlessly over her shoulder. "Sir John will call the militia and we have no wish to encounter those ruffians." Lemprière thought he had hurt his knee and matched the Widow's brisk stride with a lopsided canter down the street, offering silent thanks to his mysterious rescuer. There was something familiar about the hat. His coat had sustained a tear about the pocket which he picked at as they entered Shoe Lane, then turned into Stonecutter Lane. He was still shaken, half-expecting broad-shouldered rioters to appear from nowhere and set about him. At the end of the lane he glanced back anxiously but saw only harmless pedestrians, a crowd of children, behind them two basket-women, farther back a slighter figure, a hat which he recognized, its broad brim.

"Damn!" the Widow pulled him about. "Look there." She pointed, and through the bustle of Fleet Market Lemprière could see a squad of redcoats pushing through the crush. He looked back once more, saw the children still, the two women, but the cloaked and hatted figure had disappeared. The street was too long for him to have run back along its length, but before he could reflect further on this second disappearance, the two of them were skirting the marketplace, working their way south and east by way of Ludgate. Another squad, fifteen or twenty of them with pikes and muskets, confronted them in Thames Street. They were fifty yards away and moving toward the two of them. Lemprière moved as though to turn back, but the Widow moved forward more purposefully, only twenty yards' distance from the red-coated thugs who swaggered toward them, and Lemprière shrank against the wall, offering silent prayers to the gods of conciliation and calm.

"Here," said the Widow as she removed a key from her pocket, then turned into the nearest doorway. The key turned, the door opened, and they were safe inside as it slammed shut behind them.

"This is my home," she said. "Welcome. Perhaps you should rest here awhile."

"Yes," said Lemprière.

"And then you must meet the professors."

Some minutes later they sat in a drawing room on the first floor of the house. The furnishings were lavish, the rooms large and airy.

"My husband set sail the following year in 1766," the Widow was saying. "We had planned our course of action with care." Lemprière sipped tea from a china cup. "My husband would take the usual route as far as the Straits of Gibraltar but then, instead of sailing down the west coast of Africa, he would return to the Mediterranean—"

"And find the passage," Lemprière finished the sentence.

"Exactly. And if a school of whales could pass through it, then so could a fully laden Indiaman. He would emerge in the Indian Ocean months in advance of all expectation. The Company's monopoly would be at an end."

"And he found the passage?"

"Wait. I was left in London; I too had a part in all this. If the route were established, it would have to be safeguarded. If one man could find it out, so could another. Accordingly, I was entrusted with my husband's sketches, charts, all manner of speculations. They were bundled up and sealed, only our lawyer was to see them, and he only when a firm undertaking of secrecy was given. Only then would he begin to draw up the patents, charters, and other documents; in short, put the force of law behind my husband's claim. But we had great difficulty in persuading any lawyer to take our case.

"It was a complex business, legally speaking, as you might imagine. I must have sat in a hundred offices, every practitioner in London had an idea of what we were about. Some scoffed, some showed polite disinterest, most simply refused the commission there and then. Those few who agreed to accept the work invariably returned to me within days with excuses, prevarications, and refusals. As soon as they learned that their adversary in the courts would be the Company, they ran for shelter with their tails between their legs. I was at my wits' end. For all I knew, my husband was plowing up and down the Mediterranean, charting the last of the great trade routes, and I could not even find a lawyer. That was when I visited Chadwick and Soames, your own family's solicitors."

"And they took the case?"

"No, they did not. But they referred me to one of their juniors. He had left the firm to practice on his own some months before."

"Mister Skewer!" Lemprière burst out. The Widow looked at him in surprise.

"What an absurd notion," she said. "Skewer was still a clerk for Mister Chadwick, and was to remain so for another twenty years. No, no. Hardly Skewer. The young man Chadwick recommended was a rising star, very quick, very bright. And he was someone I knew from another time, before my marriage to Alan."

"Why did you not go to this man before?" Lemprière asked.

"Another long story," said the Widow quietly. "Perhaps I knew already that the business would turn against us. Anyway, I went to him, and when I had told him the story, he agreed to take the case. I left the sealed papers with him and went home. It had been three months since Alan's ship had sailed, three months of disappointment and failure, but now at last, I felt we might achieve something. In truth, it was still a dream. Alan was always an ambitious man, there was no secret to that. For me, the lawyer was a triumph. By the same time the next day, all those dreams, all the things we wanted, and everything I held most dear would be lost, ruined, drowned, dead. . . ." Her words just stopped. Lemprière watched as she poured more tea into both their cups. Her own rattled against the saucer as she picked it up.

"It began the following morning. The lawyer who only the day before had agreed to act for us arrived at my door. He had spent the night reading my husband's papers and his message was brief. He told me he would not take up our cause. But I knew him from before, we were more than acquaintances." The Widow twisted the ring on her finger, reminding Lemprière of Lady de Vere, the same gesture.

"There are bargains struck which should not be struck, but they must be done, do you understand me? And I knew this man from before my marriage. He had courted me. He still wanted me, you see. He would not take what I offered, but I would have given it had he required that. He knew that, and I knew he knew. It was our contract. And it was for my husband. . . ." The Widow gave a short bitter laugh.

"It is not so terrible," Lemprière said.

"No," said the Widow, "not so terrible, save that I knew he wanted me, that he was too much the gentleman to take what he wanted. Not so terrible, except that on that day, on the other side of the world—how could I know?—my husband was already dead, and all his men with him. Really not so terrible, except that the lawyer took up our cause when it was already lost and they ruined him, branded my husband a common blackmailer, his wife a madwoman or the shyster's whore. Alan was dead, floating in the seas off Ankara, and I was as you find me, provided for by the Company, not even worthy of their enmity it seems, though I would destroy them in a second had I the chance. It is," she chose her words with care, "an appropriate humiliation."

"And the lawyer," Lemprière said. "What became of him?"

"Surely you know," the Widow said softly. Lemprière shook his head. "The lawyer was George Peppard," she said.

A maid was hovering, waiting to light the lamps. Lemprière saw Peppard's face in the dingy room on Blue Anchor Lane and remembered how his voice had tightened at a mention of the Company. He looked at the Widow, his mind placing Peppard at her side, her courtier, perhaps her husband's usurper, but the husband was drowned, betrayed, and left for the fishes. That was what she was thinking. Dead men. Drowned men drifting in the slow currents of the ocean, their limbs waving slowly back and forth as they fell, and lay there riddled with arrow-worm and their mourners' dreams. They tumbled down slowly. Far above, the abandoned flotsam gathered to form a chaotic raft. The three-master was splintered planks and shredded canvas all snarled together in the rag-ends of the rigging as it lurched over the wave tops far above the dead sailors, a seaborne Ceraton calling the deep-sea sleepers to a second prayer. The basins shifted and the waters moved. Slight twitches in the still water disturbed the dead men's creeping progress as the abyssal waters began their slow convection. The bodies rose.

The lamps burned a little higher, bringing the ghosts back in other forms. The maid left the room, and Lemprière watched her until the door was closed.

"They never found the wreckage," the Widow was telling him. "Not the slightest trace. And remember, Alan had resolved to sail into the Mediterranean. Arakan is on the Indian coast. Either the ship was lost elsewhere, or—"

"Or he found the Mediterranean passage," said Lemprière.

"Yes, and that would have been the knowledge we needed, which the Company feared most of all. I knew they had lied to me, they had destroyed him somehow. They knew much more than they said, but like a fool I rushed them head on. I was mad with the lies and the half-truths, and Alan's death too. George begged me to stop, but I would not. Without Alan it was hopeless. Only he knew the facts of the matter and he was drowned. They ridiculed us in the courtroom and broke George Peppard with their slanders. I made him do it. . . . He stood up in court and spoke of whales and charters, secret waterways. Without Alan it was nonsense."

Lemprière remembered Septimus's words outside Skewer's office. Maritime insurance, a fraud of some sort. He asked the Widow if it were true.

"That was after the case. George had evidence of some sort to support it. He used it to negotiate a settlement, out of court, you understand. I know very little of what went on, but that too blew up in his face. The Company accused him and my husband of blackmail. I think it is that slur above everything else which has driven me all these years. My husband is gone, but I will revisit his death on the Company and its agents. It might seem that something so vast is beyond redress. Perhaps so, and yet for the last twenty years I have tried to prove nothing else. Come, I will show you."

The Widow stood up then and ushered Lemprière to the door. A corridor led to a room at the rear of the house where the noise from the street was replaced by the fainter shouts of the watermen on the Thames a hundred yards away. Already, it was dark.

"Look," the Widow indicated along bulging shelves which lined the room and which groaned under the weight of ledgers, account books, trial transcripts, atlases, old broadsheets, histories both official and un-official.

"The evidence," she said. "Almost every complaint or attack ever made against the Company has its place somewhere here. Every corruption, vice, every crime is chronicled and noted, including that against my husband." She fingered a thick bundle of yellowing papers. "The Neagle case," she said. Lemprière looked at the evidence, in awe at the Widow's industry. The room was one vast indictment.

"Do you know of a writer called Asiaticus?" he asked her. The Widow looked at him in surprise.

"But of course. Though your own knowledge puzzles me. How do *you* know of him?" Lemprière told of his discovery of the first pamphlet among his father's papers, and the gift of the second made to him by Lady de Vere. He mentioned the agreement only in passing.

"You do not, by any chance, have the fourth pamphlet?" the Widow inquired eagerly. Lemprière shook his head. "A pity. I have the first three. They are full of fine sentiments, but the evidence is lacking. The fourth pamphlet was supposed to reveal everything, but I have never discovered a copy. I rather doubt it was printed at all."

"Perhaps it was all just bluster," Lemprière hazarded. "He might have had nothing to tell."

"Perhaps," the Widow agreed, "but I incline to the opposite view. He gives the impression of knowing more than he tells. There is a threatening tone, damaging revelations are promised. I rather like the man."

"Who was he?" Lemprière asked.

"It is still a mystery," the Widow said. "For obvious reasons he kept his identity hidden at the time. The first pamphlet appeared some time after Buckingham's return from La Rochelle, late in 1628 or early in the following year. The other two followed a few months later, then nothing. Asiaticus, whoever he was, went to ground and never came out again."

"Not under that name, anyway," Lemprière ventured and the Widow nodded.

"Anything might have befallen him," she said, "as it might anyone who impinges on the Company's interest." She was looking at him. Lemprière stood there surrounded by shelves groaning under catalogs of abuse and recrimination, all that remained of thousands of victims. Anyone at all. The Widow's gaze was still fixed upon him, then she spoke again.

"I know a little of your own inquiries," she said. Lemprière looked back at her. "Your affairs are your own," she added quickly, "but whatever you unearth, it will not be enough, not enough to get what you desire. I wish to know no more, but when you reach that point, come back to me, Mister Lemprière." She gestured at the shelves. "I will tell you what you need. Everything you need to know is here somewhere. Remember the offer." For the second time that day, the Widow recalled Alice de Vere to Lemprière's thoughts. "All the wealth you can imagine. . . ." was the promise held out a week before in the crumbling mansion. Now, "Everything you need to know. . . ." He let the silence gather as the two women and their offers competed in his thoughts and he wavered like Paris with the golden apple; unimaginable wealth, unguessable knowledge, and beside them both was a shimmering third, not yet, a little longer and farther away, disappearing into the night.

The Widow was looking out of the window. He could see her face reflected in the glass. She turned and tapped him lightly on the arm, breaking his reverie.

"Keep your counsel, John Lemprière," she said. "Come, meet the professors before you leave." She had taken his arm. "They rarely have the chance to speak with a man of learning." Lemprière demurred at the description, then suffered himself to be led out of the study and up a tight staircase which creaked under their weight. As they reached a door at the top, a loud, staggered thud was heard from within and a babble of voices started up in dispute.

"Ah," said the Widow. Lemprière looked askance. "They are playing Jump or Die," she said, then opened the door to reveal three gray-bearded men hunched over a large table which seemed to be covered with a large stylized chart.

"Mister John Lemprière," she announced to them as they rose from their seats, then, "Professors Ledwitch, Chegwyn, and Linebarger," in turn, and pleasantries were exchanged.

"We were just beginning a game of Jump or Die," said Ledwitch to Lemprière. "If you would care to join us?" Lemprière declined politely. He looked down at the chart which was divided into hundreds of differently colored squares, bright reds, blues, and mauves near the edge of the design, less distinguishable colors, khakis, olives, and browns, near to its center. At the very center was the plan of a walled city, and at the center of the city was a winged man. Lemprière peered curiously at the figure.

"The flying man," explained Linebarger. "He is the point of the game. Every player is trying to become the flying man."

"And how is that done?" asked Lemprière. He scrutinized the chart more closely and noticed that every square had a short message scrawled in tight script upon it; the messages grew less legible the nearer they were to the center, especially on the dull-colored squares, until, up against the walls of the city, they were barely visible at all.

Professor Chegwyn turned to him. "Throws of the dice move each player from square to square," he said. "When you land on one the instructions are self-evident. For instance, if I throw a two I shall land here." He pointed to a bright yellow square and peered at the writing upon it. "Here, I would have to form a tactical alliance with the Duc de Guise. A six," he looked again, "puts me in charge of resistance at Montauban in July of 1621. Naturally, I am close to being the Duc de Rohan at this point, which gives me immunity from forced abjuration for three throws."

"Very useful if you become La Tremouille at La Rochelle in 1628," added Ledwitch.

"Do you follow?" Linebarger chipped in. But Chegwyn threw a five and the other two groaned. All three clambered onto their chairs, then jumped simultaneously to the floor, making an impressive thud.

"I landed in the middle of the Saint Bartholomew's Day Massacre," said Chegwyn, pointing to a murky square.

"It means the game must begin again," added Ledwitch.

"La Rochelle?" said Lemprière.

"This." Linebarger indicated the walled city at the center of the game. "This is La Rochelle. It is under siege. All these brightly colored squares are what we term the *Politics*, the drabber ones are the events of the siege itself, where matters grow a little confused. The city is, well, it is the city. And the Flying Man at its center is, of course, the Flying Man."

"You have to get through the politics to get to the siege," said Ledwitch.

"And through the siege to get to the city," said Chegwyn.

"And in the city is the, er, the Flying Man," proclaimed Linebarger.

"I see," said Lemprière. Ledwitch threw a four. "Bras de Fer!" said the other two and Ledwitch raised one of his arms in the air.

"He has become Monsieur La None shortly after being fitted with an artificial limb by the silversmith, Vaucanson," explained Linebarger. "It is one of the more oblique incidents."

Lemprière watched the game with a keen interest, which quickly waned. The game had been restarted twice and none of the players had emerged from the *Politics* when he asked what happened if a player should reach the city.

"He must defend it with his life, we think," said Professor Chegwyn.

"Are you not sure?"

"It is a formidably difficult game," said Chegwyn. "So far, we have not managed to reach the city."

"So the Flying Man," Lemprière pointed to the winged figure at the very center of the city, "is really irrelevant." This provoked a clamor from the professors. The Widow had taken a seat to one side and refused to participate in the debate.

"The Flying Man is everything," protested Ledwitch.

"Of course, he is relevant, he is the only survivor," explained Linebarger. "Everyone else either jumped or died; either way they died, except the Flying Man."

"You are saying that at the end of the siege, there was a flying man who escaped—"

"Of course we are," said Chegwyn. "The Sprite of Rochelle. On the very last day of the siege. It was seen by hundreds. The citadel was already blazing, men and women in flames throwing themselves from the walls, cannon going off, breaches in the walls. In the midst of it all, one of the Rochelais throws himself from the walls, but he does not fall."

"He flies," said Ledwitch. "There are numerous accounts of it. Apparently it was a child."

"The Sprite of Rochelle," Lemprière said, more to himself than the professors. "Flying men?"

"It is not so incredible as it appears," said Chegwyn. "After all, Daedalus and Icarus managed it. You should know that, Mister Lemprière."

"And the Persian king, Kar Kawus, had himself tied to hungry eagles, then hoisted a lump of meat on a spear just out of their reach. They flew up for the meat, and"—Ledwitch flapped his arms—"well, it is self-evident."

"Alexander the Great used the same method," said Linebarger.

"That was griffins, not eagles," said Ledwitch. Lemprière had forgotten the incident and now remembered that his entry on Alexander was already with Cadell at the printers.

"Ki-kung Shi invented a flying chariot," offered Chegwyn, "but does not say how."

"They all seem rather remote," Lemprière remarked. The professors nodded in accord. "Fair point, fair point."

"King Bladud!" Linebarger burst out. "He flew over this very city. Fell to his death, of course."

"Still had time to found Bath," added Ledwitch gloomily.

"What about Oliver of Malmesbury?" The Widow had joined the discussion.

"'Ie causet to mak ane pair of wingus,'" quoted Linebarger.

"A mere tower jumper," said Ledwitch.

"Do we count tower jumpers?" asked Linebarger. Grudging acceptance was given, and the talk turned to Giambattista Danti of Perugia, an unnamed cantor of Nuremberg, and the Abbot of Tungland's leap from the walls of Stirling Castle. Bolori's fatal plunge from Troyes Cathedral was passed over quickly. Burattini's spring-loaded cat-levitator was applauded by all. Ledwitch made much of Ahmed Hezarfen's flight and safe landing in the market square at Scutari. Chegwyn championed Besnier's jump over a house in Sable. Scorn was poured on Cyrano de Bergerac's attachment of bottles of dew to the flyer, who would then be drawn up to the heavens with the dew by the early-morning sun.

"You have yet to mention angels," said the Widow.

"No evidence," said Linebarger rather gruffly.

"Does not Wilkins mention angel spirits?" Ledwitch mused. "'And the Sprite of Rochelle was said to have wings. It was last seen skimming over the waves, out to sea. . . .'"

But there was little enthusiasm for angels. Lemprière's only contribution to the discussion had been a mention of Hermes (dismissed as too mythological), and "someone on a kite." He felt it was time to depart and began to take his leave of the professors, who exhorted him to stay, tempting him with further rounds of Jump or Die, but he was adamant. It was past eleven when he took his leave of the Widow on the doorstep. His route home was explained in simple terms. "Remember my offer" were her last words before they parted. The door closed behind him and he began the walk home.

Thames Street was almost deserted. His breath came in clouds as he walked quickly through Ludgate and into Fleet Street where the odd prowler heralded a more populous scene ahead. Convivial groups of 'prentices and their masters, well-dressed young women, and amiable drunkards staggered about offering toasts to each other's health and the New Year, which Lemprière only now remembered was due within minutes. Still, this realization hardly broke his train of thought which ran between the Widow, Lady de Vere, and George Peppard, whose sad circumstances were now more fully explicable. He wondered again why the man had not told him of the possibility which Alice de Vere had held out to him with such force. "Wealth, beyond your dreams. . . ." But really, he caught himself, it was as fanciful as Neagle's Whale, though he felt there was more even to that tale than the Widow had let on. George Peppard would know, if anyone did. And the Company, of course. Poor Thomas de Vere, and François who had turned on his fellow investors, something at the siege, after the siege. . . .

Questions turned over and over in his mind like tumblers never quite falling to earth. Somewhere, something like a war had disappeared. Whales, disappearing ships. False soundings. Lemprière continued along Fleet Street and the Strand until his own dwelling came into view. He jammed his hands into his pockets, heard a loud rip, and looking down, saw that he had extended the tear in Septimus's coat by another six inches. It was then that he had a good idea.

Lemprière mounted the stairs of the house, but instead of stopping at his own room, he continued on up the stairs to the one directly above his own, where he knocked on the door. At that moment, the last seconds of the year pulled the hands of the clock together and one after another the bell towers of Saint Paul's, Saint Clement's, Saint Anne's, Saint Mary's in the Strand, and Saint Mary's by the Savoy, the churches around and about and all over the city of London let loose a ringing, jangling, clanging, crashing cacophony. On the landing where Lemprière waited it was an endless deafening row. He stood with his hands held protectively over his ears, and it was in this attitude that he was discovered when the door finally opened and he faced the individual he sought, a small man with an aggressive expression and a flattened nose.

"Yes?" shouted the man.

"You are a tailor!" Lemprière shouted back over the din.

"I am," returned the man.

"I have a tear in my coat," Lemprière bellowed. He indicated the rip. "I thought I might engage you to repair it!" The tailor looked at the coat, then Lemprière.

"Trousers me," he said.

"Ah!" Lemprière yelled. "But you could just sew it up perhaps!" The tailor shook his head.

"Trousers," he said again, then stepped back into the room and shut the door. The noise from the bells was abating. Lemprière stood in his mud-mottled, rose-colored coat and regarded the tear. Only the odd rogue *dong* disturbed the peace and the night's silence was almost restored. He descended to his room where his dictionary awaited him. A new year had begun. The mob outside the inn, his mysterious rescuer, the Widow and the whales, the three professors and their flying man, all ran through his mind as he picked up his pen and began once more to write.

• • •

Lemprière: The name took hold of Nazim like a tightening hand about his skull, five steel fingers embedded in his brain's soft fiber. Bahadur was the first who had found out the name in Paris and returned with its price subtracted from his soul, *We change inside,* the voice from his dreams, never the same. The second was the Nawab, whispering it like a child, "Lemprière," in the cool interior of the palace, and his command, "Find him, find them all." All nine. Then the two women, who chatted away their misfortunes through the night of the rain, sending him the name like a guiding thread, but he had lost it outside the coffee shop. Le Mara was the blunt thumb, waiting for him to declare himself. But he had lost Le Mara too that day, caught by his own indecision between the black coach and the assassin, hampered in his search by the crowd, and the idiot in the coffee shop too. Excuses. Nazim's thoughts tracked fading footprints and half-heard whispers, the name *Lemprière* teasing out his suspicions along fantastic lines until his pursuit was of monsters, demons, and all his buried fears exhumed as dead things which looked like life. *We change inside.*

The Nine were split, he knew it. Le Mara's business with the woman in blue was no harmless prank. The Lemprière was the object of a plot. "Christmas Eve" had drifted over the wooden partition, but the place had not been mentioned. The black coach might have led him there, but he had lost the coach. The following morning he had resumed his vigil on the quay and watched Coker's men as the slow caravan of crates was started up once more. Le Mara had appeared only briefly, enough for Nazim who had followed him at a distance along the Ratcliffe highway to a house in a mews to the south of Tower Street to which Le Mara produced keys. When he had disappeared inside, Nazim had worked his way around to the back of the house. It was closer to the Thames than he had imagined. Deceptive city, a thought not followed up, as he noted the drawn curtains in every window. It was midday.

Hours had passed in patient observation of nothing when Nazim crept up to the back door and, peering through the crack between the lintel and the top of the door, saw an interior which persuaded him that he might force an entry with impunity. Once inside, his earlier assumption was confirmed. The house, from its tiled hall to the meaner servants' quarters in the attic, was completely empty, the hangings masking this fact from the gaze of the curious apart. There was not a stick of furniture, no belongings, not a possession in the building. Nazim's gathering speculation led him directly to the cellar where his suspicions were confirmed by a trapdoor set about with huge flagstones. Locked, he knew even without trying it, from within. Below it would be a shaft and somewhere beyond that, Le Mara. The house was nothing but a gateway, but to what? The time was not right for confrontations, the ghost of Bahadur's error held him back. There would come a time for that and he would be ready then. Nazim stood over the trapdoor, feeling the blood pump in his veins. They were down there, somewhere below: the Nine. Perhaps the Lemprière too.

The days leading up to Christmas Eve brought different frustrations for Nazim as the purpose behind the woman's contract in the coffee shop became no clearer. Some act planned against the Lemprière was taking place and yet he could not discover it. Le Mara's routine was unchanged, offered no clues. It was useless to him. On the day itself he could watch the ship no longer and paced the streets aimlessly in a silent fury. Somewhere, he knew, their hands were being shown and he was not there to see it, and though he controlled his nagging rage, it returned when Le Mara's customary station by the quay was abandoned for a different one. Some act had been committed to precipitate this new state of affairs, an act which might have led him to the Lemprière, but he had failed to find it out, and Nazim wondered how many errors and lost opportunities the unwritten rules of his peculiar game would permit.

Le Mara's new station was to the north of the city, an area bounded by Goswell Street to the west and Moorfields to the east, close to where the tight-packed streets around Golden Lane petered out and became the open fields beyond Saint Agnes. Once more, Nazim took up observation of the man, trailing him each morning from the house off Tower Street to posts dotted all about the area, never the same one twice, in a pattern whose significance eluded him.

Although careful to keep out of sight, Nazim knew the other man would assume his presence as a fact. The other acknowledged this in the winding, circuitous routes chosen to reach the area over which he kept watch. Further evidence were the rambling circuits of the city which interspersed Le Mara's vigils, unfathomable journeys which might take in Hyde Park, Southwark, or Wapping, which seemed to exist only for the sake of their own complexity. Nazim had accepted these as part of the push and shove of their contest, before it was engaged in earnest. It was a simple matter to track Le Mara through Clerkenwell, or Poplar, or even around Chancery Lane which was where Le Mara had led him the day his underestimation of the other man had almost cost him his life. Chancery Lane or, to be exact, the streets branching out from either side of Fetter Lane, very close to his own hiding place.

He had followed Le Mara patiently for over an hour. It was New Year's Eve and all kinds of commotion were being let loose on the streets. This should have made Nazim's task harder but Le Mara seemed to have abandoned all his earlier ploys; there were none of the sudden dashes down alleys, loiterings by shop fronts, or long sojourns in coffee shops and taverns which had bedeviled Nazim in the preceding days. Le Mara walked calmly down the street looking neither to left nor right, toward an inn outside which Nazim could see a large crowd.

They were being addressed by a silver-haired man who stood on an orange crate holding up a length of red cloth. His speech was a tirade against imports, textiles, the hardships of the poor, the greed of nabobs and foreign princes, and most of all the Company. The crowd filled the street right up to the inn which the speaker faced from the far side, and Nazim watched as Le Mara disappeared into its midst, seeming to mingle with the rough laborers and journeymen who made up its numbers. Le Mara was less visible as Nazim followed him into the crowd, odd glimpses between the crush of bodies, confusion as he edged through behind, then a huge roar from the crowd at which Nazim glanced up to see the ranter framed between two burning banners, a climax, and Le Mara was lost to view.

Nazim worked his way this way and that, but saw nothing until, suddenly, he looked back at the speaker and saw Le Mara standing directly in front of the man. He was staring directly at him without expression and Nazim could do nothing but stare back as Le Mara leaned toward a smaller man standing beside him and whispered something in his ear. It dawned on Nazim that he had been led there. He could see the whisper rippling through the crowd, gathering momentum as a wave which crested in a shout of "Spies! Indian spies!" and he knew suddenly he was in great danger.

Nazim pulled down his hat and began to shoulder his way out of the crowd. Already, a punch had been thrown. The man behind him had seen his face as he turned and was clawing at his shoulder. Nazim turned quickly, jammed two fingers into the man's eye, and turned again as the man screamed. The mob had turned on itself. A giant of a man was laying about all and sundry with a plank. A thin young man fell almost on top of him, scrabbling after his eyeglasses. The giant was coming toward him. Nazim caught hold of the thin man's wrist and hauled him forward. "He's dying, damn you, dying!" A scream aimed at the giant who hesitated, confused, long enough for Nazim to skip sideways, drop his human shield and run for the open space of the street. Le Mara was gone, lost again. Another mistake.

He had walked the few yards to Stonecutter Lane, which was almost deserted: two basket-women, a gang of children, and two more distant figures beyond them, all looking the other way as he slipped quickly through the coal hatch, except that one of the two distant figures looked about as he slid into the darkened cellar, and Nazim's last glimpse of the afternoon sun was its reflection glinting off something on the figure's face, off something which must have been a pair of eyeglasses.

The new year came, and this incident apart, the routine was as dreary as before. Le Mara's area had narrowed to focus on the streets below Chequer Alley to the east of Germey Row, principally Blue Anchor Lane. The assassin was waiting and watching for something or someone, and as Nazim was forced to do the same, he sensed the long accumulation of minutes and hours that the other would be taking on, a slow buildup toward some conclusive act. He was eager for it, even though it was not his, waiting and watching.

The weeks went by. By the middle of January, Nazim believed he knew the object of Le Mara's interest: a short man, less than five feet tall. He rented rooms in Blue Anchor Lane. The man would depart before seven each morning, and return at about the same hour in the evening. Where he went, or what he did between these hours, was a mystery to Nazim, though not, he presumed, to Le Mara. Perhaps other agents were engaged to track him during the day, but the arrangement seemed a loose one. And why was Le Mara waiting? He could finish it now if he wished. He was waiting for some other event, something more, something else that Nazim did not know.

And so the three-cornered vigil went on; the short man watched by Le Mara, Le Mara watched by Nazim. Cool evenings and cold nights, long days of rain or shine, the days trooped on one after another, uniform and eventless. Nazim would sometimes find himself exhausted, barred from direct entrance to the cellar in Stonecutter Lane by the early morning crowds who filled the street leading to Fleet Market. Then, he would gain entry to the house by the exposed back entrance, chancing an encounter with the woman who still squatted in the rooms above, alone now, abandoned by her friend, it seemed.

His nights in the cellar were silent receptions for wilder flights and imaginings. His quarry would visit him in these hours in disguise: as the winged Lemprière or the horned Lemprière, the submarine or sub-terranean Lemprière. But his most vivid dreams were still of Bahadur, whose face pressed against his own through the hours of broken sleep. As before, they would walk on the red cliff. They were silhouettes against a huge blue sky. Their shadows were blacker than black on the ground at their backs. The sun glared down. Strange gliding motions from the machine. They would continue until the scrubby terrain at the foot of the cliffs became the white stones he remembered more clearly. White stones, and Bahadur's hand about his arm. They were talking and soon the three words he dreaded would come and then, then they would rock back and forth on the brink of the cliff. He would feel the pores of his skin squeezing out beads of sweat and he would see that Bahadur's face was dry. Back and forth, rocking back and forth. His eyes were twitching under their lids. Like a pendulum . . . *change inside*. His face was wet. Bahadur became a child, a doll, a tiny struggling thing thrashing its limbs and dwindling to nothing.

The woman had returned, Karin. The gaps in the floorboards gave him a slatted view of the woman, her blue dress more filthy and ragged than before. The woman was crooning to herself in French, a lullaby. It occurred to Nazim suddenly that since the disappearance of her companion he had not seen the woman eat. Her movements in the rooms above were hesitant and feeble affairs. She spent more and more time in the house. A corpse would present problems; the dead invariably excited more attention than the dying. She was talking to herself in an accent that jumbled the street talk of the market women with baby talk, and underneath both the inflections of Paris.

"Won't leave will she? Willshe, willshe, willshe? Nooo. . . ." The sound was a mellifluous jumble of half words and phrases. It soothed Nazim as he drifted slowly back into a sleep where the faces of the Nawab and Bahadur awaited him. Behind them both the features of the Lemprière rose up slowly to arrange themselves as ciphers of his ignorance.

Answers. The following morning found Nazim at his station at the entrance to Blue Anchor Lane. Le Mara waited a hundred yards or more farther up, forty yards beyond the door from which the little man had already emerged and walked briskly off. The weather was very fine, the sky clear and cold. A northeasterly cut down the street in gusts.

Nazim had spent the night plagued with dreams, tossing and turning on the cold earth of the cellar, and throughout the day their vivid images returned, taunting him. Anyone, everyone might be the Lemprière. Even the little man, when he returned some hours after the late January sun had fallen below the gables of the roofs, excited a silent speculation within Nazim. A woman leading a toddler by the hand stared curiously back at him. A workman met his gaze frankly before Nazim was forced to look away. He looked farther down the street to a tall man who was walking toward him. Nazim recognized something in his gait, then saw the silver frames of the thick eyeglasses. He recognized him then from the mob outside the inn and shrank back against the wall, but the young man glanced neither left nor right as he turned into the lane. Nazim watched as he walked down to the door into which the small man had disappeared only minutes before.

• • •

"ABC." Lemprière sniffed. "D." He wiped his nose, then thought to do the same for his eyeglasses. "E." He sniffed again. Lemprière nursed a slight dislike of the letter "E." The look of it, but also its pronunciation which seemed to him misleading. "Eee." How many times did "E" sound like "Eee"? Its vagaries seemed to imply a new vowel, a "yur" or "er," an "eh." It was a promiscuous, fawning surd, continually merging with its neighboring consonants ("R" in particular), confirming Lemprière's view of it as a perfidious little hieroglyph: "E, ee, *eeyurgh.*" He looked at the page in front of him and noticed that the left lens of his eyeglasses was now lightly smeared with snot. He rewiped.

The page emerged as his entry on *Euripus,* a narrow strait between the island of *Euboea* (three pages back) and the coast of *Boeotia* (in the batch already with Cadell). The to-ings and fro-ings of its current were so irregular as to be inexplicable, prompting Aristotle to throw himself in for enlightenment. Either it was regular for the first eighteen days of the month (or nineteen, according to some) and then irregular, or it was the same every day, but changed fourteen times in that period. Hence, *Euripio Mobilior:* "I shift about in the manner of the waters of the Euripine Strait," meaning "fickle," which Lemprière had remembered from Cicero's letters to Atticus. "John Lemprière. Twenty-third day of January, 1788," he wrote at the foot of the entry.

The uppermost page of a thin sheaf of papers beside it lifted, slid, and seesawed to the floor as a sharp gust of wind found the crack in the window frame. Septimus had called two days previously to collect the completed entries, buoyed up with Cadell's encomia on the work so far. He transmitted these to Lemprière, encouraging him to attack "E" with a gusto that had now all but evaporated. The coat had not been mentioned. Lemprière had told Septimus of his meeting with the Widow and the professors who lodged with her. He had launched into a long recitation about the whales, secret undersea passages, and Captain Neagle's disappearance, until Septimus had become conspicuously bored and left with the wad of papers under his arm. Later it had rained.

Now, Lemprière replaced the errant page on the sheaf, eclipsing the entry on *Empedocles.* The Widow's extraordinary tale had grown no less improbable in the retelling, the whales especially, but also the strangely complete disappearance of Captain Neagle, his ship, and all its crew. Empedocles, nearing death and wishing to be thought a god, had caused himself to vanish into thin air by throwing himself into the fires of Mount Etna. Captain Neagle's vanishing act had something of the same about it in Lemprière's view. He was gone certainly, but where? Empedocles had been posthumously discovered by virtue of a charred sandal thrown up from the volcano's crater. Lemprière imagined various items of Captain Neagle's apparel and their fates: a cap washed up on the beaches of Arakan, boots navigating between the Mediterranean and the Red seas, a striped woolen singlet floating aimlessly in the Thames. The wind gusted once more, rattling the panes. Decomposing trousers cut from the stomach of a whale.

The Widow was devoted to the dead man. Perhaps the Company *had* engineered his disappearance, but despite her rage it was guilt, not redress, which drove her. His own father's memory hovered near these thoughts, approaching and receding with their ebb and flow, small ripples lapping at the pool's edge. And Peppard! The little man had begun life almost as a figure of fun in Lemprière's perceptions, scurrying about apologetically as the Widow attacked Skewer with her shoe. But Peppard had been the one to decipher the agreement in the chilly room in Blue Anchor Lane. He, Lemprière, had not understood the first word. Then he recalled the awkward moments that night, the slight silences where the man who might have been the Widow's lover could be glimpsed beneath the broken exterior of the disgraced lawyer, the menial clerk, a lost marker in the game the Widow and her husband had played with the Company.

He turned to the page before him and raised his pen once more. Peppard had concealed his liaison with the Widow, and there was the matter of the agreement. Farfetched or not, the notion that he might be heir to such a fortune should at least have been mentioned. Lemprière remembered how the Widow's rage had suddenly ceased in Skewer's office, the effort of her composure. That had not been for the benefit of Septimus or himself. That had been for Peppard. There was more to Peppard and the Widow than met the eye, and yet his suspicion was a speculative, free-ranging thing, sprung from curiosity rather than fear. Their complicity was too bashful.

Lemprière contemplated the word he was about to write, "Euripus" again, a Greek. His pen wavered over the paper, then his curiosity got the better of him. He rose, put on his pink coat and left Euripus to his own devices.

Peppard was lying under his bedstead when a knock sounded on the door. He was reading. His head came up too suddenly, colliding with the crisscross lattice of heavy-gauge wire which gave the mattress it supported its last vestige of spring. Sandwiched between the wire and the mattress, his late reading material, the page pressed down and through the gaps. Caged there and agitated over the last twenty years by the mattress's weight and Peppard's slight yet calculable bulk as it tossed and turned above, the once-soft but increasingly brittle paper had been abraided by these gentle motions so that now the wire held the page by the merest filaments.

"John!"

"George!" Fraternal handshakes were exchanged between the two before they fell to talking of the three months since their last meeting. As they spoke, Peppard concealed his unease. His various late suspicions centered on figures lurking at his back, unseen at first but then in the street, two different faces, so far unacknowledged by him but out there still, curling about him like the Company's tentacles, watching and waiting. . . . For what?

For his part, Lemprière made no mention of the murder at the De Veres', and perhaps it was these respective evasions which accounted for the overheartiness of their first minutes together. Peppard's earlier explanation came under subtle attack as Lemprière recounted his encounter with the hapless Captain Guardian and the meeting with Alice de Vere. He stressed her eccentricity but nevertheless skirted around the little man's earlier omission in the manner of a tentative besieger wary of damaging his prize. Lemprière tried to raise abstruse legal points amid the chatter and teacups, until after much circumlocution Peppard grasped both point and nettle.

"You wish to know if it is possible that you own a ninth share of the Company," he said. "And, if you do, why did I not tell you. Is that the case?" Lemprière flushed and told him that it was. Peppard settled himself more firmly in his chair. "You do not," he said. "Which answers both points. I know that the agreement was made in perpetuity, forever in other words, but it was between individuals. Forever, in that case, means so long as they lived. That, in the strict legal sense, is why you do not own the share stated in the document."

"And outside the legal?" Lemprière pressed.

"I am a lawyer," Peppard said, "or was. I can only advise within the law, but I will tell you this. If your agreement has any value it is because it tells of things the Company does not want told. Not the agreement itself, John, the story behind it. That is its value, and its danger."

"And what is the story?" Lemprière asked, leaning forward eagerly.

"How on God's earth would I know?" Peppard laughed, then choked it off and his expression changed. "Now, listen to me. If these men, these investors of whom the agreement speaks, are still running the Company, then they have survived for almost two centuries. Dangerous men to have as enemies. And if you run after them waving your piece of paper and demanding your family's share, then they will defend themselves and you will be a blackmailer. Within the law, that is. To be dubbed a blackmailer is an ugly thing, but to stand alone against the Company is madness, as we both know. I by experience, and you, John, by my example." Lemprière looked up guiltily, suddenly ashamed that he knew the details of the little man's disgrace.

"Is that not the case?" Peppard asked. Lemprière nodded. "Annabel, the Widow Neagle, visited the office. She told me you and she had spoken."

"I did not ask—" Lemprière began.

"I know," said Peppard. "But it is better you know. A cautionary tale." He smiled.

"I know only that it was something to do with insurance," said Lemprière.

"Maritime insurance," Peppard added. "But the story began a little time before that, with the whales. . . ." He spoke on, outlining Captain Neagle's discovery in the Mediterranean just as the Widow had told it, only now it seemed even more fantastic than before.

"A secret route from the Mediterranean to the Indies, and a monopoly on that route would have been a discovery indeed," Peppard was saying. "Alan Neagle would have gone down in history. In a sense, he did, of course. And the lawyer who beat the Company in court, for they would have fought it to the last, believe me, that lawyer would go down similarly. I was young and full of ambition; one great case would have secured everything I wanted. Alan Neagle had sealed up all his notes and instructions and already set sail. His wife was to engage a lawyer. The case was a gamble, but many would have taken it. I had heard of it long before she came to me. And I heard how the Company was warning people off, bribing, threatening, offering violence or reward. An old story. I was visited myself and offered a sinecure in Leadenhall Street; I threw the wretch out." Lemprière saw anger flash across the little man's face. "When the Widow came to me, I wanted to take the case just for that, but the more she told me the more hopeless it seemed."

"But you took the case," Lemprière said.

"She knew I would, she had only to ask. . . . An old promise." Peppard's voice drifted across the table. "I was Annabel's suitor, you see, before Alan Neagle. She came to me last of all, did I say that? It was desperation. I knew that well enough, and she offered . . . Oh, I took the case. That was the point. Never mind why." Peppard gulped on his tea. "Anyway, she left me with Captain Neagle's papers. They were sealed and she had not seen them."

"Evidence, about the whales," Lemprière hazarded.

"Conclusive evidence, copper-bottomed, you might say. I opened the package that night and read Alan Neagle's account of what had happened in the Mediterranean with bewilderment, then amazement. Their ship had been blown off course as they claimed, and the crew had seen the evidence with their own eyes. What they found was every bit as great a revelation as Neagle claimed."

"The evidence for the whales?" Lemprière was growing impatient.

"There were no whales," Peppard replied. "Not then, not ever. That whole story was poppycock. What Alan Neagle discovered that day was a ship, a ship which should never have been there. A ship he should never have seen."

• • •

Outside the house, the earlier gusting winds died slowly. The layered air settled calmly over the city. Far above, the astral fabric rolled silently while all the efforts below it teetered on the celestial contraption, balancing their forces, for the moment.

Nazim waited in the cold. Le Mara stood at his station farther along the street. Between them lay the object of their patient attention. Nazim shivered and pulled the brim of his hat farther over his eyes. Le Mara waited. His eyes moved quickly, sweeping the street to left and right, checking and rechecking. Waiting.

"When the storm lifted, Neagle and his crew found themselves drifting in the Sea of Alboran, as he told his wife, but the sight which greeted them was a ship. Unexceptional, and the crew paid it little mind for the most part. It lay less than a league away to port, a three-master. More than that, an Indiaman."

"An Indiaman? So there was a passage by the Mediterranean!"

"Who knows? It might have been there for any reason. The point is not so immediately why it was there, but that it was there at all. You see, Alan Neagle recognized that ship. It was the *Sophie*, though that was not the name she sailed under then."

"So it had been renamed," said Lemprière.

"Renamed, yes. And refitted too, according to Neagle's notes. But most important of all, it had been reported sunk, lost with all hands. And this was over twenty years before. It should have been rotting on the ocean bed, yet here it was plying the coastal trade up and down the Mediterranean two decades later."

"An insurance fraud, then," said Lemprière, remembering the Widow's words, and Septimus's before her.

"That was Neagle's conjecture; not on the ship but its cargo. The Company does not build its own ships. There is a leasing agreement with the shipyards, but it is very complicated. The cargo is owned outright, though; an insurance claim would be straightforward, and less quantifiable. 'A thousand bolts of cloth' could become 'a thousand bolts of silk,' 'colored stones' could be 'amethysts,' and so on. The ship could be sold as well. It would all add up, I suppose."

"You are not convinced?"

"When I read Neagle's account that night, it struck me that the sums involved were really very small compared to the risk. A few thousands, no more, and a vast scandal in the offing if it came to light. Risk and profit are two things the Company balances very finely. My own thought was that they needed the ship for some other purpose. After all, why *was* it there?"

"But they could simply buy a ship."

"Certainly, but when it just disappeared, for no visible reason, questions would follow. They must have been trying to avoid that. So, something in secret and the means to do it."

"What?" said Lemprière.

"I have no idea," said Peppard. "When I found out Neagle's real intentions that night, I could no longer take the case. It was blackmail, dressed up a little with a covenant or two and some fine legal prose, but blackmail all the same. That was to be my function. Annabel knew nothing of this, or almost nothing. She believed her husband's lies about the whales, and still does. I resolved to have nothing to do with the whole business, packed up the evidence, as Captain Neagle termed it, and presented myself at her door the very next morning. I would not take the case."

"But you did take the case." Lemprière could barely keep track of Peppard's vacillations.

"Yes, yes, I did. There was more to it than I . . . It is a long story, but the point is that I was Annabel's suitor, before Neagle, you understand? And I was in love." Peppard swallowed. "But Annabel had made her choice, the Captain. I knew the decision gave her more pain than she ever let me see. But, that day, when I returned the papers, we . . ." Peppard had looked away. "It was clear to us both, blindingly clear, that Annabel had made the wrong choice. She should have married me, not Alan Neagle. Neither of us said so, but later she wrote to me and told me of her feelings that day. They were as I guessed, and my own were as strong. We were both still young, there was still time. But the betrayal wounded her, the betrayal of Alan Neagle. I think that is why I took the case eventually. We knew what we were doing. Perhaps we thought we had to give Alan something. As it turned out, we gave him everything and we both were left with nothing, not even each other. The case began and from the start I knew it was a calamity. Whales . . . I was laughed at. The Company fought back slowly at first. Our own motives came under examination and they became anything the Company wanted them to be. Annabel hardly cared. If we had tried, that was enough. But then the news of the shipwreck arrived and I realized why the Company had been so slow to attack me. They had been waiting for a free hand, and Neagle's death gave it to them. Without his evidence, the case was a farce. They began to lay suits against me."

"But for what?" Lemprière asked.

"Everything and nothing, anything they could think of. It hardly mattered. Throw enough mud and some will stick. I held my nerve until they began to implicate Annabel, a Company widow, mind you, and then I made my mistake."

"Neagle's real evidence—"

"The ship, the insurance fraud, yes. I only wanted to end the business.

I wanted nothing else from them. In return for that, my silence. But it was blackmail, I had no real proof and they knew it. It was simple for them. A meeting was arranged, witnesses were concealed. My every word was written down as I spoke and at the end the record was presented to me. It was quite explicit. If I should ever breathe a word of the matter I would be tried and sentenced, or worse. In the meantime, I was requested never to practice law again. I was a blackmailer, and anyone who might have helped me was reminded of that fact. The disgrace still hangs over me. A blackmailer. And for Annabel, Alan Neagle was the man who had lost his life for her. She did not love him, but in death he was there between us, as if we had to lie together on his corpse. We lost everything, even each other."

"And the ships?"

"Nothing more was heard of either, and either would have vindicated me. I no longer care about my good name, but Annabel and I . . ." Peppard's voice was drifting again, into regions of what might have been, where Lemprière, preoccupied by what might yet be, could hardly follow.

"You have a family?" Lemprière asked him, changing the subject.

"Barely," Peppard snorted. Lemprière reached into the pocket of his coat and produced the brass case of the miniature of his mother. "Marianne Lemprière." Peppard read the inscription aloud. "She is very beautiful."

"She looks a little older now," said Lemprière. He left the miniature open on the table where it seemed to draw Peppard slowly back into discussion.

"You could do better than Skewer, though, disgrace or no, surely?" Peppard's choice of employment was a puzzle to Lemprière. Skewer was odium in person and for Peppard too, he suspected.

"Yes, yes, I suppose. There are compensations." Realization dawned on Lemprière that the depth of the little man's longing extended deeper than his earlier estimate.

"You stay for the Widow," he said. Peppard only nodded.

"You know she still cares for you. That is why she visits."

"I hardly think that is so."

"It *is* so," Lemprière redoubled his emphasis. "After all, if you both still feel as before—"

"After all." Peppard weighed the phrase. "Too much 'after,' and too much 'all,' " he said. "My hopes are sunk deeper even than the *Falmouth*. Neagle rots in his cabin and I keep him company. . . . John? You might at least pay attention to my ramblings. . . ."

But Lemprière was not listening. He faced Peppard across the table, his eyes directed at the other man but focused on a point somewhere far behind him, another room, another face, and most of all, another's hand. Captain Guardian's words echoed back to Lemprière from the night at the De Veres' as Peppard named Neagle's ship, the *Falmouth*, and there was the name, cut into the palm of the Captain's hand, and Guardian's shock of recognition became Lemprière's own in the room in Blue Anchor Lane. The *Falmouth*, *"lost for twenty years and here it is again"* had been the words as he came to in the wreckage of—what? A stepladder!

"It is here," Lemprière said slowly. His eyes found Peppard's face once again. "The *Falmouth*, it is here in London." More of the earlier meeting was coming back to him.

"The *Falmouth*?" Peppard's mouth was opening and closing.

"No." Lemprière racked his brains. "It is renamed, like the ship Neagle saw. It is called . . ." He caught at the name. "It is called, I believe it is called the *Vendragon*." He brought it out in a rush. "You were right, George. They have done the same thing again. Only now, their ship is not in the Mediterranean. It is here, berthed right here in London!"

Peppard stared at Lemprière, and when he spoke his words were measured. "This time there will be no mistakes," he said. He paused and thought. "I will gather the evidence patiently, I will watch, wait. We will need the records of the ship, everything."

"But how will we—"

"There is someone who owes me a very great favor, a very great recompense. He will help."

"Who?" asked Lemprière, but Peppard was already out of his chair, out of the door.

"I will send word this very minute," he heard Peppard shout from the front door. A minute or so later, he returned with a ginger-haired boy who was engaged to carry a message. Lemprière watched as Peppard scrawled a few lines.

"You know where this is?" he asked the boy. The boy nodded and was dispatched. Peppard scrawled a few more lines. "The when and where," he said. "If you could come, it would be a great help. My friend will not be easy to convince." Lemprière folded the message in his pocket.

"But who are we meeting?" he asked again.

"Someone I have not laid eyes on in over twenty years, but you will find out."

"You might not recognize him," Lemprière probed.

"Oh, I believe I will," Peppard returned with a broad smile. "And you too. His name is Theobald and you will know him the moment you set eyes on him." He would not be drawn further on the man's identity. They talked on, and Lemprière could see already that Peppard was thinking of the Widow.

"You might have told her about Neagle's lie, the whales and so on," he ventured.

"To ingratiate myself with her?" Peppard drew the implication.

"I suppose he was right after all," said Lemprière, taking a different tack.

"Mmm."

Peppard was sprawled in his chair, the image of contentment.

"No! Not at all!" he burst out. "I do not believe the affair is anything to do with cargoes or insurance. It is the ship they need. It is so plain. I wager you the *Sophie* disappeared without trace, just as the *Falmouth* did, or *Vendragon*, whichever name you prefer. They are using that ship for something, some purpose which must be linked to the Company, and they have been doing so for two decades at the least, perhaps much longer. What are they using that ship for?"

"Captain Guardian said it was moored below his house. We could simply go and look, although I do not know his house. . . ."

"We could find it," said Peppard. "But we will talk more on this in a week's time." Lemprière nodded his assent. It was late and the excitement had tired him without his realizing it. Peppard seemed just as animated as before. He rose to leave, straightening his coat. Peppard rose too, and his face became pensive.

"I am sorry I could not help you with your agreement," he said.

"Oh, no matter." Lemprière dismissed it airily, then looked more closely at Peppard. "What? What is it?" he asked.

"Nothing, probably," Peppard said. Lemprière waited. "It is just . . . Since the court case, I have posed a threat, a very slight threat to the Company, what I know, you see? Over the years, there have been various scandals, crises, attacks on the Company. The point is they have not forgotten me. In times of the Company's troubles I have been watched. That is why I ran and hid the night we met."

"Watched? By whom?"

"The Company's agents. A precaution, I believe."

Lemprière grasped the point. "You are worried they will try to silence you, about the ship. Never fear," he reassured the little man. "My lips are sealed. Not one word." He grinned.

"No, no one could know about the ship. Only the two of us are privy to that. It is your agreement, John. You see, the past few weeks, I believe I have been followed again. I am not certain yet—"

"Followed by whom?"

"There are two of them; one I have encountered before, the other is new. He wears a peculiar hat." Peppard extended his arms. "Very wide. I may yet be wrong."

"But the Company is suffering no crisis now. Why should they watch you?"

"None that has come to light. Unless . . ."

"Unless what?"

Peppard hesitated for a moment. "Unless the crisis is you."

"Me?"

"The agreement, John. Skewer knows, Annabel, Alice de Vere, her son, myself, anyone else?"

"Septimus."

213

"Of course. And yourself. Seven people cannot keep a secret. I cannot see the value of the thing myself, but it begs awkward questions, John. The answers might exceed all our speculations. Then again, I might be wrong. All I say is this: If they are watching me, then they will know of you. I will have led them to you. Be careful, John."

"I will," Lemprière reassured him. "Until next week."

"Next week!" Peppard saluted him and Lemprière turned to clatter down the stairs.

Once in the street, Lemprière looked about him in experimental suspicion. The gusting wind had died down, much to his relief. That the Company might be undergoing some upheaval from his agreement, a mere piece of paper, seemed too unlikely. He dug his hands in his hip pockets against the cold and wriggled his fingers. The street was deserted as Lemprière walked quickly toward Golden Lane. His hands clenched and unclenched in the pockets of his coat. They were empty. Lemprière stopped in his tracks. He patted the other pockets. Nothing. He looked back along the road to Peppard's house where, he now remembered, he had left the miniature of his mother lying open on the table.

Wedding bells which might have tolled two decades before, but had not, tolled now for Peppard. The future rose up, vast and static for him: an Ephesian temple of columns placed by kings and carved with the tokens of his long-nurtured love. Hail Lemprière, Ctesiphon of his new hopes. He was elated. A staircase sixty feet high carved from a single vine tree broached the dripping roof of his wants and drained a stream of years from the sky above it. The decades were moments and the moments were motes of dust circling slowly in the far sunlight of a country he had left years before. His ship, he laughed silently to himself, had come in. From the table, Marianne's painted eyes watched him sprawl carelessly in his chair.

"Annabel," said Peppard to himself, then "Lemprière," as he noticed the miniature. His friend was not two minutes gone. Peppard rose from his chair and picked up the miniature, thinking to run after its owner. But as he moved to the door, he heard light footsteps move up the staircase outside. He had been saved the trouble. A knock sounded.

"John!" George Peppard called out. He threw back the bolt to open the door.

Two shapes had emerged as the door to the house in Blue Anchor Lane was closed. Nazim hovered about his station fifty yards from the entrance into which the spectacled youth had disappeared. Fifty yards beyond that, he sensed the disturbance of shadows that was Le Mara. An hour idled by, and the earlier flow of people ebbed to a trickle of souls who wandered past alone or in pairs on obscure errands. The street was empty except for a small gang of children, whose presence farther up the street pricked him into watchfulness. Nazim remembered the earlier encounter, the sound the boy's nose had made as the cartilage crunched against his hand. They shouted and ran about, six or seven of them. As their noisy game went on, it seemed to Nazim that they should be part of a more populous and more animated scene. But for them, the street was dead.

The northeasterly gusted, then died with the passing minutes. Apart from the thin cries of the children and Le Mara's agitation, imagined by Nazim from his station, the drab peace was undisturbed. His adversary went unseen and unheard, a dark fluttering of suspicions.

A door opened farther up the street. The little man had emerged. He was standing on the short flight of steps which led to the door of the tenement. Nazim watched as he gestured up the street, toward the children. One of them trotted over, a gangling boy with a shock of ginger hair. After a short exchange they disappeared into the building. The other children went on with their game. A minute or two elapsed, then the boy emerged again. He turned and began walking toward Nazim. He was clutching a letter. Nazim moved from the concealment of the shadows into his path. The boy's feet stuttered to a halt. The two of them faced each other. A simple demand, and the exchange was made.

"Theo, twenty years is too long. Meet with me at eight in the evening Friday next at the Ship in Distress. A matter of urgency. Geo."

Nazim read the note, then folded it and handed it back. The boy continued on his way. Geo to Theo. Nazim moved back out of sight. Le Mara was still up there, still waiting.

More time: the slow accumulation of seconds into minutes. Inside the building the two of them would be talking, or thinking in silence, arguing or resolving their differences, mapping out their plans, drawing lines between disparate points.

The minutes ticked slowly by and Le Mara's presence gathered in the near distance. The door opened again and the tall youth came out. He too was walking toward Nazim, looking about nervously. He was a matter of yards away. Nazim rocked back on his heels. Suddenly the youth just stopped, blinking behind his eyeglasses. He was patting his pockets. Nazim stayed motionless in the shadows. He had lost something. He was hesitating, should he go back or go on? Still undecided. Nazim watched, and then saw him walk on, away from the house to the end of the street where he turned the corner and was lost from view.

Nazim turned his attention back to the house. For one moment it seemed nothing had changed. Then he saw the shadow moving down the street. Le Mara was running silently toward the house. Dressed in black from head to toe, he was barely visible as he flitted across the street. Then Nazim saw a flicker of silver and knew that he had miscalculated the meeting he had witnessed. Whatever had been discussed had altered the values of the players. The spectacled one's departure had brought a last visitor to the little man. Le Mara had entered the house. Now it would not take long. He had assumed the little man was an incidental player. He had been wrong.

A minute or two later, the door opened again and a shadow ran away down the street. Le Mara's work was done. Le Mara had fled. It was quite quiet. Nazim moved in turn toward the door. It had been forced. He moved up the stairs. Nazim heard the Nawab's words echo in his memory and the name which would lead him to them. The door was unlocked. He pushed it open and stepped inside.

Nazim saw a table, chairs, books, and, lying on the bed, a body. Bahadur had taught him how to do this. *Take the man from behind. Hold him about the head.* His uncle's eyes were calm as he spoke. *Drive the knife in at the side of the neck. Lower rather than higher. Hold the knife still. Pull back the head. Push the knife away from you.* There were reasons. *The knife will block the windpipe and silence your man. The first gout of blood will spray away from you. It is very powerful.*

Red dripped down the far wall. The body was on the bed, oddly hunched as though about to rise. Nazim saw that one of the hands was clenched tight about something. An object. He prized the fingers open and discovered that the little man's last talisman was a miniature. Nazim opened it and read the inscription. He sat heavily on the bed. He had come too late. The miniature showed him a woman with fine features, a wide mouth, gray-blue eyes. The inscription read "Marianne Lemprière." Nazim stood, staring down at the name. He slipped the object in his pocket and made for the door. Lemprière, he thought, and berated himself. His task would be far more difficult now. The name for which Bahadur had given everything was nothing. The Lemprière was dead.

On the bed, the dead man leaned slowly, then toppled to one side. The bedstead creaked under the slow impact. Below the mattress, held in place by the wire lattice, the letter which earlier he had read for the last time finally fell apart, diamond-shaped fragments fluttered to the floor like confetti, scraps of an earlier message. "My dearest George, my only"—"for when our time comes, and it shall"—"with all my love, Annabel." Nazim turned and closed the door. Blood soaked through the mattress and dripped down steadily onto the fragments of the letter.

. . .

It was past seven and his destination lay almost an hour away by foot. Lemprière strode briskly south, then east along the Strand. Somerset House was a white hulk to his right. He moved through and around the crowd. Observing Peppard's advice, he looked about him to left and right at regular intervals. He had done this all week. His vigilance had become an obscure point of pride. The *Falmouth* had sailed into their lives, which would be different now, and Theo, the note's recipient, whoever he was, would be the agent of that change. Past the courts at Temple Bar and the arcades of Fleet Market with the stench of the Fleet Ditch bubbling up from beneath the flagstones, up the short climb to Ludgate, around Saint Paul's and into Cheapside, Lemprière hurried through the evening traffic to Milk Street. The tavern was up ahead, where his friend and the mysterious Theo awaited him.

Being situated almost a mile from navigable water, any vessel which may have occasioned the naming of the Ship in Distress must have been subject to a very great distress indeed. If the provenance of its title was obscure, so too was its design, for the building seemed almost wholly made up of caves. Successive narrow stories overhung one another in the manner of a staircase seen from the inside, and the whole construction impended over Milk Street like a monument to the final drunken lurch before its own collapse. Despite this, Lemprière regarded the tavern without apprehension. Muddle rather than menace was its keynote. The tenements to either side fed it with a steady stream of patrons whose custom this night was augmented by a meeting of the silk-weavers' guild. Lemprière saw them to his left as he entered the door, a quarrelsome bunch set apart from the main body of clients who stood about drinking and exuding faint disgruntlement at the invasion.

A fierce debate was boiling up among the weavers. "I'll not eat rye!" yelled one fiery spirit. "I'll starve first!" Lemprière noted that the moderates among them invoked Sir John Fielding while the urgers of mayhem, who were more inclined to break some windows or torch the lascar-house, shouted for Farina. He wondered how many more such disaffected assemblies were wavering between complaint and riot within the city. The mob outside the inn had turned ugly with frightening speed. He stood there, fingering the tear in his coat. Peppard was nowhere to be seen.

The weavers had digressed into an examination of Farina's credentials, and Lemprière listened to their chatter as he looked around the dingy surroundings. Accounts of his provenance varied: the bastard son of a Whitby collier's captain, an orphan, product of a Wapping rookery or a Frenchman naturalized in his tender years from a usurped line of Merovingian kings, a soldier of fortune, an imposter, pretender, mountebank, or Moses; there was mention of his feuding with Wilkes, a shadowy role in the Gordon Riots two decades later, exile in the Low Countries after that, or Spain, the silencing of a woman in Stepney (never proved). Now he was back, claiming to fight for them and fighting to claim what was theirs, their champion, deluder, leader and mis-leader, a mastiff who would tear off the heads of kings, noblemen, and nabobs. A toast was raised and they cheered "Farina!"

Lemprière moved off nervously. The regulars were clumped together, pint pots clenched, glancing disapprovingly over their shoulders at the racket. Lemprière weaved a path through them to the far side of the room where, at one of the tables which ran along the wall, he saw a solitary figure.

Himself excepted, the man was the only patron drinking alone in the tavern. He approached from the side, still uncertain, to observe the man from behind the cover of two stout burghers who grunted to each other in guttural voices. The man's black cloak was thrown over the back of the chair beside him. He stared straight ahead with his hands clasped about a pint pot, lost in thought, it seemed. The cruise lamps gave a dim, yellowish light, but he could make out a prominent, slightly hooked nose and large dark eyes set into an oval face. Ageless, the man might have been thirty or fifty. The light darkened his skin, Lemprière thought at first, but the tavern's other denizens were ruddier, paler, streaked with dirt or soot, giving the lie to this hypothesis. Straight black hair cut short, white nails . . . a lascar. The clothes had deceived him too; he was well kempt. That was it, and Lemprière made vague connections with the general thrust of Peppard's charges, the Indies, Indians, disappearing ships, lascars worked on Company ships. Nothing was definite, but his certainty that this was the Theo of Peppard's note grew until he approached the Indian who turned and looked up without surprise as though he had been aware of Lemprière's presence for some time. Lemprière extended his hand, inquiring, "Mister Theobald?" The other rose and took his hand. His eyes flicked down at the tear in Lemprière's coat.

"Peppard is our mutual friend," he said. Mister Theobald nodded, removed his cloak from the chair nearest Lemprière, and placed it beside the hat which was on the chair to his left. Lemprière glanced at the hat. The Indian was looking at him. "Of course, how rude," he realized. "My name. I am John. . . ."

Nazim waited for the surname, but at that moment, Peppard appeared and walked directly past them both without a sign of recognition.

"George!" Lemprière called after him. The little man kept on walking.

"Mister George?" said the Indian, shaking Lemprière's hand.

"No, I . . . excuse me, one moment," and Lemprière pushed through the drinkers in pursuit of his friend. "George!" he called again. "George Peppard!" and Peppard turned.

It was obvious at a glance that Peppard's fortunes had changed. The threadbare clerk of a week ago was now a proper Bond Street lounger. A new surtout and shirt with matching collar was topped with a knotted muslin scarf. A pair of brightly buffed shoes with elaborate brass buckles adorned his feet. But the greatest change was his hair. Where before there had been a meager dark brown covering, a shock of bright yellow now hung in frizzed curls almost to his shoulders.

"Do I know you sir?" Peppard affected a mock-haughty tone. Lemprière laughed and clapped him on the shoulder.

"Very good, George," he exclaimed. "Really very good indeed. Come now, Theobald is waiting." He gestured over his shoulder.

"He is *indeed*," rejoined the exotic creature. "He awaits an explanation at the least."

"George?"

"I am not George," said the other. "I am Theobald." Lemprière felt the horseplay had gone on long enough.

"I have already spoken with Theobald," he told Peppard, and looked back to where the Indian was waiting.

The Indian had gone. "He was. . . ." he began, then thought furiously. Had he made a mistake? Peppard's face was peering at him, the lines on his forehead were gone, the eyes a little narrower. . . .

"You turned," he said. "I called your name and you—"

"You called 'Peppard,'" the other interrupted him. "I am Theobald Peppard, George's brother, and now I would like to know who on God's earth are you?"

The Indian had not exactly introduced himself, hardly said a word, in fact. *Mister George*, perhaps he spoke no English, had wandered off aimlessly, despairing of Lemprière's return. It seemed the only explanation, but the man had given a clear impression of understanding every word he said. And then there was the hat. He knew the hat from somewhere. . . .

". . . George's twin brother," the new Theobald was saying. "I received this note a week ago." He showed Lemprière the note George had penned the night he had visited him. "Where is George?"

"You must pardon my mistake," Lemprière offered. "The two of you are very alike. In appearance, I mean."

"Yes," said the other shortly. He was looking around the crowded interior. "Well, I can hardly wait here any longer." Theobald regarded his surroundings with disdain. "Already it is half past the hour."

"You have only just arrived!" Lemprière protested.

"But I might have arrived promptly and loitered a full half hour," retorted the other.

"You mean you would wait twenty years and miss your brother for the sake of a few minutes?" Lemprière was incredulous.

"If George meant to meet me here, he would have arrived on time. What is your interest, in any case?"

"He has a chance to clear his name, with your help and mine."

"Clear his name! Of course! George's ship must always go down with all hands, must it not? I have been here before, Mister—"

"Lemprière," said Lemprière.

"I refused to throw away my life for George's sake twenty years ago. I refuse again today."

"No, no. It is really very simple. We have all the evidence, we need only confirmation." Lemprière outlined the story of Captain Neagle and the *Falmouth*, its disappearance and reappearance.

"Preposterous!" exclaimed Theobald. "Am I supposed to confirm this slander? Do you have any idea who I am?" Lemprière shook his head. "I am the chief archivist of the East India Company," he announced, and threw out his chest.

Twenty minutes later, the two of them were tramping the pavements of

Golden Lane. "It is not so much confirmation we need," Lemprière had said, "but a decision: for or against. Naturally, the whole business is, as you say, preposterous. You are the only man who can prove it, one way or the other. George is obsessed, he must be convinced. We must have proof, you understand?"

Theobald Peppard had understood that he was indispensable. His grudging acceptance of Lemprière's proposal—to call upon his brother at his lodgings—had followed shortly after.

"I still do not understand your own interest," Theobald was saying as they trudged northward.

"In the *Vendragon*? None at all," Lemprière answered. "I sought George's advice on an old document, a family heirloom. We became acquainted."

"So whether this ship exists or not, whether or not it is engaged in some underhanded scheme, these things make no difference to you at all?"

"Exactly so," said Lemprière. "Only insofar as they affect George."

"Aha," said Theobald in a skeptical tone. Lemprière resisted a strong urge to lock horns with George's brother.

"When did you become the Company archivist?" he asked in neutral tones.

"What is it to you?" Theobald snapped back quickly. A raw nerve.

"Curiosity," said Lemprière.

"Shortly after George's shenanigans twenty years ago. Are we there yet?"

"Almost," Lemprière said. The dispute between the brothers was growing clearer. Theobald had taken the sinecure while his brother was silenced.

"Here," he said to his companion, indicating the entrance to Blue Anchor Lane.

They turned and began the final stretch of their journey. A small crowd was gathered ahead of them, and as they drew closer Lemprière saw that they were clustered about the entrance to George's house. They were peering through the doorway, craning over one another's shoulders for a better view. Some of them wore blankets draped about their shoulders. Lemprière edged his way through their midst and was confronted by two beadles who barred his passage.

"Excuse me." He motioned as though to pass.

"A relative?" asked one of the officers. The sinking feeling in his stomach hardened to a cold knot.

"A friend," he told them and was waved through. Skewer was standing in the hallway. He made as if to speak as Lemprière passed. The door to Peppard's room was open. An officer who sat outside did not look up as Lemprière leaned heavily against the door-jamb. Two men were in the room. The first stood between the door and the bed, his bulk partially obscuring the second who knelt, it seemed, on the bed itself.

". . . yes, about a week," the second man was saying. "It would tally with his employer's account. Mister Skewer said he failed to arrive for work on Thursday morning, is that right?"

"It is," said the other. "I would guess Wednesday evening from the evidence here. You would want to talk to anyone who visited at that time. Done professionally, that much is quite clear, head pushed away, incision in the right spot. . . ." The man who was standing turned abruptly, and Lemprière saw then that his eyes were bandaged. It was Sir John Fielding.

"You are a relative?" Sir John asked in a brisk tone. "A friend?"

"A friend," said Lemprière.

"We need a relative," said Sir John. "Mister Rudge, we need a relative, for the formalities."

"Were you here or hereabouts last Wednesday night?" he asked Lemprière. Lemprière could not speak. "Who are you?" Sir John demanded.

"No," Lemprière managed at last, thinking, they will check, find out. . . . "Smith," he said.

"*John* Smith?" Sir John's tone was sarcastic. George, thought Lemprière. George. Rudge was scrabbling under the bed.

"There is a letter here, in pieces." He was talking more to himself than his companion. Theobald arrived in the doorway.

"John, what on earth—" Then he saw the bed.

"John it is," said Sir John Fielding in a gruff voice.

"A love letter." Rudge was picking up pieces of paper, spattered with blood, which had soaked through the mattress. " 'With all my love, Annabel,' " he read aloud. "Annabel who?"

"Make a note of it," said Sir John. That was what Henry would have done. "Make a note of everything." George's body. Lemprière turned and stumbled down the stairs.

Once outside, he took deep breaths of the cold night air, his hands clenched inside his pockets, his eyes shut.

"Why?" Theobald had sidled up. "Why George?" Lemprière stared at the little man, who seemed genuinely puzzled. "Could anyone believe that nonsense of his about Neagle's ship? It was all so long ago, all finished years ago."

"A week," said Lemprière. "Not years, a week. And I will prove it too, with or without your help. George was right. I will find that ship, and the reason for its being here. Everyone will know that George was right and everyone else, yes, you too, was wrong."

"Of course, I will help," Theobald protested. "Within my powers. But let me remind you, Mister Lemprière, George is dead because he nosed about where he had no business. As I said, George's ship always had to go down with all hands—"

"But it didn't, did it?" Lemprière rounded on him. "It went down with George while you were safe in a Company sinecure, and nothing's changed there, has it? Except this time his fortunes will not rise again because he's dead, and you are alive and will not help!"

"Now you listen to me," the other man snapped. "Mister Smith or Lemprière or whatever you call yourself, I will help if I wish, but don't pretend your efforts are for any reason than saving your own hide. If George is dead because he knew of some, some *business*, then you are next. I would not throw away my life for George before, and I'll not do so now. Good day to you, Lemprière, and good riddance!" Theobald turned on his heel and stamped off down the street.

"He was worth a hundred of you!" Lemprière spat after the man.

Theobald's words had stung him, though he was wrong about the ship. George had had no chance to tell anyone of the *Falmouth*'s reappearance. Self-interest, Theobald had alleged. George's words, almost his last, came back to him: *Unless the crisis is you . . . the agreement, John, it begs awkward questions . . . I have been followed.* George had even thought to warn him: *If they are watching me, then they will know of you.* But he had been wrong. It was the other way around. He, Lemprière, had led them to George Peppard. And it was not the ship which had brought them to murder him. Only the two of them had known of its existence. And if it was not the *Falmouth*, that left only one possibility. It was something in the agreement.

In the days that followed the weather grew fine and cold. A bitter wind cut through the first half of February. Peppard was dead. Each day, Lemprière would allow the fact a little more weight, one more of its aspects. The taut membrane of his understanding dipped under the load, touching lightly on other surfaces beneath. Lemprière's thoughts led to the Widow, thence to himself and the face borne away through the night, *yes, that night*, thinking, *He might have wed, his last chance might have completed the cycle to arrive again more wanted and needed than before,* seeing his own chance veer away into an uncertain night, framed in the coach window. Lost? No, everything would come around, in the end. But there was the mess of flesh and blood, Peppard's body, an end to his own cycle. Chopped short: a broken circle, or one never drawn in the first place. As Peppard reached out at the last for the woman he sought through the years of scandal and disgrace, she fell away from him. Lemprière thought of Juliette. Peppard's body punctured the water's surface and sank slowly into the depths; a drowned sailor with the pumping flukes of his destroyer painted in his eyes, the little man shooting up papers and their explanations in streamers, confetti reeling down in a theater rainstorm. A cold truth waited. It stood in the concealment of the characters, in the slopping waters and the night. It was an agreement between dead men, a ship lost and then found. It was Juliette.

After his encounter with Rosalie, and more mindful of his vulnerability following Lydia's swift removal of his purse at the Pork Club, Lemprière had placed the gold signet ring in the safety of his traveling chest. Its jagged surfaces now caught the morning sunlight. A rough "C." It functioned as a makeshift paperweight for the letters, documents, cuttings, and scraps which Lemprière had already removed from the chest, examined, and discarded as irrelevant. The chest itself lay open on the floor beside him. A mound of paper awaited inspection in front of him. He was slumped on the floor and one of his legs had fallen asleep.

"*A* is for *Avarice* and an *Anger* that will burn John Company's ship and shrivel his paper promises and send his men to the hangman in a rude cart so that they be pelted with a raiment that suits, rotted things and suchlike. *B* is for *Bastards,* for they are all *Bastards,* John Company too who sold his birthright for a pittance for a foreign whore and her litter now robs and pilfers and murthers too. . . ."

The anger of Asiaticus against the Company; it was the first pamphlet, preceding the one Alice de Vere had given him. Lemprière skimmed through its torrent of rage. Could John Company and the foreign whore be the original merchants and the investors from Rochelle; the "birthright" their charter? The "rude cart" must indicate a small band of men. It would hardly hold the hundreds, or thousands, employed by the 1620s. They might be messages but, like the second, the first pamphlet grew vague where it should reveal, vented spleen where it should lay down charges. The identity of the mysterious Asiaticus vexed Lemprière quite as much as the tantalizing withholding of his secrets, but both were distractions to his present search which was for an address.

He rummaged on, and the pile before him decreased as he discarded more of his father's papers. The tottering mass collapsed twice, sending the signet ring skating under the bed both times. A draft crept under the ill-hung door. His angry boast to Theobald Peppard, that he would find Neagle's ship and clear his friend's name, sounded like so much wind. Besides, if George's death had a purpose, it was the agreement which would reveal it. *Not the agreement, the story behind it,* Peppard's words.

He went on with his search. A thick bundle of letters tied with yellowing string burst open, scattered, and came to rest in a static cascade. He knew the letter he sought was not among the bound bundle—he had already seen it, before the Pork Club. Curiosity alone drew letter after letter from the envelopes: *Charles Lemprière, Rozel Manor, Island of Jersey,* in faded ink on each.

The correspondents were a bewildering band of informers: priests, spinsters, seamen, bankrupts, second sons back from the Tour, their tutors and dancing masters, chart-makers and shipwrights. Without his father's original inquiries, Lemprière could only guess at the purpose behind these replies. One man had fallen through a hole in Houndsditch and broken his ankle. Another said that the harbor at Saint Malo had a draft of fifteen feet four years ago, but now he was not sure. A third had rowed across the Straits of Gibraltar and enclosed a haphazard diagram of the currents. After ten or more of these, Lemprière's picture of his father's researches was considerably more cluttered but no more intelligible than before. He barely bothered to open the remainder.

The one letter without an envelope was there by accident. Hardly a letter in truth, more a draft. Crossings-out and corrections fouled the neat handwriting, which he recognized at once. Of all the letters in the bundle, this was the only one written by his father. After the first sentence, Lemprière took off his spectacles, wiped and replaced them. At the end of the paragraph he checked the letter's signature. He moved to the desk, sat down, and continued reading. Several times he stopped and drew deep breaths. At the letter's end, so far as the son was concerned, his father was a different man. The letter read,

My dearest Marianne,

As I write you from this room in Southampton I know at once that I am your husband and your betrayer, both of these things. Would that I were only the former, with all my life I wish it, but it cannot be. I am both.

That much you know already, my wife, though not the when and where, nor the how. The why is yet beyond me, but I will tell you the rest and you may judge me as you wish with all the accidents and circumstance before you. I will tell the story in a plain way, even though the hurt it causes you hurts me too and the writing is an agony in truth. But I will do it. I owe you this and much else besides.

It was in Paris, when Jake and I sank money in the wallpaper factory (and what a foolhardy venture that was!). The last day of our visit—we had found our factory that morning and celebrated through the afternoon. We ate and drank a good deal in an eating house—Puy's (Marianne, I do not even know if you wish to learn these things but I must tell you everything now). It was the December of 1769, as you know. The night that followed was almost stranger than I can tell.

After we left the eating house I was in high spirits, but Jake was sullen, as always after drink. It was raining. We walked down Rue Saint Martin, crossed the Marché des Innocents, as the Paris people term it, and moved into all the little streets below it. As we left the market square, Jake turned and fancied he saw a figure standing in the rain behind us. He was a good way off, but even drunk I too saw him clearly enough, I thought. I had a need to find the Seine then but Jake pulled me into a drinking-shop where we drank hot wine with cloves, two glasses of it I had. The man we had seen in the Marché des Innocents a little time before appeared then in the tavern, an Indian by the look of him. I pointed and Jake took fright. Marianne, all this must seem a putting-off of the story, a prevarication, but it is all of a piece I swear. Somehow all these matters had a bearing on what followed; forgive me. Anyway, the two of us quit the tavern in a terrible commotion. I do not know why. It was raining even harder. Jake was extraordinary, pulling me along through the streets. I was quite drunk and could hardly understand his urgency. Later he told me the Indian meant us a mischief but how he knew that is still a mystery. Jake sought a refuge for us in the streets about there but all the houses were dark. We ran and ran, I remember. I was stumbling and cursing and the Indian was still at our backs. That is how we came to the Red House. It was the only one would give us sanctuary. I was soaked through and reeling from the drink. Now, while I sit here writing to you my wife, I can call to mind only parts of what took place. The Red House was a place of ill fame—a bawdy-house to put it plain—and its Madame took us for customers though we only sought refuge. There was a salon, as they call it, where the women of the house wandered about. I remember fires burning. It was very warm. I took a glass or two there. There was a woman called "the Contessa," this much I can still see in my mind's eye, clambering up the stairs but dimly. My next memory is of Jake shaking me awake and carrying me out of that place. The woman was gone and I had no memory of what had befallen me. Whatever became of the Indian who had chased us there, I do not know.

The rest of the story you know; the consequences of that night followed me from Paris to Jersey and even into our own home. The payments I have made provided for all her needs, both of theirs I should say, and so far as Paris is concerned that is the end of the matter. Marianne, I have never seen the child and I never will. I sit in this room covered in a shame which is all my own. Would that I could wash it off, but I cannot. If you wish it, I will stay here. I cannot ask you to forget, only to forgive if you can.

With all my love, your husband,
Charles

She had forgiven him, of course. Charles had returned, penitent, reformed, and now he was returned to his son, reformed again. The forbidding countenance his father had worn fell away as Lemprière read the letter, to reveal a hapless and luckless adulterer, a loving husband, a frightened man alone in a strange port. Also, he could not help but see it, there was something of the buffoon in Charles and Jake's escapade, the drink, the rain, the women. Something of his own experience at the Pork Club. Septimus had carried him out, as Jake had his father nineteen years before. He spared a thought too for the offspring—so fleeting a mention he might have missed it—lost somewhere in the Paris slums, his own brother or sister. Strangely, he felt very much the only child, as if this other had only a speculative existence, or was an invention of "the Contessa," for the money maybe. The money. That was how Marianne would have found out. She had always settled the accounts.

Lemprière rummaged quickly through the remaining papers. Yes, he was right. The receipts were sent as acknowledgments, clearances for the next payment, *reçue par Madame K., 43, Villa Rouge, Rue Boucher des Deux Boules, Paris,* a line of them stretching month after month through the years. It was almost naïve of his father to think his mother would not find out eventually, Lemprière thought, almost as though he wanted to be found out.

In her dealings, his mother reflected the certain boundaries of life on an island which had always been her home. Within them were the gentle contours of maternal and conjugal love, always given freely and without condition. But transgress those boundaries and a completely other animal arose, an embodied rage which he had seen on infrequent, vividly remembered occasions. He imagined his father looking for his wife in those gray-blue eyes as they turned red, and instinctively his hand went to his pocket. Then stopped. Lemprière slammed his hand down against the floorboards and thought again of the night he had bade farewell to Peppard, stopped fifty yards from the house, and patted his pockets. He had left the miniature lying open on Peppard's table. He might have gone back for it. But he had not. His eye had wandered over the room on his return, stunned at the sight of the body, the shock. Would he have seen it, had it been there? Surely yes. The table was right before him. So it had been moved. Taken. By Sir John? No, they asked for "anyone in the vicinity." They did not have a name. Perhaps Peppard had removed it, hidden it. But all these speculations were only an avoidance of the true conclusion: The miniature had been taken by Peppard's killer. No one else had the means. Peppard's killer, whoever that was, held the brass case even now, and on the case was his name. Lemprière. He imagined cold eyes flicking over the inscription, weighing up the threat, the need for silence.

Wait, wait, wait, he told himself. If he, the holder of the agreement, had led the killer to Peppard, then he was already marked. Already spared. He was a symptomless carrier, only those he touched suffered. He thought then of his first night alone in this very room, when he had imagined his father's ker flying up, carrying all its troubles into the ether, sending them up like so many plague signals to advert his own special pollution. Miasma. For all the exorcisms of his dictionary, all the fixing of his daemons, they were there inside him still, flying out to ring him with the blood of innocents: his father rolling over, an accusing arm lofted heavenward pleading in futility; the woman in the pit, as the molten gold poured down; and George, his friend, a mess of blood on the bed. How could he tell anyone, when even the breath of it led to death? Only Septimus had heard it and lived. What protected Septimus? *You can trust Peppard.* Those words grew heavy with significance and yet became no clearer. It was a signal of sorts. Sent to him by Septimus, received by him, imperfectly deciphered. The emphasis fell on all or any of those four words, reshaping them, pulling them this way and that. Septimus had hinted broadly that he should talk to Peppard in the first place. He had contrived both meetings with the De Veres. He had helped him with the dictionary. Septimus had arranged that.

Morning became afternoon. Lost in his own thoughts, Lemprière did not hear the midday clamor of the city's bell towers. His search continued in a listless way. Scraps of paper were turned over idly, examined perfunctorily, discarded without regret. His father had become the apex of a host of corridors which opened one by one under his scrutiny, radiating out and revealing paths the dead man had followed, all abandoned now. They all represented aspects that the son had barely guessed at. It was past three when he found the object that had prompted his search.

From his study, Charles had sat penning questions, notes, and letters to unseen recipients near, far, and wide. He had corresponded on the subject of the western coast of France, its harbors in particular and their suitability for ships displacing four hundred tons. Another corridor entered blindly.

Lemprière sat in his own makeshift study in Southampton Street and turned over an envelope. *Captain Ebenezer Guardian (retired), the Crow's Nest, Pillory Lane, Wapping* was marked in untidy script on its back, a passport to his father's earlier inquiry (whatever that might prove to be), thence to Peppard's ship, which was to say Neagle's, the *Vendragon* or the *Falmouth*, any or all of these.

So, Captain Ebenezer Guardian (retired) would clear up these confusions? He would explain the mysteries of every port south of the Cherbourg peninsula and Charles's interest in them, not to mention the significance of a ship lost these twenty years past and recently returned, which spawned it. As Lemprière donned coat, pocketed letter, and readied himself for the journey, it all seemed very unlikely.

• • •

The problem was radical. The limitations of the material (wood) created complications at the design stage. The notoriously officious Lübeck customs men levied tax on the deck-space, thus the less deck the better. At the same time, crossing the shallows of the Zuider Zee necessitated a vessel with as small a draft as possible. Captain Guardian sat before a well-stoked fire in the Crow's Nest contemplating these problems.

Clearly, a flat-bottomed ship would be needed for the Zuider Zee, if its holds were to be capacious enough to show a profit, while excessive tumble home, rising out of the water and curving steeply inward to the deck, would deny the Lübeck tax-farmers their ill-gotten levy on the deck-space. In short, a fluyt. Viewed head-on, it would resemble an upright, swollen triangle with masts: a floating hold, really. Problems abounded: with no effective deck, how would the fluyt be manned? And, even supposing its roomy hold was filled to bursting, how would the same cargo be removed? Guardian fiddled imaginatively with hinged fo'c'sles and a drawbridge mechanism, but it was an ugly brute, this fluyt. At least it had little need of ballast. The tumble home would need feathered planks, lots of them. Captain Guardian sighed. He hated planking, and was even beginning to wish he had never embarked on the project, when the small brass bell hung in the narrow staircase beyond the door jangled suddenly, announcing a visitor below.

Eben hurried his stiff limbs down the stairs, curious as to his caller's identity. At the door he was confronted with an angular individual, tall, dressed in a pink coat, with spectacles, who thrust out his hand and began talking at once.

"Sir, I am—"

"I remember who you are," Eben said. "You're Charles Lemprière's boy. John, is it?" He shook the proffered hand. "Come in, come in. We all looked for you at the De Veres', you know? Bad business, that. Come aloft." Captain Guardian indicated a narrow staircase which, as they ascended, seemed to grow narrower until the Captain had literally to squeeze himself up between the walls of the final flight, though his guest did not touch them, and which brought them finally, both puffing, to a room crammed with papers, charts, and dog-eared volumes of all descriptions, in which a small fire burned brightly and four windows looked out to all points of the compass.

"The Crow's Nest proper," Captain Guardian announced. He offered his guest a seat. Lemprière arranged his legs. Eben regarded his guest. A nervy thinness; crumpled in the stepladder's wreckage he had looked somewhat spidery, comical. The physique was the same, but there was nothing laughable about him now. Tense, he looked. Put him at his ease. Eben had liked the sound of his father, matter-of-fact sort of chap so far as one could tell. The fluyt could wait.

"My condolences on your father's death," he said, and the young man acknowledged them with a solemn nod. "I wonder, how was it he—"

"Hunting accident," Lemprière said quickly. "I am afraid I missed our appointment."

Appointment? thought Guardian. Front of the De Veres', of course. "Not at all, no, we were tramping around hunting for you, in any case." The fluyt resurfaced in Guardian's thoughts. Portcovers, like portholes, bigger though, enough to load the thing. That would do it. Ramps for access.

"I was curious," the young man was saying, "as to my father's letters to you."

"Of course. So you should be. Fascinating man, your father. Harbors he was interested in."

Charles Lemprière had fired Eben's curiosity. Building ships was one thing, and a great thing too, no doubt about that. But it hardly stopped there. Launching, floating, steering, navigating, all these actions made the ship fast to its yards, its port, the sea, the sea's vagaries, and beyond that the stars. All these were the life of the thing. Constraints too, but the balance of them all against the tonnage and the will of the men aboard, that was the real ship. A dynamic beast, breasting the headland breakers, nosing inquisitively through sandbanks, a living thing taking harbors for its homes, different from one another as an Adam town house from a wattle-and-daub hovel. Eben searched the crammed shelves of the Crow's Nest.

"Harbors on the western coast of France. Anything that would take a ship of four hundred tons. Your father had an idea a ship of that size was plying the coastal trade. Seemed rather unlikely to me." The young man looked puzzled. "Too big," Eben went on. "Coastal trade means rivers.

Difficult to navigate, and so far as France goes, no sailing. Prevailing winds are easterly, inland from the west coast." Still puzzled, it seemed. "You can't sail," Guardian spelled it out. "You have to use the currents. A big boat like that would need a big current, and anyway the draft would be too shallow. The Loire flows westward, but not from the west coast. The Rhône is good as far as Arles, but after that, well . . . The charts are useless, that's the real problem. Riverbeds move around. A deep channel one year can be a sandbar the next. It just isn't feasible."

"So what did my father actually want to know?" Lemprière asked.

"Harbor plans," said Eben, "any harbor with the right draft."

"Pardon me, 'draft,' I'm not—"

"The depth of water drawn by a vessel, the depth it needs." Eben pointed to an engraving above the mantelpiece by way of further explanation. "Anthony Deane's the man. Had it all worked out with tables and suchlike. Invaluable. Charles, your father, wanted charts which would tell him the harbors such a ship could put into."

"And you told him?"

"Well, no. I had to send to Holland for most of them, old friends over there. . . . Anyway, the last only arrived a few weeks ago. I had them bound too. All takes time." Captain Guardian gave up his post at the bookcase and marched to a plan-chest on the other side of the room against which leaned an object Lemprière had taken for a tabletop. Eben hoisted it aloft and staggered back. "The binding may have been a mistake," he grunted. The leather-bound slab was deposited on the floor.

The two of them squatted down. Eben watched carefully as the young man opened the heavy cover and glanced through charts of Le Havre, Cherbourg, and Brest. Charles Lemprière had engaged his enthusiasm and his curiosity in equal measure. The detailed queries of the dead man's letters seemed to circle about some larger question. He could not be sure, of course, but all his experience told him that a ship of four hundred tons tamely hugging the coast of France was an improbable event, if not an impossible one. Four hundred tons: That was an ocean-going vessel. It had no regular business with coasts.

Lorient. Nantes. This son of his did nothing to damp Eben's inquisitiveness. There was more to his visit than a dead man's effects. Eben regarded him sideways as he turned to the final chart. La Rochelle. The young man was staring down, suddenly intent where his interest moments before had been perfunctory. Rochelle then, thought Guardian. Was Rochelle the home of this phantom vessel?

"Beautiful harbor that, best sort too."

The young man looked up, distracted from his thoughts. "Sort?"

"Oh yes," Eben said. "A natural. You can take a good lagoon harbor, give it five years and the river will silt it solid. Rochelle's got these natural headlands." He indicated the points of Minimés and Chef de Bay. "They keep the worst of the weather out. The approach is complicated, of course. There are two islands, here and here, and a couple of mudbanks,

Pen Breton and La Longe, here and here. Then there's Richelieu's ridiculous tower which keeps the channel narrow." Lemprière looked up, not understanding. "You can see the top of the mainmast, but the rest of the ship is hidden behind the tower. The depth is good, though. Only obstacle is the remains of the mole—"

"A mole?"

"Built during the siege. Richelieu blocked off the harbor. There were ships sunk across here"—Guardian drew a line across the narrowest point—"and just behind them he built a mole, a kind of sea rampart. Stop the English ships getting through to relieve the town. It was many years ago, but there are bits of the bloody thing still there."

"Sixteen twenty-seven," said Lemprière. He was staring at the plan.

"Yes, I suppose so. But for Richelieu, La Rochelle would be one of the best ports in Europe. That's just my opinion, of course." The young man traced the outline of the harbor with his fingers. "The port itself is at the far end from the mouth; you pass between these two towers and unload in the city itself. Have to go in on the tide, naturally." He was odd, this spectacled visitor. Was he even listening?

"The shape," Lemprière said absently, still staring at the harbor. "I know it."

"What? From where?"

"Pardon me, I thought . . . I must be mistaken." The young man seemed to gather his thoughts. "And La Rochelle would take a ship of four hundred tons, then?"

"No doubt at all. A good tide would give you four, five fathoms. More than enough. Of course, that's not the real question, your father's, I mean."

"No?"

"Is it?"

"Pardon me?"

"Not at all," said Guardian. He was hard-going, this Lemprière.

"What I mean is, the real question is about the ship, isn't it?"

"Oh. Yes, yes, I see."

"A ship of that size going up and down the coast," Eben went on. "What is she doing? What, more to the point, is she carrying?"

"Quite," said the other.

"Well?"

"I have no idea. I rather thought you might know."

"You have no idea what your father was looking for?"

"None at all," said Lemprière with convincing candor.

Eben sighed, then closed the book. Another mystery. It was the sea, of course. But why a ship? Why at the bottom of everything was there always a ship? His knees cracked as he rose from the floor and walked to the east window.

It was late afternoon. The light was beginning to fail. His eyes traveled over the jostling ships crammed together in the Upper Pool of the

Thames. His spirits were strangely sunk. The legal quays were full as ever. The suffrance wharves on the southside likewise. Three-masters, little brigs and sloops, a few colliers, they were all jammed prow to stern against one another. Only the steps separating the wharves offered a space. Barges nosed clumsily about the larger ships moored in midstream like sightless fish. Apart from the *Vendragon*, of course. The *Vendragon* was not attended by anyone. Captain Guardian looked over the shambling mess of wharves, piers, stairs, and watergates, the greater and lesser vessels with their masts and rigging, their varying states of disrepair, and saw hierarchies, precedences, pecking-orders: All the intricate subdivisions and degrees of standing which were the sea's secret language made wood, canvas, and rope, different responses to its vagaries. Every sort of sea had its ship, so the shipwrights said, and the sea delivered its rebuttals without favor or discrimination. Eben viewed the vessels before him with a colder eye. So many ships and boats. So many secrets . . .

"What a lot of masts." The young man had joined him. "Is this a good harbor?"

"A port," Eben corrected him. "It would be, if they took the trouble to dredge it once in a while, didn't choke it with tanneries and mill wheels. The other side of the bridge is practically a weir. You see Dyce's Quay?" He pointed.

"The one with the big boat?"

Eben mentally bit his lip. "Ship, yes. That's lost five feet of water in as many years. Most of the others even more. The tide runs out here, and they all discharge ballast on the quiet. Bloody disgrace. The wharfingers block anyone who tries building any more quays. Bristol's got more frontage than Port of London, and a quarter of the tonnage, would you credit that?" But he was talking to himself. The young man was looking out over the Pool, this way and that. What did he want?

"Your hand healed, then?" He was looking at the relic of the incident.

"Damned tattoo," replied Eben. The automaton's wound had marked his flesh in spidery black lines, *Falmouth*, now indelible on his palm. Part of him. The young man was looking out the window once more.

"I have a friend, had a friend: George Peppard . . ." The name rang faintly in Eben's memory. Peppard, Peppard . . . The Neagle affair, of course. Peppard had been the lawyer, gone down with the ship, the *Falmouth*. This second Lemprière had seen the wound in his hand, heard the root cause of his action as he tried to take the sketch from Maillardet's contraption. *Vendragon. Falmouth.* One and the same. The boy was telling him about the Neagle affair, the whales. . . . He remembered it all.

"No one who knew Alan Neagle believed that story about the whales," Eben interrupted. "A fine sailor, the best of his generation, but ambitious beyond measure. Lied to his own wife, didn't he?" The young man was still speaking, telling him things he already knew. Neagle's ship sunk without trace, miles off course, Neagle silenced, an insurance fraud unprosecuted through want of evidence.

"The Company could not afford a scandal, they *had* to silence him, and his wife, and her lawyer. . . ." Yes, yes, thought Eben, insurance frauds. Worse things had happened.

But now the evidence was here in London, moored a cable away in plain view, the *Vendragon* née *Falmouth*, Neagle's lost ship. He had known it for weeks, and he had known Neagle when the ship first put out. Admired him. Disliked him a bit. Clever and hollow. Pretty wife. Youngest commander of an Indiaman in the Company's history, brilliant talker. Everyone knew Neagle, or knew of him.

"My friend, George, he was disgraced even though he was right, and then you told me the ship was here, and it proves he was right. They have renamed it, but it's still Neagle's ship. It's not the *Vendragon*, is it? It's the *Falmouth*."

"Glad to be of help. If I can clear a man's name," Eben began gruffly.

"You cannot. No one can. He was killed two weeks ago, the very night I told him what I learned from you." Killed him? The point of it all began to dawn on Eben. The Company killed him. . . . Yes, he could believe that.

"It was no robbery, nothing was taken. No coincidence either. I promised him I would help. That night, I promised I would help to clear his name." The voice was cracking. Lost friends, Eben understood that. Waste and grief, the sea's toll on its travelers. So they had killed his friend and this gangling specimen would bring them to book, put them before the masthead. Very well, very well. Now he knew why Charles's son was here. The proof for which he had come was visible still, touching gently against the wharf, tap, tap, tap in time with the slow swell of the river.

"There," Eben pointed to the wharf. "That's the *Falmouth*. That's Neagle's ship."

Eben watched as the young man leaned forward, his nose almost touching the glass. The porters were at work, shifting rope-handled crates along the quay as before, one man at either end. A cart was disgorging more crates farther down the jetty. He could not see the two watchers. Their attendance had been less certain of late. The young man's face was set, his gaze fixed on the *Vendragon*. He would not be able to understand the scene; see it, yes, but no more than that.

"If your friend, this Peppard, if he was killed, are you not in some danger yourself?" Eben asked. They were carrying crates over from the cart.

"I believe not, it's odd, a long story." Absent tone, his eyes fixed on the ship, and the crates. "Why have they brought it back? Why now?" Eben looked at him. It was more than curiosity, this thin face.

"It arrived empty," he said. "They off-loaded some ballast, nothing else. And they knew it was coming. That quay was clear a week before it docked. Would've cost a small fortune."

"It has been here long?"

232

"Months. Usually it would be loaded in days. The pressure on these quays is immense."

"What is going on?"

"I have little idea. Those are Coker's men working down there. Hired hands. If it was all aboveboard they would use regulars."

"I have to find out," the young man said abruptly, and he was even walking toward the stairs when Eben's voice sounded loudly in the confines of the room.

"No!" The young man stopped, looked about, already questioning. Eben thought how he might explain it, that he was not in the Strand or the Adelphi, that he was here, in the docks, at the river's edge where the laws and rules and codes of the land grew ragged and frayed as the land itself when it petered out into water and became the mudbanks which the tide said were both land and water. To the outsider, a dubious area with its own rules, its own privacies and penalties. They would throw him in the Pool, nail him in a crate and throw him in. They would not think twice. He was ignorant, he would blunder and fall foul of the laws. He did not know them. Tell him that.

"It's a rough crew, you see," he said. "You'll get no answers. Something worse most likely, you follow me? Stay clear of the docks with your questions. That's good advice, young Lemprière—"

At that moment he was interrupted by a loud crash and a volley of curses from the quay. They met again at the window and craned their necks for a view. One of the crates had fallen, a snapped handle. It lay like matchwood about the smashed crate's contents. A statue of some sort, someone carrying a pot on his shoulder, six feet or more had it stood upright. Packing straw began to disentangle itself from the statue's limbs. So that was what they were carrying. A thickset man was shouting at the men.

"That's Coker," said Eben. Two of the men ran to the ship, returning with a shroud that was wrapped hurriedly about the statue. The original carriers and the fetchers hoisted the load between them and the statue continued its journey, swinging between them in a makeshift hammock. "There!" Eben stabbed his finger, and Lemprière just saw a wiry man dressed in black, hatless, as he walked behind a row of dock cranes.

"Did you see him? He keeps watch over the loading."

"Who?"

"Don't know. Usually two of them, hiding from each other." The statue was halfway along the gangplank. "Coker takes his orders from that one, the other's more of a puzzle. But that one's the commander." They both looked again. The man in black had effectively disappeared.

"He'll be the Company's man," said Lemprière. Eben nodded, both unsure. The statue had disappeared into the hold. The line started up again. "Statues," said Lemprière. "There must be more to it than that. If I knew what statue, perhaps."

"It was Neptune shouldering an urn," said Captain Guardian. "Through which water might run, as in a grotto."

"Neptune? But he didn't carry a trident, and how can you—"

"Can't cast a trident. Too fiddly," Eben said.

"How, pardon me, how do you know? I hardly saw it myself; but—"

"I've seen it fifty times before. Every garden with running water and an owner of the middling sort has one. It's Coade Stone. They turn them out by the hundred. Yours for nine guineas, three shillings, and ten-pence, if memory serves. That ship is loaded with fake statues," Guardian laughed. "So now you know." The young man offered a tight smile in reply.

"I need more than that," he said. "They might sail at any time and I would be left with nothing." He was staring down at the men and the ship. Guardian could read his thought.

"I tell you no," he said. "Stay away. If they are working some decep-tion they will deal with you as they did this Peppard. The Company is not to be trifled with."

"The Company is a vile thing," the young man said bitterly. "A cold, creeping thing. Am I to do nothing?"

"A regular Asiaticus," said Eben genially. Diffuse this Lemprière, he thought, quieten him. Fools rush in. . . . Keep him away from the hired hands, away from the sharp end. But his guest was gazing peculiarly now, not calm but deflected. By what?

"Asiaticus, how do you know of him?" the young man asked sharply. Guardian thought back, surprised at this turn to his questions. He told him of the pamphlet which had washed up on the mudbank a little way up the quay some months before, "A. Bierce" inscribed carefully on its fly-leaf, the author's vitriol and rage all muddied and blurred, caught up and whirled in the tidal waters to fetch up sodden in his hand at the river's edge. Taken home and dried before the very fire now burning low on the other side of the room, it had amused Guardian to read of such hatred for the Company. In truth, he had little love for it himself. A late autumn evening had been enlivened, lifting him from the melancholy of the Ballast Fiasco which had preceded its arrival by a single night. He handed the pamphlet to Lemprière now, who cast his inured eye over its alphabet of anger. It was the third of four. Again, more promises of revelation than revelations themselves. Promises or threats.

"Keep it, if you have a use. . . ." Lemprière took the wrinkled, dried-out pages. Yes, he did, not quite knowing what yet, but yes all the same. Thank you. His eyes drifted back to the ship.

"Listen to me, young Lemprière. I will keep a watch over the ship. Leave her alone. If they make ready to sail I will get word to you. And, if time is short, I will take the helm myself, do you understand? You have my word." The doubt was already gathering in his guest's face. Must he offer credentials on top of his word? "I sailed from this port, man and boy, for close on forty years. If matters come to a head, I'll find the men I need, believe me," Eben affirmed. The doubt faded slowly. The two of them shook hands on it.

"I am in your debt," Lemprière said solemnly.

"Oh," Eben brushed the obligation aside.

"You said two men?"

"Two? Oh yes. The one you caught sight of, that's one. The other's an odder creature. Black cloak, hat—"

"What does he look like?"

"Couldn't say. The hat covers his face. A broad brim, like this." Eben drew a wide circle in the air above his head. "You know him?"

Lemprière thought of hats. "No," he said.

"Now, I have my own question," Eben said. "What was your father really looking for? This ship of his, what was it up to?"

"I only wish I knew, but until today I had no idea he was looking for a harbor, let alone a ship. In all honesty, I know no more than you." Eben accepted this reluctantly. He poked at the fire, then the young man spoke again.

"What was the *Falmouth*'s tonnage?" he asked suddenly. Eben smiled.

"Yes," he said, "four hundred tons, or thereabouts."

"My father sought a harbor for a ship of that tonnage."

"There are thirty or forty ships of that size sailing from this port alone. All the older Indiamen are around that size."

"So my father was looking for an Indiaman," Lemprière leapt on the fact.

"There are plenty of other ships of that size, hundreds—"

"But most of them are Indiamen. I mean, what if my father's lost ship and Neagle's are connected in some way?"

"You mean, 'What if they are the same ship?' "

"Yes."

"Because they are both probably of four hundred tons."

"Yes."

"And they both have something to do with the Company, possibly."

"Yes."

"In my opinion," said Captain Guardian, "that is about as likely as an IJmuiden cargo-boat avoiding ship tax at Lübeck. And that," he added with emphasis, "is very unlikely indeed."

Indeed. Lemprière left the Crow's Nest a short time later with Guardian's promise, his warning, and the chart book, the latter a black leather sail whose width being an inch or so longer than his reach would be carried two-handed and a foot from his face at the mercy of any gust or other urban turbulence which might blow him off an even keel, spin him about, and capsize his fragile bark utterly. There were hats involved: the broad-brimmed affair worn by the elusive Watcher No. 2 and mentioned by Guardian, a similar one glimpsed for a panicked split second when a hand of steel dug him out of Farina's mob, ripping his coat—still unrepaired—and now, as he pushed his flapping atlas against the rogue wind, homeward up the gentle slope of Pillory Lane toward Thames Street, the Indian at the Ship in Distress came to mind, his eyes flicking to the ripped pocket, his cloak (a *black* cloak) slung over the chair on which rested a black broad-brimmed hat, just as Guardian has described. Were all these the same hat? Different hats? The same hat worn by different men, exchanged tête-à-tête at regular intervals; some other, less discoverable arrangement?

A billow of wind pulled his black shroud along as Thames Street was entered, sailed through, and left behind. Lemprière lurched and stumbled, a jolly sight for the passersby. The irregular sail blocked his view. The slight irregularities of the street were keel-crunching reefs, and his fellow citizens becalmed wrecks inviting collision. A hazardous journey, and below the surface clutter an old monotone was sounding up from the hadal depths, connecting with him and then diving down once more for a long-dead Greek whose black-sailed ship brought Ægeus tumbling down the cliff, dead from that earlier son's forgetful mistake. His fingers were numb with the effort and the cold. It was dark. Hints of the coming jacquerie adorned the walls of the capital: *Their Banners Will Be Stained With Blood In The Streets*, on the wall of Rowlandson's glass-factory; then, more simply, more coolly partisan: *Farina*, chalked on the bricks of the adjoining yard, already crumbling, already being lost to the urban mulch which squelched underfoot as he forced the passage home through an unrelenting head wind. He imagined the lashing wind and rain eroding the features of idols until their noses and mouths were bland and picturesque, ready for the restorer's touch. Theseus with an idiot's grin. Neptune carrying a pot "through which water may pass, as in a grotto. . . ." There was more to it than fake statuary, more than the massed productions of Coade. . . .

In this manner he continued, pulled by sails which were pictures of the sea, pictures of harbors, a careening rattling hull veering insensibly between known and unknown coasts. The rudderless vessel, steered by a hundred different winds, lurched over a sea of old mistakes, its mainmast sinking slowly below the horizon toward the ragged mouth of its last port where it would be pincered between the headlands and becalmed within the basin of Rochelle, a lost ship.

There was a familiarity to the harbor plan, a half-grasped correspondence. Perhaps, in some other unremembered time, he had drifted within the basin of Rochelle, looked about at the jutting spurs and banks running this way and that, and then, viewing the abstract of that scene on Guardian's chart, reduced and from above, the earlier surroundings had come back to him as though he had flown above it all and seen the natural harbor with its mouth, the only access, the only break in the haven's rough circle, making its image a wide and irregular "C."

A drenched messenger boy had waited in the hallway of the brothel. They had read Jaques's note and left directly. Vaucanson recalled the teeming rain. They had found the Indian in Rue Boucher des Deux Boules, outside the bawdy-house. The lights from the Villa Rouge had blazed through the thin material of the curtains in squares of glowing red. The Indian had stood like a sentinel outside. Le Mara had spun him about, knocked the breath out of him, taken a knife-quick flash of steel to the throat. The hired men had finished it.

Seventeen: Vaucanson counted the winters since that night. They had carried him to the coach. He remembered the Indian's oval face looking up at him. They had taken him to England. From Dover to the metropolis, thence down through the hidden shafts and tunnels, Vaucanson had fetched him back to this place, a workshop littered with silver wire, copper rods, angle joints, spring-loaded governors, tiny ratchets and reticulated chains, watchmaker's and surgical tools. Here, secreted in a remote gland of the Beast, Vaucanson wasted no time in slitting the Indian's fingers and sliding in the shiny steel rods. The floor was awash with fluids, and his own arms coated to the elbows with gore. He could gaze into the Indian's eyes and see the original man interpenetrated by the machine with its gears and tiny winches, its self-governing extensors and sensors, its blank inaction a neutrality which could not be human: the peace of the Zero-State.

"Bahadur," the machine had croaked.

He had turned the Nawab's last "envoy." That night in Paris, Jaques had emerged red-eyed from the brothel with the dupe, the latest of the Lemprières slumped unconscious over his shoulder; another dangerous game, that, and who in the end, seventeen years later, had resolved it? Who had sweated long months down here with the dogs howling and spattering him with their shit, as he drew their hates and affections along filaments of steel and sutured their soft brains with silver-wire stitches so that they saw The Pool and they saw The Man, so that they passed safely by the naked girl and the boy who would be concealed in the bushes on the other side, just as he bypassed their canine affections to reach the lupine substream which drove them to tear Charles Lemprière apart?

Crude engines, the dogs. Casterleigh had shot them later and good riddance. But Bahadur, his earlier and more precious creation, was altogether different, an altogether more delicate balancing act between necessary human memories and his machining under the screw-thread, scalpel, and saw. They had sent him back, this assassin, sent him back to his master the Nawab as a silent fuse.

Somehow, they had lost him. Returned to the Carnatic and his master, they had heard nothing. The Nawab continued as before. And now

Bahadur's successor was in the city, better primed for the task. Better able to reach them.

So, for that matter, was Charles Lemprière's son. Vaucanson looked behind him at the ranks of humanoid forms. The dim light caught steel plates festooned in a tracery of wires, nodules of brass and zinc, intersections of metal and nonmetal. All this would be fleshed out in clay. An amalgam of some sort, they would cast them at the Manufactory, disguise them as garden statues. Another of Boffe's misbegotten spectacles, and he thought with disfavor of the De Veres', hauling the smelter and crane down through the gardens to the bog under the guise of drainage equipment. Drainage equipment! The Coade Manufactory was convenient, already suborned, already put to other uses, and yet. . . .

He thought again of the figures lined up behind him. Crude things, limited, built for a single purpose. The leader's plans encircled them all, baffling them, throwing them this way and that, and he too had been thrown by the request, had nodded and accepted the new parameters. Could this latest Lemprière justify this panoply, this overwhelming motley in which the eight of them cowered like puppet-masters dressed in black against a black background, all these layers of camouflage and deceptive armor? The leader encrusted them with his impossible schemes as though a connector that should have ensured a simple loop had worked free somewhere inside him and was thrashing this way and that, deluging them with its mad spray of thoughts. What function did these schemes serve when their objective was so simple?

Above his bench, the clock whirred and struck. Vaucanson carried the lamp before him as he left the workshop and edged carefully along the ledge beyond it. The Beast's own dim illumination was hardly enough. He thought again of the Indian and Le Mara, the quick scuffle in a rain-swept Paris street which seemed to play out its moves over and over again, round and round in his brain. The meeting chamber's brazier was before him now, across the gravel apron of the antechamber. Was that Casterleigh? Yes, and with him Le Mara.

Two silhouettes slipped into the chamber. His footsteps were amplified in the cavern's vaulted ceiling as the tiny dry stones settled noisily beneath each footstep.

"All they await is our ship. . . ." Jaques was already speaking as Vaucanson entered. Seven candles burned, his own made it eight. Only the ninth remained. Only the chair next to the leader stayed empty. All were present: the leader flanked by Monopole and Antithe, his two echoing sentinels; Boffe, Le Mara, Casterleigh, and Jaques, who was telling them of Paris.

"Duluc, Protagoras, and the Cardinal have already set their men in place. They understand what is required of them. They have consented to everything. The first disturbances will be minor rehearsals. Paris itself will stay untouched right up to the last moment. It can simmer for weeks, months even, before it boils over. Paris is the key. From Paris, it will spread outward through the provinces all the way to the frontier. Beyond, perhaps. That is when we must act."

"But can our funds support it? Support the whole enterprise?" Casterleigh queried. "We would be left with nothing if—"

"There are no 'ifs.'" Jaques spoke calmly. "Paris will fall. France will fall. And we shall catch her."

"And if not?"

"Jaques is right." The leader's ruined voice spoke from the shadows. "The country will be ours once more. If we lose her, then we lose everything. These matters are already agreed. We are committed. We cannot remain exiles here for eternity. We must act as one. *All* of us." The leader gave the word an unnatural emphasis.

Vaucanson looked from one to the other. Casterleigh subsided. Jaques was telling them about the ship, the rendezvous at Point Minimés, colored lights, times, arranged signals.

"Duluc will be there with his men. They will be ready to unload the ship on the appointed night." Vaucanson tried to imagine their return, the creaking of the rigging, the slop of the waves as they sailed homeward, but all that came to mind was another, more distant voyage, an ignominious flight past the palisade, the smell of their sweat as they cowered in the boat, and behind that a vile stench which hung in a pall over the broken, abandoned city. The smell of burning . . . Could they return to that? The burning, the fading screams, but all so long ago, he told himself, dead and left unburied behind them, the price of safe conduct. Now they would repay it, every last *sou*, give everything they had to regain their demesne. The choice was already made. Casterleigh was hunched silently in his seat, full of silent anger. There had been disagreements over the lawyer, this Peppard, who had buzzed about the Company, a winged irritant for twenty years, who had flown too close. "Contain him," the leader had commanded. But Le Mara had killed him, and Casterleigh was behind that. It all went back to the boy, Lemprière, whom they were to place in a fabricated world of twilight truths and compromises, of uncertainties and hallucinations, their own world, and all this circling and hedging about was in place of the old solution tried and tested over all the stubborn generations of Lemprières, and Le Mara knew best what that was. The lawyer had been an associate of this latest Lemprière and there was no more reason for their procrastination than that; his was an elimination long overdue. Vaucanson thought back as Jaques's voice droned on. The Lemprières snaked back through the years like segments of a worm which they had diced as each generation took up haphazardly where the last left off. The unequal struggle went on and on until it had seemed there was no end to their snaking enemy. Medusa-like, this John would term it. Now the last of them was here within reach, and still the leader held off. Some fear of their extinction gripped the leader, the other bond with this spectacled boy.

"He will approach from here." Boffe had his absurd plan laid out before them all, begging their indulgence, their attention so precious to him. The Manufactory was represented by a crude box. The roof came off as Boffe indicated the necessary course of events. ". . . through here, and out the door . . ."

"Is her participation necessary?" Jaques asked.

"He must follow her," Boffe began to explain.

"She is the bait." Casterleigh cut him off. "And I will distribute her as I choose." Juliette, Casterleigh's creature. "She will do as I say." Vaucanson saw that faint inflection register on Jaques's face, but he had no claim on the girl, no special interest, her accompanying him to Paris aside. Vaucanson thought briefly of the night it had rained, Jaques emerging from the Villa Rouge.

"You already have a girl for this purpose, this Rosalie, do you not?"

"She is safe enough," said Casterleigh. "No need for worry, Monsieur Jaques." It was almost a sneer.

"Clear enough, Monsieur le Vicomte," came the leader's voice. Vaucanson saw Casterleigh look away with an ill-concealed grimace. "Lemprière will play the part we give him," the leader went on. "Our friend assures us of that, and time is short now for he has found the ship."

The others looked up in surprise, none more so than Le Mara, whom Vaucanson watched as he wrestled with incompatible facts, saying, "Not possible," in his harsh monotone.

"Apparently, he saw a crate break. Our friend tells us he saw the contents. . . ." And there it was again, something like warmth in the leader's voice, pride in this Lemprière's agility at jumping through their hoops. "He knows of the ship, he knows of the Manufactory, or will do. Our own friend will see to that. Are we agreed?" The nods were hesitant, reluctant. Vaucanson's part in the arrangement was already complete, waiting blindly in his workshop far below, lined up ready, *click, click, click.* . . .

The meeting ended. Vaucanson retraced his steps across the antechamber. He heard a sound behind him, stopped and turned. Casterleigh and Le Mara emerged out of the darkness.

"A word, Monsieur . . ." A word before he turned again, with their proposal aligning itself in his thoughts, before he continued his descent through the deserted galleries and stone enfilades, along narrow ridges and tubular corridors with his decision wavering between yes and no, on and off, for and against, before he recognized Casterleigh's ambition as their salvation from the leader's schemes and mad preparations, before he answered yes, he was with them, and the leader had outlived his use.

. . .

Something was wrong with the sky. All day the gun-metal cumulus had inched across, extending its monotone to all points of the compass. Somewhere far above the clouds' fat undersides, an invisible sun had probed laboriously but without success. Now, with the onset of sunset, a drastic wound spilled freakish purples and yellows onto the congruent gash of the river.

Lemprière watched from Westminster Bridge as garish light connected the river surface with the sky. The brazen patriarch behind him would have flared into gleaming life had the light burst its banks, had the statue been polished in the recent past and been cleared of pigeon droppings and other more willful defacements. *The Streets Will Cry For Farina* was scrawled in slashes of green chalk on the pediment, the work of furtive sloganeers. Such sentiments were growing, gathering force in the city, catalyzing its low mumbles and grumbles, its cussedness and craven protests, injecting more potent terms into the rituals of discontent. Their solutions may yet involve the breaking of carriage windows, daubing of churches, burning of opera houses, acts of unfocused violence. Lemprière peered once, then again, before loping off nervously onto the bridge where the light was now the color of cheap jewelry, thinking, *they'll think I did it,* toward his rendezvous with Septimus who was late and would not show up. A woman selling apples followed him. Sky mostly gray at this point. River still purple.

Over the bridge in search of Coade, prompted by Guardian's mention of the statue material a week before at which Lemprière had remembered a previous conversation scattered through the hubbub at the De Veres'; talk of giant tortoises cast in Coade, something to do with an opera house, someone called Marmaduke. Coade Stone.

"From the Coade Manufactory," Septimus had informed him, "in Lambeth."

That was two days ago. Between his return from the Crow's Nest and Septimus's arrival he had worked diligently at his dictionary, finally halting at "Iphigenia," whose heading stared up at him with eyes accusing as Iphigenia's own, ranging through the later dreams of her father Agamemnon.

"Immolate her," Calchas had told the Greek commanders at Aulis. Unhelpful winds had fetched them up high and dry on the Boeotian coast, and as the temporary camp grew rife with explanations, offenses real and imaginary were floated as possible provocations for their ill fortune, while the soldiers cooled their heels on the beach and their commanders quarreled over who was to blame. Perhaps Agamemnon was absent from the crucial meeting, when the debate reached its conclusion and the propitiatory victim was chosen. Perhaps he was hunting and perhaps this suggested the official line to the huddled commanders. Agamemnon had killed enough stags for one of them to be Diana's favorite. *Stags, Diana, the familiar counters are gathering, another round is starting up.* . . . It was credible, and with Calchas's sanction, with their own solidarity . . .

Agamemnon took the decision on the chin, understood this particular need, sent for the girl. Word was sent to Clytemnestra, a nonsense about their daughter's marrying Achilles. Iphigenia arrived to the sight of ominous preparations, hymenal fears replaced by mortal ones, pleading with the tear-stained eyes which would later have Agememnon tossing and turning at night under the Trojan walls. And yet, when Calchas's knife was raised, swung down, seemed to slice through innocent flesh and innocent bone in a first gout of bright blood, just then, well . . . A goat, yes, standing there on the altar, bleating, blinking its yellow eyes in plain view of all. A substitution? Metamorphosis? The suppliants speculate. A divine intervention, most certainly, and in fact the story went on, though the Greeks did not know it, involving other, yet more far-flung clansmen and an extraordinary resolution which time will bring bubbling to the surface.

Lemprière saw Iphigenia torn up and reassembled by the phony cross-currents of impending war, a prevision of wider and more gruesome conflict. He imagined Agamemnon as a failed paterfamilias, persuaded out of reluctance by the nervy cabal of his confederates, offering token resistance while his wife was hoodwinked into connivance. Ghettoed back in Mycenae with the slaves, the women, and the ghosts of Argive kings, Electryon, Perseus, Acrisius, all urging gullible acceptance, grandson, son, and father to Danae, who was victim of a similar arrangement, Clytemnestra sent the girl on her way. How many daughters have been lost? How many recovered through coincidence, luck, fate, or intervention from higher up? Lemprière imagined Iphigenia as a doll, a plaything for the furtive band of heroes to while away the long, windless days, pulled this way and that by their different whims until the sacrifice itself, when they stood there mocked by the absurd goat, so obviously the product of a wider logic, an idea quite beyond even the wiliest of them. And, as mentioned, the incident had its coda.

The sky's ragged mouth was closing, sucking violet light out of the river. Lambeth confronted Lemprière. An old woman was trying to sell him apples.

"Lambeth," Septimus had said as he gathered up most of "G," all of "H," and the greater part of "I." "All signed?"

Two days had passed in outward idleness while Lemprière imagined himself leaping onto the altar at Aulis, a grinning Plautine slave facing down the massed *milites gloriosi* in their ceremonial breastplates, snatching the girl, and racing out to a waiting canoe. A stray arrow *(stray arrow?)* would catch her as he paddled against the weak coastal tide, there would be grief (convention demanded it) and revenge. He thought of Juliette, dreaming thoughts of a beautiful future which involved terrible mutual loss and long years of grieving on both their parts. To lose her was a kind of romance too. He could almost believe he had won her in the first place. But then there was the kiss, his first, bestowed lightly in the library. The actual press of her lips, her hands as she pulled him up outside the church, all these nudging his cloudy constructions until he rubbed his eyes, stretched and stamped about the room. Why could this not be enough? He awaited signs, fated meetings, an astral sanction. Septimus and Lydia, Warburton-Burleigh, even the Pug, they all had an air about them, an assurance. Everyone seemed to have it. Juliette had it. He did not.

Healing themselves aloft, squeezing the bruised light to a crack, a livid line, clouds of a darker gray lowered their bulging undersides onto the city like sinking ships. Westminster Bridge threw its details into the twilight, and Lemprière realized that Septimus was not going to turn up. It was well past six. Lemprière bought some apples, turned away, and walked south over the river for Coade.

"Funny stuff," Septimus had said. "And Eleanor's no stranger than she should be. Took the place on twenty years ago, makes ornaments, statues. You see them in gardens, on buildings, all over the place."

"But I've never seen them anywhere," he had protested. "What *is* Coade Stone?"

"That's the cleverness. It looks exactly like stone, is hard as stone, but a fraction of the price. No one's exactly sure what it is, some sort of earthenware, almost porcelain. The exact formula's a secret. They mold it, then fire it in huge kilns at the Manufactory. You know those Dolphin pedestals? Edmund has a pair. They're from Coade's."

Lemprière remembered watching from the Crow's Nest, the crate breaking open on the quay.

"So they're loading a ship with it," Septimus had continued, taking a bottle from his pocket and looking about for a glass. "So what? What does it matter?"

Lemprière had thought of a brash promise shouted after Theobald in Blue Anchor Lane that night, of George dead in a room with a scattering of cheap furniture. He thought of Guardian's caution, Peppard's warning, of his own luck running out. It would be easy for them, easy as George was. He had turned to Septimus.

"I need your help," he had said.

The river was behind him now, north through the haphazard streets of the New Road. A greenish tinge hung in the air as though Lambeth were sunk in water.

Wine had slid down his glass in films of overlapping pink. Septimus had listened to the tale of disappearing ships, reappearing ships, whales, crates, statues, insurance, and the harbor draft at La Rochelle. He had heard Lemprière's suspicions about the agreement and been told that it was already worth one man's life, perhaps another.

"Peppard knew the ship was here, here in London, but not why. That is why I must go to the Manufactory," Lemprière had finished up.

Must go? Irritated reflections on Septimus's unreliability mingled with the motives for these late disclosures. Who else might he have told? Who else would listen? The *Falmouth* was berthed in London, renamed *Vendragon;* it was being loaded with statues. François had made an agreement with Thomas de Vere, something had happened at La Rochelle, George was dead. These facts were his satellites. His father was dead. He thought again of the pool, the dogs, the great gray clouds and the girl picking her feet out of the water. The elements gathered around him. His father rolling over, one arm held up to ward off dangers that had already passed, and in his mind the same scene was unwinding like fine silver wire. The woman with her distorted face twisting away from the glistening downpour, the hiss of metal, the smell of it. These matters cohered in him. Buried legends cracked through the generations' interment, flooded back at his unknowing behest. Was it himself holding all these things together? Peppard had not died for any ship, but a piece of paper signed a century and a half before. Less: an opinion on that paper, requested by himself. Guilty.

The Coade Artificial Stone Manufactory stood in Narrow Wall by the King's Arms Stairs. Two spacious yards guarded by high brick walls flanked, successively, a large triple-fronted house, four high, narrow roofed sheds built one against the other, and a long windowless hangar which effectively doubled the size of the complex. The sheds faced sideways to the street, rising clear of the house by ten feet or more, their steep, gabled roofs reaching back out of sight. Between these sky-lit sheds and the house, itself no mean structure, an alley ran, visible through the iron grille of a gate set into the brickwork. Two larger double gates enabled access to the yards thirty or forty paces down the road, and over these the legend "Coade Stone Manufactory" was mounted on hoops of wrought iron. By day the scene bustled energetically with raw materials arriving at one yard and the finished product, crated for dispatch, leaving by the other. Workmen wheeled in clay and coke, stokers fed furnaces which turned out the grog—prefired pellets of clay—by which addition the remarkable shrinkage rate of barely one inch in twelve was achieved. China clay, sand, and glass made up the formula upon which the Manufactory's fortunes rested.

Now, as Lemprière approached the smallest, most central of the three gates, which would open to admit him to the alley beyond, the complex was deserted. He clutched his apples as talismans in his one good pocket and entered. The alley led him to a pair of high coach doors which were opened to disclose the dim interior of the first shed.

He went in, allowing his eyes to adjust to the dim light filtering down from a skylight high overhead. Large wooden hoppers stood against one wall together with a large number of hessian sacks bulging with coke. A number of oil lamps were ranged along a shelf to one side of the door.

"Hello," said Lemprière. No one answered. He picked up one of the oil lamps and began to walk the length of the shed in search of matches. The partition dividing it from the next shed ended a few yards short of the far wall. Lemprière realized that the entrances were staggered. He had to walk the length of each shed to find exits which were always at the far end from the entrance. He proceeded in a formal zigzag into the second shed, just as narrow, just as high as the first. He could smell wet clay. The floor plan of this part of the Manufactory was now clearer to him, and he moved more confidently past a row of low vats with buckets hung on the wall behind them. He skipped over some sort of stirring device, tripped on another, and fell heavily against the last vat, saving himself only by grasping the bucket on the wall behind, which slowly pulled its hook out of the wall and emptied a stream of ground glass into the vat. The unlit lamp fell softly into the glass-covered clay as Lemprière himself teetered on the edge, this way, that way, finally falling back toward a large chimney breast. He rested against it for a second, then smelt burning. His hand! The bricks were scorching hot. The chimney formed one side of a huge kiln. He blew on his palm and felt cautiously in the vat for the lamp. Undamaged.

Lemprière removed the hood and set about opening the heavy door to the kiln. A touch of the wick against still-hot coals brought it flaring into life. He returned once more to the vat and tried in vain to scoop glass out of the clay. Eventually he replaced the bucket in defeat. The lamp threw huge shadows up the shed's steep walls. On the side of the vat, the word "Stalkart" had been scrawled in green chalk, the letters "H.O." beneath it. Lemprière went on, past the kiln, picking his way around flat-bed trolleys, coils of rope, shovels, and a large water tank, into the fourth shed where the landscape suddenly changed.

Faces stared out of the walls, limbs hung inertly from indented shoulders and hips, animals inverted themselves in snarling attitudes. Molds, he realized. He hurried to pick a way through the narrow corridor between their stacked ranks. The fourth shed brought him out into a corner of the hangar he had seen from outside.

A few of the molds seemed to have spilled out into this wider space. They were large hemispherical affairs, irregular inverse domes about five feet across. Something was scrawled on each, green chalk again. "Stalkart" again, now "M. Stalkart," and "H.O." was "Hmkt. Op." He looked more closely. Inside-out tortoises, Lemprière realized, giant ones. . . .

The hangar was a warehouse. Its interior stretched away into a darkness well beyond the flickering apron of lamplight. The far wall was invisible. It was filled with statues, pale, almost luminous, effigies. Blind eyes stared at him as he held up the lamp. Hundreds of them, thousands, a petrified forest sewn from dragons' teeth. Cupids and little cherubim, gods and goddesses arrayed in a vast, disorganized tableau. He could see Pomona, Father Time, Neptune "with an urn . . ." and without, a trio of Graces, Samson, Hercules strangling vipers, Zeus with his thunderbolt, all in Coade Stone, standing there like silent witnesses. And all of them seemed to be looking toward himself. Three women held out their arms, the first veiled head to toe, the second helmeted, the third rising out of a stony spume: Juno, Minerva, and Venus awaiting the judgment of Paris. Lemprière placed an apple in each of their open hands and sniggered to himself. The goddesses looked on, unamused.

A soft clanking reached his ears from somewhere above. He held the light up and saw chains, long looping chains hung with hooks every ten feet or so suspended from heavy rails, a lattice of them crisscrossing the whole warehouse. Some sort of lifting system. The statues were arranged too closely for—

Bang! It was the door, the door to the first shed, and Lemprière was a trespasser, a thief, a spy come for the formula. He froze, then moved toward the statues, thinking to hide himself in their midst. *Click,* from somewhere in their ranks, then, *click, click, click.* . . . Something crashed to the floor in the second shed.

. . . *click, click, click,* taut mental surfaces rose out of zero-states. Lemprière heard stone grind on stone, somewhere back there, in the dark they were moving. Footsteps? Footsteps! Coming closer, in the third shed now, and he could not bring himself to walk into the mass of statues, with their limbs twitching in the half-light, stone moving against stone. He looked around quickly, thought to douse the lamp, and even as he cast around for a hiding place, even in his panic as the steps grew louder, drew nearer, a cool clear voice in his head which was not his voice said, *"It begins again, you know its outline, only your attendance is required now.* . . ." Not his head. Where else?

Lemprière pulled a tortoise mold away from the wall, heavier than he thought. He crawled under the bowl of its shell and lowered it like a trapdoor to cover him as the footsteps rounded the corner of the last shed. He stuffed his fingers in his mouth, not because he was frightened, though he was, but because as the lip of the shell had lowered he saw the three goddesses he had earlier sniggered at close their fingers on the apples and apple pulp ooze between their stone knuckles and drip to the floor. Dead. He was shaking, trying not to breathe as the footsteps halted and the maneuvers began.

An air hole. Lemprière pressed his eye to it, cowering in the tortoise mold. He heard footsteps circle about him. He could see the blank faces of statues lit by yellow lamplight. Not his light. A shadow, close up to the air hole, another, someone had walked past, ankles, skirts, long black hair as she moved farther away. Were those anklets, leather bands set with turquoise? Recognition dawned; as she halfturned, he tried to rise an inch, and something slammed down on the mold, something covered the air hole.

"Juliette!" he shouted. She was walking into the midst of the statues. "Get away!" He heard the grinding sound grow louder, penetrating the shell of the mold and then a soft exclamation, "Oh," an unsurprised tone. The grinding grew louder and he strained his back to throw off the mold but it was held fast. He kicked and shouted again. Something cracked inside the mold, a shard of Coade Stone which his feet had broken off. He grasped it and hammered blindly but it was no good. He could feel the shard cutting his hand. Outside, there was a softer sound, a sucking sound, like a boot caught in mud as it comes free, *suck*. . . . The chains began to move and rattle dully.

Click. The air hole was uncovered. The statues were unchanged, unmoved. He pushed again and found he was able to lift the weight of the mold. He rose and stood upright. A lamp was burning, placed on the floor some yards behind him.

"Juliette?" he called hesitantly, then again, louder. The chains swung softly, their links clicking against one another. He picked up the lamp and held it high, trying to peer through the ranks of statues. Somewhere, a tank was leaking. He moved a little closer, craning his head. A steady drip, somewhere in the sheds, behind him.

"Juliette?" The dripping sound grew louder, a fraction faster. He looked to left and right. Had she left? Escaped? He thought that for a moment. When he turned he saw the black slick on the floor. The indifferent light caught the drops as they fell in a quick *drip, drip, drip*. He looked up at the chains. An animal carcass hung ten feet above his head. A goat. Gutted, it formed a sort of hammock. Lemprière saw the loaders struggling with the statue, carrying it aboard the ship in its shroud. Its head hung down. Her hair, long and black, hung down. Her feet stuck out the other end, the leather bands still about her ankles. It was hard to see her face. In its passage from her throat to the cool on the floor, blood had run down the chin covering eyes, nose, and mouth. And his eyes were wrong. A door was open across the place. Beyond it was the second yard. He walked toward it, a careful step to begin, though when he passed through it he was running, faster through the yard, past the stacked crates, faster it seemed than he had ever run before. Behind him, the girl swung gently in the embrace of the goat. The links of the chain clicked softly, almost inaudibly together, *click* like nervous military heels, the massed soldiery sniffing and looking at one another, their abashed commanders frozen to the spot, ashen-faced before the sight of the goat tapping its shiny hooves on the altar where, this time, Iphigenia had waited too long for deliverance. . . . Juliette?

. . .

Accident and design. Nazim was haunted by one, lost in the other. The cellar's dark had grown populous with ghosts, telling him different stories in different dialects. Behind them all, some lambent Ur-tongue curled gently, caressing them toward accommodation, a sort of sense. Not yet, not yet. The Nine he sought were now eight. They had plotted against one of their own on the night torrential rain had washed through the streets and two women in blue satin had talked before a makeshift fire of a girl, Rosalie, and a "prank" played on the Lemprière. Three months later he was dead, his throat slit in a room on Blue Anchor Lane. Bahadur's "Lemprière," and his own: The three were caught in their own triangle. Now it was broken, the Lemprière was dead, and some link came free in Nazim with that fact, something which had bound him to his task, *find them*, words spoken in the Nawab's palace, the strange tense laughter, *kill them*.

The Lemprière was his ambiguous guest, who hovered about the paths of his thought and whose outline flickered in and out of view, recognizable suddenly and without warning.

He rolled over and felt the hard case dig into his ribs: the miniature, the woman with blue-gray eyes. The Lemprière's mother. Above him, the remaining of the two women moved listlessly. Again, she had not lit a fire. Almost dawn now.

In the melee outside the inn, in Blue Anchor Lane the night of the Lemprière's death, at the Ship in Distress a week later where he had almost discovered his name: "John. . . ." left hanging in the air— frustrations followed the tall young man in his absurd pink coat; a traveling accident, this henchman of the late Lemprière. He had slipped away as the young man engaged Theobald in conversation and waited outside. He had followed them dutifully to Blue Anchor Lane, though he had known what they would find there, and known too that their discovery would tell him nothing. Another trail followed through until it gave out on a trackless plain where he, Nazim, found himself in familiar limbo once again. He had resorted to the docks, but even the business of loading the *Vendragon* had grown intermittent. Long days of inaction greeted his renewed vigil, and the ease with which he accepted this new mode unsettled him. He thought of Bahadur, the woman depicted in the miniature, and, above him at this moment, talking a gibberish he could barely follow in a tone he could hardly hear, Karin, the woman in blue. The smell of decay filled the house and Nazim caught himself following her decline with lessening detachment. Shadows racing up the cliff. He felt the changes.

In the second week of this new phase of his vigil, a crate had broken

248

open on the quay. A large statue, someone carrying a water pot, had lain briefly on the ground in full view until a length of canvas was found to cover it and haul it aboard. Le Mara had darted out, an eel from its hole, then retreated back into hiding. The statue had been carried aboard in an improvised sling. Nazim had remained where he was, unseen by them all, following the mishap, looking around and about him. And up. The window at the top of the house was lit, a hundred yards away from the ship but barely fifty from his own post. Two faces were staring out over his head at the fiasco on the quay. It was the old man whom he had earlier taken for the building's sole inhabitant and, beside him, the spectacles identifying him, the thin curves of his face confirming it as he gazed down on the ship and the men wheezing under the statue's weight, stood the Lemprière's companion.

The Lemprière himself was suddenly present, invisible, grinning, announcing the first of his surrogates: *Meet them, shake their hands. . . .* Nazim, edging sideways behind a tangle of crates and splintered planking, kept his eyes fixed on the figure above, seeing him in the inn where he had hovered, very erect, remembering the way his head had jerked back a little at each hesitant emphasis as he spoke. He had approached ostrichlike, the rip in his pink coat still unmended. The slight tearing sound had hardly been audible in the angry din. The brawl encompassed him as Farina had shouted for calm, a postponement of hostilities, and he, Nazim, had hauled the young man out by the collar. The brutes fought. Farina shouted. Now, he was growing more significant, present in numberless acts distributed through the city, both great and small, from the rip in the boy's coat and the slogans to the tight clusters of men huddled on street corners and, less clearly defined, more urgent acts, quick meetings, referrals, tiny cracks in the city's glaze forming a slow pattern in the seismic quiet. Soon, thought Nazim, but when?

And there was the Lemprière again: chuckling, feinting, muttering *j'adoube* as the stratagem once more failed to unfold and Nazim remembered the first time he had heard the name, in the palace of the Nawab. It marked a point in time and space very distant now. The Nawab's commands were dim shouts, receding cries, ignorable complaints. The story was the same, for he would find them, and kill them, but it was about himself and others now. Himself and Bahadur. Himself and the Lemprière. Even himself and the woman on the floor above, or the woman in the miniature, or the two who had already disappeared. Even himself and Le Mara.

The boy, the pseudo-Lemprière, had later left the house overlooking the quay, staggering under a large black book. Nazim had followed Le Mara back to Thames Street where, over the following days, other events were to unfold.

It began with the black coach. He had last seen it scattering pedestrians, taking the woman in blue away from the coffeehouse. It reappeared around the corner from Tower Street and came to a halt outside Le Mara's house. Three days had elapsed since the incident on the quay. The door opened and a thickset man with a hawkish nose alighted and entered the house directly. Nazim watched as the door was closed. As the afternoon light faded, no lights appeared in the windows. He thought of the trapdoor in the basement of the house. The man did not reemerge until the early hours. The coach moved off at speed. Nazim listened until the clatter of hooves on cobbles was replaced by the night's silence. Another of the Nine, thought Nazim. Eight now, he corrected himself. The Lemprière stirred inside him, relapsed.

On the second day the same events were repeated and Nazim waited with the coach and the dozing horses. A little after midnight, a light appeared in an upper window and shortly after that Nazim shrank into the shadows for there, only twenty or thirty yards from him, was a young man, almost invisible in a black coat, black shoes, and black stockings, walking down the street toward the house. The door opened to admit him and the young man entered. When he left, an hour or more later, the light at the top of the house was extinguished. Whatever lay beneath the trapdoor had not been for his eyes; untrusted, thought Nazim, a supporting player.

The following two days saw Le Mara back at the quay where Nazim watched as the efforts of the preceding months seemed to loop back on themselves. Cases which had earlier been loaded onto the *Vendragon* were now taken off. The men employed in this task managed their loads with greater ease than before, however. It was apparent that the cases were empty. Nazim watched as a wagon was piled with the containers, then driven slowly though the streets to Le Mara's house.

Here, the foreman, his helpers, and Le Mara alighted. Two further cases, somewhat larger than the others, were added to the load. The hired hands struggled a little under the weight. The wagon moved off once more, and again Nazim followed as it trundled down Thames Street, continuing west to London Bridge, where it crossed the river. The Borough led both of them south, wagon and its shadow, until the wide highway was exchanged for a maze of tiny streets which led them into Narrow Wall Road, thence to the King's Arms Stairs. The coach turned through a pair of wide gates into a yard. Nazim read the legend: Coade Artificial Stone Manufactory. The sky was leaden, had been so all day. Now a rift opened above, an odd light was streaming through the opening, somewhere north.

The two crates were unloaded and the lid prized off the first. Nazim watched as a young girl was lifted out. Something was wrong with her legs. She looked dazed, pretty, long black hair hung down her back. The two men frog-marched her around the side of the large brick building which formed one side of the yard with several tall sheds at its rear. Beyond these a lower, more extensive building stretched away until a second yard, identical to the first, completed the Manufactory. Le Mara followed the ugly procession.

The second crate remained on the ground beside the wagon. Nazim could hear a sharp knocking, a scrabbling sound coming from within it. The noise came in haphazard bursts. Some minutes passed before Le Mara and his accomplices returned. The girl was no longer with them. Le Mara's countenance was unchanged. His assistants seemed to step hesitantly. A command was barked and they began levering open the second case. The two men wrestled with its contents under Le Mara's directions, reached in, and manhandled the occupant out. It stood there, blinking even in the failing light. A goat. Le Mara knelt quickly at its side and the goat staggered sideways. Its hind legs would not support it. It fell and twitched on the bricks until it was still. Blood ran out of its throat. The two men picked it up and carried it toward the sheds. The gashed sky was closing itself, the evening approaching.

Events accelerated then. The black coach appeared, driven at speed down the road and into the gates. Le Mara signaled. A figure was making hesitant progress watched by two pairs of eyes. It was the pseudo-Lemprière tripping toward them, stopping midway along the side of the Manufactory, entering a small door set into the brickwork. The black coach disgorged a passenger. The same girl, for a moment, the identical dress, the same long black hair. Were the features finer, subtly different? Difficult to tell in the twilight and at a distance. The pseudo-Lemprière had entered the Manufactory between the brick building and the sheds. Le Mara had the girl by the arm. The same dazed expression, looking about her as though landed blindfold from the air. The coach pulled away, down the road toward the second yard. Le Mara was leading the second girl behind the building by the same route as the first. Nazim used the coach to mask his progress down the road toward the far yard, trotting at a crouch by its side until the gates were passed and he was on the far side of the structure behind the sheds. The girl emerged. She was clutching something to her face. The coach door opened, the thickset man had caught hold of her. She fought. Nazim watched as she was cuffed, then the man looked down on her.

"The bargain was yours," he said coldly. The girl struggled. She was led quickly to the coach which made off again at speed. Nazim heard shuffling footsteps somewhere inside, moving faster and faster until the door flew open and the pseudo-Lemprière was suddenly running across the yard. Nazim ducked behind a crate. The boy stumbled, almost recovered, then tumbled, was up again running even faster out of the gates and down the street. Nazim thought for a second, then gave chase.

Later, lying in the cool quiet of the cellar, Nazim questioned his choice. He might have searched the Manufactory, its interior would surely have told him more than the events which followed. The pseudo-Lemprière had collapsed, wheezing, a few hundred yards down the road.

Passersby stared curiously at him. He seemed oblivious as he continued erratically, veering in and out of the road toward the nearest tavern. Nazim saw him order a glass of brandy, then another. Someone barged against him and he lashed out, catching the offender on the top of the head. He was hit back and fell to the ground, then was thrown bodily out the door by a group of men. He reentered and would have suffered worse, but a black-garbed figure appeared out of the rough mass and stood by the young man. The group surely might have defeated him but something stayed their hands, something in his bearing. The pseudo-Lemprière was scooped off the floor by his rescuer, whom he then tried to punch. More drinks followed. As the rescuer turned from the counter, Nazim saw that he was the visitor to Le Mara's house two days before, the untrusted one whose footsteps he had not heard. And, as he watched through the grimy window of the tavern, he fancied there was a resemblance between them, very slight, growing slighter as the bruises came up around the pseudo-Lemprière's face.

The two of them downed glass after glass and Nazim knew that he had made the wrong choice. He should have followed the coach, or the wagon, or searched the Manufactory. He would learn nothing here. Even posthumously, the Lemprière had deceived him again. He had turned from the tavern and walked home by Westminster Bridge where an old woman had pestered him to buy apples. They filled his pockets as he gained the house in Stonecutter Lane. Karin was asleep, lying on the floor above his head. Nazim had lifted the trapdoor and climbed silently into the room. Drawing the apples out quietly, one by one, he laid them next to her. He climbed back into the cellar. He had made another error, chosen a blind alley rather than the trail. More than ever before he felt at sea, awash with competing, contradictory waves, out of his depth. More than ever before he felt that he must fail for want of a single good bearing. The woman had woken, found the apples lying next to her. The sun rose finally, a bright brilliant ray. Lying in the cellar, Nazim heard the woman's teeth crunch on the apples. He listened as she chewed and swallowed. He smiled to himself, and the Lemprière chuckled at his side.

• • •

Now, strong wings unfold over the wider canvas. March peels off the African coast and spreads north over the Mediterranean up into the Adriatic's stubby pelagic isthmus. Here, where the brave tunny swims amid glittering shoals of sardines, the ocean currents have almost given up their ghost. Waters nudging the coast around Trieste, Fiume, and Venice have taken four decades to reach this point, four more will flow past before they see the Straits of Gilbraltar again. The March winds which whip fake white crests out of the wave-tops meet this collar of land and shoot up to bring weird weather systems down on the geography hereabouts. Snow still dusts the Hungarian Steppes, drifting in the Klagenfurt Basin where warming foehns blow the loose powder around before threading through the broken country of Bosnia and on through the dry valleys of Herzegovina and Dalmatia. The notorious Hungarian winter is at an end and the Campaign Season is afoot once more.

The Imperial Internuncio has disappeared without trace and the Venetians have allowed a Turkish squadron to operate out of Castel Nuovo. The Emperor himself travels to Trieste. In Vienna, the Venetian ambassador is rarely seen in public, never at court. Stories concerning his private habits circulate the city and, thinly coded, reappear in German gazettes. The Turkish squadron sails up and down the Adriatic. Hundreds of miles away, at Constantinople, the standard of Mahomet is unveiled in the seraglio to excite the warlike ardor of the people. Still no word on the Imperial Internuncio.

In Paris, divisions are less tangible, more devious. An invisible order is defining itself beneath the visible. Only the King does not know this. Placing his *arrêt* on the Official Statement of the Revenues, and again refusing to abolish the *lettre de cachet,* he soothes a fractious Parlement: "My Parlement ought to submit with respect and in silence to whatever my wisdom judges proper. I lastly forbid you to renew your deliberations on this subject." He has said this four times now. He is troubled. Someone keeps moving the orange trees and this means something he cannot quite divine. Both Himself and Monsieur are dropsical. Madame has promised to reorganize her household for a saving of fifty thousand louis d'or; it is encouraging. The King has abolished a number of tax offices; an opera is ordered in celebration. News from the Vendée is that discontented smugglers, dispossessed of a livelihood by his tax reforms, have taken to gun-running. The Assembly of the Notables announces the revenues to be one hundred and eighty-five million francs. The King is delighted. In deficit. King depressed.

And. . . . The airs above Paris are pleasant zephyrs, teasing gusts, and thermals, splendid for swooping and diving, for keeping just pleasantly airborne while the arriving warmth of spring fills the sky. The air-gods are ambient, endlessly accommodating as they body about, tumbling him downward, metropolitan angel, OK, missionward. . . . Compared to them, the city is a cracked launch-pad, a broken plate, ceramic trash with the Scum River cutting it in two, riddled with hermetic cells and insurgents' convening points, all the engrams of furtive meetings and dealings which stand out like weals, crisscrossing, zigzagging, deepening in color where they overlap. The most livid marks are his business, the places of the most intense convergence. It seems so casual that the Cardinal should call upon Monsieur Calonne, that Duluc should rent an enfilade of cellars running directly beneath the Palais de Justice or Protagoras commission a survey of the catacombs which riddle the city and give access to the most obscure and surprising parts of that city, many of these exits yet to be discovered, hence the survey. . . . What could be more natural than *les Cacouacs'* tendrillike operations, their measured expansion and gradual preparations? Monitored from this distance, it seems so clear, so obvious. How could anyone fail to see it? Especially those closest, in the thick of these whispered assents and noiseless understandings, tipped winks and clammy handshakes, almost encircled by the whole business. And who *is* moving the orange trees?

Wood delays at Cherbourg. The fortifications (called in the officialese of a now-mountainous correspondence *refortifications*) are months behind schedule for want of wood. The heights still look down welcomingly on all and sundry. They should look lowering, discouraging, at least dismal. Work has ground to a halt. (High-altitude turbulence aloft clears the sky, giving the illusion of a serenely blue infinity.) Above the channel, huge white cumulus formations bank up and around. Below, ships lie at anchor off the coast at Deal, the sloop *Cockatrice* and cutters *Nimble* and *Wasp*. Charles Mitchell of the Indiaman *William Pitt* bound for Fort Saint George sees the *Commerce* disappear over the horizon for North Carolina. Fishing smacks loaded with smelt and salmon ride the bars of the Thames estuary, the north foreland is far behind, ahead the wooded slopes of Kent rise behind a marshy acreage of shouting fowl and gravel strands. The alder, willow, oak, and birch creep riverward from nowhere to line the banks of the crowded river, and the tide pulls steadily, five or six hours at a time, on the vessels nosing upriver for berths at Blackwall and the Upper Pool. The *Countess of Mexborough* is departing for Oporto, but there is a delay, a shortfall is discovered, and Captain Guardian watches as bales of wool are off-loaded onto Porter's Quay. Captain Roy is scurrying about below. He had an idea to travel to Charing Cross this morning. Francis Battalia, alias the Stone-Eater, is performing at No. 10, Cockspur Street, for two shillings and sixpence (the captain's stumbling block) and is affirmed an extraordinary phenomenon by people of the lower sort who watch him openmouthed as he swallows pebbles, stones, and small rocks. "Persons as please may bring their stones with them," and they do. Very few notice the heavyset men who march directly upstairs and who seem to be exempt from payment. Mister Boyle (surgeon) who has examined the Stone-Eater's grosser excrements pronounces them beige in color and of a sandy composition. Doubters remain, arty snobs mostly, but even Francis can only guess at the animal-mineral symbiosis which is going on inside him, a ventral mystery about which his technique flutters, the Mouthward-Backward Flip and *gulp*, the Gravel Plume, the Pebble Cannonade (for this he currently wears a cap topped with a small Austrian flag) and the Big Rock Swallow. Even through streaming eyes he cannot help but monitor the to-ings and fro-ings up and down the stairs, along corridors aloft and all the other seemingly innocent convenings of Farina's lieutenants. Even when one trips noisily over the stumps of a nautical cripple at the back of his audience, they hardly waver. A tribute to his art, even if obscurely used by these conspirators with their studied workaday airs. Young men and women in faded calicos and garish chintz look wonderingly on. The silk-and-satin set stay away. They await the golden throat of Signor Marchesi, lately arrived in town to sing Sarti's *Guilio Sabino*. His voice is judged no less a prodigy than Gabrielli's, a tenor mezzo-bass running fluidly through contralto to the highest soprano reaches, and this is only his reputation. Excelling in portamento and expression, he runs through three octaves of semitones with as much rapidity, smoothness, and precision as Cramer's violin, so it's said. Bidding has been high, Lord Lansdowne's offer of £100. for a private recital is already turned down. Marmaduke Stalkart, caught with a bill from Coade's, was never in the bidding. He settles for Signors Morelli, Calveri, and Merigi in a revival of that comical favorite, *Gli Schiavi Per Amore*, which alternates through March with Storace's *La Cameriera Astute*. Houses are reasonable, and the dance interlude, featuring a *pas seul, pas de deux, cinq, sept, Bernois,* and *Russe,* is booed less than usual. Only the tortoises mar his composure. Marmaduke had hoped to have them installed by March at the latest but the Manufactory has delayed, suffered disruptions, offered excuses. Twenty-seven of the amiable beasts should be grinning astutely over the Haymarket Opera House, beckoning theatergoers away from Cobb's, but his roof is still bare and his balance at the bank depleted. He would like to call off the concert for the New Musical Fund (a sure loss-maker) but fears to disappoint. If only the tortoises would arrive, all would be well. What *is* going on at Coade's? And what are the slogans which keep appearing on the walls of the theater? *Take The Enemy Alive, Farina,* in green chalk?

London in March is quite cold and rainy. Much of Lincolnshire is underwater and London receives a new influx of discontented refugees, joining Cornish copper-miners, laid off following news of last year's deficit, and the still-vociferous silk-weavers. The Lottery Suicides continue. An old woman in Great Wild Street is found drowned in a tub of water, and General Carpenter, who chose the fine black horses which pull the King's carriage, has his cockaded hat pulled from the Serpentine. Nets, hooks, and poles trawl till evening when the pale body is recovered. Mister Antrobus dies. A three-act play called *Francomania* opens at Covent Garden. Cruikshank dissects a cadaver whose organs are all reversed, left mapped exactly onto right, right onto left. Mufti wins the Craven Stakes and the Queen of Naples is pregnant.

In the valleys of Croatia, lagging explosions of sound follow close on silent Turkic smoke plumes. The cannon's fractioned arc delivers a triple charge, sighted smoke-puff and cannon-report sandwiching the cannonball, *ding an sich*, which will blow the scene to smithereens. The scene is too still, far too still. . . .

But March is full of quirks, and thus the Pork Club, usually preoccupied with a glass of *Maraschino de Zara* and the Paris fashion in shoe buckles at this hour, today have murder on their minds. They are convened at the Craven Arms.

"A goat?" Walter Warburton-Burleigh's eyes lifted from a report on the Austro-Turkic conflict.

"A goat," confirmed Monsieur Mustachio and read aloud from the *Lud's Town Monitor.* " 'A girl, aged fifteen to twenty, dark hair, costly dress, was found at the top of the King's Arms Stairs by Coade's Artificial Stone Manufactory this night before last by a party of lightermen. The girl was wrapped in a hammock fashioned from a slaughtered goat—' "

"Goat!" the Earl exclaimed. "Horrible!" Septimus flapped frantically through *The World* to no avail. Lemprière did not move.

" '—throat slit ear to ear—' "

"Where?"

" 'Mister Rudge, coroner, expressed the opinion that she was killed that evening, from her variously departing signs of life.' "—Lemprière rose abruptly—" 'Neither the girl's nor her assailant's identity is known at this time.' *Hey!*" Lemprière had bumped into Monsieur Mustachio's chair and stumbled past for the door.

"John?" The Earl half rose from his seat. Septimus looked up.

"Juliette," said Lemprière. "The girl is Juliette." Then he was gone, the door slammed behind him and the Pork Club left in disturbed silence. The Pug broke it.

" 'Lady Yonge's Concert,' " he spelled out, thick digit prodding the newsprint, " 'attended by the Casterleighs, both father and daughter.' She's not dead."

"Only sleeping. . . ." crooned Warburton-Burleigh.

"What did John mean?" the Earl asked generally, his gaze alighting finally on Septimus, who looked over from behind *The World.*

"Only John knows what John means," Septimus said in dismissal. "It's his work. The dictionary makes him odd from time to time." He warmed to the theme. "He was picking fights with watermen in a Lambeth tavern night before last, had to pull him off myself." The Pork Club are faintly impressed by this.

"I cannot find the story," a man moaned from beside the fire.

"Nor I," said another, scanning the columns. A chorus of negatives was welling up, for, in fact, none of the other papers carried the story in any shape or form.

The watermen had scooped her off the King's Arms Stairs an hour before the tide and carried her like a totem, head high, back over the river to Bow Street. Five men had found her. The procession was a hundred

strong on arrival and Sir John stood arms akimbo before a mob baying
for a murderer's blood. He raised his arms and exhorted them, "Men,
you have all done well!" But he could sense unsatisfied appetites, frustrated needs, the urge to sacrifice something, someone, Sir John at Aulis
before the massed soldiery and the goat's yellow eye on him. *What to do?
What to do?*

"Justice will be done," he went on in a strong bass-tone, voice of
implacable vengeance, what they wanted. Give their blood lusts free rein,
justice could be burial alive, slicing off of the limbs, anything they needed
to imagine. Good God, was that what he was now, the mob's Pandar
handing over a sacrificial whore? But they were turning away, drifting
back. No tide would engulf him, not tonight; tonight he was a beacon
radiating order, yes, a tall beacon in his blindness shining out over the
lanes of safety.

But it was bad, this one. The symbols were in league: the goat, gold
wire sutured the slashed belly in a ragged stitch, the girl a carcass within a
carcass, coupled with it on the steps by the river and left there for the
turning tides, for fair weather and the Fleet.

"Fifteen at least, twenty at most," said Mister Rudge later, as he
snipped the wire, and Sir John heard the goat peel open to disclose its
fruit. "And pretty. Hair black, long. A little undernourished." The
throat had been, knife driven in from the side, pushed forward and
out. Sir John thought of Peppard's body, a professional killing. The same
hand?

"Yes, I would guess that is possible." Water rushed in the basin. Mister
Rudge was washing his hands. But the symbols . . . the extensions of the
act reached further. They had touched the mob, himself; even Rudge. In
the mortuary's coldest cellar, the woman in blue stared one-eyed into
darkness; gold, an obscene stump swelling out of her mouth, piercing her
sides, cooled now with the rest of her waiting for the encumbering flesh
to fall away. A sweet smell hung in the cold echoing air. She was rotting,
and Rudge wanted her buried. He dared not. That one he had kept quiet.
The young Earl could be relied upon for silence. Still, he had not chased
up the loose end from that night. Lemprière, the one the searchers had
tracked before they came upon the body. The sweet smell was stronger,
decay coming for him, for them all. Rudge's footsteps slithered on the
slabs. He must find the murderer. The mob demanded sacrifice. He must
feed their need. Farina was out there, in the rookeries and courts, the
alleys visible and invisible, waiting for Sir John's mistake. He would
know about the girl already, and if that were linked to this Peppard's
death, and the first woman's slaughter came to light, its manner, he could
fill the inarticulate heart of the ritual with whatever he chose, any type of
fear, any carefully channeled outrage. Already the air was mutating,
cross-cut with insurgent impulses and pockets of distortion, the patrician
contract was on a blocked frequency emerging in obscure and unintelli-

gible pitches. Strange acts prevailed. The much-bruited cat-eating contest between Lord Barrymore and the Duke of Bedford had entered its third round last week. Live cats too. Carpenter's suicide bothered him, suicides generally, truth to tell. And the figures were rising. The body politic was turning itself inside out, lewdly exposing its organs for vulgar fingers to pinch and prod. It was a time for moral exempla, but the better sort were dressing like 'prentices at a tannery and the 'prentices taking their coffee at Lloyds. Bulwarks were needed, barriers against Farina's scorbutic influence which was out there massing and gathering. What would Henry have done? Something dazzling and elegant, Sir John reflected gloomily. Swift notice and pursuit, his own watchwords, seemed misplaced. Swift notice of what? Pursue where? The malady was already here, in the city. Perhaps the city was itself the sickness.

The stench of decay was stronger. Rudge's grisly movements, little gristly cutting sounds and sharp tears, filled his thoughts with dead flesh. Pitter-patter of feet, the boy's.

"Sir?" Yes. A woman was waiting upstairs, had waited an hour. She had followed the body from Westminster Bridge.

"In a moment." Sir John sent him scurrying back. The boy was improving. The string about his neck was no longer essential.

"Rudge!" he called. His colleague was swabbing goat's blood off the body, working methodically over the skin's surface.

"I have a name for you, an improbable name. . . ." Rudge dabbed once, twice, looked up at portly Sir John. "A most ordinary and yet improbable name."

"John Smith," said Rudge promptly.

"Exactly." They both thought of the young man bursting wild-eyed into Peppard's room, already grief-stricken, the calmer Theobald following who had confirmed only "John."

"Not Smith?" ventured Rudge.

"Not Smith, certainly. But what?"

"The brother, Theobald, he will know. They were together. In any case, the coat is an advertisement. Bright pink."

"Of course, elem—" Sir John was on the point of saying "elementary," but the word was misplaced; irredeemably now the times were compound. "Mister *Smith*," mused Sir John.

"And spectacles," added Rudge as Sir John made his way upstairs, drawing the filaments together *currite fusi*, snip snip, solution and dissolution with the smell of decay growing inexplicably heavier in the air, the bodies were below, while the boy guided him through to the waiting woman who began gabbling to him the moment he entered in hardly intelligible accents, nonsense and sense confounded together.

"Silence," ordered Sir John. The woman shifted in her chair. "What do you have to say?"

"I saw her, sir, when they carried her back. You see, I was out, down there, you see, and thought, she's lost, sir, she was too. . . ." Sir John grasped the point.

"You mean you know the girl, the girl murdered tonight?"

"Oh yes, I know her, sir, true enough. She is Rosalie, you see, sir—"

"Feed this woman," ordered Sir John. "Bring her to me within the hour."

Outside the door, muttering and scuffing their feet, greasy-haired and inky-fingered, frowning already, awaiting bad news in worse odor for they had sensed the censor in Sir John, stood the editors.

"Not a word," said Sir John as he approached this mutinous crew. "Not a single word. . . ." which, their nine-pronged protest and the *Lud's Town Monitor*'s ill-advised indiscretion aside, would prove to be the case. The editors printed stories on the Lottery Suicides, Lades's and Bullock's Great Cock Match, Mendoza's fight at Epping, the Cornish copper collapse, imprudence in the Linen trade, diatribes against the Easter exodus, and articles on riders attacked in the Blackfriar's Road by a bulldog still at large, an expanded advertisement for Welch's Pills for Female Obstructions and Complaints Peculiar to Virgins and, among all these, a report on Lady Yonge's concert. . . .

" '. . . attended by the Casterleighs, both father and daughter.' " Septimus had taken the paper from the Pug and set off in pursuit of his friend.

"Whatever you saw at Coade's, it was not Juliette Casterleigh. She was alive and well the night before last, listening to Handel and"—he peered closer—" 'Clementi's Funeral March.' " Hunched over his desk, Lemprière laughed bitterly.

On the night in question, they had staggered home across the bridge by Westminster, Lemprière on his friend's arm, drunk and battered from his encounter with the watermen. He slurred nonsensically as they passed the point where, months before, he had first blurted out Juliette's name while the rain poured down on them both. Hardly aware of the bridge or the dulled rush of the river below, still Lemprière recognized the old woman pestering passersby with her apples and broke free from his companion. Snatching one from the woman, he held it aloft.

"Food of the Gods!" he shouted, turning this way and that, trying to give it to startled matrons and market-workers until Septimus paid the vendor and dragged him away, still shouting, cursing foully. As they approached Southampton Street, Lemprière grew calmer. At the door, his ranting ceased.

"So they have killed her," he said in matter-of-fact tones. "They have killed Juliette now."

"Who?" Septimus demanded. But Lemprière stayed silent. Juliette's face sped away through the night, a horse clashed its hooves downstream from the pool, all gone away.

" '. . . and the evening was attended with the greatest gaiety and *bon ton,*' " Septimus concluded. Lemprière's first reaction was disbelief, followed by relief. He stood up with the room unbalanced as his emotions turned. He had trodden over ice which thinned to a brittle wafer through the two days since her "death." Hour by hour the cold waters awaited a first crack, for his trapdoor to crash open. She was alive, she was brought back alive, and Lemprière sank onto his bed under the weight of this fact. His head dropped. Then came the first suspicion, a swelling kernel of doubt.

" 'This Stone-Eater. . . .' " Septimus was reading aloud, but Lemprière paid attention only to his own thoughts. If not Juliette, then who? Who had died in her place? The head hung down, slack-mouthed with Juliette's face upside down and masked in blood. He heard it drip quickly on the stone floor, the chain links click against one another as she swung in her clammy sling, the goat's corpse, her substitute. Iphigenia.

For the story went on. Leaving the goat in her place on the altar at Aulis, she was carried to Taurica; Diana's priestess now, she wielded the knife over sacrifices in her turn. Any stranger caught within that country fell to her altar until two Greeks, fast friends and Argives like herself, were dragged before her. Unsurprising that Iphigenia's long exile should fuel her curiosity, should lead her to ask them for news of her homeland. She wrote letters to her brother Orestes and told the men that one might be spared for her courier. Their friendship led each to entreat the other to go, yet, at the last, one of the two, Pylades, agreed to take the letters. When he saw to whom they were addressed, however, he told Iphigenia to take them herself. He would not go, he told her. There was no need. Their recipient was already arrived. Orestes was his companion: her own brother. Distant leagues over the Ægean, another buttress fell in the house of Atreus. All three fled Taurica together. Of the statue of Diana which the three of them bore away, "it was afterward placed in the grove of Aricia in Italy." Some references followed, Pausanias, Ovid, Virgil, though he made no mention of the sacrifice at Aulis. Lemprière signed the entry and dated it, *Friday, 14th March, 1788.*

Orestes and Pylades, Theseus and Pirithous: proverbial friendships. Pirithous, to meet with the renowned Theseus and test the Minotaur-slayer's mettle, went so far as to invade his country. The two met as instant friends on the battlefield and afterward the torments of hell could not part them. When Septimus called a day later to collect this and other entries, Lemprière paused to reflect on their own friendship. The bruising to his face had disappeared and the livid mark on his leg was spectacular but painless. The only lasting damage from that night was a cut to his hand sustained through gripping the shard of Coade Stone chipped from the tortoise mold. He had found it the next morning still clutched tight in his hand. It now resided on the mantelpiece. The cut was healing well, and certainly Septimus had saved him from much worse. Still, would Septimus have insisted on his taking Iphigenia's letter, or met him as a friend between their opposing armies? Lemprière's suspicion was that he would not and, worse, if challenged would come up with any number of dazzlingly plausible excuses for his refusal.

"Perhaps you imagined the whole episode," Septimus was saying as he helped himself to the last of a knuckle of ham. But Lemprière had not imagined it, the dead girl was real whether she was Juliette or not. The question turned. He had visited the Manufactory for clues to the nature of the *Vendragon*'s purpose and found nothing, yet as the days between then and now went by and he reflected further on the events surrounding that night, it was his own nature which began to emerge. Again, it was Septimus who prompted him.

"What did you mean, 'they have killed her'?" he asked, as Lemprière gathered up the entries. "Who are 'they'?" And Lemprière had no real answer to that question, except to recall Peppard's warning that he was watched, to think of the room in Blue Anchor Lane, the throat slashed as the girl's had been, a jumbled fear.

" 'They,' not 'me,' " he said distinctly, grasping what it meant as the words emerged. "I did not kill that girl. I did not parcel her like meat and hang her from a butcher's chain. They did that. And I believe they killed Peppard." He looked down and might have taken the thought further then, followed it to its conclusion, but at that moment it was enough.

"There is nothing insane about me." He spoke clearly and looked at Septimus, who froze for a moment and seemed lost for words.

"Well done," he said at last. "Splendid work. Now, if you intend nothing further with this ham. . . ." Lemprière felt the distance between them widen, as though they were products of quite separate orders.

In the weeks that followed, he returned to his dictionary. Rather, he threw himself upon it. Where before he worked methodically from "A" toward "Z," now he scribbled and scrawled haphazardly in a kind of fury. His working habits submitted to no particular regime, his entries followed no pattern. He chased the characters of stories which happened to hold his interest until he grew weary and abandoned them for others. He opened texts at random, chose headings by chance, followed whims, flipped coins. Discharged of any therapeutic function, the entries were guided along no course but that of their author's passions. He wrote at any or all hours and in any circumstance. It was a kind of release, the letting go of an obsession and also, somewhere at the back of his mind where a question turned outside the clutches of the dictionary, a kind of flight. He no longer fussed over the details of this or that corrupted text. He was not overworried by emendations. His cross-references grew erratic and Septimus relayed a stream of minor complaints from Cadell, all of them offset (Septimus was quick to point out) by the fact that at this rate the dictionary would be finished by July. He had begun to call more frequently than the collection of the entries necessarily justified. Often he was accompanied by Lydia. They would tempt Lemprière with a variety of excursions which he saw only as distractions. He grew irritated by their persistence. Why, for instance, should he want to watch a cat-eating contest, or view exotic trees at Burgess's?

"Orange trees, Citron trees, Jessamine trees. . . ." Septimus clutched a hand-bill.

"Arabian and Catalanian," Lydia read over his shoulder.

"No," said Lemprière.

Lydia thought his work unhealthy, morbid even. His dictionary was a contagion. She added her appeals to those of Septimus and even grew peeved at his refusals which, Lemprière thought, did not suit her. He did not wish to look at trees and had no desire to watch Lord Barrymore eat a cat. He wanted nothing more than to continue with his work and that was all. Nevertheless, their invitations continued and even intensified. When Lydia returned from Burgess's warehouse with an orange tree, Septimus having carried it all the way from Savoy Steps, his resolve began to weaken.

In truth, it was a horrible thing, five feet tall in its yellow tub with unpleasant straggly branches. Various tree-diseases had already attacked it, pustular boles and resinous sores covered its spindly trunk while its leaves, thankfully few, were brittle and papery, mottled with obscure cicatrices and parasite-scars. Several colonies of insects infested the foliage, compensating for the paucity of living space by vigorous breeding and frequent ill-natured forays about the room.

"It will brighten up the place," said Lydia. "And when it grows bigger, you can eat the oranges."

Looking at the orange tree, Lemprière sensed the refugee's stubborn resentment of its place of exile. He thought wistfully of orange groves, acre after acre of sandy sun-baked soil with long avenues of fructiferous saplings heavy with swelling gourds, et cetera, how far away they were, how much happier his invader would be there. All the same, he was touched, and when Septimus suggested they should go together to watch a man who ate stones at Charing Cross, his response was "Not this month," rather than "No."

"Excellent," said Septimus. "We shall go on the fourteenth." Lydia added her enthusiasm and Lemprière grew faintly embarrassed by it all.

"The fourteenth," he said.

He worked on furiously, and for the first time since he had begun the project he felt absorbed in his work without its being absorbed in him. He produced mounds of paper which as soon as written might go to the devil for all he cared; his production was heedless. He revised nothing. And at the back of his mind, far away from the center of this activity, the question still turned. If not Juliette, then who? The question was familiar, but come upon by him from a disguising angle. He would take no pains over it. He was busy, involved, and self-indulged. Yet, as the month neared its end, the question rolled as a ship might roll in the few seconds before it sinks to disclose a view which is seen once and never again, turned to him an aspect which would harden his suspicion and still intensify his longing. If the girl was not Juliette, then why did she resemble her so closely? An altered aspect. And in the moment before the air rushes from the hold, and the keel and scarred hull show themselves fatally before sinking into the waters, at the last in this, he asked himself what part would Juliette play?

Far removed from such concerns, in the sheltered parks and gardens of the city, a mild end to March brought the almond trees and laurustinia bushes into bloom. On the last day of the month the gooseberry bushes were in full leaf and the first of the summer's flies had appeared. Quite suddenly, March became April.

· · ·

In the second week of April, a square-rigged two-master lumbered into the harbor at Constantinople. The sloop *Tesrifati* on detachment from the Ægean squadron was captained by a fresh-faced graduate of Gazi Hassan's naval school at Midilli. Halil Hamit had taken his first command expecting a well-oiled fighting machine ready to fire off the *Tesrifati*'s fourteen-gun broadside, maneuver skillfully through the narrow channels of the archipelago, and live for days or weeks on nothing more than a sniff of the enemy and the hope of engagement. He had found a leaking tub crewed by malcontents, stocked with rotting fish and damp powder. The last was unimportant as only three of the *Tesrifati*'s twenty-eight guns could be relied upon to fire without blowing up itself, its gun crew, and, conceivably, the ship's magazine. Expecting well-drilled obedience, he had found consent by inertia at best, habitual defiance at worst. They were debtors, conscripts, petty thieves, *kif* and opium addicts to a man. Sweet fumes now lingered on the lower deck. As it limped into harbor, Hamit rehearsed his report. It was terse. "Two months sailing between Lissa and Ancona. Nothing sighted." The *Tesrifati* docked and Hamit watched his crew shuffle down the gangplank. To a man, he loathed the sight of them. Surely, he hoped against hope, surely they would desert.

Two days later and all the crew were aboard. Every single one. They had been delivered in manacles the previous night, having been caught en masse boarding a frigate bound for Trebizon. They were chained below decks right now. Hamit himself had to oversee the revictualing. He watched as old barrels of rotten fish were unloaded and new ones put in their place. A cargo of saltpeter for the arsenal at Midilli was stowed all about the lower deck, this being the purpose of his recall, as he understood it. Its destination called to him, recalling days climbing rope ladders and nights studying trigonometry under the cruel but fair supervision of the sergeants with their unusual and comforting punishments, their shaggy caresses in the Ægean moonlight. . . .

Hamit was suddenly distracted from these fond recollections by a crate swinging over the side. Roughly five feet square, it landed with a thump on the quarterdeck. An official from the Beylik section of the Office of the Imperial Divan wanted him to sign something.

"There has been a slight change of plan. . . ." began the official as he scribbled.

Within the hour, the cargo stowed, the crew unmanacled and instantly idle, the *Tesrifati* ran through the Bosporus before a gentle following wind. Hamit stood belowdecks contemplating the crate. It was to be delivered to Liverre forthwith. That was his overriding command and he was not to concern himself with its contents. After that, duty on the Ægean patrol would resume. Hamit's crew looked on sullenly. Unchaining them, he had had to choke back the impulse to apologize for their discomfort. They looked hungry. They would not meet his eye. They were waiting for a calamity. Now, Hamit gave the crate an encouraging pat. Instantly a voice from within began shouting.

"I demand safe conduct! I demand access to the Venetian ambassador, proper facilities, a translator, my possessions, an audience with the Divan. . . ." The demands went on for some time. Hamit listened to them as they grew less strident, ending forlornly with, "I am Peter Rathkael-Herbert, the Imperial Internuncio to the Sublime Porte and I demand water." Then, "Water, please," then, "Please," and then silence once more. Halil Hamit weighed up his duties, then went to fetch a crowbar, a cup, and a pitcher of clear cold water for his guest.

The crate was where the extreme ends of the debate had finally met, middle ground between sending back the Internuncio's severed head in a burlap sack and escorting him to the border with all possible pomp in compensation for his imprisonment, now explained as a junior official's ghastly mistake. Of course, the implications ran much further. Decapitation of the Internuncio would suggest reckless warmongering, in line with recent gains in Transylvania and the late Drave massacres, a strong hint that the Turkic forces were prepared to fight until doomsday. An escort, on the other hand, betokened appeasement and a quick end to a war which helped no one. The stalemate around Belgrade and various anti-Ottoman insurrections within Serbia supported this line. Within the heady atmosphere of the crate, an unstable compromise was found. If the Internuncio survived, all well and good. If not, well, he was the enemy after all.

A mutinous capsule toiling on the spread sea, the *Tesrifati* was one beacon among many as night descended over Europe. Peasant mutterings over the *robot*-labor draft, a rebellion among the dwarves of a Magdeburg circus, Anabaptist ferment in Thuringia, these too wink in and out, and off. And there are others. The configuration is still unclear in April, but as popular ferment grows, such outbreaks will become more frequent, the beacons more numerous, until a long-destined shape emerges from lines implied between one point and another, as a message sent by heliograph confirms the network of stations, relaid from mountaintop to campanile, from watchtower to platform in flashes, bright junctions of x and y directed to precise degrees of arc in accordance with exact timetables of transmission and reception. Compared to the network which supports its brief and flickering life, the message itself seems of little import, just as the letter itself is nothing to the mighty Thurn und Taxis postal system, and the leg-capsule negligible compared to the flight of the carrier pigeon. So, the message emerging this April night is secondary at best to the means of its emergence, which is the system. The problem is scale, human unit to geopolitical mass, monoculture to Euro-system. Coming volcanic eruptions will seem random and totally out of the blue to mortal observers despite literally eons of warning through regular seismic motions of the earth's plates—but how to relate the explosive violence, the rain of molten debris shooting through thousands of feet per second to the inches-per-century tectonic creep which preceded and caused it? The middle terms are missing and only primitive augury fills the gap. Can the Emperor's bed linen truly portend the voyage of the *Tesrifati* this April night? Charlatans grow prosperous on these discontinuities. For lack of a sufficiently lofty vantage point, haruspices resort to reading entrails and bird-flights, all kinds of geomancy and weird divination are practiced. Quite innocent structures and arrangements become potent as indices prefiguring catastrophe and other forms of disorder. Take, as an instance, the orange trees at Versailles.

In Le Notre's plan it was quite clear. The orange trees ran in straight lines, a double terrace on either side of the gardens, away from the back of the palace toward the artificial lake. Louis's first tutor of mathematics had told him that parallel lines met at a point infinitely distant from the observer or more obviously at the foot of the throne of God. Louis preferred the second metaphor and recalled it often, linking it vaguely with his own divine right. Looking out over the terrace after the levée, he derived a faint comfort from the neatly sculpted orange trees in their cubic slatted pots which ran in rows toward the lake. If he screwed up his eyes, the lines met and God was in the lake.

The first change came a month ago, a subtle realignment to begin with but growing more noticeable toward the end of March. By April it was indisputable. The orange trees were converging. His first thought was an overzealous sycophant busily rearranging them by moonlight, waiting only for a favorable sign to declare himself. Or herself. Accordingly, he smiled a lot in the vicinity of the orange trees, clapped his hands, pointed, said "ha!" in a joyful tone. No one came forward. The gardeners perhaps. A guard was placed on the orange trees but no underlings were caught.

The orange trees, which once peaceably affirmed his topmost position in the order of things, now only added to his worries.

The pattern repeated itself. In the Vendée, renegade tax officers had taken to brigandage, enforcing their own covert tariff system through the organization he had supposedly abolished. Officers sent to stamp out this fiscal subversion were hounded with violence, their families threatened. A clamorous Parlement had quieted itself when he announced the abolition, and afterward he had felt reconfirmed, serene in his placement. Now the business had turned on him. He heard the words "tax reform" with acute unease and wondered what disaster his next helpful measure would occasion. Standing still, he was aware that matters moved of their own accord. Moving himself, everything stopped. Orange trees again.

His plan to revive the watchmaking trade (women watchmakers) was encouraging, and at least the new Board of Marine Affairs was safely appointed. Still, events conspired against him. Reports of the Bank's directors coming to blows at their general meeting had reached the press, and the resignation of Monsieur Caburrus had seemed to endorse those reports. Various agencies took delight in recalculating the deficit from Necker's figures which rose and rose as the new amounts were published on a weekly basis. Apparently he had sanctioned taxes called "ving-tièmes" which the Parlements of Toulouse, Rouen, and Montpellier now refused to pay. Small riots were taking place in these towns and others where his *arrêt* met its usual hostile reception. The works at Cherbourg were horrendously delayed, and the costs—four, perhaps five millions—rising by the month. This at least was the Marine Board's pigeon. Vaudreuil and Bougainville had delegated extraordinary powers to their secretaries to bring the project in on time and under budget. They had left the week previously. On secondment from the Finance Office where their labyrinthine damage-limitation exercise on the deficit had drawn universal if slightly baffled praise, Monsieurs Duluc and Protagoras would proceed from Cherbourg to La Rochelle. Here some other task awaited them. Vaudreuil set great store by them, even the Cardinal gave his recommendation. The deficit was still huge, naturally, but how much worse might it have been without their efforts? He dreaded to think.

Sunlight cleared the gables behind him to shine down onto the terrace and himself, to glitter off the lake, warm the yawning palace corridors, and ripen tiny shriveled oranges on the anxious trees before him.

The same sun beat down on his trusted undersecretaries who stood now on the heights above Cherbourg.

"Folly," said Protagoras. His companion surveyed the scene with weary eyes, shaking his head in agreement. Their journey from Paris had taken a full week. It might have been done in three days, but a number of minor detours had taken longer than expected. None of these would have excited much comment in the turbulent capital, but nor would they have been readily explicable. Even with the full breadth of their extraordinary

266

powers, the relevance of minor officials from the Parlements of Toulouse, Rouen, and Montpellier to their assignment was questionable. And why should they meet at night in a village outside Argentan? Given even their almost limitless remit, informal contacts with disaffected tax-farmers from the Vendée seemed somewhat outside their official roles. They traveled in short stages, unobtrusively by public coach, and their journey had been punctuated by such diversions until the previous evening, when at an inn a few miles outside Cherbourg, they had met the contact the Cardinal had been at special pains to procure.

No introductions were made. The three sat in an upstairs room around a table which was piled with papers. The talk was in English. Duluc and Protagoras watched as the third man drew long columns of figures, underlining and marking totals in a complex system of cross-references.

"You might liken them to pools within a reservoir," he said as they watched him across the table. "The levels in individual pools may go up and down, but the volume of water within the reservoir remains constant. Only the distribution differs. Europe, and the whole world for that matter, does its business in this way. Each pool is a country with more or less wealth. Here is France, for example, with none at all, a minus value. France can still do business because, were it to be sold, lock, stock and barrel, the amount would erase the deficit many times over. Now, by balancing imported goods against exported ones, weighing foreign debts against investments and adding the per capita wealth of each of its subjects, a state can be "valued," given a number corresponding to its worth. This much is familiar. When these values are combined, they give a further number corresponding to the volume of the whole reservoir, or the wealth of all nations. My concern, however, is with the pools."

"Pools?" Protagoras interrupted.

"Individual nations. These can be calculated by subtracting repayments and expenses from borrowings and earnings, plus the cost of imports from exports of course. The final figure is the nation's wealth. In theory it is simple. In practice"—he gestured to his trunk which overflowed with papers—"a different story. Still, your Cardinal paid handsomely enough for—"

"Cardinal?" Duluc broke in sharply. "We know of no Cardinal." The third man looked bewildered for a moment, then recovered himself.

"Of course," he said quickly. "Now, your *friend* commissioned an overview of England's last three fiscal years. As I said, the calculations are never exact. Mathematically speaking, the task is tedium itself. Errors creep in. There are also factors which cannot be accounted for, smuggled goods, informal loans, goods in transit, and the like. But generally these are negligible and allowances can be made when they are not. I claim an accuracy to within two or three percent. That is why these figures puzzle me. I have rechecked them twice now. In each of the three years, there is a discrepancy of almost four percent. That represents several millions of pounds. It is as if someone somewhere is running a national bank, but quite outside the banking system. Stranger yet, the money never reenters the system, no other country shows a corresponding rise. The money is not being used. In one form or another it simply sits somewhere. Where, I do not know, and how, I do not know. But it exists, gentlemen, that is certain." He looked up then, expecting surprise, curiosity at least. Protagoras and Duluc merely nodded confirmation.

"There is one more thing," he said. "I performed the same calculation for the same years a century ago. The results were the same and I'll wager the intervening years show the same deficit. Whoever, or whatever, controls this process controls a sum greater than the capital of any state in the world."

When the man had packed up his papers and departed in a hurry for the morning pacquet-boat, Duluc sat down at the same table and wrote two brief notes. The first was to the Cardinal. It read, "All Jaques claimed for himself and his associates is true. We have our confirmation. We proceed to the final arrangements at Rochelle. Our cause is safe." The second was to Jaques himself. It merely identified their recent companion and outlined the findings of his calculation. That would be enough. Jaques, or his partners, would take the matter from there. He signed off, "Until the thirteenth," by way of his mark, and carefully sealed the letter. It would probably travel by the same paquet as its victim.

The following morning, he watched with Protagoras as the pacquet tacked gingerly past the "improvements" and out of the harbor. For larger ships, the entry into the port had become a pilot's nightmare. The reason for this was plain. A wooden monster wallowed in the harbor at Cherbourg. It was two hundred meters long, of varying width, with sprouting piles and bizarre projections running off at angles all along its length which undulated where heaps of unused building materials had been dumped to rot or warp. The first section was roughly straight, the second roughly curved, and the third roughly both. The monster lay at a diagonal across the harbor pool, ending in a squat tower which, he squinted, seemed to be constructed from wheel-barrows. This whole structure, in the officialese of a correspondence now so incumbent that it had overflowed into the offices of the Marine Board Directors and grown there until their resignations were added to its bulk, was the New Jetty. It was the sacred crocodile of the Marine Board and it had eaten its priests.

"Sheer folly," Protagoras said once more. The fortifications were more modest, spindly scaffolding and planking for the most part. It was the jetty had done the damage. The citizens of Cherbourg claimed that ships putting in there for ten or twenty years were now using ports to the north and south. The inns were empty and the wharves idle. The town was dying. A petition was being got up to be sent to the King himself. The wood shortage was contrived. Less wood, not more, was needed, and none at all in the harbor. In the fortnight that followed, Duluc and Protagoras would pay lip service to their roles by listening carefully to these complaints. They would turn blind eyes to minor acts of sabotage and deaf ears to reports of every barn for miles around being stacked high with intercepted wood-consignments. Their recommendation would be to abandon the project at the first opportunity. Far below, a league or more out, a frigate which would later feature in the petition was sailing northeast. Duluc and Protagoras turned from their vantage point and walked to the waiting coach. Already their thoughts were flying southward down the coast toward La Rochelle where a very different project awaited them.

• • •

Chased by a stiff breeze, the converted frigate *Tisiphone* sailed on up the channel for Deal. She was loaded with powdered charcoal, and her commander still had hopes of catching the next day's tide. The tail wind lasted until late afternoon, then died. When the *Tisiphone* reached Deal at four in the following afternoon, the tide had already turned. The sloop *Cockatrice* and cutter *Nimble* already lay at anchor. The *Tisiphone* joined them overnight, setting off the next morning for the Upper Pool. The fading wakes of ships farther advanced and crosscurrents shot from the riverbed's basins rebounded from bank to bank, gently rocking the three-master as it advanced with the slow surges of the tide toward the city. Belowdecks, within its close-packed barrels, charcoal shifted to form invisible patterns, prolific whorls, and unfolding carousels of black on black, slow rotations and undulations as the strata shuffled top to bottom in a secret echo of the waters' conflicting forces. Docking at Queen's Wharf on the legal quays around six that evening, the three-master drew Captain Guardian's vigilant eye fifty yards upstream from the *Vendragon* to view this new arrival.

"*Tisiphone*," he announced to Captain Roy who was peering up approvingly at his mantelpiece. "From Lisbon via Cherbourg, carrying charcoal." He had read the ship news which had reported her departure a month before. "She's early," he said.

"Probably avoided Cherbourg," speculated Captain Roy.

"Ah."

The works at Cherbourg were familiar by report. Eben glanced back down the quay to the *Vendragon*. As promised, he had kept a watchful eye on the Indiaman, though there was little to report. Loading had come to a halt some weeks back, and, a solitary watchman apart, the wharf in front of the ship had been deserted. Several times he imagined he had seen lights moving below deck, brief flashes escaping through the planking, but no one had boarded the vessel for weeks and no provisions had been taken on. It seemed an unlikely berth for stowaways. His concerns during this vigil had been of a less obvious nature, nothing he could specifically describe, nothing very particular, but still a vague anxiety gripped him in these weeks. How would he put it? The quays running up and down the river's edge were changing, their character was different from before. It was indistinct, this change, ill-defined still, but it was for the worse.

The docks had always been a rough sort of place, always had its own codes and customs, its own running feuds and vendettas. But recently it seemed to Eben that the codes and customs had fallen into abeyance and the feuds and vendettas become more virulent. A new viciousness was afoot. He had seen a man kicked to the ground and left for dead on Butler's Wharf. There were reports that a customs man had been set alight on the south bank and made to run a gauntlet. Habitual disputes escalated into fisticuffs, fisticuffs into brutal beatings. For the first time in his life he found the port a threatening kind of a place, and an important consequence of this change was Captain Roy.

The amputee was a variously respected figure along the wharves and quays of the port. Protected by rumors of a vast buried treasure, by respect for an unparalleled knowledge of the world's ports garnered in his younger years at sea, and by sympathy for the loss of his legs, Captain Roy had patrolled the docks from before even Eben's residence there. In the mornings he hawked matches around the city markets. The afternoons and evenings inevitably drew him back to the river. No one laid a finger on Captain Roy. That was the code. Then, two weeks ago, on the first day of the month, he had come upon a party of mudlarks. They were loading a wherry with cases. Captain Roy had pointedly ignored their thievery and continued along the quay. That too was the code. A few yards past and he had heard quick footsteps. Suddenly he was being lifted up and thrown into the water. The high sides of the ship offered no hand holds. His stumps pumped ineffectually. He was drowning, and the mudlarks were leaving him to his fate.

Apparently a lighter had hauled him aboard, choking and spluttering, shivering with the cold, cursing his assailants. He was dazed with shock. There was no room for doubt; they had tried, quite casually, to kill him. That was not the code.

Hearing of the incident, Guardian had asked of the captain's whereabouts and found him, still shivering, under the short pier beyond Tower Stairs. One glance at Captain Roy had convinced Eben that twenty years of solitary living must come to an end. The captain was installed at the Crow's Nest that afternoon. The docks had changed and, indirectly, his own life had changed with them. So far, his guest had proved an agreeable companion. They shared similar enthusiasms and conversed in familiar terms. Roy had resumed his match-selling, Eben his watch on the *Vendragon*. This evening was to be their first outing together. It was an experiment and also, Eben understood, a token recompense for his hospitality. At Captain Roy's expense and insistent invitation, they were going to see the Stone-Eater.

Two hours, four miles, and five shillings later, the two captains stood in a crowded room in Cockspur Street waiting for Francis Battalia, the Stone-Eater, to make his entrance. Captain Roy had caused a minor fracas outside when four heavyset men led by a smaller, colorless fellow had walked directly to the front of the queue and entered without paying. Why should he pay when they had not? It was explained that they had not gained admittance, and indeed, looking about the room, Eben could see no sign of them. A flight of stairs ran up to the floor above. The crowd were young men and women, mostly of the poorer sort. A head of pretty red ringlets caught his eye, two youths with her, he looked again, then once more. It seemed an unlikely place to find him, to find himself for that matter. The redhead said something and they both turned to her. The spectacles, the daft coat, he was right. He waved across the audience and called. "Young Lemprière!" The young man was looking around. He gestured again. "Join us," he called across. Eben watched as the three of them edged through the crowd toward him.

"Pleased to make your acquaintance, Lydia." Eben shook the proffered hand.

"And Mister Septimus Praeceps." Lemprière concluded his introductions. Eben introduced Captain Roy to all three and appraised the young man introduced as "Septimus."

"Have we met?" he asked frankly. The face was familiar. Distant, but remembered.

"The De Veres', this Christmas last," Septimus said.

"Of course, yes. . . ." But the memory was from somewhere else, and long before last Christmas. He groped for it.

"What news from the *Vendragon*?" Lemprière was asking, and Guardian wanted to tell him about the new wind blowing along the quays, about Captain Roy and his own hanging fears, but what he said was, "A few lights belowdecks, little else. She is loaded and ready to sail. What did you find at Coade's?" Lemprière wanted to tell him an even stranger tale then, confide a more pervasive suspicion.

"Nothing to advance my understanding of the *Vendragon*'s purpose."

"Statues," said Captain Roy. "That's what she's hiding."

"He knows that," Eben said.

Attendants at the rear of the room were turning down the oil lamps. Eben's eyes were drawn to Septimus's face once again.

"Saint Helier!" he exclaimed suddenly. "We met on Jersey."

"Jersey?" Lemprière looked from Eben to Septimus.

"I think not," said Septimus.

"Never forget a face," said Eben.

"Impossible," said Septimus. "I have never set a foot on Jersey."

"Sssh!" hissed a young woman in front of them.

"It is quite dark in here," said Lemprière by way of a compromise.

The crowd shifted, then parted to allow a short stout man through to the low stage at the front. He turned an ugly, intelligent face toward the crowd.

"I am Francis Battalia," he announced, "commonly called 'The Stone-Eater.' My first performance tonight is the Gravel Plume." With this, he scooped up a handful of gravel, filled his mouth, and tipped back his head. His cheeks twitched, then contracted, and the gravel shot up in a sheer column, hung there, then down, back into his mouth. Instantly, the act was repeated. The gravel shot up once more, the column a little thinner this time. Lemprière watched as the Stone-Eater's throat constricted, wrestling the gritty particles down toward his stomach. The gravel plume thinned further as more and more was swallowed, rose, and fell until only a single tiny nugget was left, held between his teeth. He blew, the particle flew up, struck the wooden ceiling, and rebounded downward to be instantly swallowed. A moment's silence, then the whole room burst into loud applause.

"Thank you," said the Stone-Eater. "Now, for the Pebble Cannonade, I must don my hat. . . ."

Eben enjoyed the performance more than he had anticipated. Only Septimus distracted him. Glancing across at the young man only confirmed his first thought. They had met on Jersey, he was sure of it. If only he could recall the circumstances, or even the year. Never forgetting a face seemed to mean remembering little else.

"For my next performance I must beg my audience for sustenance," the Stone-Eater was saying.

"Go on." Lydia nudged Lemprière.

"You brought the damn thing especially," Septimus chipped in. Reluctantly, Lemprière drew a cream-colored stone from his pocket.

"For the Big Rock Swallow, I beg of you a rock," the Stone-Eater went on. The same face, thought Eben.

"Sssh!" the young woman admonished Lemprière, who was suddenly reluctant to offer up his stone, protesting as Septimus pushed him forward.

"Sssh yourself!" Captain Roy hissed up at the woman. A small burst of applause greeted Lemprière's hesitant arrival at the front of the stage. He advanced, holding his rock.

"Ugly little man," the woman remarked to her consort, who looked at his shoes, only to find Captain Roy there.

"Thank you," said the Stone-Eater, taking the Coade fragment from Lemprière. He handled the rock, then frowned. There was something odd about it. Francis Battalia tipped back his head, carefully fitted the rock into his mouth, and began working his throat. Slowly, inch by inch, the rock descended. When only the tip was visible, he was suddenly seized with panic. Something about this particular rock was deeply disturbing.

Then, three things happened very quickly. Sir John Fielding appeared at the back of the gathering and told everyone to remain where they were, Captain Roy bit the complaining woman on the leg, and Francis Battalia swallowed the stone which would bring his career to a premature and undeserved end. Thereafter matters grew confused.

The woman shrieked and lashed out. A posse of officers rushed into the room and up the stairs. Lydia fell back against the wall. An oil lamp crashed to the floor. Septimus jumped away from the flames. Captain Roy bit the woman again. The four queue-jumpers ran down the stairs pursued by Sir John's officers. Septimus shrank back against the wall. The woman tried to kick Captain Roy. Lemprière pulled Lydia away from the smashed oil lamp. The oil extended a tongue of flame across the floorboards. Sir John's officers jumped on the four queue-jumpers. The spectators did not remain where they were. Captain Guardian saw Lemprière stare intently at the colorless little man who had accompanied the queue-jumpers. Sir John Fielding did not see the little man signal to Lemprière. Septimus seemed to be glued to the wall. The constables busy hitting the queue-jumpers did not see the little man walk casually out the door. Captain Roy bit Lydia by mistake. Lydia hit the complaining woman by design. Francis Battalia swallowed hard and asked for calm. The constables dragged the four men away. Sir John Fielding thanked all concerned for their cooperation and everyone gave Sir John a round of applause.

"Septimus?" Lemprière stepped over the dying oil-lamp flames and shook his friend by the shoulder. Septimus did not reply. He was pressed back tight against the wall, his eyes screwed shut. His face was drained of color.

"Leave him," Lydia's voice came from behind him. She was busily stamping out the last of the flames. When they were extinguished she took hold of his shoulders and pulled him forward.

"He is not hurt," she said as she led him toward the door, his eyes still closed. "It's the flames," she said by way of explanation. "Don't worry. I have seen it before." Lemprière realized he was being dismissed. He rejoined the two captains.

"Haven't seen a fright like that since my whaling days," said Captain Roy. Captain Guardian nodded.

"Fire," said Lemprière. "He has a great fear of the flames." He had not realized before. Guardian nodded once more.

"I was wrong about him," he said. "Yet he is the very image of the man I met on Saint Helier." The circumstances of the meeting had come back to him. A drinking bout.

"It was twenty years ago, at least."

"Image of the man?" Lemprière asked. "How?"

"He resembles the man I remember exactly, but your Septimus would have been an infant, either that or he has not aged in two decades."

"I feel certain he would have mentioned such a visit," he told the Captain, "had it taken place."

The three of them stood there, part of a crowd unsure whether to stay or go. Judicial footsteps thudded through the floor above their heads.

"They should have paid like everyone else, I suppose," Lemprière said, thinking of the queue-jumpers. Safely in custody now. Eben looked sideways at him. He was thinking of the little colorless man, the slight gesture of recognition he had made to Lemprière as he coolly made his escape. Was the lad part of that mob? Hard to credit really, but still. . . .

"They weren't nabbed for that, oh dear," Captain Roy scoffed at Lemprière. "They weren't in the audience at all."

"Then what? Who were they?" But even as he spoke, Lemprière was remembering the little lieutenant outside the inn the day he had spoken with the Widow, the same man, Stoltz. So the four men dragged away this evening . . .

Eben told him. "They were Farina's men," he said.

· · ·

"Five pallets, five chairs, a table, a map of the city, five half-empty glasses, five plates, five half-eaten meals—"

"How many men, Sergeant?" Sir John interrupted the inventory.

"Four, Sir John."

"Once more."

"Four, Sir John."

"Thank you, Sergeant."

Stoltz had escaped in the confusion, or arrived back in the middle of it, or had never been there in the first place. . . . No, the information had been good.

"Charge them with conspiracy, affray, anything." He dismissed the sergeant wearily. Cells were springing up all around the city, but Stoltz would have been a catch. Farina's right-hand man, his *éminence grise*, the administrator and paymaster of his rabble. Stoltz might even have led him to Farina, who was a phantom. His raids always came too late, his quarry was always forewarned and left him warm sheets, swinging doors, smoking candles, tight-lipped servants who "Never saw nothing." Tonight, once more, he had struck at the man and missed. Farina was still at large, working himself into the seams of the city, feeding on its discontents, growing stronger and stronger.

In return, the city fed him well. There were crimes looking for motives and, parasite to host, Farina would give them that. The case against Clary would collapse within days. Sir John knew him for an arsonist, the Sun-Fire office knew him too, but neither of them knew the why of the matter. Garrow and Leech were the same. The prisons were filled with deserters, luckless conscripts who had fired the Savoy Prison the week before. A turnkey was siezed as hostage and nearly set alight. The incendiaries were locked up in the Tilt-yard now, but public sympathy was with them. On the south side of the river, a customs officer *had* been set alight, then made to run the length of a jetty. A man, still unidentified, had been stabbed to death in broad daylight alighting from the Dover coach. Sir John had found out he had sailed from Cherbourg the day before, but knew no more. His trunk was filled with papers and the papers were filled with figures, but none of his belongings were named. Even his Bible had its flyleaf cut out.

That was the nub of it. Nothing explicitly named. All these troublesome events were portentous in some way, weighted with something that he could not grasp and, he suspected, Farina could. The Lottery Suicides were still rising, what did that mean? A Mister Wyatt had invented a movable hospital. It was erected on the terrace at Somerset Place, a clever affair with windows and ventilation ports. Once dismantled, it fitted onto two wagons. Clever, but it unsettled Sir John. A hospital should be fixed in place, a stable point like the Examiner's Office or the court, like Parliament, the palace, or the prison. Things that stayed in place when everything else was adrift. Henry would have grasped it, and would have known what to do. He, however, seemed to fall behind as the pace of events grew faster and faster. He was going backward. His guide-boy was regressing in sympathy; he had had to resume use of the string. Only his investigations into the strange murders (figuring now, in his private thoughts, as "The Ritual Murders") gave him any encouragement, and even here his progress was fumbling. The woman, Karin, when fed and returned to the Examining Office, had sat before him as he questioned her gently and persistently, leaving some areas alone, returning to others several times until every corner was swept out and the results lay sifted in an orderly pile before him.

She had last seen the latest victim five months before at a tavern called the Craven Arms which Sir John knew of old. Rosalie had disappeared that night and her whereabouts between then and the night of her death were still a mystery. A visit to the establishment and a number of discreet questions there had told him nothing about this missing time. A club met there on a regular basis, pigs, pork, something of the sort. Drinking games occupied most of their efforts, marshaled it seemed under the aegis of the tavern's proprietress, an incredibly ancient woman whom Sir John remembered as very old from twenty years before. Her husband was an invalid. She endorsed her patrons as good boys, on the whole. They could be foul, but in essence they were young men intent only on their cups and their tarts. The intricacies of the Game of Cups were explained to Sir John by the Crone; how it was played, how won.

"Rosalie was the prize that night," the Crone told him.

"Prize?"

"The winner would take her for the night, if capable."

"And who *was* the winner, that night?" Sir John asked slowly.

"Oh dear me, a newcomer for certain, never seen him before and only once since. The name though, let me see, he was back here a month or so ago, a Frenchman, I believe. . . ." A maid walked through the kitchen carrying a dead goose.

"Jemmy!" the Crone called over. "Who was that lad won the Game of Cups, the newcomer, had a French name?" Jemmy thought for a moment.

"Pierre," she said. "Skinny-looking sort. They called him, let me think, was it Long Pierre?"

"That was it," the Crone said uncertainly. "Long Pierre." Sir John turned his head slowly toward the Crone. A faint smile spread itself across his features.

"Lemprière," he pronounced carefully.

"Yes," said the Crone with sudden strong conviction, "*that* was his name. Lemprière."

Not half a mile away and oblivious to this invocation, its subject sat cocooned in his thoughts. Through a mild April broken only by his visit to the Stone-Eater and a snow squall on the fifth, Lemprière patrolled the kingdoms of his dictionary.

Like a future-ghost, he moved among the Isauri and warlike Lacedaemonians, the Lestrygones who ate sailors washed up on their shores, and the Mandurians who ate dogs. In Latium he pushed through thick-leafed laurels over ground where Rome would later rise and teem with painted courtesans stalking through the Suburra, stalls crammed together in the Tabernae Novae, and prisoners wailing up from the subterranean levels of the Tullianum. Over the tracts of Mesopotamia, Pannonia, and Samartia, he traced lines that were borders, marked points which grew into cities. He saw villages which would later rival Rome and Babylon: Lutetia, Olisipio, and Londinium, and stranger places which would sink into the earth leaving only disbelieved stories: Ophiodes, the topaz island, so dazzling it appeared only at night; the labyrinths at Lemnus, Crete, and Assinoe, where the sacred crocodiles lay embalmed hidden deep within one of three thousand chambers; Samothrace, where mysteries began their lives before sucking in the thoughts of men. He searched through Trapezus on the Euxine coast and out to sea where, on triangular Leuce, in a different version of the tale, Achilles took Iphigenia as his bride. But she was not there. From the enclosed *Palus Mœotis* through the Cimmerian and Thracian Bospori to the Mediterraneum, north to Liburnia, south over the Syrtes sandbanks to Melita and Utica, where the Carthaginians fled when the siege was lost and the city burned. Along the rocky shores of Seriphus, Danae's landfall, over the fertile hills of Naxos where Ariadne cried for Theseus, and inland to the Scamander, called

Xanthus by the goddesses who bathed there before the fatal judgment of Paris: Minerva, Juno, Venus. He searched for them all.

But the Xanthus was a muddy stream, Carthage debris, Zama a place where the blood of Scipio's and Hannibal's armies had long ago soaked into the soil. He was an intruder kicking through the husks. Liburnia was now the arena for a squalid border war, he had heard. Quiza was on the coast, Mauritanian something. Little of note happened on Onoeum. Taenarum was the southernmost tip of Europe. Velinus was a stagnant lake and it rained frequently in Umbria. Someone mentioned Xylenopolis. Pliny? Very little grew on the banks of the Zyras.

As the weeks of April passed, he began to believe that something was lost to these cities, kingdoms, islands, and seas. With their hold on him loosened, his own idea of them was changed. Their contours remained, but dry and paper-thin. If he chose to push his arm through the tight skin, he would find the flesh stripped away from within, heart and lungs disengaged. It was not a world which would ever be lost, but its earth, rocks, rivers, and seas were draining away, its raw substance being lost to the idea as sands are exchanged in an hourglass, the future trickling steadily into the past. Less deceived, Lemprière knew that his skepticism had its price. The fields in which his imagination had once played were drying and cracking. The old heroes were being dispossessed. He asked himself, where now was their kingdom? They wandered in aimless groups, men and women walking through ill-defined streets on private missions. He was there among them in a city of exiles, looking into their faces, turning from one group to the next, still in search of her. Iphigenia fled from Taurica with her brother and his companion. Where did she flee? The statue of Diana, their booty, later arrived in Comana, or Sparta or Aricia, the accounts were in dispute. Orestes and Pylades returned to Argos. But Iphigenia joined the bands of the lost who had forgotten their beginnings and lost sight of their ends. Beyond the city there was nothing but flat plains and drab skies. The faces were masks lifted from the features of corpses, husks of memory. Only the city held firm; Troy or Carthage, the first or second Romes, the walls held firm, enclosing the memories. The smell of burning, the first breach. He would find her before the besiegers stormed through the streets, staving in the doors, firing the roofs, searching for the prize of Paris, the jewel which sucked all of them in. Face after face reeled up to him, but they were all wrong, none of them the one he sought. Danae, Iphigenia, Helen . . . None of them Juliette.

· · ·

Five days out, five days in which his crew had sat belowdecks sucking resinous smoke from their pipes or had fished for tunny without luck off the *Tesrifati*'s stern, and Hamit knew nothing had changed. They were worse than dogs, stinking and scratching themselves, doing nothing without curses and kicks, laughing at him behind his back. They called him "boy" and he hated them. He thought often of Midilli, his comrades and the sergeants. Then he looked at his vessel, saw a hulk overrun with vermin, and his heart sank. In these moments of despondency, his refuge was the hold where he dutifully fed and watered the mysterious man in the crate. Each day, he would clamber down the well with a pitcher of water and a satchel of ship's biscuits. To be incarcerated in a crate in the Mediterranean heat was bad enough. He would not inflict the fish upon his guest. When his duties permitted, they spoke together at length: Hamit grousing about his crew's deficiencies, his guest replying in a mixture of extraordinarily bad Turkish and a language he did not understand, save for one word. This was "water." It was always his first word. The boy sat hunched with his back to the crate, the Internuncio cramped within it, while around them the *Tesrifati*'s timbers creaked, water slopped in the bilges, and rats scampered fearlessly over the barrels of saltpeter. They were refugees, bound together by different kinds of misery.

For the first week the weather was fine, the wind set fair, and the *Tesrifati* plowed westward toward her landfall. Hamit decided to abandon the Straits of Messina for a course skirting Sicily, and so enter the Tyrrhenian Sea from the south, between Marsala and Carthage. The Syrtes sandbanks were kept well to port, and the constant weather meant little work for the crew who were intent on inner demons and angels, marveling at the sea surface with eyes like saucers as they packed their pipes and sent sweet clouds of blue aromatic smoke rolling through the decks. Then, on the eighth day, the sirocco began to blow.

All day the hot wind took them north. Hamit fancied he saw the Egadi Islands slip past to starboard. When evening came and the sails were lowered, Hamit walked the length of the ship telling the crew to expect fog. The hot wind would draw up vapor from the sea and, at the first lull, lower it in dense banks all around them. The crew did not care. Some were slumped unconscious in their hammocks, others sat bolt upright, staring ahead with eyes of glass. Some moaned and flopped helplessly in the grip of private terrors, others jabbered to nonexistent companions. In the surrounding quiet of the sea, the *Tesrifati* floated like a cradle set adrift. The only lights were dim flares from the pipes, the only sounds the moans and babbled nonsense of their smokers. Night fell. One by one the stars were eclipsed. By morning, as predicted, the ship was drifting in fog.

Hamit stood alone on the quarterdeck. Fog shut the ship in a world suddenly reduced to the narrow apron of sea, a few yards at most, encircling the hull. Banks of white rose up on all sides, formless giants dissolving as the ship moved through them, or they passed over the ship, for Hamit did not know whether his vessel moved or was becalmed there. He threw fragments of wood into the water which drifted away but all in different directions, some returning, some swallowed up by the mist. He could barely see the far mast and thought the ship might be anywhere, drifting onto rocks or reefs, drawn by the tides into a hostile harbor. The cocoon of white would lift and . . . No, he would hear the breakers, the rush of water over coral, the shouts of the sailors, and the fog which surrounded himself and his vessel was soundless. Only the waves lapping at the hull broke the quiet. Hamit faced blank walls of gray, and the fog went on and on, neither thickening nor thinning, simply rolling over the still ship in wave after wave. By midday the fog had still not cleared. The sun had not been glimpsed. He fancied he saw huge shapes moving alongside the *Tesrifati*. His crew drifted listlessly about the upper deck, but Hamit paid them little mind. Standing motionless, staring ahead into walls of dissolving white, Hamit and his ship were drawn farther and farther into the mist.

Then, the dark mirage. At first it was the *Tesrifati*'s own shadow. Some strange refraction of the nowhere-light had thrown a dark double of his vessel off to port. Then it was his imagination, an image rising out of the silent hypnotic hours, now redoubled and returning. And then it was a black ship bearing down on him out of the fog. Hamit turned and began to shout. A dark form was running alongside his ship, the angle of coincidence so narrow it must have been there for hours. Hamit scrambled down ladders, through hatches, along gangways, shouting, cuffing the heads of the crew. None of the guns were primed. He could hear water rushing in the channel formed between the hulls. Two or three of the men were stirring themselves. Hamit looked and saw the black ship loom out of the fog to fill the gunport. He was hammering down the powder, tamping the ball. Lining the wales of the black ship from prow to stern were faces withered with age. Two crewmen were pulling at his arms. He pushed them away. The ship was almost on him, filling the sky, blotting out the fog, huge and black as night. He lit the taper. The crewmen were shouting at him, moving backward. Hamit touched the fuse and turned to see them running away from him with their hands to their heads, away from the cannon. The fuse hissed, he heard the first grappling hook fall with a thud on the deck above. Then the cannon exploded.

From within the confines of his crate, the Internuncio heard muffled shouting, a thud somewhere above, a deafening explosion, more thuds, a terrible grinding sound, and feet running in all directions around him. The ship was being boarded. He heard barrels being rolled along the gangplanks and manhandled out of the well. The hole through which his young friend had fed and watered him allowed a view directly overhead. Useless. Then his own turn came and he braced himself against the "walls" and floor as the crate was shifted up to the deck, then seemed to

279

hang in space before landing on the deck of the *Tesrifati*'s aggressor. He heard voices speaking in English. The grinding sound came again. The hulls rubbing against one another, he realized belatedly, and then the ships were free of each other. He could hear the crew levering off the lids of the barrels. He raised his head to shout his presence and the sound died in his throat. His crate was positioned directly below the mainmast. Looking up through the feeding hole he saw swirling fog, bare spars, and rigging. At the top of the mast, a tattered pennant flew, and on the pennant was a skull and crossed bones. They were working down the line, staving in the barrels with jemmies. Peter Rathkael-Herbert cowered in his crate waiting helplessly, hopelessly for discovery. Then his turn came. Wood splintered above his head and shattered slats rained down on him as he curled up, burying his head in his hands. The lid was prized off and a croaking voice above him said, "Aha!" before strong hands reached down to pluck him from his refuge and deposit him on the deck. Crumpled, racked with aches and pains, exhausted Peter Rathkael-Herbert looked up to see an old man, grizzled and weather-tanned, standing over him. The old man reached down and offered the Imperial Internuncio his hand.

"I am Wilberforce van Clam," he told the disheveled heap. "Welcome aboard the *Heart of Light*."

The sirocco began to blow away the fog.

Aboard the *Heart of Light*, Peter Rathkael-Herbert saw sunlight for the first time in a fortnight. Looking up into the rigging and around the deck where the crew were making ready to set sail, he could not help but notice the extreme age of the sailors. Not one seemed to be under fifty. Wilberforce van Clam was at the helm.

"Take some tea." He gestured to a pot brewing on an occasional table by his side. "Wilkins!" he shouted. "A cup for our guest, if you please!" Webley "Mussel" Wilkins, a spry sixty-year-old with a long white mustache, jumped to the task.

"You are . . . pirates?" Peter Rathkael-Herbert ventured, watching as elderly men leapt up and down the rigging.

"Pirates? Oh yes, pirates all right, absolutely pirates we are, aren't we, lads?"

"Oh yes!" came the reply from all quarters of the vessel.

"But we're Pantisocratic Pirates," Wilberforce van Clam went on. "We never really wanted to be pirates at all." He paused and sipped his tea. "It's society made us what we is now."

"Society?" Peter Rathkael-Herbert was bemused by the notion. "But how?"

"Aha!" said Wilberforce for the second time that day. "Now that is a tale worth the telling. Wilkins! A chair for my friend!"

And so, seated in a splendidly upholstered armchair and fortified by tea, the Imperial Internuncio listened while Wilberforce van Clam unfolded the story of the Pantisocratic Pirates.

"We first came together in London in 1753," Wilberforce began. "This was after the Great Comb Riots and alien dissenters were being interned under the Sedition Act, that was us, you see. We were Poles, Prussians, Serbs, Dalmatians, any nation you care to think of. Even a Frenchman. Anyroad, we all fetched up together in Newgate jail and waited for the business to blow over. Only it didn't. More tea?" Peter Rathkael-Herbert shook his head. "Very well, we thought, so we wait to be charged. Standard procedure, you see. Get charged, plead guilty, be deported, three days at Boulogne and you're back within the week. But time wore on and we still were not charged. In the meantime we kept ourselves busy, political debates, discussions, a little dialectics. We look back on those days as the birth of Pantisocracy. It was the only compromise we could reach. You see, when you've got die-hard Anabaptists and Thuringian ultramontanists in the ranks, take it from me, you need something broad. Pantisocracy is broad, if nothing else."

Wilberforce reached for his pipe and began packing it with a gluey substance. "All men are equal," he said as he lit the pipe, and Peter Rathkael-Herbert smelt a sweet scent familiar from the *Tesrifati*. "That's about it, really. The stuff about land ownership doesn't really apply aboard ship. Anyway, in the end we figured out the delay. The section of the Act we'd been charged under had yet to be passed, and with the threat of revolt over, no one was very interested in getting it onto the statute books. We couldn't be released until we'd been tried, and we couldn't be tried because the law didn't exist. We rotted there for over a year until the magistrate who'd arraigned us in the first place chartered a ship. This ship, in fact, though it was called the *Alecto* then."

Wilberforce sent clouds of sweet blue smoke wafting toward his guest. "The idea was: Stage an escape, hop aboard this ship, be charged with the escape, plead guilty, be deported to France and back in a few days. The only problem was the magistrate. He retired that very week, leaving us aboard the *Alecto*. There we were, suddenly fugitives from justice with nothing and nobody between us and the gallows. Technically, we were already pirates. After a quick debate we decided to go the whole hog. We put the master and his crew in the pinnace, hoisted the Jolly Roger, and set sail that night for the Barbary Coast. It's been thirty-odd years now and I can tell you truly that not a man jack of us has looked back since. I still think of that magistrate and each time I do I raise my glass and toast him: "Happy retirement, Henry Fielding!" Without him, we'd all be living under the English boot, but here we are and here we stay. It's the rover's life for us and a damn fine life it is too, right, lads?"

"Right, Cap'n," replied a trio of hoary-headed tars from the quarterdeck.

Wilberforce van Clam passed the pipe to the Internuncio. "Suck on that, m'boy."

Hot sweet smoke curled in Peter Rathkael-Herbert's throat. Small metal centipedes raced around the insides of his kneecaps.

"Nn," he said, exhaling and handing it back.

The sky was a vacant eye, massively blue. The sun flared low over the sea. He coughed and thanked the captain.

"Only for today," Wilberforce explained to him. "Wilkins is captain tomorrow, then Schell, we rotate, you see, all being equals 'n' all. Gets a bit confusing sometimes."

His head was spinning, slow half-rotations which blurred the ship and its aged crew, somehow making them even more fabulous than they already were. "Pirates," he slurred. The chair was so enveloping, a whole world.

"Look at it financially, morally, politically, however you like," Captain van Clam leaned across, "we're the most successful pirates these seas have ever known."

"Bar one." Webley "Mussel" Wilkins had come up behind him.

"Uh?" The insides of his knees were huge wooden cavities now. Hundreds of small metal balls bounced and sprang off the planking.

"The Indiaman's no pirate," Van Clam protested.

"The piracy's on land, but she's a pirate ship, mark my words," Wilkins retorted.

"Thanks." The Internuncio took the pipe, drew deeply, and passed it on to Wilkins. "What Indiaman?"

"Indiamen," said the captain. "When we first began she was called the Sophie. She was an open secret. Gazi Hassan warned us of her first, this was in his free-booting days, before he started founding naval academies for the Sultan, reorganizing the Turkish fleet and whatnot."

"Turkish fleet!" Wilkins spat.

"Anyway, he told us nothing came within a league of that vessel and lived to tell the tale. 'Give her a wide berth,' he said, and we did. No one knows where she docks, no one has seen her crew, and no one knows why she sails these seas."

"She makes two voyages a year." Wilkins took up the story. "Each year she appears somewhere off the coast around Jaffa, never exactly the same place, but always the southeast corner of the Mediterranean. No one's actually seen her being loaded, but on her voyage back she sits low in the water. She sails west, out of the Straits of Gibraltar, and then heads north. After that no one knows, but she's back within two or three months. Spain perhaps, the west coast of France, she might even make England, but wherever she docks that's where she unloads. West to east she rides high; empty, I'd say."

"Indiamen, you said."

"Indiamen, mm. Two of them. There was the Sophie as I said, then there was a second. We'd been sailing these seas, what, seven or eight years, I suppose, and the rumors started up about a second ship. Still an Indiaman, well-fitted, lots of guns, lots of tumble home, but newly built by the look of her. About the same time, the Sophie disappeared, just vanished. No wreckage, nothing. The *Corso* had lost ships, the corsairs had taken losses too. She was a hell-ship and good riddance, that was the feeling north and south the length of the coast. The celebrations were short-lived though. The second Indiaman took up where the other left off, worse than before even. Whoever commands her seems to know these seas better than us all, and sails that damned ship like an Argonaut."

The Internuncio let the tale blow gently about his ears. The sky was undulating, a vast eyelid of shadow creeping across the blue. He wanted to know why the voyages were made, he wanted to hear the mystery of the ship's purpose explained. Perhaps he asked these things, and perhaps Van Clam told him about the caravan which arrived on the coast around Jaffa and which was said to meet the ship and load it with the rarest metals, the most precious stones. As he slid into a dream under a sky so clear where all the stars were chances taken or missed, perhaps he asked the name of the ship, a name they had avoided voicing, as the ancients avoided mention of the Furies for fear that the name would summon its owners. But the pirates' fears were groundless, their object being hundreds of miles distant, never to return, and called by them now in syllables reaching down into the Internuncio's sleep. "*Vendragon*," said Wilberforce with a shiver. "And God help us all if we see that name again."

"*Megaera!*" The name shouted from the crow's nest, rousing the Internuncio from his sleep with the sun already high, sending elderly pirates scampering up the rigging, bowling along the gangways, diving through the hatches.

"*Megaera!*" There she was, a tiny black shape on the horizon, and the Internuncio felt the *Heart of Light* swing about as Captain Wilkins set a course for his prey.

"She's carrying sulfur," Wilkins threw over his shoulder. "We're low on powder, you see. Harder to port! That's why we needed the *Tesrifati*'s saltpeter. A few barrels of sulfur, the same of charcoal, and we'll have all we need in no time."

The sun rose higher and it seemed to Peter Rathkael-Herbert that they were gaining on their prey. By the afternoon she was less than five leagues' distance away.

"Put on more sail!" Wilkins roared aloft. A thin grey smudge hovered on the horizon, gradually becoming land.

"Dammit!" exploded the captain. They were overhauling the *Megaera*, but too slowly. The coast would reach her first.

"Third time this year we've missed her. There she goes, look at her." Wilkins shook his fist. "Next time, you bucket of worms, next time!"

But the *Megaera* had indeed escaped, and as the *Heart of Light* slackened sail to tack away from the coast, she slid safely into harbor at Marseilles cursing, for the third time that year, the lack of a squadron to protect law-abiding vessels from the depredations of privateers.

A letter was drafted and the mate posted up to Paris that very day.

They would petition the King. The master of the *Megaera* had had enough. Running Caltanissetta sulfur between Cagliare and London should be routine. The *Flota* two centuries before had had an easier time of it. And waiting for him out there, somewhere on the open sea, was the black ship, *Heart of Light*. He needed an escort, something with fire power, something to blow the *Heart of Light* to the deepest pit of hell.

"No," said Louis to the *Megaera*'s request for three twenty-four-gun corvettes, and "No" to Monsieur Necker's request to rebut the charges made by his successor, Monsieur Calonne. Louis had awoken to a radiant dawn, full of decisiveness. Already he had banished the Bordeaux Parlement to Liborne, refused the resignation of a colonel in Toulouse, and inveighed against the protests against His Catholic Majesty in Brittany.

"No," he said to a request for pay from the Switzers guarding the Palais. Today he would not be cowed. He would make at least ten more decisions before breakfast, and twenty before lunch. The dauphin, he knew, was ill again. A sickly child, the dauphin. And his wife . . . His wife was not universally loved, it was undeniable. Today was a day for looking matters squarely in the face.

"A petition from Cherbourg, sir." A secretary approached. "On the matter of a blocked harbor."

"No," Louis replied, "absolutely not. If they require a blocked harbor, they may build it themselves."

"I believe they have it already, sir. They wish it removed. . . ."

"They want it, they do not want it. What am I to think? My decision stands. No, wait, send the petition to . . ." In his agitation at the Cherbourg petition, Louis had risen from his desk.

"Majesty?" The secretary's pen was poised; he looked to his master, who now stared down out of his window. Morning sunlight glinted on the artificial lake.

"Majesty?" again, but Louis's eyes were fixed on the orange trees. The lines were broken, disordered, confused. They looked as though they had been dropped there by, by balloon. Where had his guards been when the outrage took place? Were they in on the orange-tree plot?

"The Switzers' pay," he spoke over his shoulder to the secretary. "Double it."

"And the Cherbourg petition, Majesty?"

"The Marine Board," barked Louis as he turned away from the insult which confronted him below. "Let them deal with it." He paused. "That is enough for today," he said more quietly. "I am tired of it now."

And so the Cherbourg Petition was dispatched, with other official correspondence, back to Paris and the offices of the Marine Board where, moved by stages from teetering heaps to disheveled piles, by way of neatly labeled mahogany drawers, overflowing bureau-desks, lacquered memoranda trays, and ormolu Louis Quinze side tables pressed into service by the sheer accumulated bulk of neglected requisition orders, rejected tender offers, minutes of meetings for projects abandoned years before, outline plans of schemes so far in the future that the technologies to execute them had yet to be invented, treasured thumbnail sketches and speculative costings of notions dear to the hearts of successive directors past, present, and even future (infantile executions in bright crayon coupled with the endemic nepotism of the Marine Board's policy on directorial succession support this last)—all of this filed, indexed, and cross-referenced under classification systems devised uniquely by a succession of independent-minded secretaries who had overlaid them one on the other until every item was enshrined in a category of which it itself was the only example and the whole farrago resembled nothing so much as a bone-china tea service dropped from height onto an adamantine and unyielding surface, such as a block of granite, it (the petition) quickly came to the notice of Monsieur Bougainville, who recognized at once that this was a matter for his trusted lieutenants, Monsieurs Duluc and Protagoras, en route at that moment between Cherbourg and the port of La Rochelle where, weather permitting, the petition would be waiting for them on their arrival. And so it was.

On the twentieth day of May, a coach-and-four made weary progress across the plain toward La Rochelle. The coach was red with dust thrown up by its passage along the Bressuire Road. It had passed Marans and was traveling over level terrain though the road, which twisted and turned to avoid the slightest hummock, wheeled the view about this way and that, until the two passengers wondered if they would ever arrive. Duluc peered out of the window at the plain which, a century and a half before, had played host to the red coats of Richelieu's army. A city of tents had sprung up behind the trenches and mortars, out of range of the walls which came in and out of view with the twists in the road. Behind those walls the Rochelais had fought and starved and, at the last, burned themselves alive rather than be taken by the Cardinal's dragoons. Old stories. Duluc wondered whether, in years to come, travelers to La Rochelle might look at those same walls, murmur his name, and, closing their eyes, imagine the scene as he would create it in the coming weeks. Passing at last through the gates into the city, he was struck by how few buildings had survived from that time. He knew the facts, but here the facts were stone and wood, flesh and blood, which had turned to nothing years before. The city, he realized suddenly, had never recovered from the siege.

Low tide showed them the remains of the mole which had blocked the harbor. The harbor itself was a ragged circle, broken where it met the sea. Beyond it was Île de Ré, and to the south, Île d'Oléron where a patch of water seemed darker than that surrounding it. The sea between the two was troubled with crosscurrents and strange eddies that legend ascribed to the flight of a young child over those waters on the last day of the siege.

In their roles as officers of the Marine Board, Duluc and Protagoras knew the true reason was a complex system of sandbars which moved invisibly below the surface in response to the tides. Two towers marked the entrance to the inner pool of the harbor. Casting an eye over the humble fishing smacks and lighters which crowded together along the quays, Duluc found it difficult to believe that it was from this harbor that *Les Cacouacs'* partners across the sea had first made their fortunes. It was from here the Cabbala had fled, and to here they would return. No, no one would remember Duluc. Le Mara, Cas de l'Île, Romilly, Vaucanson, Boffe, Les Blas, Lemprière, and their leader, whose identity he had not been told. Those would be the names graven on Rochelle, as the Greek commanders' were on Troy, as Scipio's on Carthage. Duluc would be forgotten, a clerk in the service of princes across the water. Eclipsed by their return.

In the week that followed, the inhabitants of the hamlet of Lauzières to the north of the city watched with diminishing curiosity as two men labored with lines, stakes, compasses, and charts on the narrow isthmus of land which ended at Pointe du Plombe. They were from Paris, surveyors it was thought. The two men walked up and down the shoreline writing figures in small blue notebooks, holding up plumb lines, even hiring a boat and paddling about to take soundings. These too were written in the notebooks.

Two days later, the news was posted in Lauzières, Nieul-sur-Mer, and Marsilly that Monsieurs Duluc and Protagoras of the Marine Board were seeking to recruit a workforce. A jetty was to be built at Pointe du Plombe. It was to be fifty yards long and at its end would be a mooring post, stout enough to secure a vessel of four hundred tons. The villagers were caught between curiosity and ridicule. With the harbor at Rochelle, no ship would dock at Pointe du Plombe. For all their measuring and noting and stamping about with tide tables and charts, the men from Paris clearly lacked sense. What could they want such a mooring for? And here of all places? Within the day, Duluc and Protagoras had all the hands they would need.

The survey was a sham. All their efforts were a charade. The jetty had been drawn and its position marked six months before. In the Cardinal's Paris residence, Jaques had leaned across the table and the girl had peered with sullen eyes as he pointed to the chart. "Here, extending to here. The ship will be four hundred tons, do you follow?" The Cardinal had nodded his acceptance before passing on the commission to his lieutenants. The Marine Board was a convenience.

"There is a channel, very narrow, the width of a man's shoulders. As it deepens, the ground closes above and it becomes a cave, a tunnel." Jaques's face had tightened. "A long tunnel." His voice was distant. "Build the jetty where the channel meets the sea."

Duluc had found the channel on the second day, overgrown and blocked with small trees and bushes. Together with Protagoras, he had forced a way through the undergrowth. They walked in single file, for the channel was as narrow as Jaques had described it. Gradually the sides of the channel rose up and met above their heads; the vegetation thinned and was replaced by gravel which crunched underfoot. They moved deeper into the chamber until the light from the entrance dwindled and Duluc produced a candle. A few paces more and the passage broadened, then opened out into a long low cavern. Abruptly, the path ended.

They were at the edge of a lake which stretched out and away in front of them and the light from their candle could find the roof, but nothing to right or left or ahead except water extending into the darkness. But what held their attention was the boat. A dinghy perhaps ten feet long, beached on the gravel shore of the lake. Someone, sometime, had rowed across the lake. Duluc took out his compass and watched the needle swing toward him. They were facing south, toward the city. The two of them stood looking out over the darkness of the lake, their thoughts reaching south to Rochelle and back one hundred and sixty years to when the Rochelais had burned with their city and nine men, now their partners, fled under cover of the carnage. As they stood on the lightless shore with the candle flickering over the dinghy, the same realization dawned on both men.

"This was how they escaped," said Duluc.

• • •

Downstream from the Crow's Nest, the *Vendragon* displaced four hundred tons of surrounding water, patiently awaiting her masters' return.

"Algae blooms off Île de Ré," read Captain Guardian from his post at the overlooking window.

"Fish?" asked Captain Roy.

"Belly up by the hundred," said Eben. His eye wandered once again from the fine print to the ship moored below. He was waiting for the watchman to reappear.

"Young Lemprière has no business aboard ships," he remarked.

"Pleasant fellow." Roy recalled his enjoyable evening at the Stone-Eater's of a month ago. "His friend was in a fine funk." Eben saw Septimus pressed up against the wall by harmless flames, white-faced with his eyes screwed shut.

"The fire," he said, and both men nodded, remembering similar scenes aboard ship. All men had their private terrors, and the sea brought them out often enough.

"It might have been the last performance." The Stone-Eater's name caught Guardian's eye in another column. "The building is under Sir John's interdiction and the King believes Cockspur Street a disfigurement to its neighbors. He wants to pull it down."

"He's sickly," said Roy. "That's the real reason. I heard he has consulted Bulwer, for blockage of the bowel." Eben thought of the final swallow, Lemprière's creamy-pink stone sliding down the Stone-Eater's throat as Sir John's men battled with Farina's ruffians. The strange signal passed between Lemprière and the ruffians' escaping leader, Stiltz, Stoltz, Farina's right-hand man at any rate. Roy bit a woman in the leg, not once but several times, and the evening turned into a scrum, a near-riot. Tonight they were to go to the theater. He could not quell the feeling of rising apprehension. He looked down once more at the ship but nothing had changed. An opera. He hoped Captain Roy would enjoy it as much as he had enjoyed the Stone-Eater. His eyes moved over the ship but there was still no sign of the watchman.

On that same morning, seated with the Dukes of Cumberland and Queensbury, Lord Brudenell, Lady Cramer, Sir W. W. Wynne, and others of the cognoscenti, Marmaduke Stalkart watched in gloom, his own and that of the surroundings, while Signors Morelli and Morigi swapped the arias of *La Frascatana* back and forth on the stage before him.

"Add the tightrope act," he called up to Bolger. "Richter, whatever his name is." Bolger nodded and wrote the instruction down.

"Yoooo-ooo-hooo!" sang Signor Morelli.

"Meee-ee-ee!" returned Morigi. Lady Cramer waved a handkerchief at her husband who led the skeleton-orchestra on his violin. He waved back as he caught sight of her. The orchestra ground to a halt.

"Very good, Morigi," Stalkart called to the tenor. "Very sweet on the *rispondi*." Morigi shrugged and began to wander toward the wings. "Could we add an *allegro* by tonight?" Stalkart asked Bolger as he climbed down from the stage. "Something short?"

"*Se serce, se dice.*" Lady Cramer rolled several nonexistent "r"s.

"Something with a bit of spirit," the Duke of Cumberland chipped in gruffly.

"It is far too late," said Bolger. Stalkart sighed. "We break, back by eleven, everyone!" He clapped his hands, rose, and took Bolger by the elbow. Together they walked through the semi-light of the auditorium.

"This opera house will go dark inside a month. Look here." Bolger pointed to the columns of figures in his ledger. Marmaduke glanced down.

"Morelli is in fine voice, did you hear him?" Lovely silvery tones banished the column of dwindling figures for a moment.

"Douse those lamps!" Bolger called back as they left by the stairs. "Do you understand me, Marmaduke? One month and"—he drew a finger across his throat—"curtains." Marmaduke climbed ahead, knowing what would follow.

"There is a time to call a halt, and I am calling it now." Marmaduke waited. "Your damned tortoises will tip us over the edge. They will bankrupt this theater and the interests of anyone with a stake in her. . . ."

There it was. The tortoises. Bolger was right, of course, but he had no vision. Marmaduke had long shouldered the burden of opening the more prosaic eyes of his partner. The dwindling audiences for *La Cameriera Astute, Gli Schiavi Per Amore*, and now *La Frascatana* were nothing new. That really was the point. The people craved novelty and so he packed the program with tightrope acts, sword fights, concert pieces, and ballets. Still, the empty seats stretched back into the cavern of the pit and the galleries were deserted. He had fallen behind their appetites. Sometimes, as he watched them from the rear of the theater, their faces would become blanks. Even shouting or coming to blows with their neighbors, the features would dissolve in the absorbent clouts of their rag-doll heads, along with the fire and life of the piece onstage before them, soaking it up in some hungry reaction, some deficiency they had to fill, they had to have more and more. It was a new hunger and he could no longer feed it with the old repertoire. At Sadler's Wells, a theater (theater? A grocer's shop with three candles and four chairs) packed them in with cudgel-fighting. A man who swallowed stones in Cockspur Street did good business up until three weeks ago and he was left with dance finales when the pit wanted tightropes, tightropes when they wanted horsemanship, and so on and so on. So he clung to his tortoises like a disbelieved prophet; they were far off but promised, and when they arrived, well, then his kingdom would be restored.

"Cancel the order," said Bolger. No, never, not in any event, not if the theater should crash in flames into the Haymarket.

"They are part-paid already," he said, and watched Bolger swallow back his riposte, which was that the part-payment accounted in large degrees for their troubles. The tortoises should have arrived from Coade's three months before. A succession of excuses—the last was a chipped mold—held Marmaduke at bay.

"No one will see them in any event," said Bolger, knowing that discouraging Marmaduke from his folly was ever a lengthy business.

"Ah, not true, you see. . . ." and Marmaduke explained how the leading tortoise would be placed on the edge of the roof, rampant, perhaps bearing the legion's standard which was the Minotaur indicating the secrecy of its battle-plan. Behind it the massed tortoise-ranks would cluster wonderfully. They would be invisible for the most part, this was true. But Marmaduke was no lunatic. Precisely through remaining unseen, his tortoises would prove a novelty the mob could never exhaust, not this season, nor the next, nor the one after that. They would be a mystery, in the best and most alluring, most crowd-pulling sense.

"I leave you to your dreams." Bolger rose and stalked out in search of Richter. Marmaduke watched him leave in silence. Of course, even the tortoises would not save the theater in a single month. He was not foolish enough to believe that. He needed a coup, a revelation, a dazzling surprise, something to shock all London into attendance. In short, he needed Marchesi.

Cobb had him signed up already, but so far not a note had been heard from the famous tenor. A variety of infections bedeviled Marchesi's throat, there were problems in rehearsal, with the scenery, with his fellow singers. . . . Marmaduke read these familiar signals without difficulty. Marchesi wanted more money and he, Marmaduke, was determined to give it to him. Damn the tightrope walkers, fancy riders, dancers, stone-eaters, and all the other charlatans, a reputation like Marchesi's was money in the bank. Money, however, was the problem. Bolger presented a persuasive case for this fact two or three times a day. There was no money. No money at all.

Marmaduke leaned back in his chair and smiled to himself. Settled there, twisting this vicious circle inside out, he heard a clattering, clanging kind of a noise scrape up the corridor outside. Marmaduke's head appeared sideways around the door as Tim, stagehand and dogsbody, side-footed a pail over the floor. Marmaduke looked down at murky gray-green water slopping in the bucket.

"More daubers?" Tim grunted in the affirmative and continued on his way. Marmaduke had noticed the slogans appearing on the walls of the theater two months earlier. At first the cryptic messages intrigued him, then they were a nuisance, taking Tim a morning or more to erase. Now he was worried. The theater seemed marked out for some kind of special treatment at the hands of Farina's men, a special defacement for this citadel of the graced and favored. Sir John had been short in the extreme when he had complained.

"Nonsense, Stalkart. Do you ever look outside your precious theater? The same slogans are everywhere. . . ." and then Marmaduke *had* looked, and it was true. They were all over the city. Farina. *Farina*.

Tim's bucket gradually faded from his hearing and he closed the door once more. A few minutes later a knock sounded, signaling the arrival of his visitors. Stalkart, who recognized one vaguely, greeted them familiarly.

"Did we meet at the De Veres'?" The taller of the two paced up and down the room while his wiry companion stood quietly and without expression just inside the door as though an attack were expected. This was comical in some way, but Marmaduke did not smile. He listened attentively as conditions and fees were outlined. Already, he was thinking of Marchesi, a fat purse of gold to free the fat gold throat.

". . . access to all areas and facilities, the wardrobe, the properties, stage machinery . . ." the big man was saying.

"A performance, splendid. The orchestra will—"

"There is no need for any orchestra."

"Of course, of course," Marmaduke agreed.

"We will hire the theater outright for a single night. You need to know no more than that." And then the figure was mentioned, which swept away all Marmaduke's obscure misgivings about the arrangement, which would later sweep away Bolger's, although, on learning that the money was already spent, even to secure Marchesi's retainer, his joy would be less fulsome.

"That will prove acceptable," Marmaduke said calmly; already the golden notes were rising, the vicious circles turning virtuous, the tortoises, Marchesi, the money, all of it falling into place.

"There remains only the date, Viscount," Marmaduke prompted his visitor.

"Two months' time. The tenth day of July," said Casterleigh as he and Le Mara walked out, leaving Marmaduke Stalkart elated at the coup and wondering, without much caring, for what purpose exactly they required his theater. In his mind's eye, the tortoises were already in flight.

. . .

No, Sir John had not taken much trouble over Stalkart's complaint. Farina's name was scrawled and daubed over every public building from Green Park to Shadwell. The green chalk—was that a clue, a message also to be read? He did not know, and in any case could only imagine green. Farina's campaign had gone to ground. His lieutenants, Stoltz among them, had disappeared, and the leader himself, well, the stories multiplied. He was gone to Paris for arms, or Amsterdam, or Lisbon. He had taken the cloth, joined the Wesleyites, he worked as a laborer in Tothil Fields, he had sailed for the Indies, was dead, or risen from the dead as an avenging angel, a cohort of the devil, an invention of himself. His skull was made of solid silver, he drank poison and did not die, he had fought with the corsairs under Gazi Hassan. He could remember his own birth and knew where and how he would die. He was Farina.

For Sir John, who felt the city's taut skin pulsing beneath his feet, he was a monster hatching in the sewers and underground courses, in the subbasements and cells, in the lightless spaces beneath the everyday townscape. Once already he had shoved his scrawny ragged neck up into the light, cawed for meat, and sunk out of sight. Next time the fledgling would be a harpy, hungry and risen to feed. He was everything that was wrong in the city. The squalor, the stench, the ruin. He was the unexplained deaths and unforeseen collapses and Sir John could not find him.

He asked for more constables, and received polite smiles. He explained the need, talking of the Linen Houses collapsing, flooding the streets with jobless workers, of a new viciousness in the dens and rookeries, of a woman who stamped her foot, broke a vein, and bled to death in the street, of the urchins who had danced around her and painted their faces with her blood, perhaps they did not know, perhaps it was innocence made them do this but he did not believe it. He was refused. If trouble broke out, the barracks were near. But Sir John told them the prisons were full of deserters from those barracks and still they would not yield. Then he realized that they would not give him the men because they feared a blind man and his force of constables as they feared their own regiments and the mob. They did not trust him. What would Henry have done? He had packed up the foreigners and sent them off in a boat, although, remembering the incident across three intervening decades, Sir John recalled it was not a success. They had escaped with the boat—ship, rather—or been lost. And that was the Comb Riots, a gentle ripple compared to his present fears. His own men were frightened and mutinous. Even his guide-boy, it was a dreadful incident, he would rather not think of it. It might have ended in disaster; ridicule, a gibe, a prod, a poke, a trip, and then a fat blind man rolling under the kicks of the Mob, kicking him and kicking him. The mood could turn like lightning. The boy had untied the string which Sir John had attached about his neck. He had tied it about the neck of a small dog. The dog had led Sir John down the steps of Bow Street toward the market and it was Mister Gyp, the knife-grinder, who had saved him, whispering in his ear, "Your boy's a dog, Sir John," as he passed. The joke so visible it could not have been missed, a Chief Examining Magistrate led by a small dog through the gauntlet of the market. He had been wrong about Gyp. The boy was padlocked now. The clanking irritated Sir John.

Troubled on all levels, he discharged his duties at Bow Street with a new perfunctoriness. A weather-eye on the coming storm and an ear to the ground which shuddered far below drew his attention this way and that as the catalogs of arson and affray mounted in the Examining Office. He needed a refuge, and found it in the cool halls of Rudge's mortuary. Rudge hardly noticed the city's anxieties. So far as Sir John knew, he never ventured beyond the doors of the mortuary. On the pretext of his investigation into the Ritual Murders (a title he half regretted sharing with Rudge), Sir John spent long hours meandering about details of the women's and Peppard's deaths, a kind of purge from which he would emerge briefly free of his cares. The investigation itself was a lonely success in the lists of his recent failures. The figure of Lemprière floated about the affair, never quite connecting with it, never far away. He had been at the De Veres' the night of the first murder and he had been, perhaps, the last to see Rosalie alive. But five months before . . .

Doubts nagged Sir John. He had a sniff of his quarry, but no more. On the strength of his visit to the Craven Arms, he had recalled the lightermen who had found Rosalie's body, and they had told him of a one-sided fight between themselves and a madman in the King's Arms tavern. That was the night of the murder, and their assailant had worn eyeglasses and a pink coat. He had asked Rudge if he remembered the boy from George Peppard's room, Theobald Peppard's companion, and Rudge had confirmed "John Smith" had been seen at the King's Arms that night, except John Smith was not his true name.

Sir John waited in the Examining Office for his summoned witness to appear. He could not fault his own deductions. There was no missing element in the causal chains by which he hooked the killings to one another. And yet something marred the composure of his logic, something which told him all his deductions led him falsely, that his steps were actually theirs, and they served other masters. Doubts and more doubts clouded the case before him, adding another layer to his troubles. A knock sounded at his door.

"Come!" instructed Sir John. He heard the door open and fussy footsteps move across the floor. "A seat, Mister Peppard." He gestured before him.

"Sir John," Theobald said by way of greeting as he sat.

"You are Theobald Peppard, brother of the late George, an employee at East India House in Leadenhall Street?"

"Chief Archivist and Keeper of the Correspondence, I am, yes," Theobald answered. Sir John leaned forward.

"On the night your brother's body was discovered, you arrived in company with another gentleman. Do you recall that night?"

"Naturally, Sir John, my own brother's death, how could I forget?" Because, by all accounts, you had not spoken to him since his good name sank with the *Falmouth* and Captain Neagle twenty years before, Sir John thought to himself.

Aloud he said, "Do you recall the name of your friend that night?"

"He was no friend of mine! Not at all, no. I met him only that evening, he was trying to force George into a terrible business. Blackmail, would you believe? I tell you I have my own suspicions about *that* gentleman—"

"Naturally." Sir John sought to stem the flow. "But do you have his name, Mister Peppard?"

"Lemprière," said Theobald promptly. "L-E-M-P-R-I-E with an accent like this." He gestured with his hand and Sir John sighed inwardly. "R-E."

• • •

A future-ghost stirred in the city of the dead, rose and walked among the shades of forgotten heroes, through streets which rose and leaned in until the sky was a narrow slat of light far above. The powerful gods were only

293

local deities here, weakened to lares, the lemures of untended graves. He saw the false prophet, Laocoon, whose errors would now lead no one astray, there being nowhere for them to be led. He saw the unheeded prophets, Nereus and Œnone, who told Paris of the outcome of the rape and his own end, but it made no difference then and never would again. Larga and Lais walked arm in arm taunting the shades of Lycurgus, who hobbled on his stumps through the streets which were all so similar with their shallow curving gradients and regular flagstones, and clean too, as though invisible sweepers were always at work over the next rise, around the last corner, erasing all traces of the inhabitants. Macco gabbled and Mandana looked askance at her groom. Manto was silent, for there was nothing to foretell there. Niobe's hybris trailed behind her, the shade of a shade as she drifted past. Odatis, weeping bitter tears which seemed to sink into the flagstones, stood by Pasiphae, who waited for the attentions of her lover with a patience borne of certainty he would not come; the Minotaur would never be born, would never be slaughtered in the labyrinth by Perseus, who would never escape to leave his accomplice wailing on the beach at Naxos. He would never return. She would never wait for him. Penelope would weave by day and unravel by night and never abandon her task, for her husband too would never reach Ithaca. He wandered ashen and insubstantial as them all, a gray man in gray streets which wound round and about and back, doubling and redoubling. Theseus and Pirithous passed without recognizing one another; Volumnius and Lucullus forgot their old friendship. Xenodice and her mother were nearby or so; over there it was Zenobia: She knew her child was lost somewhere round the twisting streets in the city doubled on itself and tiered in time, the first and second and third and fourth and all the cities of Rome, all the cities of Carthage and all the cities which had folded one inside the other until every last stone was the stone of a thousand such cities, every wall had fallen a thousand times and every gate led to the same flat landscape, scree rolling for miles under skies which would never rain or shine. . . .

And here was where his search went on, this future-ghost, for the city was counterweight to his dictionary which filled itself at the expense of these streets, and he was the agent of an exchange between different versions of the same past: the city and the book. The faces came grayer and grayer, almost transparent as the streets coiled about some unseen central node and their gentle gradients grew steeper. They were fewer now and they fumbled like blind men in the expanding light, for the roofs were drawing back and the streets opened out into broad bland swaths of gray stone. Still he noted the shrinking ghosts, although now they seemed to fade at his touch. He saw them fall away to nothing but knew they were safe, serried in columns and rows down the page like the bodies washed ashore from a wreck which are lined up along the beach. At the center of the city was the citadel and already, even at a distance, he seemed to be pounding on its doors, a huge thudding sound against the heavy iron, because she must be inside, whatever he sought had to be there for there was nowhere else but the space beyond these portals and his fists were crashing into them, *thud, thud, thud* . . .

. . . *thud, thud, thud,* "John!" *Thud.* "Are you there?" His hand jerked, spilling a tongue of ink over the entry for Xenodice. "John!"

"Yes! A moment . . ." He dabbed at the ink, then ran to open the door. Septimus walked past him into the room.

"Ah." He added his own efforts to those of Lemprière as the last of the ink was mopped away. "Splendid work." He leafed through the entries, picking one out. "Unsigned?" Lemprière scribbled a signature and date, still gathering his thoughts.

He had been at work, transcribing the ghosts into his dictionary in a waking dream. Septimus brandished the sheaf of completed entries as though to congratulate him on his industry. He was nearing completion. Another month and the strange gray city would be empty, all its citizens interred with only his entries for headstones. Septimus was talking of his work, telling him of an obscure incident involving the Pug and Warbur-ton-Burleigh. Lydia was well. He spoke of Cadell's enthusiasm for the project, the weather, a contretemps among the opera set, the Lottery Suicides, Lemprière's orange tree which simultaneously flourished and caught tree-diseases in the corner, and Lemprière, who had resolved to ask him about the night they had visited the Stone-Eater—he had not seen him in the meantime, three, perhaps four, weeks—listened instead as this compelling chatter led further and further away from that night toward far-flung matters: the shoals of dead fish floating in the Channel, a movable hospital erected in Somerset House, the defection of a dwarf troupe from the circus at Magdeberg.

"They were sighted in Perpignan a week yesterday," he said. But Lemprière saw his face with its eyes shut and all the color drained away and he heard Lydia's comment that it was a harmless fire had terrified him. He did not think of Septimus as particularly brave, but neither could he connect terror with his friend. He had faced down the lightermen in the King's Arms. He was never at a loss. Why had he stayed away these last weeks if not to hide the face behind that undaunted mask? He would ask. Now, he thought. Do not wait.

"Septimus," he interrupted, and was about to form the question when a second knock sounded at his door.

"That will be Lydia," said Septimus as he opened it.

But it was not Lydia. It was the three professors: Ledwitch, Linebar-ger, and Chegwyn, who burst in and began talking all at once.

"Mister Lemprière!" said Ledwitch. "We rushed as soon as we heard."

"We remembered your investigations," added Chegwyn.

"Flying men." Linebarger drew Septimus into the conversation. "Firm proof at last."

"What on earth are you talking about?" asked Lemprière, which the professors thought very good indeed.

"Ho, ho! On *earth*, ha ha!"

"Who *are* these people?" asked Septimus.

An hour later, Lemprière, Septimus, and the three professors sat in the room where Lemprière had once listened to the Widow Neagle as she spun a tale of her husband and her lover, a ship and a whale. Ledwitch brandished a copy of the *Morning Chronicle*. Septimus sat with his fingertips touching, his posture conveying intense skepticism as Ledwitch spoke of Turkic prisoners marching north from the Banat who witnessed a flying man.

"At first they thought it was a gull," he said.

"It was no gull," said Chegwyn. "No gull is the size of a man."

"No gull," said Ledwitch.

"We remembered your interest in the Rochelle Sprite," Linebarger spoke to Lemprière, "and this sighting is so similar, so strikingly similar."

"They saw its face," Ledwitch continued. "Blackened it was, just like the Sprite's, an infant's face—"

"You never told me those things before," said Lemprière.

"Hardly surprising," muttered Septimus.

"An infant's charred face," said Lemprière, more to himself than his companions.

"From the fire," said Ledwitch. "The fire in the citadel, when the Rochelais died. Of course the Turks took it for a Mahometan angel—"

"What else do they say?" asked Septimus.

"Nothing," said Ledwitch. "They are dead. They were found two days' march from Karlstadt with their heads caved in. A 'Sergeant Vittig' is under arrest."

"So there are no more details. A flying man, a blackened face, an infant's face—"

"The Sprite, yes. There are records, Richelieu's men saw—"

"I mean the Karlstadt sighting. You say an infant's blackened face?"

"The face of a Moor, a Mussulman. If it were a Mahometan angel as they say, its face would be dark, would it not?"

"But then it would not be the Sprite, if such a thing ever existed, would it?" Septimus came back. "And the report makes no mention of an infant, or an infant's face, and this report is taken from the Vienna dispatches, is it not?" He turned to Lemprière. "Would it not be convenient for the Austrians if such a miracle took place in this way; it does after all rather distract from Mister Vittig's massacre, does it not? And a massacre of prisoners by an Austrian renegade when the Emperor is clearly trying to extricate himself from this war, when his own Internuncio is, they say, held hostage by the Turks, would be at the least an inconvenience, would it not? And, regarding your Sprite,"—he gave the word an incredulous inflection—"how convenient for Richelieu and his friends would this Sprite have been? An angel, a flying man. So much more engaging than the squalid details of a siege. Who would talk of women and children burned alive when one could tell the story of the Sprite? Can you really give any of this credence, John?" His tone was hurt, amazed, angry all at once.

The professors were silenced by his demolition. Lemprière read quickly through the article.

"It does seem largely concerned with the massacre," he said. "You could have told me this at my lodgings."

"There is no such animal," Septimus weighed in. "Not at Karlstadt, not at Rochelle, not here or anywhere. Why do you waste my colleague's time in this way? He has business enough without such nonsense. Come John, Lydia will be waiting for us in any case—"

"No, wait!" said Ledwitch. Lemprière had risen and was putting on his coat. He turned in surprise.

"I mean, please wait," Ledwitch repeated. "If you could—"

"John?" Septimus was ready to leave.

"We did not mean to deceive you," said Linebarger.

"Deceive me?"

"We need your help, Mister Lemprière. We had to bring you here." He paused and looked at the other two, who nodded for him to go on.

"It concerns the Widow," he began.

And of course Lemprière had thought of the Widow. He had thought of her the night he had shouted after Theobald Peppard in Blue Anchor Lane, which was the night she had lost George, though she did not know it then. She might have had him; they might have had each other. Against all the odds, between them they had kept their chances alive. Against all the odds, their stock had risen, their long-awaited cargo delivered by the ship which was moored below the Captain's house. But George was dead and Lemprière had thought of the Widow and done nothing. Now he had been called to account. The professors knew nothing of his involvement in Peppard's death, nothing of the agreement which had led the killer to George's room. If it was strange the professors had not previously mentioned their hostess, it was stranger Lemprière had not asked after her. To sit in her house and talk and not say her name: It was a small lie to which a larger evasion was attached. When Lemprière asked how he might help, and Ledwitch said that he was the only one who knew "a Mister Peppard," he felt the full weight take hold of him as though the intervening months were so much slack which was now used up.

"She is much changed," Ledwitch said, "since she heard of his death. She rarely leaves her room now, and we, we hardly know what to do. We thought if you spoke to her, perhaps . . ." His words trailed away, lost somewhere in her loss.

"Of course," said Lemprière, and he began to climb the stairs, thinking of the things he might say and those he might leave unsaid.

Later, when he had bade his farewells to the professors and told them to think nothing of their slight deception, thinking of his own being so much greater, when he walked back through the noise and chaos of Thames Street with Septimus, typically his counterweight, in buoyant mood, when his gloomy silence proved resistant to all Septimus's sallies and his friend was at last forced to ask how he had consoled the Widow, Lemprière would say only that he had not told the truth. Now, as he knocked and opened the door to the Widow's room, he still entertained the thought that he might blow a little of George's hope on the ashes and she would rise up, fiery and full of the outrage which was how her own hopes had been preserved through all the years of the lawyer's disgrace. But one glance at the old woman sitting in the high-backed chair facing away from the curtained windows and he knew that it was not so.

The Widow did not look up as he entered. He began the long litany of condolence standing in front of her in the darkened room. He ended by mumbling and twisting his fingers together. He took off his spectacles and the room dissolved. He could not see her face, which was blank, or her eyes, which never looked at him or blamed him. He knew the truth and the truth had moved on, leaving her marooned in this room which she would leave rarely now, there being nothing to draw her out. No angry visits to Skewer's office, no strangers to accost and fix with her pertinent questions, no lover across the water waiting to claim her and be claimed in turn. Lemprière thought of these as he stumbled through the smooth phrases which he remembered d'Aubisson saying to his mother when they had gone to his office together. He could tell her that he was sorry, that he had liked George, that he too grieved, and all these things were true. He might have told her that George loved her, that had he lived he would have married her for he had found the means to clear his name, that George had told him exactly that and meant every word. He might have sailed off, caulked with these truths, insured against later discovery. He replaced his spectacles and looked down at the frail woman.

"George loved you," he said. "But he could not come to you. I know he understood that. Too much had conspired against you both." Lemprière thought of Peppard's jubilation at the mention of Neagle's ship, returned at last to save them both. "He could never have married you," he said and flinched inwardly at the lie. The Widow seemed to stir and Lemprière waited for a long moment, but at last turned to the door. The Widow spoke then.

"We always lose," she said.

"That is not true," said Lemprière. He was thinking of Juliette. "It is not always true," he said, but this time the Widow made no reply.

• • •

To the east, the sky was a gash of pink and gold. Dawn spread in a stain across the horizon. Morning sunlight caught the peaks and scarps and threw long shadows which shortened, then disappeared, as the sun climbed higher in the sky. The sea chopped and glittered under its rays and the moon shrank to a pale detail in a luminous blue sky.

Aboard the *Heart of Light*, Peter Rathkael-Herbert opened his eyes to the glow of a summer dawn and reflected that there was no better thing for a man than to sail the high seas in June and be a pirate.

"Aye aye!" Wilberforce van Clam greeted the Internuncio. Twenty-three days had passed since his liberation from the *Tesrifati*'s hold, and the helm had rotated back to Wilberforce.

"Where is she?" he asked. They had lain in wait for the *Megaera* outside the port of Marseilles. When her master had finally despaired of an escort, he had slipped out under cover of darkness, hoping to lose his pursuer. Her topgallants had just been visible on the horizon as the dawn came up. Another hour of darkness and her escape would have been complete, but the chase had resumed.

"Ten, fifteen leagues." Wilberforce pointed dead ahead. "She'll be passing Rochelle about now." The pursuit had taken them west across the Mediterranean through the Pillars of Hercules and into the broad swell of the Atlantic. The *Megaera* plowed north toward the western coast of France with the *Heart of Light* following in her wake.

In truth, the pirate ship was much the faster vessel, but among its mariners, in the matter of helmsmanship at least, some were more equal than others. Whole days had been lost in dead calms. Canvas had been rigged for winds that never came. All this time the *Megaera* would pull away until a better helmsman took the wheel and the gap began to narrow once more. The pursuit had now gone on day and night for a week, and both vessels stood ten miles off the western coast of France separated by a single day's sailing. Even fully laden with her cargo of sulfur, the *Megaera* expertly rode the swell until Wilberforce, speaking to the Imperial Internuncio during one of their evening chin-wags when they would sit together blowing sweet blue smoke off the stern as the sky turned orange or green, remarked of her captain that he "knew a thing or two about his tack," which the Internuncio took to be high praise indeed.

Now the sun rose higher and elderly pirates began to appear on deck. Heinrich Winkell, once Bavaria's only Jansenist, today the *Heart of Light*'s midshipman, tentatively arched his back, walked slowly to the side, hawked, spat, and greeted the De Vin brothers, Oiβ and Lobs. Amilcar Buscallopet, Smyrna mystic and ordinary seaman, dragged his bad leg for'ard. "Slim" Jim Pett emerged from a difficult visit to the heads.

"Wonderful!" he greeted the June sunshine flooding the decks, then "Aah" as his back twinged. "Dear oh dear . . ."

"Come on there!" Hörst "the Wurst" Craevisch chivvied him from somewhere below. Gradually the pirates assembled, wheezing in the cool morning air, watched from the helm by Wilberforce and the Internuncio. They scratched and muttered as brittle bones and rheumatic joints began their own slow reveille. Clearly, the mornings were difficult for them.

A scrabbling somewhere aloft and "Mussel" Wilkins descended from the crow's nest to join them both.

"Saw her around three bells," he panted, "crossing the moonlight. She's closer than we thought." Wilkins stopped to heave breath into his lungs.

"How close?" asked Wilberforce.

"Close. Eight, ten leagues. Just for an instant the moonlight caught her sails. She's showing no lights. Reckon she'll be—"

"Oi!" a shout came up from the lower deck. All three looked down and saw Hörst lying on his back, fat arms and legs pumping the air as he tried to rise from the deck.

"Is it snails do that? Fall on their backs and can't get up?" Wilkins asked.

"Tortoises," said the Internuncio. Lobs and Oiβ de Vin each had hold of an arm and were pulling him upright. Wilberforce looked north once again.

"Reckon she'll be coming up to Rochelle about now," Wilkins finished his sentence.

• • •

"*Megaera*," Duluc read aloud. He lowered the weight of the telescope to the ground. The ship was in full sail a mile or more off the coast. Protagoras took the instrument from his companion's hand and looked for himself.

"Mmm," he said, then swinging left toward Île de Ré he scanned the sea between the island and its neighbor. The dark patch of water they had spied there on their first day at Rochelle had turned out to be algae. Local fishermen had complained that it poisoned the surface fish in these waters, and indeed whole shoals had been seen floating belly-up in the broad channel between the islands. By night, the area had glowed a ghostly green as currents running off the coast stirred the cells of tiny creatures. The light reflected off the white bellies of the fish floating in their midst about which the algae seemed to cluster as if needing a center, some confirming totem. The previous night, Protagoras had stood aboard a hired lighter, communicating by lunar heliograph in an improvised code with Duluc, who arranged the specially ordered panes of green glass in front of an array of oil lamps and adjustable shutters until they were certain that the prearranged signal could be seen clearly by a ship approaching along the promised bearing. In the long intervals while Duluc directed his small work force to realign this shutter or that flange on the hillside, Protagoras had watched the algae slowly creep out from behind the low headland of Île de Ré. The smell of dead fish wafted over a black sea. Green lights flashed intermittently from the shore and he silently urged his colleague to hurry up and finish the business. It seemed as though the algae had sensed the small boat and were heading very slowly toward it, to surround it.

Now, as he searched with the telescope, the carpet of light seemed to have disappeared altogether. The tide, he supposed. If the algae had drifted around to the blind side of Île de Ré, as he suspected, the *Megaera* would pass directly through it. He returned the telescope to Duluc.

Below them both, down the hillside and beyond the dense undergrowth which ran in a strip behind the strand, their work force was hard at work on the jetty. In the fortnight since their arrival, and in contrast to the monster at Cherbourg, a simple sturdy construction had taken root off Pointe du Plombe. Rising twelve feet out of the water, a double row of piles extended for twenty yards out to sea, as if an avenue of trees had been lopped off midway up their trunks. It was low tide now, but when the waters rose they would come within three or four feet of the tops of these piles. On the thirteenth of July, at three in the morning according to Duluc's extensive calculations (checked against his own empirical observations and frequent consultation of the published tables), the tide would reach within six feet of the tops of these piles and thus within eight of the broad gangway which the piles would support. It was a compromise: enough water to float the arriving ship, but with her decks low enough to be on a par with the gangplank. Speed of unloading: that was essential. But if the ship ran aground. . . . He worried about this fine margin, checking and rechecking his calculations.

He was pleased with his jetty, and even regretted that after a single night, a crucial night certainly but still a single brief night, his effort would be abandoned to the tides and the weather. Naturally, his reports to the Cardinal mentioned only the bare facts of the work: this or that stage completed, such and such materials required and so forth. The *Conseil aux Conseils* had no interest in his enthusiasms, and in fact were liable to regard them with suspicion. Regarding his colleague, Protagoras, he maintained a looser protocol, but he was careful too. He embroidered his jetty in secret, even shamefully. It was a strong and excellent beast and his enthusiasm galvanized the work force. A low rumbling disturbed his thoughts then, and turning to discover its source, Duluc saw with pleasure two carts hitched together and drawn by four oxen, their driver up and out of his seat, pulling hard on the brake as the whole contraption descended the hill toward him. The weight was palpable. It was his mooring post. Thirty feet long and forty feet in diameter, solid oak. He walked down the hill toward his work force who waited on the strand. A good day was ahead.

Later, when the sun was low in the sky and his work force lay propped on their elbows, exhausted, with the mud on their legs drying in the last of the day's heat, Duluc was able to look out and see his post standing straight and tall out of the water. There for the next hundred years, he thought. As his eye wandered down the avenue of piles, the second ship came suddenly into view, framed perfectly in the jetty's perspective as though it were constructed for this purpose alone. Fishing smacks were passing back and forth between himself and the vessel, day fishermen being replaced by the men who cast their nets by night. The ship resembled the *Megaera* superficially, but the earlier vessel had slid behind the north headland hours before. Taking up his telescope once more, Duluc picked out the name of this second ship. Like the first, she was bound north under full sail. His eye wandered over the decks where several groups of old men stood idly. The hull of the vessel was black. Not tar-black or paint-black; absolutely black. She reflected nothing: The sea and fading sun, a red June fireball this evening, seemed to be swallowed whole. Even the water around her sides looked darker. Then he swung the telescope up to the mainmast. He looked once, blinked, again, then called "Protagoras!" On the top of the mast a pennant flew, and on the pennant was a skull and crossed bones.

"Protagoras!" he called again. "She's flying the Jolly Roger!" He was about to call for a third time, but Protagoras was nowhere in sight and Duluc knew suddenly that he had returned underground once again, to the cave and the subterranean lake beyond it.

"Pirates," he said to himself and then, still only half-convinced, he looked again. "Very old pirates."

Passing within two or three miles of the open mouth of Rochelle, Wilberforce pointed out the twin towers guarding the entrance to the inner harbor, the citadel in which the Rochelais had died, and the line across the outer harbor where, at low tide, the remains of Richelieu's mole could be seen. Peter Rathkael-Herbert saw a town where pressure of space had forced the buildings high. Slate-gray roofs crushed together in angled zigzags, and chimneys pushed higher still with their faint smoke fading against the dip of the horizon as the sun settled and the city was redrawn in shades of gray like an old stone ghost. He looked at the harbor and tried to imagine Buckingham's fleet drawn up in a crescent, the men-o'-war flying their battle flags and signal pennants, baffled by

Richelieu's barrier. They would have floated there just three hundred yards from the safety of the twin towers and the Inner Pool beyond, and to the Rochelais starving behind the walls those three hundred yards must have seemed an ocean they would never cross.

Île de Ré drifted to their stern as the *Heart of Light* continued on. They were sitting to the port side of the ship. In accordance with the rota, "Mussel" Wilkins had relieved Wilberforce at midday. It was almost sunset. A half-completed jetty ran off the headland to the north of the city, and a gang of men were walking up the hillside behind it. Beyond that the land was wooded, a few low hills and the smoke from a village somewhere behind them. Peter Rathkael-Herbert watched as Wilberforce packed the pipe, his hands shaking a little as resin was thumbed into the bowl. He lit it, drew three or four lungfuls, and handed it to his companion.

"So they all died?" he asked, taking the pipe. The smoke was hot, curling up from the bowl in dense plumes as he released the mouthpiece and drew it down. Waves slapped louder against the sides of the ship.

"Died? Died, yes. Some of them. They all died in the end."

The sea was darker, bluer too. His mouth was dry, and when he hawked his spit was thick and very white. He watched its arc over the side flatten and quicken, meters per second per second, falling into the slopping waters in a splash of blue-green light.

"Poor Rochelle," said the Internuncio. A smell familiar from the *Tesrifati* wafted over the decks. He looked over the side once more and saw its cause. Hundreds of dead fish floated upside down in the water. Toward the bows, the water gave off a faint glow as it was cut by the *Heart of Light*'s prow.

"I've had my fill." He handed the pipe back to Wilberforce.

"Hmm?"

"Enough. I've had enough now. The sea is behaving strangely. . . ." Wilberforce stirred himself to look over the side.

"Algae," he said matter-of-factly. "Glows when you disturb it. Bloody nuisance, but we'll be through it soon enough."

Thus reassured, Peter Rathkael-Herbert took back the pipe, and within the hour he was drifting in a dreamscape where, as gubernator of a judicial inquiry, he presided over the trial of his former employer for treason.

Wilberforce sat back and watched the algae twinkle blue and green all around the ship as the death throes of red snappers and incautious catfish disturbed its toxin-loaded calm. The Internuncio slumbered in the chair beside him. Occasionally a word or broken phrase would escape from his tortured dream. Wilberforce van Clam thought he heard "Guilty," and a little later, "Hang the Emperor." The algae went on and on. Must be the biggest bloom in seven oceans and a hundred years, was his last thought before the opium pipe slid from nerveless fingers, his eyelids closed, and he too was overcome with sleep.

When the *Heart of Light* reached Cherbourg sixteen days' sailing later, she still floated in the same algae. By then the crew would have realized that they were actually being followed by the billions of tiny creatures which made up the poisonous blue-green carpet. An efficient system would have evolved to clear the larger, more noxious fish from the vessel's immediate vicinity and various theories put forward to explain the algae's evident attachment to the *Heart of Light*. The algae carpet extended for fifty or sixty yards to port and starboard and almost a hundred off the stern. From time to time, portions of the carpet would break off and float away to wreak havoc on hapless icthyo-ecosystems elsewhere, but the algae would quickly regenerate and by sundown the gap would be refilled by millions of new bioluminescent cells. The reason for their attachment to the *Heart of Light* was simple. Weed.

When, as the *Alecto*, the *Heart of Light* was captured by Wilberforce and the rest of the pirates back in 1752, her hull was clean as a newly scrubbed butcher's block. Six weeks before, she had been careened and scraped at Blackwall until you might have seen the grain in her oaken sides. But twenty-six years at sea had taken their toll. Above the waterline, countless tiny carnivorous mollusks had affixed themselves and slowly spread up to the wales where they realized belatedly that the beast to which they clung was not animal but vegetable and began to die of starvation. Now dead, and still fixed there, their decayed remains accounted for the matte black of the *Heart of Light*'s hull. The pirates had often given silent thanks for these mollusks and the legacy of night camouflage which their mass self-sacrifice had left behind. Below the waterline, the story was not so happy. Weed, the curse of any helmsman, infested the hull, making the *Heart of Light* sluggish and unresponsive to the wheel. When undertows caught the thick forest of undersea tendrils, the whole vessel would list to one side. Fish approaching from below sported happily in this unexpected feeding ground. Naturally rich in proteins and nutrients, with mussels for the clamp-jawed wolf fish and juicy tuberous neritic kelp for wriggling eels, the ragged shaggy underside of the *Heart of Light* formed a compelling habitat for the algae which clung there fiercely, building up in untypically thick layers below the waterline, snuggling up to every ribbon and trailing frond until the whole hull was encased in a gelatinous and parasitic soup. Motile cells wagged their flagellae in happy self-congratulation, noctilucal lights pulsed on and off, flickering between sea and sky, water and air, between their one- and zero-states until the scintillons packing ten thousand glittering square meters of thrashing diflagellates united in one vast configuration, an expansive love letter from the algae to their reluctant host. Pursuit of the *Megaera* or no, the algae had said good-bye to their wild, floating years and decided en masse to anchor themselves here. Their compulsion was absolute. The algae were in love with the *Heart of Light.*

Love, careless love. Had they known their stubbon residence would lead, however indirectly, to the destruction of the *Heart of Light,* perhaps they would have floated off, resignedly oxidizing their luciferin to play the great game of eat and be eaten in pastures new. Certainly a vague, half-articulated melancholy pervaded the colony as massive fish-kills went on dogging their progress up the western coast of France: The algae were not without compassion. But of the *Heart of Light*'s eventual fate, how could they have known? When the courted vessel reached Cherbourg, an irreducible ten hours behind the *Megaera,* her quarry, the algae still flung themselves out like a broad lover's cape of blue and glittering green, billowing out over the ocean behind the vessel they had learnt to call home.

Love then, a hopeless trailing love. Looking off the stern, Wilberforce van Clam complained bitterly of the ship's unwanted suitors. It was foolhardy enough to have ventured so far from their familiar hunting grounds. But that leap made, to lie at anchor off Cherbourg, flying the Jolly Roger and surrounded by a sea of light, was madness. Luckily, the harbor appeared so clogged it was doubtful a squadron could get out to attack them; even so . . . Amilcar Buscallopet devoted his evening prayers exclusively to the problem of the algae, and "Mussel" Wilkins, aided by Lobs and Oiβ de Vin, made fruitless attempts to cut it away with long-handled scythes improvised from the dinghy's oars. But their efforts came to nothing, and all this time the *Megaera* was escaping toward the safety of the Thames estuary. Faced with the problems of the algae, the weed, the escaping *Megaera,* and their own dwindling supplies of gunpowder, the pirates knew they were in a desperate strait. It was in these circumstances that Wilberforce van Clam, for only the fourth time in the vessel's twenty-six-year history, convened the *Heart of Light*'s highest legislative body, in which every member of the crew had his voice, the Pantisocratic Diet of *Light,* and in this forum he proposed a simple but daring plan.

It was this: The *Heart of Light* should assume its original name and, disguised as the *Alecto* (as, in fact, herself), should pursue the *Megaera* up the Thames and there launch a full-blown no-nonsense pirate raid on the Port of London itself. Thus restocked with the desperately needed sulfur, they could then sail downriver under their true colors, pillaging perhaps a small bankside settlement or two en route, and return to their former happy existence lurking about the fat Mediterranean trade routes. Wilberforce stressed the element of surprise to his shipmates and, more subtly, the fame which so audacious an act would confer upon them all. As the protocol demanded, the Pantisocratic Diet of *Light* listened in silence to his proposal, and when it was ended, Hörst Craevisch struggled to his feet.

"Idiocy!" he exclaimed, waving an admonitory digit in the air. "Sheer lunacy!"

His stomach quivered with emotion as he went on to cite all kinds of precedents and possible pitfalls, each and every one mitigating against Wilberforce's plan. But Wilberforce was ready. When he stood up, seemingly hours later, his tones were measured and calm, bespeaking compromise, which was the form of his second plan.

"Algae," he said and stopped, allowing the word to sink in. Gray-headed pirates squatting painfully on their haunches (as the protocols also demanded) nodded sagely.

"Algae," Wilberforce repeated, "and weed. The algae is attracted to the weed on the hull. Sometime, and somewhere, we will have to careen this *Heart of Light* of ours and scrape the weed."

"And the barnacles," came a voice.

"And the barnacles," Wilberforce agreed. "Now, I share all your fears of the Port of London. We are all fugitives from that place. But all of us have suffered at the helm when the old lady swings about for no reason, or rolls in a calm sea, or snags her keel when the soundings clear a fathom." The less expert helmsmen, who suffered these mishaps even without the weed, nodded vigorously. "I propose a second plan. An appendix, if you will: Should we arrive and find the *Megaera* defended by His Majesty's frigates, well then, our story is simple. We are bound for the drydock at Blackwall and our only purpose is to scrape the hull. And it will be true. If we are to scrape the hull, why not there? And if we are to ever rid ourselves of our guests"—he gestured in a wide circle to the enveloping algae which slopped greenly all about—"this ship must be docked, raised, and scraped to the boards."

The fourth Pantisocratic Diet of *Light* was to last a further three weeks, with plenary meetings and delegatory committees leading to amendments at the subcommittee stage, then there would be talks, and talks about talks, trade-offs, discreet lobbying belowdecks, several shameless displays of filibustering, and even the odd case of vote-buying, but in the end, Wilberforce van Clam would see his dual resolution adopted by a majority of two, and only then, still pursued by her amorous escort of phytoplankton, would the *Heart of Light* set sail for Deal bound either for the *Megaera* and glory or Blackwall Docks and a week's scrubbing, but whichever (a further vote would decide the issue finally once they were in the Thames), Wilberforce was privately convinced that in all the politicking, it was the algae which swung the vote his way. Its constant encircling presence besieged the waverers, persuaded the doubters, and exerted a unique pressure on men used to an open sea who would look out over the twinkling lights of their escort and intuit a vast and diffuse purpose behind their presence, an obscure commerce of some sort which, most unsettlingly of all, seemed to have nothing to do with them, to exclude them somewhere as if they, the crew, were the escort and the algae were the true protagonists, which, from the point of view of the algae at least, was precisely the case. Thus, in his plan to take the *Heart of Light* home, Wilberforce found his most powerful allies in the algae. Without their mute intervention, the battle for the hearts and minds of the crew would have been lost, the *Heart of Light* would have sailed south on a slim majority, and the catastrophe which was to befall her might well have been averted.

And Wilberforce? The Internuncio watched him wait out the bluffers, persuade the doubters, lose long exhausting arguments, win them back, and pace the deck for hours with his eyes looking out miles over the water for England, the Port of London, and beyond them to the secret nailed into the heart of the *Heart of Light*, and after the final vote had given him the fight, he watched as the man slung himself from a cradle off the bow's rail and broke the heads of the nails with a chisel until the name-plate came away with a crack to tumble down into the algae, "*Heart of Light*," where a film of tiny blue-green creatures swamped it before his eyes and it disappeared to become part of the colony which encircled and surrounded them all. In its place, Peter Rathkael-Herbert saw the darker wood of the original plate, protected alike from the weather and prying eyes by its substitute for all those years until its removal discovered the vessel's first name, *Alecto*, now itself a masquerade, one among a rainbow of false colors which would take them deep into the heart of the Port of London, and thence a version of Rochelle.

The master of the *Megaera* thought he had lost his pursuers at Cherbourg. Having crossed the channel and hugged the coast as far as Deal, the mouth of the Thames was reached on the thirteenth of June. A barge guided her past the estuary shoals and sandbars as far as Gravesend, where the pilot met the vessel and led her upriver between the squat settlements of Shadwell and Rotherhithe, past the teeming suffrance wharves on the south bank until the Tower was reached and the river was crowded with small boats, lighters, wherries, and barges which moved about the larger vessels standing at anchor in the Upper Pool, all waiting to berth and unload on account of the Dispute. A tight space was found off Queen's Wharf, lashed up alongside the *Tisiphone*, who still awaited a gang to unload her cargo of charcoal.

"*Megaera*," Captain Guardian noted the following morning. "From Caltanissetta."

"A guinea her cargo's sulfur," challenged Roy.

"Done," Guardian took him up, and later that day paid the same to his guest as they walked slowly in the baking heat along the quay and found that Roy's guess was correct.

"Had to be sulfur," said Roy as he took his winnings. "Nothing else there."

It was late afternoon and the air was close.

London boiled in the June heat. Summer glared off every street and rooftop. Alleys and courts trapped the heat and fed it to the citizens day and night alike until they tossed and turned and rose hollow-eyed to see the same sun waiting for them the next morning. And the next. Eben rose with the dawn and ran his errands early. After eight or nine in the morning the gutters stank, the light blazed in his eyes, he sweated, grew irritable, and looked into a middle distance which was a shimmering haze of rising heat in which men and women appeared and disappeared like reflections off a moving sea. The quays were at a standstill, although this at least was due not to the heat, but the Dispute.

The Dispute had begun in the first week of June. No one knew precisely what it was over, or even whom it was between, but already it figured as a catch-all excuse for any omission or failure of duty and as such had no lack of subscribers. If wool-bales were piled up on Butler's Wharf, as they were, then it was because of the Dispute. If a collier stood three months in the Upper Pool with her load disappearing by the sackful every night as the mudlarks raided her unguarded decks—indeed, if she was unguarded in the first place—then this too was put to the account of the Dispute. There were meetings. Meetings between wharfingers and shipowners, between shipowners and warehousemen, warehousemen and stevedores, even stevedores and wharfingers. But the issues were vague, and in the meantime the Dispute spread along the wharves and quays to north and south like an obscure paralysis. Men would arrive for work, but somehow never manage to start. Goods rotted in holds and clogged the quays, spreading up and back toward Thames Street until the approach roads were blocked and Eben and Roy's afternoon promenade along the waterfront came to resemble an obstacle course of crates, sacks, hawsers, chains, planks, beams, and discarded ballast. It seemed no one could get this sluggardly creature by the tail, it had no name or cause unless, like everything else these days it seemed to Eben, the Dispute was something to do with Farina. His name had even been scrawled on the stonework of the Opera House, at which memory Eben stopped in his tracks.

"What day is it?" he asked Roy as they walked back together to the safety of the Crow's Nest, and hearing that it was the thirteenth, he cursed mildly for two distinct reasons. Roy looked up at him in surprise.

"The tortoises," said Eben.

"Ah," said Roy.

They had gone to the opera. In return for Captain Roy's excursion to the Stone-Eater (still suffering, according to recent reports, from a mysterious malady of the bowel), Captain Guardian had taken his house-guest to a performance of *La Frascatana* at the King's Theatre, Haymarket. Despite advertisements to the contrary outside rival establishments, Eben had been assured that the golden-throated Marchesi, of whom so much was being made in the gazettes, would sing the role of Cambio. The evening, as it turned out, had not proved a success.

Eben had last visited the opera house fifteen years before. He knew its proprietor slightly. Stark, Starkart. Something of the sort. He recalled a slow progress up broad flights of shallow stairs which swept left and right, an entrance into the auditorium, a greeting of half-known acquaintances, a general convivium. The performance, whose title he forgot, had been agreeable: mellifluous and Italianate with fussy strings and fat women in red velvet singing to men who sang back, then everyone together and *tout va bien*, the End, and home by carriage to a glass of port by the fireside. It was all very undemanding and enjoyable. He should have returned long before. Stalkart, that was it.

Their late visit had turned out a rather different affair. Entering the foyer, Eben knew at once that it was not a night for the cognoscenti. It was crammed with people who hooted and jostled in a ruffianlike manner. Roy's inevitably slow progress up the broad staircase drew impatient curses from this low crowd. They were barged and stampeded past until Roy began to curse and growl at the insubordinate horde. Reaching the safety of their seats, the two of them found themselves surrounded by apprentices and ladies' maids who disported themselves immodestly, got up, moved, sat down, got up again as though every possible seating permutation had to be exhausted before the performance could begin. Then it was announced that Marchesi's golden throat had a "dose of the nodules" and would not be gracing the production that night. In his place, a Signor Morigi would play Cambio.

The audience booed, and continued to boo when the curtains opened to disclose a Palladian interior of false perspectives and mirrored pilasters behind which a vast tortoise was painted with a vaguely Roman soldier astride its back. Someone threw something, the singers entered, and a story of hopeless love unfolded, or would have unfolded if they could have seen through the bodies who stood up to shout abuse, swap seats, leave, return, and engage in ribald conversation. Whole rows decamped he knew not where during Cambio's final aria and only returned to shout insults at the curtain call, which was brief. Some Irish tunes followed, and these were better received. There was a tightrope act and a dumb pantomime which drew scattered applause.

Captain Roy sat mute beside him through it all. Eben was humiliated by its awfulness and knew Roy knew it too. When they rose to leave midway through a reprise of the tightrope act, Roy said it was very different from how he had imagined it.

Leaving the theater, they met Stalkart on the stairs. Tousled, unshaven, red-eyed, he grasped Eben by the elbow.

"Did you see him?" he asked, eyes staring ahead.

"We gathered he was indisposed—" Eben began stiffly.

"Not him! The tortoise, you saw him?"

Eben recalled the fragments of the set he had glimpsed between the mass of bodies. "Ah, yes—"

"Twenty-seven of them! Imagine it! Just wait, you'll see, you'll see.

They all will. Tortoises, eh? Where, do you think? Where?" Eben shook his head, edging sideways. "The roof! We'll put them"—Marmaduke pointed at the ceiling—"on the roof. A week today, you just wait. A ton apiece they are, the beauties, hoist 'em up, stick 'em down. Come and watch, everyone's invited and"—he looked about conspiratorially before lowering his voice—"when they're up, no one'll ever see 'em again. You see? They're a mystery!" And he began to laugh softly to himself. Eben watched him carefully. When he was calm again, he asked Eben if he had enjoyed the performance and, hearing to the contrary, dragged both men down to the foyer where he scribbled quickly on a scrap of paper.

"There." He gave it to Eben. "That'll get you both in. Not a word, mind you. . . ." Eben looked down and read, "The Secret Gala. Thirteenth day of July. Admit Two." It was signed "M. Stalkart."

"Five weeks' time. Only for the cognoscenti, mind you. Marchesi will sing in a performance of . . ." He did a little dance of frustration. "I cannot tell you, it is a secret, you see? Yes, a secret. But the tortoises." He was suddenly serious again. "They are the true spectacle. The elevation will begin at two. Come!" he exhorted them. "Enjoy!" He waved good-bye as Eben and Roy shuffled out of the foyer. "Come one, come all!"

He was still waving as they made their escape. Roy was silent for most of the journey home, then, turning into Thames Street, he cleared his throat.

"Quite fancy, the sound of those tortoises," he said. Eben looked at him in surprise.

"Then we'll attend," he said, glad to salvage something from the evening's wreck.

Now, eight days later, walking back along the quay and learning of the date, the elevation of Marmaduke's tortoises was the first of two reasons for Eben's curse. They had missed it.

"Never mind," said Roy. They were passing the *Vendragon* in their quayside promenade.

"It's not only that," said Eben. He was distinctly irritated with himself. "I should have attended a funeral today."

Across the city, through the heat and haze of a blazing afternoon, over the Fleet, down the Strand beyond the sweltering rookeries of Charing Cross, the tortoises were rising. Fat pink torpid tortoises, baked twice already in the Manufactory kilns, once more in the heat of this June afternoon, swung left to right and seesawed in their slings like improbable pendulums as they rose inch by inch skyward, roofward, up to the men who manned the ramshackle derrick on the summit of the Opera House, who sweated, cursed, and pulled the beasts—a yard or more across, half a ton each—across the parapet, while the men on the hawsers below sank twenty-six times to their knees as they heard the gross statuary dunt finally on the roof far above. Twenty-seven wagons had left Coade's that morning to trundle in convoy along Narrow Wall, crossing the river at

Westminster, straining through Whitehall, pulling hard up the short rise of Cockspur Street to their destination in Haymarket. Each wagon carried a crate packed tight with straw, and in the midst of each a tortoise lay cocooned with its bland herbivore's smirk and stumpy legs and every other detail down to the individual plates of its shell perfectly realized in creamy-pink Coade Stone.

Straw and splintered crates lay scattered about the Opera House. Twenty-six carts lay empty. Marmaduke Stalkart ran hither and thither in excitement as the last tortoise emerged from its packing, was lashed about the midriff, and slowly elevated to its prime position among them all, the parapet itself, for this was the leader of the battalion, the *primus inter pares,* the only one which would ever be seen by the hordes who would now surely flock to the theater, the tortoise-rampant himself. Bolger pursued him with his ledger, but he didn't care. He didn't care that Marchesi was fleecing them, inventing maladies and contractual breaches to up his already considerable ante. He didn't care that Casterleigh's money was already spent, that there was no more and the cognoscenti stayed away in droves. He didn't care that Bolger worried over the leasing of the theater to the Viscount, thinking that on July the tenth any manner of disturbances might wreck the theater once and for all leaving him, Marmaduke, ruined, meaning himself, Bolger, liable for the loss. He didn't care about the slogans, or Farina, or the ruffians who were said to stalk the streets in organized gangs and beat passersby for nothing at all, or the heat, or the funeral he, like Eben and others, should have attended this morning (she would have understood), or the labors of Coade's hired hands. No, all he cared about, as he looked up to see the last beast clamped into place and rise rampant on one leg to grin down over the parapet, was his tortoises. Come one, come all, he thought triumphantly to himself. Come friend or foe alike, my tortoises will defeat you all!

Behind him, the twenty-seven empty carts were preparing to return to the yard. The drivers checked their horses for a moment and doffed their hats in respect. A hearse was passing, but as he turned to look, the small crowd, the drivers, the other hands, Bolger, and lastly Marmaduke Stalkart himself all saw that it was empty. Half a mile away to the north, the bells of Saint Anne's in Dean Street began to chime.

. . .

"Damn!" Rudge looked at Sir John in surprise. He saw no reason for the outburst. The bells chimed again.

"The funeral! Damn my forgetfulness!" Sir John exclaimed. Rudge waited for his colleague to subside, then resumed his questions.

"With an accent, you say?"

"Like this." Sir John drew a diagonal in the air, left down to right. "As you see it. L-E-M-P-R-I-E with an accent like this"—he made the motion once again—"R-E."

"Blackmailing George Peppard?"

"This Lemprière held an agreement of some sort between an ancestor of his and the East India Company. Apparently a share of the Company was his, a ninth—"

"A ninth? Good God!" Rudge sounded incredulous. Sir John nodded.

"My thought exactly. But Theobald insisted. George was to take the case, or forge some sort of deal, otherwise Lemprière would, well, Theobald became rather vague. Some new aspect of the Neagle affair, he thought."

"That was a dead letter years ago," Rudge snorted. He was wiping down the slabs. Sir John could hear a damp cloth moving over the marble, the slight sounds of his colleague's exertion. Drops of water falling to the stone floor.

"Anyway, George refused and this Lemprière killed him to close his mouth, so Theobald maintains." The last three words hung in the air between the two men. The street above was a faint hum, nothing more. Only the bells seemed to reach this lowest cellar of the mortuary.

Sir John wanted Theobald to tell the truth. He wanted Lemprière guilty, without doubt. Or not guilty, again without doubt. But in his heart he knew George Peppard's brother for a liar. Perhaps he told the truth, but if that were so it was only in support of some wider, more nebulous lie. Theobald had grown confused or forgetful whenever Sir John had probed his story. Whatever else this Lemprière might be, he did not seem a blackmailer. There was the question of the women too. What part did they play? So far as he knew, the murders of George Peppard, the girl Rosalie, and the older woman whose body now rotted in a casket in the cellar adjacent to this were connected only by their suspected assailant. There was no pattern to it, and Sir John, above all else these days, sought patterns with a strong passion. That, after all, was what Henry would have done.

"Another thing." Rudge spoke suddenly. "If Theobald had never heard of this Lemprière before the night on which they met and, as must be the case, there has been no contact since, how would he know how to spell the name?"

"The name? Well, it is not so hard. . . ." Then Sir John caught Rudge's drift. "The accent," he said, and made the motion for the third time. "You are right. He would have to see the name written down. A tavern, a walk to Blue Anchor Lane . . . There was no opportunity."

At that moment, in a space both anterior and distant, the noose, which had tightened about the young man's neck, was lowered very slightly, an easing which brought the hook from which he hung into view as a sickle moon, or a tiny scythe, or a cedilla.

"By the same token," Sir John went on, "if they had not met before,

312

why should Theobald invent such a calumny?" He was thinking aloud. "Someone else is involved," he said.

"One at the least," Rudge replied.

Walking back to the Examining Office at Bow Street, Sir John would resist this thought. The Lemprière case was sharp and hard. There were inconsistencies certainly, and complications, he would tell himself, but at root, in essence, it was firm. He needed to believe it, needed one single suspect. Not hundreds. One. He felt the case slipping, sliding out from under him to join the general drift which was toward diffuseness, confusion, vagueness. Disorder. Everything might be degenerating into a farrago, but he wanted Lemprière pristine and untouched by all that or, better still, all that to take on more of the characteristics of the Lemprière case.

But "all that" would not oblige in June. The city's misfortunes came in gangs, in weirdly themed spates. The heat seemed to cage itself and concentrate, building up to burn holes in the city's fabric with an eerie specificity. Children: They drowned, two of them while bathing in the Thames; were burned when a draper's house was consumed in Union Street; crushed by a coach overturning on the Lambeth Turnpike; took their own lives after viewing a hanging in Pultney Street; had their skulls caved in, a flower pot, a servant's carelessness on a third floor in Berwick Street. Collapses: A summer storm would sap the foundations of the Coal Meter's Office; cracks would appear in the paving over the Fleet River, in the cobbles of Leadenhall Street; four houses in Wapping would disappear overnight heralded by neither agitation of the air, disturbance of the earth, nor subterranean rumblings of any sort. A small earthquake would be reported in Norwood, swallowing two, and a whirlwind at Deptford would raze a cottage and four sheds, firing their contents aloft so as to cause a monstrous hazard of the air. A man would be killed by a descending fruitbarrow. Finally, limbs: Lord Chatham's foot would be taken with gangrene from a gash of his shoe buckle; a leg and thigh, female by the shoe, would be washed up at White Friar's Dock; arms jutting from the portholes of a brig at Blackwall would discover a stowage of slaves, above three hundred dead, above sixty dismembered for concealment; a single finger would be delivered to Sir John at the Examining Office, only that, quite clean and without explanation.

This then would be June and part of July for Sir John. Behind these perversely grouped events, the dock dispute would spread out further from the quays, the silk weavers would march, the heat would intensify, the arrival of malcontents by land and sea, agitators, dissenters, alien troublemakers, would be reported, flocking to the city like flies to a haunch of rotting ham; an old mistake (not his) would return to haunt him, and behind all these, even the old mistake, even the heat, he suspected, would be Farina.

So Sir John would cling to Lemprière as a single certainty in the midst of this evil flux, talking endlessly about it to Rudge and Mrs. Fielding, who would call it an unhealthy obsession and buy him Freak's Tincture of Peruvian Bark, plaguing his guide-boy with confusing rhetorical questions. And then, on the tenth of July, even that last support would be kicked away like the shoring timbers in a besieger's undermining tunnel, and the tower's foundations would crumble from the corner, spreading through walls, turrets, and bastions to the whole city, miles of stone crashing in and the roofs ablaze, when a young man would call at his office quite out of the blue, whose voice he would recognize vaguely, who would know more of the murders and of this Lemprière than Sir John himself, who would call himself a "concerned friend" to Lemprière and treat of the murders in turn and in detail, who would quit the Examining Office without leaving his name which Sir John would only recall, infuriatingly, some hours later, as belonging to one who had carried the first victim back to London on the roof of his coach and spoken to Sir John six months before, and this, naturally, would be Septimus.

He would come late, too late for Sir John and too late for the city. He was still far off as the guide-boy clanked ahead of him and Sir John sought to penetrate the opacities of the case on their route back to Bow Street: He was still almost a month away. The guide-boy stopped.

"What now?" barked Sir John. He had been hoping to remove the chain and collar. The imagery was unfavorable.

"Funeral, sir," said the guide-boy. Sir John cursed softly once again.

"The hearse is empty," he told the boy, thus adding another thin coating to his reputation for second sight.

"I know, sir," said the boy. "We can't cross, sir, cos of the carts." Sir John listened as twenty-seven heavy carts trundled slowly past in front of them both.

"Good lad," he said. Perhaps he might dispense with the chain. Try string again.

When the convoy had passed, the two of them continued. Sir John thought of the hearse's latest occupant and felt a second twinge of guilt over his absence. Then he thought of the conversation in the mortuary which had delayed him. The two thoughts mingled and he enjoyed a faint sense of serenity from a small certainty that arose from their synthesis. George Peppard's murder. Theobald's story, Lemprière and this half-cocked nonsense about an antique agreement was an imbroglio of half-truths with which Alice de Vere at least would have had no truck at all.

• • •

Dong!

Lady Alice de Vere of Braith, widow to the late eleventh Earl and mother to the twelfth, died peacefully while inspecting her son's drainage project on Friday the ninth of June at three in the afternoon.

Dong!

All attempts to resuscitate her proving hopeless, her grieving son, Edmund, arranged for the funeral service to take place at Saint Anne's Church in Dean Street five days later.

Dong!

Now, with the notices sent out, the pallbearers hired, the hearse engaged, Edmund de Vere stood in church while the vicar, whose predecessor had married the deceased to the Earl over fifty years before, recalled a life stretching over seventy-two years. Beside the Earl stood John Lemprière. Together they formed an audience of two.

The vicar addressed them, trying hard not to glance at the rows of empty pews which stretched away at their backs and which provided a testimony that, though mute and obscure in its meaning, seemed to drown out his own entirely. Other than Lemprière, nobody had troubled themselves to attend.

Afterward, Lemprière sat with the Earl in a tavern in Berwick Street. The Earl took a mug of porter, then another. Lemprière watched Edmund's faculties return and heard his vowels more clearly as he supped on the ale.

"It was very sudden," he said. "We were viewing my drainage scheme in the west pasture."

"Ah." Lemprière recalled the project from his singular meeting with Alice de Vere.

"I think she was surprised by the operation. Or the lack of it. A hole in the ground, a crane . . . Not much to look at. The crane should have gone months ago, in any case."

"*That's* the drainage project?" Lemprière leaned forward, thinking of the black arm swinging out of the night sky, the blazing pit. "That's all it is?"

"Yes." The Earl was a little taken aback. "I expected more myself, I was promised more. In fact, I am vexed with Septimus on several counts this morning."

"Septimus? What has he—"

"Recommended the engineers, made the introductions, gave the guarantees. Now they've disappeared without trace. Still, it hardly matters now, I suppose. My mother was opposed to it all from the start; she had her own enthusiasms." Lemprière digested Septimus's involvement in silence.

"She spoke of you a few days before her death." Lemprière looked up again. "The same obsessions as ever. The secret agreement, the fourth Earl, a fabulous treasure hidden who knows where, you, the Company." He drank deeply from his mug. Lemprière mopped his brow. The heat in the tavern was stifling. The outburst came suddenly, out of context. "And not one of them could bother to turn up. Not one!"

Lemprière was caught off guard. The fact had filled his thoughts in the deserted church. It was the moment he had been dreading from the second the service had ended. Now he listened to himself make excuses for people of whom he knew nothing but their absence that day. It was the heat, the summer flight of estivating gentry to the country, the erratic coaches, the clogged roads, the Dispute, inadequate notice, even Farina, any or all of these things and the same for those he knew from the merest acquaintance, Stalkart's overheard remark, Maillardet's distress, and Byrne's *schadenfreude*, a dowager's imperious glance, a gaggle of giggling nieces dismissing him from behind their fans. They were all confused, mistaken, delayed, or debarred, but when he came to their own mutual friends he ground to a halt, his invention exhausted.

"I thought at least the Club would turn up." The Earl's voice was shaking. "I told Walter the day before last. He was to see to it that everyone knew. I thought at least Septimus might, or Lydia, you know she is a caring sort, I thought she . . ." The Earl's expression had changed subtly. "I rather thought I might rely on Lydia, you know. I actually rather . . ."

It was immediately clear to Lemprière that Walter Warburton-Burleigh had not told any of the Pork Club of the funeral, and he told Edmund de Vere the same without embroidery. The Earl nodded in resignation at the fact, but Lemprière could see that his thoughts were elsewhere.

"Lydia would not have known," he added, and the Earl nodded again. He was looking up, out of the open window behind Lemprière. Lemprière turned and scanned the upper stories of the building opposite, which was a bakery. The windows were open and a maid was dusting within.

"Beautiful geraniums," the Earl said, and pointed to a row of pots on the ledge, put out to catch the afternoon sun, and it was Lemprière's turn to nod. "But how rude of me!" the Earl exclaimed suddenly. Lemprière turned back quickly in surprise. "Here I've been, bleating my misfortunes. You must be bored to distraction. Tell me now, how does the great work proceed? Where are you in your dictionary?"

Somewhere before "A" and in a place after "Z," chained at its center and clinging to its outermost border, in the margin and the text, he was halved and quartered as the dictionary neared completion. It was his own monstrous monument, an extension of himself. It was a usurping version, a simulacrum that sapped and displaced him until he was a spent host exhausted by its parasite. Lemprière would rise early and sit at his desk in the sweltering June heat, looking at the manuscript leaves before him, sometimes with pleasure and pride in his achievement, sometimes with boredom. There were days on which he might have shouted from the windows, others on which he might have burned the whole manuscript. He began to see the reason behind Septimus's prompt collections.

Septimus came twice before the funeral, and twice after. On each of the latter visits, Lemprière chided him for his nonattendance, but desisted when Lydia, who accompanied him on all four occasions and, to Lemprière's annoyance, watered the orange tree on each, took the criticism to include herself, grew tearful, and professed at length her sympathy for the Earl, who was the most couth and best mannered of Septimus's motley associates, in her opinion. Septimus made conventional noises and mouthed excuses centering on Walter's sins of omission the day before, but his expression was distant and Lemprière noticed that Lydia would look quickly at him from time to time as though to reassure herself that he was still there. His flashes of inappropriate bonhomie and roughshod energy were rarer, he seemed to look through Lemprière as he spoke, his eyes fixed on a point somewhere beyond him. When questioned on the matter, he would talk about the weather.

On Septimus's first visit, Lemprière presented him with a sheaf somewhat thinner than usual, and thinner again on his second. The third yielded a meager four sheets and the fourth only one. Toward the latter half of June, Lemprière would sit at his desk for whole days without once reaching for his pen. The heat dried the ink in the inkwell while a plague of details swarmed about his head like the aphids which invested his orange tree or the flies which settled on his forgotten meals. As the heat of June was exchanged for the still fiercer heat of July, he began to realize that the task begun eight months before might almost be ended, and as the pages and blank spaces of the dictionary grew full, so the city where his mind wandered in search of the book's subjects was emptied.

It rose out of the scree now as though it were part of the drab landscape which surrounded it; the two hardly distinguishable. At its gates, Laverna's altar was bare, robbed of her head. The streets were unchanged, the doors and windows smaller, perhaps, the interiors more opaque. He knew them to be empty. He walked, and the noise of his feet sank into the flagstones. Nothing echoed. Nothing moved in the streets. He found emblems on the gray stones. A snake skin sloughed by the python sent by Juno to pursue the pregnant Latona told him that they had passed and gone. He had them already. He thought he saw the limbs strewn by Lamia as she devoured her children. The air was laced with a scent that Lelaps would follow forever, never finding its prey, never returning with it to its master. The smell of burning. Shadows cast by the façades were the darkness in which Leucippus killed his father by mistake, the red moss grouted in the cracks of the flagstones was goat's blood from some Lupercalian rite seeping up to say only that the sacrifice was made long ago. He found Magnes's iron-clewed shoes stuck down and straining for the lodestone below, the dragon's tooth which would never become Menœceus, the tortoise on which Mercury's foot would never rest. He had them all. The well in the courtyard showed him a face a hundred times more beautiful than his own, but it was himself, not Narcissus, peering into the water, and the dim dissolving shape which sank as he reached down was the letter which Orestes would never take from Iphigenia, she would never know he was her brother, they would never

317

escape. He had them too. Not her . . . His sister. Her brother. The stench of Nessus's carcass was in the air, from which the Ozoli took their name. In the center of the square, before the iron doors of the citadel, a thousand shields lay piled. He thought of the Rutuli, first of the Romans, the Sabines, who had mingled with them till they were all Quirites. Tarpeia had pointed to the gold bracelets on their shield arms. "The ornament on your left arm for entrance to the city." They had agreed, and crushed her under their shields for her treachery, but if he cleared the pile shield by shield he would find nothing. She was gone with all of them, sucked out by the dictionary as Utica sucked out Carthage and later ate it, down to the children's cries reaching after Vagitanus, sinking into waters which hardly rippled as they accepted them, stilled, and grew stagnant as those of Velinus where Alecto descended into hell, swallowed sure as Xanthippus sailing from the ingrate Carthage he had saved to the Corinth he would never reach. It was the Saguntum where the Zacynthians had burned themselves alive rather than submit to Hannibal. It was Zama where Scipio crushed Hannibal; where the long fall of Carthage had begun.

Now he approached the gates of the citadel. He saw long dark marks run up the walls, blacker than the gray stones. He saw them spread from the high arched windows, and he smelt burning once again. As he lifted his arm to pound on the doors, the heavy iron swung in, opening away from him. He could hear, but not feel, the wind; a faint wailing within. It was the last of the city, the final page of the dictionary. If he had come this far to bury or drive out his ghosts, then he had arrived. His father was dead, the woman in blue was dead, Rosalie was dead. The ghosts which demanded these sacrifices were figures of his past, gone with their victims. If that was enough, it was done.

He walked in through the doors and found himself in a shell. The walls reached up to a block of gray sky, for the roof was gone. Smoke streaked the walls and soot crunched underfoot. Blackened stumps of wood projected from the walls where joists had supported higher floors before the floors and their supports were burned away together. The arched windows were gaps caked with black where the smoke had poured out. Fragments of charred wood littered the place. The smell of burning was everywhere. It stung his nostrils. The stone floor and walls seemed still to radiate a faint heat, but whatever had happened here, however the conflagration was begun, and whatever the fate of those caught within, the fire itself was long extinguished. The only clues were ashes, smoke, soot. Nothing, they told him nothing.

In the second week of July, Lemprière put down his pen and gathered together the last leaves of his manuscript. He thought of the time it had taken him to write, the eight months since his arrival. But when he counted through his labors, it was not from the "A" to "Z" of his dictionary which marked his time in the city.

He saw Septimus handing him the bottle in triumph when they had won the Game of Cups together at the Pork Club. He heard his coat rip when a strong hand pulled him out of Farina's brawl. He saw George's expression change from bitterness to joy at the mention of the *Vendragon*. Then he saw George dead in the same room; he saw the woman die in the pit and the girl already dead at Coade's with Juliette's face plastered over her own. He saw Annabel Neagle silent in a darkened room in Thames Street and heard the bitter outburst from Alice de Vere, her hopeless appeal to him. Last of all, he saw the coach emerge out of the darkness only to pass him by in the snow with Juliette's face framed in its window, a different appeal as she sped away from him into the dark. Then he looked down at the last of his dictionary and thought of a city burned to ashes with all its people, and knew that what he had done was not enough. There was more, and even if he had run from "A" through to "Z" he had not found it.

When Lemprière put the last full stop behind the last sentence—already nagged by doubts, certain he had left something out—he found himself at a loss. All his other projects had lain neglected during the last months of his activity and now he was unsure how to pick up the threads. He thought of the agreement which had stayed undisturbed in his traveling chest, the *Vendragon* which was still moored below Captain Guardian's house, protected by the Captain's promise to inform him of its movements. Of Juliette, whose whereabouts, whether indeed she was still in the city, were unknown. For want of anything better, he put on his coat and boots and walked the streets that night.

The city had changed. He knew it in a minute, blind not to have seen it before. The streets were illuminated only by the moon, the lamps unlit. Rubbish lay in heaps on every corner. Piles of bruised fruit and vegetables, broken crates, soiled paper, and grosser products which passersby kicked down the thoroughfares until they were littered with the same. Straw blew about when faint gusts of wind disturbed the streets, but this was rare. The heat settled in thick layers between the houses and shops. The gutters were dry as dust. He walked briskly but without aim, north through the market to begin with, then turning east and south. Gangs of men passed him, moving with purpose, their eyes fixed on points he could not see. He stepped smartly out of their way; something about them unnerved him as though they were dogs trained for a single task and were searching for it. Some of these gangs, always more than ten, rarely more than twenty, moved in a loping half-run. All their members were dressed alike as though each had an obscure uniform to go with its equally secret purpose: sashes, arm bands, angled hats. Some carried badges or emblems: a riding whip, a light cane, a short sword. He saw them everywhere. They jostled and barged the other citizens, pushing past them as though they did not exist. Standing still, they clustered to talk in low tones, and when he walked past such a group they fell silent and watched him as he went on his way. He never saw them stop finally, or discovered the point of these platoons's marches. He avoided them, crossing quickly from one side of the street to the other as they passed. Even children. Faces of six and seven blank with zeal passed him, and when he plucked up the courage to ask one, a girl in her infancy, what was the purpose of her progress, the girl looked at him as though he were mad not to know and said, "For Farina."

Then he knew that these gangs were the mutated heirs of the silk-weavers he had overheard in the tavern where he had met Theobald and his dark-faced imposter, the recent descendants of the brawlers outside the inn, and the purpose behind their marches whether they knew it or not was to find one another and fight, or unite. He returned home unsettled. When he slept that night, he dreamed of fires.

The knock on his door came in the middle of the afternoon the following day. He was certain it was Septimus and he was wrong. As he threw open the door he saw blond hair and a familiar face.

"You were right," said Theobald Peppard. "I was wrong." The words did not come easily, his ill grace was ill concealed. "Everything George said—" He paused and Lemprière gestured for him to enter. "It was all true. I have found the papers which prove it all, under my very nose. George was right from the first."

"I know," said Lemprière.

East India House rose out of Leadenhall Street, four stories high, stretching fifty feet to either side and back a farther three hundred. Lemprière had tried to persuade Theobald to disclose his information, but the other had refused and dragged him east across the city, through Fleet Market, past Saint Paul's, and along Cornhill to his place of employment. The menacing gangs he had seen the night before were in evidence again as they moved through the baking streets. In daylight they seemed less threatening, but the tension he had felt among the citizens was unchanged.

Theobald seemed nervous too, but they arrived unharmed. After tirades against the Company from George and the Widow Neagle, he had expected a lowering prison, a grim towering fortress, a vast house of evil, but East India House was bland and faceless, hardly noticeable despite its size among the houses and shops which flanked it. He was sweating in his coat from the heat and strode eagerly behind his guide as Theobald mounted the steps to the cooler corridor within.

"These are the Proprietors' and Directors' Court Rooms." Theobald indicated a vast room to the right in which Lemprière saw a horseshoe-shaped table large enough to have shod Pegasus. The strong sunlight had blinded him and his eyes adjusted slowly to the dark interior.

"These are the sale rooms." Equally vast empty rooms led off to the left. The long central corridor was crowded with clerks and other officers of the Company, all of them carrying bundles of papers and files, intent on their errands. But as they reached farther back into the building the passage began to clear. Theobald pointed out more Committee Rooms and the various offices concerned with the warehouses at the rear of East India House. He took an obvious pride in their number and his own knowledge of their workings, which he explained to Lemprière as they passed.

"The court is a popular senate," he said. "It makes no distinction between Christian, Turk, and Jew, nor between country or sex. The Proprietors elect the Directors, and the Directors appoint the Committees. Here"—he pointed—"the Committee of Correspondence meets, the most important of all the Committees. I am Keeper of the Correspondence, you see? Here, the Committee of the Treasury, and here, of Law Suits and of Military Funds." They turned then and continued along another corridor where Lemprière was told of the Committees of Buying, Warehousing, Housing, and Accounts. These were treated with less reverence by Theobald. A short flight of stairs led them down to a passage identical to the last and running beneath it.

"The third tier of Committees meets here," explained Theobald. Again Lemprière had to listen to anecdotes, about the tardiness of the Committee of Shipping, the acrimony within the Committee of Private Trade, petty disputes in the Committee of Government Troops, and the rank stupidity of the Committee of Stores. Each of these Committees had its own Chairman, Directors, Chief Clerk, and staff of officers whose various peccadilloes and bureaucratic idiosyncrasies were known to Theobald.

"But, as I said, the Committee of Correspondence is preeminent," gloated Theobald. He pointed upward. "Up there," he said.

"Is the correspondence really that important?" asked Lemprière half-innocently and then had to listen as Theobald explained how orders sent to India were prepared in the Examiner's Office, then sent to the Board of Control to be annotated in red ink. He digressed on the petty feuds between these rival departments and gave a potted history of the battle of the inks before going on to say how the annotated correspondence was sent and the eventual response read in the Court of Directors before being distributed by the Secretary among all concerned branches of the Examiners' Department, abstracted, and copies of the abstracts sent to the Directors whereupon the Examiners would begin to gather all materials and documents necessary for the reply, whereupon the whole process would begin again.

"And all correspondence is treated in this way?" asked Lemprière in frank disbelief. Theobald seemed to hesitate while he won or lost a minor internal battle.

"Not all," he said quickly. "There is a thirteenth Committee which can send orders directly to India without any authority but its own. It is called the Secret Committee."

"But you know of it? Others too, presumably. How is it secret?"

"It is secret," said Theobald, "because no one knows who sits on it, or where it sits, or even what it does."

They went on then, past long rows of glass-fronted bookcases filled with bound papers, and room after room of clerks who sat in rows, scribbling furiously. Theobald explained the precise function of each, together with its position in the Company's scheme of things, which always seemed to place the department under discussion somewhere near the bottom and himself, Keeper of the Correspondence, somewhere near the top. The corridors were almost deserted. Theobald nodded curtly to the few clerks who passed them. They took back-staircases and seemed to rise farther than the building could possibly extend, then deserted stairwells to descend below its lowest basement. At the bottom of the last flight of stairs, Theobald stopped before a small unmarked door.

"Only I, of all the Company's thousands of employees, have a whole floor to myself." Then he opened the door and they entered an office which contained two desks, one chair, and an oil lamp. "The Office of the Keeper of the Correspondence," announced Theobald.

"Your floor seems somewhat smaller than the others," said Lemprière as Theobald lit the lamp, then reached into a drawer. A large key emerged from the desk by way of an answer and Lemprière noticed a low door with a small grille set into it on the other side of Theobald's cramped quarters. Theobald struggled with the lock, which was stiff with disuse, then leaned and pushed back the door, whose hinges were stiffer still. A musty smell filled the office as it opened. Theobald took the lamp and beckoned for Lemprière to follow. They entered single file, for the door was narrow as well as low. Theobald held the lamp as high as his stature would allow and Lemprière straightened to survey the scene before him.

Theobald's domain did indeed extend the length and breadth of East India House. Rays from the lamp shone out a hundred feet or more until the gloom of the low interior defeated them, and beyond there was only blackness. It was, in effect, a vast cellar.

Rough corridors ran forward and to either side between hundreds of thick blocks. Each was ten feet or more across and reached from floor to roof. Lemprière took them for squat supporting columns. The musty smell was much stronger inside, the air cold with damp. Then he saw that the columns were paper: vast piles of sheaves of papers stacked in blocks. The cellar was an archive of monstrous proportions. Theobald walked ahead of him, turning this way and that between the moldering piles until they could no longer see the door through which they had entered, the side walls, nor yet the far end of the cellar. Lemprière heard the faint drip of water somewhere in the darkness. The smell of damp paper was all around him.

"This," said Theobald, as he came to a halt beside a malodorous pile of papers spotted with green mold and gestured into the blackness about them, "is the Correspondence. All of it. Everything. From the first venturers right up until today." Then he paused and looked about. "There are secrets here, if you can find them," he said in an undertone. "Matters the Company wouldn't wish public a thousand years from now. Some of them, terrible things . . ." Lemprière thought he heard a note of regret in Theobald's voice as though it were his brother and the unlucky players in the Neagle affair to whom he alluded. But then his tone changed and he was the bureaucrat again.

"Only I have the right to enter the Archive," he asserted. "Even the directors must apply for permission. Now look—" And he pulled a sheaf from midway up the pile and handed it to Lemprière. "The accounts from the *Falmouth*, Neagle's ship," he said. Lemprière saw columns of figures next to lists of provisions, shipwrights' bills, and other expenses.

"The end," Theobald said, and Lemprière turned until the columns ended suddenly in 1766 on a page yellowed with age and dotted with mold, but otherwise quite empty.

"What?" he asked. He saw nothing significant. "This was when she sank?"

Theobald nodded. "No total," he said. "And no payment. The insurance was never claimed. Not on the cargo, not on the lease of the ship."

It began to dawn on Lemprière that this was the extent of the "proof" Theobald had bruited on the other side of the city, and he was on the point of becoming annoyed when he saw Theobald's shoulders shaking and crocodile tears run down his cheeks.

"George was right all along," he sobbed as Lemprière joined the pantomime by patting him on the back. But his hand froze and Theobald's tears stopped in an instant as both heard the door behind them being pushed open for a second time.

They turned and saw two slight figures enter the Archive, lit from behind by a lamp held by the third, a larger man who squeezed his shoulders through the door only with difficulty. Theobald doused his lamp and led Lemprière away from them, farther into the gloom of the Archive. Lemprière looked quickly at Theobald, expecting panic, but he was cool and collected. Behind them, the three figures fanned out.

Two were lost almost instantly to view, the third only a dim shape in the lamplight sixty feet away. Powerfully built, thought Lemprière. The low tones of a conversation whose words they could not make out pursued them as Lemprière and Theobald moved noiselessly about the moldering piles. They caught glimpses of the lamp and its holder but the other two were invisible.

"What are they doing? Who are they?" Lemprière whispered. Theobald only shook his head and pulled him farther back again. But whichever direction they took, it seemed that the lamp eventually followed, slowly quartering the archive and narrowing their avenue of escape. Now and again they heard sounds which might have been the footsteps of the other two, and they would back away slowly until the sound faded. They maneuvered about the Archive in this way for what seemed like hours; only minutes in reality. Then Lemprière rounded a corner and there, only feet away, was a shape which turned at his sharp intake of breath, the head coming around, and Lemprière grabbed with both hands to seal off the cry, pulling it down and pressing as hard as he could, the lamp moving closer, only twenty feet away now and its yellow light creeping around the corner until it lit the body beneath his own and a voice came which he recognized, as he recognized the silhouette from the doorway and now the girl beneath him. The voice was Casterleigh's. The girl was Juliette. The Viscount was calling her and moving toward them both. Her eyes were wide with fright. Casterleigh called again.

"Answer him!" he hissed into her ear. She looked mutely up at him as he released his hand from her mouth. A long moment passed. Insanely, he wanted it to go on longer. The lamp was only feet away and he could hear the Viscount's footsteps moving nearer.

"Wait!" Juliette called, then rose, and as she did so whispered, "Tomorrow," only that, and he saw the fear still in her face as she slipped away.

"Come!" the Viscount ordered her, and Lemprière heard her half stumble as she was pulled forward. Then he realized that her fright was not at him at all.

He would have risen but Theobald pulled him back. Together they watched as Casterleigh's lamp moved away, its yellow light catching the corners of each squat pile whose shadows closed like teeth on one another as the three of them moved toward the wall farthest from the door. When it was a faint glow almost seventy yards away, Lemprière rose and crept slowly after it. He moved sideways, looking down the length of each passage in turn. He heard a sound like a door, the light wavered, then suddenly went out. A key scraped. He ran forward in the sudden pitch black.

Theobald relit his lamp and followed at a more leisurely pace. The lamp's rays shone out, throwing a giant shadow onto the far wall which rushed to meet Lemprière as he penetrated to the end of the Archive. It ended in a wall in which alcoves were set, hundreds of them running to left and right. A door was set in each, lower even than the one through which they had entered.

"Where is it?" Lemprière stalked up and down, peering at the doors as Theobald drew near. "The one they left by, where is it?" He pulled the nearest door open. It was heavy oak, inches thick and banded with iron. A hinge snapped as it came free. Paper. However deep the chamber he had opened extended, it was stacked floor to ceiling with paper. He opened another. The same.

"It isn't," said Theobald. "They are just little cellars, extra storerooms for the Archive. None of them go anywhere."

"You have looked?" Lemprière pulled open another, and another. He fancied the lamplight had disappeared somewhere to his right.

"There is no other way." He was working his way down the line, Theobald, despite his avowed skepticism, holding the lamp over his labors. Then he pulled and the door was fast. Again, but it would not move an inch.

"Here," he directed Theobald, and they both saw the fresh scratch marks around the keyhole. "The key," he demanded, but Theobald shook his head.

"I did not know they were locked. I did not know there *was* a key." Lemprière's head dropped, then he rose and tried the next door in line. Like the others, it was opened with some effort, and like them, it was stacked high with papers. But badly.

Lemprière was half-buried as an avalanche of paper descended on him, which he kicked away in irritation. He pulled at the locked door again and clawed at the jamb but it was futile. Then he kicked the barrier in frustration and heard a deep boom echo up from somewhere behind it. Both men recoiled from the sudden racket, then listened in the succeeding hush for the sound of returning footsteps, both poised and ready to flee. But there was only silence. The two men looked at each other.

"I didn't know," said Theobald. "I thought . . . I never looked." Theobald bent to pick up the papers which had spilled from the adjacent door. They were bound for the most part, making the task easier. Lemprière bent to help him. As his hands closed about the first armful, a familiar frontispiece stared him in the face. He stopped.

"What?" asked Theobald, but Lemprière only continued to look at the pamphlet. "What is it?" the other asked again.

"Asiaticus," said Lemprière. He picked up others of the booklets. They were all the same, thousands of them. "The fourth pamphlet," he said. Then to himself, "Here of all places . . ."

Below them both, hundreds of feet below, at the foot of the ladder pinned to the side of the shaft, the three of them stopped and looked up as the thin beam of light shone through the keyhole. Le Mara turned away first. The Viscount pulled Juliette about. As the three of them walked down the slight incline of the cavern, a pounding thud echoed down the shaft from the door, the sound rolling through the broader tunnel in which they walked. Casterleigh smiled to himself, imagining the impetuous blow. The girl seemed to hesitate at the sound.

"Move!" he barked. The command joined the dying echoes of the first report, the two mingling and ricocheting together down the throat of the Beast. He pushed her forward again. She was wavering, weakening, he knew it and he wondered how far she might be trusted. A little farther, he urged her silently. After that it would not matter. After tomorrow, none of it would matter.

. . .

"U is for the fat white *Underbelly* which hangs and sways beneath this Great Kingdom of *England* where *John Company* clings like a Savage Horseman, a Secret Rider, and on his back an *Ulcer* grows that is affixed there and draws out his strength and through him the strength of the Kingdom. And I, Asiaticus, know this *Ulcer* for a foreign growth, an unlicensed importation into this Realm, a Cabbala. . . ."

He had given up his struggle with the door and helped Theobald pile the pamphlets back into the store, retaining a single copy. They had shut it, wedged it, then made their way back through the length of the Archive to Theobald's office. Theobald had opened all the drawers in his desk to show that he did not hold the key. Lemprière had thanked the little man for his efforts. Theobald had seemed smug and not at all nervous at their discovery. The echo had died very slowly.

"V is for this *Cabbala's Venial* Sins, in the papists' term, for so they believe them, but they are mortal, thirty thousands of times Mortal then, and now *Vampirick* as the peoples of the Banat say it, for they suck Blood where before they spilled it, but I have some of that blood too and have stained my battle flag red with it for V too is for the *Vexillum* I fly to token my revenge. I shall march on them as *Vlad* and make their cellars mine. . . ."

He walked home in a kind of cloud. A hot wind shifted slowly through the streets in sluggish segments, fat blocks of heated air. It was evening. The moon was almost full. The gangs were more numerous, the citizens fewer. On one corner, a group of people had gathered and clapped in unison. He saw people exchange signals as they passed one another, strange little salutes, nods of the head. He saw a woman with a babe in arms, but the infant was still and smelt of decay. On the road in the snow, among the piles of rotting paper, he had let her slip by again.

"W is the *Wolf* I hold now by the ears and the *Worm* that twists upon my tongue. I go to *War* with them, the *Words* being near an end. To the *Web* they have wove from the guts of the dead, their own will be added for the *White Ladies* are with them now, these new *Worthies* of London, foretelling death. Soon shall I arrive to tell them more. . . ."

He had reached his home and pulled the pamphlet from the ripped pocket of his coat. Asiaticus's anger seemed more direct than before and Lemprière's earlier guesses grew firmer. Not only the Company, but the investors too were his target, "a foreign growth . . . a Cabbala," he called them. It seemed that Asiaticus had decided on some aggression beyond the rhetoric of his pamphlets. "*Worthies*": There were nine worthies, like the investors, though that would include François. He could hardly concentrate as he read on. Her promise.

"X is the initial of *Xerxes* who stood safe behind his Armies weeping false tears before their fight with the Greeks, saying, 'Of all this multitude, who shall say how many will return?' He is their mentor for only they returned while their Army perished. The Jews have a name, it is called *Yom Kippur*, it is my Y, it means their Day of Atonement and it is upon them all and most of all upon one, upon you *Zamorin* for you are my end, or I yours, and you are my last letter, my Z."

The pamphlet ended there. Lemprière tried to imagine the Cabbala of investors standing behind their fellow Rochelais, as though they were a shield, but Asiaticus implied a more deadly betrayal than that. After all, it was Richelieu who had cut off the town by land and sea, who had bombarded its inhabitants until they gave up the ghost and died rather than be captured. Asiaticus's rage suggested a far worse deed than the investors' flight from their dying city. But whatever that deed might be, the fourth and last pamphlet completed the dictionary of rage, hate, and threats without disclosing it.

Lemprière turned the pages back and forth, wondering at Asiaticus's own stake in the saga. Presumably he had gone forth to battle as promised, but the very presence of the pamphlets in East India House spelled defeat. He was long dead. They had found him and his pamphlets, and dealt with both. Or this *Zamorin* had; one of them, he supposed. Their leader.

As he pored over the pages, Lemprière noticed that the paper on which they were printed was hardly marked at all. The Archive had fairly stunk of mold but the pages before him were unblemished. Printed in 1629 or 1630; they must have lain there for close on one hundred and sixty years. They had yellowed, but that was all. He rose and lifted piles of books from the lid of his traveling chest, then rummaged within it until he found the three preceding pamphlets. A quick comparison solved the mystery. Better paper. The first three were printed on coarse stuff, the fourth on lighter, finely grained material, more like writing paper. Also, the small cellars might provide a drier home for the papers stored within them than the vaster and damper Archive proper.

Lemprière pushed the four pamphlets about his desk. Some other fact was lodged at the back of his thoughts but it would not come. Something to do with them spilling out and burying him, but his mind was drawn back to Juliette. He was already waiting for her. He saw her face pulled away from him, staring from the back of the coach, from between his own hands in the Archive. Closer each time, yet each time receding into different kinds of darkness. He heard the single word *Tomorrow* and urged it on faster to bring her back.

Strong sunlight woke him. He had fallen asleep at his desk. The morning sun streamed through the window onto his face. He rose, adjusted his eyeglasses, removed them to wash, replaced them, and resumed his seat. It was hot in the room and he was sweating. Then began a day of waiting.

The gazettes would later record the eleventh day of July as the hottest that year. By midday, the room was stifling. He opened windows, but the air hung in saturated blocks. The street was a furnace, and as the sun moved east to west, the windows opposite glared in his face. He tried to occupy himself, stacking the books for which, with the dictionary completed, he had no further use. He began to read Oppian on fish but the thought of oceans of cool water only tormented him further and he gave it up to lie on his bed, trying to think of entries he had omitted from his dictionary. So far as he could recall there were none. Septimus had come for the last sheets over a week before. Doubts niggled him. Several times, as he lay there, he fancied he heard light footsteps on the stair and leaped up then to open the door, but no one was there. It was the waiting, nothing more.

Perhaps she had meant something different. Come for me *tomorrow*. Find me *tomorrow*. Perhaps it was a warning and by tonight he would lie on this bed as George had on his. But the thought that she might come and find him gone kept him lying there, waiting. The shadow cast by his house rose slowly up the one opposing it, and Southampton Street was still as though the heat stifled even sound. From time to time he took great gulps but heat, not air, filled his lungs. The orange tree watched him from its corner, taking grim pleasure in his discomfort.

Toward the end of the afternoon the heat began to change. It grew heavier, stickier, more omnipresent. When the sun set, he rose and hung out the window but the air was sluggish and hardly moved. He splashed water on his face and was replacing his spectacles when he heard a single knock at his door, an unfamiliar signature. Lemprière took a breath, gathered himself, then walked across to admit his visitor.

"Ah, John . . ." Lemprière stepped back, his shoulders dropping in a mixture of disappointment and relief. It was Septimus, who seemed unsure whether to enter or not. Usually he banged loudly on the door; very loudly, if carrying his walking cane. Usually he walked in without asking. But Lemprière saw his expression was vague, as it had been on his last visit, and the one before that.

"Come in," he said, and Septimus wandered over the threshold, then stopped in the middle of the room. There was a short silence.

"What?" asked Lemprière. Septimus turned.

"Ah, John," he said, as if catching sight of him.

"Yes?"

"Yes."

"What?" He had had conversations like this with Septimus before. Usually he grew irritated but this time his friend seemed genuinely bewildered.

"I wondered about the entries. If you had completed the last of them, as I imagined. It would be best to collect them now."

"Yes," Lemprière said. "But I gave you the last a fortnight ago." He peered curiously at Septimus. "Where have you been? Where is Lydia?"

"Oh . . ." Septimus waved imprecisely. Lemprière looked again at his friend. He was torn between wanting to know the cause of this vague humor and needing to usher out its owner before Juliette might arrive. Septimus was looking about him as though in search of something unlikely to be there.

"Ah, John," he said again. His eye lighted on his pink coat which hung over the back of the chair. It seemed to anchor him, for his familiar bustling manner returned and he began to chide Lemprière over its condition, which was lamentable. The chair displayed its ripped pocket to peculiar advantage.

"I went to the fellow upstairs . . ." Lemprière began, rather caught off guard, and was about to tell him of the tailor's strangely narrow line of work when Septimus seemed suddenly to regain all his former spirit.

"Don't trouble yourself with that scoundrel!" he burst out. "Had a shirt sewn by him once. Appalling job, a one-handed drunk could have done better. . . ." He went on to slander the man outrageously until Lemprière laughed out loud. "What he does, sticks the needle up his ass, swallows the trousers—"

"Trousers?"

"Shirt, pardon me, though you wouldn't have known it for one. Stay clear of the knave, that's my prescription."

"Right you are," said Lemprière, still laughing.

"Ah, John," Septimus clapped him on the back. "I've been out of sorts. Forgive me." He moved toward the door which Lemprière held open. "I know I came here for a reason," said Septimus as he left, "but damn me if I haven't forgotten what it is."

Lemprière saluted and watched him take the stairs two at a time. He closed the door. Then he stopped laughing. How long would it take? Two, three minutes.

Lemprière took the coat from the chair, turned it inside out, and rolled it in a tight bundle. Then he climbed to the next floor and knocked softly on the door. He heard a chair scrape and footsteps move quickly across the floor.

"About time . . ." as the door opened. "I've waited . . . Oh." The tailor looked up and saw that it was Lemprière. His expression switched from annoyance to surprise, then back to annoyance. "I told you before," he said quickly, "trousers only. Now if you don't mind . . ." And he made as if to close the door.

"Trousers," said Lemprière, holding up the bundle and placing his foot against the door.

"Too busy!" the tailor shouted.

"Trousers!" Lemprière brandished his coat. Then he leaned against the door and nudged. The tailor fell back and Lemprière walked into the room.

"Where are your children?" he asked innocently. "And your wife?"

The tailor was silent. "The work you are so busy with? Needles? Thread?" But the tailor only stood in sullen silence.

Lemprière looked about the room. A narrow bed, desk, chair, books stacked against the far wall. It was identical to his own.

"Who were you expecting?" he asked, though he had known the answer as soon as the tailor had mistaken him for his overdue visitor. He was the same height, his clothes similarly dark. "What are you doing?"

The answer lay on the desk. The last entries of his dictionary were stacked next to an identical pile. A neat and exact copy. Lemprière stared at them in silence.

"You have copied my dictionary," he said. The "tailor" nodded. "All of it?" The nod was given again. Lemprière thought for a moment. "The signatures," he said. "How did you—"

"Left 'em out. Dates too. Don't know why they were there in the first place."

"Copyright, Mister Copyist," Lemprière replied sharply.

"Makes no odds, no difference at all," the copyist said. Lemprière digested this information, then changed tack.

"Pays well, does he, Mister Praeceps?" The purpose of Septimus's visit to the house was now abundantly clear, even if it had not been so to Septimus himself.

"Well enough. Look here, Mister Lemprière." The man's tone was earnest. "It's not so strange to make a copy. For safe-keeping, I mean. Cadell's place isn't fireproof—"

"Without my knowledge? In secret? Behind my back?" The thought that as he had written his dictionary, a clerk stationed directly above him was tracing every line of his pen, duplicating every word that he wrote, angered him in a way he could not readily explain. The action seemed somehow to mock him. Lemprière gathered up both piles from the desk.

"I don't know why he wanted them." The copyist tried to placate him, but Lemprière pushed past the man, clutching the last of his dictionary. He slammed the door and stamped down the stairs, baffled and angry and curious all at once. But then he forgot the papers and his rolled-up coat, his bafflement ceased, and his anger evaporated. His curiosity was a memory of curiosity, postponed and half-forgotten already, for Juliette was standing alone at his door.

She wore a dress of cream linen. He recognized it as the one she had worn when she first descended from the coach outside the church in the parish of Saint Martin's. Then, she had appeared as a fabulous, quite untouchable creature. An apparition. She turned to him as he approached. The hills and parched grasslands of Jersey seemed very far away, that summer a different age. She was quite beautiful. That had not changed.

"You came," he said.

She sat on the bed. He watched her from the chair. At first he had been tongue-tied. The events that had befallen him were dammed up inside him. If he extracted just one, the whole torrent would descend and drown them both. She reminded him of the afternoon in the library and they both laughed quickly, then stopped as the memory became a prelude. She had heard of his work, his dictionary. He realized that he still clutched its last sheets in his hand and released them, along with his coat.

"It is finished then?" she asked, and he nodded. They both sat very straight in their places.

"You could go home—"

"Yes, I suppose I could," he answered without really thinking. When he looked across at her, he saw a kind of appeal in her expression. "Come with me, come back with me," he said quickly. He knew what he wanted now. "We could leave this—"

"No!" she broke in. "I cannot, I cannot tell you why; that is why I came. Go now, John, simply go."

"Your father—"

"What do you know?" Suddenly all her composure left her. "Tell me!" she implored him.

Lemprière was startled. He began to tell what Walter had said, that she was held a virtual prisoner, what his own perceptions told him, her terror in the Archive only the day before. But as he spoke of Viscount Caster-leigh, he saw her expression change from pleading to resignation. Her head dropped.

"The Viscount is not my father," she said. "I am only his ward. Nothing more."

"Then leave, leave now," he urged her.

"He knows who my father is," she replied. "He will tell me soon. . . ." Her voice was hopeless. "I must stay till then, I know he will tell me. In the end he *must* tell me. . . ." She talked on in this way but more and more to herself as though she had rehearsed it too many times. At length, she fell silent. Lemprière began again to argue that she should come with him back to Jersey. Juliette sat shaking her head.

"I do not know how you are able even to look at me!" she burst out. Lemprière stopped in midsentence. Slowly, his cheeks reddened.

"I knew nothing of it until much later," she said. "Believe me, I beg you." He looked away, two images rising irresistibly before his mind's eye: his father's body, torn and bloody, rolling over in its death throes, and the body of the girl who sat before him now, naked as she was in the pool.

"I thought," he began, and cleared his throat. "I thought it was my fault, you see. It is why I wrote this." He indicated the last sheets of paper. "There were other things: at the De Veres', at Coade's . . ." The memories silenced him for a moment. "But it was not my fault." He gathered himself.

"No," said Juliette.

"The dogs, they would have known you, of course, and not my father. Perhaps if he had lain still as I did, then it would not have happened. Such things do happen, I understand that, and I suppose we have to accept them. . . ." Now he was the one to address himself as he explained the accident to her. When he looked up again her expression had changed. Juliette's face was aghast and amazed at the same time. "What is it?" he asked. "I could not help but see you—"

"I know you saw. It does not matter," she said quickly.

"Then what?"

"Nothing," she said. "John, nothing keeps you here. Go, please go." She rose and Lemprière rose too.

"Come with me," he said.

"I cannot. Do you not see how I am here? I must return."

"Then I will come."

"No," she said. But Lemprière's mind was fixed. "No," she said again as Lemprière made to follow her. He opened his mouth to protest and she closed it with her own. She kissed him, then he felt her pull him forward. They sank together down onto the bed.

"Damn you." She was pulling at his shirt. His hand was tangled in her hair.

"Damn us both," he gasped. Juliette put her hand over his mouth.

"Yes," she said. . . .

The air in the room turned to heat and circled slowly over them both. Twice she whispered, "Do you sleep?" Twice she heard him murmur in reply. She lay by his side, still half-dressed. The third time he was silent. She whispered, "Can you really not know?" He shifted in his sleep. Juliette rose silently and stood at the foot of the bed, looking down at him. He slept with his knees pulled up to his chest. She bent to gather her clothes and he stirred. She froze, then went on with her task. She crept quietly from the room and dressed on the landing outside. His ignorance was a miracle. A gift to her. If he knew what had truly befallen his father, he would never give up. Yet he did not know, and as she crept downstairs, she thought of her own father, whoever he was. His usurper, the Viscount, would be waiting with his partners. It was her own ignorance which bound her to them. She looked down once again at the sleeping form. His, she thought, might still keep him away.

The stair creaked as she descended and she stood still for a moment, listening in the dark. Then she went on, out of the door and into the street where their different kinds of unknowing parted company. At the very top of the staircase, a pair of eyes opened, and a body cramped from the long wait stirred in the darkness.

Lemprière fell back panting, exhausted, emptied. He felt her body fit itself to his own. Her breathing slowed. He heard her voice whisper to him. She was warm even in the warmth of the room. A faint breeze entered through the windows and circled slowly over them both. She whispered again, perhaps, but her voice was more distant this time. His own breath fell into rhythm with hers, rocking them gently toward and away from each other, toward sleep.

The sound from the staircase would have to reach very deep to find him. When his eyes opened it would not be only at that sound. Her going would be felt as a disturbance along the axis of his body. An imbalance, a dream as his arm reached across for her. It would become true and his breath would stutter. His eyes would open and already he would know she had gone. Then he would rise and run to the window and catch a glimpse of her before she turned the corner. Then, when he awoke, she was gone.

Lemprière was pulling on his coat and boots, half-running, half-falling down the stairs, half-dressed, half-awake, stumbling and running after her down Southampton Street, turning into the Strand and seeing her already a hundred yards away in the half-light of the full moon which bleached her dress from cream to bright white, a moving beacon which he ran for down the empty highway. She had fled once again. It must be the early hours. The moon was low in the eastern sky; the breeze a little stronger now. She turned, saw him, and ran. At the top of the staircase, the figure rose slowly in the dark and rubbed aching limbs before moving down the stairs after them both.

Lemprière ran past white stucco arches and bow-fronted windows, railings and brickwork pitted with shadows cast by the moonlight. He skipped low piles of rubbish and skirted larger mounds of market debris in his pursuit. She ran ahead of him, and in every street he gained on her until she turned a corner and then, when he rounded it himself, she would be farther away than ever as though the streets themselves were stretching every time he lost sight of her. She took narrow alleys and passages which zigzagged west across the city and he kept after her, closing and falling back, while the silent buildings rose up and around them. When he rounded the corner from Cockspur Street he thought he had lost her. He was in Haymarket and the citizens abroad at that hour were shuffling slowly. None of them were she. The broad steps of the Opera House passed to his right, then he heard a door swing shut behind him. He turned but saw nothing. He stopped and walked back a few paces. A narrow alley ran down the side of the theater. It was pitch black. Lemprière let his hand guide him as he walked down the alley's length. Suddenly the stones of the wall gave way, he pushed and a door swung open. He entered and found himself in a corridor which curved away to left and right. A faint light glowed from one direction. Lemprière closed the door behind him and moved toward it. He heard a low noise which became a dull roar as he drew nearer. The corridor led him in a long curve to a flight of stairs. The noise was much louder, a cacophony of shouting and screaming. He pulled aside a curtain and jerked his head back, shielding his eyes.

The auditorium was a blaze of light. Oil lamps and candles were ranged all around the tiers and stage. He had entered from the side, between the pit and the first row of seats. The auditorium was a heaving mass of costumed humanity crammed with bodies that shouted and cursed one another as they surged forward and back, clambering over and between the seats, filling the stage and pit with hugely confused conflict. Swords and spears were being waved; the garbled din was deafening. Lemprière shrank against the wall as revelers careered toward and away from him clutching bottles, makeshift weapons, and one another. He seemed to be ignored as he looked over the reeling horde. Of Juliette, there was still no sign.

He stayed back and saw that there was some order to the scene before him. His first thought was of a factional masquerade. It had started well enough perhaps, with polite conversation and genial unmaskings and all the paraphernalia of the *bon ton*, but something had gone wrong, convention succumbed to the bottle, acerbic wit descended to abuse, reasonable doubt to madness. Everyone wore dominoes—loose enveloping smocks of black or white linen—and crude wooden face masks with holes for the eyes and mouth. Inept fighting was breaking out in the pit between black smocks and white smocks, clumsy blows being struck by bottle-wielding warriors of both colors. Then, as he watched, a number of the black smocks turned tail and the white smocks pressed forward, clouting them with ineffectual swords (wood? he wondered) as they retreated to the back of the auditorium where, under the first of the rising tiers, a man in black stood with crossed arms. He was a giant.

He looked again for Juliette but she was nowhere in the auditorium, nor in the orchestra pit, nor on the stage where the white smocks flocked (some of them seeming oblivious to the conflict below) and toward which he was now swept as the white smocks also retreated. An uneasy truce held all in check. The black smocks gathered in a chanting, shouting line in front of the foremost seats. The white smocks similarly, on the edge of the stage. They had their own giant, not as large as the black smocks', who seemed to lead them, and then Lemprière felt himself being manhandled by his neighbors up onto the stage and toward the giant who thrust a long wooden sword into his hands and clapped him on the back, at which the white smocks cheered before taking him by the arms, struggling hopelessly as he was thrown from the stage into the pit, acutely conscious in his pink coat of being on display, his sponsors still cheering and looking up to see his challenger from the black smocks standing in front of him holding a sword just like his own, except that the challenging giant brought it down on a chair lying between them both which splintered as the steel blade hit six inches into the floor. Among all the props and shoddy machinery of this sham, the sword was real, and his challenger, he saw now, wore horns, and behind his mask his mouth opened to roar the cuckold's challenge at him. "Paris!"

Lemprière rose to his feet. For a moment he held his wooden sword up before him, then he thought, "I am insane to believe this." Menelaus advanced. Lemprière dropped his lolling weapon to scramble back onto the stage where the black-smocked giant berated him for a coward and a soft seducer but Lemprière ignored his taunts and pushed his way through the crush to the back of the stage where he began pulling the masks off his fellow Trojans. He found faces caked with rouge, smeared with paint and paste, pockmarked faces, toothless mouths, and eyes rolling in their sockets from the drink. Even as he scraped the greasepaint off the shoddy illusion, he thought of the sword shuddering in the wood of the floor and wondered, "Where was Aphrodite with her cloud of mist to carry me to safety?" But the answer to that lay an hour past and a mile back on the narrow bed in his room where she had shown him once and for all that she was flesh and blood, and human as himself, unless that too was all illusion. He shouted, "Juliette!" But the clamor drowned him out and no one turned to claim the name.

Behind him, the white-smocked Trojans surged forward again and the black-smocked Greeks fell back behind barricades of seats, hurling empty bottles and wooden lances and bits of seating at their attackers. The Trojan leader, Lemprière's scolder, Hector, crashes through and lays the Greeks to waste, throwing one against the wall, another over his shoulder, a third into his fellows. The black giant is unmoved, a brooding Achilles, as Hector finds himself surrounded, then driven back to the foot of the stage. He seizes the brave leader of this counterattack by the throat until he crumples and lies still. The black-smocked Achilles moves at last. Dashing aside white-smocked warriors with either hand, casually swatting off the Trojan missiles, he reaches Hector, who races up and down in front of the stage. Olympian trapeze artists swing down from the gods, back and forth, whispering for him to stand and fight. The advice is taken—a mistake. Achilles catches him and brings him down with a single terrible blow. Auditorium left, two pantomime horses trot in, drawing a chariot with one damaged wheel and gilt paint flaking off the cheap coachwork which disintegrates under Achilles' bulk, and he drags Hector around the auditorium himself. (Grief-stricken ululation from the Trojans and the exposure of Hecuba's breast.) Achilles tires, stops, and uncorks a bottle, while on the stage, Paris sees his Helen escaping through the screen to the rear of the stage and shouts "Juliette!" over the din. Her head turns and she mouths "Go back!" once more over her shoulder as he struggles to push the Trojan bodies aside.

So the pursuit began again. Backstage, the props department was already hard at work on the shattered chariot. The pantomime horses had divided about the midriff, and their occupants, red-faced and sweating, were refreshing themselves with cold flannels and beer. Costumes were strewn everywhere about the floor, bright chintzes and gauze, animal heads and unconvincing armor. He looked up and saw that the ceiling extended to the height of the building. Ropes and pulleys hung down, together with swaying ladders which reached up to flimsy platforms and catwalks a hundred feet or more above him. Odd bits of scenery hung suspended in midair: a triumphal arch, a mountain, several trees, and a contraption of irregular tubes painted blue and white with handles to rotate them which was, he guessed, the sea.

Juliette was high in the rigging already, a tiny blaze of white in the high shadows. As he watched, she pushed open a hatch in the roof. He saw a square of night sky, her body silhouetted against it, and then the hatch was closed. Lemprière started up the ladder after her. Halfway up he paused and looked down. The ground was much farther away than he had imagined; too far. He went on, moving slowly up to the highest of the platforms, then along a catwalk which swung freely on its ropes until he reached the hatch. He pushed it open, pulled himself up through the opening, and lay panting on his back. Sky, stars, the night. He was on the roof of the Opera House.

A warm wind blew. The flat roof stretched for forty yards in front of him. It was leaded, but salts deposited there by the rain, the moonlight and oxides of the air, combined to bleach it almost white. He was standing to its rear, and ahead of him the flat surface was dotted with curious humps, creatures of some sort. Twenty, perhaps thirty of them. Tortoises! A single creature reared up on the low parapet farthest from him. They were huge, standing waist-high at least. Apart from himself, the scene was quite still. He called "Juliette!" again. There was no response for a moment, then, on the other side of the roof, he saw a figure rise and stroll toward him.

"Good evening, Lemprière! You come for what is mine," the figure called as he drew nearer. It was the Viscount. His boots thudded over the lead. Lemprière edged sideways.

"She is not yours," he called back. "She told me. . . . You are not her father." The Viscount drew closer.

"True, Lemprière, so true . . ." He laughed shortly to himself. "She is not at issue here. Something greater detains me, something far more difficult to grasp." He stopped, and the two faced each other, still yards apart. The moonlight threw distorting shadows over Casterleigh's face. He had sought Juliette, only her. What else was there?

"Your share, Lemprière! Your ninth of the Company!" The Viscount hurled it in his face. He saw Juliette's expression when he had mentioned the dogs: astonished, aghast. "The thing your father sought," roared the Viscount.

"My father!" he gasped.

"Your father, your grandfather, and his father and his before him, all of them. They all sought what you seek. As fast as we cut them down, they sprang up again. All of them, Lemprière. And your father . . . Could you really believe it was an accident?"

Lemprière saw the dogs running low over the ground, springing as his father turned to flee, his arm raised, falling, rolling over and over. . . .

"All of them accidents, Lemprière?" The Viscount was moving toward him.

"Even François?" Casterleigh stopped in his tracks. Lemprière edged sideways. His back was to the parapet now. The Viscount advanced again. His bulk towered over Lemprière.

"Everything in time," he said, and lunged. Lemprière fell back. The first tortoise bumped against the backs of his legs. He scrambled up and the Viscount lunged again. He moved almost casually after his victim, skirting the tortoises, herding Lemprière toward the parapet.

"This time it is you, Lemprière." He drew a short dagger. Lemprière stepped back again, shaking his head. Snatches of his father's letter came to him. *If my mode of passing follows the precedent set by our ancestors . . . doubts and unanswered questions. John, pursue them no further. . . .* The Viscount came at him again. *Your curiosity will not be appeased.* He sensed the parapet close at his back, the sheer drop beyond it, *your vengeance never enacted.* Fool, he cursed himself. The dagger swung in an arc before him, forcing him back. He retreated and knew that he could go no farther. The Viscount grinned and swung again. Lemprière jumped back and up, onto the parapet. *Of my papers, burn them.* Fool! Casterleigh thrust at him for the last time, the knife an inch from his face, his mouth moving as though about to speak; the parapet slid out from under him and his center of gravity had already left his body, it was behind him, racing down to the stones a hundred feet below. He was falling backward into space. He had lost and he was going to die, like all the other Lemprières, and for nothing, because he was the last.

And Casterleigh's expression froze on his face.

Lemprière would go over the elements of what followed many times, but he would never be sure of the exact order. He heard a loud rush of air behind him, deafening and rising from below. He saw Casterleigh fall back, staggering as though he had been hit, his eyes focused somewhere above his own head. He tasted salt. He felt a hard hand against his back, sure it was a hand, pushing him forward with extraordinary strength. Strangest of all, he smelt burning.

But the wind had not risen and no one had hit the Viscount. Salt? His own mouth was full of spit, fear, he supposed. Nothing was on fire, though, and the hand at his back, it *was* a hand, he was quite certain, and yet how could it be? The hand of God? He was flung forward off the parapet with great force. The roof was rising to meet him as one huge sheet of lead that seemed to melt and disperse in a fine light mist as his head came down, filling his vision until the Viscount, the tortoises behind him, the hatch behind them, and even the sky were sucked away and replaced with lead that was white, then gray and then black.

John. Hands were around his neck, pulling him forward, upward.

Pursue them. . . . His face was being hit from side to side. He tried to hit back.

"John." Waves of gray were rolling back and lightening. He was asleep, he thought, being hit.

"John! Wake up!" The grays were sharpening. He looked up and saw a face above his own. It was upside down. He groaned and tried to raise his own head. The blows stopped.

"Get up, for God's sake. We have to move, come on, John!" It was Septimus.

He was lying in the alley beside the theater. Septimus was kneeling beside him.

"John, we must go! You have to get up." He tried. His head pounded.

"Good, now move."

"Septimus, what are you . . . How are you here?" He was rubbing his forehead. The bone felt soft.

"I saw the girl enter as I left, waited on the stairs—"

"Juliette! Where is she?"

"I don't know. I followed you both, found you lying on the roof. . . . We have no time for this. Look." He pointed up the alley to the Haymarket, where Lemprière saw groups of men moving past in purposeful gangs, shouting to one another, rallying, gathering. "The city's going up, don't you see? Now, come on!"

Their journey back took them through all the streets Lemprière had traveled earlier. But now, instead of the solitary girl fleeing ahead of him, he saw gangs of men and women who swirled about carrying staves and torches, wearing strange face-paint and shouting "Farina!" They moved in all directions, clashing, mixing, and joining, but the general drift was east. Lemprière and Septimus were carried along, and as his head cleared, Lemprière began to look strangely at his friend. The farther they went, the more Septimus seemed to lose his earlier purpose and urgency, and down the Strand, it was Lemprière who hustled them both through the menacing clusters of the mob. They reached Southampton Street unscathed and Lemprière ushered Septimus through the door and up to his room, where his friend slumped down as though some inner reserve had brought him this far, but no farther.

The warm wind blew through the open window, rustling the pages of the pamphlets which lay on his desk, stirring the air which had lain in the room since his departure. Juliette's scent and his own were mixed together as its heavy volume was disturbed. The street sent up odd shouts and the sounds of footsteps moving quickly over the flagstones. Septimus was slumped in the disorder of the bed. Lemprière stalked about the room, casting glances down at Septimus, who seemed deep in thought.

"So you waited at the top of the stairs?" He broke the silence at last. Septimus propped himself up on his elbows and nodded wearily. "By the

338

door of the copyist?" Septimus looked up in surprise, then resignation, then nodded again.

"Why?" asked Lemprière. "If you wanted the dictionary copied, you might as easily have told me as concealed it." Septimus opened his mouth to speak but the other put up his hand for silence. "So you waited, and you followed me, and I suppose you watched the whole pantomime. Was I meant to believe all that? Was I meant to think I was Paris? I am not mad, do you understand?" He was standing directly over Septimus, who tried to wave him away, but Lemprière had taken hold of his theme and would not let go. "It was all a sham, wasn't it? Tonight, at the theater, and before . . ." His mind was racing back, his voice suddenly colder and more certain. "Why were you late the night we were to go to Coade's?" he asked. "At the De Veres', who arranged for a pit to be dug and a crane to be placed in the middle of a bog? Come, come, Septimus. A drainage project?"

And then Septimus's explanations began to tumble out: Juliette had become an obsession with Lemprière, he might have done anything. The night at Coade's? He was delayed, distracted, he had forgotten, had arrived too late, and as for the crane and the pit, he knew nothing. He had merely recommended someone to the Earl, and if the fellow was a rogue, he was sorry, but that was all. Septimus rallied somewhat as these excuses were offered. He sat up and dealt with Lemprière's questions in turn. But he was improvising, seeming to form his answers as they fell on Lemprière's skeptical ears, and they were weak. Before, he knew, Septimus would have blustered and bullied until he, Lemprière, was convinced. But now he was vague and hesitant, stopping and changing tack in midsentence to Lemprière's snorts of disbelief. He seemed unable to concentrate on the matters before him. This unsettled Lemprière. He almost shouted at his companion.

"What is wrong with you? You have been this way for weeks, even before then. . . ." He thought of Septimus's terror at the Stone-Eater, when tiny harmless flames had ringed him and his body had seized up in fright. Then, before that, at the coffee shop, when he had seemed to drift away leaving only a shell, a husk that was and was not Septimus. The husk spoke to him then.

"I . . . I am not quite myself, John, that is true. I suppose I should have left you there, but I wanted to bring you back. Here, this is where we met most frequently, this room. I thought, after tonight . . ." He paused and stood up. "You might think, well, anything. I believed you were in danger and so I followed. We have been friends, I believe. Friends of a sort, no?"

"Casterleigh tried to kill me," Lemprière said. His back was to Septimus as he spoke. The moon had risen higher, its light streaming through the window onto the desk. The wind had risen too. "Tried to throw me off the roof." Pages stirred in front of him.

"His daughter," Septimus said behind him. "I told you."

"No," Lemprière said. "She is not his daughter; and she was not the reason. It was the thing which brought you and me together first of all." Septimus moved behind him. "The agreement," he said. "George was wrong after all. It is still good, though how I do not know. It has been a curse for all of us, all the Lemprières. Even François. I think they tried to cheat him out of his share, after they escaped."

The wind lifted and turned the first page from one of the pamphlets in front of him. The moon shone brightly, and for a moment both sides of the text appeared garbled together as the light shot through the paper. He was thinking of François and Thomas de Vere, their chance meeting after the siege. The note in the fourth Earl's diary recalled itself from his encounter with Alice de Vere. He had taken her for a fool, a madwoman, just as one hundred and fifty years earlier her ancestor had taken his own for the same. Thomas de Vere had quit their meeting with François's promise ringing in his ears: ". . . soon I will be richer than any man bar himself, for he made an Agreement with me and will keep it." The fourth Earl had written those words clinging to his hope, even while noting, "All this was said in a grete rage like a madness. . . ." And then François had disappeared.

Lemprière thought of Casterleigh's words on the roof. They had found François and silenced him, and he had left that promise as his legacy. A ninth of the Company was the Lemprières', and one by one they had all gone after it, even his father, even himself. One by one they had suffered the same fate as François. Somewhere, somehow, the fortune had survived while its true owners had died in its pursuit. Was that the last secret? Was that the reason for the feud between the investors and the Lemprières? It was not enough. Not enough for his father, nor his before him, nor any of them. Not enough for François:

"I asked him if he mourned his fellow merchants yet for it is now some months since the final slaughter he told me nay, for they lived yet and were they burned to death with the rest his answer would even then be nay for he detested them as he would birds who eat their young and worse. All this was said in a grete rage, like a madness. . . ."

Madness. Something in the siege. The wind gusted a little harder, and on the desk in front of him the pages of the fourth pamphlet began to turn through the last letters of Asiaticus's lexicon.

"X is the initial of *Xerxes* who stood safe behind his Armies weeping false tears before their fight with the Greeks, saying, 'Of all this multitude, who shall say how many will return?' He is their mentor. . . ."

Mentors, foul birds, kings who slaughtered their peoples. The Company piling up its profits year after year, somewhere a vast hoard. The moon was even brighter as it sucked heat from the sun's rays and threw freezing beams onto the desk. Not enough for François:

"I believe he means mischief to his old fellows the other eight merchants but talked only of marking their papers, or having marked papers, saying *mark you* in his accent and winking. For myself I kept my peace and we talked of other matters, like the vile attacks by hacks on the Company. . . ."

"The Jews have a name, it is called *Yom Kippur*, it is my Y, it means their Day of Atonement and it is upon them all. . . ." Mischief, revenge, atonement. For what? Their theft? It was not enough. There was more, something beyond the investors' hoard, something more behind the words on the page which tumbled over slowly as the light drove through it and the answer stared up at him. Then he knew.

As the moonlight streamed through the paper, he realized that the pages of the fourth pamphlet were the "marked papers" that had so puzzled Thomas de Vere. Lemprière held the pages up to the light and turned them one by one. Each held a watermark, a rough crescent.

"It was never the money," he said, half to himself, half to Septimus. Lemprière stared at the watermark. The identity of the symbol before him was unfurling its secret. He knew it already, had seen it twice: as a wide banner and a tight emblem, both greater and smaller. Only the scale had held their correspondence at bay.

"Septimus," he said to the figure behind him. "In my chest there is a ring, and by its side a large book. Could you . . ." He heard the figure shuffle across the room behind him. He was already sure as he took François's ring and held it next to the watermark and saw the ragged "C" of its signet reproduced in the watermark in Asiaticus's pamphlet. François's "grete rage" and the rage of Asiaticus were one and the same. François and Asiaticus were one person. Their hate shared the same object. Septimus was turning the pages of the book on the desk before him. Harbor plans of the western ports presented themselves: Le Havre, Cherbourg, Brest, Lorient, Nantes, ordered by his father, gathered and bound by Ebenezer Guardian, eventually collected and carried home by Lemprière himself.

"There." He stayed the other's hand. The same symbol appeared again, but larger. The ragged crescent was the outline of a harbor, the break in the circle its mouth. As Lemprière read the legend above the plan, he realized that this was the real significance of the watermark embedded in the pages of the pamphlet. This had been François's real threat to the investors. Not the abuse against John Company, not his ABC of hate, but this symbol, sent to them in the pages of the fourth and last pamphlet. Whatever crime François Lemprière's former partners had committed to excite his rage, it was somehow tokened here. Its disclosure had frightened them enough to have him killed, and all the Lemprières who followed the trail he had begun. The three images, ring, book and watermark, coincided in sudden sharp focus before his eyes. The roots of the feud lay in the place whose plan was before him now.

"I know the design," he murmured to himself. Septimus drew back.

"Here," he pointed to the place, and then the name came. "It began here, here at—"

But he did not finish. Septimus caught him under the arms even before he crumpled from the blow and lowered him to the floor.

"Rochelle," he whispered in Lemprière's unconscious ear. "All of it began at Rochelle."

ROCHELLE

The anticyclone moved east from the Azores toward Portugal, then north as dawn rose on the thirteenth of July. Gradual isobars channeled a sweeping breeze inland east and north in a crescent of summer turbulence. Rippling over the flat plains and mountain ranges, the anticyclone began its passage inland as sunshine fell on the broad waters of the Danube whose banks sucked in the shadows of night. Its pressured heart tightened as the sun rose higher and the winds blew a little harder. Still air over Mitteleuropa began to spin in sympathy, setting off further eddies in turn, and more beyond them as the process began to replicate itself in ever fainter and more numerous twists, clockwise and anticlockwise, each frontier more complex and less definite than the last as they spread north and east, kicking up dust and shaking leaves from the Golden Horn to the Hook of Holland. Local prevailing winds—the mistral, sirocco, tramonta, various foehns—disrupted and contributed until the currents and crosscurrents, interference patterns and pressure zones, were jumbled together in a weather system whose complexity outran its observers and left them adjusting windblown instruments. Whole orders of information wafted and gusted past in secret sweet abandon rippling through the billion blades of grass, grains of sand, motes of dust, and if there was an instrument to register the effects of this system, from its merest nanospan to greatest gigascale it was a land mass nothing short of Europe. Its needles were already twitching, its ports wide open and circuits humming with a music so confused it could only be heard as a monotone. But, for the perfect observer, for the single invested overseer of this straining engine . . .

The anticyclone moved closer. Its center shifted north, nudging the edge of the landmass as though searching for an entrance. Inland and out to sea, the curved winds got up and pulled against the central pressure zone. The sun rose higher and the sluggish warmth of the preceding days focused itself in a hot breeze. The engine hummed a little louder. In the perfect spheres and cylinders of the topiary trees, along the precise lines of clipped privet, leaves and stipules twitched their lighter undersides in and out of view, light and dark. The mirror of the lake gave way to a new corrugated surface whose diagonals ran west to east and zigzagged as the wind broke through the restraining surface tension. Lawns flashed indecipherable messages as individual blades of grass flattened themselves this way or that, all in concert, all collaborating against the mown squares and trimmed rectangles. The sun turned them into heliographs, reflecting new and confusing ciphers that seemed to curve away from within the straightforward logic of the gardens toward a wilder perspective and a different destination.

Taking the levée, His Majestry traced the gliding movements of pomaded and powdered figures across the parquet toward him. A bow or curtsy, a rustle of finished silk and away. He thought of the escapement of watches, the movement up the tooth of the cog, a soft trip, and down. Then the next, and the next, around and around forever.

"Ah, Monsieur!" A sleek figure floated toward him, paused, and then away to be replaced by another. Around and around, like the earth about the sun, or the moon about the earth. When he stood up and made his way out, everyone stood up and he advanced through their neat human corridor to the door, whereupon they closed behind him. Take the sun, he thought. It radiated out, drawing all the planets about it for a retinue. Without it they would fly off who knows where on quite incalculable paths, detrimental ones possibly. The authority of the sun was, in this model, a kind of largesse. One *gave* commands, *gave* orders, for example. So far, so good. The planets and their satellites behaved in a certain way, flew along certain paths at certain speeds, reappeared here and there at certain intervals. . . . This was homage and was needed, he supposed, to keep the sun in place. Now came the difficult part.

He felt sunlight hot on his face and a hot wind as he stepped onto the terrace. The day was beautiful and breezy. Garden people scattered and melted away. As the planets and so forth went around and around, their lines never met, but their forces (centripetal, centrifugal, gravitational, the pulls of competing masses, in short the *sum*) were the sun. Or rather, the lines drawn across the diameters of their orbits all met in the sun. That was better. All in the sun.

He descended the steps and advanced on the orange trees. Behind him, his retinue came to a halt on the last step above the parterre. The lake glittered enticingly in the distance. He waved at them and they retreated backward up the steps. Possibly he should have continued on around the terrace. All lines met in the sun, even the most divergent. The lines of orange trees drew nearer now and he moved among the slatted pots admiring the sculpted spheres his gardeners had created about him. The wind had risen, and though the outward forms of the trees remained serried in long lines stretching off into some other quirk of perspective, the leaves within these bulbous globes were all confused as breezes and gusts deranged them, flipping them about until they were all higgledy-piggledy and Louis frowned. His retinue disappeared around the corner of the terrace, following some nominal version of himself. The leaves rustled. He looked again down the long lines, fancying he saw a slight curve. Louis advanced farther, then frowned again. He had thought his orange trees had got beyond this, but the rows curled into one another and his vista of the lake was quite spoilt. Behind him, it was the same story. Still, he had come this far. . . .

He turned and crossed into the adjacent row, but the orange trees were placed very close together, and when he struggled through he found them quite as disorderly as those he had left. He advanced again, or thought he did, but only found himself back where he started. He paused, then moved off. Much better. Any moment now he would emerge in front of the lake. But he grew confused when he seemed to strike a path that led him at right angles, then in a tight arc, then it narrowed, and he might well have been back at the starting point yet again. It was difficult to tell. He moved off again, but had hardly taken a pace this time before the orange trees clustered so thickly he was forced to stop. The sun shone down unhelpfully. The leaves rustled in relays up, down, and across, from all directions and angles. He began to take a step, but the resistance was strong, the impedance high. He stopped, on the point of setting off again. The orange trees shifted behind him. He would set off again soon, or even now. The leaves, the invisible ripples on the artificial lake, and the blades of grass on the lawns all jiggled in disorderly concert. Quite soon now. Orange trees moved and closed around like satellites. The sun was fixed above. Quite soon. He stopped. The heliograph-lawns blinked on and off, chattering in staccato binary, the lake made tiny troughs and peaks, and the leaves signed on and off, faster and faster until the message was a blur and every port of the machine hovered, every gate swung both open and shut. The difference between its one- and zero-states narrowed to the State, and within the State, trails crisscrossed and spread, interacted and commingled, acted and countered one another so that the field of operations became a field of possibilities, the lattice of trails a cloud in which any event likely to take place was almost as likely not to, and now, from this perspective at least, the whole ergodic panoptic salmagundi appears blindingly, abundantly clear.

The airborne pressure zone hovered off the Iberian peninsula, nosed inquisitively about the Bay of Biscay, and moved north. Up the Atlantic coast, past the mouth of the Gironde, the anticyclone spun toward Île d'Oléron. Brisk winds preceded it and followed in its wake. Its center was quite still. Sitting on the hillside, overlooking the jetty, Duluc and Protagoras felt the novel sensation of an easterly breeze at their backs. The sun was in their faces and still high. They sat patiently. Soon the carts would arrive. Then night would fall. Sometime after that they would ready the signal beacon, and sometime after that the signal would be answered. Out of all their frantic efforts and those of their partners across the water, out of all the freak and engineered meetings, chance collisions, when all the values were weighed one against the other and almost every force had met and countered its opposing force, *then*, a single supercharged particle would emerge from the carnage and make for them along a single possible vector, and when the *Vendragon* finally docked at their jetty, this force too would be canceled with all the others and the final trail would have come to its end.

Now the wind began to die away, and presently the two of them found themselves sitting in a strange calm. They looked at each other, then both turned their gazes out to sea. The engine had reached its most precarious state and the eye of the coming storm looked down on them all. The still center of the anticyclone rested directly over Rochelle.

. . .

As the months of summer dragged by, Nazim felt his mission drift away from him. He stood in the baking heat behind the tackle of Butler's Wharf and watched the *Vendragon* loll in the water for days that stretched into weeks. Sometimes, for variety as much as purpose, he would hang about the back of Thames Street and stare at the lightless windows of Le Mara's house. But the *Vendragon* was loaded, or forgotten, or abandoned by her masters—his enemies, he reminded himself—and Le Mara seemed to have disappeared into thin air.

There was no doubt they knew of his existence. He had advertised his presence on the quay to Le Mara from the outset. He was an alien body, a resistant particle that jammed and fouled the smooth workings of their machine. He tried to believe his watchful presence was a kind of pressure under which their operations would buckle and break, spilling the information he needed like so much oil. But it was not so. Their actions, if he were truthful, were no more apparent to him now than when he had walked down the gangplank of the *Nottingham* nine months before. They were making ready, they *were* making ready. But for what?

The night at Coade's had revealed their hands more naked than before, and still the incident was opaque. Two girls, seemingly twins and dressed alike, the black coach, Le Mara and his larger partner, the young man in black at the inn: The actions he had witnessed seemed to refer to nothing outside themselves, like a complex and bloody board game or a machine that assembled and disassembled itself. At the center of these pointless acts stood the pseudo-Lemprière. Player? Prime mover? Pawn? He did not know, and the real Lemprière was dead, slaughtered in the room on Blue Anchor Lane.

Nazim fished in his pockets for the memento of that night. Did the woman whose gray eyes stared up at him from the miniature know her son was dead and replaced by an ambiguous imposter? They must know he knew these things, yet they ignored him, and their inattention diminished him as though he were an irrelevance thrust out on the periphery of their actions. Similarly, the Nawab's sphere of influence had shrunk, his commands to Nazim were only faint suggestions now, tendencies of behavior. He remembered his original purpose clearly enough. Find them, kill them, recover what is mine. . . . The urgency was gone and he was left as a spectator in a dream, between two faltering gyres where he drifted not quite caught up and not quite held by either.

So he floated in the heat of summer, and the sluggish months wore on. When he noticed the dispute which spread through the bustling quays, bringing them gradually to a standstill, he saw it as the outward expression of his own creeping paralysis. His world contracted to the dark haven of the cellar where he would lie and listen to the feeble movements of the woman above. Nazim retreated further, into sleep where dreams of blinding sunlight and red cliffs gave him a different vista and a different vision of mortality. Bahadur's unsurprised face was always waiting for him there. He would wake with the smell of human decay in his nostrils, invading the clean silence of the dream. Decay, death, different forms of death. Something told him the two were opposites. Something in the woman's too-human frailty was missing in Bahadur's long plunge down the face of the cliff, something in the coldness of his uncle's face as he pointed to his chest. "We change inside. . . ." Was that what had happened to him? To them both?

Toward the end of June, with the heat rising a degree or two by the day, he began to note changes in the city. All the pent-up energy of its streets seemed to flow around and around without effect. The citizens, for all their variety, seemed to wear the same face with only the expression varying to distinguish them from one another. He saw the same transactions and heard the same exchanges in the markets. The restlessness of the city seemed always to turn in on itself as though all its energies were required just to keep the engine moving as it did.

But as June edged closer to July he saw new features pressing through the stucco and brickwork. Slogans began to appear on the bland walls. A more restless creature was emerging, though it looked like simple neglect as rubbish piled up in the streets and the lamps were left unlit. The night patrols passed over the cellar with less and less regularity, eventually ceasing altogether. He ventured out more frequently then and wandered the streets by night, drifting unnoticed through the inns and taverns, listening to the casual metropolitan gossip. He saw new coalitions spring up around brilliant talkers, cells form about a well-turned phrase. July filled the courts and alleys with foreign accents and groups of men who glanced at him suspiciously as he passed in his cape and broad concealing hat. Their muttering followed him until he disappeared from sight. The second week of the month brought a slow hot wind and the gangs grew larger. They began to hang about the main thoroughfares and move down the streets as single units. A new sense of purpose, still suppressed, still unclear, was palpable in the heat. He felt it rise with each succeeding day as though any number of different desires were converging to find their satisfactions in the city. All becoming the same . . . It was a familiar concentration. Familiar from where, he did not know. He felt himself focus, even draw from it. He resumed his vigil at Le Mara's house and at the deserted docks which, he realized, were not idle but only waiting, just as he was waiting. The streets hummed with undisclosed purpose, like his own, and the feeling of familiarity grew as the city tensed and stretched around him. His anticipation gathered in a knot inside him, tightening until on the night of the twelfth the first strand broke.

He was outside Le Mara's house. The mews was deserted. A livid sunset was daubing pinks and darker blues over the western sky. Heat rolled like a millstone through the streets and Nazim sweated beneath his hat, for the slow hot wind offered no relief. He had been watching the house for over an hour when the black coach drew up. Nazim shrank back and watched as it came to a halt. No one got out. It waited there for several minutes, its driver muffled despite the heat and motionless on his seat. Then the door of the house opened without warning, no lights, no sound, and four figures emerged. Nazim recognized them all from the night at Coade's. First came the girl, dressed in white and seemingly reluctant as the broad figure behind her pushed her forward: Le Mara's partner. One of the Nine. Next came Le Mara himself, expressionless as ever. Last of all the one he had seen only twice, before and after the incident at the Manufactory, first here, outside this house, and afterward at the King's Arms tavern where he had faced down the thugs who threatened the pseudo-Lemprière with their clumsy violence. The others addressed him as Septimus.

The first three disappeared inside the coach, which moved off slowly. Nazim made as if to follow, but Septimus still stood outside the house, turning this way and that. Nazim could only watch in frustration as the vehicle turned the corner west into Thames Street. The young man dawdled a few minutes more, then began to walk slowly up the street. Nazim followed. Like the coach, the young man headed west. He walked as far as Bow Street, where he seemed to hesitate before the door of an imposing building, then, some inner decision resolved upon, he advanced up the steps and entered.

When the door closed, Nazim drew nearer and read the plate set to one side: "Chief Examining Magistrate" and, underneath, "Sir John Fielding."

He looked about. The streets were quiet, almost deserted. Strange for this hour. Again he felt the odd sense of familiarity. The changed city was brooding, waiting for something. Underneath Sir John's name someone had scrawled "Farina." Only a few minutes had passed before the door opened once more and Nazim saw Sir John himself, bandaged eyes somehow directed at his informant, thanking the young man, shaking his hand and saying, "Yes, very helpful, Mister Praeceps, very helpful indeed. A thing eliminated is another found . . ." and the words that followed were on the edge of his hearing, but he heard the name that followed, certain he was right, though the sentence was a low mumble: ". . . Lemprière . . ." Not even sure which of them had said it, and then the door closed and he was following this Septimus across the Piazza and down into Southampton Street, where he realized he need not have worried about losing the coach. It was waiting for him at the top of the street. Nazim watched as Mister Praeceps nodded to its occupants, then walked down the street and disappeared into one of the houses.

He took up a station above the coach with a clear view down the street and settled down to wait. The streets were still quiet. After an hour or more, he saw the door of the coach open and the girl get out. The moon was up, shining brightly on her white dress. She walked down Southampton Street and entered the same door as Mister Praeceps. The coach set off once again, moving west. Again Nazim was caught between staying and pursuit. He stayed. The night wore on and he had begun to think his decision an error when the door to the house opened and the girl crept out, picking up her heels as she walked noiselessly over the cobbles. When she reached the top of the street, she looked back. Both of them saw the door thrown open. The girl abandoned all attempts at stealth and took flight. A disheveled figure in a pink coat stumbled after her, and in the moonlight Nazim thought at first it was Septimus. He waited until the young man had passed before he too gave chase. Somehow, he was not surprised when he saw that it was not his earlier quarry at all. The pseudo-Lemprière attracted confusion as a dog did fleas.

A strange chase ensued, three sets of footsteps clattering through the streets. Nazim shadowed Lemprière, knowing that he shadowed the girl in turn. Their paths zigzagged west as far as the Haymarket, where both of them disappeared. Nazim walked up the thoroughfare looking to left and right. He found the black coach waiting for him again in an alley that ran off the road down the north side of a theater. An identical alley ran down the far side but it was empty. The Haymarket itself was less deserted than the smaller streets through which he had passed. Men and women walked up and down it in twos and threes. The moon had risen higher and in its cold light their faces looked as though they were carved from chalk. He patrolled the alley at the back of the theater. He remembered the girl's role at the Manufactory as a kind of lure, drawing in the pseudo-Lemprière much as she had drawn him to this theater tonight.

And this Septimus, he had appeared later as a guardian angel of sorts, protecting the goods from damage. But tonight the girl had tried to wave him back, to warn him off; and Praeceps had gained entry to the house with ease. He was trusted by the pseudo-Lemprière, though clearly in the pay of the Nine. Two of them at least . . . Only eight now, he corrected himself, remembering the real Lemprière's body in Blue Anchor Lane.

More than an hour had passed. A noise to his right, toward the coach, footsteps, and the girl's voice as he edged around the corner and saw the coach door close, muffling the voice. He drew nearer and heard some kind of struggle taking place inside, the girl's voice sharper than before.

"Let me, let me go! You said he would come to no harm. You swore, damn you," and the struggle resumed.

"Cease." Le Mara's monotone barked after a minute or two. Then "Cease" again, and whatever threat had been offered in the darkness of the coach was proved effective, for the sounds suddenly stopped. Nazim crouched down by the side of the coach, expecting it to move off at any moment, but the horses waited impassively in their harnesses. He heard a rushing gust of wind somewhere above. The hot wind was getting up, and more people were appearing in the thoroughfare, moving back and forth in small groups. His attention strayed, recognizing something in the gatherings. The heavier footfalls moving up the alley were almost upon him before he turned and saw the broad frame of Le Mara's partner moving toward the coach and himself.

He thought surely he would be seen, caught between the advancing figure and the street beyond, bathed in moonlight, but the man shambled like a sleepwalker and Nazim saw that his head was tilted back, looking up at the sky. The face was gray and the mouth gaped as though its owner had begun to say something and suddenly found himself struck dumb. The bloodless face passed him unawares as the man stumbled toward the coach. The door was opened and Nazim saw the vehicle shift slightly as its suspension bent beneath his slumped weight. He crept closer and heard Le Mara's voice grate out a question.

"Is it done, Viscount?" But the Viscount said nothing and Le Mara was forced to repeat the question.

"No." The answer came then. "He lives still." The girl gave a short cry of surprise and relief.

"I will finish it."

"No!" the Viscount shot back.

"I will find him—" But the Viscount held him back. His voice shook.

"Our past has come back, now. Up there, I saw it. It found me. You know the thing I speak of—"

"Praeceps will deliver the boy as instructed unless we find him."

"Leave it, I said. Understand me now, leave it. We have bigger fish to fry, and if the boy appears he can share their fate. Let us go."

Nazim found the boy with ease. As the coach moved off, he followed into the Haymarket and watched it turn north. Praeceps and the pseudo-Lemprière were lying in the alley on the other side of the theater. The Haymarket was filling with people who milled about in confusion and Nazim mingled with them. Presently the two of them emerged, first Praeceps and then, supported by him, the pseudo-Lemprière blinking behind his eyeglasses, conspicuous as ever in his pink coat. They moved off together through the gangs of men and women. Nazim followed. As they approached Southampton Street their roles seemed to reverse and it was the pseudo-Lemprière who guided the other through the more aggressive groups. The citizens of the city were appearing from nowhere, banding and disbanding as a gradual drift east began to establish itself among the bodies. Some had painted their faces. One gang carried short clubs which they swung and slapped in their palms. The name "Farina" was everywhere.

As the two of them reached the house in Southampton Street, Nazim felt the tense purpose which rushed through the streets. So it begins, he thought to himself.

He paid only cursory attention when the two emerged once more, their roles reversed again. It was inevitable. Praeceps was supporting his companion as though the other were drunk. The gangs were gathering in the street. He saw Praeceps hail a carriage from the Strand and bundle the unconscious pseudo-Lemprière into the cab.

"Leadenhall, East India House!" The carriage moved off into the mob and Nazim let it go. If the pseudo-Lemprière had followed some parallel path of his own against the Company, he had reached its end now. His own had a little farther to run and it was clear at last. The city had reached its brink and beyond tomorrow there would be no more time.

He made his way to the docks and broke open a store on Hythe Wharf. The tool he needed found, he returned to the cellar. All through the next day's uneasy interregnum he lay with his eyes open, staring into the darkness and thinking on what he was at last about to do. When night fell, he rose and walked through the gathering mob to Le Mara's house. Its windows were dark. He entered by the back door and descended to the cellar. The hatch set into the floor was locked, as he had expected. Nazim pulled the crowbar from his belt and drove it down. He leaned his weight against the bar, levering open the hatch. It groaned and cracked and at last splintered under the assault. Nazim gathered himself, then threw the trapdoor open and looked down. The shaft dropped down into darkness. Down there, he told himself, they were waiting for him.

• • •

He was alone. It was dark. He was trapped.

Lemprière opened his eyes, bent his neck, and a dull pain spread across his shoulders, then up into his skull. His mouth tasted foul. He put his hands to his face and found his spectacles still in place. His body was laid out with his feet and head slightly raised by the curvature of a tunnel. He was underground. As he grew more conscious, he realized that the darkness was not absolute. If he put his hand up to his face, he could count the fingers. A diffused light drifted in the gloom, its source obscure, showing him that he lay in a tunnel which curved and twisted away in both directions. Lemprière pulled himself upright and sat quietly, thinking on what he should do now.

Septimus had betrayed him from the first day in Skewer's office. Casterleigh was his father's murderer, and his grandfather's perhaps, and his father's before him. Casterleigh was one of the Cabbala, the refugees from Rochelle. Together with Septimus (one of them too? a hired hand?), they had pulled him this way and that like a puppet. And he had believed it all: his father's death, the woman in the pit at the De Veres', at the Manufactory, believed everything as he forced his mad constructions on the killings. Actaeon, Danae, Iphigenia, and then himself as Paris, who in his own words "fought with little courage," whose infatuation brought the siege to Troy and the massacre to its people. Perhaps his courage had been slight. Perhaps he might have seen the truth for all its trappings a little sooner. But he was not Paris. It was more than infatuation.

The air in the tunnel was warm and still. Even with his spectacles he could make out only the most general contours, and the strange light was very dim. He fancied he saw a darker form some yards to his left. The ache in his head was a dull throb. He began to crawl through the dust toward the figure, but as soon as he moved, the whole vista disappeared in a dense black cloud. The dust was so fine, the least disturbance sent up great billowing plumes, and he coughed as it bit the back of his throat, which sent up more clouds. The powder swirled around him, blinding and choking him. He stopped and sat very still with his eyes closed for some minutes. When he opened them, the dust had settled and the faint light had returned. He brushed gingerly at the fine coating on his face. The light was yellower than before, and brighter too. He saw that the dark form rested in the tunnel and made a shape similar to his own. The light grew stronger and he might have made a clearer identification then, but as he looked into the gloom he saw small billowing waves of powder roll around the curve of the tunnel. Someone was approaching, carrying a lamp which was all but engulfed by the particles sent up by his or her footfalls. And presently he could hear these too, soft regular thuds in the dust. The lantern moved closer and closer. The screen of dust advanced and Lemprière was engulfed once more. His eyes watered and his nostrils were clogged. The dust was a dry black fog and the lantern swayed nearer until it hung directly over him. Miasma. The soft footfalls stopped. He tried to speak but coughed instead. The lantern hung there in silence. Gradually, the dust settled once more and Lemprière was able to look up. He had expected, perhaps, Septimus. Or Casterleigh, or even Juliette. The face he recognized was none of these. If he had thought of all the people who might conceivably find him in this place, the man he greeted now would not have appeared among them. Yet it was the man who had found him wandering in the fields above Blanche Pierre an age ago and a world away, the day of the killing by the pool on Jersey. And it was the man whom his father had set out to visit that day, whom he had never reached, who had known Charles would call that day, the last day of summer.

"Jake!" he said as the face emerged from the dust, yellow in the lamplight, quietly looking down at him and unsurprised.

"Jaques," said Jaques, as he bent to help Lemprière to his feet.

There were questions, certainly there were large questions to be asked now, and yet Lemprière did not ask them. As they walked through the twisting passages and vaulted caverns of the Beast his queries would die on his lips, as though Jake's mere presence here was a self-indictment which overtook and answered everything. How else could he be here, unless. . . .

But now, with the dust settling around them both, it was the dark form he had glimpsed before which held his tongue. In the light from the lantern it emerged as a human figure lying across the tunnel ten yards away from him. He moved toward it slowly. Black powder swirled up to his waist in billowing layers, covering the corpse as he drew near. Lemprière stood over the still figure and waited for the cloud to settle. As the layers grew thinner and fell back, a face rose up like a drowned man's rising too late to the surface; he saw white teeth and lips drawn back tight and thin as ribbons. The eyes were shriveled to peas and the skin pulled tight over the skull as though the arid tunnel had leached the water from the corpse and left only skin dry as paper stretched over porcelain bones.

The cadaver had been laid out with its limbs splayed, still in its clothes. Lemprière could make out tufts of white hair, a kind of ruff about the neck, and the buttons of a coat, but the clothes were dry as their wearer and the two were barely distinguishable now. Lemprière thought of the rage of Asiaticus which he had taken for empty rhetoric, and the wild talk of his ancestor, reported by Thomas de Vere. He looked into the face of the corpse and knew that those emotions had found the same end here in the dark, alone. They had found François, or he had found them. They had killed him and left him here. Lemprière looked down at his ancestor and wondered if the same fate awaited himself.

"John," Jaques called to him. "There are matters to be settled." Lemprière glanced once more at his ancestor, then turned to the man who stood waiting for him.

"You are one of them, Jake, are you not? You are one of the Nine."

"I am," Jaques replied. "Just as you are, John."

. . .

Nazim knelt amid the wreckage of the trapdoor and looked down. A long vertical shaft descended into the darkness. He saw that the sides of the shaft were bricked for the first twenty feet or so and thereafter they had been cut from solid rock. An iron ladder was set into the bricks. Nazim replaced the crowbar in his cloak and drew a short knife from its sheath, gripping it between his teeth. He checked his pockets for candles and matches, then took a piece of splintered wood and dropped it down the shaft. He was able to count to six before a muffled thud echoed up the shaft. Warm dry air rose up from the opening and mingled with the more humid vapor in the room. Nazim pulled his hat on tight, then swung himself over the lip of the shaft to begin the descent.

The shaft was narrow and seemed to reach down forever. The iron rungs went on and on. Above him, the entrance shrank to the size of a penny and still the shaft went down. He paused to draw breath and felt his heart thud in his chest. When he looked down, he saw only darkness. Somewhere, down there, they were waiting for him. He went on, hand over hand, farther into the depths. His feet found a rhythm and moved steadily down the rungs. His teeth clenched about the knife. Several minutes passed. Then suddenly he seemed to slip, and the rungs were gone. He was hanging in space. His legs were swinging, then kicking against the side of the shaft before he could pull himself up and find the last rung once again. He looked up and saw the top of the shaft as a pinprick of light. Below him, nothing. Nazim crooked his arm around the rung and ferreted in his pocket for the matches. As he pulled them out, his weight shifted, his foot slipped out, and he had to grab for the rung again. He pulled himself back onto the ladder and cursed. He had dropped the matches. Nazim rested there a few moments and considered what to do next. After a few seconds' thought, he tensed his legs, let go of the ladder, and jumped into darkness.

As he had guessed he would, he fell three or four feet and landed safely. The ladder had stopped a few feet short of the bottom of the shaft. He was standing on a slope and realized that the shaft dropped into the side of a much larger tunnel. His matches had come to rest where they fell, and he was about to light the candle when he noticed that he could see two faint shapes. His hands. The absolute darkness lightened further as his eyes searched the gloom. A very faint glow seemed to come from everywhere and nowhere, from the rock itself. The tunnel was several times his height in diameter. Its sides curved up and around him, ringed with thick ribs of petrified muscle which formed slight troughs between one another. He found that his stride matched their intervals and began to walk comfortably over the humped ridges, thinking that Le Mara's stride would match them by the same token.

His senses sharpened as he moved through the tunnel. He could see perhaps twenty yards ahead of him. After a minute or more, he noticed a gradual incline as the tunnel began to rise, and soon after his path was blocked by a mass of crudely buttressed planking. The barrier extended to the roof of the cavern but the wood was dry and brittle. Nazim pulled the crowbar from his cloak, prized out two of the planks, and squeezed himself through the opening. He found himself in a much larger cavern, contiguous with the last as though it had suddenly widened and opened out. He was standing on a long platform of stone seemingly suspended in space. Twenty feet below him, a small lake of black water had collected, but the strangest features were the rows of curved and sharpened obelisks that ran in rows to either side of him, jutting clear of the water and extending down from the roof, each one thirty feet or more in height and resembling nothing quite so much as huge teeth.

A barrier similar to the first lay twenty yards ahead, and Nazim trod gingerly over the tongue to reach it. It was constructed much like the other, although here the timbers were not dry, but sodden. Nazim began to realize he had made a mistake. He pulled at a plank which disintegrated at his touch to expose a wall of red clay packed behind the timbers. As he watched, the slick red surface bulged slightly, then began to glisten as the first waterdrops forced their way through the plug. Nazim thought of the shaft, the position of Le Mara's house, the direction he had taken through the tunnel, and realized then that he had walked south, underneath Thames Street to the river. The water seeping through the clay plug he had unwisely disturbed was the Thames itself, and as he watched, he saw a steady drip begin to run in a thin trickle down the rotted planks. He turned and began to retrace his steps through the mouth and down the throat of the Beast to the foot of the shaft which he passed, and behind him the trickle turned into a fine spray as the clay began to break up. Nazim walked more quickly now, not thinking what lay behind him, only what waited ahead.

• • •

"Where are we?" Lemprière asked.

"Beneath the city," Jaques replied, from behind him. "You have been dead to the world for fifteen hours or more." They were passing through a succession of caverns so high that even the rays from the lantern could not find their ceilings. Looking up and around him at this series of natural cathedrals, Lemprière could hardly believe that above them the humdrum streets were filled with ordinary men and women who moved through them quite unaware that the solid ground beneath their feet was riddled with tunnels, passages, and vast chambers. He remembered the echoing boom which had answered his kick against the locked door in the Archive and thought of that sound careering through these same chambers.

"You knew my father would die that day." He threw the accusation over his shoulder.

"Truly, no," came the answer. A heavy silence followed. "But when he did not come, I knew it had been done. You cannot understand, John. Not yet."

"He believed you were his friend, his partner. You always failed him. Even your business failed him."

"I tried to save him, to discourage him. Don't you realize we *tried* to ruin him? Don't you think I did all I could to stop him before he found us?"

"But he did find you—"

"You have all found us. Every Lemprière has inherited the mystery, every one has solved it, or come close enough to spur us to action. All of you have perished and passed the obligation on to the next, or somehow found something. We do not know why you persist, or how each Lemprière comes to follow the same path. That is your mystery, but something drew Charles toward us just as it drew his father, and his before him—"

"And me."

"No. The circumstances have changed. We drew you in ourselves. You see, we anticipated you, John. We have been waiting for you for some time."

They crossed slender bridges of calcites and granite, passed beneath stalactitic needles tipped with quartz, and scrambled over smooth sloping plates, sliding down into troughs of powdered stone whose motes spiraled up into hollow spires and honeycombed minarets. Deep boreholes opened to either side of them, and filaments brushed their shoulders as they began to ascend a winding sinew of stone which led them into space. The lantern shone out in all directions and found nothing but the path ahead hanging in the middle of a vast darkness. Lemprière kicked a loose stone off the edge and listened for its impact. He heard nothing. They were rising steadily through the dark, and presently Lemprière saw the underside of a vast flange of rock above them, but whatever it was joined to remained invisible. They approached it slowly from beneath, and as his line of sight cleared the lip, he saw a wide flat apron covered with gravel and small stones. The lamplight found the ceiling of this greatest of caverns at last, a hundred feet above them, sloping down and away to form walls which remained in darkness. Their feet crunched on the gravel as they left the path and the walls loomed out, solid rock to left and right, but formed from strange-waisted columns directly ahead of them. Jaques indicated that they should veer to the left, and presently Lemprière saw a heavy door set into the wall. They walked across the gravel, and when they stood before it, Lemprière stopped and turned to Jaques. He thought of the desiccated corpse lying in the dark tunnels behind them and the city left burning long before his birth.

"What did François know that all of you feared so much?" he asked. Jaques's face stared blankly into his own. He reached over to the door and pushed it open. Candlelight flared from the room. Lemprière heard voices which grew quiet as the door swung open. An expectant silence took their place and he knew that within the chamber they were waiting for him to enter.

· · ·

His mind was racing, his feet skipping quickly over the thick ridges of the tunnel. Bahadur's face kept coming at him out of the darkness. The calm of the expression haunted him; an inhuman resignation, cold as his body when they grappled on the cliff. He was looking down over the lip of the cliff. He was waiting in the palace. He was walking down the gangplank of the *Nottingham*. The crew were calling to him. A bundle of white rags was tumbling down hundreds of feet and he was saying *yes* and the Nawab's laughter echoed through the corridors of the palace. Bahadur was tumbling to his death, down and down. Why could he not see the impact?

Shortly after he passed the shaft through which he had entered, the cavernous passage began to slope down. It twisted and curved to left and right as he moved deeper into the Beast. Perhaps half a mile from the shaft he stopped suddenly and a lunatic voice inside him said *Here is where he fell, here he is.* A bundle of white rags lay in the center of the passage ahead of him. But as Nazim moved closer he saw that they were not cloth, but paper. Small booklets of some kind. They lay spread in a heap in the middle and to one side of the tunnel. A shaft identical to the one he had descended dropped into the tunnel directly above him here. The pamphlets had fallen down, or been thrown, and had come to rest in this spot. Nazim peered up this second shaft but saw and heard nothing. By his own reckoning he was somewhere beneath the Exchange, hundreds of feet below its foundations. The shaft might emerge anywhere at all, he thought. He was about to move on when he remembered Praeceps's instructions to the driver of the carriage the night before. Leadenhall Street. East India House. He looked up the shaft once again and marveled that an entity as vast as the Company could be controlled through so narrow a conduit, for this was surely the passage by which their commands were passed to the organization above.

The tunnel began to descend more steeply and Nazim used the ridges as steps. The air grew warmer and drier. Eventually he found himself walking levelly once more. The passage broadened farther, funneling out until he could no longer see the sides. The ridges grew less prominent and more broken. Strange conical humps rose out of the rocky floor, and their mirror images protruded from the ceiling. He began to step around them as they rose higher and those in the ceiling hung lower. The cones began to meet, their thick bases reaching stalactite to stalagmite, joined by attenuated filaments of stone so fine he could pass his hand through them and barely feel them splinter. The spaces between these thin-waisted columns suggested hundreds of spherical chambers, bubbles of darkness through which he passed as he traversed the spongeworks. Nazim looked up and saw that the ceiling had risen out of sight. In its place the honeycombed stone spread its thick junctions and filaments far above him, from side to side, forward and back. Then, just as it had risen, it began to recede, and before long he was again skirting the stumpy pyramids which had heralded its appearance. The dust grew coarser underfoot and he trod more carefully. He seemed to have emerged onto a flat plain of gravel. Walls curved away like cliffs to either side and he was about to follow one when he heard two sets of footsteps moving across the gravel on the far side of the apron.

Nazim stopped and crouched down. The footsteps moved closer, passed before him, then receded to his right. He scanned the gloom and fancied he saw the gravel simply stop more than sixty yards' distance from him. Beyond it there was darkness, nothing at all, an abyss. The footsteps stopped, and presently Nazim saw a crack of light far away to his right that widened until it was a doorway, and light was streaming out from the chamber behind it. He saw two figures who seemed to pause there for a moment before they entered and the door was closed once more. He turned and walked back into the spongeworks where he would wait. He hardly knew what to make of what he had seen. The eyeglasses, the pink coat, who else could it have been? The pseudo-Lemprière was one of them after all.

. . .

The flames of eight candles flared and sent a maze of shadows racing over the surfaces of the ceiling. He saw Juliette, standing with her back to the side wall. Her eyes never moved from the candlelight. She seemed to see nothing. Not the stems of the candelabra, nor the flames from the candles, nor himself, not even the eight men ranged about the table who sat impassively, staring at him as though he should be the one to break the silence. He held his tongue and glanced again at the lamp and its tapers. One was unlit.

The table was shaped like a horseshoe. He stood almost between its pincers and looked about the waiting men. Before him, to his left, Jaques settled in his chair. Next to him a thin-faced man stared coldly forward without expression, and beyond him slumped an obese figure, red-faced and breathing audibly through his mouth. Casterleigh sat opposite Jaques with Juliette standing behind him, and beside him a fifth man whom Lemprière did not recognize. At the head of the table, a chair deeper and higher than the others was flanked by two identical cohorts, gray men with faces of stone, standing still and silent as caryatids. Someone sat in the chair, but Lemprière knew this only from a pair of hands which grew out of the darkness and rested on the table before him. The shadows seemed to cluster more thickly there and the high sides of the chair enveloped and hid the figure's face. Between his hands, a book bound in black leather rested on the table. Lemprière looked at the book and the men who contemplated him from their seats. He noticed that the table, though smoothly cut on the outside, was fantastically irregular within with all kinds of indentations and projections jutting in and out. He recognized it from the device on the ring, the watermark in the pamphlet, the map of the harbor; all of these, but exceeding them in scale and only exceeded itself by the original, which was the harbor at Rochelle. The figure in the chair seemed to shift. The leader, thought Lemprière, and remembering the last words of François's last pamphlet, put the name Zamorin to the man. The shadows moved once more and then the leader spoke.

"Welcome at last, John Lemprière," he said. The voice sounded as though stones were grinding together in his throat. "We have waited some time for you."

The fingers of the hands were moving. Casterleigh stared up at him with disguised hatred and something else, some vestige of his expression on the roof, frustration, amazement, fear. He had seen the thing which terrified him there, and looking back at the man now, Lemprière knew that thing was not himself. The leader's fingers twitched again, then took the book and opened it. Lemprière squinted over the length of the table as the pages were turned. He saw handwriting, deletions, blots, and marginalia. Dates and the same signature, over and over again. The signature was his own. The book was his dictionary.

"A fine piece of work," the leader's voice rumbled out of the shadows. Lemprière broke his silence.

"My dictionary! What are you doing with it? Why is it . . . Why am I here?"

The leader turned the pages of the manuscript. "Everything in time, John Lemprière. There has been so much time, after all. I hardly thought it would take so long, yet you are here and your dictionary with you. . . ."

"Who are you?" Lemprière broke in. The hands stopped.

"You know who we are, John Lemprière. We are the descendants of the investors you found at the De Veres', the refugees from the city sacked a century and a half ago, the men your ancestor hunted whom you have cornered here. We are your quarry, Lemprière, and now you have us. We are the Cabbala." The hands moved from side to side, indicating the men ranged about him. "Jaques and the Viscount you know from their guises in the world above. Messieurs Le Mara and Boffe to my right, to my left, Monsieur Vaucanson, and behind me Monopole and Antithe Les Blas.

"Your dictionary is here," he paused and breathed out heavily, "for so many reasons. Some of them you know already, but there are so very many reasons, John. You could never have known them all. It is here because you knew your mind was not your own; because you believed yourself mad; because the Lemprières have run at a tangent to us for too long and we need you back. The dictionary is here for all these reasons. Even before them, events of many years past, matters which seem distant even to us. Your dictionary began long before you yourself, John, long before you, or we, had conceived it. It began with a voyage. A voyage and a siege."

"Rochelle."

"Rochelle, yes. And the voyage was the first expedition of the Honorable Company of Merchants trading to the East Indies; and it was a disaster."

Lemprière looked across at Juliette, but she remained motionless, staring into space. She was a shadow. Her real body was elsewhere and this abstraction would not acknowledge him. He looked away, and as he did so he saw Casterleigh's eyes flick across the table to Le Mara.

"The year was 1600, the century new-struck, and our ancestors were here, in this city, when the ships set sail," the leader began. "They heard the Queen's Charter cried from the dais and watched four ships float downriver on the tide loaded with nothing but hope and daring. They watched all this and thought of their own sovereign's mistrust. Those ships should have been their own ships, those men sailors from Rochelle; and the cargoes they were to bring back . . . But you know something of that already."

"The voyage was to fail," said Lemprière.

"Naturally; else we would not be here, nor you, nor your dictionary. Our ancestors suspected it then, even as they set out. Returning to Rochelle, the expedition never left their thoughts. They were traders and merchants, shipwrights and bankers, nine men who saw what their English counterparts saw, and the Dutch had seen for decades. The East was a bursting pot of gold and all that was needed were ships, men, and sanction. A charter. The nine of them knew it was possible, but the Catholic court would grant nothing. They were of a different persuasion,

Huguenots. Rochelle was their fortress. Had they mounted such an expedition, and they could have done, it would have brought the King's frigates to anchor off the coast and his dragoons to their doors. Perhaps they should have launched the venture come what may—the warships and dragoons were to come in any case—but they did not, they were cautious. They waited.

"Two years passed by and nothing was heard. Normal business continued, running goods up and down the coast, plying the river trade. They were wealthy, but unsatisfied. They wanted more, and when the four ships returned fully laden late in 1603, they got what they desired."

Lemprière listened as the tale of the Company's pepper and the collapsing market unfolded for the second time, but where Alice de Vere's voice had dropped in gloom and despondency, the leader's rose with excitement. Once more, Thomas de Vere twisted and turned under the weight of his failure, his creditors came after him like hungry dogs, and his finances sank into the pit of the whole venture's foolhardiness. The investors were left penniless and their charter was worthless paper.

"Not the Cabbala," the leader went on. "Our ancestors coveted that charter above everything and would have it too, but the matter was beset with troubles. They saw the investors as kindred spirits, Philpot, Smith, De Vere, and the others. They had been proved right. Their Dutch rivals had rigged the market, the glut stank of policy, but it gave them the Company. The voyage was possible, the trade was there, and when they calculated the profits, they dwarfed all previous ventures. They pooled resources and set sail for London the following May. When they arrived, it did not take long to discover the Company's plight. Every shipwright, victualler, and chandler from Deal to the Pool seemed to hold a debt. There was not a financier in the city would commit a farthing to a second venture. They knew at once they had them.

"The nine matched themselves one to one with the first investors. At first, none knew that the others were being approached. They must all have suspected. Our ancestors offered them terms they could not refuse: their debts settled, the Company relaunched, and a second voyage undertaken. In return, each would take a ninth of any profit or loss and pay each investor a tenth of that sum. They would act as agents of the Cabbala. Naturally, all these negotiations were conducted in the strictest secrecy. They may have been Protestants, but they were Frenchmen still, and our countries then were all but at war. It was this fact which bound them together. Neither party could withdraw from the arrangement without risking exposure from the other. For an Englishman to sell the Queen's Charter was more than sharp practice. What they did was treason. The agreements were dressed up in all kinds of rhetoric to mask the fact, but it was there and all knew it.

The fourth Earl held out longest. He knew what it meant. But in Norwich, in April of that year, Thomas de Vere signed, and when he did, the Company was ours. Our ancestors returned to Rochelle like conquering kings and celebrated for a month. A club was formed. They thought the skulduggery and secrecy a kind of joke, a huge prank, and called their club "The Cabbala," thinking that was a kind of joke too. They never dreamed it would become the truth."

The leader's voice was almost disbelieving, almost appalled. The present Cabbala stared at him from their seats. Their eyes chilled him. Of course it became the truth. They had taken what they wanted. They had become masters of their dreams, like himself. Now they sought to disown them. He felt nothing for them. Their disbelief was a lie. The leader sighed in the shadows and then his voice came again.

"The years that followed brought all the Cabbala hoped for and more. They mounted other voyages with other ships, drove the Dutch from pillar to post, and their trading posts were such horns of plenty they spilled over with spices, silks, and gemstones, rare metals, silver, and gold. They had only to lower the bucket to scoop wealth from the sea itself. They grew rich as Croesus, and richer with every passing year. The Company's ships wallowed back so low in the water, a heavy sea would all but swamp them, and every ton paid them back a hundred-fold.

"The partners in England benefited accordingly. De Vere, Philpot, Smith, and the others, they all became forces to be reckoned with in this city. The sums were fabulous, exorbitant. Once every year, an Indiaman would moor off the coast a few miles north of Rochelle. The cargo would be taken off in ketches and stowed in a cave near the point. It was bullion and gemstones. Jewelry for our barbarous god. It was simple. Once a year, nine tenths of the Company's profits would be paddled over open waters from ship to shore. No one ever knew. No one ever found out. Our ancestors' fortune mounted until their calculations could hardly measure it. It was all so preposterous, so out of scale. They wanted to invest, or lend, but any projects which might have gone unnoticed would not have reduced their fortune by a thousandth, and anything larger would have brought attentions they could ill afford. They had everything, and nothing to do with it. That was a problem they, and we, would never truly solve, until now perhaps. Back then, they hardly cared. The agreements held firm and the Company grew. Our forebears looked out on a sea that gave them everything they had dreamed of, and all that time the nightmare waited. They never looked back, never turned and looked over their shoulders. Perhaps if they had they might have seen it in time, for when the nightmare came it came by land."

"The siege," said Lemprière.

"Yes," said the leader. "The siege of La Rochelle; where we went wrong."

Flat salt marshes spread inland from the fortress of La Rochelle in all directions like a vast glacis concealing nothing. Small waves lapped in the harbor, subdivisions of the Atlantic swelled beyond. The coast ran like a

362

ragged seam stitching Armorica to the Aquitanian basin, marking the abutment of land and sea. Two possibilities, two opposites, and the city a point on their buffer zone. Advancing armies and advancing storms, droughts and ergot creeping through the corn; these could be seen clearly as though Ptolemy's lens were mounted atop the citadel. They might advance, but measurably, observed from the watchtowers by sentinels who took that distance for security. But it was false; all these stealthy advances, armies or storms, came in camouflage, second skins for a beast which moved across the plains that summer like inevitable weather.

Just as the pack moving fast and low over the ground announces the advancing flurry of the hunt and behind that the design of the hunter, so the weather signals its own cyclonic stillness, its dead center which is so much hot air, behind that, deep swells and troughs of pressure, behind that the globe's own whirling momentum, the periodic flashes of the sun called days which are the measures of shrinking distance as the horizon shifts from a far-off violet smudge to a red gash of misfortune spilling down on the heads of the besieged who look up for a familiar sky in vain. The rain is not quite rain, the sun not quite sun. The advancing system has its own biases and probabilities, which remain discreet, only visible very suddenly when the rolling swell of corn and the waving vines and faint scarps and slopes of the plains about Rochelle and elsewhere are suddenly pumped high by a surge of energy, when they overload and fold in upon themselves. Then the leeway is swallowed, the distance disappears, and energy gathers on the wave's turbulent cusp. At once it is obvious. Hector realizes he is alone, tricked, and defenseless. Achilles raises his spear. The worst is arrived.

The flat marshlands unwrinkle, and the folds disclose rows of tents, zigzagging trenches, forward emplacements butting up to the bastions, and thousands upon thousands of tiny points of red swarming toward the walls while the cannon send smoking prophecies of ruin, fulfilled in a split second when the first cannonball bursts the first wall, explodes into the street, and the first of the Rochelais are killed by debris that seems to fall from a burning heaven which has already abandoned them to the sword and musket-ball, the powder-mine and torch, to the creeping earthworks which coil and tighten about them month by month, to their hopeless defense, their betrayal and ultimate defeat. The siege has begun and already it is over. The real victors are already inside the city.

The chamber was quiet. Lemprière saw Le Mara look across the table at Vaucanson. Jaques looked to the chair, then turned as if some signal had been given.

"The siege was a means to an end," he said. "Richelieu meant to take away their privileges, in particular their trading privileges. He meant to charter new companies to take the trade. For his part, the King meant to have La Rochelle for himself one way or another. There is more, but . . ."

"Tell him," Casterleigh broke in. "Tell him everything, the other reasons."

"What reasons?" Lemprière searched the faces around the table. Vaucanson spoke.

"Rochelle was no ordinary city. It had its own laws, own counsel, own church. For the Huguenots in France it was a model. What might be, you understand? Louis knew and Richelieu knew. Every reformed congregation in the kingdom looked to Rochelle for guidance. And gradually the guidance became more than that, more like a scheme. A plot even. The Rochelais had no truck with regicides, but the King was a monarch of Jesuits and *dévots*, a supporter of the League, of our enemies at home and abroad. Do you follow?" Lemprière shook his head.

"A coup!" Boffe burst in. "A grand coup! It was years in the planning, went back to the massacre on Saint Bartholomew's Day, to Duplessis-Mornay and a whole troop of sponsors. Oh, it was a glorious piece of skulduggery. . . ."

"But it brought the siege to their walls," Jaques went on more soberly, "as our ancestors knew it would. Trade and state were what the siege was about. The King's forces finally came within sight of the walls in the first week of August 1627. Buckingham's fleet had arrived from England and landed on Île de Ré the week before. The good duke was already pressing his case against Toiras and the rest of the garrison in Fort Saint Martin. The royal army dug itself in and repaired the forts to the east. . . ."

"Such a spectacle, Monsieur Lemprière." Boffe shook in his chair. "The men, the horses, the cannon. The stage was set with trenches and earthworks, thousands upon thousands of them. And the Rochelais. The gallant besieged, heroes. All Europe knew of their plight."

"And all Europe ignored it," Casterleigh sneered. "The English were never to take Fort Saint Martin, and even if they had it would have proved of little consequence."

"There had been sieges before." Vaucanson spoke. "But they were formal affairs. Exchanges of words. Terms were agreed upon and matters would stand much as they had before. Our ancestors had little enough reason to believe their own predicament would prove any different."

"But it *was* different," said Jaques. "Perhaps the King knew their plans were more advanced, perhaps their trade was more valuable than they knew themselves. Whatever the reasons, the royal army grew and grew until by September of that year there must have been twenty thousand troops camped around Rochelle. Still they looked out from the walls untroubled. With their own and the English fleets they held the seas to the west, and supplies were ferried in with ease. Naturally there were batteries on the points of the outer harbor, but their fire was inaccurate, the mouth too wide, the ships too fast. Then, midway through October, a strange construction began to take shape. Day by day, little by little, the points of the headlands seemed to be extending farther across the mouth of the harbor."

"Richelieu was building a mole," said Casterleigh. "To close off the harbor."

"A kind of rampart," Vaucanson expanded. "Two rough jetties made from piles and rocks. A storm, even a strong tide, these would have washed it all away. But they sank ships filled with stones to either side and filled the space with boulders. They left a gap in the middle for the force of the sea to expend itself. If this table were the harbor, the space in which you stand now was eventually no more than inches across. Even then the Rochelais felt it would never withstand the winter storms. They placed a new battery on Pointe de Coureille and began to harass our ancestors' ships. The mole was still hardly advanced, though, and the last months of that year held few terrors for the besieged."

"To the east," said Jaques, "the King's lines were impregnable. There was nothing to be had by land. The sea had always provided, and now it was our ancestors' lifeline. They began to understand why, with only twenty-five thousand souls in the city, there had been no great assaults on the walls. They meant the Rochelais to starve. That was the purpose behind the mole.

"Buckingham sailed for England in November. He left his promise to return and Saint Martin in the hands of the King's men."

"And did he return?" asked Lemprière.

"He was to meet his end at the hands of an assassin later that year, but the English needed the Rochelais if they wished their ships to pass unhindered along the western coast of France. They understood what Richelieu wanted well enough. The Rochelais imagined Richelieu's mole and the King's fleet would be swept away for flotsam. But then, a few days into the new year, a huge storm blew up from the south. It raged all night, and in the morning they looked out over the harbor and, for the first time, began to worry."

"Why? What had changed?"

"Nothing, nothing at all. Perhaps it was a freak, a piece of the Cardinal's luck, but the mole was still there. It was untouched when they expected every trace of it to lie five fathoms down. They knew then that the city might fall, and that was when our ancestors sent François to England." Vaucanson had been staring at Jaques during this recital. Now he turned to Lemprière.

"If the mole could withstand the storm, it might withstand the fleet. The Cabbala needed to know what the English planned and plan accordingly themselves. They needed to know if and when to run. That is why they sent François."

"He left on the last day of January under cover of night in a dinghy." Jaques took up the story from Vaucanson. "His scheme was to rendezvous with some Hollanders coming up the coast with salt. But he was sighted passing through the mole. There was musket fire from the walls. Our ancestors could do nothing and did not know if he lived or died."

"He lived, though," said Lemprière.

"Oh yes, he lived," Casterleigh answered.

Jaques glanced across at him and cleared his throat. "The other eight were left inside the walls. No boat larger than a pinnace made it past the mole after that. They had sunk ships to block the opening, and their masts rose above the surface like a palisade. The Rochelais fired on the mole from the walls but to little effect. They were trapped and knew it."

Lemprière looked in the shadows for the leader, who had remained silent throughout. The others had grown animated as the events of the siege were relived, survived a second time. But the shadows were still, the human pillars behind him were still. Even Le Mara seemed more animated and Le Mara had not uttered a word.

"The Cabbala numbered eight then," Jaques went on. "They waited for word from François, from a nuncio who might have been dead or alive. The city waited too, cut off now by land and sea. Our ancestors already knew the means of their own escape should it become necessary, but it was hazardous. There were factors beyond their control—"

Lemprière broke in. "How could they escape? If they were cut off as you claim—"

"Wait, for there is more before that. The Rochelais began to realize that they might lose. The city began to change. A series of fires swept through the merchants' quarter, started by cannon fire, it was thought. They were the work of incendiaries, arsonists hidden in their midst. Everything that would burn—straw, hay, faggots, powder from the magazines—was carried to the citadel and stored in the cellars there. Soldiers were seized trying to cross the lines carrying passports signed by Richelieu himself. The traitors were uncovered and swung a dozen at a time from gibbets in the square. Toward the end of January a sickness spread through the city causing jaws to blacken and gums to bleed. It was scurvy. Food became scarce. The Rochelais began to kill the horses, then the asses and mules, cats and dogs, rats and mice at the last. Before then there would be cannibalism in the poorest quarters. Anything that lived was killed. Anything that could be swallowed was seized upon for food: ox hides, leather scabbards, and boots boiled in tallow, even cinnamon and licorice from the apothecaries. They made a kind of bread from straw and sugar, or wood pounded in mortars, plaster, earth, even dung. They hardly had the strength to cheer when May brought Denbigh's expedition off the coast with fifty ships. But the batteries mounted on the mole fought him off and the Rochelais fireships drifted harmlessly into the banks. Still there was no word from François. By the end of May the silos were empty and people took to gathering cockles along the coast under the enemy's guns or foraging for purslane between the walls and the King's lines. Inside the city, the old and the very young began to die."

Juliette's face was perfectly still, almost inhuman in the candlelight. The energies of the Cabbala were beginning to ebb. Lemprière listened as Jaques conjured images from the last months of the siege: hollow faces on consumptive bodies, bodies like anatomies, the smell of the unburied dead, flat skies, the dull *crump* of the cannon which went unanswered though there was powder in plenty, for the soldiers could no longer traverse their own guns, skins shining with a mockery of blooming health. So few children. The quiet streets. Sentries posted for the night halved in number by daybreak. The great bell silent. No one had the strength to toll it by then. The outer walls were already cold, and people moved like ghosts toward the center of the city. Rumor and hearsay brought them by the thousand to the iron-banded doors of the citadel. The city was dying, they knew this, but the manner of its death was still unknown. There were stories, intimations of the revenge to be exacted by their King. These lead them through the drab streets and into the citadel where the doors are shut and barred behind them. High arched windows look down on the mass of bodies. They have nothing to lose, so the story goes. Nothing at all.

"By October the Rochelais were dying in their hundreds. Deputations were shuttling back and forth between Guiton and Richelieu, trying to arrange terms. Bras de Fer was talking of a suicidal charge for the lines. There were fewer than eight thousand left from a city of twenty-five. In the last week of the month, François's message arrived coded in a dispatch addressed to Guiton, the mayor. François's message read: *There is no expedition. No quarter will be given. Save yourselves.* The city was to be sacked, its walls razed. There were no terms, for the Rochelais had nothing to offer and everyone in the city suspected as much. They had nothing to lose. Nothing at all. So our ancestors planned their escape." Lemprière looked down at Jaques, but Jaques would not meet his eye. Vaucanson was watching the other man too.

"Why wait?" he asked. "Why not before?"

"Their lives were there." Jaques would look at him now. The shadows stirred in some kind of affirmation. "Everything they had built and worked for was in Rochelle, its ships, walls, houses. . . . They knew they would lose all that. But the main hoard, the wealth from the Company, all of it cached and hidden over twenty-five years, that they thought might still be saved, until François's message. Our ancestors had waited too long and now had to run for their lives." Jaques stopped again and Lemprière saw the leader shift in the darkness. Vaucanson spoke.

"There was a passage. Land and sea were denied them. There were only two ways out of Rochelle: by the air or through the earth. Beneath the citadel there was a kind of cavern, a tunnel which ran from the cellars under the foundations of the city to a subterranean lake. It was their own discovery, a vast lagoon, and at its center a tiny island which they used for their cache. The lake spread undergound, north for two miles or more, and on its far side a strip of gravel formed a kind of shore. A second tunnel led from that secret shore to the known coast of Pointe du Plombe."

"Where they unloaded their cargoes . . ."

"This would be their route and it would have been straightforward but for the Royal Camp."

"Up and down the coast for miles. Vast!" Boffe unfurled his arms.

"There was a field hospital nearby and perhaps a barracks. They might emerge face to face with the King's Dragoons, or they might have found the tunnel and the lake—"

"And the gold."

"That was as good as lost in any case. They could not take it with them. Above all they needed a diversion, so they passed on François's message to the survivors. Rumor of the impending massacre ran through the city like . . . Almost as if people wanted to believe it. They convened a meeting in the citadel on the night of the thirtieth. They came in their thousands. Men, women, their own wives and children. They barred the doors. . . ." Jaques's voice had dropped. "They believed François, they believed Rochelle and everyone in it was doomed." He stopped, as though some central obstacle had been reached, and looked about him at the other members of the Cabbala. No one spoke.

"So they escaped, through the passage under the citadel—"

"Yes!" Jaques spoke quickly. "They escaped that night. Through the tunnel, over the lake in a rowboat, all eight sick with hunger. It was almost dawn when they emerged at Pointe du Plombe. The Royal Camp was in chaos, strings of horses loose, soldiers running this way and that, leaderless brigades arguing and splitting into platoons, a happy rabble all cheering and pointing south to Rochelle. Our ancestors watched with them. A thick column of smoke stood in the dawn sky over the city, rising out of the citadel. Smoke and flames were pouring out of the windows. Human fireballs plummeting out of sight. It went on for almost an hour. You could see quite clearly even from that distance. It was like a display of fireworks, but soundless, of course. Every time a body fell the troops would cheer. They were moving in. They knew the city was finished. Then suddenly they fell silent—".

"That is none of his concern." Casterleigh's voice broke in harshly. Boffe looked anxiously from Jaques to the others. Jaques ignored the outburst.

"They fell silent," he repeated. "Everyone saw it: a fireball tumbling down from the window, a burning figure smaller than the others. Perhaps a child. They saw it dip and rise. It fell again, toward the sea this time, and the seawater doused its fire."

"An illusion, a trick of the light," growled Casterleigh.

"It rose again, the story goes, a black point speeding away until it was no bigger than a gull, a fly, and then nothing at all."

"I know of it already," Lemprière said. "It was the Sprite, the flying man."

The others shifted uneasily. "Afterward, they would say its face was charred and it was winged, like an angel," murmured Jaques.

"A dark angel," said Lemprière. Jaques seemed to recover himself.

"It was a survivor, like our ancestors," he said. "Every other soul in the citadel either jumped or was consumed by the flames." Again he seemed to reach the same obstacle and came to a halt.

"François had been . . . mistaken," he spoke carefully. "The city was not sacked. It was true no expedition was planned, he was right about that. But Rochelle was never going to be sacked. Neither Richelieu nor his King had any intention of reducing it to rubble. But our ancestors believed otherwise, you see? Their own wives and children, hundreds, thousands of others. . . . They believed it would happen in any case, that they had nothing to lose. The citadel, then the whole city. And if the Royal Army believed them dead too, why should they hunt them? They thought the Rochelais were as good as dead already. Why should they die too?"

The realization began to sink in. Lemprière watched Jaques stare at his own clasped hands, or the table.

"They gathered the Rochelais in the citadel," he spoke deliberately. "They barred the doors. They escaped and left them behind. They emerged at Pointe du Plombe, looked back, and saw them jumping from the windows, a column of smoke rising." Jaques nodded slowly. Lemprière went on. "The city was not sacked, yet the citadel and the people gathered within it were burning. The troops were still outside the walls, yet the fires had begun."

It was Le Mara who spoke, and Lemprière heard his voice for the first time. "Our ancestors burned them," he said.

"And for nothing," added Jaques.

Again he looked to Juliette and again her face gave away nothing. The eight candles burned steadily and their reflected flames fanned out over the surface of the great table. Jaques was mumbling, rambling about sacrifice and necessity, their own wives and children lost in the fire for the greater good.

"And François?" he asked. As Jaques began to nod his confirmation, Monopole and Antithe shifted slightly behind the leader's chair as though responding to some movement within it. Jaques was looking across the room at Juliette.

"The Cabbala made its escape," Vaucanson took up the story, "and by the end of November its members were installed here in London, in these same caverns. Our ancestors drained them and set about rebuilding their fortunes from nothing." But as Vaucanson spoke, Lemprière's thoughts were pulled back to the fire, to the last throes of the Rochelais as the atrocity in the citadel unfolded. Two miles distant, the eight could watch coolly, elated perhaps at their escape, and the ninth, François, would see nothing at all.

"What of François?" he asked, cutting Vaucanson in midsentence. No one answered him. "Surely the fault was all his? It could hardly be your own ancestors! They were misled after all," he goaded them, but still no one answered. Vaucanson looked to the leader, and Lemprière heard him speak for the first time in an hour.

"Tell him of François," he commanded.

"Our ancestors met with François in London in late November," Vaucanson said. "His leg had been injured by the muskets at Rochelle and the wound had still not healed. They had not laid eyes on him in over a year, but from the first it was apparent he was changed, of a different disposition from before. They told him everything, the course of the siege, the plight of the Rochelais, the effect his message had had. He told them frankly that he had been in error, but that it was his last such mistake. Then they told him of their escape and began to tell him of his own wife and children, and their fate." Vaucanson stopped.

"Go on," the leader said. The tale seemed as much addressed to him as to Lemprière.

"He grew wild. He shouted that he knew them now for mercenaries and murderers. He vowed then and there that the Lemprières would have their revenge."

"So it began," murmured Lemprière to himself.

"After that he seemed to vanish into thin air. He was on Jersey, of course, with his new family; your family, Mister Lemprière. There was a great deal to do at that time. The Company had drifted rudderless for the best part of two years. The Cabbala's arrangements were in disarray. Without Rochelle it had no base, and if the profits were to flow agin, it needed new routes, new hoards. In the midst of all this they ignored François and his talk of revenge. He had disappeared. They held his share in trust and thought no more of the matter. Then, in January of 1629, the first pamphlet appeared."

"Asiaticus," said Lemprière.

"At first they did not guess its author, but in February a second appeared and they began to suspect. March brought a third and with that they were certain. Their antagonist was François. The pamphlets alluded to events which, outside themselves, only he could know of: the buying of the Company, the agreements, the system of agents, the manner in which the profits were diverted, all these and more. You have seen them, you know how they were organized. The fourth would run from 'T' to 'Z,' it would be the last, and it promised to expose the Cabbala as the real masters of the Company and, for good measure, the butchers of Rochelle. We knew that he had met with Thomas de Vere in late March, and some days after that, our ancestors received word from him directly. He was coming for them, to settle the matter finally."

Lemprière thought back to the dried corpse lying in the cavern far below them and tried to imagine the confrontation which had taken place before the killing. He saw François, the revenger, the true Sprite of Rochelle, crawling through the tunnels and galleries to reach the eight of them, who waited patiently as they had for himself. He would come in time. Everything would come in time. Then they met and the quick bloody flurry would end it, or was it more drawn out than that? Perhaps they had tried to reason with François, to enclose him once again inside the fold.

"He was not the man they had known before." Jaques was speaking, choosing his words with exaggerated care. "He seemed to see only conflict, know only anger. His old partners were the murderers of his wife and children. After that fact, there was nothing."

"But he knew the others would follow, that the Lemprières would go on throwing themselves into this pit until their bodies filled it—"

"Yes." the leader's voice brought Lemprière up short. "Yes, he did know that." His hands were turning the pages of the dictionary again. With more purpose this time. Lemprière watched as a folded sheet of parchment was taken from between the center pages of his book and handed to Monopole, from him to Boffe, then Jaques, Le Mara, and finally himself.

"It was written shortly before the meeting. It is meant, I believe, for you." Lemprière unfolded the document and glanced down the close-written body of the text which filled much of the page. Above it was a legend: *I, François Lemprière, merchant, to you my descendant, wherever you may read it, whosoever you may be. Welcome.* He angled the yellow-ing parchment toward the candlelight and began to read. *Perhaps you are my son or grandson, but I think not. I fear this business will take many generations and many more years to reach its settlement, but should you read this, then that settlement will be close, and writing to you here in this City of London, my refuge and my place of exile, I rejoice that you have come at last.* Lemprière looked up from the testament.

"He knew what he was about to do?"

"He knew," the leader replied. Lemprière bent his head once more. *I ask myself how much will you know? More I think than I know myself. Tomorrow I go in search of them to take back what they took from me at Rochelle. Tomorrow too I begin my search for you. I left my first family at Rochelle, my six children and their mother pregnant with a seventh. Now I must leave my second family on Jersey to settle the account. I must leave you, my unborn descendant, and now, while I write these words, I can only hope for your return.*

Of my partners and our Company I will say little here. If you are reading this you know already how we took it from the Englanders. They were good years, when we stood firm together and fought our battles as one. But they are finished now, finished with the siege and forgotten with the dead at Rochelle. I will not lose my heirs a second time. Lemprière read further of the siege and François's mission to England. The English had never broken through the mole. The Cabbala had escaped and the Rochelais died in the citadel, François's wife and six children among them. François knew them for murderers and would have his due. The account did not seem to Lemprière the ravings of a madman. He read, *Tomorrow will see the account begin to be squared. When you read this the final tally will be made.* Then he found himself addressed directly again. *You have traveled a strange road to read this, my message to you, strewn with the corpses of those who fell before you and trammeled with trials and hard labors. Most likely you have come from Jersey, perhaps the very house I built at Rozel. Like myself, you have left home and family and perhaps you have grieved for them as I do now. Now you have come to join me. Together we might still keep the promise I made. Together we may yet return to Rochelle as conquerors. Once again, to you my heir and successor, welcome.*

Welcome to you too, Lemprière thought, remembering the corpse. He folded the parchment carefully. He felt the leader's eyes upon him.

"How do you come by this?" he asked. François's testament had touched him. It made few appeals, its confident hopes and anticipations appeared doomed with hindsight.

"It was written the night before the meeting, the same one threatened in the last of the pamphlets. You read of it there, I believe."

"You led me to them, you placed the pamphlets there for me?" Lemprière thought back to his discovery in the Archive, something about the way they fell out . . . naturally. They had been stacked against the closed door, stacked from within. The disappearance of Casterleigh, Juliette, and their companion grew a little clearer.

"Of course," the leader answered. "You have not come this far unaided. In that respect you differ from your ancestor."

"He came for his wife and children. I come for my father, and for George, and for the others of my family—"

"And the women, John. Remember the women." The tone was caustic, harder than before. "And all the other innocents who elect you their champion. Ask yourself why they are dead while you still live. Why is that, John? Why is George dead? Or your father? Or the women? You come for no one. You were brought. You are not François. François came for recompense and we settled—"

"And after that settlement he was never to leave this place," Lemprière rounded on him. "That settlement left the corpse I woke alongside, your handiwork, is that not true?"

"No one denies these things, John, but you have not yet heard enough." The leader's tone was calm again, emollient. "Wait, listen. With the settlement came a new remove, a different phase of existence. The

372

Cabbala occupied these chambers and shrank from contact with the world above. As you will have guessed, or suspected from Theobald's indiscretions, we formed the Secret Committee. From this chamber and in that guise we ran the greatest Company on the surface of the globe. We set about restoring our fortunes and those of the company, which had drifted in the time of the siege. In the Indies we sponsored petty rulers and despots, extending credit to them through the Company and recouping it directly ourselves. In this way, the Company's profits were diverted to ourselves before they ever reached England. Each year a caravan would leave the court of this or that provincial tyrant bound for the eastern coast of the Mediterranean. Each year we sent a ship to meet it that would wallow under the weight of bullion. The ship would sail west, the length of the Mediterranean, then north along the western coast of France to our old cache at Rochelle. In essence it was a simple procedure. In practice it was fraught with difficulties and once at least was almost to prove our downfall. Acquiring ships in secret drove us to fake shipwrecks, small armies were needed to guard the caravans, and the loyalty of our Indian agents was always questionable. However we arranged it, the whole business seemed designed to advertise our existence. We used Indiamen supposedly lost with all hands. We renamed them. The *Vendragon,* in which you and others have taken such an interest, was only the last in a long line. Captain Neagle stumbled across her predecessor more than twenty years ago, and though he mistook what he found for an insurance fraud his blunderings almost brought the whole arrangement to light, ourselves along with it. But we silenced Neagle and took his ship, as you know. The *Falmouth* became the *Vendragon* and the gold flowed again. Now she sits laden and waiting for us here in London, waiting for us to come out. But I run ahead.

"From the first we directed everything from here. Having chosen secrecy, it became our cross. We might emerge if we wished, but never as ourselves. Inside and out we have become exiles, different, only really belonging here. We began to change, John, as the years passed, we changed in here." A hand was pulled back into the shadows. Lemprière heard it tap against the leader's chest. Vaucanson was watching intently, and it seemed that he was about to say more, but then the hand rested again on the covers of Lemprière's dictionary.

"After the siege and its settlement, as our predecessors took stock of their new surroundings and set the Company back on its feet, in the midst of these difficulties and with so much yet to do they thought at least the feud with the Lemprières was resolved. They were wrong. It was only beginning. One after another your ancestors came after us, and one by one we cut them down. We asked ourselves what led the Lemprières to us, one after another? How could you know?" Lemprière shook his head as he thought back and asked himself where it had begun. He saw his father roll in the water at the edge of the pool.

"The agreement," he said.

"No. We led you to that, and only you. Something else, John. Some other hand has guided the Lemprières. But whose? Whose is the third hand, John?" The Cabbala had turned their heads to him and were staring as one. He thought, are we Lemprières not alone then? Do we have an ally? He racked his brains for some remark of his father's which might throw light on the matter.

"François told his family nothing," the leader said. "Nothing of ourselves. Yet, generation after generation came in search of us, and as we stopped one, another would spring up in his place to come at us from another direction. At first it was Rochelle. The first Lemprières knew more of the siege and our part in its aftermath than they could possibly discover alone. Why should they ask in the first place? After them, your ancestors moved closer still, to the Company itself, and after that wherever a chink opened in the veil we put up, it seemed a Lemprière was waiting there, peering through the crack, trying to tear apart the fabric. With your father it was the Neagle affair. How could he know its significance? What led him to the western ports of France? Had he lived to search them as he planned, he might have found our depot at Rochelle and all that it contained. How did he know?" A few seconds passed before Lemprière realized he was expected to answer.

"I was never privy to my father's reasons," he said stiffly.

"No," the leader said in resigned tones. "Perhaps it no longer matters. Inevitably some ends are left loose."

"Is that why I am here? Was my father a loose end too?" Lemprière's voice was bitter.

"The central cord, John. To bring you and your dictionary to this point has not been easy." The book again. The leader's fingers were twitching about its corners, lifting the cover a fraction and letting it fall. Abruptly it was flicked open and the unseen figure read aloud, "Aarassus. Aba. Abacenae. Abadir. Abae. Abaeus . . ." As the recitation went on, it came to seem a mockery of his labors. The dictionary. Was that why he was here? ". . . Abagarus. Abala. Abali. Abalus . . ." Lemprière tried to think of its beginnings, the day of his decision to embark on the project when Kalkbrenner had produced the notion like a skeleton for himself to clothe with flesh. Septimus had been there and Septimus was in their pay. Was Kalkbrenner? ". . . Abana. Abandus. Abannae . . ." The leader's voice was being overtaken by his cohorts, Monopole and Antithe parroting their master. Kalkbrenner, Septimus, or before them both. He thought back to the island, to an ambiguous dusk and himself staring from his window out across the fields of Rozel which shifted in the gloom and deformed themselves about an old faith, an old body pulling itself out of the roots and wiry turf, stalking across the distances to his neglected chambers: Vertumnus. The first figment of his madness; but how could they have known? ". . . Abanta. Abantes. Abantias . . ." Actaeon, the second. Danae in the pit. Iphigenia at Coade's. ". . . Abantidas. Abantis.

Abaorte. Abaratha. Abaraza . . ." Paris. He looked again at Juliette and thought of her as she had stepped from the coach outside Saint Martin's. How far back must he go? When had they caught that glimpse inside his head? He tried to think back to that night, to the vision seen from his window and the troubled sleep which had followed. He had shouted something into the night. Had someone heard and understood? He could not believe it. When he awoke he had visited the priest and been dismissed as a fool. He had climbed a tree, fallen, Juliette had found him on her way to, to the church? Yes, the church.

"Calveston," he said, and behind the leader the recitation stopped. His neck was beginning to throb once more. He wanted to sit down. "Father Calveston told you I saw demons, phantoms in the dark. He told you I was mad."

Juliette walked down the path to the church, leaving him to his confusion. He walked home. The invitation to the library had arrived and, a few days after that, the edition of Ovid in thanks for his services. There in the book was the singular illustration: Diana in spectacular undress, Actaeon in the first of his agonies. That was the tale he had read, which they would have anticipated and counted upon. Glaring reds. Steel grays. The horse had turned and walked upstream.

"Very good, very good." His father's body was still. The leader was speaking very far away. Calveston had told the girl, the girl the Viscount, the Viscount the man who addressed him now.

"You thought yourself deranged, a helpless conduit for your monsters. You gave up your books and shut your eyes, but by then we already had you, John. When you came to this city we gave you Septimus, your *fidus* Achates for the voyage ahead, and where Septimus led, you followed. To Kalkbrenner, where our dictionary was first put to you. To the De Veres, where its pages came to life. To Coade's, where we hung Iphigenia. The dictionary was ours, John, Danae's death our doing, and Iphigenia, she was my gift to you." He was turning the pages.

"Here are your monsters. Here is where you shackled them. And underneath each is a date and your signature. Each time you put your name to the catalog, we drew a little closer. Exact descriptions, exact dates, your exact name. Why do you imagine Septimus had you sign and date each entry?" Lemprière's whole head was throbbing. The earlier blow, Septimus's blow, seemed attached to him like a thick collar of flesh. He said, "Septimus?"

"A young cadre in the Company. He showed initiative in a difficult situation; suggested himself . . ." He could hardly follow what the leader was saying. Sign and date each one, absolutely of the first importance. Make 'em laugh, make 'em cry. ". . . the victims were real, John. With or without your help, they are dead." Make 'em pay. "Murdered, in Sir John's view . . ."

Sir John's name brought him round. Septimus and Cadell faded into the past, into nothing. Sir John, who caught killers and thieves and hanged them. His name sounded out of place, resonant with a rule of law which was suspended in this place, in this company. Sir John, whom he had lied to in Peppard's room, who was behind the searchers he had fled over the snow-covered estate of the De Veres, who now sought the young man seen running from Coade's that night, namely himself.

"You are the murderer, John. Your dictionary is the key, the proof." The collar was thicker, a cord of muscle tightening about his neck.

"It is your signed confession."

His hands touched the ends of the table to either side of him. They would never believe it, never give him credence as a murderer, not ever. . . . But the evidence piled up: his presence at, or near, the murders, his subsequent silences, his lies to Sir John. (Smith? Lemprière!) His dictionary. He imagined his appearance before the court: myopic, withdrawn, odd. Guilty. Unbalanced, perhaps, Ladies and Gentlemen, by his father's sudden and suspicious death, to which he was also a "witness," alone in the city he took a terrible revenge on the women who shunned his advances. . . . He would hang. They would hang him and then the feud would be finished. Welcome to you, François. Welcome, John.

For a second time he felt the parapet slide out from under him. Casterleigh's face was staring up, tilted, as though Lemprière himself, here and now, were whatever apparition had appeared behind him on the roof of the theater. Then, for the second time, he felt the hand behind his back push him forward.

"But you will not hang, John.

"Many years ago I made a vow." The leader spoke, and though he could not be seen, his words were for Lemprière and no one else. "I would return the conqueror. Tonight, this night, I mean to keep that promise. I intend for you to keep it with me. You have done well to come this far, Lemprière. Come farther. The *Vendragon* waits for the Nine of us to take us back to Rochelle. The country we fled a century and a half ago now waits in ignorance to welcome us rulers. Join me, John. That is your choice. Become as I am." And with that the leader leaned forward, out of the concealing darkness, into the candlelight, and Lemprière saw the shadows peel away from his face and seep out of its folds and lines like blood running off meat. "Or hang."

There was something wrong. Not on the skin's surface, nor within the head, but between the two. The skin and flesh on the leader's face hung and moved as though the sinewy threads which twitched and shifted the lips, cheeks, chin, and nose were snarled up and so delayed those movements. The mouth was shapeless, and Lemprière saw that when he spoke his neck puffed out and the sound seemed to come from his stomach. The muscles had collapsed. The face hung slackly as though his head were a bag of skin irregularly filled with flesh.

"The candles, John." A slight movement of the head indicated the lamp in which they burned. "Eight for the eight of us here and one unlit." Lemprière saw Casterleigh glance away from him and make a signal across the table to either Jaques or Le Mara. "The ninth is for you, John. Light it."

He caught Vaucanson in the corner of his eye looking across the table to Casterleigh, but nothing was said or signaled. Vaucanson and Casterleigh. Jaques or Le Mara. Two possible triangles. All of them in their different ways were watching the leader without seeming to, as though, like himself, they had never seen his face before; and Lemprière thought of the man's solitude through the years since the siege, waiting for the last Lemprière to arrive and take up the ninth place. But why? Still that question wrote itself over his face, and the leader's face began to lift in approximation of a smile, acknowledgment of his unspoken question.

"Why you, Lemprière? Because you were part of François's settlement. We did not know your name then, except it would be Lemprière. You were still unborn by a century or more, but I knew you would come finally. Your place has been kept. Your share held in trust. The girl is yours if you want her, and in time my own seat at this table. All of it yours, if you will join with me."

"You did not come here for revenge." Lemprière spoke carefully. "You did not come for the Rochelais. You came for the Company."

Le Mara looked from Casterleigh to the leader and back. Casterleigh's face was frozen. The leader stared at him and Lemprière met his stare. When the man replied, his voice was changed, the warm tones stripped away from the cold fact of his action. The pretense was abandoned.

"Yes, I wanted the Company and I got it. I wanted you and I got you too. You do not have the luxury of judgment, Lemprière. You have a choice. Tonight we return to Rochelle and France to expel those who drove us out. Join with me, or hang."

With that, his hands closed about the book and flung it across the table.

"Take back your dictionary, Lemprière. Come with us." He gestured to the lamp. "Light the last candle."

Lemprière took the book and slipped his ancestor's testament between its pages. It felt heavier than he imagined. Le Mara's posture was unchanged, still coiled in his chair. But his face was different. Lemprière moved toward the lamp with the book in his hand. He saw that the expression on the assassin's face was puzzled, as if something had happened or had failed to happen and this was inexplicable to him. Eight candles flared out of the lamp. He looked away for a moment and blinked. The same expression was on Vaucanson's face. He took the taper in his hand and was about to turn. They were both looking across the table, both watching Casterleigh. They were waiting for him. The taper burned higher and brighter as its flame ate into the wax. He looked up and saw Juliette's face turn toward him at last. Her face was tight. There was a movement below him and to his right where Le Mara sat, where the frames of his spectacles ended and the world became a blur. The lamp was a blaze of light this close to him, and as he moved to ignite the ninth and last candle he heard Casterleigh say "Yes," as though in answer to a question, and Jaques said "No," as if it were a question. Le Mara had already moved, half-risen, and thrust his arm forward. Lemprière looked down and saw it. Le Mara's knife was buried to the hilt. Jaques was rocking back and forth trying to lean forward with a puzzled expression on his face. The hilt knocked against the back of the chair, *tap, tap, tap.* The knife was lodged in Jaques's back. It seemed to take hours for the leader to protest.

"You dare!" Vaucanson had risen too and had hold of Boffe. Le Mara cradled the head in his arms and pulled back suddenly so that the thick neck cracked loudly in the stone chamber. Boffe's hands twitched on the table.

"How dare you!" The leader's voice had filled with rage. The two figures behind him had not moved. Nor had he, though his arms strained to push him up. He could not stand, Lemprière realized. Jaques was trying to speak, but the words were a gurgle in his throat. Lemprière froze.

"Light the candle, John," The Viscount regarded him casually from his seat, his accent a mockery of the leader's. Juliette was behind him, staring directly at Lemprière, her eyes wide, her expression urgent. She was telling him something with her eyes. He raised the taper like a pathetic sword.

"You are mine, John," said the mockery again. But serious too this time as the Viscount rose from his seat and Lemprière remembered the size of the man, his physical bulk, and his own terror on the roof. Jaques choked and spat a gout of blood from his throat.

"Juliette," he began to say, but the rest was lost as his mouth filled again. She was staring at the candles, signaling to Lemprière. Casterleigh tossed a chair aside and began to move around the table. He stared back at Juliette, his gaze flickering to the Viscount, who advanced toward him. The candles guttered. Casterleigh grinned and flexed his hands as he approached. Juliette began to move, and then suddenly, Lemprière understood. At the same moment, Casterleigh saw her and understood too. Lemprière gulped air, filling his lungs to bursting, and the Viscount threw himself forward, the huge hands reaching for him too late.

• • •

Stretching first one knee, then the other, arching and straightening his back, rolling his neck, flexing every joint down to his fingers and toes, Nazim waited outside the chamber in the darkness. When the pseudo-

Lemprière and his companion had disappeared into the chamber, Nazim settled at the edge of the gravel. His limbs moved rhythmically as the minutes, then hours, passed by. His mind raced and once again the pseudo-Lemprière was its quarry. He rehearsed the young man's encounters to himself: the winner of the woman in blue's protégée at the Pork Club, buffeted by Farina's men outside the inn, confiding with the real Lemprière the night of his murder in Blue Anchor Lane, mistaking himself for someone called "Theobald" at the Ship in Distress a week later, running like a madman out of Coade's, running after the girl to the theater the previous night, hustled unconscious into the coach a matter of hours later by Mister Praeceps, the same man who had spoken to Sir John that night, and their discussion had centered on "Lemprière," although the man was dead months ago, killed by Le Mara, and they all seemed in league against his bespectacled successor who was at once the drunken butt of a practical joke at the Pork Club, the near victim of Farina's mob, betrayer or loyal lieutenant to the true Lemprière, a myopic fool in the Ship in Distress, a lunatic at Coade's, inamorato at the Opera House, colleague of Praeceps, then corpse in Southampton Street, and now it seemed he was allied with, perhaps even one of Nine whom he, Nazim, was here to dispatch.

Nazim wrestled determinedly with these pseudo-Lemprières, trying to trace them back as affects to some single Ur-Lemprière, but the adversary he constructed was still too awkward with his thin arms and legs and his strange angular body which defied all attempts to pin him down as definitely this or certainly that or possibly something else entirely. It was neither dark nor light and Nazim wanted to be clear. Real or not, the Lemprière would not fit. Now of all times, he wanted to be single-minded, but the Beast was as ambiguous as the Lemprière, gulled or guileful, guilty or innocent as he was, and its sourceless light drew strange shapes from the wavering hollows and high, vaulted spaces which drew his eye in turn. Had the blackness been absolute he might have dismissed them as phantoms, as patterns seen when the eyes are screwed too tightly shut, freaks of the brain's idling engine. Undefined objects and figures seemed to hover and flit in the half-light above him.

Once or twice he fancied he heard disturbances in the air, wind rushing over some alien body far above and away across the gravel, over the abyss from which the Lemprière and his companion had emerged an hour or more before. Freaks and phantoms: the Beast sent them to beg his unanswered questions and feed on his doubts. He thought back to the wide, ribbed tunnel he had followed to the chamber blocked off with planks and buttresses, to the stalactitic teeth and petrified tongue which seemed to lap at the water pressing behind the wall of clay. He remembered the water seeping through the wall whose supports he had kicked away without a second thought, the tiny glistening beads, then a silver trickle as though the Beast were a vast water clock measuring the time to its own destruction. A trickle, a rivulet . . . And then?

And then his anxieties flew back into the dark spaces above him. He heard the air there rush suddenly as though a gust of wind had found its way through the tunnels, a particular kind of gust—he had heard the sound before—and he wondered, a bat? But the shape that swooped in and out of his vision in a blink was larger than that, much larger as it disappeared away to his left and he heard an audible *crunch* as something landed on the gravel fifty or sixty yards away. The theater, minutes before Le Mara's companion had staggered into the coach, he had heard it then. He rose and squinted into the gloom. He saw nothing. It was nothing. Only the scree shifting of its own accord, the air's susurration, a convection current set off by the heat of his own body, a deferred version of himself, nothing, nothing at all. But he could not rid himself of the suspicion that on the far side of the gravel, away from the entrance to the chamber, someone or something was watching and waiting in the dark, like himself.

The minutes trickled by and nothing more was heard. Gradually, Nazim's attention swung back to the chamber. He began flexing his muscles and joints once again, back, neck, shoulders. . . . A bubble of sound burst into the darkness, a gabble of voices disgorged from the door to the chamber and suddenly bitten off short as the door was closed. Nazim heard a man's voice barking orders, a choking sound, a deeper voice raging, then silence, and out of the silence the sounds of unguarded footsteps approaching from the chamber. No lights had shone. Two sets of footsteps, he realized as they drew nearer. The door opened again. It seemed the lamp within was alight now. Silhouetted in the light from the doorway behind them, two figures were moving toward Nazim, while in the doorway itself, cast like shadows by the stumbling pair ahead of them, two further figures were framed for a moment before they too began to move in pursuit. The door closed, the darkness resumed, and there were only the sounds of overlapping footsteps crashing toward him. Nazim clutched the miniature in one hand and his knife in the other, then moved toward them. The first pair were very near now, the noise so loud it seemed impossible he could not see them. Suddenly two faces came out of the gloom, scared unguarded faces, first the girl and then, a little behind her wincing with the effort, the pseudo-Lemprière. The sight of himself brought them both to an amazed halt. The pseudo-Lemprière's eyes narrowed in recognition.

"You!" he gasped. Behind the pair of them, the steadier footfalls of their pursuers stopped too.

There was a brief complete silence as the three of them, Lemprière, Juliette, and Nazim, looked at one another, and the pursuers behind paused, baffled suddenly by the absolute quiet. Then into that noiseless moment dropped a sound, a toneless *pop* which was followed by something like air but more substantial this time, more forceful, and Nazim knew that far behind him through the spongeworks and the broad tunnel, beyond the rotten planking he had disturbed, the clay had failed, the clock had run out, and now water was pouring down the throat of the Beast toward them. The girl's arm was about the pseudo-Lemprière. They looked quickly at each other as he raised his knife hand and stepped forward.

· · ·

It was simple. As Casterleigh threw himself forward, Lemprière blew out the candles and the chamber was plunged into darkness. He heard the Viscount's bulk crash against a chair, a grunt as he fell, then a strong hand closed about his wrist and pulled him suddenly toward the door.

"This way," Juliette's voice urged him. She was guiding him out of the chamber and then he felt gravel grinding under his feet; they were out and running, their footsteps echoing like gunshots around the vaults of the cavern. Her dress appeared as his eyes adjusted to the faint light, a wavering area of white ahead of him. At his back he heard at once a match strike and the door open again. The lamp was being relit. Two figures appeared in the doorway, one broad and tall, the other shorter and of slighter build. Then the door closed again and there was darkness. He could hear the practiced footsteps of their pursuers as they began to come after Juliette and himself.

They had gained perhaps forty yards, crashing forward together over the gravel, her hand still about his wrist, his breath already short. The ground seemed to slide out from under him, dragging him back with every step he took. He heard Juliette's breath coming more quickly, and underneath the sound of their own footfalls, those of Casterleigh and Le Mara drawing closer. Suddenly Juliette's body slammed into his own. She had stopped dead in her tracks, and as he collided with her, her arm sought his own for support. The footsteps behind them stopped. Lemprière looked up and saw a man dressed all in black with a black cloak and hat whose broad brim was raised to disclose a face he knew from the Ship in Distress, the Indian who had been Theobald until the real Theobald arrived.

"You!" he exclaimed. And the hat . . . The hat he had seen in the midst of the brawl outside the inn, a strong hand pulling him away from Farina's thugs, and somewhere else. His rescuer there. The three of them were silent. Lemprière heard a sound somewhere in the distance ahead of him, like a cork being pulled and the wine rushing out of the bottle. Running water. Juliette looked up at him and her arm tightened about his own. The Indian had raised his arm and begun to move forward. His eyes seemed to look through them both. His hand held a knife. The footsteps behind them began again. Lemprière moved sideways, pulling Juliette with him. The footsteps were faster and louder. The Indian advanced, as though they had not moved, toward the spot they had occupied, and over it toward their pursuers who could be heard plainly now. They watched for a moment as Nazim advanced to meet his quarry. They were passed over, spared, and again it was Juliette who pulled him forward, toward the haven of the spongeworks. As the two of them moved off and the cloaked figure went forward to engage their pursuers, a sixth player, unseen and unheard by the other five, rose from his position on the far edge of the gravel apron and turned his eyes toward the chamber where his own quarry lay.

The gravel behind them, Lemprière and Juliette ran quickly over hard rock. Their pace slowed again as odd humps of stone began to rise up and obstruct their flight. Behind them Lemprière could hear the footsteps of the three converging, coming to a halt. There was a flurry of sound as the battle was joined. Ahead, the rushing sound was louder and more distinct, more obviously water moving toward them. A pair of footsteps detached itself from the melee to his rear, growing louder then abruptly silent as their owner reached the harder ground they now traveled themselves with greater difficulty.

The humps had grown taller, more like spires, each the height of a man, dividing the area into open chambers as though bubbles had been blown in the molten rock and solidified to leave a honeycomb. The sound of water was louder. Lemprière wondered whether it was Casterleigh or Le Mara who had taken up the chase. Casterleigh, he thought. It would be the Viscount. Juliette was ahead of him, weaving a way through the spongeworks. The dull roar was directly ahead of them both, drowning out any sound from behind now.

Gradually the waisted columns began to shrink to hummocks once more, to swellings, and then to vague irregularities in the stone floor. The spongeworks was behind them and they were faced with a wall of rock rising up out of sight. At its center a gaping mouth broke the sheer cliff—the entrance to a broad tunnel twenty yards across and as many high—from which the roaring of the water was clearly audible. Lemprière began to cast about for an alternative passage, but Juliette pulled him forward hissing, "This way!"

"The water," he protested, but she seemed to pay no attention.

"The river has broken through," she threw over her shoulder. "This place will flood. We must reach the shaft before the water rises or we are drowned."

"There must be another way." Lemprière looked about desperately.

"There are only three entrances to this place. Two of them are in there." She pointed into the tunnel.

"The third, then—"

"Miles distant. It comes out under the Opera House, back there." She pointed behind her. "Le Mara will be guarding that, once he deals with the Indian." Juliette took his wrist and pulled him forward.

For the first time since he had fled the chamber, he remembered his dictionary was still in his hand. He jammed the bulky volume into the ripped pocket of his coat and hurried after her. Almost as soon as they had entered the tunnel, Lemprière felt the first tongue of water curl around his boots and seep through their soles. The floor of the tunnel seemed to undulate. The water was collecting in each trough. He stumbled over the ridges. The roar of the water echoing down the tunnel was so loud they could barely hear their own feet splashing as they stumbled forward. Juliette kept glancing over her shoulder as though expecting their pursuer to catch them at any moment. She pulled up her skirts and led the way. Soon the water had risen to their knees and Lemprière could feel the current pushing against him. The tunnel began to rise and the water was a broad flood cascading down the ridges which they used as steps.

The river water stank. As they clambered up, Lemprière felt something soft and clammy wrap itself around his legs, then another and another, something white, like cloth. They were racing down toward him, dozens of them carried down by the flood. François's pamphlets, he realized. He picked one off his leg. Juliette turned back to him.

"Not far now," she gasped. The water had reached her waist. As she resumed her struggle, they both heard the sound which grew out of the tunnel behind them: the bellowing of an animal filled with inarticulate rage. Both knew then that it was the Viscount who had followed them. They redoubled their efforts but the current was stronger, the torrent ahead even louder. They could no longer walk in the center of the tunnel and had to cling to the sides. The water rose higher and Lemprière thought: Of all the deaths inflicted on his family by the Cabbala, to be drowned underground like a rat would be the most dismal. Then Juliette gave a short cry.

Lemprière looked up and there, a mere ten yards ahead of them and projecting from a shaft in the ceiling, was the ladder. Juliette turned and pointed to it and tried to speak over the noise of the water. The roar was deafening, impossibly loud. Then, as they struggled and reached the ladder, quite without warning, the noise stopped.

Lemprière and Juliette looked at each other in complete bafflement. They were sodden and panting. The waters even began to recede. Lemprière grinned and was about to speak, but Juliette put her hand to his mouth. Both of them heard the quick irregular splashes and grunted curses of their pursuer. He was close, not visible yet, but moving at speed.

Juliette had him grasp the first rung. As he climbed up, his boots rang on the metal rungs. Juliette followed, urging him to climb more quickly.

The water was almost silent, a placid thing swirling in lazy whorls and framed below them in the circle of the shaft. Above there was only the dark. He heard a creak, and at first he thought it was his own weight on the ladder. But the creak seemed to go on and on, getting louder and louder. The sound rose up the shaft, an ear-splitting racket of tortured wood on rock which reached its crescendo with a hideous cracking sound, and the water exploded down the tunnel once more as though pent up and suddenly released. Juliette shouted to him to climb faster. The water at the foot of the shaft churned and frothed. It seemed to glow as the torrent was renewed, a phosphorescent white, almost blue-white, almost green. The water was glowing green. Juliette was tugging at his leg. Bright green, and in the light he saw a vague shape moving below. She was shouting at him, pointing down the shaft.

"Green!" he shouted back. But that was not her message. The light glowed brighter and in it he saw suddenly that the vague shape below was not so distant as he had thought, nor so vague. It was Casterleigh moving up the ladder. He was climbing powerfully and with purpose toward them. Even then Lemprière hesitated, transfixed by the sight below as the circular frame of the shaft was filled with another still stranger prospect. The green light dimmed to a corona about its edges, highlighting a triangular shape that Lemprière recognized though it seemed impossible, moving unmistakably down the tunnel through which they had passed. It was the prow of a ship. A three-master, though the masts were snapped off a yard above the deck and the sides were at once scourged and held together by the tight embrace of the tunnel. Then the water stopped. Once again the creaking noise sounded down the passage and Lemprière realized a second ship was straining to enter the Beast.

• • •

Tonight, London is an outpost of the Europe-machine: a place where Rochelle is possible again. The preludes to its end are buried: Troy, Carthage, the first and second Romes. Its echoes search now for resonant surfaces, places fit to replay the old drama: the siege about Belgrade, perhaps, or the riddled foundations of Paris, Constantinople, or even Vienna, where the Emperor Joseph's indecision still hangs over the city. Or London. Tonight, London is the choice, and an imperfect translation is already underway, echoes and correspondences are being pumped through the ports and circuits. They are straining under the load. The engine of Europe hums and spins, twitches in and out of its possible states as congruent details are fed out of the old city, away from the still center of the anticyclone and into the new metropolitan template.

Already the cognoscenti are filling the Opera House, huddling there like the doomed masses in the citadel. The streets are lit with torches, thousands of them as invaders gather in the east. At Rochelle, a green beacon shines out along the agreed bearing over a dark sea, waiting, and this too finds its distorted version, its reversed echo as the translation takes ahold and advances upriver to the city. Aboveground, as below, the players are poised. London is ready for Rochelle.

The sunset was unusually lurid. Eben looked west from the Crow's Nest as the dying light shot ribbons of color into the gathering blue-black night. Reds, pinks, and golds he had come to expect—the skies this summer were disturbed and erratic—but never more so than tonight. Even the sky's wildest palette rarely extended to green. Nevertheless, there it was. A fat glow in the upper air refracted from God knew what meteorological freak, probably miles away, probably Africa, he thought, and it was not a muddy green either. It was bright, this green. Leaf green.

"Green," he said.

"Green," confirmed Captain Roy. He was stationed opposite, looking east.

"Probably Africa," Eben went on.

"Perhaps to begin with," said Roy. "Shadwell now, though," and he pointed downriver as Eben came to look for himself. The Thames's meanders curled away through the eastern districts, a dark flood until Shadwell, where Roy pointed, and beyond which Eben saw that the coils of the river were indeed bright green as though a lurid serpent had crawled inland in search of a latter-day Laocoon, and its head, silhouetted against the iridescence which snaked away to stern, was a ship. The ship was moving upriver on the last surges of the tide, and its lagging escort of green was following, fanning out across the width of the river.

"Extraordinary," muttered Eben.

"Algae," said Roy.

It was; and the ship was the *Heart of Light*. Renamed *Alecto,* the three-master moved slowly upstream in the baleful glow of its suitors. As far back as Tilbury, the algae had broadened to touch the banks on either side. The river was luminous, molten, uncanny. Green. Peter Rathkael-Herbert watched from the bridge as the lighters and smacks moored downriver gave way to larger vessels, brigs and colliers, then frigates, Indiamen, and ships of the line as they neared the Port of London.

"So much for surprise," muttered Hörst "the Wurst" Craevisch, who stood beside him. They were marooned in a sea of green light that filled the river behind them for as far as they could see. The tide pulled them steadily into the city and their glowing escort followed. Of their mission's object, the *Megaera* (and specifically her cargo of Sicilian sulfur), there was as yet no sign. The Imperial Internuncio moved forward and practiced a tentative thrust with his newly issued cutlass.

"Jolly good, Peter!" Wilberforce van Clam called encouragement for'ard from the quarterdeck. "Now lunge, lunge! Yes, yes!"

Dead fish bobbed up and down in the luminous carpet which encircled them. He had yet to get used to the stench, and at night still dreamed of his time in the *Tesrifati*'s hold, horrible dreams of suffocation and decay. Wilberforce was waving for him to continue but he had lost the urge.

"Pass the pipe." He reached over to Hörst, who handed it over. Blue smoke rolled thickly around him as he puffed, banishing the redolent fish for a minute. The algae seemed to roll like waves around the ship and Hörst's voice was far away and tinny as he shouted, "There she is, Wilberforce! The *Megaera*, dead ahead!" Pirates were gathering around Wilberforce on the quarterdeck, adjusting bandanas and stuffing braces of pistols down their trousers. Most held cutlasses in their teeth. Peter Rathkael-Herbert essayed another lunge. Not good.

"Where?" he asked Hörst and looked to starboard as directed where, among the clutter of masts and jostling hulls that was the Upper Pool, he saw tied up to a long wharf a barge, then what looked like a scaled-down Indiaman, beyond that a cargo vessel, *Typhoon*, *Tisiphone*, something of the sort, and last of all, the *Megeara*. Lobs de Vin was already practicing throws with his grappling hook. Peter Rathkael-Herbert pulled deeply on the pipe. The port seemed deserted, neglected almost. Odd piles and heaps, impromptu depots and careless stacks of bales littered the quays as they drew nearer. The first hooks were flung out over the glowing water to land and snag in the *Megaera*'s lower rigging. The *Alecto* swung about and moved toward her prey. A little shudder ran through the vessel as Peter Rathkael-Herbert jumped down to join his fellow pirates, then another.

The prow collided gently with the stern of the *Megaera*, the ropes were made fast, and then he was leaping forward with the rest of them, feet clattering over the decks of the boarded vessel, cutlass in hand and pistol at the ready while all around the algae glowed greenly and further shudders began to run through both vessels. Peter Rathkael-Herbert looked over the side, frowned, then looked again. The ships began to move more violently, straining at the hawsers. The river swirled. Its surface dipped. No, he thought. He turned to his companions.

"Abandon ship!" he cried. "Wilberforce! Hörst! The water, look! Oh, God, no . . ."

The luminous river surface was massing, piling up in heaving ramparts of green; solid walls of rising water teetered all about the ship, whose deck pitched forward as though old Father Thames was suddenly a muscled giant sporting with the *Megaera* as a whale with its tub. The pirates skated down the deckspace, sliding and tumbling toward the prow as the first trough opened in the water, an embracing wound which pulled the vessel to itself, sending shudders through her timbers to the elderly pirates who now scrambled over the bow's rail, all thoughts of brigandage lost for the moment in a desperate tangle of arms, legs, heads, short swords, cutlasses, cudgels, and pistols, a great heap of human panic spilling from ship to shore as the *Megaera* began to roll.

The trough deepened, and a terrible sucking sound filled the air. The green light throbbed in deep pulses around the vessel which turned blindly, hawsers snapping like thread as she seesawed crazily, pitching up and down, yawing in a wild destructive spin. The river was a vortex, sucking the ship down below the pulsing surface, her masts insane fingers pointing to an empty sky. Within her hold the barrels of charcoal were shattering. The *Megaera* whirled about as the river got a grip on her, the whirling pool spun faster, and with a great belch of escaping air she was dragged below the surface. As she disappeared, a wailing sound, a howling of tortured timbers, cut through the murderous gurge, as though the ship were not yet dead. Then the sound stopped. For a brief moment the waters were calm before the ship was swallowed down, and the abysmal undertow surged again. Watching from the quayside, Peter Rathkael-Herbert and the pirates saw their own vessel swing about and turn its blind nose toward the whirlpool. A hole had opened in the riverbed, a hungry mouth to swallow ships.

What could they do? They stood in silence on the quay, frail spectators to the unfolding catastrophe as their ship was tossed up now and plunged stern-first down into the crashing green waters which tightened about her and pulled her under.

Again the pause, again the moment of stillness, the shriek of splintering timbers, and then from farther down the quay the *Tisiphone* pulled like a maddened beast to join her furious sisters. The indraft sucked down the third of the sisters, drawing in more of the algae's carpet of love, dragging that down too. Perhaps they went willingly, as heedless lovers, carrying down a flaming torch of green to the sister-ships, for they will need that too. The whip of scorpions alone will not suffice for the vengeance these Furies have been sent to enact.

The last luminous green rivulets sank from sight. The waters were black, whorls ceding to eddies, eddies to faint shivers, until at last the river was calm, darkly languid, and viscous below the pirates' disbelieving gaze. Peter Rathkael-Herbert, Wilberforce van Clam, Amilcar Buscallopet, Heinrich Winkell, "Slim" Jim Pett, "Mussel" Wilkins, Lobs and Oiβ de Vin, and all the remainder of the *Heart of Light*'s gouty, hoary-headed crew stood together on the quay.

Hörst turned to Wilberforce.

"Now what?" he demanded of his captain.

" 'Straordinary," adjudged Guardian from his post at the east window of the Crow's Nest. "Never in all my years . . ."

"Saw something like it off Malacca once," rejoined Captain Roy. "Turned out to be . . ." His voice faded away. Perched atop the plan chest by the north window, he leaned forward suddenly.

"What? What did it turn out to be?" But Roy was not listening. He was looking up the short passage which connected the legal quays to Thames Street above.

"You remember the Stone-Eater, Eben?"

"What? The Stone-Eater at—"

"That evening. When Sir John's men raided the—"

"Ah! Yes, yes of course."

"The furtive little devil, slipped out in the confusion, remember him? Signaled to young Lemprière as he nipped down the stairs." Eben remembered, remembered too his hasty promise to Lemprière, made here in this very room, and his own misgivings as their tiny alliance had seemed to widen that night to include Farina's loyal lieutenant and beyond him Farina and God knows who else, the Mob itself even? Yes, perhaps even the Mob, if it should come to that, but certainly *this* individual, marching along the quay toward the pirates about now at the head of a dispirited corps (forty? fifty? certainly no more than that) who followed in a straggling line behind. There was the *Vendragon*, still safely tied up and seemingly impervious to the river's late assault, still affirming that earlier pledge. And did Eben remember? Of course he did.

"Stoltz," he said. Roy nodded sagely and thought for a moment.

"So where's Farina?" he asked.

• • •

Now what?

"We defend ourselves," said Wilberforce, and Hörst's head swiveled aft as he pointed to the gang of loping desperadoes who now strolled, staves in hands, toward them, and at their head a leader who, as he approached, glanced nervously over his shoulder as if to check that the contingent he had set out with half an hour before was still up to strength, present, and above all, correct. Stoltz.

"Two to one. Bad odds, Wilberforce," muttered Hörst as he drew his cutlass and adjusted a raffish bandana. Should've worn the eye-patch, he thought privately, then winced as his back gave a twinge. Lobs and Oiβ de Vin clutched a brace of pistols between them, and behind them Peter Rathkael-Herbert dibbed halfheartedly at an imaginary foe. He thrust, foot forward in the improved manner, and turned to Wilberforce for approval. But Wilberforce paid no attention, not to himself, nor Hörst, nor even the motley mob who had drawn themselves up in a pedantic line, staves perfectly aligned not ten yards away from them.

"They don't *look* like the Militia," murmured Amilcar. "Perhaps we should parley? Wilberforce?" But Wilberforce was looking east down the quay, past the late berths of the *Tisiphone*, *Megaera*, and their own *Alecto* to a ship which, had the whirlpool persisted, must surely have followed that hapless trio.

Along the quay away from the mob went Wilberforce, drawn by bewildered curiosity toward the ship which sat expectantly in the water. Can't be, he thought. Stoltz's mob drew closer and raised its staves in readiness. Peter Rathkael-Herbert aimed a tremendous cutlass. It *is*, thought Wilberforce. He looked back for his men and saw a big-looking cove followed by a smaller one (no legs?) hurrying along the quay into the back of the mob who were poised as the pirates were poised, yes, no legs, he confirmed as the first sword was raised and he looked back and saw the hell-ship's name writ plain over her bows.

"She's the bloody *Vendragon!*" he roared, but no one heard, not Hörst, or Amilcar, or the Internuncio, not Stoltz or his mob, not even the Captain stumbling down the quay (though his identification of the vessel Eben is pledged to defend, even if reluctantly, is surely the main-spring of their determined haste), for at that moment the very ground on which they all stood gave a great percussive shudder, and from deep within the bowels of the earth a terrible pandemonic shriek exploded into the upper air. All stared as one at the river's surface, which broke open now as if the Charybdis that had swallowed the ships now sought to spew them up once more.

· · ·

Love, desperate love. Three times Lemprière heard a ship's tortured sides scream against adamant rock, three times the waters stilled, then surged again, backing up behind the vessels and rising up the shaft. The viscous escort of algae sought vainly to shield their lover from the Beast's raking outcrops and jagged stipules which scourged and smashed her timbers as her hellish descent went on. The toxic waters rose, and in their glare he saw the Viscount pulling himself up the ladder, an engine of steel clothed in flesh, grunting and roaring behind them.

"Faster!" he shouted to Juliette. Her limbs moved slowly now. They had climbed a hundred feet or more. His own lungs were burning, his hands numb as they closed about the next rung. The rush of water filled his ears and above him there was only the pitch-black of the shaft. He looked down and saw the waters welling up once more, thrusting up the shaft, overtaking the Viscount, their toxic glare reaching almost to the girl who labored below him. They fell back and the Viscount was still there, clinging to the ladder, his body a ghostly green from the dunking, still coming after them. Juliette's energies were beginning to fail her.

"Not far!" she gasped. Lemprière reached down and felt her hands close about his arm. He hauled her up like a rag doll, the muscles screaming in his shoulders, feet unable to feel the rungs, each one a mountain as they neared the top. But the Viscount was close. Lemprière hardly dared look down, each rung telling him, stop, breathe, rest, sleep . . . a kind of trance filled with pain, up, again, and then his hands were scrabbling among papers and digging into dry earth. He was at the top of the shaft. A heavy iron grille loomed above him as he scrambled over the lip and reached back to pull Juliette after him. They looked down and saw the Viscount climbing powerfully, the waters rising. Together they heaved the weight of the grille upright until its massive hinge groaned, and it fell with a crash across the opening of the shaft. Juliette dropped to her knees.

Lemprière ran forward into the cellar. He saw the door he had kicked in frustration and beside it the one he had opened with Theobald. But it was blocked behind a great mound of pamphlets, François's pamphlets which now he kicked away, tossing them aside to reach the door beyond. For one moment he thought it was locked; he kicked furiously and the old wood grated on its hinges, swinging open at last. Behind him, he could hear the water rising in the shaft.

Through the bars of the grille Juliette saw the Viscount's face turn and look up. He was only yards below her. He climbed more rapidly but the water was already at his ankles. Juliette watched his progress calmly, then, as he neared the top, she rose and moved forward deliberately to add her own weight to the iron grille. The dark form below rushed up the final rungs of the ladder. The Viscount's hands closed about the bars. The water was at his waist. He pushed once and the grille shuddered; again, but he could not lift it. His straining face pressed itself between the bars. The waters rose more slowly now. His eyes found hers through the bars of his cage.

"Your own father?" His tone was almost reproachful. "You would kill your own father?" His face disappeared for a moment, then returned.

"You are not my father," she spoke flatly, looking down at him. The water inched up his chest. When it touched his neck, his composure seemed to leave him.

"Help me," he whispered. Juliette knelt quickly.

"Tell me," she hissed. "Give me the name. Tell me my father's name."

"I will tell you. Please, closer. I want to tell . . ." His hands were struggling to reach her through the bars. The mouth swallowed, tried to form itself; then he whispered into her ear.

Lemprière heard her cry, "No! You lie!" He ran to the shaft as Juliette stumbled back and ran to the door. The water had reached the bars. The Viscount's face was distorted against them, mouth working to pull air into his lungs. But the water rose inexorably, closing over the mouth, eyes, and nose. Lemprière watched as the Viscount's body plummeted silently down the flooded shaft until it was swallowed by the black waters of the Beast.

He turned and walked out of the cellar, into the Archive beyond. He looked left and right down avenues of moldering paper and was about to call when he heard the door slam shut on the far side of the Archive.

"Juliette?" he called. "Juliette!" He ran forward into the gloom of the Archive but she was gone. She had fled him again. Why?

. . .

Three times Jaques heard the waters stop. Three times he thought he might not drown. He thought there was still time; still time to find her, time to reach the ship, to escape, to live. But the waters surged again, a deep roar rolling inevitably through the caverns and chambers toward him, dashing his false hopes against hard truths. He would not find her, or the boy. The Viscount would find them both. Perhaps he would spare them. Perhaps he would tell them the lie of his own manufacture which Casterleigh knew for a truth and would tell them with such flat conviction that they would believe it too. They had all believed it. Even Charles.

Jaques had hardly felt the blade, had hardly moved as Le Mara drove home the knife. Now it was a shard of ice lodging against his spine. He leaned forward and heard the hilt knock against the back of the chair which held him prisoner. Below the waist he felt nothing. Boffe's head twitched again on the table to his left. The leader muttered in his chair. Behind him, Monopole and Antithe were still as statues. Vaucanson had got to them, tampered with something inside. Now Vaucanson had fled and they were left to wait while Juliette and the boy scrambled through the tunnels with the Viscount at their backs brandishing the lie he had furnished like a cudgel above their hopes. Fathers and false fathers. There had been no time.

His stomach heaved and more blood ran into his throat. Any moment now his partners would throw open the door and free him, coming for him as angels of mercy, agents of deliverance, as they had that night, the night the lie had begun. Soon, he quelled his fear. They would come as they had before. Or the boy! Yes, he would return to help old Jake, help his father's old friend, just as Charles himself would have done. Charles would not leave him. Not Charles, with his obstinate decency, his refusal to shrug off the onus, though he should have when the letter came and he, Jaques, had told him so, told him to ignore it. The woman wanted money, nothing more, and he should give nothing. He saw the lie swelling her belly. Return it unopened: He heard his own vehement

391

advice and might have said more then, but Charles believed the child was his and the onus was his too. So he paid and the Viscount had given his dogs the scent and they had led him back down the trail of receipts to the house in Paris, its windows glowing in squares of red and the rain pouring down on them both as they stumbled dripping into the hallway.

Casterleigh had found her a dozen years later, had twisted her to the shape he wished and dangled her before them, here in this very chamber, fashioning her as the bastard-Lemprière he would turn on the father and son both. His delight at the prize, at the neat triangle they would form. He might have spoken out then, but he had kept silent, thinking back to the night they found refuge in the Rue Boucher des Deux Boules, in the Villa Rouge; the night it had rained.

The business with the Indian was over. Vaucanson had him trussed in the coach already. The rain still poured, pounding like the waters outside the door. Inside, the candles burned as they did now behind him and the women moved like beautiful ghosts, wheeling about him in their finery, paste glittering on their fingers and about their necks. It was almost dawn. He had walked upstairs in search of Charles. Outside the door, the first crash sounded. He was opening doors, peering in to find his friend. Again, a crash, louder this time. He felt the blood heaving in his throat. Candles glaring behind him. She was sitting upright in the disorder of the bed. Charles was slumped beside her, dead to the world with the drink. The room was red, but that was not how it had been. His head spun and she moved slightly. She was saying something and the rain was too loud, the water roaring outside the door. The sheet which had covered her fell away. Charles stirred and she looked down sourly. Her whole body was red, and his own, as though the house were burning down around them. Her legs parted in invitation. The ceiling was a dark circle swelling out above them, folds unfurling and eyelids peeling back, a blackened face looking down on him. Not simply black. Charred. The door swung open. Charles stirred beside them. A baby's face, its charred lips moving and eyes blinking behind peeling eyelids, but not in the bedroom now. In the doorway to the chamber.

It seemed that time had stood still, pent up behind the remembered scene and now released, it sped forward as the door crashed back, splintering from the force of the entry. A figure stood amid the wreckage of the door. The sound of roaring water crashed over Jaques's head. His own blood was filling his eyes with red but the raging torrent beyond the door glared with green light, forcing aside the crimson film until he saw the three ships being tossed and mangled in the torrent rising outside the chamber. The figure in the doorway turned its charred face to him, an avenging angel whispering inside his head of matters they both already knew. The ships were crashing into one another, hulls splintering and spilling their cargoes into the air, barrels which burst open and loosed clouds of choking powder to swirl above the tortured vessels, their work all but done. Now the avenging angel turned from Jaques to the one who sat at the table's head and Jaques watched as he knelt before the leader. He seemed to speak but the words were lost in the cacophony of shattering spars and the pounding of Jaques's own heart. He choked and struggled but he was drowning, dying, and no one would come for him. The light seemed to fade. Juliette? No, she was lost to him now. The angel had risen and the leader's mouth was working, trying to speak as the torch was plucked from the wall and the clouds of dust swirled thicker, great swaths of yellow and gray with every combustible surface exposed, only waiting for the spark. *Tisiphone, Megaera, Alecto.* Matchwood, spent vessels. Jaques gulped for air and found only blood. The dark angel turned, an infant's smile burned across his face. The leader was screaming at him but the words were lost. The black figure turned. Jaques saw the arm draw back, then hurl the lamp and its eight flaring candles into the heart of the powder.

• • •

The Europe-machine grows confused. Duplicate messages are crashing through its ports, lagging copies of one another which lap the control-loops in decaying orbits. The congruence is inexact, the once-strong signal breaking up. The beacon pulses from the hillside north of Rochelle, but the bearing is off by fractions of degrees and a skewed version is the result in the streets of London tonight. At the Opera House, the luckless cognoscenti await Marchesi with hungry ears. On the quayside there are rough rapprochements going on, pirate-ague crossbreeding with Stoltz-fever to derive a new resistant strain. Subterranean vectors lead away from one another, not toward as they should. It's all going wrong. The assassins wheel away, thrust meeting counterthrust, westward into the darkness. The Viscount is already spent. Lemprière runs through the echoing corridors of his lost love, up and out of the buried circuits which still wind down and hum with nascent surges as the ships commingle their cargoes, and the most-knowing player, the nearest we have to a perfect observer, takes the candles in his hand, waiting to send his signal up, to bridge the two orders and shunt the greatest of all these players forward. Hundreds of feet above this ignition the charge is waiting to go off. The Mob is massed in Leadenhall Street.

The day's preceding blazing heat, the whole heat of summer behind it, has baked the fat black ground. The surging river has filled the riven trenches, and the saturated mulch has bubbled and thickened to a foaming broth which crystallizes in the parching sun. A vast *salpeterflöz* lies fallow and waiting for the coarser elements of sulfur and charcoal to bring the mixture right. The proportions are shifting, racing each other up and down the columns, small arms, cannon, and blasting powders aligning themselves in ratios of saltpeter, sulfur, and charcoal, 75:10:15 edging closer toward the magical 75:12:13 where the compounds and elements can recombine and blow apart. The powder is tinder dry, the mixture is close enough. In the entrails of the Beast the match is already lit, is poised above the fuse. A vast powder-mine sits below the city, and perhaps the city knows this, for the buildings are voiding their interiors into the streets which fill with refugees from the old order, seekers after the new. The alleys and byways contract and expand as if the guts of the monster below have come to life and broken through its stony skin to form a supple exoskeleton here on the crawling surface above. Jostling bodies cram the city's conduits, and the torchlight is a deep red glare after the darkened interior behind him as Lemprière bursts on the scene and runs down the steps of East India House, drilling his way into the mob which stretches away down Leadenhall Street, pushing aside the rioters-in-waiting in his desperate search, for he has lost her again, and now he calls, "Juliette! Juliette!" but she cannot hear him, she has gone, and all he finds are vulgar insurgents.

Men's faces, orange and yellow in the torchlight, fill the street and snake back out of sight, all looking west to the cowering beadles and the Militia who oppose them from a safe distance at the far end of the thoroughfare. So far, the rabble is a torpid beast, its main body still digesting the options, but at the squamid head of this hydra is Farina. A wind is blowing, a hot wind strengthening by the minute. His hair flies out behind as he addresses the mob.

Lemprière elbows his way through the sluggish body, drawing curses and the odd cuff as he goes, craning his head for a view, still shouting her name. The crowd shifts and murmurs around him. There are groups who are shouting and groups who are silent in face of the gathering thought. Farina is pointing. The crowd's mood is beginning to turn. Lemprière looks about him, his urgent gaze sweeping the faces who are all intent on something farther up. Four men at the front of the crowd bend to pick something up. The mob's attention focuses on their efforts, its own desires clotting about this new spectacle. Lemprière looks over tousled heads as the four men advance carrying an object he dreaded then, has imagined since, and dreads again now. Could it be?

Farina's voice lifts over the crowd, over the howling wind.

". . . and this, this is what they conceal from our justice!" The mob focuses as the four men lift their load into plain view. Yes, Lemprière thinks numbly. A part of his nightmare is hoisted up to face him once again, the obscene stump still lodged in her mouth, the tattered blue dress shredded and flying in the wind. The air is close suddenly, the smell of decay strong, and he is back at the De Veres' staring down into the pit as now the corpse seems to stare only at him. But only for a moment.

Somewhere beneath his feet, somewhere beneath all their feet, a low rumble starts up. The ground itself begins to shake. Lemprière looks around in a panic as the sound grows and grows until it is not a sound but a physical force. Then, somewhere behind him, from somewhere deep below his feet, the full force of the explosion erupts into the street.

. . .

So it begins, thought Sir John in the dingy brass and varnish of the Examining Office at Bow Street.

"Arm yourselves," he enjoined his beadles in tones instilling urgency and calm. "The Militia will join us at the Fleet." His guide-boy shuffled beside him. Nervous beadles sweated in their tunics. He could smell it. All day the reports came in of people gathering in the east. A hot wind blew and the streets were oddly quiet. Sir John thought of his old adversary. The boy shifted again, tugging on his chain. Farina.

"On!" he intoned, and heard his beadles wheel about obediently to follow him forth to war.

He marched at their head, leading his token force east from Bow Street to cross Drury Lane and continue on through Lincoln's Inn Fields by Portugal Row into Cursitor Street with the boy clanking a short chain's-length ahead and the pattering steps of his beadles bringing up the rear. The Fleet reached, the Militia are added to his band which marches more confidently now through Ellarden Street to the north wall of Saint Paul's and along Cheapside to Cornhill. The streets are all but deserted, according to the boy who keeps up a running commentary along the way. Sir John is heartened by this.

"The Militia behind us," he ventures to his guide, "they would number perhaps a thousand men?"

"Thousand, S'John? I'm not rightly sure on the counting, sir. Not sure about thousands at all, sir."

"Several hundreds, then. Several hundreds added together, do you follow, boy?"

"Oh, I knows my hundreds, sir. S'only my thousands I'm unsure on. I'll take a look, sir. . . ." Sir John feels the chain jerk as the boy swivels about. "Yes, that'd be about right, sir."

"Several hundreds?"

"About a hundred, sir. Perhaps a few less. That'd be enough to sort that Farina out, eh, sir?" But Sir John does not answer. "Sir?"

"Yes!" barks Sir John, thinking, no, a thousand times no. The boy falls silent at this outburst. The chain feels terribly heavy in his hand and the wind is against him, blowing hard into his face.

The boy is cowed momentarily. He soon pipes up again. "There they are, sir! Right ahead of us, sir!"

"Halt!" Sir John raises an arm to the beadles close behind. "Fall in!" He hears the shuffling of nervous military heels. So few, he thinks. Too few.

"These rioters"—he bends conspiratorially toward his boy—"they would number, let me guess, hundreds?"

"Hundreds, sir? Oh yes, hundreds easily, I should say, sir. More like thousands . . ." Sir John hears movements to his front and rear, the one a massed grumble, the other a timorous fidget as the resolve of the Militia begins to melt.

"Hold steady!" he calls over his shoulder, but he knows it is already too late. It was too late months ago. The wind rises again and he can hear Farina's voice as it is carried down Leadenhall Street toward him.

". . . and this, this is what they conceal from our justice!"

Sir John thinks of concealment, a thing devoutly to be wished, the things concealed, and he thinks of Rudge. The boy is saying, "They're lifting something up, Sir John," and Sir John already knows the thing Farina has unearthed to goad the mob to fury. Henry is silent within him and the chain clanks as the boy says, "They've got her, Sir John. That woman you's always talking about, the dead one. . . ." Sir John already knows, in his mind's eye he can already see the blue dress, the blue flesh which even the coldest and deepest of Rudge's crypts has not preserved from decay and the prying eyes of his adversary, Farina. She is being raised as a gagged totem to their own tongue-tied resentment. She is an outrage they can understand.

"Raise arms!" he commands in stentorian tones and listens behind for the sharp intake of breath, the rustle of starched uniforms, the cocking of musket-hammers. But the sounds he anticipates are overtaken by another.

A deep rumble sounds from below. The cobbles beneath his feet seem to ripple as the explosion rips its way into the street somewhere ahead of him. He hears water falling to earth and then silence.

"Take aim!" His own voice sounds tinny and distant after the din of the eruption. He pauses for a brief moment, imagining the raised muskets, then gives the order. "Fire!"

Silence.

He starts, as if the reports have indeed gone off behind him. He begins to turn, but checks the movement as the boy's voice sounds beside him.

"They're coming toward us, Sir John."

"Fire!" he commands again. Again there is silence. Sir John feels panic rising from his stomach. He pulls on the chain but it seems to come loose. He can hear footsteps, thousands upon thousands of footsteps all moving toward him. Suddenly he is a fat blind man. He is far from home. He is alone. A faint noise at his side.

"Boy?"

"I'm still here, Sir John."

"Good lad. You, you took the collar off?"

"I did, Sir John." He can hear their voices now, the scrape of advancing feet.

"Are we alone, boy?"

"The men's crept off, Sir John." Alone. "The other lot, they're quite close now, Sir John," Close. The other lot. He has lost and Farina has won.

"Don't leave me here," he whispers. He waits. "Boy?" There is silence. "Boy! Where have—"

Someone takes the free end of the chain from his hand. "Not to worry, Sir John."

• • •

The wind seemed to carry the scent of decay, forty, fifty yards down the street as the corpse was raised before the mob. Somewhere behind him a woman's voice cried "Bet!" and the crowd about her fell back as she slumped to the ground. He saw Farina with his hair streaming out behind him, face turned into the wind and roaring for justice. The redcoats were melting away beyond him and only Sir John remained. The ground shuddered and quaked, then split as the Furies below took their revenge.

The waiting has been too long, has become too charged in the years since Rochelle, and its unexpended force needs fault lines and fissures, needs access to the real arena now.

A vigorous wound opens along the length of Leadenhall Street as the detonation below splits the resistant earth. The mob spills to left and right and it seems that the fissure is directed at Farina who raises his arms in defiance. The jagged mouth tears up the street toward him, widening to swallow him whole but still he stands there, proud and isolated and doomed. . . . No. The fissure stops inches short of its insolent challenger. Farina is suddenly victor, leader, healer, all of these and more to the mob who begin to creep forward, picking themselves up and relighting those torches doused by the spray. They are all his followers now, even Lemprière, if for other reasons. Sir John is slipping away down a side-street led by a small boy on what looks like a length of string. The mob inches forward, then swaggers, then runs toward its leader who shouts, "To the Opera House!" as he is swept up and along in the furious surge westward in pursuit of the Militia.

The rag-ends of the mob, its stragglers and wavering followers, walk either side of the water-filled crack which runs the length of Leadenhall Street. Soon the thoroughfare is deserted. Water slops in the fissure. The force of the explosion below has peeled back the surface of the street to form a lip on either side of the crack. Odd bubbles rise through its surface and the wind drives ripples down its length. The water grows agitated. There are other bodies and they are rising now. The liquid shifts more urgently. A dark shape is rolling and rising through the blind waters, snagging and freeing itself on the jagged sides of the fissure. It surfaces as a corpse, slick and shiny, the arms waving vaguely. The street is silent and deserted. East India House looms above. The waters stir again. Farther down the fissure, a second body is rising to the surface. For a moment it seems to hang suspended in the water, then the head lifts and its arms reach for the air.

• • •

He could not believe the scale of it, the measureless expansion of candle-light to inferno in a split second and the blistering heat, the black sheet of force which swept out from the explosion as the ships flared like lucifers and dashed the chamber to a paste of wood and water and flesh. *Good-bye, my leader.* His old fear raced against the flames but the flames won, as they always had. His victim's throne was splinters, his throne-room crushed. The leader was melting flesh and it was finished at last. The earth and rocks were his laurels and the cracked passage to the air above was his progress through the applauding ghosts of Rochelle. The earth peeled open and the sky above was his. Why should he linger now? Why waver between water and air? The fires were doused and the screams of the burning were whispers telling him to rise up and leave, to join them at last. Why then should he think of Lemprière?

He pulls himself out of the water. The dead man's head bobs gently. He recognizes the corpse as his fellow-traveler through the earth's tonnage. But as he watches, the waters begin to recede. Jaques's body begins to sink. The waters fall faster. A gibbous moon hangs low in the sky. He sees Jaques's face, an answering moon staring up out of the black water and a flurry of silver about him, then even these small signals disappear as the corpse sinks into the fissure's darkness.

• • •

The smells are of waxy torch-smoke, sweat, and excitement, a localized *sudor anglicus* as the mob heads west after the Militia. Along the way, piles of dried straw, dead trees, and various other desiccated garbage crackle into mysterious flame as frustrated rick-burners make an arsonist's *rus in urbe* of the stony urban envelope. Gangs of feral children run about shrieking. Linen-workers and copper-miners laid off from the late collapses in their trades wave banners. Barbers, waiters, tailors, shoe-makers, cabinet-makers, milliners, dress-makers, artificial flower-makers, saddlers, coach-builders, farriers, cooks, confectioners, and cab-men find themselves united here and now by a lack of work so complete after the late estivation of the gentry for the country that their usual rivalries are irrelevant; somehow the Opera House is an irresistible target for their unvented spleen, a symbol deluxe of their late and fickle employers.

Surrounded by his praetorian guard of silk-weavers, Farina leads the jacquerie on. Mountebanks and their merry-Andrews, gambling-house captains and combination-boys, ply their trades as the mob floods west through Fetter Lane and Lincoln's Inn Fields. Hawkers of pie and porter pass through the moving columns. Fish are available too. Cries of righteous anger and fervent curses mix with the traders' calls and together drift up toward the moon. Torchlights flash in zigzags down the staggered windows. The railings are slats in a phenakistoscope, rolled out along the route to count the passing tens of thousands of legs. Four and a half million cobblestones register the tramp of dissident feet, jackboots, sabots, clogs, and the map they could draw between them would cover Europe in a wriggling lattice of lines that all converge on London until that city was black with tracery, a sucking mouth pulling them in toward Stalkart's squat turret of culture. . . .

Lemprière pops up, gawky-limbed and squawking, outstanding amid a zone of short people a hundred yards or so back from the front. He sees the mob stretched out behind him while the vanguard hoofs its way along Fleet Street and the Strand, hooting and jeering, drawing its loose assemblage tighter, throwing the odd rock after the fleeing Militia; a traveling city-state going to war. At Charing Cross it divides to filter through the confusion of little alleys thereabouts but reforms to march as one unit into Haymarket, where the last of the Militia are spied disappearing into a large building on the right. The ad hoc alliances have become a single compound, a disgruntled and volatile alloy. Lemprière feels bodies jarring and swirling about his own. He wants a clear idea of what's going on. He shouts her name again but the mob is baying about the Opera House, banging on the doors which seem to be barred from within. Vague wailing noises drift out of the building and are answered by the antiphonic wind. A tense semicircle opens in the crowd, spreading out from the high doors and down the steps. Lemprière steps into it and surveys the mob from the raised perspective. He sees upturned faces nearest him which, as he overlooks them, spread back through the surging crowd until every visible eye is angled up to the rooftop. Lemprière wonders vaguely why all these people should fix their attention there, and then a body slams into his back, knocking him forward, flat, and winding him as a stunning thud dunts on the spot where he stood.

Lemprière wheezes and looks about. He sees his tackler, arms still locked around his legs, looking forward at him. Then the grin fades.

Lying behind them on the steps, an asinine grin on its face, its squat tonnage pinkly complaisant at this precipitous downturn in its fortunes, is the tortoise-rampant. Lemprière barely registers the tortoise. On its back is a body. Its chest is split open from the force of the impact and there is something in the chest, something moving insensibly, something not fully human. Little pistons are twitching among the detached ribbons of flesh and a smooth lozenge of brass is trapped in the wrecked machinery. Lemprière looks around him, but the faces of the mob are still looking up, away from himself on the ground, toward the roof. And this time he looks up too.

• • •

From the entrance to the spongeworks deep within the Beast where the battle was joined, Le Mara and Nazim have thrust, parried, and counterthrust their way west through galleries, tunnels, and caverns along a subterranean vector exactly matching the howling progress of the mob, hundreds of feet above. Their own conflict is played out in silence. Only their sudden exhalations and short grunts of effort betray their presence. They are armored insects rehearsing the bloody rite of courtship, tiny horns locked together, segmented legs scrabbling for a footing on the lightless stone. Their motions match each other, question and answer swapped back and forth in arcs and quick lunges, feints and retreats, as Nazim is forced backward by his unblinking foe. It looks equal, but it is not. Only once does Nazim match his strength against the Cabbala's assassin, bearing down on his knife hand with all his weight. The arm is cold and hard as metal. The force of the rebuttal astonishes him, tossed aside like a doll before he rises and resumes the struggle. He looks for weaknesses, errors, unguarded moments. There are none and they go on. The rush of water behind them fills their ears; their eyes stay fixed one on the other. His opponent never blinks or stumbles, only advances on him, driving him back.

Through the deadly semi-light of their struggle come his ghosts, Bahadur and the pseudo-Lemprière. The miniature is a tight lozenge in his hand, counterweight to his knife. Her gray-blue eyes, soft smile . . . mother to a false son. The real one is dead already by the hand that turns on him now, and the wavering outline of his successor is lodged inside him, playing a shadow-game, ducking behind his body's contours as they shift and whirl away from the assassin. And Bahadur, a more coincident presence guiding his motions, once more the tutor arranging his teenage frame, *like this, yes, drive it in at the side.* . . . The pseudo-Lemprière chuckles at his antics, offering spurious and contradictory advice. Shape-shifter, self-contravener whom Nazim spared, allowed to walk past, wished well in his flight. Why? Why did he do that? Was there something precious back there, something in the way the girl's arm curled about the boy's waist as he looked down at her? Let them pass. Something to be preserved in these shifting times of ours. Foolishness, nonsense; Bahadur's voice breaks in, cold and urgent. He is returned from Paris, the magical city which has worked its metal spell upon him. He is different, changed. They are walking along the cliff top. The pseudo-Lemprière is spared, disappearing into the dark behind him. Le Mara comes at him again. Bahadur is flying down away from him, he has crawled to the very edge of the cliff and looks down but he cannot see, cannot hear. He only has the cold press of his uncle's body against his own and the arm pointing to his chest, *we change. . . .* The tunnel is sloping upward. Le Mara's face is blank. *Change inside.*

Suddenly the ground seems to jolt, and a split second later a heavy report sounds up through the tunnel. For a single moment, Le Mara's eyes leave his own. Nazim lunges forward, driving his knife into the assassin's chest, already twisting the blade as it pierces skin and flesh, throwing his whole weight behind it. But the knife penetrates an inch, then stops, skidding sideways off something smooth and hard beneath the skin, tearing a great flange of flesh away from the underlying surface. Nazim staggers back, staring at what he has uncovered. Le Mara walks toward him as though untouched. For a moment his mind is frozen. Then he sees the dust begin to lift behind Le Mara. A dust cloud is driving up the tunnel behind the assassin, a soundless rose of powdered debris overtaking and engulfing them both as the explosion's blastwave shoots forward through the Beast's every pathway, capillary, and aperture. In the moment before it blinds him, Nazim turns and shoots his glance up the tunnel, gray sloping sides curving away, something hanging down. He runs. The dust chokes his nose and mouth. Le Mara's footsteps sound dully in steady thuds at his back. Already the dust is clearing as the blast passes over, he is being revealed in flight, being overtaken and caught. Something hanging down . . . A ladder!

A trapdoor opens and he emerges amid shoddy stage-properties and moth-eaten wigs and costumes. Rope ladders hang down like rigging. Murmur of conversation, music, someone singing, a girl . . . They are in the Opera House and Nazim begins to climb, Le Mara after him, two battling spiders in the web of their own making, scuttling up the ropes and gangplanks to the roof. Fat moon. A warm wind is blowing and the street below is in turmoil, heaving with the men and women whose slow coalescence he has monitored over the past weeks and months. Tiny insects crawling a hundred feet below. The trapdoor slams behind him. His adversary is here, very well, very well. He turns and watches as Le Mara approaches. Now he knows how it will end. He turns again, his back to the man, and walks toward the edge. A low parapet is surmounted by a statue like a turtle. Other turtles lie dotted about the roof. Le Mara is coming after him, footsteps sounding heavier than they should. He ignores them. Bahadur understands his intention. *Yes, good, like that.* The pseudo-Lemprière is silent and puzzled inside him. Le Mara follows as he weaves a casual path through the bulky statues. Properties of some unrevivable production. Be clear, careful steps now. The assassin's footfalls quicken to a run. Don't turn, wait, wait, *yes.* . . .

The parapet is suddenly upon him as the footsteps close, running at him now. He turns as Le Mara leaps at him, ducks, feels something burn across his face, and then the assassin is past him, flying toward the parapet and the statue as Nazim throws his weight behind the assassin's flight, urging him over the parapet's edge.

The tortoise-rampant saves Le Mara. A single hand of steel closes about the statue as his body swings out into space. For a moment the sight of that gashed, exposed body stays Nazim, then he is on his man, standing on the parapet with the Mob as silent spectators far below. Something hot trickles down his face and he is blind on that side. His knife comes up and his victim twists away. He stabs and feels the blade enter some unprotected joint. The neck, he urges as he turns, let it be the neck. The body is cold and hard. But it is the jaw. His knife has only found the jaw. Le Mara's mouth is jammed open. He can see the blade inside the mouth, slicing the tongue as it goes into spasm. Le Mara's face is pressed up against his own, his arm moving down. He has lost. He knows it even before the assassin's own knife finds his stomach and begins to tear a path up his chest. The pain is like a black wave covering them both. His teeth grind, his nails dig into his palms as his hands clench about the knife and, still, the miniature. *Yes, now, like that* . . . Nazim brings the miniature up and feeds it to the clacking mouth, forcing it down the throat. From somewhere inside the assassin's chest a screaming sound starts up. Nazim steps back heavily. The assassin is shaking, his limbs juddering uncontrollably. His own are made of lead. He feels very cold. Le Mara's hand is still fastened about the ludicrous statue. The other is trying to pull Nazim's knife from his face. It comes free suddenly and Nazim watches as the assassin drives it slowly into his chest. The blade disappears below the breastplate. He is searching there for the resistant lozenge of brass within. The sound is horrible. For an instant the shaking stops. The assassin's head turns to Nazim. The statue seems to sway. Le Mara is leaning forward, still for a moment, then pitching into space as the base of the statue splinters and takes him into thin air, down to the street a hundred feet below. Nazim sees sticklike limbs waving and falling away into the clean silence of his dream. *Now you see* . . . Bahadur? The chest splits open far below and the gaping wound discloses rods of brass and steel, couplings of copper, tiny valves all pumping below. Now he can see the change, the things they did to

Bahadur. *Change inside* . . . He stands on the parapet and looks out over the moonlit roofs of this city. The heads of the mob are nothing to him, filled with nothing-dreams. He puts his hand to his chest and feels the cold seeping into his limbs. His head is heavier than before and the sky blacker. He sees the street far below. Black sky and the rooflit city. He leans out over the edge and feels his center of gravity pull him forward into space.

. . .

The mob is silent, every man and woman gazing up at the figure who stands on the parapet above. He looks very calm, all alone up there. Perhaps this is where Farina loses them, where the particular vein he mines gives out. They are so quiet suddenly, so intent on the man above. He folds slowly from the waist, as though bowing to his audience. He leans out into space. He falls. Disappointment and sadness move around the crowd as he pitches forward. For the moment the Militia are forgotten. The Indian's body lands with a muffled thud beside that of his adversary on the steps of the Opera House. Nazim, Le Mara, tortoise: different challenges to the mob's comprehension. Silent faces streaked with torch-smoke ring the bodies on the steps. Lemprière clambers to his feet, drawn back to Le Mara's smashed cadaver. The chest is split from neck to groin. He bends to pick out the object which has caught his attention, a lozenge of brass not belonging amid the other twisted machinery. Somehow he is not surprised at its presence here. He opens the miniature. Gray-blue eyes meet his own spectacled stare.

"Mother . . ."

He speaks aloud as though her painted image might answer him. Nazim's eyes open. Why should Lemprière turn at this moment to find the Indian's eyes looking into his own? There are unspecified debts wielding influence between them, something about crowds and gates swinging open for the lovers, lights hung in the lightless spaces. All too late now. Too many mistakes. *Like that, yes* . . . The Indian's eyes track the secret unfolding before him. His lips move.

"Lemprière . . .?" Lemprière moves toward the Indian but the eyes remain fixed on the space he has left, a faint outline he has left behind to hover and break up in the gusts of wind and weird torchlight, self-usurper, pseudo-Lemprière, he moves his hand over the oval face and the eyes never flicker. The breathing has stopped. Lemprière closes the dead man's eyes and stands upright. The minature is closed and dropped into his one good pocket. His dictionary sags from the other. The Viscount's body sinks away into darkness, he turns and she is gone again. Lemprière pushes aside the nearest bystanders to resume his search for her.

Now the mob's energies begin to turn; passive contemplation is not a natural mode for this animal. Eight or nine burly men lead the way, striding through the tight-packed ranks to cluster about the tortoise. A collective grunt and the tortoise is shouldered. They advance up the steps to the doors with their impromptu battering-ram and commence dunting. Colossal thuds ring around the crowd, galvanizing them to surge forward as the men find a rhythm and the doors begin to shake under the assault. The Indian was interesting, they feel, but this is more what a good mob is about, banging things, shouting, being numerous and overwhelming. They quake back and forth in time with the rhythm of the assault-party. As the door shudders under the bashing, their whole rapt attention focuses on the point of impact, the irregular creamy-pink ovoid with its fatuous grin now smashing against the stout theatrical portals, the smirking head of the tortoise-rampant which will lead them forward into battle against the cowering Spartans within.

*   *   *

The Rochelais could never have known, streaming through the drab streets of the dying city far away, long ago, almost forgotten, almost consumed utterly that night, for the memories which recorded their burning would prove selective and politic to the replacing order. Other lives would fill the charred space left by their betrayal, the shadows on the walls, other versions of what took place would betray them. Here's one now. . . .

Gluey yellow candles mark constellations in the dark domed roofspace of the Opera House, auspicious conjunctions, happy portents for Stalkart. There are gods above, huge ones, heavy ones which bear down on the groaning structure like tortoises. Tortoises! Yes, and the Opera House glows with life tonight, for the lamps are lit and the wheezing orchestra tunes up in the pit, and every lobby, aisle, tier, and stair is jammed with the cognoscenti. Lord Brudenell is here, and the Dukes of Cumberland and Queensberry, Mister Edgecumbe and Sir W. W. Wynne, Ladies Harrowby and Fawcett in purple crêpe embroidered with green-and-silver foil, and the Honorable Miss Petre in her Sleath's Improver for Defective Shape. The Duke of Norfolk isn't talking to the Marquis of Lansdowne after that bruising over the Declaratory Bill, and Charles Fox, Lord Loughborough, Mister Gray, and Miss Sheridan are generally acknowledged, but curtly, for it is widely believed that between the opera and the howling of dogs they don't much care one way or the other. From behind tiny glasses of crême de Canelle and Barbados citron water, Lady Frances Bruce and Lady Clunbrassil eye Mister Hanway, whose wealth exceeds that of many provincial towns. Fresh from his triumph as Colonel Downright in *I'll Tell You What!*, Mister Aiki consoles the widow of Morris Morris, merchant, dead that afternoon.

"I don't know *why* I came," she wails. "I feel *awful!*"

"There, there," pats the solicitous Colonel Downright.

Stalkart hops up and down Fop's Alley pressing flesh and greeting his patrons. He basks in the warmth of his convivium as delicious gossip and anticipation ripple through the eager assembly. What *is* the opera tonight? He won't tell, no, not even when Miss Manners gives her most winsome smile, not even when Mister Edgecumbe takes him discreetly aside, and certainly not when several of Captain James Hay's obnoxious nephews surround him and become mildly abusive.

"It's a secret," he smiles, and ducks under an arm, only to be accosted by Count Trautmansdorf, who keeps inviting people to have dinner with him at his residence in Brussels. He spies Bolger waving to him over the heads of Ladies Villiers and Digby.

"Another one," confides Bolger, showing him the latest terse message from the Examiner's Office. They've been arriving all day. Sir John's neat handwriting stares up at him. *Expect Trouble*, it reads. "I've posted Tim in the foyer," says Bolger, and Stalkart nods agreement. Expect trouble. What else is there to expect? Trouble has been the day's keynote: trouble with Marineri's scenery (which won't go up), trouble with Signora Schinotti's descant (which won't go down), with Lupino's soldier-costumes (which won't come off), but most of all with Signor Marchesi, who won't come on. A papier-mâché seascape, Marmaduke shouting, needle and thread, and a further payment to the temperamental tenor have respectively solved these minor crises. Now the seascape is mounted, Schinotti is tearful, the soldiers are sewn into their tunics, and Marchesi will perform in the second, if not the first, of this evening's productions. Yes, not one but two operas: a double bill. What, though? Cramer turns to Stalkart and Stalkart nods. Cramer taps his violin and the music starts. Stalkart looks heavenward, up into the twinkling dome where bright junctions of candlelight tell him a story of false sacrifice and fierce, destructive love. He thinks of Troy and Sparta and their fates. He thinks of wooden horses. Tuneless strings swell mournfully before him. Stalkart dreams the flight of tortoises.

As the opening andante cedes to some heavy octave passages and thence to a dismal quarrel in G minor between oboe and flute, Sir W. W. Wynne leans back in his seat and thinks of a night in Paris fourteen years before when the same music played about his ears, and as the first line of Du Roullet's execrable libretto is uttered, he exhales in appreciation.

"Ah," he murmurs, "Gluck. I remember it was Paris—" Charles Fox tells him loudly to shut up.

Marchesi is walking on, and most of the audience is on its feet, cheering so loudly he misses his cue. Cramer steers the players back and comes at it again. Again, Marchesi misses it. A couple of the chorus fall into the orchestra pit. The audience grows silent, waiting. Cramer is nodding to the tenor; then, into the silence of the auditorium, Marchesi begins to sing: A heavenly beautiful sound, delicate silvery notes stream out of his golden throat and the audience sits in hushed wonder. . . .

BANG! A crude thud crashes through the glissando. *BANG!* Marchesi seems to stutter. *BANG!* The audience turn in their seats. What on earth is it? *BANG!* Marchesi seems to be clutching his throat. Why? *BANG! BANG! BANG! CRASH!* By now the sound is quite unmistakable. A door is being broken down, and succeeding this cacophony comes many a rude shout and curse as the mob enters from the back and floods in and up the stairs wielding staves, torches, slogans, and crude banausic sensibilities. Stalkart watches in horror as the aisles fill with tousled ruffians who swagger up and down; they seem to be searching for something. The music grinds to a halt, and onstage, the chorus huddles together nervously. There's someone in their midst who doesn't quite fit, who got swept up in their earlier retreat down Leadenhall Street, wandering about there in her distraction, collared and dragged west by order, some half-baked thought about hostages because their captain just knew things would go bad tonight. They've forgotten her but Juliette is still there, not waiting or even thinking very much, just there.

People are standing up in their seats as more and more of the mob pour in. Even more are massed outside, ringing the building and the streets around. The silk-weavers at least know what they're looking for (the Militia), but the others are only spoiling, prodding Stalkart's patrons and pushing them aside as they surge up and around the tiers and aisles. A posse of equerries take exception to this treatment and lash out, which is the start of the mayhem.

The fighting spreads from its central tussle into adjacent rucks and mauls, tough little skirmishes and general fisticuffs. Two scrawny harridans take a grab at Lady Brudenell's gauze cravat and Count Trautmansdorf gallantly threatens them with transport to Brussels and dinner. Tom Willis aims a punch at the Honorable Miss Petre but only bruises his knuckles on her resilient Sleath's Improver, reels around in agony, and is laid to waste by a tactical alliance between the Duke of Norfolk and the Marquis of Lansdowne who, victory assured, engage each other in half nelsons. Albert Hall, vintner, thuds to the ground, stunned by a clout around the earhole from a sock weighted with Welch's Pills for Female Obstructions and Complaints Peculiar to Virgins, and soon everyone's involved. People are spilling over the balconies and rolling around in the aisles, falling to the ground with great theatrical groans, then getting up and whacking their opponents when their backs are turned.

Caught up, swept in, and stranded amid this amiable pandemonium, Lemprière ducks and weaves a crisscross path through the combatants, straining and craning for the better view he needs. Toward the front of the auditorium, nearest the stage (so far untouched by the conflict), the melee seems less frantic, more considered; calculated, even. The battle is dying here, its participants are separating and standing off, eyeing each other warily. More and more of them break off as Lemprière skirts about. They're standing quite quietly now, most facing the stage where the chorus stand nervously together. Lemprière smells smoke, coming from somewhere behind them. Realization is dawning. The chorus turns and sees flames begin to lick up the wall at the back of the stage. Furtive rick-burners sidle away up the right-hand aisle. Suddenly the papier-mâché storm-scape catches and the roar of the flames turns everyone's heads; surprised, startled faces watch the fire spread up into the rigging, all attention focused on *that* part of the theater as the chorus turn back slowly, nervous military heels grinding on the boards, those uniforms just a little too realistic for one of Stalkart's productions, the faces just a little too anxious. And far too many of them . . .

The first gangplank comes down in flames and the Militia crack. They spill forward off the stage, a panicked undisciplined herd into the waiting boots and fists of the mob. Thick black smoke is already filling the dome far above and the upper tiers are draining down into the pit. The soldiers are running a gauntlet as the stage empties and huge plumes of smoke waft from the wings. Abruptly a sheet of fire bursts up the wall opposite, and mob, Militia, and cognoscenti alike grow sensible of their peril.

Someone thinks of water and shouts, "The river!" but the cry is taken up as a second call to arms, "The river! The river!" A brutal scramble for the doors begins. Thick waves of choking smoke roll down from above. Men and women cough and hold handkerchiefs to their faces. Flames spread from one side to the other and the air is hot, whirling with ash and burning fragments. Lemprière splutters and pushes through the bodies, staring into faces streaked with smoke and ash, almost indistinguishable from one another now. None of them hers.

Sad putti stare down from the proscenium, their gilt blackening in the heat. The plaster cracks audibly above the noise of the fire and begins to rain down on the last of the fleeing bodies below. Stucco angels wither and weakened joints begin to groan. The weight is too much. Smoke comes at Lemprière in waves, engulfing, choking as he moves toward the stage. A shape is moving there in the blistering heat, framed and lit by fires to either side. He passes Stalkart standing in the pit, arms raised to the failing roof and crying up, "Fly! Fly!" The roof is blazing. He moves past, eyes watering, skin crackling in the heat. Great jets of flame are shooting to right and left. Ahead he can see the white dress drifting, visible for brief moments as the waves of smoke and ash roll across. He reaches her with his lungs bursting, pulls her about and to him. But her face is blank, uncaring. Above them both, the first joist breaks and crashes down into the theater. He grasps her and drags her forward but she will not walk, looking back into the inferno and resistant to his efforts, without energy or will.

"Leave me," she says. He pulls her face up to his own.

"Why?" he shouts over the roar of the fire. Her eyes look anywhere but his own.

• • •

The explosion blew an arm of water, reaching up fifty, sixty feet, a swelling column which hung, then broke into droplets of sudden liquid raining down on the river's surface below. On the quayside, pirates and mob all stare at the falling column. The commencing battle is forgotten and its combatants frozen in place as the river accepts this last of the nights's weird benedictions. Pieces of wood drift to the surface: splintered plants, barrel-staves, mollusk-encrusted timbers of one sort or another, most of it charred beyond recognition. Some weak regurgitation from below . . .

Walking back toward his crew-mates, Wilberforce van Clam looked down at the sad raft of flotsam gathering on the surface and doffed his hat. The other pirates followed suit. Peter Rathkael-Herbert lowered his cutlass and Stoltz's men began to stand easy.

Huffing and puffing up the quay came Captain Guardian, followed at a distance by Captain Roy.

"You'll be Stoltz," he addressed the most nondescript of the gathering. Stoltz nodded. "Good, good," the captain went on. "Now, I've already spoken with young Lemprière and the plan is this—"

"Plan? What plan?" broke in Wilberforce as he rejoined the disconsolate pirates.

"And who on earth is 'Young Lemprière'?" added Stoltz. "Who on earth are any of you, for that matter?" Wilberforce took his pipe from his pocket and began to pack the bowl with resin.

"Well now," he said, "that is a yarn certainly worth the telling. Perhaps you remember the Comb Riots back in Fifty-three." He patted his pockets. "Does anyone have a match?" A handful were proffered from below. "Thank you."

"That'll be tuppence," said Captain Roy.

An hour later, perhaps, the pipe had made a couple of rounds and no one was exactly sure; Stoltz's men and the pirates sat intermingled together in little clumps dotted up and down the quay. From time to time, someone would clamber to his feet and carry the pipe to an adjacent group, swap a word or two, and wander back. The wind was lighter now, the river quiet as the tide began to turn. To the west, an orange halo glowed above the city. Pieces of the *Heart of Light* tapped gently against the jetty below. They were becalmed. Behind them, the Pool was a dim chaotic sculpture of masts and spars. The compact bulk of the *Vendragon* rocked gently in the tidal swell.

". . . so here we are," Wilberforce ended up. Stoltz nodded lazily. Peter Rathkael-Herbert sucked on the pipe and handed it to Eben, who refused for the third time. Wilberforce glanced over his shoulder at the darkened vessel behind. Eben watched him.

"You know her?"

"After a fashion," said Wilberforce. The two men eyed each other warily. "Thought I might take a look belowdecks," he offered. Eben nodded. "We're rather in need of a ship. Our own was, well, swallowed."

"We saw," said Eben. Wilberforce rose to address the pirates who lolled about on the quay.

"Men," he began. "Once again we find ourselves in something of a desperate strait. . . ." He spoke on, outlining their position and its attendant perils. ". . . and so, I propose the following plan." One or two of the pirates looked up as Wilberforce pointed to the ship and argued his point. "After all, what have we to lose?" Hörst struggled to his elbows and focused wearily on Wilberforce.

"Wilberforce," he said, "enough is enough," then collapsed. The others were shaking their heads. It was late and they were tired and too old. Eben looked about the retiring crew.

"Looks like just the two of us," he said to Wilberforce.

"Three," said Roy. Eben rose and looked back along the waterfront. The Crow's Nest stood like a dark turret against the orange sky. Thick plumes of smoke could be seen rising up out of the glare. The roofs of the city were a drab mosaic.

"Fire," he said.

"Opera House," murmured Stoltz from the depths of an engulfing dream. There but for the grace of God, thought Eben. Wilberforce was moving among his comrades, bending to pat shoulders, shake hands. Presently, he straightened and nodded to Eben and Roy.

The three captains walked down the quay together toward the waiting ship. As they reached the *Vendragon's* gangplank, footsteps were heard behind them. They turned as one. Peter Rathkael-Herbert stood there, bleary-eyed, a little self-conscious.

"Thought I'd better, you know, come along. If that's all right . . ."

"Good man," said Eben. Wilberforce clapped him on the back. The four men grinned at one another. "Come on then," said Roy.

The decks were deserted. They crept over the poop and down onto the quarterdeck.

"We should split up," suggested Roy, "and—"

"No!" Wilberforce almost shouted. Eben looked at him in surprise. "I mean, stick together, all right?" he added in quieter tones. Roy nodded.

"If you like."

Peter Rathkael-Herbert lifted the hatch and together they looked down into darkness. Eben smelt Stockholm tar and warm stale air. He thought of the procession of months and the men he had watched from the safety of the Crow's Nest, his rash promise to young Lemprière. Crates, statues . . . Not enough. They climbed down, waiting at the foot of the ladder for Roy, who declined to be lifted. Moonlight poured down the open hatch, showing them the bulky column of the mainmast. Beyond it there were only cleared cabins and neatly stowed gear in both directions. They moved along carefully, pushing open hatches from below, but the middle deck was empty as the upper. They climbed down once more, to the lower deck. The moonlight did not reach down this far. Wilberforce felt his way forward by the breaches of the Indiaman's guns which reduced the deck to a narrow gangway. His head knocked against the timbers of the deck above, then on something which swung. A lamp.

"Matches, Captain Roy," he whispered over his shoulder. Roy moved forward. A match flared and Roy shouted suddenly, loudly, in the confined space. All four looked about the illuminated deck. The cannon stretched away to either side, fore and aft, until the light from the lamp gave out. Beside each cannon stood a man, and as the light fell on their faces the eyes opened, *click, click, click, click, click.* . . . They were surrounded by weather-tanned faces.

Then, heavy footsteps moved toward them, and out of the darkness came a man. His face was tanned as those of his fellows, his beard as full and his eyes as dead. Eben looked once, then again. It was impossible. He pushed past Wilberforce as the figure halted before them. It was true.

"Alan?" he blurted in disbelieving tones. "Captain Neagle? Is that—"

"The command," the figure spoke. His eyes were fixed on Guardian. The voice was flat and uninflected, almost metallic. The four looked at one another, puzzled and dumbfounded at once.

"I think it's a question," said Peter Rathkael-Herbert. Roy looked at Neagle and the crew lining the gunports.

"Cast off," he commanded and stepped smartly back as the *Vendragon*'s crew jumped into long-awaited action.

. . .

She was dead weight, a lifeless thing, as he dragged her through the smoke and flames. The roof was a pyre exploding above them, hurling down beams into the burning pit below. The structure groaned, then began its final collapse. Lemprière looked up and saw the buckling roof give way. Something massive crashed down through the tiers, cutting through them like matchwood, then another, and another. From their stations far above, the tortoises were plunging earthward, bringing down the last of the roof as they smashed through the rails and balconies. He felt flames lick his back as he skirted the bombardment. The stairs were a blazing corridor where the smoke spiraled and sucked the air from his lungs. He pulled her along behind him, choking and heaving, never looking back until he saw the street beyond, where he knelt suddenly, feeling faint, his chest tightening. He heard glass shatter somewhere behind him. Men running after the soldiers. He closed his eyes and the black smoke seemed to roll over him again in thick protective waves, darker and darker. . . .

She was standing above, looking down at him. He rose slowly and began to cough the smoke out of his lungs. When he sought her eye, she had turned away.

"Juliette?" She did not turn back. He took hold of her and pulled her to him, but as she realized his intention she twisted free.

"My own father . . ." Her voice was quiet. He barely heard her.

"What do you mean?"

"Dead. All dead." A whisper.

"But you said . . . You told me he was nothing to you, nothing. . . ." She turned on him, her face full of anger.

"Not the Viscount, you fool! Don't you understand? My father! Can you not know? Can you really not guess what we have done?"

Behind them both, the blackened walls of the Opera House began to crumble inward. The high arches of the façade broke, and flames roared through the openings. The whole construction seemed to melt, not fall, sagging, then collapsing in on itself, sending a mushroom-cloud of ash and dust up into the sky as notice of its destruction.

• • •

Carried downstream on the ebbing tide past Shadwell, the Isle of Dogs, the yards at Blackwall, and the drifting lights of Gravesend, through the shoals and sandbars of the estuary to the open sea beyond, the crew of the *Vendragon* labored in silence with the creaking rigging, as the gyring wind caught her sails, and the race of Alderney thrust her forward, a destined capsule, south with the channel currents toward Rochelle. Eben, Roy, Wilberforce, and Peter Rathkael-Herbert stood together on the quarterdeck and watched the crew at work. Neagle strode up and down the vessel's decks, passing by them without acknowledgment. The sea was black and silver. Moonlight caught the wavelets, and the lights of the western ports were distant beacons, ignored and passed by as they sped south. Water rushed against the hull, and Captain Guardian thought of nights in the South China Sea. The air was so warm and laden, the sky so clear.

High above the deck, the *Vendragon*'s crew shinned along the yard-arms to put on sail. The canvas swelled above them and the ship sprang forward, prow cutting the water to leave a shimmering wake behind. Wilberforce watched as familiar landmarks slid by to port. The last voyage of the *Heart of Light* was being reprised, but accelerated and in reverse as Cherbourg and Lorient glimmered out from the low coastline. Spurs, points, and cliffs were smudged together in the darkness, but he remembered each one. He thought of the journeys undertaken by the vessel which surged beneath him now, the repeated dogleg, east to west, then south to north and back. He imagined the waters where the Mediterranean became the Atlantic, sea became ocean, and in his mind's eye they were scored over like ice on a skating pond as the *Vendragon* turned there year after year before finding its bearing and continuing along its second axis. Could the sea ever become too traveled, ever become worn? Huge zigzags ran across the ocean's surface as the voyages of possible ships scored their fading trails. Mats of phosphor and water-spouts were the true coordinates, shifting things. A school of whales was an island; invisible junctions of latitude and longitude marked every scrap of flotsam. The mysteries were not polar, but diffuse, dissolved in the corroding brine. Wilberforce looked out over the stern and saw the last voyage of the *Heart of Light* reaffirmed in the *Vendragon*'s glowing, then fading, wake.

The dark territory of the Vendée passed by to port and presently the land fell back as the coastline swung away. A low island seemed to weigh anchor and drift out from the shore as the *Vendragon* headed in. Presently, Peter Rathkael-Herbert squinted, then pointed to a faint glow shining out from one of the points. As he did so, the ship lurched violently to port, changing bearing and heading for the spot as though complying with his signal. All four men watched as the faint glow drew nearer. A green light was signaling to the *Vendragon*, a beacon drawing her in toward the coast.

"That's our landfall," said Eben with conviction.

"Where are we?" asked Peter Rathkael-Herbert.

"If that's Île de Ré," Wilberforce pointed to the dark island now to starboard, "then we're about four leagues out from Rochelle."

. . .

The Opera House was a smoldering pile. Men were running down the street carrying buckets. It was too late. The mob had gone. In its place, bewildered clumps of men and women, streaked with smoke from the torches and the fire, drifted in the street. They seemed puzzled, as though some expected result had failed to materialize from their efforts. Ash sent up by the theater's collapse was returning to earth now, falling as black confetti on Lemprière and Juliette.

"The Viscount told you? He told you the name?" he questioned her. She nodded. "Who?"

Paper trails formed and dissolved in the air around his head. The smell of burning still stung his nostrils. Little trails formed lines between them, receipts "*reçue par Madame K.,*" *forgive me, Marianne* . . . the short span of her years tracing a shallow arc back to Paris and a house in the Rue Boucher des Deux Boules the night it had rained. Could Casterleigh have drawn these lines right? He saw her dropping down from the coach, slap her hand against the table in the library. Absence of light. Ignorance. He let her go in the Archive, lost her at the top of the shaft. Her face was pulled back from his own behind the glass of the coach-window, receding into different kinds of darkness. She was a shifting presence beside him, a hungry mouth feeding on him in the narrow bed, suddenly his lover. His need was quick, easily satisfied there. Charles sat in rented rooms writing to his wife. The ideogram assembled itself as a monstrous engine, a cipher of them both, but counter to their pairing, Casterleigh's engine, gears clacking as it chases them to the point where she would turn to him dead-eyed and answer: "Your father. Yours and mine both."

• • •

The boy led him in a stumbling run north along Bishopsgate, then west into the maze of alleys below London Wall and after that he did not know. He felt soft mud, packed earth, cobbles, flagstones, and boards underfoot. He heard the boy's light footsteps running ahead of him, and from time to time the distant roar of the mob. He was lost in the twists and turns of his guide's elected path and hardly knew if he were hurrying through some narrow and overhung rat-run or striding in full view down the center of the Strand. When he called ahead to his guide, the boy answered in terms that meant nothing to him. They were close by that alley by the Magpie, or rounding the corner fom Silvero's. Magpie. Silvero's. The boy's city was incomprehensible.

"Wait here, Sir John." He stopped and heaved breath into his lungs. The boy ran on ahead. A minute or two passed while he listened to his thudding heart. Then the boy returned. "All clear, Sir John." He suffered himself to be led around a corner into the silence of the street beyond. Again the boy stopped.

"We're here, Sir John. You'll be safe here." They climbed a short set of steps and Sir John felt his hand being guided to the handle on the door.

"Where are we?" he asked, as he pushed and opened the door. The cold interior air drifted out as he stepped within. "Boy?" There was no reply. "Are you there?" A faint, familiar smell of carbolic reached his nostrils from the cellars below. The boy was already gone. He was alone in the mortuary.

"Good lad," he murmured as he made his way down the familiar stairs. The months of waiting were over. He had faced Farina at last, and now, even in defeat, he felt the weight of his enemy's presence lift from his shoulders. He had led his men to battle and they had fled. Only the boy had stayed to lead his defeated general to sanctuary.

The stairs gave out onto a smooth stone floor. At the back of Rudge's dissection room, he recalled, stood a high-backed chair. Sir John fumbled a path to it about the slabs and tables. Henry had never faced a night such as this, and if he had, what could he have done? Nothing, thought Sir John. Nothing at all.

• • •

As the *Vendragon* drew nearer her beacon, the crew worked hard aloft to slacken sail. The three captains and Peter Rathkael-Herbert watched as the coast came into view. The green light was set halfway up a shallow slope. A jetty ran out to sea, off the point. On the strand behind it, Eben was able to make out a long line of carts, twenty or more, and assembled loosely about them, a large crowd of men armed with jemmies and long-handled hammers. The jetty was coming up faster than he had thought, and for a moment he felt that the ship must collide with it, but no, the broad gangplank was sliding safely to port, the hawsers running over the bitts below, and lines thrown to waiting hands were being made fast. The gang of men ashore began to march toward the ship. Two better dressed than the others were walking ahead up the jetty toward the *Vendragon*. Wilberforce looked at the forces ranged before them and turned to Eben.

"Don't like the looks of this much." Eben nodded.

"We'll parley with them," he said.

The four men trooped dutifully down the gangplank to meet the approaching pair, who turned to each other and whispered as they drew close.

"Evening!" Eben greeted them.

They whispered again, then one extended his hand. "Welcome to you all," said the shorter of the two. "Monsieur Jaques is still aboard?"

"Jaques? Don't think I know any Jaques. We're here for young Lemprière," Captain Guardian affirmed stoutly. More whispering followed this statement. The jetty was filled with men who stood behind their two commanders as they conferred between themselves. At length, Duluc turned from his companion to address the crowd behind. He spoke in stirring tones with much pointing to the four of them but all in French, so that only Peter Rathkael-Herbert had the roughest notion of his message.

"They're congratulating us," he relayed. "Without our sacrifice, all would have been lost. Something else . . . We are the unsung heroes of, of the Revolution."

"Very nice," said Eben.

"Now he's saying something about the carts. I think they want to unload the ship. Yes, that's it. The cargo . . ."

Almost before he could finish speaking, the first of the men had moved forward, up the gangplank and down the hatch to the hold.

"What is the cargo?" asked Wilberforce.

"Statues," said Eben.

Neagle and his crew had disappeared belowdecks. The four of them looked on as the first of the crates was manhandled up from the hold, lowered over the side, and carried up the jetty toward the carts lined up along the shore. Here the men set to work with their bars and hammers, and soon the area was littered with splintered wood. The statues were lifted from the wreckage of their containers and stood upright along the shore. The stevedores worked without pause, and soon a host of figures were clustered about the carts: Minerva, Juno, Venus, Diana surrounded by her nymphs, Hercules strangling the vipers, Jove with his thunderbolt, Neptune with an urn, satyrs, dryads, and hamadryads, all looking blindly to one another as other gods, goddesses, and heroes emerged from the broached crates to join their ranks.

"Why don't they load them?" asked Peter Rathkael-Herbert. Wilberforce shrugged in ignorance, but as he did so this small mystery began to be resolved.

Those men carrying hammers gathered around the still figures and, at a signal from the man who had earlier addressed them, advanced on the huddled statues. They swung the hammers like axes. Limbs and heads were broken off. Torsos which fell to the ground were cracked open, and soon a cloud of off-white dust hung over the carnage. At one point, a pitcher of water was passed around. Each man took a draft and then the work went on. Faces and fingers splintered under the hammer-blows until every figure lay smashed. The dust began to settle. Eben saw the first man bend and lift something heavy from the rubble. Another joined him and helped lift the object onto the nearest cart. Presently the whole workforce was picking similarly through the demolished statues. The carts were loaded in sequence and driven off up the low hill behind.

"Gold," said Captain Roy. One man had emptied the pitcher over the irregular lode before him, and as the dust was washed off a familiar glint could be seen in the moonlight. The last of the carts was clearing the brow of the hill. The men sat about the smashed evidence of their labors, catching their breaths. The two men approached once again, the first of the pair addressing Eben as before.

"Our arrangements are complete now. Send Lemprière, Jaques, and the others our thanks and greetings. We expect them at their pleasure a year from now." Both men raised an arm in salute. "The fourteenth!"

"The fourteenth!" the four of them answered, saluting likewise. They turned and found Neagle standing in silence behind them.

"What now?" asked Wilberforce.

Inland, the landmass stretched away into darkness. The green light was extinguished. The *Vendragon* sat high in the water, knocking lightly against the jetty as she was rocked in the swell. The eastern sky was growing light, dawn only an hour away now. Captain Guardian looked out over the starboard rail to where Rochelle stood like a silent sentinel marking the boundary between land and water. Peter Rathkael-Herbert thought of dawn in Constantinople, of the day's first sunlight glinting off gilded domes high above the city. Wilberforce and Roy shivered beside him. A thin, chill wind was getting up from the north.

"South," said Eben, and the others nodded agreement. South.

• • •

A bright sun rose over London on the morning of the fourteenth of July. High winds blew from the northwest and descended upon the city in cold gusts. In Leadenhall Street, the engineers were already at work with their barrows and shovels, filling and cementing the crack which split the road. Odd wisps of smoke curled up from the smoldering debris in Haymarket. At the Examiner's Office in Bow Street, Sir John Fielding berated his beadles and listened to the reports as they came in from around the city. The Militia had been chased from the Opera House through Saint James Park to the river and there thrown in. Unsympathetic wherrymen had charged half a guinea a head for their rescue. There had been looting and there had been arrests, but the mob had become dispirited, divided, leaderless at the last. It had dispersed sometime before dawn and the streets had grown quiet. The city was the same city as the night before.

As he walked from Bow Street through Covent Garden market to the Tilt-yard, Sir John listened to the noise and chatter of the fishwives and haggling traders. Gyp's whetstone was a low whirr in the east corner as he passed. A woman was selling turbot from a basket. He smelt fish, vegetables, the unwashed bodies of men and women. Nothing had changed. Now, in the cold light of morning, his fears seemed extravagant, almost fanciful. What could he have been thinking?

At the gate to the jail he was met by the turnkey and escorted through the yard to the cells below. He heard keys jangle, doors being locked and unlocked. Gates clanged shut behind him.

"Mixed bag, Sir John," offered the turnkey as they came to the first of the cells where Stoltz and his men sat in sullen silence. "Found 'em on Butler's Wharf."

"Very good. And in what practice were they engaged when come upon?" queried the magistrate.

"Sir John?"

"What were they *doing*?"

"Oh, I see, sir. Well, they was sleeping, Sir John. Couldn't wake 'em neither. Had to load 'em in the wagon like coal-sacks."

Sir John nodded sagely. "Carry on," he said.

The second cell was as crowded as the first.

"This lot was with Stoltz, and them," announced the turnkey, "claim to be pirates, sir."

"Pirates? There are no pirates in London. . . ."

"There's us, sir," came a voice from within the cell.

"And who might you be?" questioned Sir John.

"Hörst Craevisch," replied the voice, "and the crew of the *Heart of Light,* known onetime as *Alecto. . . .*" *Alecto.* Pirates . . . No, it was impossible. Thirty years if it was a day.

"Tell me, Mister Craevisch, how did you come to be a pirate?"

"Ah now, sir. Now that is a story worth the telling. You may recall the Great Comb Protest of Fifty-two. Well, there was a magistrate around then—"

"Thank you, Mister Craevisch," Sir John interrupted the recitation. "I have heard enough. Turnkey, release these men."

"Sir John? Piracy. I mean, 'tis a serious change. . . ." But Sir John was not listening. Here at last was a conundrum not of his making. Pirates indeed. Here at least the blame was not rightly his. He thought of his half-brother and his clever solutions. He turned his blind eyes to the cell as the pirates began to gather their belongings. No, this was not his fault at all. This was something Henry had done.

Sir John waited as the pirates filed past, then followed the turnkey to the last of the cells.

"Bit of an odd one this," the man announced.

"Is there a charge?"

"Affray, arson, and murder, Sir John. He's already confessed. Matter of fact, he asked specially to see you."

"And the basis of these charges?"

"Well, sir, he's punched a number of your constables who was restraining him at the time of his arrest, claims he burned down the Opera House in Haymarket, and says he killed these women, kept on and on he did. Horrible it was, Sir John. Filling 'em up with metal and wrapping them in dead animals. . . ." Sir John sighed inwardly.

"Does he wear spectacles?"

"Why, yes."

"And a pink coat?"

"Yes, Sir John, he does. Very nasty it is . . ."

"And what exactly was he doing when arrested?"

"Well, trying to walk into the Opera House, Sir John. It was blazing away and the lads thought they'd best pull him out before—"

"Mister Lemprière!"

Sir John addressed the cell's occupant. There was a pause, then a voice he recognized addressed him in desolate tones from the corner.

"I killed them, Sir John. It's all in the book, dates, methods, all signed up. I'll tell you how too. . . ." Sir John heard him leaf through some pages.

As he drew breath to begin reading, Sir John raised his hand for silence.

"Mister Lemprière, I have spoken with your companion on both those nights. By his account, you were already several miles from the De Veres' when the murder took place. As for the Manufactory, you were seen and remembered from the tavern at King's Arms Stairs by your friend and up to a dozen watermen. He came to warn me of your obsession not two nights ago. Now, I know—"

The young man erupted suddenly.

"You blind fool! Why should I confess it if it were not true? I killed them. I? I did it. Don't you understand?"

"Mister Lemprière, to the best of my knowledge you came to this city to settle a will and stayed to write a dictionary. You have killed no one, and whether or not I suspected you in the past does not alter the fact. Your friend Mister Praeceps did you a great service when he came to me. Now, take your dictionary, Mister Lemprière, and go home." And with that, Sir John motioned for the turnkey to release his prisoner.

• • •

The young man sat on the jetty with his traveling chest and a book held open in front of him. He had been there since midmorning. Every so often he would look up as though expecting someone, then, finding the waterfront deserted, would go on with his reading.

Captain Radley of the pacquet *Vineeta* watched from the stern as the young man removed his spectacles and wiped them for the umpteenth time. His appearance was extraordinary: hair uncombed, face streaked with soot, a coat which might once have been pink all stained and torn. As he watched, the young man wrapped it more tightly about him. The wind was cold as it blew across the open water. A nor'westerly, odd for

July. The sun shone down onto the boat. Stacked beside him in their crates, chickens fought noisy, private battles.

"Watch out there!" he called to the woman tottering down the gangplank. She stepped gingerly onto the deck and Captain Radley looked back to the young man. He had dropped his book, which now lay abandoned between his feet. His spectacles hung idly from one hand and his lips moved slightly as he mumbled to himself.

Upstream from the pacquet, the *Nottingham* hove into view. The huge Indiaman dwarfed every other craft on the river and the wherries paddled furiously to clear her path. Captain Radley turned back and watched his crewman stack the last of the crates toward the stern. He heard the water begin to rush against the sides of the boat. The tide had turned already. The *Nottingham* crept past with her pilot and began to round the bend. The far bank shimmered. The woman was settling herself behind the wheelhouse.

"Is he taking the passage?" he asked his passenger, pointing to the figure who sat alone on the jetty. The woman shrugged in ignorance.

"All aboard!" he called up. But the young man made no sign that he had heard. He called again and the figure moved as if startled. Captain Radley watched as he heaved the chest up shoulder-high and carried it along the jetty to the gangplank.

"Saint Peter Port?" The young man nodded. "No cabin, mind you." The young man nodded again and offered him the fare in silence.

"Cast off!" shouted Captain Radley. The boat began to swing out.

"Wait!" The young man was pointing toward the jetty. "My book. I've left it."

"Hold the rope!" shouted Radley. "Be quick," he cautioned his passenger and watched as the young man jumped ashore. He turned to the woman.

"Forgot his book." The woman shrugged again. Captain Radley watched the gulls which sped over the water, gliding, almost touching the surface. Three of them were pursuing a fourth which fled downstream, all of them shrieking together, then up, higher and higher, until they were tiny dots in the enveloping blue of the sky. He looked down once more, to the jetty, but his passenger was almost fifty yards away, miles past his damned book which still lay where he had dropped it.

"Oi!" he shouted and waved. The young man turned and waved back. Someone was with him. They were talking and gesturing to each other. Both of them started running back along the waterfront.

"The bloody book!" he roared as both of them ran past it. The girl stopped and retrieved it. The young man jumped for the deck and fell clumsily into the chickens. The girl was more surefooted. When he had picked himself up, Radley saw his demeanor was changed. He was smiling. So was the girl.

"What?" he demanded. "What's so funny? Are you coming too now?"

The girl nodded. If anything, she was in a more disreputable state than the other.

"No cabin, mind you," he said again. They were paying no attention. The boy was asking, "How did you know?" and the girl was saying, "Septimus . . ."

• • •

The city stood behind him, his old arena, with its courts and alleys, the cracked mosaic of its roofs and streets. Scorched and split by the night's upheavals, London rested in its new permanence while engineers attended to its wounds. He had watched them at work in Leadenhall Street on his journey here. Overseeing their efforts was East India House, which he knew for an abandoned hulk, a tomb. His late masters were dead and he had reached the last of his stations.

The river snaked away before him, fattening and glittering in the sunlight. The *Nottingham*'s tonnage slid downriver as the tide began to turn, wood displacing water, her crew shouting and their shouts fading into silence as the bend was reached. Wherries and other smaller craft paddled back and forth. He could hear the water moving faster. His eyes roved back and forth, and farther down the long quay, he saw Juliette emerge at last. She was looking up and down the waterfront, searching for one he had assured her would be here. Hurry, he thought to himself, then glanced down the waterfront to the boat.

Downriver from the girl, the captain of the pacquet moved toward the stern. He seemed to call to the young man on the jetty, for the angular figure rose and shouldered his traveling chest. Juliette had seen him and was taking her first steps forward, moving faster and then running. The young man stepped aboard. The pacquet was casting off and preparing to move out from the jetty. The girl was running faster. He thought he heard her shouting, but she was fifty, sixty yards away. He thought she would not reach the boat. Then the figure aboard the boat stood up and he knew that she would reach him, the boat would wait and his own efforts were not wasted. From his vantage point on the quay, Septimus could see Lemprière running up the gangplank.

It had been near the end. Sometime after the events at Coade's, perhaps. Jaques had taken him aside before. This time he confided in him. He believed the business was a madness, the boy was saner than any of them; he feared the success of their plan more than its failure. He had listened as Jaques's tongue flapped. Jaques's nerve was failing, his resolve running out; his partners were unsound, untrusted by him, and there was more. Something hid behind his anxieties that he did, and did not, wish to tell. And as he talked, Septimus watched the swings of Jaques's indecision slow and come to rest about a minor player, one he would not have guessed so significant: Juliette.

Septimus had thought the girl no more than bait, a lure to draw this Lemprière out. And of course he had followed: through the freezing night of the De Veres, in the darkness of the Archive, across the city to the theater on the night his own hand was revealed. But the girl was more than that to Jaques. The man spoke of a night in Paris seventeen years before. He and this Lemprière's father had stumbled into a brothel. Sodden and drunk, Charles Lemprière had collapsed into willing arms. Charles was insensible of his actions, or lack of them, afterward remembering nothing and accepting all on the word of his companion. But Jaques remembered perfectly. He had climbed the stairs to find his friend and found the woman unsatisfied with Charles unconscious beside her. They had left the city on the following morning. Nine months later, the demands began to arrive at Charles's door. But Charles was never the father. Jaques's secret.

Septimus had nodded and said nothing. Lemprière's antics had continued under his false guidance. He watched his companion stumble forward into their traps, toil over his dictionary, which was theirs too, and all the while it was the girl who consumed this Lemprière's thoughts. He was awkward, gullible, lacked common sense, held out the hand of friendship to any convincing stranger. Hardly a worthy adversary. He had played the false Achates to an overtrusting Æneas. Lemprière had told him everything the night of the Pork Club, on the bridge and in the rain. The task was simplicity itself, and as the net closed, Septimus had asked himself why it should come to trouble him as it did. He played the consoling friend to his companion's grief after Coade's, the witness to his delusions. His roles sapped him and at the last he was left mouthing platitudes and vague appeals. *Friends of a sort* . . . Lemprière placed the ring to the watermark, the watermark to the map, and found Rochelle staring at him in the room in Southampton Street. Septimus found his ebbing sense of purpose replaced by a strange resentment as he moved forward behind Lemprière's back. Why should he think of Jaques's words then, of the girl and her hopeless admirer? He was a hired hand demanding credence, no more than that. He never asked this Lemprière for his friendship.

The Opera House burned. Septimus watched from the crowd as he confronted her and she turned away from him. Jaques was already dead, but his deception was pulling them apart. His own custody of the lie urged him forward, but he could not face Lemprière. He saw Sir John's men carry the young man off. The girl was lost in her distraction. He followed and found her wandering the streets, smoke-streaked, uncaring of his presence. They were failed conspirators, alike only in their complicity. But the truth could redeem her, as it could not himself.

"It was never Charles. . . ." Her eyes fixed themselves upon him. He

spoke her father's name and saw her face come alive. "Always Jaques
. . ." The father who had failed his daughter; and Septimus had redressed
that failure as, perhaps, Jaques had guessed he might. She turned away
and he was left alone. But it was not for Jaques he had come forward.
Nor even for his daughter.

Now Lemprière was running up the quay. He saw the two of them
embrace quickly, then turn back toward the boat. The captain shouted
and the young man bent to pick up something that was lying on the jetty,
a book. They jumped down into the stern of the boat; the rope was
thrown and the pacquet swung out into the river. Suddenly he wanted to
tell them that he was here, that he knew they had found each other. He
waved, but the two of them were settled, already engrossed in each other.
The tide ran faster now, pulling the boat into midstream. Septimus
watched until the *Vineeta* reached the bend of the river, but the lovers did
not look up. The far bank swung across his line of sight, a closing door as
the boat slid behind it. The surface of the river seemed sluggish and oily
now. Septimus stood at his station, still gazing after the departed vessel.
Other ships were following, crowding one another as the Thames's flood
carried them downriver. His eye was drawn this way and that by the
exodus. The river pulled them away. They were gone. He turned and
made his way up to the road which would carry him back to the city.